A GRAVEYARD FOR HEROES

MICHAEL MICHEL

CHAINBREAKER BOOKS

ALSO BY

MICHAEL MICHEL

DREAMS OF DUST AND STEEL
The Price of Power
A Graveyard for Heroes
Banners of Wrath (Forthcoming)

TALES FROM DREAMS OF DUST AND STEEL
War Song
Death Dance (Forthcoming)

OTHER WORKS
Way of the Wizard
Sing no Suns, Sing the Night

For Ella. My world. My heart.
A true Hulka'skara.

And for the ones who suffer...
It is a doorway in the soul.
Desire shouts, "I demand the other side!"
Fear whispers, "You must never step through."
Despair claims, "It won't matter—all places hold pain."
Love says nothing.
It is content to dance wherever it is.

CONTENTS

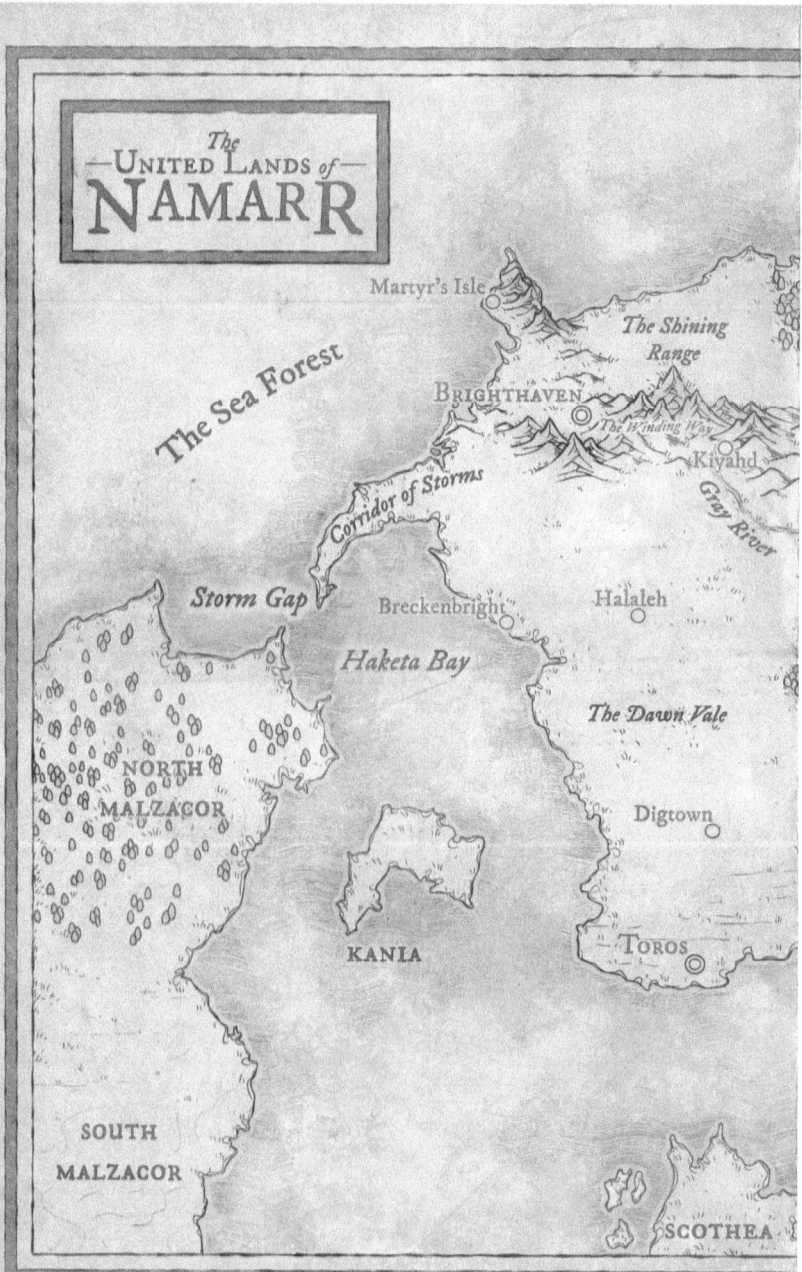

C'DATH

C'Datban
Straits

Akulsa
"The Antler"

The Fringes

Twilight Cape

The Ice King

Shadowheart

JARIK

Blue River

The Dolgn Ocean

Prav

White Plains

Summerforge

Bleeding Point

Ghastiin

Baen's Handle

ALISTAR

The Ardent
Heart

Unturrus

Nine
Lakes

Carthane

South Setton

VALAT
The Mighty Isle

Sea of Psollus

HD
2023

THINGS TO NOTE

1. If you're interested in engaging with the author as you read, there are a number of ways to do so listed in the back of this book. Please note that while he tries to respond on his socials, his discord server is best for keeping in touch.

2. If you would like regular updates and/or bonus content like the **free prequel novella,** *War Song,* make sure to sign up for his newsletter. **If there's trouble with the link, you can go to michaelmichela uthor.com.**

3. If it's been a while since you read book one, or you'd like a refresher of past events, **it's strongly encouraged for you to read a summary of the story thus far which can be found on the author's website:** michaelmichelauthor.com

4. *Dreams of Dust and Steel* **is a five book epic fantasy series that continues after** *A Graveyard for Heroes* **with** *Banners of Wrath.*

DRAMATIS PERSONAE

Ishoa Ironlight – Princess of Namarr. Descendant of Danath Ironlight.
Rakeema – Ishoa's willful anjuhtarg. An ice tiger.
Arick Quinn – A knight of Jarik.
Old Borry – Former Shadowheart holdguard.
Damsel – Former Shadowheart holdguard.
The Fly – Megalor Bog's personal bodyguard.
Mittens – A crone from Threehills.
Leena – A crone from Threehills.
Okki – A young refugee from Womunger.
Rigga Hine – The Lady of White Plains. Matriarch of the shepherds.
Hollem Hine – A lord and knight-captain of White Plains.
Adus Hine –A lord of White Plains.
Krhalka – The High Hand of the Jurati.
Gaern Yorek – A beastmaster from Akulsa (The Antler).
Wiir – Gaern Yorek's mysterious servant.
Gossryk Orr, aka the "Knight the Hallow Moon" – Lord Protector of Bleeding Point.
Lodecka Warnock – Scarborn leader of the White Wolverine Alliance. Defacto Lady of the Fringes.
Ularis Warnock – Scarborn leader of the White Wolverine Alliance. Defacto Lord of the Fringes.
Huun Korpa – Scarborn captain.

Golthius Narl – Baker lord of Prav. Lord Protector of Deephollow Prison.
Gestryn Narl, aka "Sweet Ges" – A young lord of Prav.
Enkita Vulkuu – Lady of Twilight Cape and matriarch of the hunters.
Velvet – A prisoner at Deephollow Prison.
The Dread Knight – Leader of the Knights of the Wolf Banner.

Barodane Ironlight, aka "Kord/Mal" – Former Crown Prince of Namarr.
Garlenna Renwood, aka "Ren of Fairfield" – Prosort of the Sempyrium.
Scab – A once-dead warhorse.
Pyr Syat, aka "The White Flame" – First Sword of the Kanian Remnant.
Barodane's former combat instructor.
Wolst, aka "The Beast of Anjuhkar" – Warmaster of Anjuhkar.
Malath Ironlight – Barodane's older brother. A prince.
Kordin Ironlight – Father to Malath and Barodane. A Crown prince.
Omari D'Alzir – Younger sister of Marus and Malus D'Alzir. Once betrothed
to Barodane. Whereabouts unknown.
Kaitos Barabi – Former Knight of the Crown.
Wynna Marwen – Lady of Halaleh.
Mag Marwen – Nailmaker lord of Halaleh.
"Black Blood" Vanavel – A half-Scoth drug dealer.
Horse – A hardened criminal.
Tohar – A former priest of the Sempyrium.
Merique Inari – Former Kanian Remnant turned chainman.
Nserthes the Sophophant – Former prosort to Kordin Ironlight. Defacto lord
of Martyr's Isle. Head of the Initiates of the Obsidian Hand.
Saieed – An Initiate of the Obsidian Hand.
Amoni'Alu – An initiate of the Obsidian Hand.
Bellator Gova – Valatian professor at the Academies turned bounty hunter.
Las Furio – Valatian marksman and assassin.

Gyr Renwood – Prosort of the Sempyrium. Personal counsel/protector to Duke Malus D'Alzir.

Sir Raius – Knight-captain of Brighthaven.

Sir Qel – A knight of Brighthaven.

Tabboz, aka "Mighty Boz" – Awakened in the employment of Duke Malus. Supernatural strength.

Malus D'Alzir – Duke of Lah-Tsarra.

Kaltes Kasjeri – Spy and captain of the pirate ship, *Anthera's Revenge*.

Caltheo – Gyr's cupbearer and successor.

Halladorn – Houndmaster of Brighthaven.

Velal – Duke Malus's servant.

Fullor – A bandit from Kiyahd.

Durn, aka "The Hard Heart" – A bandit from Kiyahd.

Bubinga – A Kurgish warrior.

Yashuu – A Kurgish princess.

Ikarai Valka – General of the Scothean legions.

Yanos – A Grimshield captain in Valka's honor guard.

Essuhd – Master of the Shadii.

Rhul Guhlkov, aka "The Red" – Raeklord of the Scothean cavalry. Descendant of the Red Count, Ravin Guhlkov.

Gravequeen – Rhul's monstrous mount. The jewel of the Scothean military.

Siddaia, aka "The Arrow of Light" – A child prophet.

Gishek Ghuul – A former Baron of Stormwal. Now, an Awakened in Siddaia's Blessed Cadre. Manipulates earthen elements.

Daimos – A footless cat burglar from Valat. Now, an Awakened in Siddaia's Blessed Cadre. Manipulates the air.

Zantheppi - A Malzacy-born caravan guide. Now, an Awakened in Siddaia's Blessed Cadre. Manipulates water.

Warro Herd, aka "The Void," aka "The Black Hand Marionette" – A mercenary and Namorite Awakened, turned member of Siddaia's Blessed Cadre. Generates deadly vortexes.

Nera – Ikarai Valka's daughter.

Rathon – A Scothean king.

Paranthese – A Grimshield captain.

Thephos of Carthane – A former pig farmer, now Awakened.

Syn Backlegarm – Proprietor of the Numbers gambling den. Manipulates the mind.

Ash Backlegarm – A swordswoman.

Pintarian – A Dominarri bladesworn.

Pintarith – The Holy Sword of the Dominarri's Skyfire Council.

N'Zara – The Holy Flame of the Dominarri's Skyfire Council. Manipulates the mind.

Shadowfox – A Ruptured poet also known as the Wordfox. Travels through shadows.

Zadani Innan – A master cook and head of Marus D'Alzir's kitchen. Married to Hadir.

Hadir Innan – A hunter in the employment of the banker lord of Kiyahd,

Marus D'Alzir.

Jasso Jackolo – The smartest man alive. Philosopher, professor, and unrepentant hedonist from Valat.

Marus D'Alzir – The banker lord of Kiyahd.

Rizel D'Alzir – Lady of Kiyahd.

Daran D'Alzir – A young lady of Kiyahd.

Genjin Hyrix, aka "Bloodrot" – An Awakened in service to the D'Alzir family.

Nymon the Lech – A former mercenary in the employment of Marus D'Alzir.

Vallabathus – Malzacy-born knight-captain of Kiyahd.

Thruna – A foul-mouthed crone on Zadani's kitchen staff.

Elmarie – An innocent maiden on Zadani's kitchen staff.

Akaitys, aka "Lightfoot," aka "The Dancing Knight" – A knight of Kiyahd.

DANATH'S SHADOW

NORTHEASTERN NAMARR – YEAR 64

P eople misunderstood.

A battle didn't end when bloody mouths stretched with shouts of triumph. Nor did it end when the enemy was rounded up in shackles, or when the ink of surrender dried and the gore had washed away. For those willing to fight them, battles never ended. They persisted, one haunting dream to the next, a tensed muscle waiting to be loosed in the interval between.

Over a decade had come and gone between the Great Betrayal and the battle for Jarik, but for a soldier like Huun Korpa, the fight raged on. The images were carved into his mind, stained red and brown and corpulent black.

When swords stopped singing, when blood stopped flowing, that was the moment the worries set in. Today, Huun Korpa lived, and to the living went the burden of keeping it that way.

"Those pavilions needed to be up yesterday," he rasped.

A nearby soldier saluted. "Yes, Captain." He pivoted and turned to go but hesitated. "Congratulations on the victory."

Huun Korpa gave the hint of a shrug. "Save your sentiments for the wounded."

The soldier departed and set to barking orders at clusters of men maneuvering poles into position. Hammers clanged as they drove spikes into the hard-packed earth of Jarik's bailey. Canvas snapped taut, ropes gripped by faithful Scarborn who hauled them into place. In short order, they'd have a ward erected for the wounded.

Huun Korpa swung around. A soldier was helping another past, his brother-in-arms sporting a gaping wound in his side. "Captain," they said, the voice of the latter hoarse and weak. Huun Korpa touched his shoulder. "Heal quick, soldier."

In the distance, the last of the storm bears were being put down. The beasts roared at the deluge of arrows and then moaned at their dying. Huun empathized with any creature forced to die in chains.

The hunters of Twilight Cape had been formidable foes. *Bloody work, but necessary.*

A spasm of pain originated at Huun's hip and shot up his back, lodging behind his shoulder blade where one of Bloodhorn's dagger-sized fangs had scraped him. He sucked in a breath but otherwise ignored the sensation. He wouldn't honor the dead raek by thinking of it. *Rest cold and comfortless, you wretch.*

A blood-slathered Golthius Narl plodded toward him, a gluttonous ape with a gut for gold. The knights and holdguard of Prav trailing him weren't breathing half as hard as their lord but it didn't stop him from speaking in a rush. "Took them down, eh, Korpa! Just like Lodecka said would happen. Took the whoresons down!"

The Scarborn captain nodded.

The lord of Prav laughed and jammed the butt of his long-handled mace into the mud, crushing a winter blossom. "Now where's that bitch, Belara Frost?" Golthius Narl peered over Huun's shoulder.

"My men took her into custody."

Golthius drummed fingers on the immense iron ball of his weapon. Blood rolled down its smooth surface and into the engraving of a slavering mouth. "Lodecka said she's mine to execute. I want to see her." He hooked a thumb in his belt and pulled downward, presumably providing more room for his blubbery paunch. "Right now."

Huun scratched at the patch of scars along his neck where Bloodhorn's bite had peeled the flesh off in a ragged strip. If the raek had gotten hold of Golthius Narl, the captain imagined few feasts would have been more filling.

Narl's pudding cheek oozed around a half-smile. "One thing Syphion Muul and I shared was a lack of patience. Listen to your betters, Captain. Bring me Belara or go get your master so I can remind her of our deal. Whichever you decide, do it quickly."

"Haven't you heard?" Huun Korpa's gaze wandered to the hard-eyed men with slavering mouths stitched onto their tabards who clustered behind their lord. To the ash-darkened sky snuffing out the clear blue. To his Scarborn brothers and sisters rushing prisoners to their cells beneath the Ice Maiden's Keep. "Don't you see it, Narl?" A croak of laughter escaped him. "The Scarborn have no masters. No betters. Not anymore." He let his misty gaze settle on the baker lord. "You were never one of them, anyway. Count yourself lucky to be alive and pray Lodecka still has use for you."

"Scarborn fucking scum!" The handle of Golthius's mace slapped into his palms, its smooth head of steel glinting in the fading sunlight. "My son lies wounded. Might be he'll die for your cause, and you dare threaten me?"

Silence settled around Huun. The hold lord's retinue held their breath, preparing to fight, and the bustle of activity surrounding the altercation slowed to a standstill. Scores of Scarborn watched the exchange, tendons jumping along jawlines. Hands closed around weapon hilts in quiet readiness.

We are unified, you simpering glut. It matters not who you are nor what you were. We have risen.

Throat apples bobbing, the Narl's men seemed to notice the burgeoning threat on every side. Golthius gulped and lowered his mace, unmanned by the wolves now corralling his sheep.

Now that it was clear who was in charge, Huun's cheek twitched, the closest thing to a smile he could muster with his ruined face. "You're soft, Narl. Softer than a loaf of bread fresh from your own damn ovens. You have no fucking clue what power is." A dagger whispered from the sheath at Huun's hip. He closed the distance to Golthius Narl in three hobbling steps and brought the point of his dagger to rest against the glutton's belly. "You think your men are loyal because you're some great leader?" He grunted, a gob of loosened spit sliding down his throat like steel wool. "You think they'd die for you if you weren't paying them? They wouldn't. They follow you because you were the fattest fish in their tiny pond. Now they see the truth. They see the sharks circling, and know their lord is little better than chum."

From waist to double chin, Huun Korpa traced the knife tip over Narl, its edge brushing against the hold lord's neck stubble and emitting a light rustle from the friction. Then the captain replaced his dagger in its sheath.

To his credit, Golthius didn't balk. The lord of Prav and Deephollow Prison was a notoriously hard-handed ruler. The Narls were no strangers to threat and intimidation. Size and aggression were the law of their land. "So I'm to take my orders from you now, is that what you're saying?" The oaf grunted. "Where's Lodecka? Blood for blood, that was the deal. I pledged my men to Revocation in exchange for Belara Frost's head. You think I'll be cowed by some salty speech from a stitched-together mercenary?"

Huun Korpa studied the fat man. People misunderstood—the rich most of all. They saw reality through the mirror of their own desires, oblivious to the rest of the world holding rocks and waiting for the right moment to equal the playing field.

For men like Huun, acts of bloodshed were a way of life. Not a thing done once or twice. An entire life lived with mud sucking at the ankles and shackles hanging from the wrists. "No. You're not easily cowed. Not when you think my threats empty. You require...more." He flashed a look at Golthius Narl's gut. "Stay here. I'll bring you blood."

The lord of Prav twisted in either direction, a smug look on his face. His soldiers chuckled as if he'd put the Scarborn captain in his place. They'd seen Golthius win dozens of contests of will, no doubt. The fat man postured well enough.

Unfortunate for him, Huun Korpa did not deal in empty threats.

He sent the soldiers closest to him off with a whispered order.

A few moments later, a scream, more panicked than the others coming from the freshly erected medical ward, cut the air. Sweet Ges was dragged from within, dangling between a pair of Scarborn who handled him roughly. Lips of flesh swelled around a gash in his side. Lazy spurts of blood splashed down his thighs. A Sister gave chase but was turned back—clearly she'd been tending to the boy when the captain's mercenaries had jerked him from his cot and stripped his dressings.

The boy moaned, his knees skirting up snow with every bobbing heave of the Scarborn lugging him along.

Huun Korpa turned back to the lord of Prav and the nearby Scarborn encircling them. Golthius Narl's breath had quickened. His brow hardened into bricks with a thin gap between.

Captain Korpa patted Sweet Ges's sweat-drenched, lolling head. "You're soft, Narl. Lodecka sacrificed her only son for our cause. As soon as Frost livery touched his skin—as soon as he took hospitality from Ishoa Ironlight and her family—his fate was sealed." He growled the last bit. Lodaris needn't have died. He could have been saved and should have been. Huun had tried to convince Lodecka that the boy would grow into the cause over time. That the moment the princess Ishoa was pledged for marriage, he'd come to his senses. Ularis, too, had jockeyed for compassion but Lodecka was unrelenting. "I loved that boy like he was my own. But Scarborn brook no softness. Whether we like it or not, we cut the fat away. Our lives depend on it. That's where we differ, Narl. For you, this was an opportunity. For us, it was birth. Our lives...finally ours."

Korpa's hand balled into a fist, tangles of Sweet Ges's black hair poking between clenched fingers. "If you think us unwilling to cull our own for weakness, you're mistaken." He jerked back, angling the boy's face at his father. Piggish eyes rolled upward toward a single, unbroken monobrow. Huun kicked Gestryn's wound. The boy yowled and writhed in the Scarborn captain's grasp. Sweat ran down the sides of his face as he whimpered, lips trying to form words—a guppy gulping for air.

Golthius Narl cursed. "Honorless, shit-mucking coward!"

"Honor did not give us Jarik." He threw another kick at Gestryn's side, his knee clicking with the effort. "Neither will it spare your son's life. Loyalty,

Golthius." Sweet Ges's tear-brimmed eyes rolled back in his skull—he passed out. "Loyalty gives us everything."

Huun could trace his bloodline back to a tribe from the deep north, to a time before the reign of Ice Kings in Anjuhkar, to a strong people—a fearless people—far surpassing the worthiness of the entitled louse before him.

The lord of Prav blustered, hissed a curse, then dropped to his knees. "This! Is this what you want?" His mace thudded into the frozen mud beside him as he bowed his head, arms thrown out wide.

Huun Korpa hobbled back a step, hooking thumbs through belt loops. "Yes." Every part of him itched. Any time his blood started flowing, his skin tingled with the memory of being gnawed on, and his lungs set to wheezing.

He nodded to the men of Prav who stared at their lord groveling in the mud. "Remember it, boys. Soft as the mud he's kissing. If we're to win back the rest of Anjuhkar, we'll need hard men." He thrust his chin at the unconscious Gestryn and motioned for his soldiers to put him back with the other wounded. "Today was just the beginning. More battles await. No room for weakness if we're to win. You can be at our side to see it..." He turned away. "Or under our feet."

He left Golthius on filth-caked knees and went to find Lodecka Warnock.

Lodecka watched the Sister of the Rose carry a white-hot iron from the coals, a streamer of smoke wafting an acrid scent throughout the room. Eyes squeezed shut, Ularis moaned on the upraised palette, his knees alternating bending and straightening from the agony. A handful of Lodecka's men held him down.

"Wait." Lodecka hovered over the bedraggled sister, bearing down on her with an iron gaze. "You already lost my son."

The implication was understood, evidenced in the sister's throat as she swallowed back fear. Lodecka had made sure every servant left alive in Jarik saw the examples in the bailey: bodies mounted on wooden stakes along the battlements, planks nailed to their chests with the word "dog" inscribed in ash.

Hours. Hours had changed the course of the future. Bloody hours that saw the Scarborn's kotarg restored.

"The shock may kill him," the sister said. A pathetic attempt to excuse herself if things went poorly.

"He is Scarborn," Lodecka said with finality. The healer's lack of understanding of what those words truly meant wasn't her fault. The woman's flesh looked infused with coffee—a Lah-Tsarene, most likely. A different, yet greedier, flavor of dog. Since the dawn of Namarr, when Danath and Malzai had joined forces,

Ironlights had always favored the D'Alzirs of the northwest. And comfort made ignorance for those under its spell.

The sister couldn't know what it was to be Scarborn. She'd been born free. But the ones splattered in blood and holding down Ularis knew. The ones who'd slashed and stabbed and slaughtered their way to freedom. The ones who'd ignored the spilled guts and gurgling cries of their brothers and sisters in the mud so they could keep fighting. To the Scarborn, pain was fuel. Wounds were honor and pride. Death, for the success of the whole, a welcome end if it meant a new beginning.

To be Scarborn was to be *one*.

That, the healer could never understand.

The sister nodded to Lodecka and then swiveled back to the oozing stub of Ularis's hand. He was lucky. If the Beast had aimed any higher and struck off part of his wrist, he would have severed an artery. No chance of survival. Lodecka admitted her husband was unlikely to be the type to absorb a wound so grievous. His enfeebled blood had been the poison that condemned their son.

Lodaris was dead, Lodecka reminded herself. She searched for the grief she thought she should feel. The hurt in the void of love lost. When she failed to find it, she thought perhaps guilt might follow, but she hadn't known that feeling since her father had let one of the Keeler's knights rape her mother in front of her.

She shrugged a shoulder. There had been three of them, all armed. Her father, a simple dockworker bending keels in the cold wasteland of the Fringes. A powerless man.

No. Lodaris was dead because it had to happen. All things were fate resting in Lodecka's palm. She had but to pull it closer and accept what it brought.

Heat shimmered above the glowing iron in the sister's hand, splashing Ularis's face with gold. She could do without the show of weakness. Now more than ever, her Scarborn needed to see strength in their leaders. Taking Jarik by force was a mad gambit wrought by Syphion's pride but keeping it would require political finesse in addition to a steel-clad strategy. If gossip arose among her mercenaries about the womanish sounds Ularis made in the midst of surgery, it could present a fatal chink in their armor.

Iron met flesh in a sizzling chorus. Ularis's eyes flew open. He loosed a hissing scream before his head dropped back and he went unconscious. "It's done," the sister said.

The soldiers released his arms and legs and stood at attention. Lodecka inclined her head at one of them. "Watch over the healer as she cares for him day and night. Sleep in the corner when you must. Your food will be delivered."

Before these men ever returned to the ranks, Ularis needed to be healed and strong once more. She didn't fear sedition. A lack of belief, however, could rot them at the roots. That, she could not allow.

"You two are my emissaries now. Dragga Omenfaen flees to the Crucible at Summerforge, and Rigga Hine will gather strength at White Plains for a counterstrike. You will go to them bearing a message. Speak to no others."

If either of them felt a certain way about their unfair duties, they did not show it. One asked for the message as the sister dressed Ularis's steaming wound.

In turn, Lodecka met each of their flat stares. "Death to tyrants." One shifted his weight from foot to foot. "Study their inner circles and pick your targets wisely. Wait for the right time. You'll only get one chance."

Boots slapped together as they saluted. "It would be an honor to bring you Dragga Omenfaen's half-eaten heart," said one with a rust-dusted beard.

Lodecka put little stock in the man's lofty declaration. She'd seen first-hand how hard it was to kill the man-boy of Summerforge. For any but her, maybe impossible. But her mercenary's bluster did warm her. To seize control of all Anjuhkar, she needed her soldiers to have a lion's hunger and a fool's hope.

"I expect no less from the rest of you. You're killers of a different make. Scarborn royalty will sing of your exploits for decades to come. Dismissed."

The two assassins saluted and left the infirmary.

Lodecka nodded to the soldier she'd tasked with guarding Ularis. "If the sister gets out of line, you have my permission to take her in whatever way you wish without punishment."

The sister's lip quivered, and she shot a terrified glance at the hard-faced man in the dimly lit corner.

"He won't hurt you unless he's given a reason," Lodecka said. "See that he doesn't." A square of light stretched across the room as she threw open the door of the infirmary. Cold winds had picked up—as they often did at dusk—carrying the stink of the dead. The smell would get worse when they set fire to the corpse byres. In a month, the winter snows would come, heavier than those of autumn. Come to lay a pristine blanket over Jarik's stained earth.

"You can't." The sister's voice was hoarse.

Lodecka stayed facing forward. "You are my enemy. I must." The sister started to sob. "You don't wish to be my enemy? Is that it?" She eased the door closed and turned around. The sister had drawn herself up, hunting deep within for courage. Lodecka liked that. The woman had a little steel in her spine. It took a great deal to stand up to a Scarborn of Lodecka's make. She thought of Ishoa Ironlight and the way she'd spat at her and insulted her and drew her blade with the intent to fight. In that way, this sister reminded her of the Ironlight whelp.

While Lodecka's respect for the former princess waxed at the thought of her, so too did her frustration. Her soldiers still hadn't found the girl.

The sister lifted her chin, defiant. "High Mother Tanghelka will not tolerate—"

Lodecka snatched a knife from the sister's surgical table and whisked the blade past her face. Stricken, the woman stumbled back, a hand shaking over her cheek as she knocked into the pallet holding Ularis. He moaned, head twisting side-to-side.

A drop of blood beaded along a cut on the sister's cheek. A second later, more welled and then it was dripping from her chin. The sister smudged the blood with a fingertip, drew it back. Bright crimson rather than a darker shade. A shallow cut. The woman's shoulders drooped with the realization that she hadn't been killed.

Lodecka smiled. "Haven't you heard, sister? United Namarr is no more. That means your High Mother Tanghelka holds as much sway as a stalk of wheat." The Scarborn leader placed the knife back on the surgical table. For Lodecka Warnock, the object was as sacred as the scars it left. "If you don't wish to be my enemy, then I must make a Scarborn of you. Consider this your baptism into the fold."

The sister took up a cloth to press against her wound.

Lodecka surged forward, grabbing her wrist and yanking it down to her side. "We wear our wounds with pride, sister." The woman shied away. She stank of sweat and smoke and hints of winter blossom. Lodecka released her wrist. "My older brother died when the Jurati came to exact their sentence in flesh. He succumbed to festering. 'A better fate than most,' my father had often proclaimed in later years when my mother would weep for her stolen son. I always thought it an empty sentiment when a Sister of the Rose could have easily saved him." Lodecka brushed the woman's cheek, smearing it scarlet. She stepped back. "You're one of us now. Wear it with pride."

Face frozen over a shoulder, the woman's eyes were pinched shut. "I'm a Sister of the Rose. We serve all in need but I—I don't want to be Scarborn."

Lodecka looked at the man in the corner who watched, unmoving. "It's never been a choice."

Beyond the infirmary, the sun was setting.

Captain Korpa stood a dozen paces from the door. "The others await you," he rasped and fell in behind her.

Veils of gossamer ash filled the bailey as she ascended the ramp to the High Hall. *Her* High Hall, she reminded herself. There, her allies congregated, standing on the stains of yesterday's tyrants.

An odd sensation struck her as she entered, the door's hinges groaning. A thought she would have never predicted. A sense of kinship unique to those few who managed to change the course of history. She felt, perhaps, the same as Danath had the night he'd given his famous speech at the Uron Grove before the end of Scothea's reign.

PART ONE

Ishoa Ironlight, Thephos of Carthane, Ikarai Valka, Zadani Innan, Gyr Renwood, Barodane Ironlight

Three makes one and one makes three. In the shadow of great power will come the end of things unseen.

First the Eye, bringing evil into the light. Then the Hand, ridding the world of its plight. Last the Fire, that in darkest hours unite.

Three makes one, but only one makes free.

– Prophecy of the Long Silence

Chapter One

TREACHERY

Scothea, Year 595 AR - After the Rains

A t least a score lay dead.

Blood pooled beneath them, a half hour old at most. Tabards once white and gold and proudly worn, were now soaked a deep scarlet. Vacant eyes wreathed in serpent tattoos fixed on Ikarai Valka as he approached. Axes lay out of reach of limp fingers. Shields embossed with suns and falling comets were deeply scored. Horned helms and broken bits of chain littered the ground.

A sudden wet sputter.

The men behind Valka hefted their weapons. Shouts of alarm had drawn them to the archway leading into the interior of Darkfall's keep. Prior to that, Valka had been on course for an audience with King Rathon in the Holy Chamber.

Now, he crouched over a man propped against a brass serpent statue. Entrails snarled his fingers in his lap and fresh blood leaked from his slack mouth. Valka watched the man another moment as he died, then lifted a slab of armor from the chest of a twisted corpse beside him. There was a long rent through its center. "Darksteel breastplates...cleaved by darksteel blades."

He let it drop with a clatter.

Warm wind carried crescents of dust over the sky-terrace from the surrounding cliffs, forcing him to squint. "It's the boy. The false messiah." Valka stood, quick despite his age, like a bow bent then released. "He's here."

Captain Yanos stepped close, speaking in hushed tones. "General, these were Grimshields."

Valka knew the meaning of the worry in Yanos's tone. It was a fear they all shared. A single question slithering through every mind. The answer threatened to stick in Valka's throat but he spat it out all the same. "We are betrayed." For bloodshed to penetrate so far into Darkfall's keep before the outer defenses had been alerted could only mean one thing: there were traitors in their midst. A good many of them. *High-ranking traitors.*

Wind slammed the sky-terrace, inserted among the cliffs like a fungal disc growing from a tree. Valka turned to address the fourteen soldiers awaiting orders, their faces dour masks. The furl and snap of their cloaks was the only sound; the lean of their greased mohawks from angry gusts of wind, the only movement.

He nodded to Yanos. "Take three of your men and get a message to my daughter, Nera. Tell her to take the gilded box from my wardrobe and go to—"

Shouts and the clash of arms echoed from a nearby hall then dissipated once it met the open air. Yanos slid into position beside Valka with expert poise, ax upraised.

No time. I must trust my household guard with Nera's safety. "Strike that. We make for the Holy Chamber." He dispatched two men down the outer stair to the raek burrows to find Lord Rhul. "Tell him we gather strength around King Rathon."

A pair of soldiers departed. Yanos wrung the haft of his ax as he turned back to Valka, eyes darting toward the broken bodies all around them. "We are still with you, General."

Still with me?

Never before had Valka needed to worry about his men's loyalty. Nothing in his life had ever been more ironclad. The weight of implication buckled his knees. He followed Yanos's gaze, sweeping the terrace littered with dead Scoths. He'd trained the men who'd been killed, and he'd trained those who had done the killing. If not for the evidence at his feet, it would have been incomprehensible to imagine that the boy-turned-messiah could override the decades of psychological indoctrination it took to be one of the revered Grimshields.

I underestimated the boy. We all did. He poisons every ear that hears him.

Anger simmered in Valka's chest. Just like the children starving in the lower terraces or the elderly succumbing to plague out on the plains, Valka laid blame at King Rathon's feet. But his allegiance to his country didn't allow room for disobedience. To turn his ax against his own was unthinkable.

While Rathon's weakness had turned a mild famine into a widespread disaster, it was the fault of a devastatingly hot summer as much as the king's. But with the false messiah pointing a finger, the rage of the masses had found their villain.

Valka surveyed the dead one last time. The men who'd done this had younger brothers and sisters bloating in the streets; mothers weeping over their children as they decided which one they should feed; fathers forsaking their faith to join raiders in attacking farms on the open plains. Many, it seemed, had found the boy's cult.

Atrocities motivated by circumstance make an afterthought of morality. There was the truth of it. Family was the first loyalty. Only a hardened few could elevate allegiance to their country above that of family. *Oath before ethic. Fealty before family. Death before betrayal.* Valka recalled that part of his pledge at the feet of Acramis II before the Second Invasion of Namarr but it was quickly replaced by thoughts of Nera.

He prayed that his duties wouldn't conflict with keeping her safe. His heart raced.

Nera above all. The anger for those who would betray one love for another was leached away as understanding settled in his bones. He found it hard to condemn the lowly in light of their plight.

"General," said Yanos.

In battle, seconds were more precious to survival than air. Valka could tell Yanos thought his commander wasted them now. Doubt rose cold at the nape. *Nera will be okay.* He exhaled. *I'm still the general of Scothea.*

He gave the reins over to the part of him that was trained to snatch victory from chaos.

"To the Door of Khaldis." He drew Mournfang from a belt loop. A gilded, steel raek coiled around the grip; its head and fangs formed a counterweight at the back of the battle ax while its six-inch horn served as a spike. The legendary weapon hummed and gave off a wave of simmering heat. "We protect King Rathon at all costs."

They made their way at a jog along the sky-terrace. A handful of scouts sprinted ahead, each one leapfrogging past the next at three second intervals. There was a honeycomb of archways peppering the cliffside terraces. At every one, Valka's troop slowed until a scout waved them onward.

Three entrances came and went. At the fourth, a scout paused. Valka's guts twisted up worse than a nest of mating vipers. The seconds dripped by. A half minute later, Valka touched Yanos's pauldron and motioned for him to see what transpired.

The captain crept forward, silent as a ghost, conferred with the scout, then returned.

"He sees the backs of Grimshields in diamond formation—they're under attack. He can't make out the enemy."

The last was reported with a hint of hope that it might not be their own fighting them. Valka knew better. "How many of ours?"

"Ten in reserve. A score in the thick."

Valka stared at the archway. Other forces were making their way to the Door of Khaldis. If he were the messiah, he would purge the interior palace while the element of surprise was strongest before assailing the king. The dead Grimshields at the first archway had been taken unaware, which meant friends had turned to foes in a blink.

It's a race to King Rathon now.

He considered the men fighting in the hall ahead. A rear rank of ten in diamond formation meant the Grimshields were at least twenty strong. The fact that they were on the defensive meant they faced a larger force. *How much larger?* If his unit joined forces with those in the corridor, they could make a push, slay the traitors, and make their way to the Door of Khaldis with more men.

Valka cursed. Without knowing the enemy's numbers, it was too great a risk. "They will hold. We proceed." A sour taste filled his mouth. In all likelihood, they would fight to the last man. *And to the last man, they will die.*

Yanos nodded.

The sky-terrace bent around Darkfall's Keep. Empty space and pressing winds harried them as they ran at an even pace. Valka's lungs ached, his breath becoming ragged as they went. The rigors of time had humbled him, reducing his physical abilities to that of a sophomore recruit. He fidgeted with Mourn-fang, questioning if its legendary bite would help him survive the day. Fourteen years had passed since he'd seen live combat during the Second Crusade, and though he still sparred like all soldiers in Scothea's army, he did so infrequently. Age and higher priorities had devoured his abilities. What seemed a lifetime ago, when he was a captain, he could have crossed axes with any of his shock troops and bested them. With the exception of maybe Yanos.

Valka glanced at the man hustling along beside him. When it came to violence—and it would—he hoped his captain's ax and those of the men trailing them would be enough.

If the men sent to fetch Lord Rhul succeed, our chances of victory will drastically increase. Rhul the Red and his Gravequeen were worth fifty Grimshields. Possibly more.

A chill ran up Valka's spine as he recalled seeing the pair in action a year prior.

Raeklord Rhul had invited King Rathon and Valka to the raek burrows to discuss hatching issues. An alarming number of defective stock had been yielded, all incapable of one day bearing riders. "It's the food stores," Rhul had claimed. "Pestilent cattle feeding on impure grain."

"Nonsense," said Rathon. "My agriculturist assures me he provides what is needed." Rhul knew as well as Valka that the agriculturist the king referenced was a cousin who'd been appointed to the position for aggrandizing Rathon's accomplishments.

"My King," Rhul said. "It is not as you say."

Rathon sneered, twisted toward Valka for some validation that wasn't forthcoming. When none came, he laughed and spoke in mocking tones. "So you're an expert in farming now, is it? Rhul the Red..." Rathon spat. "They say you are fearless, that you charged a column of the White Flame's knights alone with your Gravequeen and sent them into retreat during the Second Crusade. Yet you fear a little moldy grain."

"I would do anything for my country." Rhul had narrowed deep-set blue eyes at Rathon. "In that pursuit, my fears come last."

Rathon purpled. "You dare push your king!" A short man with a wide constitution, he planted thick fists on his hips. His voice fell low. "For that insult, I call on you to prove yourself."

"Your Grace," Valka started. "The raek cavalry are the backbone of our army. It may be wiser to—"

"He's going to prove his prowess right now!" Rathon rounded to a cadre of servants who cowered under his ire. He gave them orders to fetch his new toy, which turned out to be a decrepit cave bear he'd purchased from a circus. "Merit. Our kingdom lacks it. *That* is why our raeks wither. The man tasked with their care has lost his touch." Rathon rubbed his palms together. "I propose a wager. Wrestle my bear to its back and I'll give a tenth of my personal food stores to your hatching mothers."

"I accept." Rhul hoisted his famously jutting chin into the air.

"Fool!" said Rathon. "I've not told you what you stand to lose. If you're injured or killed, or you fail to put the bear on its back, your Gravequeen will forfeit her meals to the hatching mothers for a month. And you, Lord Rhul, will resign."

Valka stepped into the space between Rathon and Rhul, attempting to disrupt the conflict. "Your Grace, the Gravequeen is our army's greatest asset. To gamble her health, or lord Rhul's in such a way, is folly."

"Quiet now, Ikarai." A self-satisfied grin split his broad face as he waved away Valka's worries. "Lord Rhul is the strongest of the strong! The mightiest warrior in Scothea! Have some faith." The king snickered. "It's only a bear. But I'll give our raeklord some wiggle room here. If he doesn't wish to take the wager, he can come down from those high heavens where his pride lies and grovel to me instead. I've seen plenty of strong men fold under pressure when—"

Rhul's tidal frame moved past them, encased in seven feet of darksteel from neck to heel, and took up position opposite the bear. The dusty floor formed a haze around his ankles in the dimly lit caverns at the heart of Darkfall's keep.

His golden cape piled onto the ground behind him as he lowered into a crouch. "Release it," he said to the animal-tamers. The four of them glanced at one another, then withdrew the long poles hooking its manacles and spiked training collar.

The bear roared at its freedom and then lumbered toward an exit but the raeklord circled to cut off its escape. The bear swiped at the man and huffed. Valka had seen bigger bears but it still outweighed its human opponent by double. Despite the immensity of the wager, Rhul appeared calm as he barred the beast from leaving and waited for it to close with him. It rose onto two legs and roared—the moment Rhul had been waiting for, Valka realized.

The raeklord shot forward and clasped his hands around the bear's haunches, dust swirling. The creature gave a startled whine as Rhul hoisted it into the air with a grunt of his own. It twisted in his grasp and bit an armored shoulder. Fighting for purchase against the man raising it aloft, it clawed at the chain covering his back. Sparks spit into the dim.

With a dip of his hips, Rhul heaved upward then slammed the bear onto its spine on an upthrust stone. There was a sickening crunch. Rhul rolled away, glanced at the injured creature, then disappeared into the pitch black stables at the back of the cavern.

Rathon gaped at the cave bear writhing in the dust, useless legs flopping back and forth as it struggled to leverage its upper body to rise.

There came an echoing hiss. The bear thrashed harder, efforts rendered futile by its injury. In dawning horror, Valka watched the Gravequeen materialize from the shadowed stables, Rhul wordlessly directing her. The colossal war snake loomed over the bear, midnight orbs assessing its broken prey.

The Gravequeen struck. Fangs the size of short swords pinned the cave-bear's torso between its jaws. Three more bites in rapid succession and the bear lay motionless. The entire time the Gravequeen worked her mouth around her meal, Rhul the Red watched his king impassively. A normal raek would be incapable of ingesting something so large, but like her rider, she was anything but normal.

If Rhul can get here in time, we could hold the Holy Chamber for months.

Valka returned to the moment at hand. He wiped sweat from his brow and hot air filled his lungs. A dull ache emanated in his legs under the weight of his armor. The oldest among the unit by a decade, he refused to call for a stop. *Just a little farther.*

A pair of bridges came into view, spanning the distance between Darkfall's keep and the Holy Chamber. Cliffs disappeared to either side of the great square structure sitting on a pedestal of naked rock in a sea of cerulean sky. The

Door of Khaldis, a foot thick and banded with iron, was sealed. *If King Rathon is within the Holy Chamber, he's safe.*

The terrace curved around the keep and terminated at the bridges. Valka brought his men to a slower pace in case another force lay in ambush. None came. Nevertheless, two scouts were dispatched to the other end of the bridge while they waited.

A pang of sadness assailed him. *Will I ever see Nera again?* Outside of his service to his country, she was the most important thing in his life. In part, she gave him the necessary impetus to fulfill his duties, for there was little point in protecting Scothea if the only good he'd ushered into the world was gone.

I have to get to her. Even now, men of his once loyal legion could be raiding his home. Hurting her. Binding her. Preparing to use her as leverage. *Or worse.*

He grit his teeth, suffocating the dire ruminations. Such vagabond sentiments were the death of strategic clarity. He needed his wits. Already, he'd been woefully outmaneuvered. *Rathon's head could be on a spike within the Holy Chamber. Maybe we've already lost.*

His mind sifted through the list of potential traitors. The kings of Scothea had rarely faced challengers to their rule. It wasn't like Malzacor, where Imperial Lights cut the throats of their cousins or siblings every decade or so. But Valka was a historian of some acumen and Scothea didn't stand outside of history. Where one held power, another most certainly coveted it.

What fanaticism could sweep my ranks without my knowledge of its magnitude? Pockets here and there, yes, but those had been dealt with harshly and without delay. Valka still heard the eerie quiet murmurings of those soldiers charged with heresy. He'd expected screaming when they were stripped naked, slathered in goat fat, and then chained to a post. Criminals condemned to the same blubbered and wet themselves. Not the boy's cultists. At least, they should have wailed or gone white with fear when the raeks descended for the feast. But the only sense of dread throughout the process of such executions had been the one that gripped the living, that silent, widening pit at the backs of their minds after witnessing such a testament of devout fanaticism.

The common people, with little but their suffering to rely on, were easily culled into dangerous beliefs. Agents of the Shadii reported that none was better at this than the false messiah. The Arrow of Light, his followers called him. Loosed from the heavens to strike evil from the world. The Shadii suspected he was Awakened but it was never confirmed. Outwardly, he displayed no signs of power. Valka's knowledge of the messiah had waned since King Rathon had begun shouting down reports from the Shadii Master, Essuhd. He'd not wanted to hear of the boy unless he'd been dealt with.

News that never came.

His sermons swept the canyons. Then the plains. When the first royal farm was ransacked, the Shadii sent assassins to kill the boy. None returned. A month before today's treachery, Essuhd had warned of a possible uprising.

How could I know the boy's influence had spread so far, so fast?

It was the Shadii who were tasked with gathering intelligence, but Ikarai Valka was no slouch when it came to spying. He'd rooted out his share of heretics and fed them to the raeks. Outside of those rare instances, reports had claimed his legions were unmolested by the boy prophet's ravings.

Lies and more lies.

The scouts returned from across the bridge and signaled for safe passage. Valka led them across, stealing glances over the parapet as he went. Columns of smoke rose from the lower terraces, dark stains smudging the sky. Cries of battle bounced around the canyon—whether it came from within the keep or somewhere far below, he couldn't be sure. Scotheans, little more than spiky blots, moved through the streets like ants charging over spilled honey. It was unclear whether they were fighting against or celebrating an outcome Valka dreaded.

Perhaps Rhul has secured the keep and launched a counterstrike against the mobs.

The niggling intuition in Valka's gut that had served him more times than he could count said it was otherwise.

They came to a flight of marble stairs leading to the Door of Khaldis, a monstrous thing with a golden emblem at its center. A pair of raek statues faced outward on either side, their horned heads pointing at the rising sun. Only the Dawn Tower of Alistar had been built higher in the world, a point of frustration for all Scotheans ever since the Namorites had slain Count Ghulkov and taken it for their own.

"Hold here." Valka's men fanned out and took up a defensive position at the mouth of each bridge, facing back the way they'd come. He took a deep breath and hurried up the steps, heart hammering in his chest. The frightening image of one of his men burying an ax in his skull from behind sent cold tingles down his spine.

He crested the final step, then made for the Door of Khaldis.

A silk-smooth voice from behind froze him in place. "Sheathe your ax...that's a good general. Take one step back—now one to your right. Another. Turn around."

Valka complied without hesitation. To disobey would be death. A poisoned dart-sling, or thrown dagger, or Mimborean night powder—the Shadii used them all in the ways of the silent kill. None was more capable than the owner of the voice. Their master. "Greetings, Essuhd." He turned to lock eyes with the Shadii Master.

A moon-pale face hung in the shadows of one of the titanic raek statues. Placid eyes regarded him from a cleanly shaved skull.

"Your men cannot see you, nor can they save you if you shout." The Shadii Master spoke fast and pointedly. "If I so wish it, you will die before your next breath and I will be gone before you strike the stones."

CHAPTER TWO

HOPES DEFERRED

NORTHWEST NAMARR – YEAR 64

G yr Renwood ignored the soldiers at the back of the chapel, hoping they weren't there to interrupt his delivery of the rites.

But that hope quickly evaporated.

Sir Raius, knight-captain of Brighthaven, slid through the doors, making no sound, just another inky blot on the wall in a carousel of shadows cast by guttering candlelight. Sir Qel, a lanky knight with blond, slicked-back hair and a scraggly russet mustache, remained by the door.

Gyr's mind churned. Duke Malus wouldn't call on him during rites unless it was a matter of great importance.

Sir Raius swept past the benches filled with Followers, forest-green cloak trailing. The small man moved with a vigilant strut, hunched forward and swaying, one arm secreted away as if gripping a weapon out of sight.

"Followers of the Sempyrean, open your hearts in reflection and seek the wisdom of the gods," he intoned.

Before the gods, before himself, before even his own daughter, Gyr Renwood was a man sworn to duty. Every second of every day for the past thirty years, he'd served the banner of fist and chain snapping over Brighthaven's battlements as Duke Malus D'Alzir's prosort.

Without question or delay.

Of late, time weighed heavy across his shoulders, soaked and steeped his bones with age, bearing him to his knees. As a result, prayer had become easier—more sought after—but that was the only thing. Rarely did he expend energy without purpose or necessity. Trained in the ways of war by the Kanian Remnant, Gyr had once been very capable of defending Namarr with mace and shield. Weaker physically, but stronger in experience, he was now acutely aware that his value rested more so in the espionage taught to him by the Sempyrium.

Leave the fighting to Sir Raius.

Playing the priest had always come last. The closer to death he came, however, the more the sands of time shifted, and with them, his focus. *I'm worn like old leather. So very tired.*

Sir Raius gave him a dutiful nod. *Time to go.*

Lifting his arms, Gyr's voice was smooth, resonant. "Rise as one. Stand with the gods of light. Allow the dark one's waters to leak away without exception."

Followers—servants and their families, with a smattering of other important city officials and merchants who'd bought their way into the duke's private chapel—stood.

Gyr coughed, cleared his throat and attempted to speak again, but it ended in a violent bout of hacking. His cupbearer, Caltheo, stepped close and touched his back. "Water, Father?"

Gyr subdued his fit long enough to catch his breath. Sweat broke across his bald forehead, and the armpits of his priest's robes. He gripped Caltheo's shoulder and whispered into his ear. "Take over."

Concern knit Caltheo's brow as Gyr pressed the wooden icon of the Sempyrean into his hands: an onyx stone anchored the carving of arrows, denoting the dark god, Taker of Light, Scion of the Abyssal Sea, Lord of the Eternal Maw.

Stepping from the dais, Gyr reminded himself there were more ways to lead Followers from Nacronus's clutches than being a priest. In most cases, politics served a far more functional pathway to the Sempyrean's light. If Gyr was anything, he was pragmatic.

He coughed into a fist, opened his hand, then closed it. Blood glistened in his palm. He wiped his mouth, then hid the evidence of his ailment by wiping it on the inside pocket of his cassock. Showing vulnerability had never been his strong suit.

Gyr followed Sir Raius from the chapel.

He'd ditched his priest's cassock in favor of a doublet, trousers, and a leather jerkin. A ceremonial prosort's mace made of wood hung from a thick belt. Finding the banded oak door to the library locked, he knocked. Three sharp reports echoed down the stone hall.

A pair of iron braziers to either side of the door illuminated a familiar face as it opened.

Barely a head taller than the door's heavy ring-handle, Tabboz squinted at him. Eyes once golden were now clouded with cataracts, something she'd earned growing up under the merciless sun of North Malzacor. "Who is it?"

"Only me, Boz," Gyr said.

The Awakened woman stepped back from the door. She snorted. Shadows hid in every wrinkle of her red-brown skin where it wasn't covered in drab, grubby clothing.

Light washed over Gyr as he entered, blooms of candle wax dripping from iron stanchions at every table. As he passed Tabboz, a cloud of sour body odor punched him in the nose.

"Are you taking care of yourself?" he said. The grimy woman found little purpose in keeping herself clean or well kept. Despite Lord Malus's urgings, she made it into the bath less than a few times a year.

"What do you care, priest?" she muttered, words low and quick.

Gyr had always appreciated the old woman's candidness. Despite decades of serving the duke together, she had never warmed to him in the same way. "Never trust a priest" was all she ever said on the matter.

Lord Malus suspected her past had something to do with her withdrawn nature. Over the years, the duke had pieced together a theory on her origins. He placed her in the mountains of Northern Malzacor amongst a brutal patriarchal cult just before she had journeyed to Unturrus. As an adult, Tabboz's head came up to Gyr's chest, making her one of the smallest women he'd ever seen. As a child, he imagined, she would not have fared well in a male-dominated group of spiritual fanatics.

Little did it matter. It wasn't Boz's personality or her story Malus needed. It was her power.

Gyr smiled. "The Mighty Boz is a great asset to the Duke of Lah-Tsarra. It's my duty to ensure she remains healthy and strong."

Tabboz tensed. "Strong?" Cataracts gave way to a flash of jet black vapor. Ink spilled from her eyes, rose from her shoulders, clogging the space overhead.

Gyr's heart skipped as he watched her Locus stir to life. He stepped back, hand instinctively moving toward the ceremonial mace at his belt, but he stopped it, realizing she didn't mean him harm. Against the Mighty Boz, it would be useless anyway.

With a mean, muddy smile, the tiny woman used her pointer finger to slam the heavy oak door closed, so forceful it shuddered against the frame and a chip of wood flew into the air, twisted then fluttered to land on the floor between them. Dust shook free from the rafters in more than a few places. "How's that for strong, priest?"

"Right." A chill worked its way up Gyr's spine as he left her to guard the door. "Noted."

The Duke of Lah-Tsarra, when he was not sitting at the Collective table in Alistar, took his official business in the library, an ever-present stack of books at his side. As an agent of the Sempyrium, Gyr was well read. Malus D'Alzir, however, was a horse from another stable. "I live to learn, and I learn to live," the duke would say. Gyr could find no argument with the sentiment.

An unsettled feeling crept across Gyr's chest as he came to attention at the back of the room. Seated behind a table, Malus watched him approach. A stranger stood off to one side.

Malus leaned forward onto his elbows. "Apologies for interrupting the rites. I know you've grown more attached to spiritual matters of late."

"The gods are willing to wait, my lord," Gyr said. "Their patience is infinite ...especially for something important."

"It is that." Malus sighed and stood. Shadows peeled back to reveal a slender frame and an attractive face, accentuated all the more by lustrous dark hair pulled into a knot at the back of his head. Despite strands of gray creeping over the duke's ears, he was aging well for a man just past forty.

With a look to the stranger at his side, Malus's expression turned serious. Gyr's jaw clenched as he took measure of the man, wishing he'd opted for steel over wood just to be safe.

"This," Malus said, "is Kaltes Kasjeri. A spy."

"And a pirate," the man added with a smile that would cause the father of any young maiden to hide her away. Kaltes's hair was short in the way of Kanians, his skin a tarnished bronze. Tattoos wound up his neck from the collar of a leather vest, reaching toward a perfectly trimmed salt-and-pepper beard. He swept aside his cloak and bowed to Gyr. Knives lined his clothes—his boots, a strap across his chest, his belt.

Definitely a Kanian. But a pirate and a spy? Gyr's eyes narrowed. "This man is not one of mine, my lord."

"He reports directly to me." Malus smiled. "Don't worry, Gyr, I won't make it a habit of doing things behind your back. Your counsel helps run this country as much as my policies do. Which is why I need you to hear what Kaltes has to say."

"Please." Torchlight glimmered over a silvered tooth in the Kanian's broad smile. "Call me Armada. I've summited Unturrus, so, I think I've earned it."

Gyr frowned, wondering where he'd heard the name before. The man felt neither trustworthy nor malicious. Only exceedingly confident.

"Armada then." Malus clasped his hands behind his back. "Tell my prosort what you've told me."

"Gladly." Kaltes Kasjeri, or Armada as he would have it, proceeded to recount a dangerous mission that Malus had sent him on. Steal across the Sea of Psollus. Stalk its coasts. Capture a Scothean ship. Return with information.

And information he received, from not one, but two ships' crews.

Once finished with his account, Armada's silver-toothed smile disappeared. "My only regret is that the torture of the crews did not last longer. They were weaker than expected. Even for Scoths."

"Torture is not to be relished," Gyr glared at the pirate. "A necessary evil to bring about the greater good of the Sempyrean's will, but no more."

Armada spit onto the floor. Malus eyed the spot, stoic in his displeasure. The pirate seemed to care little for what pleased the duke. He locked eyes with Gyr. "I relished it quite a lot. In fact, I hope to relish it again soon. Mind you, I don't risk my life or that of my crew for gold, nor for *your* gods." He made a fist. A gust of wind swirled through the library, toppling an inkpot and tossing open a book on a nearby table, its pages flipping madly. The Awakened's eyes dimmed with coal light. "I do it for revenge."

Malus raised a hand, beseeching calm. "Thank you, Kaltes. That will be enough. Your payment will be—"

"No." The pirate released his balled fist. The wind died, and the light dissipated. "The pleasure was all mine." In a jangle of leather and steel, the man shouldered past Gyr on his way out into the hall.

The door banged closed.

Gyr shook his head. "Are all pirates so sensitive?"

Malus laughed. "I only know the one, but I can certainly claim him to be the most useful. His hatred of Scothea outweighs all else. Kanians have lost more than we could ever understand, but he...he has lost much."

History hung over the room like a strung up carcass, a bloody thing, laid bare. For a moment, they were smothered to silence by the horrors of the past.

Gyr lifted them from their ruminating. "So, it is as we feared."

"Indeed." Malus's brow jumped as he loosed an exasperated sigh. "Scothea is in upheaval. This boy prophet could herald a third invasion."

They stared at each other, the dread of those implications swirling like a storm.

"We cannot be the only ones with spies," Gyr said.

"The question is, why didn't anyone bring it up at the last meeting of the Collective?" Malus cocked his head. "Where are the messages between holds? Why hasn't the Collective been called into an emergency session? What motivations might cause such dire information as this to be hoarded? Suppressed?"

A hollow feeling entered Gyr's stomach. "It's possible we're the first to discover it."

Malus pursed his lips. "Perhaps..." His eyes took on a distant look as he stared at the place on the floor where Kaltes Kasjeri spat. "I fear it something more insidious. Namarr was founded by risk-takers and opportunists. From Valat and Malzacor mainly—but from all over the world—they flocked to the

Land of the Endless Coast by the thousands. It didn't matter that Kurgs slew them. The opportunity was too great." His fingers drummed the table. "A land free of rulers. Kingdoms waiting to be built need at least a little blood for the mortar, they thought. Churches, like the Sempyrium, too, thought the same. One could go from gutter to throne if they said enough was theirs and then convinced the men to their left and right to take up arms to help them defend it. All predicated on the tenuous promise of some future fortune, mind you. Why fight a king when you can wander into a forest and name yourself one? Sadly, that's not how it panned out, is it?"

Going to a bookshelf, Malus touched a number of bindings before selecting one. He leafed through the book's contents. His voice fell low, matter-of-fact, as if disinterested in what he said next. "And then Scothea came along and put a stop to all the little dreams in all the little minds of all the little men. We feared losing our patch of grass so much that we forgot. Lah-Tsarra forgot. Peladonia forgot. Anjuhkar forgot. The Kurgs didn't forget, but it made little difference at that point. The rest of us had forgotten for them. You see, Gyr, wolves don't attack an entire herd. They separate their prey out one at a time. Out of fear, we refused the treaties of our neighbors and chose instead to face Scothea alone. And in that pride born of fear, we were subjugated. Prey to the wolves, one by foolish one. All because no one wanted to give up their right to be the ruler of everything they thought themselves entitled to. The first Scothean invasion taught us one thing if nothing else..."

He snapped the book closed, raised its cover insignia so Gyr could see. "Greed is a poor defense strategy. It took a man born into slavery, born into suffering, born without a copper wheel of wealth to his name. It took Danath Ironlight's birth, in the shadow of tyranny, to remind us about the power of unity." The book bore a gauntleted fist snapping a chain on its cover—the Ironlight sigil. *To Crown a Slave,* the title read.

"The United Lands, we're now called." Frustration entered Malus's voice. "And yet, my friend, I fear the nationalism we once shared, the very adhesive keeping this great nation together, has frayed. Greed and opportunism long latent in our bloodlines bubble to the surface. The powerful withhold information so they might use it to their advantage. *That* is why we've heard nothing from anyone else. They broker information for power, even at the price of everything we hold dear."

Gyr cleared his throat. "You fear a traitor?"

With care, Malus pushed the book back into its place on the shelf. "Yes. I fear the highest level of sedition at the highest level of government. The magnates plot their campaigns for princehood. One could say they've been doing so since Barodane left it vacant fourteen years ago. As you know, the most recent meeting of the Namorite Collective was of an unprecedented duration. This period of having a Shadowcrown will not last."

Gyr raised his chin. "What about the girl in Anjuhkar?"

"Belara Frost is besieged in a war of ideologies. The spark of Revocation, I'm afraid, has caught on like wildfire under Syphion Muul and spreads quickly. The duchess has convinced herself that she has it under control, but she doesn't. If Anjuhkar fractures from the rest of Namarr, Ishoa Ironlight's claim will be no more. She is young, still four years from being crowned and that is four years too far from now. Our last vote to await her ascension was perfunctory at best. For many, it now seems a hollow gesture that's run its course."

Gyr took a seat to give his legs a much-needed rest. "If Revocation gains enough traction, there could be civil war. Or worse."

"Scothea could invade," said Malus. "Belara and I have spoken of such. Which is exactly why you must see a traitor's hand in this. It's happened once, during the Great Betrayal. That sets a precedent. Surely, it can happen again. Namarr is a massive land, second only to Malzacor in size and second to none in resources. It does not lack for enemies who would possess it."

"Who are we left to trust?" Gyr crossed his arms and leaned back. "Roddic Olabran is the Magnate of Lah-Tsarra, voted in by your own holds."

"From what I saw at the Collective, the Hammer of Breckenbright seeks to strengthen the Masonry and little else. We should trust him about as much as a highway bandit." Malus inhaled slowly. "As of now, my brother Marus is our best bet."

"Agreed." Like his twin, the banker lord of Kiyahd shared a discerning hand for rule and a utilitarian approach to politics. Few showed themselves to have the interests of the people more at heart than the duke's brother, Marus. Except for what had happened with their sister, Omari, little could separate the twin lords' loyalty to one another. "I'll draft your brother a letter as soon as I'm able."

"No. I will tell him in person," said Malus. "The fewer birds we must send with this information, the better. Daran's nameday falls within the next couple of months. Tell my brother Marus we come to celebrate my niece. I wish to be on the Winding Way within a fortnight."

"Of course, my lord." Irritation rode the line of Gyr's jaw. *Nothing I wanted more than a long journey through deep snow and rugged terrain.* Guilt followed, routing further complaint. "Your brother is but one ally. If it is a traitor at the highest level, we'll need more. What about the Golden Silos? I know you dislike Haydees Cotter, but the man—"

"Is the same as Roddic Olabran," Malus scoffed. "Though he keeps his ambitions hidden beneath a veneer of benevolent devotion to the Sempyrium."

"Since when does being a follower of the Sempyrean make one unworthy of trust?" Gyr shifted his weight from one foot to the other. "Is this why you've begun recruiting spies behind my back?"

"Please, Gyr. You are like a father to me. I trust you more than I trust myself."

Pride swelled in Gyr, which surprised him since he'd never been a father to his own child. *I'm sorry, Garlenna.* Shame clawed at him, the cold hands of Nacronus. A fiery tingle wound through his chest, causing him to cough.

Malus went to a steaming pitcher, poured a cup of hot tea and forced it into Gyr's hands. "We can resume in the morning if—"

"No. A minor cold. I'm fine." Gyr panted, regaining his composure enough to dive back into more important matters. "You underestimate Haydees Cotter. He's a good man."

"I hope you're right. For now, though, we keep him at a distance. Archprelate Alcor was the single vote in favor of crowning a new prince and ending the Ironlight line," Malus said. "And he has too much of Haydees Cotter's ear for comfort."

Gyr recalled Alcor's views on Kurgs from their time spent training together at the Sempyrium. The word "extermination" had come up far too often.

"You are right, Gyr. Marus is not enough. We need an ally, one whose lands aren't in turmoil. A Peladonian." Malus wrung his hands. "Duke Onai Saud's blood ties to Valat are suspect, but besides my brother, I'd trust him above all others. You should know it makes me wary, for there's no more dangerous man in Namarr. If you still agree, I say we risk our position and bring him in on this."

"Yes," Gyr said, suppressing a grunt of pain from the burning in his lungs. *Tonight will be a rough one.* Lying down always worsened the coughing fits. "I agree. I believe he has Namarr's best interests at heart. I'll see to it."

Gyr made to leave but Malus stopped him, a hand wrapped around his arm. They'd already spoken of secrets no ears could hear, and yet, the duke lowered his voice for further measures of secrecy. "There's something else."

He stared into the duke's eyes, less than a foot separating them. Malus hesitated. Spoke in the way of one restraining emotion. "I've had word...Barodane may be alive."

Gyr blinked. Blinked again. "What did you say?"

"I know. I thought I was being taken for a fool at first, but..." Tears formed at the corners of his eyes. "Barodane... He may be alive."

"How can that be?" *The Mad Prince died. It can be no other way.*

"I don't know." Malus's shoulders drooped. "If Barodane lives—"

"He can unite Namarr." Awe tumbled forth with Gyr's words.

Malus nodded.

Not yet convinced, Gyr cast about. "This is ludicrous. Where did this information come from? I'm sorry, Malus, but Barodane died fourteen years ago."

A scroll, no larger than Malus's index finger, slid from his pocket and into Gyr's hand. "The source's reliability," he said, "is beyond question."

With a crinkle, Gyr unrolled the scrap of parchment. The message was brief: *The Mad Prince lives. You may find him in Digtown.*

The signature at the bottom sent a shock through Gyr. "Locastri," he muttered. *The Mistress of Time.* The image of a spider web sat beside her name, the thinly etched strands comprising it undulating with gray light.

"The very one," Malus said.

Gyr rolled up the magic-touched scroll and handed it back to Malus.

"The person I trust most to find Barodane is you. Unfortunately, I cannot spare you." The duke grinned. "I'll need you and your wisdom at my side on our journey to Kiyahd to see my brother. There is, however, another equally suited to the task."

It struck Gyr like a dagger in the gut. "Garlenna."

Malus nodded. "Who better?"

My daughter...I've not spoken to her in years. Not since the Great Betrayal. Not since Rainy Meadows. The room dimmed as Gyr fought to clear his mind. He lifted his chin. *Duty first.* "It will be done."

"Thank you, Gyr." A somber expression fell over Lah-Tsarra's duke. "I know it isn't easy for you. But we need her. She's the only one we can trust. Furthermore, she is who Prince Barodane trusts most."

Malus's arms fell to his sides. He stared at the vaulted ceiling of his library. "Can you imagine?" His voice, barely a whisper. "Barodane alive."

Back in his quarters, Gyr felt the weight of his age in every fiber of his being. Scothea in turmoil sent ripples across the world, and yet no one in Namarr seemed to know of it. War brewed. Traitors plotted.

Rest, it seemed, would have to wait.

His lungs ached but it was nothing compared to the pain he felt in his heart as he put ink to parchment and wrote Garlenna's name.

Once the letters were finished, he tossed fitfully until dawn, sleep becoming a hope deferred for some future day.

CHAPTER THREE

THE WORLD IN ASH

NORTHEASTERN NAMARR - YEAR 64

W inter had come. The transition from autumn changed little but for the ever-soiled gray sky. The air still chilled to the bone, and snow fell, now daily rather than weekly.

On the run and traveling in the open, there was no reprieve from the pressing cold. No surcease to the acrid tint of smoke in the air. No distraction in that silent expanse from the memories that dogged her.

Ishoa flinched. The first flickers of pinwheeling flakes poured from the sky. Since the Battle of Jarik, she startled easily, shot through with heat and an urge to flee at the merest sound or motion. Even falling snow.

She raised her face to the waning light in the sky. She plucked a flake and rubbed it between thumb and forefinger, smearing it into powder. *Ash*. Sometimes ash mixed with the snow. More than just Jarik had burned during the Scarborn uprising.

Another flake settled onto Rakeema's fur and began to melt. *Gone in seconds, like everything and everyone I love.*

Something crashed through the nearby underbrush. Ishoa whirled, dagger clearing its sheath. Rakeema crouched beside her and growled.

Twice during their flight from Jarik they'd run into soldiers. First, a trio of Joffus Kon's men, garbed in plain clothes but for purple neckerchiefs their comrades might identify. She and Arick had hidden from them, watched them set fire to a small fishing village on the shores of a huge lake.

The second encounter—with a pair of Scarborn—had been an unavoidable and bloody affair. Ishoa swallowed bile at the memory. The effort of hewing a tendon...the feeling of it severing beneath her knife set her fist shaking. Vibrations had run up her arm when the blade had grated against bone, but she'd been too scared to stop sawing. Arick had dispatched the other before pulling her away from her victim. Afterward, they'd stolen their supplies, for they'd run out of food themselves.

The thing in the woods rustled. The scant warmth Ishoa felt leaked out of her. She shifted her weight into the balls of her feet, steeling herself for a fight.

Branches snapped as undergrowth gave way to the intruder—whoever it was didn't seem concerned about being heard.

Arick hobbled into the ring of trees, favoring his injured leg. He glanced at Ishoa's gleaming blade, then at Rakeema as the anjuhtarg dropped to her belly. A clutch of carrots dangled from one hand by the stalks.

"You're better off hiding," he said. "If I'm not here, don't try to fight."

She stared at her cousin flatly, his already lean frame further hollowed out by ten days or more on the road afoot. Burs and twigs tangled in once regal, snowy braids cascading down his back. If the obscured reflection in Rakeema's eyes could be trusted, Ishoa looked similarly unkempt.

Best that I don't look a princess.

Having Rakeema was bad enough. Arick told her as much daily. "We need to get rid of her," he would say.

"Touch her and I'll kill you," she had replied. While Ishoa doubted she could do any such thing, Arick left it alone after a handful of such exchanges.

Now, she turned from him, rammed her knife home, and then sat. If not for Arick forcing her to flee before she attempted to kill Lodecka Warnock, she and Rakeema would both be dead.

Arick reminded Ishoa daily of why he'd saved her. Certainly, he hadn't risked his life for her out of an abundance of love. No, he sang the same fool's song about the necessity of maintaining the Ironlight bloodline. For the good of Namarr, he claimed.

But cousin, Namarr is gone. The thought never passed her lips, but it never rested either. *It's gone...because I wasn't strong enough to keep it together.*

Syphion Muul's insurrection had closed like a trap around Anjuhkar, a screaming doe with its leg caught. Soon, the predators would arrive in droves.

Arick handed Ishoa a carrot with soiled grooves and mold on one end. Her stomach gurgled as she set to, eating around the worst of it. Rakeema rose and bounded off in search of a mouse or squirrel. Ishoa watched her go, then said, "Where did you get it?"

"A farm a half mile off."

Ishoa slowed, licking parched lips. "Could we shelter there?"

Arick chewed—a score more times than seemed necessary. Striated jaw muscles writhed under his skin. "Syphion Muul's dogma moves faster than we do."

The cloak Arick had pilfered from a butchered courtier outside the walls of Jarik had a fresh spatter of blood on the hem, the last traces of daylight making it a deep maroon. "You fought?" Changing their attire had been the first thing they'd done after Jarik but it was difficult for a Quinn to disguise themselves.

He stared past Ishoa into the stretching, evening shadows of the trees ringing them. "She had a pitchfork."

Ishoa's stomach lurched. She knew the rest. She flexed her hand, now a purple hue with spots of white from the cold. "We can't go back, then?"

"Too dangerous."

Ishoa hurled the last nub of her carrot at Arick's face, struck him in the chest. "So we keep on running?" Sobs gathered at the base of her throat. Each day she woke hoping the horrors that had followed her from Jarik might stop. That she might not see Wolst's bloody teeth, nor the holdguard's flesh melting and crackling outside their barracks, nor the slack look on Othwii's face as a spear jutted from his chest.

But the thoughts didn't stop. And that meant Ishoa had to keep going, even when she wanted to rest. Desperately, she wanted to feel that something—*any-thing*—was normal again.

"Yes. We run." Frozen eyes regarded her. "As fast as we can, we run. The common folk don't care that it's Scarborn leading the rebellion. They see stability in strength. Syphion Muul's promises of greater prosperity under a sovereign Anjuhkar have swayed many." Ishoa recalled something Othwii had said in his library. *Let a barn burn long enough and eventually all the rats are sure to emerge.* Arick continued. "And not just the Scarborn. We have to get you to Alistar safely. With an army at our backs, we can retake—"

"While the Scarborn purge the duchy of detractors and gather strength to bring down our allies?" Ishoa stood, upper lip curled. "Every second I'm running validates my people's opinion that I'm weak. You think you're saving Namarr, cousin, but in truth, you're helping Lodecka Warnock carve out Anjuhkar for her own."

Arick winced as he stretched his injured leg and laid on his side. The wound needed treatment. They were covering less distance each day, and whenever they inevitably called a halt before nightfall, Arick made excuses as to why—like needing more time to hunt for food or ensure that they weren't being followed. But Ishoa knew the truth. She smelled it with growing alacrity.

"Ishoa." Sweat beaded on his porcelain brow. "This is Namarr's war now. The common folk need to see the knights of the Crown, and you at their head. They must be reminded that they are a part of a greater whole. Anything else is folly."

I could also die while on the run. Ishoa saw her gravestone, the words "Died Fleeing" etched in the stone.

The blinding fear that had gripped her at Jarik had faded some. In the heat of battle, she'd fled for her life while Wolst fought and died at her heels. All she'd done was weep, hug her pet tighter, and leave her people to their fates. The shackles of shame and anger dragged her back to that decisive moment with increasing frequency. Arick had driven her to the choice, but in truth, it hadn't taken much to convince her. Cowardice compelled her, and now, she was trapped in its unrelenting jaws.

Torn between her duty as a princess to survive, and a deeper calling to do things her own way, she sought any escape. *Is it my way to die sword in hand?* Revenge seemed a distant dream. *Against half the holds of Anjuhkar and a dubious populace, I'm one girl. I'd die just like Wolst. Worse, they might use me to bargain for peace...*

The idea of Lodecka Warnock being granted Anjhuhkar as a result of Ishoa's folly sent a shiver down her spine.

No. Arick was right. For now, they had to run—and that made her hate it even more. She had no clever plan and no allies to execute one if she did.

She was helpless.

The sobs in her chest broke loose, quiet and deep. Arick ignored her as she huddled into her furs. Rakeema returned, the gray fuzz around her maw smeared pink and covered in tiny brown bristles from whatever small prey she'd found.

I'm tired of being so damn special. Others decided what she would do. How she would do it. They made her decisions for her in service to the greater good—as they saw it to be. She was a princess, yet she seemed to have no power at all.

Her sobs subsided. She ran her hands over cheeks, brushing away the tears. Despite completing the Trials, she still felt like an impetuous child. *Can I truly blame my family for choosing what's best on my behalf? My failure with Lodaris cost him his life, and it cost me Jarik. More...*

The list of her inabilities was long. The catastrophe brought about by her weakness, expansive. Syphion Muul was right. Namarr was better off without her.

CHAPTER FOUR

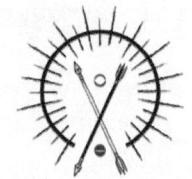

THE WAY UNSEEN

The Ascendant's smock hung around Thephos's waist in tatters, exposing scuffed skin and purple and yellow bruising. As so few did, he descended Unturrus, each step an unfolding mystery.

He smiled to himself.

The Mother had come, and *he* had disappeared. He recalled the feeling of unraveling into her warm embrace. Of floating on a sea of light. In that place, he knew he could be anything he wanted to be. Anyone. Not just Thephos of Carthane, an accursed pig farmer filled with shallow regrets and memories of shallow graves. He could be the things he'd never dared acknowledge. Things he feared to desire.

A man—that above all. A man worthy of love and respect.

The bitterness surrounding his past was gone. He'd done what he'd done in order to survive under a cruel tyrant. The painful weight he'd heaped onto himself for not fighting back was undue, for the man who was meant to teach him about courage, and care for those weaker, had never exhibited such qualities himself.

Thephos the pig farmer was a learned tool. A father's hate and wrath had fashioned him—made him into an object rather than a human. His existence had served the whims of a coward. Too weak for love, the old devil had been a tunnel, incapable of holding onto whatever good happened through it.

The thread of such realities had drawn Thephos deeper into the web of the Mother's understanding.

Numb oblivion followed. The eye of consciousness closing...

The first sensation thereafter was a soft caress at Thephos's back, like he lay atop a bundle of furs fit for a king. He had squirmed against the feeling, attempting to burrow into the ecstasy of it, an infant newly born that was desperate for soft, fleshy bosom.

He'd blinked. Bolted upright.

The world had changed. The way he saw it...somehow more distinct. Every plane and curve held a firmer edge. Every leaf, rich with vibrant hues. The ground itself sang of complex artistry. Stone eroded by the rigors of time set his soul to thrumming when he placed a palm against its roughness to rise.

Dense air filled his lungs to bursting.

He had awoken on the Cusp. Right where the shamans had disappeared. Just before his first journey on godsthorn...

Rubbery legs carried him downward. The sun moved at a regular pace and any trace of snow was gone. Wind like a lover's breath bowed around him as he went, footsteps thudding in tune to the ticking seconds. He'd missed the pulse of time.

Tears slipped free. He wasn't afraid of his emotions anymore, at least, not like he had been. It wasn't that the unpleasant ones were gone. They'd simply withered. Made room for others he preferred. Joy had carved out its space within. The joy of living. The joy of being free from numbing horror.

The joy of possibilities to come.

Though few, I never appreciated the comforts I had.

Warmth. Life. Breath. The sunrise of another chance, and the sunset of days better past.

Tears of joy—the first he'd ever known—streaked his cheeks.

Down he went, weeping and walking until he could do so no longer. Then, he curled up under a solitary elm tree.

A clawed hand dragged down Thephos's calf.

I'm here for you, Theffy.

His eyes flew open. Stars filled the sky around a hulking silhouette blotting out those directly overhead. His heart hammered. Panic gripped him. He choked on spittle and blinked, but the specter was gone.

He sat up to find Unturrus deadly silent.

Crossing his arms over his naked chest, he scanned his surroundings. Nothing.

Arms drifting back for leverage, he scooted himself deeper into the inlet of the elm's root system; it did little to make him feel safer.

Memory of the voice crawled up his spine...into his ears. He slapped his hands over them. "It's nothing," he murmured. An hour passed, spent convincing himself that he was sane. That everything that had happened made sense. Unturrus had exposed him to impossible horrors and mind-shattering truths.

He'd watched other ascendants be torn apart and bisected and driven mad. He'd heard things and seen things that weren't truly there. He'd been taken to a different dimension by a benevolent being from another reality, though he recalled almost none of what he'd experienced there.

As long as the nightmares of his waking life dwindled, he decided, he could handle the occasional disrupted night of sleep. It certainly wasn't the first time he'd woken to dread illusions in the middle of the night.

The thought that all of his problems—all the demons he'd struggled with—might be forever gone, seemed ridiculous. Olthr had echoed as much. He'd told Thephos that ascending Unturrus was only the beginning of an Awakened's journey. "One doesn't simply acquire powers and set off on their merry way. There is a great deal to learn about honing such gifts. Awakened must find their place in a world that no longer sees them as normal, that fears them as much as they revere them."

The thought of anyone revering Thephos made him laugh.

Echoes bounced around the mountain slopes, a strange and alien sound. Thephos froze. Not since early childhood had he heard himself laugh.

Thephos eased onto his side, head pressed onto a root worn smooth by time and the elements. Eyelids heavy, body weary, he nevertheless laid awake until the sun slashed the horizon, its amber glow bleeding over the branches of the elm and stretching across the earth. Warmth leaked onto his face as a scintillating crest of light shimmered in the distance. For as long as he dared, he stared at the spot, letting it burn its ghostly likeness into his vision. Then he closed his eyes.

In the rusted dark, it danced, a single spark to start the world ablaze.

He came slowly to his feet, then proceeded down again.

He wasn't sure how long it would take to reach Eastshadow. But the threat of demons worried him not at all.

A bell clanged to life, downslope and to Thephos's left just as he spotted the Corpse Gate. The blackened bone archway marked a break in the fifteen-foot wall like a decaying tooth. The moment Thephos had first walked through it, a shiver had rippled through him, the body's visceral understanding of its doom. Much had changed in the interval between that day and the one he'd woken to the day before.

Fear had a purpose now that truth accompanied it. He was Awakened. There was something to live for. Something to stay alive for. A reason to deny death.

For nearly two decades, his body could conceptualize little beyond its suffering—the aching, whimpering weakness of it—and so saw relief in oblivion.

That body is gone now. I am what is left.

He rubbed his hands together in wonder. Faint hues of indigo light glimmered at the corners of his vision. Like flickers of motion or shadow at the peripheries, when he swiveled his sight to uncover more, the indigo light was gone.

But it was enough. The lasting mark of the Mother. He stood straighter, balling his fists knowing they possessed some mysterious power. *If my father tried to hurt me now, I could strike him.* And yet, the petty desire to do so had fled, a bitter flavor leached from him.

More bells took up the call as he descended toward the gate, some so distant, they winnowed to a low tapping. Those closest pealed a half dozen times more and then stilled.

That's a good thing if I remember it right.

The old man at the Numbers had told him Ruptured got the black bell—that is if the crownguard could tell it was a Ruptured. That alarm was a constant and panicked one, but anyone else whose descent took them back through the Corpse Gate got a more ceremonious reception.

Three rings, then a pause. Three rings, then a pause.

It was melodious, but at the same time, foreboding.

Will I be seen as a monster? A hero? A man?

A thrill palpated Thephos's chest. A knot tightened in his stomach. For once he would be seen as something more than a pathetic worm.

I'm an Awakened. Gods...I am Awakened!

Warm revelation dripped through him, spurring him quicker toward the Corpse Gate. A small crowd was forming beyond, dim silhouettes in the waning light. He hoped to see Syn Backlegarm among them.

A sliver of pride brought a smile to his face. If the owner of the gambling den had told him the truth, the man was about to make a fat profit on his bet. The crownguard who was a father, too, would hopefully benefit from Thephos's unlikely chance at success. *Take your profit and spend it on your son. Give him a gift. Tell him he's worth more than the dirt he stands on.*

As Thephos passed between the Corpse Gate's black bone arches, the air was sucked from his lungs. He gasped and dropped to his knees on the other side. Buzzing filled his ears—the ever-present cloud of flies hovering before the gate.

Someone laughed.

Still heaving, Thephos lifted his face. Ballooning pants, striped black and white, were tucked into maroon leather boots. Syn Backlegarm grinned down at him. "Hey buddy. You made it."

Thephos nodded and claimed his feet. "I'm lucky, I suppose." True as they might be, the words felt strange coming from his mouth.

"Nonsense!" Syn threw an arm around Thephos and started to walk him into the gathered crowd, much like he'd done the first time they'd met at the Numbers. "Luck is a pessimist's reckoning of fate. I knew you were special. You've got no evidence to deny it now."

Thephos let himself be guided by the bigger man. "I suppose you're right."

"Of course I'm right." Syn pointed at a hooded figure in the crowd. "Ash my love, congratulate my friend, Thephos of Carthane!"

Warmth spread from Thephos's heart into his limbs. *Friend.* He lowered his face, a sheepish smile plucking at his sallow cheek. *Friend.* He shifted, letting his shoulder slide deeper into Syn's embrace. The movement sent a prickle down his neck, for it seemed a risk to sink deeper into comforts never known. Heart-pounding seconds sauntered by at an agonizing pace as he waited for Syn to shove him off or glare down at him in disapproval.

No such thing occurred.

Hands rose and fell against Thephos's arms, shoulders, and back as he was led through the clutch of Eastshadow citizens, flinching at the majority of congratulatory blows.

Scores had gathered. More than a few wore disappointed expressions—those who had bet against him, he assumed. The face of the crownguard who'd been kind to him sprang from the press, unreadable but for an arched eyebrow.

Did he lie and bet on my death?

The man was swallowed up by the press of spectators and disappeared. The uncertainty he'd seen on the man's face clung to him as he parted from the crowd, heading for the Numbers.

"Come! We gotta toast your success!" Syn thrust a triumphant fist in the air as the boisterous swirl of sound from the gambling den hit them. "You know what though, let's stop at my place first. That's where I keep the good stuff. Malzacy gold-wine."

Thephos had never heard of it. He glanced back the way they'd come. Ash followed them, happily engaged in discussion with a rail-thin man that was taller than Syn by a few inches. Others he didn't know trailed along, too; most were seemingly deep in their cups given their staggering steps. "I've never drank before."

"Never is a word for a past life. You're Awakened now." Smiling broadly, Syn leaned down so that his mouth was a pinky finger's length from Thephos's ear. "You'll be in high demand and drinking the finest stuff from here on. Wealth isn't hard to come by for those with your gifts."

Thephos blinked. A slight frown creased his brow. *What gifts?* Despite a bone-deep understanding that they existed, he had no clue what they were, nor how he might access them.

As if reading Thephos's thoughts, Syn said, "Don't worry about the confusion. It can take minutes, hours, even weeks to get a feel for them. Ah! There it is!"

"I'm glad one of us knows what's going on," Thephos said.

They turned down a side lane a short distance past the Numbers. A lone yurt sat at the end, isolated from the structures around it by a good twenty yards or more. In appearance, it looked like a smaller version of the Numbers, painted black-and-white, and covered in random numerals.

Syn released Thephos from his avuncular embrace, then unbuttoned and swept aside the flap. "Man of the hour goes first!"

Thephos stepped through.

Given Syn Backlegarm's ostentatious appearance, he expected something more grandiose. The room, however, was sparse, well lived-in, and plain. Clothing scattered over a stuffed mattress absorbed most of the space, while a writing table with a chair and ink pot beside a large chest filled the rest.

Thephos turned slowly around. "Thank you for—"

A sharp ring—steel swept from a scabbard—came first. A sharp blade touching his flesh, second.

One sword point jabbed him in the cheek. Another lay in the concave of his throat. Suddenly, the earth opened at his feet and sucked him down. A heartbeat later, it solidified, clamped around his submerged calves. He cried out but didn't dare move as something cold slithered around his torso and squeezed. He looked down to find chains cinching tighter—tighter—until breathing became a dire effort.

He gasped, looked to the tent opening.

Inside, Syn Backlegarm stood at the head of a group of five. His wife, Ash, was beside him. Gray and white light wept from the eyes of the other three. Ash and another leveled blades, odd lettering etched into their length.

All of Syn's friendly demeanor evaporated. "I'm sorry."

Light flashed. Thephos's head snapped back. Fire shot from his brow through to the back of his skull.

He screamed.

CHAPTER FIVE

THE FIRES OF LOVE

T he kitchens of Kiyahd belonged to Zadani and Zadani alone.

Her space. Her canvas. Her power.

She fueled the bodies that defended the walls of Hawk's Keep. She teased the palates of would-be lovers. She nourished the Lord of Lending, Marus D'Alzir himself.

Zadani Innan. Master cook. The heart that beat the city of Kiyahd and the hand that fed its power.

With a fist resting proudly on her hip, Zadani stirred a potato, leek, and mussel soup, its warm steam damping her face as she leaned over it. A savory coastal scent rushed into her nostrils. Only one thing brought her greater joy than the moment a perfect dish was born.

Hadir, my love.

That morning was not long ago now. Her husband, Hadir, had cradled Zadani from behind, broad forearms wrapping over her rounded belly, coarse face and soft lips brushing the back of her neck. Slow, like she liked. He'd nibbled at her ear and growled like a dog, his playful nature stoking her arousal.

Remembered passion rippled through Zadani. She smiled and waved at a sweat-drenched old woman hunched over a spit. "It's ready, Thruna." She indicated the bubbling pot. "Into the trenchers—quickly now."

Gobs of fat sizzled from the crackling boar. A thick pall of smoke built under the low ceiling. Thruna gave the spit a final turn, then shuffled over, picking at a tumescent wart atop her nose. "Me and quick parted ways a decade ago, young lass." She sucked at a broad gap in her teeth. "'Before you're dead' would be a more realistic goal."

Zadani rubbed Thruna's wrinkled arm. "Don't be so grim, my love. Here..." A kitchen fit for a lord ran on good cheer, so Zadani let the love pour out of her. Like the first coils of a warming cookpot, a song rose to drown out the flurry of activity. "With a soul unafraid and a hand for the blade, came a fire-hearted man with ice in his veins."

The head of every kitchen maid turned her way. If Zadani was in the mood to sing, then all would sing. If she was in a mood to storm, all would wither beneath the downpour.

Today, luckily for them, it was a song.

Hadir's strong jaw and gentle eyes swam before her, claiming her with love.

In the next verse, Thruna's hoarse voice joined Zadani's. All knew the *Eyes of Love*. Belara Frost's betrothal to Danath Ironlight had given birth to Namarr. Zadani hated the way tales of fighting and heroics so often overshadowed the equally important love stories throughout history. Love played its part in war as much as hate and violence. *Without love, we'd all be praising some Scoth King.*

Zadani raised a wooden spoon, beckoning her staff into a call and response as they worked to prepare the midday meal for court. "Who do I see?"

"I see me in your eyes!" they intoned.

Zadani had been told the D'Alzir family liked when they heard mirth coming from the kitchens, so she liked to think of song as the first course to a splendid dining experience. She thrust the wooden spoon at Elmarie, the newest member of her staff. "Who do I see?"

The girl's chest turned beet red as she stammered out the words. "I see me in your eyes."

Zadani shook her head. "Who do I see?" She pointed at Elmarie again, motioning for her to sing louder.

"I see me in your eyes!"

The rest of the verses slid by like butter over warm bread. Zadani smiled. When it came time to finish the song, a voice surpassing her own in quality claimed the last line. The intruder started low and then brought the piece to a ringing culmination that left Zadani's skin tingling.

"And the fires of love burn bright!"

Daran D'Alzir stepped through the door to the kitchen. Zadani greeted the young lady of the hold with a bow as the rest of the staff bent to their tasks. "Lady Daran."

The young highborn tossed flaxen hair over one shoulder. For the past eight years, Zadani had watched Daran grow from a snotty brat into a slightly less snotty brat. A stunning beauty, with talent and intellect to match, Zadani had no doubt she'd be preparing a wedding feast for her within the next couple of years. "Was our singing pleasing, my lady?"

Daran rolled her eyes the way one dismisses a playful accident. "I joined in, did I not?"

"Expertly so," Zadani said.

The girl gave a weak smile and clasped her hands behind her back. "Father wanted me to inform you that our honored guest, Jasso Jackolo, has arrived. I expect the boards to be out in short order."

Zadani bowed. "Consider it already done."

Daran surveyed the room with a flat affect. "A difficult request considering it clearly is not."

Pride wounded, Zadani tensed. If Lord Marus's wife were less interested in her wine and more interested in being Daran's mother, she might have curbed some of her daughter's ruder tendencies.

"Oh!" Daran cried, causing Thruna to jolt at the sudden outburst. Mouth parted in unbridled elation, the young lady of the hold accosted a board of pecan rolls. "My favorites. My seventeenth nameday will be here soon, Mistress Zadani. You *must* make these for me."

Zadani inclined her head. "It would be my pleasure to do so."

With a delighted giggle, Daran plucked up a roll and took a bite, scattering crumbs across the wooden plank before she left.

"Gah. Dessert before lunch." Thruna shook her head. "It ain't right."

Zadani swept Daran's leavings from the board with a frown. "We have the wisdom of years on our side. What better use for it than to forgive the young their faults?"

"I'm older than the stones they used to build Kiyahd," said Thruna. "But I'll never get used to the arrogance of the rich. Lord Marus has money enough to buy his whelp some manners."

"You're not wrong, but they pay us for food." With a singular clap, Zadani set the staff back to work with a fury. "Not our opinions."

Elmarie carried a plate of cut apples past. Zadani caught the girl gently by the cheek with a cupped hand, then lifted a spoon to her mouth. "Taste."

After a moment's shock, Elmarie obliged. Her eyes lit up.

"That's what I like to see. Thank you!" Zadani propelled Elmarie onward.

Not long now. After court came clean up, and after clean up came Hadir. He would be waiting for her. There were two moments in every day Zadani loved most: when she walked into the kitchens, and when she stepped into her husband's arms.

Wiping her hands on her apron, she went to ensure the first of the boards were ready to go out and found them less than satisfactory. She beckoned Elmarie over with a goading finger. "You will not remain in the kitchen if I see honey smears like this again. If Lord Marus himself wanders in here and makes a mess, it is still your duty to fix it. We must be meticulous." She rotated an apple slice by a half an inch. "We must be perfect. Understand?"

Eyes downcast, Elmarie nodded.

The first course went out and then returned minutes later, laden with gossip.

"The scholar from Valat is a frosty old wraith. But handsome."

"Jasso Jackolo? Too bad for you, he's a lover of men, much like our Lord Marus's own Awakened."

Thruna grunted as she and another girl hoisted the spitted boar onto a table. "If I were the smartest man in the world..." She scratched the lip-pink wart on the end of her nose, carving knife in hand. "I'd hound after cocks too. Life's easier lived without yearning for maidens."

From there, Zadani's staff devolved into speculation.

"I swear I saw Genjin Hyrix and Jasso Jackolo making eyes!"

In the kitchens, the line between truth and baseless rumor was thinner than a knife's edge. Zadani questioned anything that slid into her ears from one of her staff. She wasn't one to take part so much as listen. Complaints made a mind weak, whereas absorbing information made it strong. It was a simple choice for Zadani. One which saw her giving the commands rather than taking them.

A pat of butter slapped down amid a ring of fresh cheese and pepper scones. "Talk later, ladies," Zadani said. "These must go out. I care less about who this scholar likes and more about whether he's a picky eater."

With a self-satisfied grin, Elmarie said, "If he's picky, we can always feed him Thruna's wart."

The old woman stroked her nose. "Not my wee baby." She took up one end of the board piled with steaming meat, Elmarie the other.

Zadani led them out for the main course. A resounding bang preceded her fleet of kitchen maids into Hawk's Hall. The domed ceiling of the hall hung over the D'Alzir family positioned beneath, a single high table flanked on either side by a series of lower ones.

History was Zadani's favorite subject at the culinary school of Alistar, so when she had been hired as master cook eight years prior and first seen the hawk depicted in the stained glass dome overhead, she needed to know everything about it.

The first Lending Lord of Kiyahd, Malzai D'Alzir, a Lah-Tsarene born trader, had struck it rich in the Shining Range, only to risk his entire fortune by funding Danath Ironlight's rebellion. Some said the two became best friends. Others, out of earshot of anyone loyal to the D'Alzir, called Malzai "Blackwind," claiming his decision was all business, no patriotism.

Nevertheless, when the Unity Wars ended, the newly crowned Prince Danath made the explorer-turned-moneylender the Duke of Lah-Tsarra, giving him strongholds at Brighthaven and Kiyahd—which his grandsons now ruled.

To celebrate, a renowned painter from Valat had been conscripted to install the massive stained glass mural.

Now, Zadani walked beneath it. A soaring hawk on a vibrant purple sunset—the crest of the D'Alzirs. Marus carried the tradition of their great-grandfather as the Lord of Lending and defender of Kiyahd. Eight minutes the elder, Marus's twin brother, Malus, had been given the duty of Duke of Lah-Tsarra and lord of the stronghold at Brighthaven.

She faced the former as she came to stand at the center of the horseshoe of tables.

Lord Marus waved her forward. A half dozen kitchen staff followed, boards piled with food carried between them.

The lord of Kiyahd was a diminutive man but not unattractive. The whispered debate in the kitchen was the immense size of his squarish head and if it in any way reflected his male-member. A healthy man in his later-middle years, he had a shock of dark hair saturated with silver, which lent him an air of elegance and power. A short, wiry beard and darker tint to his skin gave him away as a Lah-Tsarene. Word had it the Lady Daran was the mirror image of her father's sister, Omari, once betrothed to an Ironlight prince. A rare blond but with the olive complexion of a D'Alzir.

Delighted throat clearing from the highborn greeted Zadani's staff as they laid out the boards.

Dish by dish, Zadani told them what they were about to eat, observing her patrons as they inspected their meal. The look on their faces during that first taste was most important.

She listened.

Sighs of bliss. Simple pleased declarations. Complex reviews. No words—that was best.

Most folk said a thing was good regardless of whether they thought so, and a cook who gathered no criticism couldn't grow their skill. Thusly did Zadani discover her own methods for improvement. In order to become the master cook of a major hold, she'd needed to develop a keen eye for reading people. She dealt in expressions and emotions as much as she did spices.

She watched.

Eyebrows raised, then a quick look at the person to either side, seeking confirmation of the quality.

A smile. A confused frown—something not quite right, or maybe just different than expected.

A slowing down...movements frozen as flavor broke across their palette.

A pang of sorrow rose in Zadani's breast. *Hadir, I wish you could see their faces.* It was the one love they could not share, though that didn't keep her from trying. Part of Hadir's greatness was his ability to sit and listen to her describe the reactions to her meals. She did her best to paint the picture. Just once, though, she wished he could see the scene unfold with his own eyes.

Lady Rizel alone left her food untouched. Ever since the woman's first daughter, Raiya, had died following her aunt Omari up Unturrus, the woman had fallen to wasting. Cheeks sunken and corpse-like. Teeth stained blue from rivers of wine. Near white hair pulled back into a ponytail, exposing a pinched face and a neck swollen by grief and drink. Many said she had looked like Marus's younger sister, Omari. Golden hair, dark skin, almond eyes—one of the jewels of Lah-Tsarra. The kind of beauty that stole a man's soul at first glance.

Now she's lucky to steal a moment of sobriety.

Sitting beside Lady Rizel was her daughter, Daran. She possessed all the budding promise of her mother's legendary beauty, as well as her father's sharp mind.

Lady Rizel knocked over a cup of wine with the carelessness of one far too drunk.

"Perhaps you should return to your chambers, my lady," Marus said.

Lady Rizel slurred her words. "Not good enough for you, am I?" Her eyes lost focus...drifted elsewhere. "Maybe I should run off to Unturrus...like Omari. Like—" A sob choked down the rest.

Marus flicked a look at his daughter, Daran. The young lady rose and then led her weeping mother by the elbow from Hawk's Hall.

Servants hurried forward to clean the mess, which drew Sir Vallabathus over as well. The menacing knight-captain watched and stood between them and Lord Marus until their task was complete.

Golden eyes marked him as one born to the Corridor of Storms, the land bridge connecting North Malzacor to Namarr. The man's eyes never stopped assessing. Never had Zadani seen the muscles under the man's cinnamon skin relax. Always at the ready with a hand resting on the pommel of his sword, he was a serious man with an armored disposition.

I suppose those are ideal qualities for a knight-captain.

Sir Vallabathus's narrowed eyes darted toward Jasso Jackolo, their honored guest from the Mighty Isle of Valat.

"If you please, Mistress Zadani," said Marus.

Zadani explained the main course: potato, leek, and mussel soup garnished with thyme and a touch of scorpion venom from the Corridor of Storms. Crackling boar, stuffed with an apple and sage slurry.

"What is your favorite dish you've brought?" Jasso Jackolo interrupted.

The man's eyes were a startling blue. Gems cut from clearest sky. A white beard and mane of thick silken hair framed his face beneath a wide-brimmed hat of Val style. He wore a multi-colored brocade doublet of silk. Earrings jangled in a row down one earlobe, and the other held a solitary emerald the size of a sparrow egg. Though well into his fifties, he'd managed to stay provocatively handsome.

"Usually, we let her speak uninterrupted so she may attend her many duties, Master Jackolo," Marus said.

Jasso grinned, eyes fixed on Zadani. There was nothing intimidating about the way he looked at her. Nothing sexual. Just curious. She felt at ease as he slung an arm back over his chair. "But look at her Marus. Is she always this proud when she tells you about the food? I've been in more courts and councils and assemblies and gatherings and congregations and convocations and cabals—"

"Jasso." Marus's tone was pinched. "Please."

"This woman truly loves her work." The scholar smoothed his vibrant brocade doublet. "And you never think to ask her about it? I say we tell these others to piss off for the rest of the day while we figure out where she gets the godsthorn she's so damn high on."

Zadani's hand flew to her mouth.

"Oh, stop it." Jasso Jackolo puffed his cheeks then blew a mighty raspberry. "We know you're not high. Anyway, I've a better question. *Why* do you love what you do? I assume you do love it?"

"I do, Master Jackolo." Zadani beamed and looked to Marus for approval to continue, which he gave. "I've but two loves in this world. Cooking for the D'Alzir family, and my husband, Hadir—he's one of Lord Marus's hunters. I live to give as much as I can to both. It brings me joy to bring joy to others."

"Great," Marus said. "Now, if you're finished with her Jasso, we can move on. I have a busy day ahead. You said you wished to observe my court, not interrogate my cook.

Jasso Jackolo scrunched his face and wagged a finger. "One more question. This one's for you, Marus. Do *you* love what you do?"

The lord of Kiyahd watched the scholar, one side of his mouth quirked into a smile. He raised his voice for all to hear. "Master Jackolo's inquisitive nature transcends the pages of his books, it seems."

Jasso laughed with the rest of them. "How else would it work? One does not gain powerful insight without daring inquiry. I ask the questions others fear. I cannot balk with worry if I'm to understand the elites of the world." He gestured at Zadani. "Nor think myself above those who feed them. The entire picture matters."

Despite a lack of hostility edging the scholar's words, Zadani was acutely aware of the discomfited expressions of those gathered. They looked at one another, faces creased in confusion while she remained front and center, drowning under waves of nervousness. *I've never wanted to be dismissed more in all my life.*

Casual as a king, Jasso Jackolo plucked a fig from a board, and then tossed it into his mouth with a wink. "If you wonder why I sit at the high table and the rest of you at lower ones, look no further than the discomfort of your silence. Your tongues, imprisoned by the fear of exposing yourself as a dullard, a weakling, or a bore. Your mouths clamped desperately tight, as if you could attain greatness by having no opinions of your own...if you just sit down in the right place and nod at the right moment to the right people." Jasso rose from his chair and bowed to Marus. "I apologize if I've offended your court, my lord. It has come to my awareness that those of a similar station to your own oft seek me out for such diatribes as you might find in my writings. If you're displeased by this, I'll leave Kiyahd immediately."

Marus D'Alzir leaned back in his chair. "Absolutely not, Master Jackolo. My people require a healthy dose of humbling if they are to better themselves."

With a flourish, Jasso plopped back down in his seat. "Grand!"

"However, some may need time to adjust to your..." Marus's words dripped out molasses-slow as he surveyed the room. "...Abrasive style."

"Fair," Jasso said. "But I doubt you are one of those you speak of, so I return to my original inquiry. Do you love what you do?"

Marus frowned. "I imagine the degree to which one loves to be lord of a hold is dependent upon their capacity to be certain that what they do results in the most good for the most people. Since no one population can ever be pleased equally—especially one like Namarr which is made up of numerous ethnic groups—I neither love nor hate the responsibilities laid at my feet. But there is little quite so difficult as the burden hold lords must endure."

Jasso Jackolo clapped. "A damn fine answer! And here I thought the great intellectuals of the world lived solely at the Academies of Valat."

"You're too kind."

"Even so." Jasso snatched up a pecan roll, tore off a small bite. He stared at it a moment, then shook the pastry in his fist. "Now, this is true power. Tastes like gods rutting in my mouth."

"Please, my lord." Blushing and embarrassed, Zadani stared at her feet. "I'm just a cook. May I be dismissed?"

"Alright, she's had enough, Jasso," Marus said. "My apologies to the kitchen staff. I know you have important duties to attend. You're excused."

Heart thudding like a drum, Zadani positioned herself behind the high table to ensure proper management of the feast as court progressed.

A dozen armed and grizzled-looking men filed into Hawk's Hall. Some had the black enameled honor plates of shadowguard strapped to their shoulders.

They stopped twenty paces short of the high table.

A man with a clouded eye where a scar ran through it stepped forward. A blond beard streaked with white covered a jutting chin. He was balding fore and aft, with a wispy strap of hair between, yet he walked with immense confidence. *As is the way of tall men accustomed to the attention of others.*

"Lord Marus D'Alzir, it is an honor to finally stand in your court."

Marus dipped his head. "I'm glad to finally have you here in the flesh, Master Nymon."

Zadani frowned. The man with the milky eye appeared to be nothing more than a common day mercenary.

"Aye," Nymon licked a corner of his mouth. "We gave it our best, but those damned Warnocks have a grip on the caravan guard business that's hard to break. Last year was tough on my men, so here we are, a hundred and nine strong, offering ourselves ass-up on the cheap. Minnows feeding a bigger fish."

Marus laughed. "I promise not to eat you. You'll find it more suitable here than the open road."

"What about training?" Nymon said. "Your letters mentioned an opportunity for myself and my best men to be trained as knights."

"That promise stands. Over the next decade, I could have a third of you knighted. I'm sure you're aware that means double your pay."

Nymon rocked back on his heels, eyebrow raised. "And here I thought myself a smart man. Could have been a knight already."

"Perspective holds more power when it's shared. You should have come to Kiyahd long ago." Marus indicated his knight-captain. "You'll be put to immediate use. Sir Vallabathus will escort your men to the barracks for outfitting."

On the way out, Nymon locked eyes with Zadani. A tingle rode up her spine as the man grinned, his tongue probing the blond and white beard-hair surrounding his lips.

Twilight fell over Hawk's Keep. Braziers and ensconced torches lit the hallways beyond the kitchens. Last to leave, Zadani locked the larder, then tucked the keys under her dress beside a cloth-wrapped pecan roll for Hadir. Besides the Lady Daran and others, the pastry also happened to be her husband's favorite.

Zadani turned—gave a start.

Jasso Jackolo was waiting. "As a traveling scholar, I meet many people. Few so interesting as you, Zadani Innan."

Instead of shrinking away as many women talking to powerful men might, Zadani gathered her breath and stepped toward him. "I'm a simple cook," she declared. "There's little interesting about it."

He straightened and folded his hands behind his back. "Just a cook? Come now, you've figured it out, I think."

She felt a scowl form across her brow. "Figured what out?"

"Life," he said. "People."

"I'm not sure I follow."

"Life is about people. Humans fear what we don't know and cannot understand. Given we're surrounded by others, we have a need to understand and know them. Otherwise, we're surrounded by fear," he said. "But you understand people. That means, you have less to fear. You know who to avoid, who to trust, and most importantly, who to love. That last part is what makes life decent, as I'm sure you've discovered."

I do. Her hand rose to fidget with a moonstone necklace lying on her chest, luminous gray when it caught light. Hadir had given it to her upon his return from a hunting trip on their fifth anniversary. "To what do I owe such effusive compliments?"

Jasso Jackolo swept the wide-brimmed hat from his head. Given the ponytail and abundance of hair cascading from under the hat, Zadani was surprised to find the man sliding a velvet gloved hand over a shining bald pate.

"I am...on the hunt for something. I find the kitchens typically possess it. Before I share more, I'd appreciate your trust and confidence on the matter." Flashing a broad, white smile, he replaced the hat. "If you're willing to lend a hand, I'll be in your debt."

"If it is in my power to help, I may." She shrugged. "You should know though, most secrets make their way into the kitchens at some point. But if I choose to help you, I'll ensure they go no further."

"Excellent," he said. "I require—"

Pain lanced through Zadani's gut. She winced as if stabbed.

Jasso touched her shoulder. "What's wrong?"

"Nuh—nothing," she grunted. But the pain came again and doubled her over. A whine started deep in her belly and worked its way to her lips. Sweat broke out between her shoulder blades. Pressure filled her face. "I'm fine."

"You aren't." Jasso Jackolo frowned, placed the back of his hand against her forehead. "Though, you're not fevered."

An oppressive weight landed on her chest, stealing her wind and bearing her down. Tingles shot into her fingertips and toes.

Jasso said something she failed to hear.

Boots rang off the flagstones of the hallway ahead. A pair of holdguard hurried toward Jasso and Zadani.

"What's this?" the scholar said.

The men stopped, saluted, fists crashing against bronze honor plates. Blood spattered their purple tabards. Their expressions were hesitant. Smeared with dirt and sweat. "Mistress Innan." One cleared his throat. "We uh—we're sorry to inform you..."

Meaningless, impossible words crashed into her like bolts of lightning.

She was falling. Light retreating. Not realizing she had swooned, she found herself in Jasso's arm. Her feet fought for purchase, heels prodding at stone as the hallway spun. A dim world pressed in around her.

Half-dragged along by Jasso, half-carried by her own feet, they followed the holdguard to a room. A woman from the Sisterhood of the Rose bent over a table, a familiar form beneath her.

Zadani pushed Jasso away and fell toward the table, her hands shaking over a mouth incapable of sound. Not even a scream. Insane thoughts came and went, asking her if she'd perhaps forgotten that she was asleep.

Perhaps it was just a nightmare.

It can't be him.

Knees weak, her body shook.

Not my Hadir. Not him.

Please don't be dead, my love.

Hadir. Please.

CHAPTER SIX

SHADII MASTER

Death stared at Valka, demanding he think fast or die. "I'm a friend, Essuhd." He spoke at a measured pace. "Let us talk first."

The Shadii master stepped from hiding. Shadow peeled back from an egg-like head nestled atop a coif of black chain mail.

Valka scrutinized the smaller man. "You never struck me as a zealot. So why betray our king?"

Essuhd chortled. "You would bait me into trust by claiming me the traitor." The dart-sling was steady in his powder-pale hand. "I will not be duped."

Valka shook his head. "If you're on the right side of this, then lower your weapon. I am no traitor."

Essuhd cocked his head, hairless brow bunching. "You're not bloody. Clearly, you've found something better to do than fight."

"My honor guard and I were on our way to an audience with Rathon. We heard fighting. Found a score of slaughtered Grimshields shortly after." Valka spoke hurriedly, not wishing the Shadii room to doubt his allegiance. "We've been rushing to the king's aid ever since."

"The king isn't here."

Valka flinched. "You have him somewhere safe, then?"

"Wouldn't you like to know."

The general leaned slightly. Yanos and the others held their position across the bridge. A warning hiss from Essuhd straightened him as soon as he'd glimpsed his men. In the shadows near the Shadii's waist, the dart-sling clicked. "Don't do that again, General. It makes me distrust you, and the seconds you breathe are fleeting. Convince me."

"That I'm not the Arrow of Light's pawn?"

"Something like that."

Valka picked his words carefully. "Present him to me and I'll show you what I think of him."

"How long have you worshiped the great dissembler?"

"Never," Valka growled. "I'm here to restore order and turn back the cultists."

"Oh?" Essuhd cooed. "And who's order would you be restoring? The boy's? Maybe your own?"

"Rathon's!" Valka hissed. Essuhd's eyes narrowed, and he decided to lose the edge in his tone before proceeding. "I swear to you upon Nera's head, I had nothing to do with this."

Valka held the Shadii Master's gaze. He stared at the general like a tomcat deciding the trajectory of its pounce upon prey. Valka inhaled, holding onto the life in his lungs as those facing impending death so often did.

"You understand," Essuhd said, "I can trust no one."

"And how can I trust you?"

"I have yet to kill you."

Valka nodded. That went a long way toward trust. Essuhd was innocent, and that made him a valuable ally if they were to survive. Confidence restored, he spoke plain but firm. "Listen to me, Essuhd. If I were the traitor, you and Rathon would be dead at my feet. That's a fact. I assume the same would be true if you and your Shadii turned your coats."

"The Shadii are not mine. They serve Scothea."

"So it is," Valka said. "Let them do so now. We can retake Darkfall—together."

Essuhd lifted what one might debate was a chin and then stepped fully into the sun's light. A portly, stunted figure, he looked out of place in plain sight. Truly, the Shadii Master was born to live in the shadows.

The poisoned dart-sling was wrapped around his wrist. A thin missile nestled on a leather pad on the back of his hand pointed directly at Valka's heart. The man lowered it. "You speak true. Neither of us would see a need for wide-scale violence like this."

The tension in Valka's shoulders abated with a slow exhale. "Is Rathon safe? We should go to him."

"He is within the Holy Chamber as you thought. Hiding in the inner sanctum with a dozen guards and the Void. A hundred Grimshields hold the throne room." Essuhd's dark little eyes shot to his peripheries. "I've not had reports from all my Shadii agents, but from those who've managed, it does not sound like it will be enough. Not by half."

"What do you know?"

"Little more than you. I fear my agents are depleted—they were the first target. Our enemy is clever. They knew the Shadii were the key to taking Darkfall. I slew three of my own in getting to where I now stand." He paused then spat onto the marble floor. "Information trickles in by bits and pieces. There are hundreds of invaders. Officers, servants, Grimshields—Scoths cut from every cloth stand on the side of the Arrow of Light. And every position they overrun wins more to their cause."

"How?" Valka searched the Shadii's face for answers that weren't there. "How is this possible?"

Essuhd's gaze fell to the ground. "As protectors of Scothea, you and I have failed. If I were not among those most capable of seeing the messiah killed for his crimes, I would throw myself into the sky in dishonor this very moment." He raised a shaking fist. "The Shadii will not rest until the betrayer is punished."

Fire erupted from a window on the other side of the bridge. Distant screams accompanied a shower of shattered glass.

"We tarry. Let us join forces in the chamber." Valka stepped into the light and whistled to Yanos. The captain brought the rest of the men hustling up the steps. They eyed the Shadii Master as they passed through the towering Door of Khaldis.

General and Shadii followed into a vaulted chamber and came face to face with a statue of Uhlvath I, the Seer King, who foretold the fall of the Rains of Fire. Marble pillars soared from floor to ceiling around the legendary monarch. In 595 years, no figure in history had rivaled the Seer King's skill at prophecy. Growing up, Valka's father was the royal librarian and did his due diligence to ensure his son was well-read. A memory flashed in Valka's mind.

"Ikarai, come." His father had beckoned him near. "Read this." It was a prophecy made by Uhlvath I.

Valka had slipped in beside his father where he hunched over a massive tome and then read aloud. "Three makes one and one makes three. In the shadow of great power will come the end of things unseen. First the Eye, bringing evil into the light. Then the Hand, ridding the world of its plight. Last the Fire, that in darkest hours unite. Three makes one, but only one makes free." The last word trailed into a whisper in the hushed library. Something momentous lay there, a mysterious truth sealed in a tomb. That young Ikarai had known. Yet the lack of specificity tilted his curiosity toward a deep foreboding. "What does it mean?"

"Well," his father said, "what do you think it means?"

Ikarai had read the prophecy again. Then a third time. "The Lands of the Endless Coast were three and then became one. Maybe we are the 'great power,' and we are the 'one' that will make them free."

"A most perceptive interpretation. But who are the eye, the hand, and the fire?"

Again, Ikarai puzzled over the text. "Uhlvath I, the Seer King is the Eye... Jathos Wrathhand, the Hand."

"And the Fire?"

A long pause ensued. "I don't know."

His father sighed. "What happened to Acramis when he was a child?"

Excitement overtook Ikarai. "He burned his hands falling into a brazier!"

"Exactly." His father had smiled and messed up Ikarai's dark hair. "You have a bright future ahead of you, my son. When you're of age, you'd do well to join Acramis's army. As we speak, he builds our military back to the glory it possessed during his father's years." The librarian's smile faded. "When we retake the Lands of the Endless Coast, you'll be a part of history. Wouldn't that be something? To be a part of a prophecy foretold."

Ikarai had beamed with pride. Twenty-five years later, he'd been there to witness firsthand his late father's misinterpretation of the prophecy. Luckily, his father had passed before the failure of the Second Crusade. Ikarai hadn't been there, but his mother claimed the man had died swearing that freedom would come to all the world when the young king, Acramis, prevailed.

Despite the lies Valka was fed as a child, he'd developed a love for history. In time, he came to uncover truths of his own. One in particular had oft rankled him. Scothean scholars wrongly accredited the origins of the Seer King's prophecy to Uhlvath I, when in fact, Mavis Ippolo had conveyed it to King Jathos before the First Crusade as outlined in her tome, *A History of Lands Near and Far*. In her words, it was a Kurgish shaman who originally spoke of the prophecy.

She had called it the Prophecy of the Long Silence.

Now, with the Arrow of Light working to seize Scothea, the recollection of the text scythed through Valka. The boy had a flame tattooed on the palm of his left hand...an eye in his right. *In the shadow of great power will come the end of things unseen.* In the years since its catastrophic defeat during the Second Crusade, Scothea had been reduced from its once mighty dominion.

This can't be. Disbelief made Valka sluggish as they continued toward the throne room. The thought that the false messiah might not be false clamped to the back of his mind, a rabid dog that wouldn't let go.

Essuhd grabbed Valka by the arm, holding him back as Yanos led the soldiers within the throne room. "This room has no ears." His tone fell to a whisper and his eyes flicked to the corners of the chamber. "And caution is a free resource."

Signaling Yanos to continue on without him, Valka waited, and then leaned in close to hear the assassin lord.

"I must leave you here, General. I've just received word from one of my agents. The messiah has taken Darkfall. We are all that is left."

Valka arched an eyebrow, shocked that a message had made it to the Shadii Master in the short journey through the Door of Khaldis. He eyed his men as they disappeared into the outer sanctum of the Holy Chamber. *One of them? Or perhaps a coded message planted in here?* He scanned the room.

"Listen!" Essuhd hissed. "They cannot be allowed to take the Shadii. You must join the cultists. Play the part of convert. If they imprison Rathon, my agents *will* free him. We'll gather strength in the shadows and find a way to kill the boy. Then we'll reinstall the Smith-King's bloodline. My Shadii have already secured Rathon's sons."

Valka let Essuhd's words sink in. *Play the part of convert...*

His gut churned with despair. To do that, he'd need to pledge fealty before all of his soldiers. Worse, he'd need to have them betray their king. He seethed with distrust of Essuhd. *Am I playing the pawn? Is this how they decayed the core of the military?* It was possible the Shadii Master had spared his life in a show of camaraderie only to fill his ears with misinformation and leverage the act for a victory not yet assured.

Valka stared down his nose at the stunted man who had risen from lesser, plains dweller stock to unimaginable heights of power. A skilled assassin and spy, yes, but was he also a sympathetic cultist who harbored decades of resentment against Scothean royalty? Had he been waiting for an opportunity like this all along so he could orchestrate the fall of a nation he reviled?

Or is he simply a devoted servant to Scothea, like me?

The dart-sling was a few feet away, still wound tight and ready about the Shadii's wrist...

To speak out in opposition to his proposed plan might make Valka seem a traitor, if Essuhd truly was an ally. But if he was with the foe, to follow the plan was utter folly.

The dart-sling was within reach. Valka's skin itched under the leather jerkin beneath his darksteel chest plate. A harrowing option remained available, hovering for a few heartbeats. They were twenty years apart in age, Valka the older, his hair gray wherever it still managed to grow, but he suspected he was stronger and a better fighter, man to man. Of sneaking and silent murder, Essuhd was second to none.

I could grab the Shadii's wrist before he understands what's happening. Killing Essuhd would send the Shadii into disarray—an invaluable blow to the messiah if he'd already converted them to his fanatical cause.

The words of Jathos Wrathhand came to mind. "In battle, fear kills swiftest. Confusion a close second. The ax, only third."

Valka chose. His hesitation caused Essuhd's expression to register danger for a fleeting moment. Eyes flickered towards Valka's fist as he brought it to his heart in a gesture of solidarity and saluted the Shadii officer.

With no plan of his own, Valka had to trust the man. Joining the false messiah's cult might be their sole chance of retaking Darkfall. The alternatives were grim. Above all, he wished to see Nera at least one more time. A sharp ache pinioned his heart at the thought of never looking into her deep brown eyes ever again.

"We are in this together now, Ikarai. Scothea depends on us." Essuhd made to leave.

"What if I'm killed? What if they do not believe my pledge of fealty?"

The Shadii turned halfway around. "You're the general of the Scothean legions. None is more loyal than you. Our soldiers trust you—the boy knows that. He'll need your help in transitioning the rest of the army to his cause."

None is more loyal. The words slid through him like a Shadii's poisoned blade. Would a loyal man betray his oath even if necessity demanded it? If Essuhd's plan went awry, history might not remember General Ikarai Valka for being a dedicated father nor a loyal servant to his nation.

Regicide and treachery will be my legacy.

Stars swarmed the outskirts of his vision. He swallowed a lump in his throat. "I'll do what I must...for the good of Scothea."

My submission might be the only thing that keeps Nera alive.

Nubbed yellow teeth and purplish gums filled Essuhd's mouth as his face split into a smile. "Worry not, General. My agents will attend you soon. Until then, we'll be in the shadows. Watching and waiting. Death in hand."

Valka returned a half-hearted smile. The Shadii slipped through the Door of Khaldis.

I will do what I must for the good of Scothea.

With an image of Nera firm in his mind, he turned and entered the throne room.

CHAPTER SEVEN

THE THING IN THE WOODS

G yr had accompanied Malus D'Alzir on numerous trips over the years. The Freedom Road to Alistar was the longest, but the journey to Kiyahd along the Shining Range's treacherous pass was the hardest.

Moments of peace and solitude were hard to come by. What shreds of it he could find were available only at the cusp of dawn. His ability to breathe unfettered by the yoke of command disappeared with the sun's rising.

Soon, he would drown in duties.

He walked past a sign that read "The Winding Way," and knelt beneath a blasted gray sky. The first panes of sunlight filtered through the forest canopy.

He sat, let his mind wander into the recent past, a frenzy of preparation, turmoil and strategy. Gyr and Malus had tirelessly planned. The contents of their letters had been strategically crafted. "Precision is essential," Malus had said.

Who to take and who to leave had also been a point of discussion. Brighthaven would be left in the care of the Mighty Boz, a duty Gyr suspected she enjoyed, though "covet," might have been the more fitting word. "Queen of the unwashed masses, eh? Who better than me?" she had said.

Although he wished otherwise, Gyr wasn't allowed to remain at Brighthaven. That would require his cupbearer, Caltheo, to be ready to give counsel, a skill honed by experience the man lacked. Sir Raius could manage the duke's physical protection sure enough, but where politics and shadow games were concerned, the duke needed Gyr.

So it is.

He sighed and lifted his gaze. A series of abrupt switchbacks and heavily forested slopes trailed up into dense mist. The Winding Way came to life. Perched on a dripping pine branch, a robin sang its song, inciting its fellow birds to take up the chorus. Across moss-strewn earth, squirrels raced, pausing at intervals to inspect a nut in a flurry of paws.

Wind whistled through the steel pauldron riding Gyr's shoulder. The honor plate bore four white arrows facing outward from the center, and a black one facing inward. He ran a hand over the fall of chain covering his torso. These days, he much preferred to give counsel in his priest's cassock beside a warm hearth rather than in battle dress and surrounded by a small army.

He placed a hand over his breast with his fingers spread, then cupped a second over the first, assuming the customary position of prayer for Followers of the Sempyrean.

Straighten. Breathe. Think nothing at all.

He closed his eyes—allowed a space within for the Sempyrean's voice to guide him.

The feel of Srah's wind rustling his cloak.

The smell of smoke from Ozoi's fires.

The sudden sound of stacking wood; a gift from Payon's bountiful earth.

The melting snow soaking his pants at the knees, Maletha's doing.

Breathing steadily now, he drifted from his frustrations. The robin's song tickled his ears. Calm washed over him. The chatter of his mind slowed, shifted with graceful intent from one thing to the next as if his thoughts were the slow swirl of a spoon through steaming porridge. His heart beat, strong and full.

A moment of complete attunement with the gods. That which all Followers yearned to achieve.

A moment without worry.

Gyr's body betrayed him, shattering the beautiful moment. A bout of wracking coughs set his lungs ablaze. He covered his mouth. Pressure pounded in his skull. His neck muscles strained, then softened as he swallowed moisture back into his throat.

Once the fit passed, it took him a moment to regain his breath. He shivered and huddled into his cloak. Determined to conceal his malady for as long as he could, he searched the area for witnesses. *Two years...*

Knees that had kissed the prayer bench before a thousand altars—that had carried him through a dozen campaigns spanning thirty years—creaked louder than the leather vest under his chain as he rose from the snow dampened duff.

Smoke coiled into the frigid mountain air from cook fires as the first of his soldiers shambled from their tents to seek the latrines, squinting against a haze of rain that had just begun. Walking to the fore of their retinue's camp, Gyr surveyed the fortifications.

Every protocol must be taken when the Duke of Lah-Tsarra travels.

One could never be too cautious.

As Gyr had instructed, the supply wagons served as a fortification along the side of camp with a downhill slope. A line of warhounds and sharpened stakes lined the uphill slope. The hounds had been a late addition to the retinue.

"A score of knights and fifty crownguard is more than enough for a short trip over the Winding Way," Malus had said. "Besides, I don't wish to tip our hand by appearing overly wary."

The day before they'd left, a crownguard found a scullion boy in the woods with his throat slashed. A messenger pigeon had been shot down nearby—the one to Onai Saud. The scene was grisly to behold, but the bird's missing message was most worrisome. The assassin had made a hasty departure, taking only enough time to shovel dead leaves onto the boy's corpse.

Malus had ordered all subsequent messages to be delivered by hand, then added fifty crownguard and a score of warhounds to their host for the journey to Kiyahd.

A fellow Namorite orchestrates our downfall.

The conclusion still staggered Gyr. *Who could be so mad that they'd invite Scoths back to our doorstep?*

Hours of debate had taken the place of rest as Gyr and Malus sought to locate their enemy through endless scenarios. In the end, Gyr decided it mattered little. Unity's death knell had been struck. If this traitor didn't succeed at destroying Namarr, another would. A crack in the door would eventually lead to its being kicked open.

Unless Prince Barodane returned.

With a wild prayer in his heart, Gyr wondered if his message had found Garlenna. *You have a difficult task, my daughter. Without you, our nation is lost.*

Rain turned to snow, blanketing the ground in a thin layer. The trail widened as they worked their way along a bluff lined with evergreens and pines. At midday, Gyr called for a halt, and then ordered warhounds and scouts to run a perimeter patrol.

Men wandered into the woods to relieve themselves, while others lined up beside a supply wagon to receive a ration of hard bread and fill their waterskins. Once most had finished, Gyr was about to order the scouts' return so they too could eat and drink before the march resumed.

A hound barked in the distance, causing him to hesitate.

What's this? Gyr pulled his horse's reins off the trail in the direction of the ruckus. He peered through dense branches. On the other side of a frozen pond, a crownguard with a warhound waved and whistled.

Caltheo appeared at Gyr's side, fresh from relieving himself and fumbling with the laces of his breeches. "A scout, Father." He finished buckling his belt.

Gyr urged his horse forward. "Caltheo, stay with Lord Malus."

Joined by Sir Raius, Gyr's horse churned powder and mud under hoof. They steered their mounts around evergreen branches that dumped snow from their boughs, and then emerged into a clearing.

Just past the frozen pond, they dismounted. The crownguard with the hound snapped a salute. The dog jerked at its leash.

"What is it?" Sir Raius looked everywhere but at the man he spoke with, his left hand wrapped around the hilt of his blade, vigilance unceasing.

"I don't know, captain." The crownguard cursed as his hound lunged, teeth gnashing in the direction of a cluster of trees. "Could be something. Could be nothing. I've never seen its like. Don't wish to again, either."

A putrid stench wafted over them. Gyr's stomach lurched.

Raius sniffed the air, a corner of his mouth bunched. "What's that?"

Somewhere behind them, a horse whinnied. *A trap.* Gyr whirled, reaching for his mace. Raius's sword sprang from its sheath, a far faster blade, but when they saw who it was, he cursed and thrust it back in the scabbard.

With a growl, Gyr named the rider. "Caltheo."

Like Gyr, his cupbearer's head was shaved. Unlike Gyr, he had the tan skin of a Lah-Tsarene and a tight brown beard. Eyes like a lizard's bulged from a baby-fat face. He dismounted and approached.

Measured anger tinged Gyr's words. "I told you to stay with the duke."

Caltheo's tone was pleading. "Father, the duke is surrounded by over a hundred others. If I'm to be prosort one day, you'll have to trust me with more than guard duty."

Gyr watched him, reluctant to admit the truth of what he said. He wasn't a teen anymore. Quite the opposite. The last couple of years, Gyr had watched him grow into his frame. Broad shoulders bore his slight excess in weight well. In addition to the Sempyrean practices, Gyr had made sure his cupbearer knew his way around the fighting yard. That which transpired in the shadows, though, Gyr doled out slowly. Some secrets were better left in the ears of those who knew what to do with them. The maturity and wisdom necessary for such things came with time.

Time I have little and less of. I must remember, it is Duke Malus I serve, not my preferences. Caltheo will be ready or he will remain a cupbearer forever. Gyr coughed, curt and crisp. He waited a moment, then cleared his throat. *Two years at best.*

He gestured for Caltheo to follow him in the direction of the warhound's fretting, and Sir Raius fell in behind.

"About a hundred paces," the crownguard shouted. "The smell should guide you."

As they walked, Gyr's chest ached. He recalled his meeting with the Sister of the Rose. Heard her words echoing in his mind. Felt his face flush with disbelief as he repeated them with numb lips. "The crimson curse?"

"Yes," the Sister had said. "You have two years at best. I'm so sorry."

Gyr rubbed a hand against his chest where it hurt worst. *If Malus ever finds out, he'll make Caltheo take my place before he's ready.*

Over the last few months, the crimson curse had grown increasingly painful. More than once, Gyr had coughed up a pinkish slurry with the blood. That's when the idea of his own mortality had truly set in; it painted scarlet messages across his palms and started funeral pyres in his lungs. "Don't die with regrets," the bloody gobs seemed to say.

Garlenna, I'm sorry. You deserved better. When her mother had died, instead of taking over his daughter's care, Gyr had delivered her into the arms of the Sempyrium, thinking they might make her a priestess. Or a cook, with a decent life in a convent's kitchens. Perhaps she could start a family of her own, a thing Gyr had never been willing to do.

But fate proved a fickle master.

Archprelate Alcor had had different plans. Training began shortly after she arrived at age six. Garlenna followed in Gyr's footsteps—surpassed them as she came to be the youngest and most highly exalted prosort in Sempyrium history.

It's my fault your life is no longer yours. I gave it away...gave you away.

Regret clogged his throat. He tried to feel proud of her success but couldn't, not when he knew she chased his approval. Not when she sought worthiness behind the same shield he'd never been able to put down. By spurning her, he'd shaped her life. A life of danger and death, of suffering and lies, all in the name of duty.

The slaughter at Rainy Meadows...just duty.

Despite enough gold to purchase land and a host of servants, Gyr tarried onward. Meanwhile, Garlenna no longer had the choice to resign her position. For the next decade, her life belonged to the Sempyrium, and so, he made sure his would too.

Over the years of estrangement from Garlenna, Gyr had found others to fill the breach in his heart. Malus D'Alzir, for one: any father would be proud of such a son. And Caltheo, Gyr's cupbearer. Though if Malus were the son whose success shined brightest, Gyr admitted that Caltheo lingered in the shadows. To appreciate his cupbearer required...practice.

Gyr considered the young man's progress, measured it against the current state of threat. *He's improved a great deal, but he's untested. I will resign when I know Malus is in capable hands. Then and only then.*

Cynicism was ever his weak point. *Hopefully, I'll live to see the day.*

The crownguard wasn't wrong about the smell. With a fury, it shocked Gyr back into the present moment. What had only been a gentle waft of putrescence was now a thick, fetid curtain he could not sweep aside. It pervaded Gyr's senses as they passed through a wall of boughs bearing clotted snow. He had smelled roadside carcasses plenty of times. This, however, was closer to the scent of a battlefield's aftermath than the corpse of a single dead animal.

Gyr choked back bile. The three of them drew green and gray tabards up over nose and mouth as they stepped inside a ring of trees. At its center, flies circled a pile of flesh and glistening offal.

Caltheo stole the words from Gyr's mind. "By the gods, what happened?"

Sir Raius ignored the comment. "It's not yet frozen."

Gyr squinted at the surrounding wood, then back at the pile.

Blood had sluiced across the grounds and coagulated in the cold. Hair scattered in matted clumps formed tiny islands amid swaths of maroon, tossed hither and thither by the wind.

A thin layer of frost and snowflakes gathered atop the rotting pile like a pastry dusted with sugar. More concerning still was that some of the mess appeared to have been dragged a short way, giving the violent scene the shape of a comet hurtling across the sky.

"What animal could do this?" Caltheo breathed. "A bear?"

The stench made Gyr's eyes water something fierce. Made him dizzy, too. Glittering shapes stole in at the edges of his vision. The pile and trees and snow started to twist away...spin...

He caught himself holding his breath—it was all he could do not to wretch.

"No clothes. No weapons." Raius's tabard fell from his nose, but he quickly recovered it. "Whoever it is, they're not one of ours." He had stopped looking at the pile and his gaze now jumped from shadow to shadow, his hand never straying from the hilt of his sword. "If it's even human."

"Not one of ours," Gyr confirmed. "We ran the count when we stopped. Everyone accounted for." Taking up a stick, he eased into a crouch to prod the gory husk. Kohl patches of bruising ran at the edges of jagged tears. *Claw wounds, perhaps? The marks of torture?* "Maybe Kurgs," he mused. "Though whatever they've done to this...traveler...would be a first for them."

"Could it be one of theirs?" Caltheo leaned over Gyr's shoulder. "A clan war?"

"No. The mountain enclaves have a golden hue. This..." He hooked a scrap with his stick and lifted. Purple blood raced along pallid flesh. "...Looks Lah-Tsarene. Or Kanian."

"How can you tell?" Caltheo stepped back, giving the mass a wider birth. "It smells as if it was conceived in Nacronus's twice-cursed loins. Could it be a swine?"

With a hand on his knee for support, Gyr rose from his crouch. An uneasy feeling settled between his shoulder blades. *Perhaps Caltheo's right. A bear attacking a pig might leave such a mess. Kurgs, too, deal in such savagery. But to whom? And why here?*

Gyr stared at the carcass, debating its importance. *The smell...so strangely potent.*

As if invoked, the vile scent poured into the back of his throat with his next inhale. He coughed wetly. Sharp pain raced up from his lungs. He hacked, grunted, rasped, chest thrumming with the strain. Vision dimming, he swooned and fell onto hands and knees in the snow. He eyed the rotting stack of meat sidelong, breath reduced to wheezing sucks.

Caltheo and Raius rushed to his side. Worry lined their faces. The latter handed Gyr a waterskin. A cool rush softened his gullet. The tightness in his chest loosened. The burning subsided.

Heaving like a mother in labor, but confident the fit had passed, Gyr sat back in the snow. Sweat riddled his pate. He ran a palm over his face, then rubbed the gathered moisture on his tabard. He looked up, found a worried expression on Raius's face, and a confused one on Caltheo's.

"Blood," Caltheo said.

Fresh scarlet painted the snow where Gyr had been. He wiped his mouth with the back of a hand. Warm. Sticky. A red ribbon laced with pink sputum clung to his knuckles. Head bowed, he flung it away.

Sir Raius's tone was hushed. "Are you—"

"It's nothing." Gyr's head snapped up. He glared at the pair. "And you'll say as much to anyone who asks. I'll have your word on it."

A grim look passed between knight-captain and cupbearer. Raius shrugged. Then the two nodded.

Caltheo helped Gyr to his feet. "We've lost none of our own. Let us be satisfied with that for now. This was the result of a bear. Or Kurgs exacting justice on their own. Neither is of consequence to us." Little would change if Gyr told Malus D'Alzir about the carcass. The retinue was already on high alert. No sense in fueling panic with yet another mystery. A traitor in the Collective was more than enough.

We must get to Kiyahd as quick as possible. That's all that matters now.

At the pond, they mounted then rejoined the retinue. During a conference with the duke, Gyr assured him it was nothing to be concerned about. *Maybe Caltheo is right.* "Animal remains. Nothing more."

Gyr gave the command to resume their march. As one, the wagons jerked forward, knights leading crownguard in files two abreast.

Even as the distance between Gyr and the thing in the woods increased, he failed to shake the image of rotting horror from his mind. Nor could he shake the guilt that maybe he'd just lied to his duke.

Very concerning, indeed.

CHAPTER EIGHT

DAMSEL IN DISTRESS

When they rose the next morning, Arick's brow was slicked with sweat. Ishoa made no mention of what she sensed had caused it. They both knew. For half a day they traveled, Arick with gritted teeth and a paling complexion, Ishoa with dread budding in the pit of her belly.

When they stopped to rest, Arick lurched against the base of a tree. Brow knit, he eyed her sidelong and wheezed. Ishoa couldn't bring herself to leave his side. Not even to search out food to stave off the hunger scraping at her spine. Rakeema, at least, would be okay. Ishoa wished she could command the ice tiger to hunt something bigger and bring it back. Their training had been cut short, however. So much had.

She took a shallow sip of water then gave the rest to Arick. He choked and sputtered, half of it going to waste. Through the latter part of the day, and all night, Arick slept. Ishoa watched. Worry set her to rocking on the stump where she sat. Starvation wormed its fiery coils around her insides. *Two rotten carrots in two days...*

It wasn't enough. Not when they were constantly on the move.

Sleep tossed her about, no comfortable place on the frosty ground where her stomach didn't scream her awake. *Do I refuse to leave Arick for his safety or am I afraid to go out on my own?* The latter, she decided, wasn't something she was willing to live with. *Too many have already died on account of me. I won't let him.*

Groggy, she woke to the sound of Arick's weakened voice. "Isha." She turned to find his eyes had become slits. The first rays of dawn slashed his face. His lips moved, but slower than they should. "Water."

Inwardly, she cursed. He'd been sweating all night it seemed, his clothing a shade darker with dampness. Lines were etched under his eyes and dry flakes mounded his lips, the hallmarks of dehydration.

Two days leaked past along with the last dregs of color from Arick's face.

On the first day, Ishoa had gone in search of water but found nothing that wouldn't kill him faster. A fetid bog, and a running stream with a dead body in it. Where it had come from, she wasn't sure, so she made haste from the area. With Arick down, she was susceptible to attack and anyone this far from the road couldn't be trusted.

On the second day, it dumped snow. She stripped off her filthy cloak and laid it out to collect flakes. After an hour, she funneled them into a waterskin. It was a significant amount of work to fill it just a third of the way. A majority of the snow tumbled off the spout until she thought to mash it inside with her pinky finger. She spit into the waterskin a handful of times and then shook it until all within was liquid.

She took a fraction of it for herself, then gave the rest to Arick. She repeated the action all day, but by the time night came, it was clear her efforts wouldn't be enough. Hydrating him was one issue. His fever, another. With Arick's teeth chattering as violently as they were, she wondered if it was possible for him to dislocate his jaw.

He needs a fire. I have to risk it. Usually, they reserved open flames for times when Arick killed a rabbit or squirrel but those days were behind them now.

She knelt in the snow over a pile of tinder and shavings that they'd been keeping dry in pouches on their belts. Flint and steel scraped and sparked. She paused and looked over at Arick.

Deadly still. She wondered how long she'd have to wait for him to get better. She swallowed hard. His mouth hung open. His flesh, waxen and sickly. *No...I'm waiting for him to die.* She loosed a growl, startling Rakeema.

Ishoa glared at Arick's inert form. "Enough! You're not dying!" Tears crowded her eyes. "I won't lose anyone else."

A spark arced onto the shavings and caught. Ishoa threw her fists in the air with a celebratory shriek, and then, taking fistfuls of his cloak and furs, she dragged him closer to the fire.

She returned to her stump, arms folded across her belly, and leaned forward to watch him with pursed lips. *You have to get better, Arick.* Besides Rakeema, he was the only family she had. If her great grandmother wasn't dead, she soon would be. Othwii had been killed by Lodecka. And Wolst had sacrificed himself so she might live. The scar left by her parents' early deaths had been freshly opened.

She balled a fist and punched her thigh. "You have to live!"

Arick's dry throat clicked. He gulped, choked on air, then returned to a piteous slumber of shallow wheezing. With each exhale, his chest stayed deflated for longer intervals. Ishoa watched, her breath catching as she stared, waiting for his inhale.

What will I do? What will I do if you die? I don't want to be alone.

As much as she disliked her cousin, Arick reminded her of the picture of her mother. The one she'd left behind. The one she'd never see again.

She glanced back in the moonlit dark. Trees and stones and rolling snows. Far from the Prince's Highway, she guessed they were somewhere between Jarik and White Plains. Arick had said as much a week prior.

Alarm whined through Rakeema. Prickles sprouted behind Ishoa's ears. She wrapped a hand around the knife sheathed at her belt.

Crunch.

A boot on snow. Not far off.

Arick moaned in his sleep.

"Who's there?" Ishoa's voice cracked. "I'm armed."

The soft crush of snow accompanied the swoosh of cloth as the intruder approached the ring of firelight. Ishoa rushed to Arick's side and shook him by the shoulder. Futile.

She stepped back. "Sajac."

Rakeema ignored her, snout fixed on the sound five paces ahead.

"Sajac!" Tightness edged Ishoa's command. The tiger's youth coupled with two weeks spent without training had seemingly made her heedless. Her tail swished as she crept farther from Ishoa. "Rakeema!"

Arick's eyes fluttered open, focus diffused. "Auntie Ishra?" he rasped. "Play another...please."

The mention of Ishoa's mother caused her to scowl at her cousin as his face went slack once more. Delirious and in no condition to fight, she was on her own.

"Hey there, girl." A man's voice. "We mean you no harm."

An unfriendly female voice added, "Call off the tiger."

"Are you armed?" The dark figures met Ishoa's question with silence. *Confirmation.* "Throw down your weapons and I may."

A few tense moments followed. The fire crackled and spit, sending a jolt through Ishoa. She hoped the strangers couldn't see her fear. She was a lone girl but she wanted to appear at least somewhat formidable—unworthy of the effort it might take to rob or rape her.

The man grunted. A rusty hand ax clanged off a rock ringing the fire, followed by a dagger and broadsword.

Ishoa shifted her weight onto the balls of her feet and adjusted the grip on her knife. "Just the two of you?"

"That's right." The woman started to sidle past Rakeema but the anjuhtarg sent her stumbling back with a swipe and a hiss.

"Sajac dammit!" This time, Rakeema's haunches twitched as if struck by a whip and she came to her master's side. Ishoa scratched her cat behind one ear and spoke in soothing tones, half-attempting to convince herself to be calmer as the intruders stepped into the light and took a seat on the other side of the fire.

"We're all good now, kid." A crooked grin peeled up one side of the wrinkled man's face. "You can stow the blade."

Ishoa spit a response. "Great advice but I think I'll keep it."

The strangers exchanged a look. The woman, at least twice Ishoa's age and sporting a pulpy bruise high on one cheek, shrugged. "Makes no difference to us. We ain't worried."

No. No you aren't, are you? Ishoa resisted a frown. Wolst had taught her to respect naked steel, no matter how rusty, notched, or dull it may be. No matter who held it. A broken sword pierced skin easy enough and these people didn't have shields. It was possible they weren't afraid of her because they didn't mean her harm.

Arm relaxing, Ishoa's knife hand dipped. Rakeema's hackles still bristled though and her ears were perked.

"So," the man said, "got any food?"

Ishoa shook her head.

"Dang." The woman sucked at her teeth and took in the campsite. She started talking about how long it had been since they ate last but Ishoa only half paid attention.

One of Wolst's stories reminded her where to focus instead. "In my youth, when I got a bit overzealous with my godsbrew, there was always some hard-hearted bastard—usually tall with an ego full up to the rafters—who would get to thinking I was a bit loose-lipped for a grizzly cub my age and that it was his job to teach me a lesson. Never strike last—I learned that quick enough. In a scrap between behemoths my size, it only takes a clip of a fist this size to fell a man." Wolst had held up his knotted knuckles and cracked them before Ishoa's face. "To make sure I was always first, I talked a little nonsense to distract them, and before they knew it, they were snoring on the floorboards." That big, mischievous, love-filled smile spanned the breadth of her memory. "Violence is a feeling in your bones, Isha. If someone really means you ill, they rarely announce it."

They carried weapons, and judging by the woman's face, they'd fought recently. Both sat. Neither crossed their legs, nor leaned back at ease. Their feet were still planted on the ground, their hands resting on their knees. A dark substance—blood or dirt—crusted their fingernails. There were faint lines ringing their brows where sweat had streaked through soot. *Helmets?* The man's chest swelled and contracted more rapidly than it should. Ishoa watched the woman intently. Her nostrils were dilating in rhythm. The woman was subtly employing furnace breaths like Wolst had taught her to do in the heat of battle. The woman did well at covering it, for an untrained eye would have never noticed.

"Well?" The woman had asked her something.

"Well what?"

The woman leaned forward, elbows on knees, shadows pruned away in the firelight to reveal unmucked rows of ocher teeth. "Is he bed-bound?"

"Can he move?" asked the man.

You mean can he fight. After a moment's hesitation, Ishoa nodded. "Went hunting earlier today. Having a moment is all."

The man grunted. "Sure he is." He must have noticed the grim expression on Ishoa's face because he pumped palms in the air. "Easy girl. We're the same as you. Nothing to fear from Old Borry and Damsel."

"Damsel?"

The woman nodded. "Aye."

Rakeema's head jerked, emerald gaze sweeping toward something else in the dark, then swiveled back to Old Borry and Damsel. Ishoa's gut clenched. "What do you want? I have nothing. If you mean me no harm—"

"Strange days." Damsel cut in. "Strange days, these. Anjuhkar overthrown. High-handed holders fighting alongside Scarborn scum. The Ironlight's fall ...old guard fading before the new. World's a wild place to be right now." She fixed Ishoa with a haunted look. "Can't trust anyone anymore, can you? Not with this damn plague of greed bleeding all over us."

"Strangers looking to share the warmth of a fire are enemies now," Old Borry said. "A sad generation we've raised. No chance of peace nor friendship."

Rakeema thrashed under Ishoa's hand, forcing her to grip the ice tiger by the scruff.

Damsel turned her head and spat. "No chance at all."

A tattoo on the woman's neck peeked from her collar. The top of an oak tree. An oak tree Ishoa was exceedingly familiar with. "You're treekin...from Shadowheart." Elation filled her, causing the tension in her shoulders to melt. "You were there, weren't you?"

Rakeema twisted, attempting to free herself from Ishoa's clutches as the strangers stared at her, their faces unreadable.

"Ain't many folk with a cat like that," Damsel said.

"Almost none," Old Borry confirmed.

Do I tell them who I am? She watched their expressions. They seemed suddenly more guarded but perhaps that was to be expected, given she'd guessed their hold. She glanced at Arick, sweating and murmuring. Without help from a healer, he wouldn't last much longer, but without his sword, none of them would.

Before she could declare her identity, Old Borry whistled sharply and wagged a finger at her. "You're the fucking princess, ain't ya?" His mouth fell open and he slapped Damsel with the back of his hand. "Course she is. Look at her...the fucking anjuhtarg and the eyes and everything Ironlight you ever heard about."

Damsel didn't move. Attention sucked in around the woman, a declaration of swift movement made imminent.

Eyes darting between the pair, Ishoa's grip on Rakeema loosened. "Megalor Bog is a loyal servant." The knife in her hand rose at her side. Sweat broke out across the back of her neck. "Faithful to the Ironlight line. Faithful to Namarr."

"Faithful to a dying dream, you mean," said Damsel. "We won't be eating his shit no more. That's concrete now."

"Fuck Megalor." Old Borry eyed his weapon on the ground, and then he looked to the dark wood surrounding them. He raised his voice. "Warnocks'll give us a fortune for the last Ironlight."

Deserters.

Wolst's warning screamed from the past. *Never strike last!*

"Heeti!" Ishoa released Rakeema's scruff as she dipped down to Arick, grabbing the hilt of the sword belted around his waist.

She heard the pair stumble back, Old Borry's curses shifting to a pained whine. Ishoa freed Arick's sword and spun. Blood flooded the anjuhtarg's mouth where it latched onto Old Borry's wrist. The ice tiger whipped her head side-to-side like a dog with a bone, and the former Bog holdguard shrieked.

Ishoa managed a single step before strong hands yanked her backward by the hair. She reeled, sword lashing wildly at the unseen attacker—nearly cutting herself as she stumbled and fell ass first, hands flinging out behind to keep her from cracking her head. A knee landed on her wrist, neutralizing her sword and crushing the hand holding it. A fist thudded into her gut from above. Spots of light dilated at the corners of her vision and vomit rose in her gorge. They dragged her flat.

A bearded face snarled down at her. "Get her legs!" Two more sets of hands pressed down. Someone sat on her thighs. She raised her head. Loops of rope were being cinched around her ankles. She thrashed. Hissed through clenched teeth. She bit to either side seeking exposed flesh, but as soon as she made contact with a forearm, it withdrew. "Watch it now!"

Somewhere in the dark, Rakeema snarled.

"Sajac!" If Rakeema could force the men off her, maybe she could get her weapon back.

Her anjuhtarg never came. She heard them cursing and slashing. A sword struck wood—the stump she'd been sitting on. When the deserters were done binding her, they'd kill Rakeema. "Go!" Ishoa cried. "Rakeema, go!" She wished she knew the command to make her ice tiger flee.

Those binding her flipped her over and forced her hands behind her back to tie them. Ishoa's mouth was pressed into the cold, wet dirt. She glanced sidelong, barely making out Rakeema's haunches as she danced back from a sword thrust. The battle frenzy was on her now. She would never retreat. Rage pumped through Ishoa. *Please, not another.*

"This one's a Quinn!" A silhouette worked hastily over Arick's inert form, binding him the same as Ishoa. She took a bite of earth, filling her mouth as the rope around her wrists was pulled burning tight. "Should do. Haul her up."

They did.

Ishoa spewed the dirt into the first face she saw. They flinched, giving Ishoa enough distraction to smash her forehead into their nose with a satisfying crunch. She hopped toward the fire, making it to the edge of its glowing nimbus before she tripped. She twisted midair and came down on her shoulder. Pain stabbed up her neck and through her ribs. She rolled over, breath clutched in her lungs, unable to release.

A face covered in dirt and spittle, beard caked in blood, loomed over her. The man heaved with malice. "That'll cost you a tongue, bitch."

Ishoa stuck it out at him. He snarled and lurched to grab her—she kicked out, heels slamming into his knee and folding it backward. He gasped and then keeled over like a felled timber. Two more dark figures replaced him, approaching more cautiously. Ishoa tried to roll away but they grabbed her and sat her upright.

"Rakeema!" Ishoa craned her head around. Bark stung the inside of her mouth. She screamed. "Go!"

The ice tiger dipped beneath a swing of Damsel's hatchet, then sprang, outstretched claws raking the woman's hip. Damsel grunted. "Someone help me with this thing."

Pale-faced Old Borry came to stand cradling a tattered hand that looked as though it was dipped in blood. He dragged a rusty sword along behind with his good hand. "I'll do for that fucking cat alright."

"Leave her!" Ishoa struggled against the other deserters' grips. "Lodecka Warnock wants her alive, you fool!"

Spittle flew from Old Borry's face as he circled around behind Rakeema. "You think I give a fancy shit what—"

His head leapt from his shoulders then rolled into the fire. It started to smoke, the scent of greasy hair clogging the air. The hands holding Ishoa moved to draw steel as Old Borry's corpse collapsed.

Damsel stumbled sideways into the firelight, a wild look in her eyes. "It's—it's him. Oh fuck."

"Who?" shouted a man behind Ishoa.

A seven-foot shadow materialized from the dark. A long haft with an ax on either end rotated in one of the towering figure's black-gloved hands. Ishoa's blood ran cold. Her mouth worked for words that never came.

She was shoved aside as the five remaining deserters fanned out.

The Fly was motionless as if wholly unconcerned. Rakeema jumped at him from behind. He spun about, dizzyingly fast, foot snapping around in a level arc to catch her full on the snout. Ishoa cried out as her ice tiger was flung across the earth by the blow.

A deserter rushed the Fly before he'd completed the motion. The ax-staff whirled upward, splitting the man's face in two. Hands a constant blur, he looped the weapon around his waist to block a sword thrust from a second attacker. The other end of the ax-staff spun around and relieved the man of his guts. They splashed to the ground, spattering the fire and sending up sizzling gouts of smoke. Cradling his innards, the man dropped and started to convulse.

The Fly remained locked in a fluid, relentless attack. Like a magician performing a trick, a dagger appeared in one hand while the other twirled the staff. He threw the knife at the man whose nose Ishoa had broken. The hilt sprouted in the man's gullet.

Damsel turned and ran into the darkness. With a curse, the last deserter kicked the fire, hoping to blind the Fly.

But Megalor Bog's bodyguard twisted, embers bouncing off his back as he avoided the worst of it. If they burned him he gave no indication. He dropped to a crouch, weapon whooshing the air in an orbit around his torso. Unpredictable. Undefendable in the hands of one so capable.

The last deserter lunged. One of the Fly's ax-heads flashed in the gloom, lopping off the former holdguard's foot at the ankle. The wounded man's momentum carried him forward, gory stub smashing into the dirt. He yowled until the Fly buried an ax in the back of his skull.

Then he moved on to the man with the knife in his throat. He was making a glucking sound and his eyes widened as the executioner approached. With both hands, the Fly raised his ax-staff moonward and then dropped it onto the deserter's forehead with a wet *schunk*.

A chill swept down Ishoa's arms as the Fly stepped past her.

He located a rope on the belt of one of her assailants and used it to tie Rakeema's mouth closed and bind her paws. The anjuhtarg's tongue lolled as she came to, wriggling in the Fly's grasp. He wasn't gentle with her, but it didn't seem like he meant to kill her, either. For that, Ishoa was grateful.

"What do you mean to do with me?"

Not even a glance in her direction.

Some of the dirt she'd held in her mouth had worked its way into her throat, leaving her voice scratchy and hoarse. "You kill your own to save me yet you leave me bound?"

Megalor Bog's executioner slid a hand into his belt and withdrew a pouch. He bent over Arick and used the knife Ishoa had dropped to cut away the clothing around her cousin's wound...then he started to carefully flay the rotted flesh surrounding it.

Arick whimpered.

"What are you doing?" she shouted. "Stop!"

A tremor of acknowledgment—a fractional slowing of the Fly's movements. Then he continued. A grainy substance was pinched between his fingers, taken from the pouch at his belt; this he daubed into Arick's wound.

He was helping them.

The featureless black mask turned to regard her. *But why?* Unalor said his uncle kept the Fly close in times of duress. Given the fall of Anjuhkar, it seemed the Fly should be glued to his master's side. She looked around, half expecting Megalor Bog to step from the trees.

But no one did. They were alone. At the Fly's mercy.

Is he a deserter, then? A friend?

A sudden realization buried itself in Ishoa's chest like an ax-blade.

Or has he just slain his competition for my bounty?

She watched him. Unmoving. Silent.

And he watched her in turn.

CHAPTER NINE

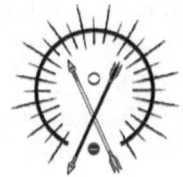

BENEATH THE SURFACE

A black sea held him. The muffled lapping of waves was a quiet rush in Thephos's ears, similar to the sound he'd come to know whenever he had submerged his head in the pigs' drinking trough to cool off on hot days.

Yet here, he could breathe. Something soft but dense encompassed Thephos's hand. A tingle ran up his spine. There was a presence beside him in the dark place. The thing wrapping around his hand, a far larger one.

The thought shot fear through him. He started piecing together the events that had led him to this place, though somehow, he knew the entity at his side meant him no harm.

"Thephos." Syn Backlegarm's voice. Garbled and distant, pinwheeling from the darkness. A point of light sprang to life and the inky waves melted back from its center. With light came silhouettes, angular forms—images.

A sudden intensity of blinding white light.

Thephos shielded his eyes as it dimmed and diffused into a world full of color. He glanced down at his hands. No chains. No larger hand holding his own. When he looked up, Syn stood before him.

"You betrayed me." Thephos recalled the stony look on his so-called friend's face...just before he took him prisoner. "You lied to me. I thought..." *We were friends!* "I thought you cared."

"Listen carefully," Syn started.

Thephos cut him off. "You're a liar."

"I'll show you the truth if you just—"

"The truth?" Wrath bubbled in Thephos's chest, but his voice still trembled with self-pity. He let his hands fall to his sides. "Why?" A desperate word echoing through the empty place surrounding them.

Syn's image distorted, shifted. The trappings of a gambling den owner seethed, color and shape a boil of sudden motion—and then it was gone, replaced with a drab cloak, vest, and breeches. Gone was the flamboyance, the guise of imitative royalty, the blaring distraction from who, or what, the man truly was.

Thephos blinked at the man. *Impossible.* He scanned his environment again. "Where are we?"

"A safe place."

A discerning man with a mission in his eyes now stood before Thephos. *Not evil though. I know what that looks like.* "What happened to your clothing?"

"Fine clothing with exotic origins, but a fake persona," Syn said. "Just a ruse. Should be obvious by now."

As the veneer dissipated, understanding settled into Thephos's brow like a brick slapped into mortar. "You're Awakened."

"That's what they say. I just feel more like myself. I still question and worry and all that human stuff. People seem to think Awakened have the voice of gods in their ear, when really, I just hear myself louder and clearer." Syn spread his hand. "Being honest, I was pretty loud to begin with. Got shushed a lot." He swiveled his torso to either side. "Safe place. Very different than when I became Awakened."

Thephos studied his captor.

"What?" Syn's arms drifted apart as he looked down the length of his body. "Not what you were expecting one of us to look like? Well...I am a Dominarri, so that's kind of the point."

Thephos frowned. Olthr, the unimist monk, had ascended Unturrus with the hope of one day joining the secret order of Dominarri. Other than the fact that they held a seat on the Namorite Collective, and that they had played a pivotal role in Danath's rebellion, Thephos knew little about them.

Save one thing.

"You're going to kill me." Shoulders slumping, Thephos gave a stuttering exhale. "I'm Ruptured, aren't I?"

Syn's chest swelled, clearly discomfited. "That's what we're here to find out."

"You're not worried?" Thephos thought of the voice that had followed him from the slopes of Unturrus.

One of Syn's brows arched.

"That I might...kill you."

The Dominarri laughed and waved his hands. "By the Triune God, no. Worry you might go mad, sure. Worried you'll kill me? Not at all. Watch."

Syn's eyes flashed, burst into pooling pits of burning white. Pain stabbed the back of Thephos's skull. He squeezed his eyes shut.

The light ebbed enough for him to lower his hands and look. A titan loomed before him. He lurched backward and fell on his ass. The laces of Syn's boots were as broad as Thepho's chest. Clumps of dirt from a moment before that

Thephos could have flicked away with a finger were now densely packed boulders he would struggle to lift.

Mouth agape, his gaze traveled upward. Syn's mountainous stomach blocked the rest of the man's face from view. That is, until he bent forward. Air whooshed around Thephos. The rustle of fabric became a landslide in his ears. Syn smiled, eyes still aglow, a face the size of the moon absorbing all sight. "All I gotta do is spit! Haha!"

Thephos's fingers jammed into his ears, protecting him against the Dominarri's thunderous voice.

"Oh," Syn whispered. "Sorry about that. But truthfully, I don't need to spit."

Thephos's body stiffened and went cold. He glanced down to find himself dissolving into a pool of rippling mirror at his feet. A reflection of his horrified face looked back at him as he inched down deeper, legs gone at the knee. "No! Please!"

Syn snapped his fingers and Thephos's body was fully restored.

He fell to his hands and knees, heaving and shaking. Only a part of his distress had been Syn's doing. Just before the mirrored pool had disappeared, Thephos glimpsed a pair of gigantic horns curling above his temples, and dots of blue flame flickering in each eye...

What was that?

Terror clamped around him, its claws sinking into his belly and squeezing. *I'm Ruptured?* He gasped.

"Looks like you get it." Syn returned to his normal size in a blink. "I have to do all that to show you how powerless you are. My mind, my rules."

Thephos struggled to his feet, shaking off the doubts that threatened to overtake him. *Stay focused. Let him decide.* "I'm in your mind?"

"Kind of. Your body is wrapped up snugly in my tent with a handful of very deadly Dominarri watching you. Your consciousness, however..." Syn tapped his temple. "Safe and sound with Mr. Backlegarm until we find out if you're dangerous."

Thephos gave a solemn nod. Horns and blue fire flashed across his mind. "If I am?"

I'm here for you, Theffy. Thephos jolted at the voice, neither his nor Syn's.

The Awakened's gaze hardened, suspicion shading his words. "I'll make it quick. You're a good guy who got dealt a bad hand. If you're Ruptured, it's not your fault." Syn's head wobbled back and forth. "Well, I guess it sort of is, but that's a big picture question. I'm just a watchdog and spy, and once in a while, I'm forced to play executioner."

The way the man said the last, Thephos could tell it wasn't something he was proud of. "So what now?"

Syn shrugged. "You take a test."

Thephos screamed.

Flames consumed his toes. Crackling flesh split and blackened as fiery tongues licked up his calves. Sweat burst across his chest and scalp as he dropped backward, pelvis striking the ground with bone-rattling force. He paid it no mind. Searing pain absorbed all.

He scooped at the ground hoping to cast dirt or water or anything he could at his burning skin, but nothingness filled his palms.

"Nope." Syn Backlegarm's voice was a distant dream on the other side of his crippling torture. "Not going to work, friend."

Thephos begged for mercy.

"Use your powers," Syn said. "Stop me."

Rage eddied through him. A shadow loomed behind Syn, four times his size. "I can't! Please! I—I don't know how..."

An acrid stench filtered into his nose. Scorched flesh filling his nostrils. Tears stung his eyes.

White light pulsed in Syn's eyes. The fire dissipated. Thephos moaned and sat up—his body unburnt. A heartbeat later, the searing agony had gone, leaving him with clenched fists and a subtle yearning to exact revenge.

"Before I took this post with the Dominarri, the process was far less safe," Syn said. "We had to do all of this in reality. Luckily, I was the last to undergo *physical* Provocation." He swept back his cloak and lifted a foot. The boot disappeared. A pinky toe was missing. He did the same with the other foot to show it too had been mutilated. "Loved those little things."

A growl built in the depths of Thephos. Energy pulsed inside him, making his shoulders ache and his hands feel as if they were swelling, hardening, until they felt like he could crush Syn's skull as easily as a beetle.

The Dominarri straightened. His mouth became a flat line, his eyes filling with sorrow. "You wish to hurt me back, don't you?" He gulped back hope.

Smooth hands slithered up onto Thephos's shoulders. Darkness crept in at the edges. Warmth, the kind that rolled off an open mouth, brushed up to one ear. *I'm here for you, Theffy.*

"No." Thephos jerked away and let his fists go limp. "No."

"I pray that you might one day appreciate the necessity of what I do." Syn stepped to one side. "And how much I hate doing it." Behind him, a hulking mass padded forward from white mist. The bear's charcoal fur was matted and its red eyes were fathomless and dull. Viscous beads of drool hung like nooses from rows of gleaming teeth.

Thephos turned to run—too slow.

The bear charged, hammering Thephos to the ground from behind. Fangs sank into his butt cheek. "Ah!" He was hoisted into the air and flung—landed hard—elbows and knees striking the unyielding, blank plane.

"Come on, Theffy! Kill it!"

He had crawled only a few feet before the bear was on him again. Its jaws gripped his calf and crushed, bone snapping. Thephos gasped. Blunt claws pinned him flat to the ground, squeezing his torso to breathlessness as the bear tore a chunk from his hamstring. *Gods! Gods no!* The mangled limb went numb, pain fleeing before shock. In the vacuous, all-consuming horror of his death, his body became a distant entity. *Am I on godsthorn again?* The veil between physical vessel and conscious awareness thickened, becoming an expansive haze. Somewhere else, he heard the labored growls of the bear. The ripping of rubbery flesh. The crunch and grate of bone.

Light dilated, then winked out.

Nothing.

Thephos drifted, ears abuzz with keening and vibration.

Syn's voice sliced through the illimitable din. "How about now?"

Dazed, Thephos rubbed his face. Vague comprehension told him he was prostrate on his belly on the ground. He sent a shaking hand down his leg. The bear was gone, as were the damages it had wrought.

"I wronged you," Syn said. "And I'll continue to do so. Loose your powers or suffer!"

"I don't know how." Thephos's tone was hollow, despondent. *You lie,* the voice cooed. *Release me.* "And I don't want to," Thephos added quickly as the fog from the bear attack retreated.

"Alright." Syn stepped close. "You don't follow your impulses. That's good. I almost killed the Dominarri who performed my Provocation. Sucked him into my mind and dropped him into an ocean with a big stone tied to his feet. Surprised the shit out of him. Luckily, I pulled my wits together before it was too late. Ruptured usually can't deny their desire for retribution. Righting wrongs or wronging rights, makes no difference so long as they come out on top." His voice was solemn. "However, some of them can, on rare occasions, suppress that insidious call, so we're going to have to keep going. Maybe something a bit more...ingrained."

The world rotated around Thephos as if he looked out from the inside of a rolling wagon wheel. When it came to a stop, his little brother stood before him, the willow tree and an open grave behind.

A sword of purest ice plunged into Thephos's heart.

Rot had set in. His little brother's eyes were sunken and shriveled. Worms writhed here-and-there where sheafs of graying flesh hung open. Dark-lipped and pale, the dead boy seized Thephos by the wrist. "You could have saved me! But you're weak. A coward!"

"I'm sorry." Thephos froze in place. "I'm so sorry."

"No you're not."

The old devil rose up behind Thephos's little brother. "Come on! Back you go, you little cunt!" His father jerked the boy off his feet and dragged him toward the grave.

Thephos snarled, then lunged after them, hands wrapping around the old devil's neck. With all his might, he squeezed. With all of it and more, he hauled backward, screaming with panicked fury—to no avail.

His father laughed. "Pathetic." His younger brother wailed as he was dragged to the edge of the grave under the willow tree. Tears streamed down Thephos's cheeks. He dug his heels into the ground, but got no purchase and the old devil was impossibly strong. A string of indecipherable words flew from his mouth as he struggled to stop the bastard.

And for the second time in his life, he failed.

"In you go!" The old devil propelled his young son into the open grave.

Heat buzzed in Thephos's ears. Bursts of blue light—the same as the Mother's wings—descended. Power expanded within Thephos. Filled him to brimming. The tether of Syn's mind seemed to lay across his open palm for a moment, a puny and fragile thing he knew he could easily destroy.

I'm here for you, Theffy.

All he had to do was squeeze.

Thephos's balled fists pressed against the sides of his head. *I can't!* He unleashed a guttural roar and then fell to his knees in a whimpering pile.

A hand touched his shoulder—Syn. The Dominarri crouched beside him. Thephos wept as the large man pulled him into his chest and held him. "You're okay. You're okay."

Exhausted to the core, every piece of him tingling with hate, power, and sorrow, Thephos leaned back to search the Dominarri's face.

"More than okay, actually," Syn said with a sad grin. "You, my friend, are an Awakened."

CHAPTER TEN

THE TOMB

Hadir's lifeless eyes were fixed on the ceiling.

Zadani flinched. *A nightmare, that's all this is.* She took her husband's hand. "Come on now, love," she pleaded. "Come on..."

She waited, hope more burden than buoy, and squeezed his hand. No pulse, nor familiar pressure in response. No smile. No tug at her fingers to coax her into scratching his back.

Nothing.

So stiff.

"I am sorry, Mistress Innan," said the Sister of the Rose. "He passed before I could do anything."

A muck of cold sorrow filled Zadani's belly. Sobs clutched the back of her throat. Mouth hanging open, her eyes searched Hadir's body in disbelief.

Deep wounds covered him. Blood soaked the tan linen and brown trousers he'd worn that morning, turning them nearly black. Hadir's olive skin, so pale now, was drained of anything that made him who he was.

This is but a husk. A dead thing. My Hadir was full of life.

Zadani dropped the rigid hand. "That isn't him."

One of the holdguard jerked his head in her direction. "Mistress Innan, I assure you—"

With a sharp intake of breath and a wave of her hand, she silenced him. "I know! My husband is dead...I know."

Tears flooded her eyes. She gripped Jasso Jackolo's shoulder to steady herself. She sobbed, a shaking hand shielding her eyes. Snot trailed onto her upper lip and she wiped it way. "How?" she managed to ask, though more than how, she wanted to know why. *Why? Why my Hadir?*

"A bear attack," a holdguard said. "We came upon him during a sweep of the north wood."

Jasso Jackolo shifted. She searched his frowning face. *He disagrees?*

The scholar shook his head and threw an arm around Zadani's trembling frame. "I'm sorry for your loss."

She pushed off, brushing the wet from her cheeks. "You had a thought and I will hear it."

Jasso seemed to recognize the implacability of her command. He nodded. "Only an observation, mistress. It is late harvest. There should be plenty of food for a bear. And if it had been keen on prey..."

"He must have run afoul of some cubs," said a holdguard.

Zadani swallowed at the rawness in her throat. "But he was so careful."

The other holdguard shrugged. "Perhaps it was a storm bear. Food's a bit scarcer this time of year...in uh...in Anjuhkar."

Jasso scoffed. "Storm bears are migrating from Twilight Cape these days, are they? My knowledge must be dated. I'll have to applaud Lord Marus for teaching only the best and most recent scientific developments in *guard* training."

The man purpled at the slight.

"No storm bear has ever been sighted beyond Shadowheart." Jasso twisted his knowledge into the man like a knife. "That is what we refer to as a fact."

"It could be that he shot the bear and then it charged him, mistress," said the other holdguard. "We really can't know."

This can't be right. Zadani's chin fell to her chest. "Please, if you would, a moment alone."

They filed out.

Jasso was last to exit, but before he did, Zadani grabbed him by a flowing sleeve. "I would speak with you. Not now, but..." Tears came unbidden.

"Take your time, Zadani," the scholar whispered. Then, he left her alone.

She fell to her knees beside Hadir's body.

"Come back. Please come back." For how long she wept and begged at his side, she wasn't sure. Like everything else, time had lost its meaning.

No amount of tears can reverse what is.

The thought made her furious. Hadir was good. She was good. Neither deserved such a harsh goodbye.

Eventually, the candles waned and the room grew chill. It didn't feel right, grieving in there, where death was the focus. *It is not our place.* Fingernails left scratches where she wiped at her tears. *I want our place. I need it.*

An immense courtyard led to a gently sloping hill surrounding Hawk's Keep. Moonlight spilled over the garden's maze of hedgerows, giving them silvery tops. She weaved between them on her way to the back entrance of the servant's wing. It was a more difficult walk than going through the halls of the keep but far quicker. By the time she arrived at the room she shared with Hadir, her lungs burned and her heart thudded—the only two things telling her she still lived.

Most nights, light spread under the crack of the door from candles Hadir had lit.

Tonight, there was no such light. Never again would there be.

Disappointment snatched the pleasant memory from her. A simple emotion, now stunning in its pain.

Keys rustled in her pocket, then filled her hand. Unlocking the door, she felt it before she could even name what *it* was. A stale wind of wrongness that rushed to greet her as she stepped inside. The room felt foreign—not hers—and her skin crawled with the unreality of it.

A hopeful but false thought told her to check the bed. That maybe, Hadir was playing a joke. That he hid under the furs.

She shook her head. Denial was the herald of madness, they said. From pit to throat, emptiness yawned within her.

He's really gone.

Fighting through rapid breaths, she lit a candle. She turned in a full circle at the center of the room, searching every shadowed corner. This was a place of life. The place they shared. The place they made love and laughed and held each other. Smiles full, eyes drinking the other's joy—reflecting it in an endless and perfect cycle they'd vowed to never break.

This is Hadir.

She climbed into their bed. An image of his ruined body came to mind, jolting her.

He was so careful though.

Dread settled into her bones.

No. Something is wrong.

Three days came, a timeless drip of faces and flowers, of whispered condolences and shuffling feet.

Three days went, a murky dream bereft of feeling. A reckoning between a past and future irrevocably changed.

There was no anchor to any of it, and so, she floated along in a thick malaise until the burial. The quiet touch of emotions returned—most of them unwelcome.

The first feeling she'd experienced in days was surprise. Swathed in black velvet and wearing hawk brooches, Lord Marus and Lady Daran were in attendance. Their presence was an honor few servants were given. The greater surprise was that Hadir would be given his own tomb rather than sharing one with the other commoners as dictated by tradition. A tomb tucked against the eastern garden wall among the D'Alzir family's ancestors.

"The least I could do. He was a great man." Lord Marus presented Zadani with a wreath of azure sentinel roses, a gift of surpassing beauty and worth. "He will be missed."

Despite the momentous gesture, Zadani had barely the energy to muster a bow. A pair of tears slid to the end of her nose as she dipped forward.

A bell rang, beginning the burial ceremony.

A procession of hunters bore Hadir's palanquin past the tomb of Lord Blackwind and the rest of the D'Alzir family's ancestors housed at the fore of the grounds. These ornate tombs towered over the rest, shining with colored glass under the midday sun. Farther back, a network of walkways led to simpler, squatter structures. The procession drifted into a narrow file onto a path pinched by houses for the dead.

Zadani stared at her feet, vaguely aware they'd come to a stop. She looked up. A Sempyrean priest intoned over Hadir's linen-wrapped body. Thruna and Elmarie hurled wads of flower petals over his form. His bow crossed his chest, the wreath from the D'Alzirs lay at his waist and the moonstone necklace he'd given Zadani was twined around his hands under the linens.

Familiar faces. Strangers' faces. At the edges of her vision, they swiveled toward Zadani, toward Hadir's body, toward their own feet.

Genjin Hyrix, the comely Awakened on Lord Marus's council, shot a glance at an unaware Jasso Jackolo. The women of Kiyahd swooned for him and his tangled mop of wheat gold hair that now stirred before a strong breeze. A young man with a kindly disposition. Unfortunately for the women of Kiyahd, he didn't swoon in their direction. Genjin sucked back a sniffle then drew his lower lip over a honey-colored mustache. A second glance at Jasso lingered.

Hadir was always one to inspire love in others.

Jealousy followed, dashing the smile that had stolen onto Zadani's lips. Genjin caught her watching him, blinked, and then nodded, a solemn gesture.

"Let us speak well of the dead," said the priest.

And they did. Oh, how they did. No matter the sweetness or reverence of the story, Zadani could not help but feel bitterness closing around her. All of it felt a charade. A hideous lie.

This is wrong.

Zadani denied the chance to speak. Instead, she sang, voice hoarse from her long nights of grief. The strength to fill her lungs was elusive, but she drowned her pain in song, unconcerned by its quality.

"With a soul unafraid and a hand for the blade, came a fire-hearted man with ice in his veins.

"Who do I see? I see me in your eyes.

"Snap go the whips! Ring go the bells! From battlefield to chapel, history does tell.

"Who do I see? I see me in your eyes.

"The snakes are gone, the land is reclaimed, and the two who would rule see their love finally named.

"Who do I see? I see me in your eyes.

"Who do I see? I see me in your eyes.

"Who do I see? I see me in your eyes..."

The last verse fell to a breathless whisper. "And the fires of love burn bright."

Silence hummed across the cemetery.

A handful of dull heartbeats later, the priest concluded the ceremony. "Hadir Innan, though you have passed through darkness, those who loved you will carry your light...always and forever."

The hunters lifted the palanquin of their peer and carried it into the tomb where Hadir was put to rest. Stone ground against stone as the door closed.

A door within Zadani closed with it.

Like a stranger's voice calling out in the night, the dreadful feeling returned to warn her.

Something is wrong!

Zadani returned to the kitchen, less herself than before.

Thruna gave her a pat on the back. Elmarie, a desperate hug. Their words rang hollow, a pointless string of nattering. Their gestures were a reminder of things stolen.

To be comforted was to defile her memory of Hadir. Without him there to offer reassurance, another voice preyed upon her, stoking dark thoughts every minute of the day.

Meanwhile, duty compelled her to work, though her passion for it abandoned her. The kitchens did not sing, nor gossip. Zadani was slow, clumsy, more burden than boon, she thought. Sometimes she caught herself muttering.

Something is wrong.

Her day at an end, she made her way through the central garden rather than the keep. Avoiding the pitying eyes of others had become an integral part of her routine. At dusk, the garden was a dreamlike place. Enclosed by winding paths of hedgerows, any who sought a moment of peace could find it there.

As Zadani passed the fountain statue dedicated to Marus's dead daughter, Raiya, a voice caused her to whirl around.

"You've a gift for song." Jasso Jackolo stepped from behind the young maiden's statue, the moon lighting half of his aquiline face.

"Thank you," she said.

"A beautiful song for an equally beautiful ceremony. From all I've heard, your husband deserved no less." Lips pursed, brow knit in curiosity, Jasso approached. "I would be remiss if I didn't follow up with you. When it first happened, you mentioned wanting to speak with me."

A lump rose in her throat. She glanced in either direction. Downslope at the edge of the garden, a holdguard patrolled—out of earshot.

The scholar arched a slender white eyebrow. "Crowded is the mind and heavy the heart of those in grief. There can be a great deal to talk about." When Zadani didn't respond, Jasso added, "While I cannot fathom what you're going through, I have had my own struggles with loneliness."

Loneliness was the least of Zadani's concerns. Since Hadir's entombment, her focus had latched onto the creeping sense of wrongness she felt. "I had heard you kept a stable of companions about you."

"Lovers?" Jasso cocked his ear to a shoulder. "My tastes make them a bit harder to come by. In Valat, such forms of sexuality have been openly accepted for half a century. But in Namarr...well...where the Sempyrium shines its light of displeasure, the common folk are quick to find the nearest shadow."

"You're in luck, then." Zadani swelled with her next inhale. "I've heard it said in the kitchen that our resident Awakened, Genjin Hyrix, fancies you. I saw it myself. The way he looked at you is unmistakable. If you find him to your liking, perhaps I could arrange a meeting."

"Can't say I've ever bedded an Awakened before." Jasso ran a velvet-gloved hand the length of his snowy beard. "Which comes as a surprise to me."

"Genjin is a good man." Zadani glowered. "Not some novelty. Deserving of more than a feckless cretin twice his age, that's for sure."

With a sharp inhale, Jasso made to retort but hesitated. He wobbled a hand. "Fair assessment. For you, Zadani, I promise to treat him with utmost respect." They milled in silence for an awkward heartbeat. "That wasn't what you wanted to discuss with me though, was it?"

"No." Zadani fingered a ringlet of her thick, jet hair. The tug of distrust, of things out of place, pushed a plan to the fore of her mind. "Before Hadir died, you spoke of needing something in exchange for a debt."

He stiffened, brow creasing. "I assure you, it was nothing important." It was clear the man disliked the idea of hounding favors from a widow. "I wouldn't dare to—"

"Please, Jasso." She took his elbow. The colorful silk there was the softest she'd ever felt. While the scholar wasn't highborn, he was world-renowned, which made the act feel like she'd just committed a crime. "I'd welcome the distraction." She stared into his eyes. "Please."

"You've been through a lot." He blinked at her hand resting on his elbow. "I don't wish to add undue pressure on—"

"Just ask me!" Anger and desperation escaped with her words. "Sorry."

He eyed her. Sighed. "Very well. But for the record, I came here to help you and see that you are okay. Not to corner you into helping me meet my own selfish needs."

"If I'm ever interrogated as to your good nature, I'll be sure to set the torturer straight."

Hands clasped behind his back, Jasso smiled then leaned forward until his mouth was at her ear. "What I ask for *is* dangerous, so I will not hold it against you if you say no."

Zadani waited.

"Godsthorn. I need it. It keeps me sharp and I've run out recently. A single thorn here and there. I won't fully ascend. Such surrender might make others suspicious." He scratched the side of his mouth. "I assume you make godsbrew for the barracks?"

She shook her head. "The holdguard keep a tight watch during our processing. You're better off finding a dealer in the city. I've heard gossip that there are those who sell it at the Salty Maid. An unsavory tavern."

Disappointed, Jasso raised upturned palms in defeat. "To do an unsavory deed, one must sometimes consort with unsavory people. Though I see the deed to be taboo rather than sin. While I'd hoped for a simpler transaction, I am sure I can find what I need at the—what was it?"

"Salty Maid."

Jasso wagged a finger. "Yes, of course. Optimism has long been my favorite drug of all. I'll head there now." He made to walk past.

"Before you go." She added honey to her tone. "And since I've steered you toward both a lover and godsthorn, I could use a favor. Now."

Lips parted, he eyed her sidelong.

"You said I would be in your debt if I helped, did you not?" Zadani swallowed hard. *Careful now. I can't do this without him.* "I do believe I've just helped."

He reached for a pouch at his belt. "Right. Compensation."

"Not money." Zadani watched a dubious expression spread over his fine features as his hand froze at his belt. She played up the pity. "My grief has made me forward. I ask too much. Go. Find your godsthorn." She turned to go. "I'll do it on my own as I'm destined to...forever."

"No, no." Two steps and he was behind her. "I vowed a favor and you shall have it."

"Thank you," she said. "It should only take a moment."

It wasn't until they stood before the tomb that Jasso struck flint to steel. For what Zadani intended, she did not wish holdguard or anyone else to know of it. The torch in Jasso Jackolo's hand came alive with flame, and with the other, he grabbed the iron wrung to the entrance of Hadir's tomb.

"You are certain?"

Zadani nodded.

Wood and stone grated, but the iron hinges were silenced by the pig fat Zadani had slathered them with. She hoped it was enough to keep anyone from coming to investigate.

The smell of dust, mildew, and decomposition sent them fumbling to cover their noses—Zadani for her homespun dress, and Jasso for the collar of his silk doublet.

Wrapped in white linen, Hadir's body lay atop a slab of waist-high stone.

"Here he is, just as he was." Jasso turned to her and waited.

"I need to see him." The kitchen knife she'd pilfered from the kitchen gave a dull scrape as it left her boot. "Would you?"

Nervous as one should be when asked to cut away the funeral dressings of a loved one, Jasso took the knife, doublet collar dropping from his face as he did. Flame flickered down the knife as he slowly rotated it. His throat tensed, looking like a snake's gullet as it swallowed an egg. *Shame.*

"I used to do dissections at the Academies." He passed her the torch. The knife hovered over Hadir's body. Jasso's tongue darted across his lips. "But this...somehow, I feel I'm getting the fool's end of our agreement."

Zadani wouldn't disagree. The only thing that mattered to her now was whether he continued.

If one of the presumed smartest men in the world could not figure out her husband's true cause of death, then perhaps her grief *had* driven her mad. Perhaps there was nothing wrong at all, and the feeling of dread was naught but paranoia fueled by denial.

Either way, tonight, I will find out.

Layer after layer of linen parted under the knife as Jasso sawed from crotch to crown. Once finished, he pulled the cloth aside.

Chills and tremors rolled through Zadani. Sweat filled her palms, pooling in the creases of flesh around her waist and beneath her breasts. The hair at the base of her cascading mane was soaked through. "I tell you, I do not believe Hadir was attacked by a bear. I *know* he wasn't." In the flickering torchlight, the scholar made a face. She fixed him with a flat stare. "You're the smartest man in the world, aren't you?"

"There are both men and women whom I would deem smarter," he said. "Alas, those same people have claimed the title for me."

"Then tell me the truth." Her tone was low. "What does my husband's body say about his death?"

Jass inspected Hadir's chest. "Was he involved with any criminal activity?"

"Of course not."

"Then what explanation could there be for his death but what you've heard? Unfathomable as it might be, there are no logical grounds for anything but what the holdguard said."

"My intuition is not wrong." She fought to quell her agitation. The wrongness she felt threatened to take control, to scream Jasso into a corner. She managed a shuddering breath, then a second, smoother one. "If you please, continue."

With a sigh, Jasso bent to the task. First, he looked at the bow Hadir had been buried with. The arrow tips from the quiver, as well. He carefully replaced both, then slashed the silk doublet—a burial gift bought by the combined coin of the other hunters. Bruised and battered skin surrounded by deep gashes lay beneath.

Cold stone met Zadani's hand as she turned away and tried to steady herself against the wall. Before Jasso could inquire, she said, "I'm okay. I'm fine. Please...just continue."

Muttering under his breath, Jasso probed each laceration, fingertips massaging the surrounding bone. He frowned. "Well it seems..." His frown deepened. "It seems you may be correct."

Anger boiled to the fore. Zadani shoved off the wall and nearly bowled into the scholar. The torch whooshed through the darkness as if the flames, too, had been stoked to rage. "What? Tell me!" she hissed, barely recognizing the voice as her own.

Jasso begged her for calm, then said, "A bear is a massive creature, capable of not only clawing a man to death but causing a great deal of internal damage while doing so. Were it to attack a man, the bones would be broken in numerous places, if not shattered. Hadir's damage is isolated to the wound sites, most of the bones broken clean. Not only that, if it were a bear, the cadaver's skin would likely have patches missing rather than crescent shaped slashes like these. These wounds are more consistent with what one might see from a sword or spear."

Zadani breathed like a rabid animal. *They lied to me! I'll kill those holdguard!*

It wouldn't be so hard. There were dozens of mushrooms and herbs she cooked with that were safe for consumption, and that required her to also know which were lethal. The kind. The amount. She knew the precise dosage necessary to sicken or kill a man.

Like they killed my Hadir.

Wounds, not long sealed, broke open inside her. Blots of darkness filled her vision where torchlight should be. The tomb and Jasso started to spin.

No, she told herself. *I must be calm. I must figure out who has done this first, and why. It's possible the holdguard only found him and assumed it was a bear out of ignorance.*

"There's more." Jasso held up an arrow. "The tip is flattened at an angle. That means it struck something hard. Compared to a few of my peers at the Academies, I'm no expert at physics, but that's my opinion, nonetheless."

"Hard like armor?" Zadani said.

Jasso shrugged. "Or a rock. Zadani, you look..." One glance into her storming face silenced him.

"Remove the linens and flip him over," she said. "I want to see something."

No longer begrudging, Jasso did as he was bidden. The corpse was stiff as a board as he rolled it onto its stomach. There, beside Hadir's spine, was a deep puncture wound.

Jasso squinted at it. "He...was run down from behind. First, I assume. It's likely that the wounds to his torso came after."

The scholar's voice was distant as Zadani stared at the spot between her husband's shoulder blades. A lover's unquenchable rage burned through her. Something *was* wrong. Very wrong.

Hadir had been taken from her.

Murdered.

Zadani vowed, whoever did it would pay.

CHAPTER ELEVEN

LOYALTY

G rimshields crowded the back of the throne room in the space around the Holy Chamber's outer sanctum. A banded door sat off to one side of the raised dais. Valka's eyes fell there. Accompanied by a dozen guards and the Void, King Rathon was sequestered within. Few uses had been found for the inner sanctum over the decades. And now, somewhere inside, Rathon hid in the dark, counting the seconds until hubris came hacking at the door rather than face the cultists and their leader.

I can almost see him trembling, a scared and spoiled child of a man.

Valka seized command of the Grimshield sachar—a formation one hundred strong. Their mistrust had been supplanted by obedience after a short but furious debate at the massive, barred double doors leading into the throne room.

Once inside, Valka paused to stare at the throne while his smaller force integrated with the much larger one. An immense depiction of Unturrus wrought from a single slab of darksteel hung over the Scothean seat of power.

His eyes fell to his feet where a map of the known world stretched across the floor. *Is this to be the last time I approach the throne an honorable man?* He exhaled. *If it is, I'll do so with dignity.* Chin aloft. Shoulders back. Mournfang in hand.

That's what he intended to do. But as he crossed the map and the blank, unexplored wilds of C'Dath into Namarr, his shoulders slumped with the burden of sacrifice.

His boots scuffed over the Sea of Psollus. He'd been defeated and deceived. And now, he would give away the rest of what he had to a child conqueror.

Grimshields moved out of his way, their questioning expressions dogging his periphery.

At the base of the steps leading to the throne, he stopped, standing on Scothea. From cave tribes battling for sustenance, to conquering distant lands,

Scothea had always found a path to greatness. Despite scarce resources and a small population, she had become the mightiest military power in the world.

And now, we vie against ourselves like a starving raek eating its own tail. He pivoted on his heels. *I will do what I must for the good of Scothea.*

Mournfang slapped onto his shoulder plate. "Diamond formation!"

Weapons, armor, and hurried footfalls raised a deafening clamor. A few seconds later, Ikarai Valka stood at the fore, Captain Yanos beside him. "Close the door."

A detachment of Grimshields cranked a windlass to lower an iron bar into place. It rumbled into position, sealing the defenders inside.

Maybe there's a chance I won't have to besmirch my name, yet.

Essuhd had been wrong before. The scope of the false messiah's influence, for starters. It was possible the insurgent's victory wasn't so assured as he claimed. Not only that, if Rhul the Red and his knights had managed to launch a counter attack, it wasn't a stretch to think they could tip the balance in the battle for Darkfall.

Valka ran his tongue around arid gums. Excitement bled into strategy.

The granaries weren't far from the burrows; if Raeklord Rhul were thinking clearly, he could deny the cultists food stores while Rathon hunkered down in the Holy Chamber.

Let attrition defeat the false messiah's forces. The faintest hope buoyed him.

An hour passed in sweaty silence before they heard them coming.

Slender and hard-faced, Valka noted Captain Yanos's eyes locked on the barred door to the throne room as the marching enemy rumbled over the stone bridge outside. "General," he said, "you should join King Rathon in the inner sanctum."

Valka stared sidelong at his captain a moment, then snorted, a smile stealing across his face. "If we survive today, I'll grease you for a raek myself."

The captain grunted. Adjusted the grip on his ax. "It's been an honor, General."

When the young officer turned his attention back to the throne room door, Valka's smile melted from his face. His lips twitched in a flash of frustration. *Will it be an honor when I betray our king?*

Row upon row of sweaty faces met Valka's backward glance. Mouths set in hard lines, white knuckles gripping ax handles, shoulders bunched in anticipation. Most were Grimshields, the embossed suns and comets on their shields shining. Each time their unpleasant fate flickered through their minds, Valka could tell. The tattooed flesh around their eyes sockets spasmed.

There was solace, at least, in knowing they didn't have to die so long as Valka did what he must.

The clank of armored skirts followed by the unified stomp of orderly, un-hurried march echoed from the chamber beyond.

Leather creaked and chain clinked as Valka's soldiers shifted their weight from boot to boot. His knees ached from running so hard before, and the muscles spanning from elbow to wrist had grown painfully tight, as if they might snap. Forgemaster Hashuuk had created Mournfang to be a powerful weapon but that didn't mean it was light.

Voices could be heard just outside. *They're in the Seer King's Chamber.*

Plate armor screeched as axes were rebalanced atop pauldrons. General Valka hefted his own. Warmth leached from him and into the ax, leaving cold prickles in his gut. Mournfang started to smoke.

The cultists beyond the door held their position in silence for a dozen heartbeats. General Valka ground his teeth, the pressure at the hinge of his jaw pinching like a vice. His chest boiled, ushering heat from his heart to his hand, and from his hand into his smoking ax. The golden coils of the raek affixed to the steel haft glowed white hot.

A terrible grinding sound echoed throughout the throne room. Shocked murmuring among the sachar died before it started as the iron bar on the door snapped in two and clattered to the stone floor.

The door crashed open, shucked from its hinges. It landed on the map of the world, throwing up a cloud of dust.

Valka avoided the worst of the stinging wave by shielding his eyes with his arm. Before he opened them, he heard a hiss from Yanos at his side. "We're doomed."

Scoth shock troops filed into the throne room, victory flashing in their smiles. A relaxed confidence in the muscles around their eyes. A seemingly endless stream of them poured into ranks that formed thirty paces from Valka's defenders. All had stripped off their white tabards bearing Scothea's crest of a raek coiling around the sun. Such a simple ploy. That was how they'd differen-tiated their own from those loyal to King Rathon.

Soon Valka's forces were outnumbered two-to-one, then three-to-one, then four-to-one. There seemed no end to the rebels.

But that hadn't been the source of Yanos's harsh portend. The fight faded in Ikarai Valka as he, too, saw the nascent hope for victory dashed. Mournfang cooled in his palm.

A silhouette hovered ten feet above the cultist force as their ranks parted, admitting him to the fore, his knights in tow. Snouts climbed the air, halfway to the vaulted ceiling, horns and twenty-point racks of goring death rising with them.

Rhul the Red and his Gravequeen. Six mounted raek knights flanked their commander.

The Gravequeen's tongue lapped the air. Her scarred bulk slithered over the map of the world and stopped at the center of the room, covering Namarr.

"I'm glad you survived, Ikarai." Rhul rose in the narrow saddle, spurred boots hooking into elongated stirrups. He pressed down on them. The Gravequeen responded by flattening a loop of coiled body against the stones. Raek knights to either side followed suit, though none dismounted.

The reins relaxed in Rhul's gauntleted fist. Encased in darksteel from head to foot, gold-enameled sunbursts gleamed on his pauldrons and poleyns, and a white cape descended from his shoulders to pile up on top of his mount's bulk. He slung his hakat butt-first through a metal link clasped to the Gravequeen's bridle, and then removed his great helm.

Rage boiled in Valka. *You swore oaths!* Did it mean nothing to them? Had he taught his legions to be so brittle of mind and weak of spine? Mournfang pulsed to life, framing Yanos and the men around him in a ruddy glow. The general's accusation came out low and hoarse. "You're the traitor."

Pale gray eyes scrutinized Valka. Rhul stroked his horseshoe jaw, fingertips brushing a long wheat-colored mustache. "I am aligned with the light." He shrugged. "You will come around in time. In that, I have faith. The hurt of this day will ebb and you will see—"

"Truth? Isn't that what he says? Your messiah?"

At mention of the cult leader, Rhul's face slackened. He flicked his placid gaze over the assembled sachar of Grimshields at Valka's back. "Lay down your weapons and none of you will come to harm."

"I've already seen what that promise will get me," Valka said. "A score of slaughtered soldiers, butchered by their brothers. Tell me, will it be an ax between my shoulder blades when I least expect it, as well?"

"You speak of the unfortunate collateral required for our Light's transition to power." Rhul sniffed. "You are the general of a dead thing, Ikarai. A new Scothea rises this day. If you desire, you will see it thrive."

A Grimshield parted a step from the formation and shot a gob of spit in the direction of the raeklord but fell short.

"Ranks!" Yanos roared.

Valka swallowed hard, never taking his eyes off his former comrade. *I will do what I must for the good of Scothea.* "Your promises ring false."

From the corner of his eye, Valka saw Yanos flinch. The captain's furrowed brow broke his heart. *Yes, my faithful soldier, I negotiate. It is the only way to keep you alive. The only way to see my daughter again. The only way to save Scothea.*

"If you seek evidence, look no further than your own men. They are arrayed before you in good faith, not killing but waiting for a peaceful resolve. Are they not sufficient evidence?" Rhul stared out one of the twenty foot windows in the wall. "Darkfall is ours, General. Two thirds of your soldiers have stepped into the light. Thousands more will follow in the days to come."

Valka stifled a gasp. The number, if true, was staggering. *Two thirds? Two thirds of my men's loyalty stolen from beneath my nose without so much as an inkling...*

Rhul continued. "Please, Ikarai. You can end this bloodshed. Right now."

"We'd rather die than bend the knee to your false prophet." Yanos spoke low and fast so only Valka might hear. "Give the command, General. We are with you."

Indecision forced a stone into Valka's gullet.

"What's your decision, General?" boomed Rhul.

The life of every man around Valka became an itch under his skin, like maggots harrying a fruit rind, each nibble a barely perceived disappearance of a thing once whole.

The throne throbbed with silence. The air burned with fear and the mounting heat of imminent violence. Rhul pulled on his great helm, then snatched his hakat from his mount's bridle in a mighty fist. The Gravequeen's neck segments writhed to life as her bovine skull ascended.

"Advance," Rhul said.

The cultists took a slow, wary step.

Body clenching, no words left Valka's mouth.

Yanos filled in, bellowing with the conviction of a legion unto himself. "At the ready!" Grimshields invoked blessings from the Holy Instruments. Aurghov, god of good fortune. Acramis, god of justice and vengeance. Valka's namesake, Ikarai, the god of unity and honor was uttered most of all.

Raek flesh slid over stone with a constant hush, drowning out all sound.

A jewel of sweat dripped off Valka's nose. Mournfang smoked, layering his vision in a haze. A hundred resolute faces moved toward him, and yet, Nera's was the only one crowding his mind. *For the good of Scothea...and you.*

For the love he bore her, his loyalty shattered.

He recognized it had always been a fragmented thing, made whole only in the absence of significant challenge. There was fealty to his king, duty to his men, but above all, love for his daughter. In that, Ikarai Valka might still be seen as a man worthy of honor. The will to defy the conditioning of oaths sworn and burdens willingly carried bubbled to the surface with urgency.

"Hold!" He threw down Mournfang, the crescent blade burying into the stone floor. The advancing force stopped twenty paces short. The grins of victory on the faces of his enemies, who had earlier in the day named themselves brothers, burned into his memory.

Yanos rounded on Valka. For a heart-stopping moment, he thought the man might fell him. They stared at each other, eternity in the span of a second, and then the captain huffed and lowered his ax.

"My men keep their weapons for the moment." Valka straightened. "First, I would speak with your messiah. Afterward, you may do with me what you must."

Rhul the Red maneuvered the Gravequeen broadside, her scales creating a deafening hush. "I celebrate your first step into the light. Soon, you will see the truth."

I mean to. And then, I'll kill the little bastard.

The raeklord ushered his mount to one side of the throne room. The rest of the cultists shuffled back to form a pathway down their center. Three robed figures flanked a fourth, smaller one, as they made their way through the press of shock troops. As they passed, Scoths laid their axes on the ground, bent and kissed the marbled floor.

Valka's breath caught.

One of the figures, a woman without feet, floated into the room. White light poured from the eyes of all three. *Awakened.*

"Please, Gishek. The ax." The melodic, saccharin voice of the fourth, a teen boy.

It has to be him.

Siddaia, the Arrow of Light. The false messiah. Valka matched him to the description of the cult leader stirring up the countryside that the Shadii had given so many months ago.

One of the Awakened, a portly man with familiar, stony features, flung out a hand. Mournfang ripped from the ground and flew into his palm with a slap. He glanced it over, then handed it to Siddaia.

Valka stared in disbelief. The boy had gathered Awakened to his cause, yet no spy had mentioned it. *That's because no spy had known. You were outwitted, fool! Essuhd, too.* At this, his faith in the Shadii Master's plan took a wound. Time would tell if it was fatal.

The boy was barefoot, the soles of his feet caked in gray dust from stone walkways and fissured as if he'd never worn a shoe in his life. Excepting that, Siddaia had a softness pervading his countenance that gripped Valka. *This is the Arrow of Light? This is who Rhul the Red bows to? This* boy...*has felled my nation?*

Siddaia wore no clothing but a simple linen smock that reached mid-calf. Hair as dark as a raven's feathers framed onyx eyes as they inspected Mournfang.

Valka wasn't sure what he'd expected. Surely not some soiled street urchin, though.

"The Forgemaster, Hashuuk, made this?"

"That is correct, my Light," said Rhul.

Siddaia blinked at the weapon. "You may give it back."

The heavy-set Awakened swung an arm. Mournfang hurtled toward Valka as if shot by a giant crossbow. It slammed into the ground at his feet, blade submerged to the haft.

Valka's lips parted in disbelief. The one who'd taken his ax must have also broken the door and snapped the iron bar—an Awakened with the power to manipulate metals. Another of them could fly. Three Awakened. *Three makes one. But only one makes free...*

Valka shook his head. *I'll not be easily swayed like these others.*

Siddaia smiled. "Are you willing to approach me, General?"

Valka left Mournfang where it lay and crossed the map of the known world. A pair of cultists stopped him a dozen paces shy of their leader. "Kneel, General."

He flinched.

One of them stepped back, extending their ax as they did, and placed it against the juncture where Valka's neck met his shoulder. "You dare *stand* before Siddaia, the Arrow of Light, Lord Illuminate, and Son of the Sempyrean?"

Valka went numb. Yesterday the man had been one of his own, and now, he dispensed threats of death to his general.

Born by the weight of defeat as much as desire, he sank to his knees. Flanked by his Awakened, Siddaia padded closer and pushed the ax's blade away from Valka's neck. "Brother, we do not force them to kneel. If the general so chooses, he may do so. For now, he will be treated as a guest." He stepped past the man to touch Valka on the head. "Stand, Ikarai. Your suffering ends here."

When Valka looked up, obsidian pools stared down at him. Chills rippled across his shoulders, yet he could not look away.

"You war inside," Siddaia said. A long second passed. "Do not think less of yourself for surrendering, Ikarai. You are a hero this day. Without you, hundreds more would have died." A fat tear rolled down the boy's cheek. *He weeps for men he killed!* Siddaia's voice quavered. "I'm sorry. The cost of lives lost is staggering." He sniffled, blinked as if seeing something for the first time. "You worry about your daughter?"

How does he know of her? Valka shot an apprehensive look at Rhul, then nodded.

"She is unharmed. You may return to her when you wish." Siddaia half-turned toward his cohort, eyes still fixed on Valka. "Do you see it?"

In unison they responded, "We see."

So he trains them much as I did.

The boy bent at the waist to bring his mouth close to Valka's ear. "You are still needed, Ikarai. Your men *still* love you. They would see you remain their general...if you allow it."

Valka shook his head. "But I oppose you."

"Now is your chance to change that. Your title and your duties will remain yours if you'll keep them. If not, you may renounce your oath to King Rathon and leave in peace." Siddaia raised his voice so all of Valka's defenders could hear. "All of you. Wherever peace calls you, you may go if you vow to shed no blood in your going. But before you leave, I request that you listen to what I have to say."

Grimshields shifted, their eyes darting to one another in confusion and distrust.

"Fear is a tool for rulers who have nothing to offer but lies and illusions. I offer no such thing," Siddaia said. "I offer—"

"Death!" Yanos's voice. "Hundreds dead—because of you!"

Siddaia appeared unshaken by the accusation. "When a soldier brings a notched blade to a smith to be fixed, would you also blame the smith for the damage? I wished no one to die. If King Rathon had transitioned us to peace, I would have gladly accepted it. But this is the cancer we must excise. Greed and lies—Scothea drowns in it." The boy's voice rose, echoing from wall to wall. "I am the truth and I have come to free you."

A chill ran across Valka's shoulders. *First the Eye, bringing evil into the light...*

Siddaia strode across the map of the world, from Scothea to the shores of Namarr. Near Unturrus, he slowed. Bare feet tracing a circle, he stared down at the Mountain of Power.

Valka surveyed Siddaia's cultists. None seemed concerned that their messiah approached armed men unguarded. Even now, Yanos stood closer to Siddaia than the boy's followers.

Pulse rising, he watched the false prophet wander farther into the raek's mouth. He held his breath. *So long as Nera lives, I can't risk it.* He would follow Essuhd's lead and let the Shadii Master do the deed.

Siddaia whipped a smile back at Valka, then stepped before Yanos—within ax reach.

"Scothea was once great, they say. I say, it still is. I say it could be greater still. In the shadows of your mind, you know it can be so. You know the might of the brothers at your side, and the history of an unstoppable nation chosen by the gods. It is not your fault we have faltered. None of this is your fault."

Somehow, Valka doubted their gods, the Holy Instruments, endorsed the Arrow of Light. All but Niriti, the goddess of malice and death, had shared bloodlines with Rathon. All but she had been kings before their shrine of godhood had been erected.

The defenders exchanged confused looks.

"Kings tell you what to do and how to do it. You sacrifice your loyalty upon their throne in exchange for gold. You leave the best parts of yourselves at their feet. Love siphoned from your families in exchange for trivial honorifics. Your skill, your strength, your courage...all shackled to their whims by a lie they name tradition and patriotism." Siddaia paced across the front rank of defenders. "That is what you were born to but it is not how you must die! I can show you the way to a new beginning. One that *you* choose. Those who follow me do not do so because they've been paid, manipulated, or tricked. They give their loyalty freely. They throw their love into the light because they wish to see their families thrive. Their strength and courage honored, put to more glorious endeavors than kings could fathom! The will of the Holy Instruments themselves! Scothea can be born anew...by your hand."

Valka stared, entranced. King Rathon and many before him fell into their role unchosen and treated it like a personal coin purse while the common folk descended into ever-worsening poverty.

The ranks of defenders straightened, gazes plastered to the prophet as his voice turned harsh. "And if you do not see it, then you are complicit! You. Are. Responsible! Every starving mouth and sickly relative sits at the altar of your making. You think my followers have betrayed Scothea? *You* did so when you would not stand for justice in your home. You took what was given because it was the easiest path." He drifted forward, almost touching the weapons of the defenders as he searched their faces. Few returned the boy's gaze. These were Grimshields, the most hardened soldiers in Scothea, and yet, they were being stripped bare.

Valka felt himself shrink as the boy continued.

"Will you go on, suckling at the illusion fed to you by gold-fingered kings so long as you must not make hard choices? Or will you choose the right? Will you stand in the light with us and see Scothea reborn? Better than ever! Stronger than ever! What say you, brave soldiers? Would you have a thriving nation, or a thriving king? Would you walk in the light of the gods, or would you skulk within their shadows? I say the crimes of your past stop here so that the accolades of our glorious future may begin!"

Siddaia swept up before Yanos. When the captain's face lifted, tears streamed down his cheeks. All the hardness had wilted away, revealing a soft-faced young man Valka barely recognized. The change in expression was unbelievable—open and vulnerable as if all of his fear and worry had been rendered impotent.

Yanos's ax clanged onto the marbled floor. Valka flinched. In a rain of steel, the rest fell with it. They knelt in a wave before their impassioned messiah.

Last the Fire, that in the darkest hours unite...

Valka shook his head. *Can it be true?* As the boy spoke, a quiet whisper of desire had sparked to life in him. A horrifying thought pushed to the fore of his mind. *I agree with him.*

A nudge at his shoulder whirled him around. Rhul and the Gravequeen loomed over him. "What say you, brother? Will you make Scothea strong once more? Or will you waste your loyalties on the weak?"

He glanced sidelong, first one way, then the other. All eyes watched him now, waiting for him to bow or kneel. To show some form of allegiance to the Arrow of Light.

Play the part.

One set of dark eyes drew him in, their intensity freezing him. Siddaia. Gentle but expectant, he watched Valka.

Watched him lower...

Watched him stretch out his upper body on the floor.

Heard him speak. "I choose a glorious future."

Ikarai Valka could not tell what was a lie anymore.

CHAPTER TWELVE

INTERLOPERS

The canvas flap of Gyr's tent swept aside with a whoosh.

He bolted upright from a dead sleep, snatching his mace and kicking his leg free of the covers. Sweat sprang from every pore. Blood rushed to his face. Light poured through the tent's opening, framing a featureless silhouette. Gyr squinted, knuckles popping as he squeezed his mace.

The intruder was short and hunched. A thread of silvery daylight glinted off their honor plate—a knight. Gyr relaxed as the fog of sleep dissipated. The shifty-eyed Sir Raius stepped inside.

He looked at Gyr with a slight frown. "Prosort?"

Gyr tossed his mace on the bed, then threw his other leg out to join the first. "As you can see, I'm awake and alert." Sir Raius twitched at the jest but didn't laugh. "You may report." *The one night I manage a little sleep. Rotten luck.* Gyr pressed palms against his brow then dragged them down his face.

"Your presence is needed," said Raius. The majority of camp still slept, which meant outriders had found something on their pre-dawn sweep.

Gyr shot to his feet. His version of the act, anyway. It took a few seconds for his hips to line up under his torso. "Wake Caltheo," he grunted.

Raius whipped the tent flap aside and left, black cloak swirling around his ankles.

After dressing, then giving instructions to a bleary-eyed Caltheo, Gyr mounted his horse. He checked the straps on his arms and armor and set out, Sir Raius at his side.

They climbed a slope, crossing one running stream and then another, both long dried up. River rock poked through drifts of crystalline snow.

Gyr fought a chill. *When life leaves a thing, the cold settles all too swiftly to claim it.*

A handful of days had passed since their discovery of the stinking pile. This time, when the call to investigate another possible threat came, Gyr forced Caltheo to stay behind with Malus.

The Winding Way is proving interesting.

If anything were to befall Gyr, he wanted to make sure a representative of the Sempyrium remained at the duke's side. There was safety in numbers when marching with the column. Smaller groups were vulnerable. Gyr glanced at the grim-faced Sir Raius. We *are vulnerable.* They moved at a brisk pace, mounts belching steam and flinging mud as the sun climbed free of the horizon. *Day comes earlier on the mountain.*

Under normal circumstances, the idea of an attack was easily dismissed. But the dead scullion and messenger bird pounded at Gyr's nerves like a musician beating a banha drum. The pile of stinking death, too. There was no scarcity of fuel for his burning caution.

Maybe they seek to isolate us. Lure us away in groups? The strategy was one Gyr might be proud of if he were their enemy. At the very least, the tactic would test their defenses and teach him a great deal about how his target behaved. A more worrisome thought hooked his attention. *Perhaps a trap set by that scoundrel pirate, Armada.* Whenever Gyr was reminded that they now acted on information from the Kanian, his stomach felt like he was digesting glass. *What if he works for our enemy? What if his job was to force us out of Brighthaven and onto the open road? What if he killed the scullion?*

Gyr ground his teeth. In moments like these, he knew it best to seek calm in faith.

In the absence of certainty, the loss of control, the dissolution of comfort, fear takes hold. Let go these mortal notions. Let Faith in the Sempyrean guide you, and with it, transcend all fear.

Despite reciting the words of the prophet Peladon, Gyr was on high alert by the time they arrived at their destination at the top of a bald hill. Raius's scouts had formed a crescent, mounts facing outward, spears leveled and ready for anything.

The knight-captain gestured. "There."

Dozens of cloven hoof-prints honeycombed the hilltop where the ground wasn't churned to muck. A handful of broad footsteps accompanied them.

"About ten riders," said Raius. "Twenty mounts, all ebhor by the look of them."

"Kurgs." Gyr got down from his horse to survey the spoor. He reached down, knees popping, and lifted a displaced chunk of turf. "Could be one day old...could be four. Hard to tell."

"No sign of fire." An ugly scout with a hooked nose shot spit from a gap in his teeth. "Maybe they were just passing through."

Gyr pursed his lips. "We're close to the mountain enclaves. They could have a hundred reasons for being here." Gyr rose, swung up onto his horse. "This is Kurgish land. We might be looking at the tracks of a family out for an afternoon ride. A meeting between shamans of the Moon and shamans of the Hawk. Or an Outclan raiding party."

"Twenty ebhor for ten riders," Raius said. "I don't like it."

Gyr turned his horse in a circle. "We ride the Forgotten People's borders. If I were one of the mountain enclaves, a retinue as large as ours would catch my attention. I'd send a group to observe. Fresh mounts included."

"You think they only wanna watch us?" The ugly scout spoke out of turn, drawing a stony stare from Raius.

"You question the eyes, ears, and voice of the duke," the knight-captain said. "More respect is due, soldier."

The man looked away. "My apologies, Lord Renwood."

Gyr waved a hand in dismissal.

Sir Raius mounted and led his horse over to Gyr's. He spoke so only the prosort could hear. "What would you have us do?"

The hilltop settled into silence as Gyr considered the words of Peladon once more. *Let faith in the Sempyrean guide you, and with it, transcend all fear.* Gyr was a spiritual man, not a foolish one. *Caution is more likely to stop a spear point than prayer.*

"Sweep the tracks for three miles. See if they parallel our march. If they do, send riders back, but continue your pursuit until you find their location. A raiding party will be equipped as such. Return to us in four days." Gyr fixed Raius with a flat stare. "If you don't, we'll assume the worst." He gestured at the half-dozen outriders. "Sir Raius, you will lead these men. Fully armed and armored, fresh horses, provisions for a week."

Sir Raius saluted, fist slapping honor plate with a sharp ring. "It won't be easy. Kurgs are better trackers."

Let Faith in the Sempyrean guide you, and with it, transcend all fear...

Offering little assurance beyond a hesitant smile, Gyr turned his horse toward camp. "Have faith in yourself, Sir Raius. As I do."

Having hobbled his horse, Gyr trekked past a row of latrines dug along a hedge of winterberry bushes and then entered a bark-strewn clearing. A series of poles had been driven into the ground and fixed with long leather leashes around which a dozen dogs sat at rapt attention.

Their singular focus was a short, barrel-chested man. The hound master waved and the dogs barked wildly, and with another wave, they fell silent. Gesturing again, they barked with increased vigor, then fell silent once more.

One dog blinked, brow twitching as it glanced sidelong at Gyr.

"Dammit!" the hound master rushed forward to slap its snout. Warhound and master locked eyes. Gyr held his breath. A bite from a dog that size would puncture flesh and break bone. A ribbon of drool hung from drooping black jowls.

The hound master bent closer, broad, flat nose touching the hound's wet one. In a low, harsh tone, he said something, and the tension fled. The dog licked the man's face. The hound master patted its head, then turned to Gyr.

"Ah, Prosort Renwood, just in time to fuck up my dogs' training this morning."

Gyr rubbed a gloved hand over his smooth crown. "Greetings, Halladorn."

The hound master crossed the clearing, and as he did, the head of every dog turned to follow him.

"Impressive." Gyr gripped the man's forearm in greeting, had his own embraced in return.

"What?" Smiling wickedly, Halladorn stroked a tumbleweed beard the color of autumn leaves. "Your soldiers don't do the same?"

"Apparently they curse at me for interrupting them." Gyr laughed. "If I commanded men as you do dogs, I could take Darkfall in a day. What's your secret?"

Halladorn crossed his arms, then turned his back on the warhounds.

Leaning forward conspiratorially, Halladorn said, "No secret, Prosort. Resources and timing is all. Feed a dog at the right moment enough times and they'll kill for you. Men are no different."

"But not all are starved such that food will force their hand to murder."

Halladorn leaned back. "Food is only one thing you might feed them. There are plenty of things men hunger for such that they'd barter their loyalty for it. Love, for those starved in matters of the heart. Money, for those hungry for power..." Halladorn winked at Gyr. "Faith, for those without direction or certainty."

Gyr raised an eyebrow. "Is it always your aim to rankle others? I see now why you prefer the company of dogs to humans."

The stodgy hound master rocked on his heels. "Because they're more likable in every way?"

"No. Because they *have* to listen to you."

Halladorn patted his broad chest as if Gyr had awarded him some great honor. "'Tis true. I *do* prefer to be the one talking. Besides yourself, humans rarely say anything worthy of my interest."

"Prosort." Caltheo hustled up to them. "Lord Malus is ready for your report."

"Excellent." Gyr turned to his cupbearer. "How go the wagons?"

"They progress much as usual," Caltheo said. "Though one broke a wheel spoke in the night. The quartermaster had to do some temporary mending. But they have assured me it will hold until we reach Kiyahd. If it doesn't, we'll divvy the load up among the others. They'll be light enough in a few days to bear extra. Otherwise, we'll need to abandon the wagon."

Gyr inclined his head, brow wrinkling. "Sounds like you've taken care of it, then. Good. We'll want to make sure we don't break more wheels. Now please, I'll need a moment alone with our illustrious hound master."

When his cupbearer was out of earshot, Gyr spoke in a grave tone. "A wheel spoke breaking at rest..."

Halladorn reflected Gyr's concern in his expression. "This worries you?"

Tone barely a whisper, Gyr leaned closer to Halladorn. "Indeed. We've just run across ebhor tracks as well. I want your hounds staked out at intervals—as far apart as you can get them. If Kurgs attack, I want warning long in advance."

"Brought this lot just for that." Halldorn hiked a thumb over his shoulder to indicate the dogs. Only the slightest shift in their haunches betrayed their statuesque repose. "I've been smell-training them with ebhor coats since the day they were shat forth."

"Needlessly colorful," Gyr grimaced. "Yet, in the matter of hounds, I trust no other. And Halladorn..." The hound master looked at Gyr, a grin splitting shaggy beard. "Keep this between us. Caution is one thing, fear another. I won't have our soldiers confusing the two because of a little conjecture."

Halladorn shrugged, then looked back at his warhounds. "Oh, I think they are one and the same, but if you insist, I give you my word."

"Thank you. Good day, Halladorn."

The hound master returned to training his dogs. His chest jolted as he shouted in Fjordsong, "Imadeh!" As one, the dogs rose from their haunches and spread out, growling.

Caltheo joined Gyr. "I don't like dogs."

"They serve a purpose regardless of your preference."

Caltheo stared at the ground as they went. After a while, he said, "Hopefully they won't need to."

I couldn't agree more.

Outside their tents, crownguard donned padded surcoats, and pulled ringed mail overhead, followed by deep green tabards sporting the gauntleted fist and chain of Namarr.

The sigil of the Ironlights. Gyr recalled Malus's words about the last of Danath Ironlight's blood. Princess Ishoa stood in the eye of Anjuhkar's political storm, and it was one the duke feared she wouldn't survive.

Garlenna. Gyr sent a prayer to the Sempyrean. *May the gods guide you to Prince Barodane.*

Cooks drained breakfast pots and doused fires in a gush of smoke. A pair of crownguard saw Gyr and Caltheo and saluted, right fist to left shoulder. Sunlight spilled across the forest. Veils of steam wormed toward the sky from the pinnacles of warming tents. The camp hummed with activity. Shouts and the whinny of horses told Gyr they were on schedule. Soon, they would march.

Lord Malus's pavilion loomed ahead.

Caltheo cleared his throat. "I apologize, Father Renwood, but I must ask. Do you think it wise to keep what we found in the woods from Duke Malus?"

Gyr slowed a step. "What has you asking?"

"I only seek to learn, Father. If I am to replace you one day, I need to know what circumstances might require me to withhold truth from the duke."

Gyr studied his cupbearer. *Still young. Still soft.* Dark eyes greeted him from a tan face free of the wrinkles brought on by years of service and hardship. *It's time I shatter this innocence.*

Gyr cocked his head and sighed. "There will be times in your service—rare moments, really—when holding back certain information is prudent." He clapped an avuncular hand on the young man's thick shoulder. "We burden the duke with what's necessary, no more. That means keeping unfounded paranoia in check. Our own, especially. We do *what* we must *when* we must, for *his* own good, even when he might not recognize it as such."

The cupbearer nodded. "Understood, Father."

Gyr patted Caltheo's shoulder. An area of twenty paces had been cleared around Malus D'Alzir's pavilion, guards posted in four directions. As they approached the edge of the clearing, Caltheo said, "But I disagree."

Gyr stopped short. Chain armor jostled as he spun around.

Caltheo licked his lips. *At least he has the decency to whisper.* "The duke should know of the thing in the woods. Of your illness, too. And the Kurgs—"

Rage flooded Gyr. "The men will know of the Kurgs after my report to the duke." His tone was stern. "It seems you don't understand, after all, Cupbearer. As I said before, I say what needs to be said *when* it needs to be said. I should think you heard me with such keen ears."

The fact that Caltheo had disobeyed Gyr's command to be out of earshot when he was speaking with Halladorn frustrated him.

"I apologize, Father. I heard only a few things. Still—"

"Still." Gyr stepped close, so close he smelled oats from the morning meal on Caltheo's breath. "Still what?"

"The duke should know." Caltheo's chin dropped to his chest. "The broken spoke in the wagon wheel could be sabotage. He needs to know all that occurs."

Gyr gave an incredulous laugh. More than a few crownguard were gathering to watch, which only added to Gyr's mounting anger. The lanky Sir Qel stood guard at the entrance to Duke Malus's pavilion. He wiped his bristly russet stash, then ran a palm over his slicked-back hair. Seemingly doing anything to avoid the tense exchange unfolding before him.

"You are not wrong." Gyr inhaled slowly. He spoke in measured tones. "And yet, your intractable manner is unacceptable. You need to understand your place if—"

"I'm to be Prosort," Caltheo finished. Dark eyes met Gyr's. The cupbearer's bearded chin thrust forth. "I understand, Father. I simply take your lead in defying my superiors. Duke Malus should know."

Gyr's mouth fell open. "Is that a threat?" His hands furled into fists, any semblance of calm shattered. He closed the gap between them, their booted toes almost touching.

Caltheo will back down or he will face the consequences of his insubordination.

The cupbearer looked away, over Gyr's shoulder. "No threat. But I will do what I must for my prosort's own good." Dark bulging eyes fell into Gyr's. "Even when he might not recognize it as such."

The back of Gyr's hand thudded across Caltheo's brow. The younger, larger man stumbled sideways. He stared at Gyr, mouth open, fingers probing a fast-forming welt over one eye. In all their years together, Gyr had never struck him.

He thought of Halladorn's dogs, how they were trained to obey through fear by hands doling out slaps. A wave of anger crested with the strike—faded as quick as it came. *What have I done?*

He went to Caltheo's side, but the moment he got close, the cupbearer stood at rigid attention, straight and sharp, like a spear. "I'm a priest of the Sempyrean Way, Father." Caltheo's voice was firm, louder than Gyr wished. "Your cowardly strikes do little to dissuade me from what is righteous and good in their eyes."

Cowardly! Horrified by the rebuke, Gyr struck again. "Do not take the Sempyrean in vain! They do not exist for you to load glory on yourself as a better to any other!"

Caltheo puffed out his chest, hands relaxed at his side. Using his tongue, he appeared to probe at a cut inside his mouth, cheek bowing around it. He spat, flinging beads of blood onto an errant patch of snow.

"Are you feeling righteous now?" Gyr said.

When no reply came, Gyr let fly a third strike...

Caught only air. Caltheo dodged the blow with a quick lean to one side. "Yes," he said. "*Now* I feel righteous."

"Prosort!" The voice was shrill with urgency.

Cupbearer and mentor whirled toward Malus D'Alzir's pavilion. The duke's body servant, Velal, stood outside the entrance wearing a perturbed expression. Fire flooded Gyr, whipcord tension from fist to neck. He heaved, chest bristling with rage.

He took in his surroundings. Crownguard, as far as the eye could see...

Waiting. Watching. Witnessing the punishment being delivered.

With a grunt, Gyr started toward the duke's pavilion, bootsteps heavy. Brick and mortar filled his hands, his feet, his gut.

Caltheo's voice brought him to a stop. "I'm sorry, Father. What I said... all of it was misguided."

Gyr did not turn around. His chest and shoulders rose and plunged with his racing heartbeat.

"Please, Father Renwood," Caltheo pleaded. "I beg your forgiveness."

After a long pause, Gyr nodded and then continued past Sir Qel into Lord Malus's tent.

CHAPTER THIRTEEN

A PROSPECT OF
VENGEANCE

H adir still lived.

Hand in hand, Zadani strolled with him through the north wood. Warmth spread from her chest into weightless arms, plunged down into her belly to the root of her sex. Throat thick with the pleasure of it, she traced Hadir's callused palms. The grooves of her fingertips brushed his, vibrating like the strings of a plucked lute.

Rays of dawn light punched holes in the canopy. Zadani looked down and found the forest's topsoil occluded by a fast-forming layer of mist.

Hadir gestured, mouth moving, but Zadani could not hear him.

Crouching, she attempted to peer through the vapor. She reached down...

Hadir pulled her away from it by the hand, worry creasing his brow. He spoke in a rush.

Zadani touched her ears. "I can't hear you, love."

Lantern jaw swiveled side to side.

Their hands separated as Hadir tried communicating with her using signs. A chill shot through her veins as if the mist itself had found a way inside of her. Shaking cold, she crossed her arms.

Hadir started to sink. Fast and faster. He flailed, gesticulating at her, at the mist, neck tendons bulging. Wild-eyed and red-faced with desperation.

Horror sucked the joy from Zadani, left her a vacuous husk. "It's okay, love." Faithless lip service.

A curtain of gray swirled around Hadir's waist, his legs now buried. Palms planted atop the mist to either side, he strained, pushing down to prevent it from swallowing him further.

A roughened hand rose to hers. Zadani snatched it and hauled with all her strength.

Still, her husband melted deeper into the earth.

"I'm so sorry!" She wept. "I can't! I can't help you!"

Mist traveled up his chest.

"Why?" she whined. She screamed. "Why is this happening?"

Hadir's mouth opened, worked out her name—that much she saw. He pointed at a squat maple tree a few arm spans away. Tears rolled down his cheeks.

His shoulders sank.

"I'm just a cook." She wrung her hands. "I can't."

His neck...

Chin hovering over the mist, he shook his head, gaze unwavering. He shook it again. Opposing waves of mist lapped over his dark hair like closing lips.

She was alone, pounding on the blanketing fog with the side of her fist. Impossibly thin, impossibly hard. Pounding. Pounding.

She woke in a pool of sweat.

A candle at her bedside beat back the last vestiges of night. Dawn, and her work in the kitchens, crept closer. She stared longingly at the place in bed where Hadir should have been. His hunting dagger lay there now, a comfort she'd claimed since the night she and Jasso had desecrated his tomb and discovered he'd been murdered.

Yes, I'm just a cook. And Hadir was just a hunter. Why would anyone kill him?

She dressed then made to leave her room, but before she could, her attention drifted to Hadir's hunting dagger again. Unsheathed, it glimmered in the reflected light of the candle she held. Facing carrots, onions, and leeks, no one cut faster than she. Shaving lamb or dicing beef, no one was defter with a blade. But as far as violence was concerned, Zadani didn't know the first thing about how to defend herself, a thought she'd never considered until Hadir had been...

Murdered. Never forget. My husband was murdered.

Zadani gritted her teeth. Sometimes, sadness drove her to her knees. Sometimes, fear set her lungs to a breathless tempo. And sometimes, rage made her do things like slip the knife into a sheath, place it in her boot, and hope Hadir's killer showed up to confess.

No matter how unlikely, the idea of vengeance buoyed her, the hope of wrath exacted, a comfort all on its own.

Hawk's Hall bustled with activity in the moments leading up to the day's court. Lit by the midday sun, the stained glass raptor burned bright, casting a purple hue over those gathering for the business of Kiyahd.

Marus D'Alzir wore a gray doublet trimmed with glittering silver that accented the aging wings of hair over his ears. A golden hawk pinned a fur-lined cloak to one shoulder, a silver honor plate on the other. From what Zadani understood, Lord Marus had served alongside his twin brother, Duke Malus, and the Mad Prince during the Great Betrayal. Though it was common knowledge the man was not a warrior, for official proceedings such as these, it made sense that he wear ceremonial attire. Nothing garnered the respect of Namorites more than an honor plate earned in service to the Crown.

Such a great man.

As the boards clunked down on the tables, Zadani wondered why the world chose some as deserving of greatness, while others—like Hadir—were chosen for short, happy lives with brutal ends. Sorrow clamped around her heart. A bolt of agony struck her gut. If alone, she would have doubled over, spilling grief into the cradle of her arm.

At court and her work in the kitchens, Zadani summoned a smile, a rigid mask without a shred of truth to it. But that's what everyone wanted to see. They didn't want to feel her pain, or see it, for that matter.

When Marus D'Alzir thanked her for her fine meal, she resented him.

When Lady Daran asked how Zadani was faring, she grew jealous. "I fare as well as one could expect." Such decency, such kindness. Zadani stretched the smile of her mask to the limits. "Pouring my love into your food has been a relief from mourning, milady." Bitterness leached to the surface.

Such a great family.

She hated them because she smiled to appease them; hated herself for wishing them ill when they'd done nothing wrong. Envy filled her. Envy for the living, for the order and chaos of life where fate and chance bestowed gifts and stole boons without reason or care for those it left forever damaged.

Zadani gave a curt bow to Daran and Marus, and then took her place near Sir Vallabathus to manage her kitchen staff.

During court, the D'Alzirs ate slowly, and so, the rest followed suit. Usually, breakfast faded into lunch, and then dinner, but only on particularly full days.

Today looks as if it will be just that. How lucky I am.

A silk trader went first, beseeching Lord Marus for increased safety measures through the Corridor of Storms.

"Apologies," said Marus. "But you must understand, the duty of protecting trade internationally is a duty of the Crown's Justice. You're better off petitioning my brother on the matter."

"Bandits have taken two caravans in the past year," the man said. "Your brother has failed."

"Yes, well, I'm sure you'd do a better job than he, if the roles were reversed." Marus smiled. "I suggest charging more for your silks so you can hire guards. Moving goods without protection is foolhardy. I hear the Scarborn are some of the best. And reasonably priced."

The dark-skinned trader snorted. "Why should I pay taxes for protection on our country's roads when I receive nothing for it?" Rather than wait for an answer, the trader left.

"I was going to buy some silks to help him recoup his costs," Marus announced. "I suspect impatience plays a factor in his ill-fortune."

The highborn court laughed.

The rest of the breakfast hours were consumed by a group of men from Breckenbright. They went back and forth with Marus on a building contract for repairs to the outer wall of Kiyahd, as well as to the Sempyrium's chapel. Eventually, they hashed out the details and Marus signed a sheaf of papers.

Breakfast at an end, kitchen staff cleared the boards and then brought out lunch. Marus dismissed Zadani from announcing the meal so they could continue proceedings, much to her relief. Her joy for the duty had shriveled like a tomato overexposed to the sun.

The next person to address the court had her sitting bolt upright. The look on the woman's face reflected the feeling in Zadani's own heart. Her pulse quickened. Tears streaked the woman's cheeks, and her eyes were red and swollen. A lost, helpless look shrouded her as she wrung her hands. It turned out, she was the lady of a small hold east of Kiyahd that was responsible for growing potatoes.

She fell to her knees, sobbing, hands twined in prayer. "Please, my lord Marus, release my husband. They said he sold godsthorn, but I swear, he never did. I swear it!"

Marus remained stoic.

"Please...I had just been in the barn when the soldiers found it. I—how could it be there? We don't even need the land back. If you'd just release him—"

Lord Marus proceeded solemnly. "Milady, you know such large quantities of godsthorn could have no other use than distribution for profit. I trust my holdguard and they have informed me about the situation. Your barn had over a hundred times the legal amount allowed for the purpose of making godsbrew. I am sorry. If I were you—"

The woman wailed and clutched her stomach. Empathy triggered, Zadani found herself cradling her belly. She didn't care if the woman's husband was guilty. She knew the hollowness there. An all-too-real despair. If Zadani had learned nothing else, it was the way suffering grounded one in the experience of being human. Despite wanting nothing more than to console the woman and tell her she understood, Zadani choked back a sob and slid behind her mask once more.

"I was there, my lord," said Nymon. "Enough godsthorn to ascend the whole damn court."

"He's lying!" The woman's lips twisted into a disbelieving snarl. "Lying..." Her eyes were glossy as she stared at her own hands. Her wailing resumed.

Marus raised his voice to cut over the din. "If I were you, I would count myself lucky that I wasn't imprisoned alongside my husband. All holds, both large and small, are too important to be squandered by those willing to violate Namorite law. You will be allowed to dissolve your marriage so you may go on with your life." Marus pressed his hands into his laps and shifted his weight. "This brings me no joy. I *am* sorry. Next."

Holdguard in black tabards dragged the woman away by the elbows, careful with her but unrelenting, her face in her palms. The doors of Hawk's Hall banged open as they left.

My situation is no better. My husband was murdered and I am without recourse. She chewed the inside of her cheek, fingers winding ringlets of her hair, wishing she could do something to help the woman.

Until that moment, Jasso Jackolo had been scribbling notes during the proceedings, but as soon as the doors closed, he slapped down his quill and stood. "By all that is sacred, Marus, do you have three bladders? When do we take a recess?"

Fits of nervous laughter circulated Hawk's Hall. A sheepish Lady Daran responded. "Master Jackolo, if you'd please refrain from such crude manners, I'd be awfully thankful."

"Oh, Daran, I don't know," said Marus. "I am growing fond of Jasso's levity. When he propositioned me for this visit, I had no idea I'd be receiving a court jester for free."

Jasso grimaced. "And nothing could be more hilarious than making me piss myself, right? I brim with far more than jokes at the moment."

"You may come and go as you please, Jasso," said Marus. "If you can hold it, we'll only be seeing one more."

Sighing, the scholar took up his quill and muttered, "A ruptured bladder is never funny."

Voluntary coughs stifled the most involuntary bouts of laughter.

A stiff-necked woman of middle years and abundant freckles entered Hawk's Hall flanked by two men. "Oh good, you're happy." Her tone dripped with contempt. The laughter died. "We stand before you as victims, the heads of small holds."

A heartbeat of silence followed.

A metal decanter clattered to the ground, Lady Rizel fumbling after it.

Daran ignored her mother. "Victims of what crime?"

"Glad you asked," said the woman. "Robbery, plain and simple. Lord Marus, you must relent your violent tax hikes before—"

A heavyset man at one table chortled, drawing the woman's ire.

"The tax increases are equal across all of Kiyahd," said Marus. "And yet, only you and your *friends* stand in court. Perhaps you mismanage your ledgers. I'm happy to offer you one of my accountants. Or have a contract written between us for a loan if that would help."

"Save your slap for another face, D'Alzir. You know these taxations are unlawful."

"Unlawful?" Zadani could tell from Marus's placid tones that he'd become angry. He was not one to run hot. Quite the contrary; he became quiet. Cold. Rarely had she seen it, though. He leaned forward. "I should have you thrown into cells for your accusation."

The woman's eyes went wide. "You dare threaten us with arrest?"

Marus folded his hands. "I suppose now is as good a time as any. Sir Vallabathus, if you please, share for the court our most recent reports."

The sinewy knight-captain stepped forward and announced in a tone as flat as his affect, "Word has come from our outpost at Staghill. The Kurgs of the mountain enclaves are mobilizing." The knight-captain stepped back, boot heels clapping the flagstone floor.

"With our borders under threat of Kurgish attack, I've raised taxes to hire more men," Marus said. "More protection for people who don't just stand to lose their possessions but their lives. And you have the gall to whine at me in my own court?"

"Phantom reasons for very real theft," the woman said. "I sometimes hear howling at night—wolves in the woods around Kiyahd. Shall we be taxed to walk abroad for fear of the danger they pose as well?"

Marus waved a hand. "If that is an example of your capacity to listen with discernment, I pray to the gods of the Sempyrean you bribed these other two to be here. I could not stomach knowing Kiyahd is home to more than one of Namarr's greatest fools." He stood and pointed to the door to Hawk's Hall. "You know nothing of the responsibilities I bear. Now, leave my court in peace knowing your taxes may save the lives of *true* Namorites."

Beet red, the woman angled to retort, but a holdguard stepped before her. Freckled lips pursed, fists balled at her sides, she pivoted and left. Her peers followed, affording a few backward glances from beneath lowered brows.

Jasso Jackolo stood with a flourish. He bowed to a still-fuming Marus D'Alzir. "You have my respect, milord. I'd have ordered her publicly spanked for such behavior. Now...glad I stayed. Gladder still to be going. Where might I find the nearest chamber pot?"

Marus settled back into his chair, exuding agitation.

"You sure you don't want to arrest her, my lord?" A wicked grin split Nymon's blond beard. "I wouldn't mind interrogating her a bit."

A sour taste filled Zadani's mouth and her lip curled. She pressed her thighs together.

"That's not how I do things." Marus rubbed his brow. "I prefer you focus more on preparing to fight Kurgs and less on impressing your men with lewd jests unbefitting a man in my service."

Nymon shrugged. "Kurgs it is then. My boys can't imagine a better way to pass the time." He whistled to a handful of gruff and grizzled men standing behind. "Whore houses or Kurg killin', boys, which is it you prefer?"

They laughed.

In a swirl of colorful cloth, Jasso returned to his seat, as did a few others.

Marus rocked back in his chair then came to his feet. "If there are no more pressing matters, I think we shall adjourn for the day."

Before she knew what she was doing, Zadani ceased fidgeting with her hair and rose. *Something is wrong.* She stepped to the center of the encircled tables.

The insides of her cheeks stuck to gums drier than the deserts of Malzacor. She felt the eyes of the highborn court shift in her direction. Their frowns and their shock were a deep ache in her heart.

Head bowed, she watched Lord Marus as he assessed her.

A flush crept up Zadani's neck and into her face, her chin and ears tingling with the sudden rush of blood. Words she could never unsay tumbled out. "My lord...I have something I wish to bring to your attention."

"This is highly irregular, Mistress Innan, and I daresay inappropriate." Marus crossed his arms, then shot a look at his daughter and wife. "But it is without question that we trust and rely on faithful servants like yourself to run Kiyahd. Further, it's no secret you are a grieving widow, so I will ignore the break in protocol this once. Proceed."

Not a good start. But what do the good graces of my lord matter when I have no husband to share it with? Why worry about a fall from favor when Hadir isn't here to suffer it alongside me?

"Thank you, my lord." She bowed. Warm sweat seeped from her crown and down the back of her neck. "I believe my husband was..." A rough, burning lump of coal worked its way from her throat. She lifted her chin and spat it steaming into the space. "Murdered."

The court stiffened. Once disinterested lords and ladies of minor holds, and lickspittle officials of the Crown, came swiftly to attention.

"My Hadir...he was murdered."

A somberness fell over Lord Marus. "There is a Malzacy proverb I offer you, Mistress Innan. 'Death steals the one life but grief is far greedier and takes from the living.' I know your husband's death is fresh, so forgive me my asking, but what is your evidence of his murder?"

Jasso Jackolo shifted in his seat. Telling Marus the truth could cause problems for the scholar. *In exchange for information about illegal drugs, he helped me desecrate a tomb in your sacred burial grounds, my lord.*

That way lay a prison cell for both of them.

"When I saw the body, it didn't look like a bear mauling. Hadir was too careful. A hunter of twenty years making such a mistake..." Zadani shook her head. "It could never happen."

Marus's fingernail clicked against the table. "This conversation saddens me. I wish you had more clear evidence, Mistress Innan. Again, I only push because duty compels me to be thorough in my dispensation of justice. Have you seen many bear attacks?"

"I haven't." Frustration edged Zadani's voice. "Is my intuition not good enough for investigation, then? Or my husband's skill—is it presumed he didn't know his trade? The holdguard who found him—these men are better at identifying a cause of death than my husband was at avoiding it?" A snort of scorn-laced laughter escaped her.

In cool tones, Marus said, "The holdguard of Kiyahd speak with my voice and act with my hand. I trust them with my life. Not only that, but they also keep you and everyone here safe, so be careful with your unfounded accusations."

Like they kept Hadir safe?

Jaw clenched, she inhaled through her nose. "Surely, you understand what it's like. If someone told you your daughter was killed by a bear when you knew it to be bandits—"

Lady Rizel covered her mouth, eyes welling with tears. A series of heavy sobs began to shake her as Lady Daran led her mother from the hall.

Zadani derided her foolhardy comment as Lord Marus's face went slack but for a twitching lip. "Mistress Innan, I would advise more grace, even in your grief. You've violated the boundaries between your duties and my court. Your interruption has cost everyone their time, heaped doubt on my men, and sent my beloved wife weeping from the hall. All this without evidence."

Shoulders sagging, Zadani's chin wilted to her chest. Silence poured into her, numbing her with shame.

"Even so, justice shall be explored to its fullest." Zadani's head snapped up.

Marus scanned the room. "When Raiya passed, I was near frothing at the mouth to find her killers, so I'll not deny your request. The two holdguard will be detained and questioned to ensure there is no corruption in my hold. Master Nymon, you are tasked with investigating these allegations further, though it should not interfere with your other duties."

A mix of emotions struck Zadani through the gut. She'd gotten what she wanted but hated the idea of interacting any more with Nymon than necessary. The man's offensive tongue seemed to be tasting every hair rimming his mouth as he smiled at her.

She shivered, rolled forward over her waist into a deep bow. "Thank you, my lord."

Despite his off-putting nature, Zadani hoped Nymon was capable. Maybe, just maybe, he might find Hadir's killer.

As she walked back to the kitchens, she became aware of the knife in her boot, warm steel pressing against her calf, comforting in its prospects for vengeance.

CHAPTER FOURTEEN

DEAD RECKONING

Leaves gathered the moisture held by the forest for a pristine moment of peace. The nourishing jewel trembled against its own weight, then fell to the earth at Barodane's feet. The rain had stopped hours ago, when they were on the open road, but here in the forest, it fell in a predictable rhythm as it made its way down from the overstory. A score of drops sped toward him, nature's erratic drumbeat of things acquired, things kept, things released.

Release...that's when new life was made.

"Riders coming." Garlenna pulled Barodane into a crouch.

His cloak was sodden and a chill leaked through his gloves to numb his fingertips. Disoriented days lay behind them, layered in the fog of cold and hiding at every turn as Barodane adjusted to his new life. *Damn soggy one, isn't it?*

He looked up—squinted and blinked against the bright patches peeking through the canopy. Sunlight bent around his fingers as they entered a lonely band of it. *Not all bad.*

"Crown's Justice," Garlenna said. "Most likely on their way to Brecken-bright."

He barely heard her as he studied the tranquil battlefield of nature.

A glimmer of motion. A gentle plop. A wet jewel shattered on his leather palm. All around, a thousand twitching fibers and snatches of sound. The unobservable stretch of things growing and things dying—nature's many be-coming one in a frantically slow, chaotically quiet race for root space.

Which parts of me have been eaten, and which have done the eating? He feared the answer more than death. *You've lost yourself, Barodane. You think you can come back? You're just going to disappoint everyone again.* The voice in his head was his own now, and sadly, he noted it was little kinder than the dead had been.

Garlenna eased down beside him, her mace handle hushing as she slipped it into the leather thong at her belt. Since they'd left Digtown, she'd been all strategy. "We'll have to dodge every town from here to Martyr's Isle. Roddic Olabran will have all the chainmen and holdguard in Lah-Tsarra hunting his son's killers."

Hooves on hard-packed road faded into the distance. Barodane glanced to his right. What looked like a series of tiny bones and scattered fur surrounded a patch of mushrooms. Death dealer mushrooms if he had to bet on it. And a squirrel's remains.

"Barodane..."

He stared at the mushrooms. It would only take one nibble to lay the burdens of both past and future to rest. A lot like ascending, he'd heard. *One last high...*

A familiar woman's face floated before him, concern creasing her brow where her leather eye-patch didn't cover. Tangles of ruddy hair—made brownish by the wet—framed his attention.

"Hey," she said, "look at me."

Barodane blinked, grunted, then sat straighter. He hadn't realized how slumped he was. The twinge between his shoulders told him he should have been more mindful. Two weeks in the saddle after a fight for his life had left him aching and stiff in places he didn't know existed.

"Sorry, Gar. I'm fine." He wasn't so sure. "Promise."

His prosort huffed a laugh. "You're a terrible liar."

He frowned. *Cheeky bitch.* Fourteen years of separation had done little to deteriorate her ability to see straight to the heart of him. He hated how well she knew him, but at the same time, riding with her again...it was like a warm fire after a long walk in the cold and dark.

Garlenna's smile drifted to one side. "Your heart may beat, but you're anything but alive. It's going to take time."

To return to my old self, you mean. But what if he isn't there? What then? He stood in a rush and started brushing himself clean. "Oh, is it? What a joy." Meckin's dead face staring at the ceiling flashed across his mind. His movements slowed. "You're sure you want him back?"

"It's not about what I want. Not about what you want, either. That's what you fail to learn. It's about what's needed. Whether you like it or not, Namarr needs you. Our wants come second."

Namarr needs a broken prince with a shaky sword hand? I wonder if its people know that.

"We better get going then." He walked to Scab, hobbled thirty yards deeper into the forest. "I suggest we stop at every tavern from here to Breckenbright."

Garlenna shook her head. "You know we can't."

"I thought the people needed their prince."

"Alive." Garlenna followed him to the horses. "Best to stay off the main roads and—"

Barodane rounded on her. "If you want me to go along with this facade, I need to know it's true. I've been in Digtown too long..." He looked away, shocked to find that he agreed with what he was saying. "It could help. Maybe it'll remind me that there's something worth saving."

Garlenna sighed, producing a cloud of steam, then rubbed the flesh under the leather strap of her eye patch. Raindrops plummeted around her in asynchronous rhythm as she stared at a stump covered in ocher and umber leaves. She sighed again, then drew the dagger from her chest-sheath and stepped toward him.

He backpedaled. "What are you doing?"

"You don't think I'm letting you go in like that, do you?"

"Have you forgotten I used to wear my hair close-cropped?"

"Your beard is what I'm after." She waved the knife. "You can't look like Barodane, but you can't look like Kord, either." She cocked her head, eye narrowed. "Perhaps a mustache."

"Like a Malzacy?" Incredulous, he stroked his facial hair.

"Given how you look, I'm stunned you have a scrap of vanity left. Have you seen yourself lately?" She shivered mockingly. "Terrifying."

He growled, "Fuck you," then snatched the knife from her.

They navigated the forest. Barodane rubbed his cleanly shaved skin with a gloved hand. It felt odd, unreal, like a stranger's hand touching a stranger's face. Scab flicked his head back and gave Barodane the side-eye.

"What?" he said to the horse.

"You're far gaunter than I realized," Garlenna said from beside him.

"Yeah?" Barodane pulled off his glove and brushed a cheek, skin feeling thin over the prominent bone beneath. He traced his jaw. "A steady diet of godsbrew and bad memories will do that to a man."

"Indeed," Garlenna said.

Face still angled, Scab stared at his rider a second then whinnied.

"Stow it," Barodane sneered. "You're not the worst stallion in Namarr, but you better hope he doesn't die. Ugly bastard."

Just before dusk, Garlenna led them to a stream. They were traveling parallel to the main road, and the dense thicket surrounding the spot they made camp looked to have been used at various times by others over the years. Bandits, criminals, drug runners. *Us, essentially.*

Barodane maneuvered his sword to catch the light. He lifted his chin. Once tan, vibrant skin had fallen to an ashy hue. The flesh around his cheeks sucked tight to the bone. Dark bags cupped his eyes. "Triune God," he muttered.

"Sempyrean gods, too." Garlenna carried firewood into the small clearing encircled by dense shrubbery. "It's bad. If I were you, I'd invoke as many deities as you can." She set about starting a fire before a thought seemed to catch her attention. She turned to Barodane. "In case you were wondering, it's not only okay for you to help with the horses and the campfire, but also preferred."

He lowered his blade-turned-mirror. "I wasn't wondering." Slid his sword into its scabbard then huddled into his cloak. "I prefer the cold."

"Very funny." Garlenna stretched to her full height, lifting her arms overhead and then dropping into a squat. Since they'd been on the road, a day hadn't passed where she didn't perform strength exercises. "I'm off. I expect the fire to be built when I return."

She disappeared into the thickening gloom.

Barodane eased onto his side in the dirt. He glanced at the stacked wood but couldn't muster the urge to build the fire. The Dregs burned in his memory. For his friend, he'd fought the blaze, though the man hadn't said a word to him even after the inn was saved. Meckin's bitter words, some of his last to Barodane, rose from charred remains. *Some friend you are. Selfish fucking bastard.*

Regret spun a sour web in his belly, connecting all the wrongs he'd done.

He sat up and stared at the stack of wood. *I promised the boy I'd be better.* Still, he couldn't bring himself to start the fire. *I'm about as useful as my promises.*

Garlenna returned, arms trapping a large stone to her midsection. She thrust it with her hips and released, letting it thud to the ground. From the sound and look of it, it had to weigh at least half as much as Barodane.

"You're weak." She squatted, hefted, straightened with a wheeze of exertion, then dropped it again. She repeated the process a dozen more times until she was breathing heavily. "Pick it up."

Barodane scoffed.

"Your body needs to remember who you are just as much as your mind. Look at you. You can't even build a fire. You cut the real you off with drugs and drink for too long. Now that you're sober, you're in your head." She crouched, patted the rock. "The body does not lie. You need to *feel* like Barodane again. It will help."

He leaned forward. "Alas, had I been hoisting stones weeks ago, Jennim and Meckin might still be alive."

"Cynicism is a poor defense for a cowardly heart. It erodes an already weak sense of willpower." She placed both hands on the stone and rolled it toward him. "Even in short supply, optimism accomplishes far more."

"Mmm." He lay back down. "We can't all be Garlenna Renwood, greatest prosort who ever lived."

"It brought me to you."

He raised his head to look down the length of his body at her. "What did?"

"Optimism," she said. "It brought me to you. If I'd let cynicism guide me, I would have stayed in Alistar. I would have accepted a pressing mission from the Archprelate. I would have never seen you again. When my father's letter reached me, I didn't doubt its truth for a moment. I knew..." She cleared her throat. "I knew you were alive."

The skin at the base of his skull tingled at seeing her rising emotion.

She swiped lank hair from her face. "I've never been happier than the moment I saw you at the Dregs. Something long dead inside came back to life. A hearth of cold ash at the center of me now roars with fire again. We *can* do this. Your grandfather's dream doesn't have to die. Namarr can be united once more."

Your dream is my nightmare, friend.

The trickle of water from the nearby stream filled the silence. As convincing as her words were, Barodane could not shake the creep of self-doubt. "I'm already going with you to find the Slave Banner, Gar. Isn't that enough? Or must I heft rocks and spout happy thoughts to meet your expectations?"

"You don't understand, do you?"

"Probably not but do go on."

Her voice took on a worried edge. "I'm not just preparing you for Solice-rames, Barodane. I'm preparing you to wear the crown again. For good this time."

The former prince's chest wound tight as a crossbow winch. His heart started to race. *Rule Namarr? Face the people I abandoned? Hold court and council and...what about my crimes?*

A laugh slipped past his lips. Garlenna shifted. She was right, the thought of ruling hadn't gained traction yet, his mind too clouded with past regrets to consider the future. It was a ludicrous idea sure to fail, and for some reason, that made the entire course of their mission more palatable. "And they call *me* the Mad Prince." He rolled so that his back faced his prosort. "Another suicide charge it is."

Garlenna responded in the most predictable way he could imagine. She did what was needed and built the fire. *Duty seeps from her damn bones, and I'm over here wanting none at all.* The Sempyrean gods made up the elements of the world, but they'd seemingly missed one, for everywhere he looked, it seemed a divine comedy of sorts.

After she finished the fire, she returned to her exercises. Round after round of a dozen squats with the stone weight, her breathing focused and consistent, trained to an optimal rhythm. Barodane had been surrounded by the strongest, most elite soldiers in Namarr for his entire life. Only the Beast of Anjuhkar had ever rivaled Garlenna's physicality.

But mentally, none did. Her attitude and focus were ironclad. As insane as it was to hear her suggest that he could rule Namarr again, it almost seemed plausible simply because it was *her* suggesting it. She had committed horrible acts on his behalf, and seemingly, she'd dealt with it. The courage and strength that might take—he struggled to fathom it.

Proud of his friend, Barodane's mouth tugged into a half smile. *Good on you, Gar. After what I did, I wouldn't listen to me anymore either. I lost that privilege, and rightly so. I suppose you want me to earn it back now.*

A scowl tightened his face as he drifted toward sleep. Garlenna continued to work out with the stone. Curiosity seized him, batting his confidence around like a mean drunkard disciplining their child.

I could lift the stone at least once...couldn't I?

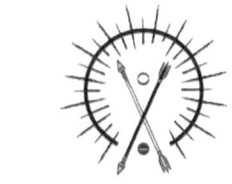

CHAPTER FIFTEEN

DOMINARRI

Thephos held no grudge against Syn Backlegarm. The Provocation was a necessary rite all Awakened had to experience and it made Namarr a safer place. Such a necessity, in fact, that when Syn had told the other Dominarri in the tent that he would be taking Thephos to Enshai himself, it came as a shock.

"Not the time for jokes," Ash had said.

"I'm not joking."

An older, weathered Awakened said, "We'll be hard-pressed without you if another one saunters into camp."

Syn waved a hand. "I'll be back before that's likely to happen, and if I'm not, Radiance knows what to do."

"Long as he's not balls-deep the lady of the moment," Ash scoffed.

Syn rolled his eyes. "Why do you always assume the worst? I've trained the man myself. He can do the Provocations in the old way just fine. This is more important."

"More important than Ruptured being set loose in the world?" Ash stared flatly at her husband, lips curled back. "One already slipped past us..."

"We'll catch him." Syn's tone rang with finality. "I go to Enshai to arrange it personally, in addition to introducing our new friend." He slapped Thephos on the shoulder.

The newly Awakened winced. The spot where Syn had slapped him was raw from where the chains had chafed in physical reality. "I'm to go with you?"

"You gotta choose, actually." Syn waved a hand. "You can either become a Dominarri like us, or you can go your own way."

"Why would I want to go with you?"

"More fun," Syn said. When Thephos gave no reaction, he continued. "Now that you're Awakened, you've got two paths ahead of you. One, you go your own way. Do that and chances are a highborn will try to hire you. It's not a bad life, though a little boring and shallow. Hardly puts your powers to use where they're most needed."

"And path two is where they're needed?"

Syn snapped his fingers. "You got it! The Dominarri provide a home for the largest population of Awakened in the world. You'd be a part of something meaningful, something that saves lives. You'd have a chance to do some real good."

The others watched Thephos, scrutinizing him, judging what his decision might be before he made it. He looked at his feet, feeling the heat of his skin flushed with embarrassment. "For the Triune God, right? I'm not religious..."

"It's not about that," Ash said, her ire flaring. "We aren't the Sempyrium, counting our gold and maneuvering our pawns for greater influence and power."

"She's right," Syn said. "Our order prevents catastrophe. You join us and you join the fight against evil."

"Me? I'm..." Thephos swallowed, shook his head. "Are you sure the Dominarri want me?"

Laughing, Syn brought his palms together in mock prayer. "Listen, friend. I know you think you're worthless, but you're an Awakened. The Mother chose you. You get that right?"

Thephos frowned. *Not really.*

"You may have been a pig farmer yesterday, but today, there's no one else like you. In Enshai, you won't be alone anymore. We'll see you for who you are—now—not who you were in your past. Who you could be in the future." He affected a pleading tone. "We need you."

Me? Who needs me? No one had ever needed Thephos before. Quite the opposite. It seemed everyone he'd met prior to Syn would have been better off without him. Better off with him dead.

"What about my brothers?" Thephos moved out from under Syn's hand. "If I worked for a lord and made money, I could make their lives better. Maybe earn enough so they wouldn't need to farm anymore."

"You'll be compensated," Ash said. "We'll send money to your family. Three gold wheels a month."

"Five." Syn shot her a look.

Thephos's jaw hinged open. Five gold wheels was a small fortune. The most his father had ever made on a sow at market was one. And that had lasted months.

Ash arched her brow at her husband. "That isn't protocol."

"No," Syn said. "It isn't."

Thephos tried to remember the last time he'd seen a gold wheel. "You want me to be Dominarri that bad?"

"We do."

Thephos searched the faces of the others. *If this is a joke, they'll laugh as soon as I say yes.*

Deep down, he knew it wasn't. He thought back to Unturrus. To the horrors he'd faced. It had taken courage not to give up—to keep going. It took courage to decide he was worth something after all. The voice seemed to think so too.

"You don't even know what power I have yet," he said.

"It sometimes takes a while to unlock, but I know it's there." Syn's cheek twitched. "I felt it. There's something extraordinary in you, Thephos. Even for an Awakened."

Syn had never told someone that before. It was written on his face and in the stunned and confused expressions the others flashed at one another.

More than anything, that scared Thephos. He didn't want an extraordinary power. Until a short time ago, all he'd wanted was to die. Now, he was being offered a fortune to fight evil for a mysterious order that had so far only tortured him and lied to him.

You want this, Theffy. They'll make you stronger...make us stronger.

The voice receded before Thephos could question it. It was seeping beneath his awareness more and more every time it spoke. Becoming almost like a part of him.

His pride swelled at the realization that he *was* unique. He was desirable. Powerful. "Yes. I'll do it."

Syn clapped him on the shoulder. "Good choice. We leave tonight."

It took a handful of days for Thephos to get the hang of riding a horse. In truth, he'd have preferred a pig. That was an animal he knew. And what was known was trusted. For all the change happening for him in such a condensed period, he longed for the familiar. Even the worst of it.

The despair of his past had lessened since summiting Unturrus, but it wasn't completely gone. Instead, it seemed to be integrating into a newfound sense of himself. He had worth. He had value. He was not, in fact, a worm. *Nor am I a coward.*

They reined in at the edge of the Ardent Heart, the journey to get there made slower by Thephos's poor riding skills. A line of trees extended to the horizon in either direction. *A coward wouldn't be here. A coward would never say yes to becoming a Dominarri. A coward would have taken the easy road.*

"Big trees, right?" Syn's horse sidestepped, brushing up against Thephos's mount.

Ash sat behind, exuding impatience. "We have to gawk at it all day?"

Syn leaned over to Thephos and whispered, "Al'Ushari makes her nervous, no matter how many times we go through."

"I can hear you," she muttered.

Thephos stared at the densely packed trees. They were ancient, each a potent entity with a power unto itself. Some were so large, it would take ten men linking arms to enclose their base. "Al'Ushari?"

"It's what the forest enclaves call the Ardent Heart. Long before the missionaries of Peladon settled here, that was its name. If we run into any Kurgs, it's probably best if you call it that, too."

Thephos searched Syn's face for humor. Even when he was serious, his tone oft made it sound as if he were joking. Thephos decided, this time, he wasn't. "How far to Enshai?"

Syn shrugged. "A week, maybe less if we—"

"It'll take as long as it takes." Ash wedged her mount between those of Syn and Thephos, then rode ahead. "Let's go."

Syn rolled his eyes. "So impatient. More days on the road with her will be a gift."

A half-smile crept up Thephos's cheek. The pair had grown on him. Syn: cheery, positive, a beam of light shining through any storm. And Ash, the storm. Yet they seemed to love each other unconditionally. At night, they cuddled close. Thephos would watch them, perfectly still, contented bodies breathing in unison until sleep came.

Thephos realized he'd never been in love. Never even considered it. For a man of nineteen years, it seemed a tragic truth.

I love you, the voice cooed.

Thephos stared straight ahead and entered the dense forest.

CHAPTER SIXTEEN

THE WHITE WOLVERINE ALLIANCE

S he dreamed of Othwii.

A soft hand gripped her shoulder as they walked together in sunlight, talking of her parents. He smelled of books, rose water, and a tang he sometimes had from the exotic teas he drank. The stories he told her were pleasant. Her uncle Barodane had a love of life that was unrivaled. Always armed with a ready jest, no matter how crude. Her father, Malath, had loved none more than his brother.

"Until you were born, Ishoa," Othwii said.

"Me? Why?"

Othwii didn't answer. He stared and stared and stared, stoking her insecurities. "Can't you just tell me why?"

Then Othwii was gone and she stood alone, the earth an unreal bowl with silhouettes of trees lining the rim.

Her question echoed back to her.

Why...why...why...

She woke in the night, cheeks slick with tears. Hot throughout her torso, the cold nipped at her face. The Fly moved about in the dark, hacking at something. Ishoa craned her head, trying to see and hear, to discern what he was doing but she was too exhausted to stay awake and fell back into the unpleasant world of sleep.

Wolst was alive. Blood dripped from matted beard and clenched fists. He drank from a clay pitcher—drank blood from it. It lined his teeth and dribbled down his chin.

Muffled words vibrated through the dreamspace. He spoke to shadows in garbled clips. Every so often, he glanced her way, more beast than man. Ishoa was exposed before his primal visage...vulnerable to the shape of his legacy. And the shadows honored him, praying from their corners to their beastly god. He was war embodied. A creature of magnitude, and she, less than a trembling leaf unwilling to depart from the branch it was birthed upon.

He turned a savage expression on her. "Isha..." he growled. The shadows moaned.

He clapped his hands and smeared them together so that his bloody, greasy fingers slimed between knuckles. "Isha!" He clapped again. Gory droplets burst in every direction.

Clap. "Isha!" Clap.

Clap! Clap!

CLAP! CLAP!

She sucked in the world with a gasp. Smoke and frigid air pierced her lungs.

The damages from the fight the previous night woke with her. Raw throat, tight neck, sore legs, tender hip, and a half dozen other injuries she couldn't remember getting. Another pointed clap made her jolt. She rolled to her side, arms and legs bound, and found the source.

The Fly.

He'd stripped from waist to neck, keeping his face covered by the black executioner's mask. Billowy trousers remained tucked into his leather boots and his gloves creaked around an ax-handle. A sheen of sweat lathered his chest as he worked. Tumescent scars latticed his shoulders and back. Lean muscle tensed into a tan-canvas of angular ridges as he dragged what he'd been working on across the ground.

Rakeema panted on her side a few spans away, paws and muzzle trussed up like a swine. Rounded eyes watched her master, the sweat of stress damping the area around her ears. A white slaver rimmed her black-gummed mouth.

Ishoa searched the ground around her for a weapon lost in the skirmish, or a piece of slate sharp enough to sever her bonds. Nothing but snow, smooth stone, and brittle sticks.

The Fly slipped his arms under Arick and lifted, bearing him as easily as a mother carrying a toddler to bed, then deposited the knight of Jarik on the makeshift stretcher. He took his time looping rope over the rudimentary contraption, making sure that if Arick came to, he would be secured and unable to fight.

Next came Rakeema. The Fly lashed a length of rope around her waist, then dragged her to where Arick rested on the stretcher and tied the leash to the back end. Once she was secure, he dipped to a knee and sawed the bindings around her paws so she could walk.

She jumped up and scrambled away, pulled to the ground when the rope around her waist yanked taut. Ishoa tried to calm her, but the ice tiger didn't give up trying to win free until she was panting.

The way the Fly had set her up, the anjuhtarg would be capable of doing little beyond walking and vocalizing her displeasure, which she did in earnest.

He set his sights on Ishoa, dagger drawn.

She wriggled backward on the frosted turf, kicking up puffs of dust as she dug her heels in to shove off. Frantically, she searched for anything that might help her defend herself.

The Fly seized the bonds around her ankles and hoisted. She tried to fight but his grip was unyielding. When she noticed he was severing her bonds, she went still and waited.

He rolled her onto her side and set to work behind her. As soon as her wrists came free, she twisted around and grabbed for the dagger. The Fly eluded her mad gambit by raising the knife far above her reach. *I'll cut you down then!* She threw a punch at his crotch.

Sliding one heel back, he avoided the attack while simultaneously striking her in the chest with an open palm.

She wheezed, the air knocked from her. Vision darkening, she saw his finger wagging side-to-side as if to say, *don't try that again.*

Ishoa struggled to breathe, sounding like Rakeema whenever she dislodged a hairball.

The Fly relaxed his defenses.

She lunged at his leg, prepared to sink her teeth into anything she could reach. A burning sensation spread across the side of her head. Snot released from her nose at the sudden, blinding pain.

The world fractured into three parts, blurred at the edges, and slowly merged back into one. A beetle scuttled past, hurrying over the snow mere inches from her face. She tried to push up onto hands and knees but couldn't.

She found her wrists had been bound. Tighter this time.

The Fly flipped her onto her back and delivered a gentle slap. Ishoa blinked, the world whole and distinct once more.

A finger waved in her face. The Fly gestured at Arick and Rakeema, then drew his fingers across his throat.

Ishoa went wooden. She nodded, letting him know she was ready to comply. He pulled her to her feet then turned his back. She thought about kicking him, an exceedingly foolish idea. She'd seen what the Fly could do on two separate occasions now. During the first, he'd singlehandedly threshed half of Ollo Bael's cattlemen, and on the second, he'd dispatched five former peers from Shadowheart within a couple of minutes. With relative ease, no less.

I could run. That was the coward's path. With Rakeema and Arick bound, she could get away, but she would do so alone. For them, there was no chance of escape. *Since fighting and running are out of the question, let's try a different approach.* "Why are you doing this?"

After slinging his ax-staff onto his back, he pulled a rope over his shoulder so he could tow Arick on the stretcher. Rakeema would be forced to follow on her leash. He motioned for Ishoa to walk in front of him.

"I want to know why you're doing this. I am your..." *Duchess. In the absence of a Crown Prince, duchies fall to bloodlines.* The word wouldn't come out. *Is grandmother dead, too?* She summoned what little confidence she had left. "Fly, you're my subject. I *command* you to release us."

The Fly grabbed her by the back of the neck and propelled her onward.

A pair of hen-like women and a girl had stumbled onto the path behind them earlier in the day.

The Fly stopped, sliced some cloth into a strip and gagged Ishoa.

By eve, they'd come abreast of a vast stretch of the Blue River. Stripped of their leaves by oppressive cold, skeletal oaks and maples lined the banks. Hats of snow rested at the juncture where branches split. Gloom thickened with every steaming breath in the waning light.

Still, the Fly urged Ishoa forward.

She glanced back. Her captor's head remained down, unconcerned by the women who hurried to catch up with them. Ishoa walked twisted around, snatching infrequent looks at her path to keep from tripping.

Breathless in their efforts to reach the stretcher, the two crones—decades older than their third companion—slowed once they'd come within a few spans. The girl tugged at their wool shawls and nodded at Ishoa. From a distance, they probably couldn't see that the Fly transported prisoners. The women crowded together behind the stretcher, undeterred by the revelation.

Their reasoning was laid bare when the Fly finally stopped for the night. Tucking the stretcher under a cluster of evergreens, he had swung around and stared at the women.

They matched his wordlessness, pulling food from one of the packs they carried and offering it to him. He took it, nodded, then set about starting a fire.

From what Ishoa gathered, they carried what was left of what they owned.

One of the crones, wearing hat and mittens but otherwise looking like an exact replica of the other woman her age, stepped over to the fire, breaking the unspoken boundary between them and the Fly. "We come from Threehills."

The Fly ignored the crone who spoke but for a slight tilt of his head. With her hands bound behind her back, Ishoa plopped down beside the fire, the action awkward.

Seemingly lent courage by her sister, the second crone joined her twin across the fire from the Fly. "Stories abound of rapes."

At least they have the awareness not to ask him questions.

"I'm no jewel, but that's never stopped a hungry man afore," smacked the twin with mittens.

Ishoa cringed. Othwii had once told her, "In times of unrest, the morality of average men dissolves with stunning speed." She was seven at the time and he was educating Ishoa on her family's history. That day, he'd needed to give some context in order to justify the darkest stain of the Ironlight line. He'd told her the nascent tip of atrocities carried out on behalf of Namarr during the Great Betrayal before finally explaining her uncle Barodane's transgressions. "A loving and carefree soul, given over to murder and madness for a sad but final moment at the peak of his grief," Othwii had said.

The girl close to Ishoa's age watched the Fly warily and took up a position as far away as she could without losing the fire's warmth. *That one is cleverer than the crones.*

One of the twin's eyes darted from the Fly to Arick on the stretcher and then to Ishoa. She cleared her throat. "Good on you getting these dangerous bandits off the road, kind sir."

After a brief pause, the Fly nodded. Ishoa shook her head and glared, but the old crone refused to meet her gaze. Little did it matter. What would these women do if they knew the truth? Fight the Fly? No. Ishoa had seen how that ended. These women were survivors and would remain so by any means necessary.

How can I blame them for their voluntary ignorance when it keeps them alive?

"They're callin' him the White Wolverine," the twin with mittens said. "Syphion Muul...they're callin' him a hero."

Ishoa chewed at the gag stymieing her ability to speak. *A hero?* The thought sickened her, and she couldn't help but hate the people she was supposed to love and protect a little for it.

"Word of his defiant speech is spreadin' across the land like wildfire. I didn't want to hurt anyone, nor be hurt. But bein' a clerk for the lord of Threehills put me on the guttin' block," said the other crone. "They come in the night for him. Lowborn folk like me...but not like me, either."

"Give someone you've slighted the chance and they'll repay the kindness."
Mittens nodded, facts of life confirmed. She threw a thumb at her sister. "Leena
knows."

"I do. Heard my lord's screams in the dead of night. Won't forget any time
soon." Leena fell quiet, huffing out a steaming breath. "Ain't just the Scarborn
who's bitter about being called Namorites. Probably just an excuse to do some
score settlin' though. These hold lords and ladies, they all got where they are by
capitalizin' at the right time. The ones who called the Unity Wars a righteous
rebellion—I ain't disagreeing that they were, but they got themselves quite the
reward from it, didn't they?"

Ishoa watched the Fly for a reaction, for any indication of his allegiance or
intentions, but he gave no sign that he was even listening.

Mittens patted Leena's knee as she continued. "Just sayin' that's the mind of
some people. Why shouldn't they call this uprising a righteous rebellion if it
gets them ahead? Some so poor, they got nothin' to lose."

"Willing to kill for it," said Mittens. "Willing to kill anyone associated with
the old Namorite system if it gets them on top."

Wolst. Othwii. Grandmother...Lodaris. Suddenly, Ishoa tasted every sour bit
of the gag shoved in her mouth.

The fire crackled. Leena gazed out over the nearby rushing river. "Tale older
than the Blue River, that."

The twins drew out a pair of blankets and gave one to the girl. The Fly did
the same and placed it over Ishoa as she shrimped up beside Rakeema, still tied
to the stretcher.

The crones went to sleep, but the young woman kept her eyes on the Fly all
night, or at least for as long as Ishoa was awake.

The princess dreamed in fitful bursts, forehead bunched in consternation as
lowborn killers with dirt-streaked faces and rusted knives came for her. There
was but one escape from their dauntless hunger for change.

Ishoa woke, snow and dawnlight greeting her.

The crones were more chipper toward the Fly. Seemingly more comfortable,
as if by not raping Ishoa in the night, he'd confirmed himself as a good man.

The Fly smothered the fire before they left, prying up frozen hunks of dirt
from beneath an evergreen that smoked briefly as he ground it to nothing. Ishoa
had watched him do it the night previous as well. *He worries that we're being
followed.* While they'd come a ways south, it was still early winter in Anjuhkar,
which meant enough regular snowfall to cover their tracks each day. The Fly
scuttled and mixed the fire to ensure it stayed that way, she realized.

The girl hissed. "Ships."

The Fly jerked around and sprinted for the stretcher, dragging it behind a dense row of bushes. The rest of them didn't hesitate. If someone as intimidating as the Fly hid, everyone else would be wise to follow suit. They did so, hunkering and panting, and waiting for a sign of safety from the executioner from Shadowheart.

Bent over at the waist, the Fly watched the Blue River. Four cogs glided upstream, their fore and stern castles bristling with scores of archers. A war galley followed, a hundred oars or more to either side, all manned by Scarborn mercenaries. The black flag of the Warnocks flew from the ships' masts beside a white wolverine paw on gray.

As they drew closer, Ishoa noticed the pop of red on white...blood-soaked bandages, borne by many of the soldiers. The ships, too, had taken damage. Arrows embedded in the railing. A crippled prow, the planks bowed from a heavy projectile of some sort. Scorch marks smearing hull and deck. The main sail of one of the cogs was a flapping ruin.

The ships' crews made no sound except the dip and splash of their oars and the ripple of flag and canvas amid the changing winds.

Change is inevitable. That's what grandmother always said. Ishoa shivered. *Have I doomed us?*

"The White Wolverine Alliance," said Mittens.

Ishoa frowned at the crone. The woman licked her lips and said, "The ones who threw down the Ice Maiden: Kon, Bael, Narl, and Warnocks and the rest."

The Fly's covered face craned back. Ishoa stared at him. *Not the Bogs though? Had Megalor's bodyguard gone renegade?* The men of Shadowheart hadn't done much to instill trust in her during the Trials, nor the Battle for Jarik.

There was some hope that the Fly did Megalor's bidding now, a single strand of it woven into a darker tapestry. Conditions being what they were, she assumed the lord of Shadowheart merely secured his bargaining chips. He would wait until the matter was closer to being decided before he made his allegiance known. *Grandmother always said Megalor Bog was predictably self-serving.*

The ships passed.

They struck a path that took them from the river and ascended a ridge. Banks of fog inhibited visibility beyond fifty or so feet. Ishoa led on, silently beseeching her fallen family members for better luck in the days to come.

Arick slept, occasionally rousing when the Fly stopped to dress his wounds, though still delirious. The duty of care eventually fell to the crone named Mittens. "My hands are no strangers to the wounded. Used to aid a Sister of the Rose in my youth and never lost the touch. Here now—aye, a nasty wound." She raised an eyebrow at the Fly. "Your doing?"

Arms lax at his side, he said nothing as he watched her work, rooted more firmly to the earth than the oak on the Shadowheart crest. Wind stirred the folds of his tunic and breeches.

The crone shrugged then bent to her work over Arick. He moaned, mumbling something incoherent. Sweat swamped his brow and soaked the armpits of his stolen, homespun tunic.

Please, don't let him die. So much of her family was gone now. She had been raised praying to her ancestors for good fortune. For once, she yearned for them to answer her pleas.

The Fly set the tone for their journey. Words weren't wasted where breaths might be.

At night, seated around the campfire, the moratorium on conversation came to an end. The girl kept her distance, stealing looks at the Fly and Ishoa when she thought no one watched. *If I'm catching you, he is too.* She was clever, Ishoa decided, but not as clever as she needed to be.

The next time the girl's gaze found Ishoa's, she tried to communicate to her that she should be careful if she wanted to live.

The fire-haired waif seemed to take the princess's meaning and scooted closer to the others. During a break in one of the crones' yammering, she spoke. "My name is Okki. A week ago, I fled Womunger, a tiny town you've probably never heard of if you're not from the Threehills area." One of the crones hummed agreement. "When word of the Ice Maiden's fall came, the lowborn rallied in the streets. The White Wolverine Alliance must have sent pigeons to every stretch of Anjuhkar."

"From what I saw, it seemed like planted men," said Leena. "Waiting for just such a scenario. A few months new to town, there was a nicely dressed fella who come through on some such far-fetched business. He led the rabble in Threehills."

Okki brushed back a strand of red hair then nodded. "You're probably right." She turned her attention back to the fire. "They killed my neighbor. It isn't just the poor folk. My neighbor owned a salt mine but the man leading his killers was richer."

Mittens raised a withered finger. "There it is! Chaos provides equal opportunity. Just as I said."

"Syphion Muul is no folk hero," sneered Leena. "A covetous prick is all."

The girl from Womunger spoke with conviction. "Greed disguises itself with many different cloaks yet always stinks the same underneath."

The three women drifted into speculation, the youngest hanging back and leaving the older to bear the burden of carrying the conversation as the fire devolved to smoldering coals.

Each of the women had lost someone to the uprising. Namorite patriots, slain for belief in the institution founded by Ishoa's family. Leena and Mittens had lost their husbands. The girl, Okki, a father and brother. On the road, people sometimes lied about such things, but Ishoa saw no reason for the crones to do so, a thought validated whenever they cried out the names of men in their sleep.

What are men good for anyway? Ishoa wriggled onto her side. *Bloodshed and warfare and suffering...*

She stopped herself, recalling that it was her great-grandmother's idea to create the Jurati and their scarring rituals. *We all pay for our wrongs one day.*

Ishoa wondered how her own demise might unravel and counted the sins of her past as she battled herself to go to sleep. She'd betrayed Lodaris. She'd lied to her family. She'd let Stirrma die for her rather than fight at her side.

Worst of all, I didn't kill the one person I should have. Lodecka Warnock still lived and that was unforgivable.

Where cold earth and the raw bite of rope had kept her awake for hours, fantasies of vengeance lulled her to sleep.

In the dead of night, she woke to someone creeping over her.

Panic brushed away the numb haze of dreams, freezing Ishoa in place. It wasn't the Fly—the smell of the man would have given that away. Weeks, if not months, had passed since he'd bathed.

In that, there was a relief. Thoughts of his indecency had crossed her mind as a possibility, but her better senses told her he wasn't the type. Whatever his job was, he was doing it, and it didn't involve harming her more than necessary.

So who is the stranger?

They moved like dripping butter—slow and smooth—up to Ishoa's side, their shadow blocking her view of the glowing remnants of the fire.

"Princess," they whispered.

The girl from Womunger. She loomed over Ishoa, her face materializing as Ishoa's eyes adjusted. Okki hooked a finger over the gag and drew it down. She leaned into Ishoa's ear. "I'll untie you."

Ishoa hesitated. If the Fly woke to find this girl trying to free her, it wouldn't go well. Megalor's bodyguard already toted a stretcher, a prisoner, and a hobbled ice tiger. His patience had limits. Whoever he worked for had undoubtedly given him explicit instructions. He didn't seem capable of disobeying orders, nor tarrying in their completion. The girl would die. Ishoa knew it in her bones.

Her hands slid over Ishoa in search of the knot. *I won't let anyone else die for me.* Ishoa pinned her shoulders to the earth, preventing the girl access to the bindings. "No. It's not safe."

Edged in moonlight, the girl stared down at her for a few heartbeats. Then her shadowed face swiveled toward the place where the Fly slept. Ishoa's pulse hastened. *Is he there?* He could be standing right behind her, invisible in those black robes of his, ax-staff in hand. The girl would never know it.

Besides, what would she do if the girl freed her? She was no protector. She was barely older than Ishoa. And Rakeema and Arick were bound, the latter in no condition to do anything beyond rest. As much as Ishoa hated to admit it, she *needed* the Fly. *Otherwise, Arick will die.*

"Go." The word shuddered free of Ishoa's lips, so quiet, she wondered if it reached Okki's ears.

The girl replaced the gag and then crept back to her place among the crones.

Morning came, panes of sunlight laying atop the fog like a white-hot blade. Ishoa glanced at Okki and she was smart enough not to look back. *Unalor said the Fly sees everything.* The girl knew who Ishoa was...perhaps she had also heard of the Fly.

At midday, the sun became a scarlet orb behind a wall of gossamer gray, a wounded eye weeping blood over the atrocities wrought in the name of Anjuhkar. Ishoa sniffed the air. *Smoke.* Yet another malignant thread woven into the rug of broken dreams. Ishoa felt she'd been walking over it all her life.

They steered onto a tributary road of the Prince's Highway.

One of the crones, Mittens, clicked her tongue as she hobbled after them. "Risky."

The pace the Fly had set with them thus far had brooked no room for interpretation of his intentions. Whether or not the crones ended the day at his camp was of no concern to him.

"We'd be best off heading for Ghastiin," said Leena.

Most of the time, the Fly hung his head as he drew the stretcher. Now, it flicked up. He turned to the side bringing the woman behind him into his periphery.

"Joffus Kon joined the White Wolverine Alliance and that means Ghastiin will be stable. Now that we know what those loyal to Namarr face, we just pledge ourselves to the new ruler of Anjuhkar...whoever it may be."

Ishoa flinched. *Who?* She skewered the girl with her stare. *Lodecka?*

"If they're smart, they'll make it Joffus Kon," Mittens said. "He's no Scarborn."

"Which is why he ain't gonna be it," snapped Leena. "You think those savages intend to throw out one greedy monarch and invite a second to dinner right after?"

Greedy monarch? Belara Frost was a hero of the Unity Wars! No one has sacrificed more for the good of her country and its people, you hag!

Rakeema mewled and thrashed against the leash around her midsection.

The Fly stopped, released the rope and took up his weapon. The stretcher banged to the ground, bringing the group to an abrupt halt.

Arick whined. A fox darted across the deeply rutted path a hundred feet further on.

The Fly paid it no mind. He faced the direction it had fled from. A wall of gray billowed into them, carrying the stench of smoke and clouding Ishoa's vision with tears.

"What is it?" stuttered one of the sisters.

The Fly scanned the area. Veils of mist wound around sparse, scraggly trees.

A shirtless boy with a ragged hide thrown around his shoulders leaned out from behind a tree. He was a few years younger than Ishoa, and he'd clearly seen the worst of some recent raid. Grime smeared him and sweat had made a series of cleansing lines across his ribs and temples. A split lip, angry and red, marred his otherwise colorless pallor. Wringing his wrists, he bore himself like a thief condemned to death and preparing to make one final plea for his life.

And that was not far from the truth.

He drew closer, and as he did, his eyes became less innocent, more dubious. They darted around to each member of the group in ceaseless, cautionary assessment. "Need food if you got it. Been out here a couple of days."

His lips were ringed a dull blue. the veins on his fingers a stark maroon amid mottled patches of white.

Mittens went to him, motherly hands outstretched. "Come here, ma' boy."

The young man recoiled, keeping her at arm's length. "Food's what I need."

The Fly retrieved his pack from the stretcher beside Arick, rummaged within, removed a biscuit, and tossed it into the road. His fist nudged Ishoa in the shoulder blade. *Back to it, eh?*

Ishoa had taken to communicating with the Fly in her head. While she knew none of it was being received, she felt like it helped her understand him better when she played his game. She glanced back.

The Fly had returned to dragging the stretcher.

Mittens frowned at his back, then draped an arm around the boy despite his protestations. "Come now, you'll be safer with us. Where'd ya come from?"

"Tyrnii," the boy said. "Two days south. I think."

"That far," Leena said. "You must have been so scared."

"I'm fine, hag," the boy spat.

Leena clucked her teeth. "Mannerless country boy."

"Sorry," the boy said. Ishoa thought it fifty-fifty on whether he meant it. "Just feelin' bad for going the wrong direction is all. Wish I'd known when I fled but I didn't think about nothin' but my life." The boy fidgeted and rubbed his wrists.

They looked raw, as if he, too, had been recently bound. "Should have known I was heading north by how cold it was getting. But I just ran and didn't stop."

"What happened?" Leena's ire appeared forgotten.

"Everything," the boy's voice cracked. "Everything you never want to see. We heard the news about the Ice Maiden in the town square...about how she'd been taken captive."

Ishoa swiveled around. Her toe caught a stone and she stumbled, barely catching herself in time. *Grandmother lives.* At least, she did when this boy fled Tyrnii. News didn't always translate from the source to the people. Hold lords manipulated it in whatever way they saw fit, of course, but there didn't seem a reason to do so now. A weight rolled off Ishoa's shoulders. The pressure of being the last of her family lifted. If she could somehow see her grandmother restored to power, all might not be lost.

She looked back at the Fly to wonder at his allegiance yet again. It was then that she realized why he allowed the others to join their group—why he fed them and lent them warmth. He needed the information they shared. Never speaking but always listening.

The boy was still talking. "...Our lady is—was—no slouch when it comes to battle, so she led out her sortie to fight the Kons demanding her allegiance. Then a hundred men the size of teenage girls came out of the forest on all sides and shot our lady full of arrows. Their skin was dark, darker than a Lah-Tsarene or a Kanian's. They were all wearing collars like a highborn's hound and their faces were kind of...dead."

Based on the description, Ishoa knew who it might be, though it made little sense. Ti-Cora, the Orenese Empress, enslaved the male tribesmen of Mimbor, and forced them to be expert archers. Dragonclaws, they were called. *But why are they in Namarr? And how?*

"Then this woman brought our lady's head to the gate and said to open it. She was yelling at the holdguards in some weird accent. We heard most of it, but some of the words were all fucked—"

Ishoa was facing forward to pick her way along but heard one of the crones smack the back of the boy's head.

"Knock it off! I ain't yours! Ancestors be good." The boy coughed. "Anyway. Called herself Sen-Ashoki the Fury. Said we better open the gates or she'd burn our fort to the ground. Cowardly ingrates, our holdguard. Dumb too, so they did it. Seconds later, I was running. People I'd known my whole life dropping dead all around, fletchings sprouting from their chests and backs..." He sniffled and went quiet for a while. "Shoved through the gate with a mass of others, all of us fleeing like a spooked sheep herd. Most of us got cut down by the Kons in the field. They'd been waiting while Sen-Ashoki did her worst."

Joffus Kon. There was Ishoa's answer. *He hired the Orenese.* It must have cost the man a fortune to plant Revocation sympathizers in cities across Anjuhkar. *Years of planning.* He was another worthy of Ishoa's wrath.

The crones had closed in on the boy to console him but a few sharp curses from him warded them off.

The Fly tapped Ishoa's shoulder and indicated for her to go into the forest. She complied, entering a dense thicket. She was forced to duck under branches and maneuver through heavy shadows for a couple of hours, focused solely on not injuring herself. If it were warmer, her feet might have found some reprieve and dried out from the wet since snow didn't reach the forest floor there.

When she emerged on the other side, she came to an abrupt halt. Smoke was thick in the air, a blond haze in every direction. She hacked into her gag as the rest of their party filled in behind her.

"Ancestors save us," said Mittens.

They'd come to the crest of a long ridge line overlooking an expanse of fields that stretched all the way to the horizon.

Most of the fields were ablaze. Plumes and plumes of smoke poured into the sky like milk filtering through a vast bowl of water. Tiny figures scurried about at the edges of it. Some looked to be on horseback, all too far away to identify as friend or foe.

"Dastardly Scarborn." Mittens placed a hand over her shocked mouth. "They'll starve us all before this mess is over."

"It's not the Scarborn," said Okki. "My father used to meet with the smaller holds in charge of these fields. This is White Plains."

"Ah," said Leena. "I've heard Joffus Kon's always had a score to settle with Rigga Hine. He'll starve her into a treaty, I'll bet all that I own on it." She patted herself down with a sour expression. "Not much to sweeten the wager at the moment."

The girl gave a rueful smile. "A wager you'd lose." None of them had taken their eyes off of the smoldering landscape as they spoke. "Rigga Hine did this. She burns her crops and shelters her flocks to keep the White Wolverine Alliance at bay. If they're smart, they won't attack until spring. The Manger is too strong to fall to anything but a dedicated siege."

"How do ya know so much about warfare?" asked the boy.

The girl shrugged, turned from the fields, and threw Ishoa a sidelong glance. "My father often dealt with the Lord of Womunger. Supplied his garrison with provisions. He used to take me with him. I heard things. Soldier talk." She stared into the distance. Ishoa sensed her struggling with something.

One of the old crones coughed.

The Fly pulled Ishoa to the lead.

"Why's she like that?" the boy said. "The guy in the stretcher's all tied up too."

Ishoa looked back. The Fly had stopped and seemed to be hanging on a decision. An ax poised above a criminal's neck.

The crones exchanged worried glances. "Criminals, we think."

"Think?" The boy gave a harsh laugh. "Criminals with an ice ti—"

Okki stepped in front of him. Ishoa couldn't hear her, but the girl from Womunger succeeded in diverting the boy from a dangerous path. In this group, the unspoken ruled. To name the obvious was a grievous transgression. One, Ishoa assumed, that was punishable by death.

Seemingly satisfied by the boy's accepted ignorance, the Fly turned and shoved Ishoa into motion.

TRUST

G yr fought to relax his shoulders as he entered Malus D'Alzir's pavilion.
The back of his hand stung. Almost as much as his pride.

Candles burned at various points inside the Duke of Lah-Tsarra's lavish tent.
Malus sat on the edge of his bed, an open book on his lap.

He snapped it closed. "I've been expecting you."

Eyes locked with Malus, Gyr tilted his head toward the body servant, Velal,
in a silent request for privacy.

Malus frowned and brushed a strand of hair over the shoulder of his sleeping
gown. "You're being a bit over-cautious, don't you think?"

"It is exactly when others think such that I must be."

"Fine." Malus dismissed Velal to fetch his riding boots from the supply
wagon. The body servant ducked through the pavilion's opening, light flashing
through a cloud of swirling dust in his wake.

Once the man was gone, Gyr spoke in hushed tones. "Lord Malus, you know
as well as I that these are not the safest times. Someone plots the downfall of the
United Lands and they know that we have entered into their game. We should
be exceedingly careful."

"I am well aware." The Lord of Brighthaven rose with a groan, stretching thin
arms overhead. He doffed the nightgown, revealing a series of distended ribs
along a slender frame.

For one with Lah-Tsarene blood, he's paler than he should be.

"In truth, I thank you for requesting Velal sent out." Malus donned a padded
surcoat of thinner, yet stronger, make than those of his soldiers. Then, he
yanked on riding breeches. He threw a shirt of ringed mail onto the bed,
followed by a darksteel honor plate and a long green tunic with a slit up the
sides. "I hate when he wants to dress me. He can do so when I'm a drooling, old
cretin and not a second sooner. I simply couldn't live with myself if I let this
nubile body waste away in the shadow of another's efforts."

"You're sharp-witted," said Gyr. "But maybe less nubile than you think."

Malus shot him a glare, his mouth a crooked grin. "Funny."

"Would it hurt you to train, my lord? I fear what little muscle you once had threatens to wither completely."

"Writing keeps my wrists strong." The duke tapped the book on his bed. "Reading, my mind."

"And young maidens, your hips and back?"

Malus filled a cup with water. "If I cared to put in the effort for such distractions, perhaps. But a warm book is always within arm's reach. A maiden, however, if I were to be an admirable husband, takes far more energy. Fortunately for them, I've decided to forgo the whole affair."

Gyr cleared his throat.

Malus plopped into a chair at the pavilion's center. "I know, I know. You want me to marry."

"And?"

"That is all. I know you want that. I do not." Malus rolled his eyes. "This isn't the type of morning report I was looking for when I sent your cupbearer to find you. How is he faring, by the way? Tales from Velal at the tent flap tell me you're beating him now? That doesn't sound like you."

Gyr grimaced. "I'm not proud of it but there was..." The tent plunged into silence. Shame vied against justification as he sought the right explanation. When neither won out, he simply rubbed the back of his hand where the blows had left them aching.

"I've not seen you raise a fist in anger since...well...never, come to think of it." Malus gathered his hair into a tight ponytail.

"There are some lessons that must be delivered swiftly and without preamble."

"I understand." The drum of fingertips on wood filled the tent as Malus narrowed his eyes. "Well, please inform me if you ever intend to give me one of these lessons. I'd hate to be slapped about."

"On that account, you have nothing to worry over. May I?" Gyr took a seat on a stool across from Malus. "If Caltheo had even a thimble of your wisdom, he might help reduce my stress rather than add to it."

"Stress?" Malus arched an eyebrow. "Something to do with your morning jaunt with our knight-captain, I presume?"

Gyr nodded. "Evidence of Kurgs on a hilltop less than a mile away. Caltheo took objection to how I handled the information. He thinks the men should know."

Malus cocked his head. "Why worry them when it's most likely nothing? Since Bacot One-Eye's treachery during the Great Betrayal, the Steel Embargo has hamstrung their capacity to wage war. If they incite Namarr, it will mean the destruction of their people. That aside, I have maintained good personal relations with the major enclaves. Have we any evidence to believe these Kurgs hostile?"

"No," said Gyr. "Which is why Caltheo and I disagreed so strongly."

"I see." Malus stared into the shadows of the tent. After a moment's pause, he snapped his fingers. "From now on, I'll take on more of your cupbearer's training. If he is to one day be my prosort, I'll make sure he understands how to serve me best."

He was mine to train. If my lord needs to bear the burden, does it mean I've failed my duty?

"What else?" Malus watched Gyr.

"I've dispatched Sir Raius and a half dozen outriders to follow the Kurgs."

The duke drew back. "I do wish you'd consulted me first. I'd rather not strain our relationship with the mountain enclaves by chasing them around in their own territory."

"I would agree with you, my lord, but this is not our normal trip to your brother's home. Do not forget what—"

Malus stood, chair tipping over backward in the process. His expression washed over Gyr like a bucket of ice water. "I assure you, prosort, I have not forgotten." Brow furrowed with disappointment, Malus's grating tone struck Gyr like a bolt. "Caltheo told me about the thing you found in the woods. Could this be why you think a small band of Kurgs is some advance force? Perhaps *this* is also the reason you strike your cupbearer?"

"I...my lord. I..." Gyr looked away, head hung. *Caltheo told him!* He crossed his arms, jaw tight, refusing to feel ashamed. "With the news of what's happening in Scothea, and evidence of a spy, I thought it a distraction. I did not want to concern you with something inexplicable."

"Yet here I stand, concerned." Velal returned, boots in hand. Malus picked up the chair, sat, then threw up a foot. Velal hurried to put the duke's riding boots on for him. "In times of uncertainty, the one thing I rely upon without question is my prosort. His loyalty, truth, and counsel. A lack of any one of those creates fissures in the ground our relationship is built upon. And *that* sows uncertainty."

Caltheo told him.

Rage faltering, Gyr watched his wrath redirected to his own actions. *Wasn't it I who betrayed Malus's trust first? An eye for an eye, they say. Or a lie for a lie.*

Throat thick with emotion, Gyr uncrossed his arms. "My lord, I beg your forgive—"

"Granted." A smile flashed across Malus's face. "And now I must ask for the same from you."

Velal glanced over a shoulder at Gyr as he cinched the duke's boot laces. Silence filled the pavilion. "Velal," Malus said. "Round up the men to pack my things, would you." The servant bowed stiffly, then left. "I've made a decision. The kind that requires your thoughtful consideration. Your forgiveness, too."

Gyr waited, anticipation stamping his chest like a bull. Weakened lungs threatened to erupt in a fit of coughing, but somehow, he managed to suppress it.

"When Caltheo told me of the thing in the woods he told me of something ever more harrowing." Malus sighed, chin dipping. "He told me of your illness. The crimson curse, he said."

With an exasperated huff, Gyr leaned back on the stool. His forehead found his palm. *Caltheo betrayed me.* Gyr shook his head, staring at a rug with the D'Alzir hawk on it while Malus spoke.

"You're like a father to me, Gyr Renwood. And I will not allow your life to be cut short by the stress of unnecessary command." Malus's eyes glistened in the candle flame. Words measured with kindness, but words that stabbed like a dagger in the back all the same. "Because of this, I'm reducing your duties. They'll be divided between Caltheo and I."

"Malus!" Gyr flew to his feet but a barking cough forced him to stumble, vision suddenly swimming, hand flying toward the center pole of the tent for support. Twice more, he tried to speak, but his words shattered like a rock through stained glass.

Malus proffered water. Gyr denied it, let slow breaths return without soothing. He swallowed a bit of saliva, rasped, "My lord, please...he isn't ready." The duke's eyes flitted over him, assessing him, judging his capabilities. *Or lack thereof.*

"Do you know what I was reading when you walked in?" Malus stepped to the bed.

"No, my lord."

Malus snatched the book from where it sat on silk covers. "I was cross-referencing the reports I received from Kaltes Kasjeri about the Arrow of Light with one of the more reliable texts that exist about the Awakened. More specifically, the Ruptured." He thumbed through the thin pages, and then jammed a finger into the center crease. "Here we are...

"Those who seek to control Unturrus's power acquire a false Locus. Release into oneself is the only pathway to true power. To claim control within is to let go of it without. One must do so entirely and without hesitation. One who does this denies the assault of fear-based delusion. They find a Locus where one always existed. These are Awakened." Malus held up a finger. "For those others who gladly feast at the table of madness, who chase the need for power over their external world by giving themselves fully into its care, the fabric of self is sundered. Illusion is left to reign as their king and conqueror. These are the lost, the Ruptured few, and they have denied the mirror. They sacrifice sanity for a false reality that adheres to their egoic whims. Those who seek to control an ocean are sure to drown beneath its waves. The Ruptured thirst infinitely for power through control...the greatest fallacy of all."

In the silence that followed, a breeze whipped the flap of the tent's entrance aside to usher in a frigid breeze.

"Locastrii had many pertinent things to say, it seems." The book snapped shut. Malus drew one arm up behind his back, and with the other, tossed the tome onto the table with a thud. "When first I read that, it was because I suspected the Arrow of Light to be Ruptured. Something I still believe to be true. That, I will save for later discussion. Now, I see the wisdom between the pages has more widely applicable merits."

Gyr shifted on the stool. "Gaining peace of mind by relinquishing control is not a new concept."

"Though I hope it to be a new practice. One which *you*, my prosort, will willingly engage."

So I'm to fade into uselessness rather than resign with dignity. A coughing fit doubled him over. Hot pincers poked his rib cage. The edges of his vision sparkled as he stared at the luxurious rugs sprawled across the floor. Tightly laced boots slipped past. A gloved hand rested on his back.

"Please," Malus said. "It is for your own good. I would have you at reduced capacity and well rested for years rather than see you worked to death within months."

Spasms fading, Gyr stood. "It...is getting worse. Perhaps you're right." A shuddering breath came and went, then another. He swallowed. "We should begin marching soon."

Hand still cupped to Gyr's shoulder, Malus gave a smile born of fondness. "You've served faithfully and boldly, Gyr Renwood, but you are by no means done. I only ask you to let others carry some small part of the load. For all our sakes."

CHAPTER EIGHTEEN

JUST A C⚬⚬K

I t took Zadani three weeks to realize she was on her own. Three weeks of begging after that cretin, Nymon, for updates on his progress. Three weeks of stomaching his vile, careless demeanor.

Three weeks of nothing at all.

In that time, the dreams continued. Night after night, Hadir came, his pleas hovering at the edge of hearing, his fear bleeding into her own, right up to the moment he was swallowed by the mist and left her yet again. Sometimes, he pointed at the squat maple tree, desperation lining his face as he mimed writing.

Haunting as they were, the dreams sucked the life from her. Each day, she woke more tired than the last. The walk to work grew more difficult, her grief a rotting deer carcass across her shoulders making her sodden in body and mind.

Another disappointing day loomed, an expectation formed from now famil-iar momentum. She'd go through the motions. She'd put on a false smile. She'd pretend to care about other things besides finding Hadir's killer.

Worst of all, she would wait for Nymon.

The courtyard of Hawk's Keep had been turned into a training yard. Nymon and his men sparred, swords and axes and shields, clanging and grunting and cursing like eloquent animals.

Zadani had watched and waited.

A D'Alzir holdguard scrambled for his blade. Nymon growled, kicked the man in the ribs, then punched him behind the ear, dropping him cold. Cheers for the victorious, jeers for the lesser, rained.

Zadani sniffled with disinterest.

"Looks like you'll have to go about drubbing yourselves, boys." Nymon had pointed at her with his ax. "The Lech has a lady waiting for him."

"The Lech?" Zadani said as the man approached with a pronounced strut.

"You heard it." He sucked at his teeth, eyes lingering overlong on her chest. "Known the world over by brothel maidens as Nymon the Lech."

Zadani grimaced. "I can't fathom why."

"Oh, ho, ho." Nymon probed the inside of one cheek with his tongue. "I bet you could do more than fathom."

"Unfortunately, my imagination isn't strong. I recall Lord Marus tasking you with investigating my husband's murder. I've not heard anything about the holdguard you were to question."

Nymon grunted. "They're off on a scoutin' mission...huntin' for Kurgs. I'll talk to 'em when they're back. Your husband ain't going nowhere."

He turned his back and that was that.

A week later, Zadani had tracked him down and found him at cards in the barracks. "Ah boys, you know I like a determined woman," he'd said.

Most laughed. A few remained quiet, a keen focus on their cards the only show of ethical disagreement with their leader. *Barely gentlemen. If Hadir heard you talk of women like that, he'd have beaten you senseless.*

"It's been over a week," she said.

"And I'll find the sap who done for your husband." He hunched around his cards, smiling, watching the game unfold. "Don't you worry, sweet woman. Nymon the Lech always gets his man." He eyed her sidelong, jaw cocked to one side. "And his woman, for that matter."

A landslide of wrathful insults swept all rational thought from Zadani's mind. She stared at him, saw a man devoid of compassion. *So unlike Hadir.*

Nymon stared back, a smile stretching across one cheek. "You'll get more from me with honey, sweet woman."

Zadani left vowing to give the man nothing, and went in search of Sir Vallabathus.

The Malzacy-born knight had been moving so quietly through the halls she almost bowled into him coming around a corner. A firm hand jutted out, blocking her shoulder. She gasped, stumbled, and stifled a scream. "My apologies, sir."

Vallabathus was motionless as his swirling black cape settled onto the flag-stones. "Be more careful," he said in a flat tone, then started to go.

Before she could think better of it, Zadani grabbed the man's elbow. A blur of motion. She yelped—a fist suddenly enclosed her fingers, crushing them together. "Sorry! I just needed a word!"

As if holding a snake by its venomous head, Vallabathus inspected her hand, then released it. He was close enough for her to smell his breath, a scentless, stale warmth. Golden eyes narrowed. "What do you want?"

She cradled her fingers, aching but uninjured. "I know you're a busy man, but you're also an honorable one. I wondered if you might support the efforts to find my husband's killer."

"Lord Marus has already given the duty to Nymon. I have other responsibilities." He swayed forward, predatory. "Don't bother me with this again."

So you're as stony on the inside as you are outside.

The knight-captain swept down the hall, cape trailing silent heels.

When she went back to Nymon the Lech at the end of three weeks, she worried it might seem like she was crawling to him on hands and knees, so she strode up to him with her shoulders pinned back as he and another holdguard waved vintners towing handcarts into a cellar.

"So," Zadani said, "has Master Nymon found his man?" She'd meant it mockingly, but the man was incapable of hearing anything but compliments from her mouth.

"You're back again." His lone good eye crawled over her. "They always come back."

A barb came to mind but Zadani lost her chance to say it.

"Hey you stupid fuck!" Nymon lurched, grabbed a vintner's apprentice by the collar as he tried to cut the line, then violently redirected the boy up the hill. By the time Nymon returned, his mask of rage had been replaced with a lecherous grin. "You been cheatin' on me girl."

Zadani blinked. "I'm sorry?"

He tapped the skin beneath his milk-white eye. "I seen who you been talkin' to. Tried to get that charboy, Vallabathus, to help."

Zadani flinched. She hadn't heard the slur for Malzacy natives used in all her life. In fact, the term hadn't been widely used since before the Unity Wars.

"I ain't good enough for you?" She shied away as he went to brush a dark ringlet from her face. "Sure. I've got information for you. Meet me tonight at the Salty Maid." He winked at one of his men. "We'll talk in private. Maybe steal us one of these casks, eh?"

The laughter had echoed through Zadani.

Echoed through her still.

Does my misfortune bring him joy?

She spat as if she could relieve her mouth from the bitter taste of the past weeks.

The kitchen was ahead. She paused outside the entrance. Fists clenched, she leaned back against the cool stone of the wall. Her hand unfurled and she rested a sweat slicked palm against her chest, attempting to calm herself. *What am I waiting for? No one is going to help me.*

The tiredness she'd been feeling dissolved. The helplessness, too, disappeared. With a sharp inhale, she straightened, rolled her shoulders. Fire stoked to life in her breast and spread into her arms. Vengeance demanded answers. Demanded action. And she was resolved to give it by any means necessary.

I'm on my own.

No sooner had she ducked into the kitchens than a bug-eyed, frazzled Thruna scuttled over, waving skeletal, maroon-stained hands. "Elmarie is a fine kitchen wench when it comes to yeasty things but doesn't know fuck all about cooking duck livers. We need you to take over."

"Of course," Zadani said. "That's why I'm here."

Thruna scratched the wart on her nose, left a garnet smear there, then returned to chopping beets.

Emotion, Zadani was learning, could be suppressed in one moment for later use in another. She let sorrow breach the surface of her placid exterior. "Thruna," she said in a hushed voice.

The old woman swiveled, her ruffled flesh gathering at the brow. "What's it, deary?"

It felt shameful to use guile with a friend, but Zadani's goal was all that mattered now. The haunting dream persisted. Lord Marus's justice had failed. And Nymon the Lech was useless, more motivated by his cock than his heart.

I'm on my own.

"I need some time to myself—just a day. I'll leave you with a menu. Elmarie can read it to you. All things you know how to make."

"Good." Weathered skin creased around a gap-toothed grin. "Good on you. Two days may be better."

Two *would* be better. She wasn't sure how long it might take to find the maple in the north wood that Hadir's specter had been desperate for her to see. If it existed. "Thank you, love." Zadani rubbed the old woman's arm.

"Ack. That's enough now." A tear trembled on one of Thruna's eyelids. "About to make an old hag cry."

A thud echoed at the entrance to the kitchens as a holdguard slammed spear butt to flagstones. At his side, Lady Daran beamed. "Ladies of the kitchen."

Hands falling from her hips, Zadani bowed, shallower than the rest. Her stomach for observing status had soured.

"I'm pleased to inform you that my uncle, the great Malus D'Alzir, Duke of Lah-Tsarra, will arrive within a fortnight to celebrate my seventeenth nameday."

Today, Lady Daran's hair was piled into a nest of gold curls on her crown. "My father expects it to be a special visit, as do I. He brings a retinue of over a hundred. Prepare yourselves accordingly, for we aim to serve Namarr's best, and our board should reflect that."

The last sounded a touch too rehearsed for Zadani. A flicker of annoyance passed over Daran's face as she surveyed the room, no doubt looking for glimmers of astonishment at her great oration. The girl left without another word.

Thruna nudged Zadani with an elbow. "Good thing you're taking the time now. Once Duke Malus arrives..." She probed the gap in her teeth with her tongue then clucked. "None of us will see the outside of the kitchen for a month."

The sun was nearly gone by the time Zadani heard Jasso Jackolo strolling up the path. The late autumn cold stole into her fingertips, her toes, the tops of her ears. Her breath came as a splash of steam that rose into the stony face of Raiya D'Alzir's statue.

The memorial fountain's euphonious trickle eased into Zadani. Of late, calm had been in high demand but short supply, so the release of tension was welcome.

The scholar from Valat whistled as he went, taking in the sights, a sheaf of papers tucked under one arm. His other whipped back and forth in long, languid, arcs.

The tune he whistled, Zadani noted, was the Eyes of Love. A wave of jealousy boiled through her. *Things with Genjin must be going well.* She stepped from behind the statue.

With a clipped shriek, Jasso stumbled into the hedges grasping his sternum, eyes agog with fear. When he saw it was Zadani, he pressed out a growl between heaving breaths. "To what do I owe the pleasure of this near death experience?" He plucked a twig off a shoulder and huffed.

"How are you faring?" She flashed him a smile. "Genjin?"

"Things are going well." He scratched the back of his neck. "We've, uh, met a few times."

"It's okay, Jasso. I don't expect life to stop simply because mine did." Despite the placating words, Zadani felt her frustration mounting, a levee of unmitigated jealousy threatening to rupture.

"Yes, well." He rocked onto his heels, then toes. "We spoke of you, believe it or not. We agree you are a very strong person."

Zadani brushed a strand of hair behind an ear. "I find it difficult to hear your words. I've grown attached to swimming in the darkness of Hadir's death. It's a comfort...of sorts. I never want to let the pain go. It's all I have left of him." She sniffled. "And if I'm strong, it could mean I may one day force myself to do just that. Let go. So forgive me, Jasso, but I don't want to be strong. I want to be weak, to be held, to feel his callused palms in mine and have him whisper in my ear again. But no...I must be strong. It's as much expectation as necessity now."

"I—uh." He swallowed. "I hear you."

Tears broke, raced down a cheek. She glanced up at the face of Raiya, voice cracking. "Do you know who this is?"

Jasso cleared his throat. "Marus's eldest daughter. I understand it that she's passed."

"And you heard what I said to Lady Rizel?" Zadani turned to Jasso. "Before she fled court?"

"Yes. Though I can't say I'm privy to the whole tale."

"Oh, the D'Alzirs have made sure of that. Raiya's aunt, Omari, was to be wed to the Mad Prince, Barodane Ironlight. But after he died, Marus wanted her to marry one of Roddic Olabran's sons. Omari hated the man, and so, refused. I cannot blame her." Zadani ran a hand through her mane of dark ringlets. "Five years ago, Omari left with a knight—Kaitos Barabi. Some say he kidnapped her. Some say she seduced him. No one knows the true story. What they do know is that her disagreement with Lord Marus had increased in fervor for a decade and that's why she ascended Unturrus. The entire D'Alzir family was affected by their clashes, but young Raiya most of all. Omari's fierce refusal of Marus's marriage proposals inspired his eldest daughter to become an Awakened like her aunt. And so, Raiya set out to conquer Unturrus."

"I'm guessing she died there," Jasso said.

"Close. Her body turned up a short time after she left. Bandits, they said. Lady Rizel has been drunk ever since. She blames Marus for driving both daughter and sister away. And when I say Rizel has never forgiven him, know that she withholds it with the bitterest of hearts."

Jasso smirked. "Highborn or low—one fills a bucket of night soil just as fast as the other. D'Alzirs die like any human."

"Yes. A touchy subject, the death of a loved one." Her next words came clipped, more spat than spoken. "Because of that, I've managed to offend Lord Marus, as well as his wife and daughter. In the process, I cut an image of madness for myself before the entire court, claiming murder without evidence. And for these stumbles, my call for justice has been answered in the form of Nymon the Lech, a most disgusting man who does nothing at all."

"This is a difficult journey for you." The scholar pulled his gloves on more tightly to fight the cold. Zadani, however, let it wash over her, yet another layer to numb the pain.

"Patience is recommended," he said. "Master Nymon—"

"Is worthless," she hissed. "I'll find Hadir's killer on my own."

Jasso's eyes narrowed. "I don't intend to go traipsing about in tombs with you again."

"I don't expect you to." Hadir's specter filled her mind's eye. "I ask a far simpler favor. I've seen you scribbling notes at court. I need paper. A few sheets of parchment should do. A charcoal stylus as well."

"Of course. Simple indeed." Jasso scoffed, staring at her like she was a puzzle. "May I ask what you intend to do with them?"

"You may." Mist curled around the base of Raiya's fountain...Hadir's head sank under it. "And if I knew that answer, I'd tell you." Then she stepped clear of the reaching mist.

CHAPTER NINETEEN

'INTO THE RAEK'S MOUTH

A blood moon filled the gap in the canyon between Darkfall and the cliffs a quarter mile to the east. Black skies swallowed the rest.

The hour was late.

Ikarai Valka hurried to the upper terraces. The guard post had been overrun. A handful of soldiers with their throats slit slumped around stone pillars.

With Yanos and his honor guard in tow, Valka continued on in silence.

Despite the dead guards, it appeared the manor terraces had been spared the worst of the fighting. Soldiers turned cultists, loyal to Siddaia, lined the entrances of each villa's avenue. Blood-spattered and holding nicked axes, they nodded to Valka as he moved past them at a dubious speed. It was clear they'd been given explicit instructions to allow him through.

But no others.

Valka wasn't the only one who'd been betrayed.

The sickly, bony frames of a hundred dead low dwellers dotted the grounds. *They fought for Siddaia...all the way to Darkfall's interior only to be cut down by those who'd incited them to rebel in the first place.*

Skeletal hands clutched sticks, sharpened bones, or broken cart handles. Dark stains soaked the dust around them. Valka stepped over one—a teenage boy, not unlike Siddaia—a gash splitting his side. Vacant eyes, bathed in torch-light, seemed frozen in questioning, begging to understand why the Arrow of Light's soldiers would kill him. Why they would protect those terrace dwellers the prophet had promised to lay low.

You were misled.

None of them saw the truth.

But do I?

While the battle for Darkfall had come to a definitive end, the effects of it still raged inside Valka, heart, mind, and soul. *Do I fight for an ideal that is no longer right? An institution that's run its course? Do I stand against the change necessary to make Scothea thrive once more?*

He'd smelled the rot at his nation's core for years. Rathon's line was a fetid wound, and the Arrow of Light promised to be the boiled wine to purge it of infection. *So why do I fight the new in equal measure to the old?*

The unknown—the handing over of power to those claiming a new and better dawn—was a rubbery piece of gristle in his mouth. Hard to chew. Harder to swallow. Harder still, for an old cynic like Ikarai Valka. He was a historian, after all. No greater body of knowledge existed to make a man rife with doubt. Especially in regard to prophets promising paradise.

Besides, for a lifelong soldier like him, loyalty often outweighed logic. For the Scothean military machine to operate, it had to.

He'd snatched victory from Ti-Cora at the Battle of Thundermount with a force half the size of his adversary's in AR 589. Five years before that, he'd hunted down and entrapped the Malzacy pirate-lord, Muggangen the Laughing Knife. When he hanged the man with rope from his own rigging, six fortunes filled the hull of his flagship, all of which Valka gave to King Rathon. The other hundred and thirty ships belonging to the pirate lord, they'd burned. And when the Hunger Riots started the summer before last, it was Valka who brought their leaders to the table for talks of peace. To do that, he'd needed a wealth of information about the men, which Essuhd had provided. Without knowing their motivations, their fears, their vices, it would have been impossible to turn them against their own in favor of personal gains and quell further unrest.

But the Arrow of Light...

I could never have known. Even Essuhd was fooled.

When Valka bent the knee, it wasn't the Awakened protecting the boy that worried him most. The Blessed Cadre: that's what the soldiers were calling them. They had torn apart the Holy Chamber where Rathon was hiding and scattered the forces within. The king had stumbled out, fat lips quivering as he blubbered for his life. Despite the dizzying show of power and the ease with which the Awakened had defeated Rathon's forces, it was Siddaia who filled Valka with awe and fear.

When the Black Hand Marionette had emerged from the Holy Chamber with spiraling onyx vortexes in each hand and eyes pooling with midnight smoke, the false messiah had stilled him with a single, gently uttered insight. A handful of exchanges more and the intractable Awakened was on his knees swearing fealty with the rest.

Flying. Manipulating metal. Paralyzing orbs of void. Stunning powers. But none were a match for Siddaia's words.

He brought soldiers to heel at his whim. Bound supernatural beings to his cause with a look. Toppled nations armed with nothing but truth.

Confidence and calm poured from the boy. Valka swore he almost saw it manifest as a faint nimbus of light trailing his hands and wreathing his face. Perhaps anyone who acted without fear or self-doubt might look the same, but Valka had never seen its like. In his mission for liberation, Siddaia was undeterred.

A childlike Rathon had begged for his life at the youth's feet.

"The throne," Siddaia had said. The stout Awakened with wild tufts of gray above each ear flung out a hand. The throne blossomed with a deafening screech, flattened at the center and bent outward at the edges to form a steel flower.

Siddaia had strode up the dais and sat cross-legged at the foot of the sundered throne while his forces clustered around Rathon like an ant colony hemming in a lone termite. "You may go," the boy said. "You are no threat. None of my followers will harm you."

Valka had exchanged stunned looks with a number of his soldiers freshly won to Siddaia's side. Niggling doubt had clicked into place, unsure if the boy's authenticity was but a keen strategy.

The Arrow of Light could not appear as any ordinary conqueror. His power lay in his mystique, his transcendent and untouchable superiority. Otherwise, the power of his illusion, of being a prophet that acted as a living god, might shatter.

A desert wolf with its leg in a trap, dragging it inch-by-inch toward safety—that's how Valka felt. Progress in any direction left him bloodier and more damaged.

The boy is an insidious genius, manipulating the unlearned masses. Even if he does so with good intention.

Yet, each time Valka thought such, a quiet voice at the back of his mind shrugged. *What if he is what he claims? What if he's the one the prophecy speaks of? The one who ushers the Long Silence. The one to bring peace.*

The injured wolf sat, for now, content to wait and see if others from his pack came to the rescue. His frantic drive for answers mattered little in the face of concrete circumstance. Whether he liked it or not, Ikarai Valka was a cultist.

Of all that had transpired on the day of Siddaia's rebellion, one thing at least had gone the way Valka hoped. When he was finally given leave, he'd taken Yanos and his honor guard to his manor nestled into a remote section of Darkfall's upper terraces.

The homes of the rich and powerful were carved into a bowed recess nestled far from Darkfall's shieldwalls. A network of expertly carved terraces honeycombed the cliffside. Each manor presented as a single panel of stone beset with numerous windows along the flat-facing gable to admit light. Each manor doubled as a fortification. Scoths had never developed a sense of trust for their neighbors. Too many years of tribal warfare in the dark days before the Rains, when warlords in caves slaughtered their enemies and were slaughtered in turn. Blood remembered, it seemed, except when it came to the Arrow of Light's rapid rise to rule. With such history in mind, the feat was all the more stunning.

But has he kept his word that Nera is unharmed?

Valka's heart raced as he quickened his step to his manor.

Just above the rows of cavern-carved villas, massive bored-out holes were ringed in ensconced torches to allow light.

Valka stared up into the windows of his neighbors, living lavishly without fear of hunger or sickness. Without hate for those chipping away at their humanity. Their dignity.

But now they knew.

Now they feared what they'd wrought. Their eyes were wide as they looked down at Valka and his troops passing by the flat stone-fronts of their manors. Their voices whispered down at him, futilely hoping for pleasing news. He was vaguely aware of their deeper fear. That, maybe, he and his men were there to kill them. To make obsolete their riches. To deliver Scothea into the Arrow of Light's hands without reprisal from the aristocrats of yesterday.

Valka ignored them. They were prisoners now, himself included. That's what the dead could never see. As much as the cultists had protected them, they also held them hostage. The Arrow of Light needed them to obey.

Sparing Rathon cultivated an image. Ruthless subjugation was effective as a short-term tactic, but those most tormented by the fall were bound to one day revolt. A more balanced approach of diplomacy and brutality was more effective in the long run.

Is it Siddaia who is the strategist or is it Rhul? Perhaps one of the Awakened. Whoever it was, they were exceedingly clever. If Valka and Essuhd were to make their play, they'd need to know who posed the greatest threat.

Valka sighed relief when he made it to his manor. All of his guards were alive. They'd simply done as they were trained to do at any sign of threat: hunker down and protect Nera with their lives. A hundred days of rations were stored in the manor, and the dozen empty windows had been secured and fortified—the same for the door.

Nera. After a brief exchange with his household guard, he stepped past the banded oak.

Then she was there, falling into his chest, bare arms clammy, words flying at him in a rush. "What happened? The guards said it's a battle. They said the Arrow of Light has taken the city. Has King Rathon..."

She pulled back, let the question plummet into the space between them.

Valka couldn't respond. He squeezed her to him, her heart beating against his chest. Memories that wouldn't be tainted because she still lived flooded him. They carved wooden figures together; "little heroes" they'd called them. She'd been far better at it. He drank with his friend Lorkav, the general who'd held the post so briefly before Valka, while Nera begged them to tell her stories of their battles. Lorkav had always obliged, but Valka preferred his secrets and didn't like glorifying violence. His daughter loved the tales of sacrifice, of heroic charges, and harrowing odds. Lorkav embellished most of it and Valka hadn't the heart to tell Nera the truth when he saw how much joy it brought her.

A joy he'd long held sacred.

His body tight with emotion, he pushed her back and assessed her. "You're okay?" He touched her forehead and gripped her shoulders, harder than he'd meant to. "You're unharmed? Have Siddaia's followers come?"

"Father." Her gaze flickered over his white-knuckled hands.

He drew back, leaving fingerprints. "I'm sorry. I just..." Head bowed, he took a slow inhale, then looked at her. "I was worried about you."

She smiled and nodded. "I'm fine, father. And I'm glad to see you are as well. Though I have questions. Please, tell me."

I thought I'd lost you. Even the memory of that harrowing possibility was enough to send a jolt through his innards. Valka swiveled to one side. "Captain Yanos, from now on, you will be Nera's personal protector. No one but..." He hesitated, unpleasant reality shoving to the fore of his awareness. *Yanos knelt to the messiah.*

If he was to play the part of a cultist, he could not be setting boundaries that might be deemed suspicious. "No one but our brothers in the light. Keep all low dwellers clear of her, do you understand? They're not to be trusted. You saw the guard post."

"Indeed, General. Gruesome work our brothers had to do."

Our brothers?

"Yes. A necessity." Without them, Nera and scores of his neighbors might have been raped and murdered. Begrudgingly, he gave thanks to the Arrow of Light's foresight.

"Father," Nera said, impatience showing.

He turned to her. While Valka had the pale skin and narrow-set eyes of a cave dweller, Nera was tan, her eyes rounded in the likeness of a plains dweller born on the outskirts of the Radiant Stretches.

That's where I told them your mother was from. Valka swallowed hard.

After so many years, she was the only person he'd broken his oath to his country for. He lied to everyone—betrayed them. And now, he'd done it again.

Maybe I'm not the man I thought I was. Maybe I deserve to be known in the history books as a traitor.

He pushed away the thought. "Come." He took Nera to the night-garden at the back of the manor. Torchlight filtered into the den, coating the towering mushrooms to either side of the path they walked in a dreamlike hue of dusky gray. Spirit lilies lined the quarter-acre perimeter, the edges of their translucent petals shimmering rainbow amid the heavy shadows enrobing the garden.

Nera clung to her father's arm as they stopped before a man-sized stalagmite thrust up from the cave floor. The file of glowing rock cast Valka and his daughter's face in a warm honey color. Yanos's boots crunched to a stop at the entrance. "Leave us and seal the door."

The man's expression was unreadable as he shut the round door with a whispering thud. *Does he play the part as well?* Silence pressed into Valka's ears, womb-like and heavy, the density of a thousand tons of rock in any direction surrounding them.

Nera's exhale cut the quiet.

"The Arrow of Light has seized Darkfall," said Valka. "King Rathon has been deposed."

A subtle twitch along her brow, then a crease. She was more beautiful than her mother had been, with a spirit to match. Valka would never forget her. "How is it you're not in chains or dead?"

Valka nodded, knowing the question would come. He spoke in hushed tones. "I swore allegiance to Siddaia." Saying it aloud made his skin prickle. A bitter taste filled his mouth.

"You?"

"Duty demands I play the part of cultist. Essuhd lives. He's loose in the keep. His Shadii, too." Some of the iron in his blood returned. Much had happened to sap him of his confidence, but the words tumbling from his lips brought back a renewed vigor. "We will bide our time, assess our resources—wait to strike. We *will* restore the line of kings."

Nera crossed her arms. "Father." She looked away. "We could flee instead. Why not do that?"

"Run?" *Abandon Scothea to a usurping, false messiah?*

Nera knew him better than anyone, and still, she could not see the necessity of his mission. He ran his fingertips over the ethereal stalagmite, washing them in its honeyed glow.

You war inside. That's what Siddaia had said. To leave with Nera, to let his duties fall to rust and dust and memory...the thought brought him no peace. A passing desire, yes, but he knew himself well enough. He was not meant for a nameless life of menial tasks hiding in alien lands, his back to a fading sunset of purpose.

But if it kept Nera safe, it would almost be worth the risk. Almost. "No. We cannot run. There's too much at stake."

She took him by the elbow. "More than our lives?"

He glanced down, drew his arm free. "Yes. More than our lives." *First the Eye, bringing evil to the light. Then the Hand, ridding the world of its plight...Three makes one, but only one makes free.* He looked at her. "This may yet end in peace."

She drew back, lips parted, studying him. "You think he could serve Scothea better than Rathon?"

"I don't know." His brow furrowed. "So many have chosen him. And he let Rathon go free, along with any soldiers who wished to leave. He's done things...they've surprised me."

"So he's everything the low dwellers have said and more, is that it? Another Holy Instrument. Another man who claims he's an equal to gods." Nera scoffed. "What will it take for this nation to learn its lesson in hubris? We'd crawl one after another into a raek's mouth if it told us only Scoths were chosen to enter." The back of her hand slapped into her other palm. "We are not special!"

"What if *he* is?" Valka raised his chin. "You have not seen him, Nera. He's different."

Nera slowed, hands easing back to her sides as she straightened. "You believe him?" Outrage swept her expression. "Were you a part of this?"

"Of course not," he snapped. "But that doesn't mean I'm fool enough to disregard what I've seen. The messiah—" His mouth clamped shut. *False messiah. I forgot to say false.* "Nothing is certain yet. That is all. I must know my enemy better if I'm to defeat him."

Valka watched Nera staring at him, a gathering storm of feeling under that calm surface. "It doesn't sound like you plan to defeat him at all."

Something crumbled and slid, echoing in one of the bored-out holes hanging over the night-garden. A few seconds later, dust swirled out into the diffused light overhead.

Valka whispered, "Like I said, nothing is yet certain."

"What am I to do?" Nera crossed her arms. "Suck the dirt from between his toes like all the rest and act like he's my savior?"

Valka paused, letting her sit with her petulance before answering. His daughter was smart but furious, a line she often straddled. Someday soon, she would be the treasure and woe of whoever married her. "Better if you stay out of sight and mind. I want you forgotten so that, when and if the time comes, we can flee if we must. Drawing unwanted attention will hamper our efforts."

"Pointless planning when we could flee right now." Her tone was incredulous. "You said it yourself. He gave everyone a free pass to leave. Yet here you stand at the crossroads. Are you a father, a follower, or do you hope to be a martyr?" She cleared her throat in the way of those freshly come to hard decisions. "You'd do well to stay out of sight yourself. Specifically, mine."

She sidled past him on her way to the door. "Captain Yanos!" The oval door swung open. "Please, accompany me to my chamber."

The hard-muscled Yanos took Nera's arm in his. Before they closed the door behind them, Nera rounded. "I'm grateful you're alive, father." The way she said it, Valka understood the implication, her disappointment in his actions springing up in the subsequent silence.

Yanos leveled a stoic look his way, saluted, then shut the door behind as he left.

Into the raek's mouth indeed. Step by foolish step.

CHAPTER TWENTY

EVER THE WINDING WAY

G yr could not find the calm required to speak with his cupbearer.

He rode at the fore of the line of knights and crownguard as they ascended another of the Winding Way's switchbacks. Snowflakes clung to their heavy coats, frost to their arms and armor. Steam rose in gouts from red-cheeked faces, brows damp with sweat earned from climbing their way through deepening snows.

Dusk neared, a cluster of rays on the dim horizon. Gyr pulled up the hood of a fur-lined cloak from Ghastiin, soft over his bald head. It had been a gift on his fiftieth nameday from Malus.

He turned in the saddle just as Sir Qel approached. "Trouble?"

"Lord Malus wishes for Caltheo to take command of the rear half of the column," the lanky knight said. "In addition to the wagons at the center."

The back half of the retinue. He'll have more crownguard under his command than I do. Gyr stared forward, taking in the evergreens and pines lining the slopes of the pass. It helped to be reminded of the Sempyrean's presence while receiving ill-news.

"You'll still command the forward column, the hounds, and outriders." Sir Qel hesitated. The apple of his throat bobbed. "From dawn until dusk, the entire retinue will heed your voice. From dusk until dawn, it will heed Caltheo's."

Gyr shot a sharp look at Sir Qel. "He takes full command at evening?" Sir Qel's expression was solemn. *That's answer enough.*

Gyr let his gaze wander upward, squinting against the sky. Snow drifted onto his face in a pleasant rhythm, though whenever it struck his narrowed eyes, he flinched. He didn't care. The coolness was comforting. *How many beautiful moments do I have left before the crimson curse takes me?*

"Lord Malus wished you to rest after long marches. For sleep or prayer." Sir Qel spoke hastily. "He said—"

"Thank you, Sir Qel." *With my duties so drastically reduced, I'm sure I'll have time for all of that and more.* "I don't need the explanation. My orders will suffice. If that's all, you may go."

Russet mustache poking over pursed lips, the knight gave a respectful dip of his head, pulled the reins of his mount about-face, then trotted toward the column's rear. *Now under Caltheo's command.*

He sighed. *Maybe I should be thankful. The blood in my mucus has been darker of late. Can I fault Malus for wanting me to live longer?*

The next day passed in much the same way. Quiet but for the breaking of camp and the occasional call to halt before resuming their march. They cut through the snow, leaving a slurry of mud in their wake like some monstrous snail.

As day trailed to night, worry drew taut across Gyr's chest. His reduced command left more room for the mind to roam, to play out scenarios most dire. With this came increasingly intense bouts of coughing. *The sister said stress makes it worse.*

It was the third day since the departure of Sir Raius's outriders. The third day since he'd struck Caltheo. Two days since his duties had been pried from his grasp. More since the stinking horror in the woods. The twenty-first day since the library at Brighthaven...since the yawning pit of despair had opened in his gut as Kaltes Kasjeri reported the Arrow of Light's rise to power in Scothea. *And every day since, my hope for a brighter future has been chewed away.* Cynicism was ever Gyr's weak point.

Remembering his letter to Garlenna tasking her with finding Barodane was the only thing keeping him from surrendering that final shred of optimism. *There is no one better suited to carry the burden of Namarr's future than my daughter.*

Yet, as Nacronus's dark hand closed around the sky, Gyr couldn't help but think it reflected some malevolent portent drawing closer. His desire to keep undue panic from the rank and file disappeared. Timely, considering Malus had tasked him with bringing the retinue to high alert later that evening.

The temperature dropped sharply with the sun as they made camp in sight of the Hook in the distance, nothing more than a blue triangle wreathed in cold mist at the end of the range.

Gyr stifled a groan as he swung a leg over his horse to dismount. His legs, back, and lungs all begged for rest, but it was nothing compared to the weight of bleak possibilities resting on his shoulders.

Once camp was set, Gyr took up position amid the evening cook fires. Malus had tasked Gyr with informing the men of a heightened alert later that night. It wasn't necessary to have the ear of every crownguard—at least half had important duties to attend—but when a large enough portion had gathered, he summoned his voice of command to address them.

"Many of you have wondered at the absence of Sir Raius and his outriders. They are out ensuring the friendliness of the locals." A beat of laughter. "While we do not have cause to believe any harbor us ill-will, we did find bodily remains in the woods. Human or swine or something else. As easy as it could have been Kurgs who left it there, it could have been animals or poachers. Nothing to fear."

Between the dry cold and the crimson curse, Gyr's throat was raw as he strained to be heard. "Nevertheless, I want you on high-alert until we reach Kiyahd. No man is to remove their armor but to relieve themselves. And no man is to leave the perimeter alone. Latrine lines will be cut *inside* of camp..." Groans rippled among the soldiers. Leaving their armor on was bad enough, but the smell of fresh waste added disgust to discomfort. "Bulwarks are to be constructed as battle-ready. As if lives depend on it." Up to that point, defenses were being made to the standard of a quick march.

As Gyr gave the last order, a busy quiet fell to dead silence. "Make sure weapons are within reach even when you sleep. Enjoy your dinner."

The assembly broke apart, a lethargic dispersal to the tune of unhappy murmurs. But before long, men were shouting, laughing, passing wineskins from hand to hand and seeking distraction from the gnawing fear of reality.

Such is the life of a soldier.

It brought him no satisfaction to make their lives harder, but he also wished to see them all reach Kiyahd alive.

Before Gyr turned in for the night, a familiar face found him amid the bustle of activity around the cook fire.

"Father." The welt above Caltheo's brow had faded to a discolored yellow. Firelight gleamed along his bald pate when he bowed—danced within onyx eyes as he lifted his gaze.

Much like a crownguard wears a bronze honor plate, and a knight wears a steel one, Caltheo's own pauldron reflected his station. *You're no prosort yet.* It wouldn't be long though. Not at this rate. The fist and chain of Namarr, and the five arrows of the Sempyrium, glittered russet on the young man's shoulder. It looked newer, more polished. Far fewer dents and scars than Gyr's own.

"You've been keeping your armor well." Pride stuck in the back of Gyr's throat. *Is it the luxury of one with less responsibility, or is he just the shiny new prosort, more capable and useful than the old?* Gyr forced himself to relax. "I'm glad to see you, Caltheo."

The cupbearer cocked his head. "I assumed the opposite might be true. I admit I took measures to steer clear of you. To give you...time."

Time to adjust to my new role, you mean.

"Prudent. Your wisdom grows." Gyr wiped the damp from his nose. "A quality that I have, until recently, chosen to overlook. Come, let us inspect your wagons."

Gyr led the way. Crownguards saluted as they passed, fists clanging against bronze. The occasional knight slapped steel as well. Those soldiers who didn't see them were busy knocking back trenchers of stew, or gnawing at hardened bread, while others were setting to their armor and weapons with rag, spit, and pumice. Around a dozen more foraged the woods to fashion defensive stakes, and another group dug earthworks around the encampment.

They arrived near the line of wagons situated at the rear of their force. Stones had been jammed under the wheels and one of Halladorn's hounds was stationed with each. Gyr stopped beside a dog-legged pine, out of earshot from the nearest crownguard. Caltheo turned to face him.

"My anger has passed, leaving me with curiosity." Gyr pinned his shoulders back and folded his hands at his waist. "I want an explanation, Caltheo. I deserve to know why you didn't come to me first. If you had, I would have liste—"

"You truly believe that, Father?" Caltheo shifted his weight from one foot to the other. "We do *what* we must *when* we must for his own good, even when he might not recognize it as such. *You* told me that."

"In regard to Lord Malus only," Gyr said. "Besides, I told you that after you'd already betrayed me. You told him I had the crimson curse."

"With but one soul to give, we serve the highest good of all." Caltheo recited words from the Prosort's Creed. "I did my duty and I do not regret it. How do you expect me to serve if I go against the code given to me by the Sempyrium?"

Despite Gyr's attempts to keep frustration at bay, his temper flared. "I've lived the Creed longer than you've been alive. Do not think to quote it at me. You gave your word and then betrayed it. Damn your reasons."

"Even if it means our lord's life?"

A cold tingle gripped the base of Gyr's neck. Legless words, shaped in stunned breathlessness. "You presume that I am unable to protect him?"

Caltheo glanced at the wagons. "Of course not." Tears welled in the cupbearer's eye. "But...you're dying."

The sounds of the bustling encampment seemed louder in the shared silence. Crisp night sky pressed down. Snow sparkled at their feet. A moment Gyr could have reveled in if he were alone, his soul brushing that long sought-after peace. *I rage for a world that no longer wants me...no longer needs me.* Gyr felt himself softening. *What if I let go?* The question wore no trappings of fear. Just possibility.

Caltheo sighed. "What was I supposed to do? I've been training under you for six years—"

"Seven," Gyr corrected.

Caltheo gave a curt laugh. "You refuse to let me make even a small mistake such as that one. Was I supposed to wait until you died to take responsibility for my training? I'm trying to give you peace of mind, Father. To assure you Lord Malus will be in safe hands. I had to do it. You know you never would have given me a chance otherwise."

"You're right." A sudden tightness in Gyr's throat caused his voice to crack. "You and Malus both." A violent cough shook him. Bursts of pinkish steam shot into his fist. Ears ringing, the fit abated as quick as it came. "I should go. Maybe...maybe I do need rest."

He'd only made it a couple steps before a truth dawned on Gyr. He rounded. "I trust you, Caltheo. I know you'll do right by me and by our duke."

A smile tugged a corner of Caltheo's mouth.

The image of pride stamped across his cupbearer's face was the last thing Gyr thought of before sleep welcomed him. But it wasn't the first.

Those thoughts were reserved for all the fears his imagination could summon: Garlenna's task. Sir Raius yet to return. The thing in the woods. The crimson curse dissolving his lungs, slowly, methodically, and without surcease.

And hope.

For decades, his daughter had bent the impossible to her will in the name of the Sempyrium. And on the morrow, Raius might return with his outriders having seen their duty to its most thorough end. The thing in the woods was likely nothing more than a slaughtered pig, like Caltheo said. With his duties reduced and rest ahead of him, the crimson curse might not take him for years yet.

He might see Garlenna again. Might see Caltheo grow into a successful prosort as well. Might see Malus happily married.

Gyr imagined them smiling.

Then, the wild bark of hounds dragged him awake.

CHAPTER TWENTY-ONE

THE NORTH WOOD

Z adani spent the morning gathering wildflowers into a bouquet, picking only Hadir's favorite blossoms: dark green turtle's foot and sunburst iris. The song she'd been humming trailed away as she realized her husband would never see them.

Bitterness clung to the roof of her mouth.

Hadir's killer walks freely around Kiyahd. Arrow slits scarred the towering stretch of wall and huddling stone bastions of Hawk's Keep behind her. She worked her tongue against the wretched taste in her mouth—spat. *I wonder if they've smiled at me this week.*

Nails dug into the skin of her palms. The flowers in her hand crunched, a foamy white substance oozing from the stalks.

I can't trust any of them. Not until I know who killed my Hadir. Jasso Jackolo was the lone exception, for it seemed an impossible stretch of logic to think the scholar had helped her uncover his own bloody crime. *Nevertheless, from here on, I operate with impeccable caution.*

She dried the sweat on her palms, then worked her way along the low wall that encircled the keep.

A holdguard posted at the path leading into the north wood propped a foot against a stump, a spear loosely cradled in the crook of his elbow, both forearms slung crosswise over a thigh. A downward twist at the corners of his mouth told Zadani he wished to be anywhere else, doing anything else, but hated himself for lacking the ambition necessary to do so.

Zadani passed the hedgerows to either side as she approached the break in the wall.

"What?" the holdguard said tersely.

"Greetings." She smiled. "We've not met. I'm Lord Marus's personal cook."

The man screwed up one side of his face and shrugged. For a moment, Zadani questioned whether she would get what she needed, that being, to know exactly where Hadir had died. Soldiers gossiped as much as kitchen ladies did. If Hadir was killed by a bear in the north wood, this guard would surely know the details of it.

"If you enter the wood, be back by sunset," the holdguard said, his tone making it clear he preferred she come and go without bothering him. "Easy to get lost out there in the dark. Dangerous."

"Oh yes, I'm aware of the dangers." It was no act when her smile faded. The best lies were layered in truth. "My husband was killed out here last month."

"Oh." He scratched the back of his neck. "You're *that* cook. I'm sorry. I—uh. Gods...my condolences."

That changed your tune, didn't it? Zadani was learning that a crestfallen expression and a story about one's dead husband brought others to heel rather quickly. With vengeance burning within her day and night, it was easy to overlook any guilt she might normally have about lying or manipulating others.

Justice for Hadir. That's all that matters. "He loved these flowers. I wanted to lay them at the place where he died, but I don't know where that is. Could you guide me there?"

"I'm sorry, mistress. I can't abandon my post even for something so noble as that."

"No, no." Zadani clutched the flower bouquet tighter to her chest, her tone pleading. "I wouldn't ask you to be there. I want to be alone with my husband."

"Ah. Of course." Cheeks reddening, the holdguard loosed an exasperated breath. "How can I help?"

The poor man is floundering with embarrassment. By pulling the strings of sympathy as hard as she did, it made others vulnerable and all too ready to complete whatever task she gave them to escape the feeling. *I could compel him to do anything right now.* Zadani stared at him expectantly, letting him writhe in the silence a few moments longer.

Affecting a serious tone, she spoke quickly, directly. "I need you to tell me exactly where my husband died. In fact, if you draw me a map, that would be best." She handed him a scrap of parchment and a charcoal stylus.

The holdguard laughed nervously. "Right...right."

Once he finished drawing the map, Zadani thanked him.

The man shrugged. "Here to help."

Zadani leaned in close. "Would you do one last thing for me?"

Doubt flickered across his expression, but he nodded. The chance that he might share their interaction with another made her uneasy.

Hadir's killer could be anyone. Even this man.

"I want to do right by my husband's spirit. The gods of the Sempyrean, too. I intend to leave some things of value where he died as an offering. Hadir was very devout." In truth, Hadir had a healthy disdain for the Sempyrium. "I hate to say this, but there are those in Hawk's Keep who have few scruples when it comes to thievery."

The man straightened, chest puffed with pride, his good deed done for the day. "On my honor as a holdguard."

"My hero." She patted his tabard, palm falling against the black hawk of D'Alzir. Tucking the map in her belt, she gathered her skirts and strode into the forest.

Zadani ditched the wildflowers in a passing stream. She wanted to cover as much ground as she could as quickly as possible. That meant having her hands free. For good measure, she tied her skirts into a knot on one hip.

Bands of light pillared her path in errant bursts from ground to canopy. Fallen leaves from cedar, birch, and oak created a deciduous skirt around the ferns to either side of the path, though it was still too early in autumn to hear their brittle crunching under foot.

In determined silence, she walked.

It took less than half an hour for the pommel of Hadir's hunting knife to start digging into the bone above her ankle. After an hour, a sharp tingle radiated from the raw indent of her flesh and she was forced to move the sheathed blade from boot to belt.

If anyone found her, she'd decided her excuse as to why Lord Marus's master cook strolled through the forest bearing steel. *I am afraid of bears since one killed my husband. This was his knife—it makes me feel safe.*

She repeated the words in her head so that if she needed to speak them, they would sound like truths. It was a paradox, rehearsing so as not to sound rehearsed. Anyone innocent in the matter of Hadir's death would understand her sentiment about the knife, but any who troubled a grieving widow over her safety might be the very person she sought to sink the dagger into.

With vengeful fantasies occupying the fore of her mind, shame slapped at the back of it. She had lied. Manipulated. Even used her grief to garner sympathy and control. Now, she carried a dagger in hopes of using it. *Who am I becoming?*

No one Hadir would love.

Even when it had hurt, he had never lied to Zadani. Early in their courtship, he took a tumble with a singer at a tavern. It brought both of them pain to discuss it but discuss it they had, and as a result, grew closer.

I miss you, my love. Tears blurred her vision of the leaf-strewn path ahead. *You were too good to die.* Maybe that's why she reveled in her subterfuge, her deceit and contempt. Good people got used. They got murdered. While the worst—they seemed to get what they wanted.

I want vengeance! Zadani raised a linen sleeve and soaked it with her tears. The leather vest cinching her sternum felt suddenly constrictive. She hooked thumbs through the laces and tugged it from her breast, gulping down a handful of breaths in the process. *And if I have to be the worst to get what I want, so be it.*

Hadir stood for good in a world that couldn't care less about the means by which one achieved success, and that was the very reason Zadani was willing to bend her morals to see him avenged.

She consulted the map the holdguard had given her and found she wasn't far.

Sunlight marbled her path. The trees thinned and let out into a meadow. She held her hand up to the horizon, judged there to be less than a couple hours to search for the maple tree before she needed to return. Outside of the danger, there was another reason to return by dark. The holdguard's silence—she wouldn't give him reason to break it by failing to return when she'd said.

Impeccable caution.

Crossing the meadow, she wiped sweat from her brow. Having spent ten years in a kitchen, she was used to sweating from the heat of cook pots, smoking spits, and brick ovens. Neither old nor young, Zadani also wasn't light by any stretch of imagination. The rugged journey was difficult. A dull ache in her low back caused her to shorten her stride on one side, and her breathing sounded like a ragged bellows.

The leather vest hadn't been such a good idea, either. Better than heavy robes, certainly, but she couldn't go on with it squeezing her, so she undid the laces.

Breasts liberated and swaying freely beneath her linen tunic, Zadani picked her way along a ravine and then found the outcrop of rock the holdguard had described as "shaped like the bottom row of a gaffer's teeth" at the top of a nearby hill. "Somewhere near there is where they found him," the holdguard had said.

With a despairing sigh, she clambered up the slope. As she went, her thighs and backside started to burn. A pinch jabbed at her chest, and the back of her neck became unbearably hot. *Damn men and their short hair. If I could, I'd shave mine off!*

Without Hadir, her massive dark mane felt like it lost its purpose. He'd loved the way it felt, tight curls looping around his fingers as they cuddled in bed after lovemaking, rosy-cheeked and grinning ear to ear. *If I cut it, people will think I've gone mad with grief.* She couldn't have anyone thinking such things if she wanted to remain master cook. The position held some power, limited though it may be.

She reached the top of the hill. Looking back to where she'd started, it appeared a far easier climb and shorter than it felt. She worked her way around the crown of columnar stone, stepping over rock where wind and time had toppled it. At the bottom of the slope were great slabs resembling broken teeth.

A sea of verdant tree tops stretched away to the northeast, toward Shadow-heart. A hazy veil of cold obscured vision beyond that into deeper Anjuhkar. Zadani turned south, in the direction she'd come from. On a squat hill, Hawk's Keep overlooked Kiyahd. It seemed small from her vantage, the place she'd called home with Hadir for so many years, smaller than expected given how large it felt when she walked its halls. To the west lay the Shining Range. Somewhere on the snowy slopes of the Winding Way, Malus D'Alzir, the Duke of Lah-Tsarra, traveled. When he arrived, Zadani would be busy.

Too busy.

Dread accompanied the realization. If she didn't figure out who murdered Hadir soon, she would not get a chance while the Duke of Lah-Tsarra stayed in Kiyahd. The idea of putting her search on hold for an unforeseeable amount of time made her feel ill.

Time is wasting. I have to stay focused.

In widening circles, she walked in rings around the hilltop, thankful to be heading down rather than up. It made sense that Hadir might have been here. Often, he painted as clear a picture as he could of the views he'd seen while out hunting.

Zadani froze.

She looked back toward the broken teeth of stone jutting from the hilltop, astounded that she'd failed to recognize it. Hadir had described the view a handful of times. *This is his favorite spot.*

To fight the hollowness yawning at the pit of her, Zadani quickened her search. Hadir's voice echoed through her, explaining what to look for while tracking. Footprints, disturbed earth...*blood.* The thought sickened her. His swaddled corpse in the tomb had been easier to stomach since it was not *her* Hadir. But here, where he'd last been alive...where he'd been murdered in sight of his sacred place...

Zadani bent over, palms on knees, and retched. *No. Do not think of it. Malus D'Alzir arrives soon. With all of my duties, that leaves no time. No time, Zadani!*

She wiped her mouth, swished water from a skin, spat it, then continued.

The sun fell lower.

Near the base of the hill, she found an upturned stone covered in dirt. Although the dirt was dry, the small pit it came from had yet to be filled in—the stone had been moved, and somewhat recently. Like a chicken inspecting corn, she hunched forward, searching for a second sign. *There!* A crescent of compressed earth a few strides away—possibly left by the front of a boot. She opened her arms wide and formed a line with her body from the boot track to the overturned stone. Hadir hadn't taught her this, but she knew the idea was sound. The trajectory of evidence led her into a dense cluster of trees.

Within it, everything was a humming grayness. A thin mist crept around the torso-thick trunk of a maple—*the* maple. A painful lump lodged in her throat. Cold sweat lathered her from toe to crown. She trembled, eyes lowering to the spot where the layer of mist always swallowed Hadir. Right where the fog was about to roll over were hoof prints. Different than the tracks left by a horse. And deep—mount *and* rider.

The parchment crackled as she drew it out; the charcoal stylus followed. To calm her shaking hands, she pursed her lips and exhaled a slow, stuttering breath. As best she could, she copied the hoof prints. Once finished, she stared hard at the tracks, burning the image into her mind in case her skills as an artist were lacking.

She rolled the parchment, inserted it in her boot. *I must go before—*

A horse whinnied.

Panic rifled through Zadani. Her first instinct was to run like a criminal fleeing arrest. Her second was much cleverer. The rolled parchment jumped into her hand as she barreled toward the base of the maple and the gaping hole there.

"Hey!" came a shout.

She jammed the paper inside, stood, wiped away sweat and smoothed her attire. Rehearsed lies came to mind, a false smile to her lips.

I mourn my husband. I give respect at the last place he drew breath. I am a grieving widow. I may need an escort back to...

The last thought withered when she watched the silhouette of a rider materialize from the mist, two others trailing him. Goose-flesh stiffened along the backs of her arms.

As they approached, Zadani untied the knot at her hip, letting her skirts fall back to ankle length. Nymon the Lech eased his horse to a stop and leered down at her, cloudy eye probing the opening of her unlaced vest and exposed cleavage. The corner of his mouth curled.

She was no fool. She knew that look. What it said. What it wanted.

He dismounted. "What are you doing out here?" He tossed the reins to one of his men. "Alone?"

He swaggered close. The toes of his boots almost touched her own, his breath hot and acrid, as if he ate meat and only meat. She stifled a shudder as both good and bad eye roamed her sweaty breasts. He licked his finger then held it up as if testing the wind. "Gettin' chilly with this breeze. Best we get you warm quick."

Fear and disgust threatened to show but she pushed them down deep. *For you, Hadir. I do this for you.* Zadani affected her most coy smile.

One glance at Nymon the Lech's men—the way they inspected the trees with indifference—told her all she needed to know of the situation. *A blind eye to their leader's crimes.* Her heart hammered.

"You've such a sweet face." Nymon probed his inner cheek with his tongue.

"It reflects the sweetness I put into the meals I serve the D'Alzirs." *I belong to the D'Alzirs, not you.* "Lady Daran so loves my pecan rolls."

"I like rolls." Nymon ran a hand along a fold of belly on her side. Everything in her wanted to recoil. Instead, she met his gaze, neither defiant nor inviting. Calm and powerful.

He flicked aside the laces of her leather vest then adjusted his breeches. "So what's a beauty like you doing out here by yourself?"

"My husband was killed here. By a bear. I mourn at the place he last breathed."

The Lech nodded. "Dangerous to walk these woods alone."

He was right. She *was* in a dangerous place—one he created. There was a dance to keeping him intrigued. Too little and she lost power and courted suspicion. Too much and she risked being brutalized.

She planted her hands on her hips and rocked forward to project some strength. She flipped her hair back, then reminded herself to make no more flourishes of femininity. "Is there something besides animals I should worry about?"

Nymon threw his men a smug look, then stepped closer. "Only animals here." His stomach brushed against her breasts. "We patrol for Kurgs. Orders from Lord Marus."

"This close to Kiyahd?" *He lies.*

Nymon nodded. "My thoughts exactly. I thought Marus was a smart man. Waste of fucking time."

"Speaking of time, I've a holdguard expecting me back at the wall." If her heart wasn't threatening to beat out of her throat, Zadani might have been clear minded enough to summon a false name for the guard to give the lie more impact.

"Don't go so quick now." Nymon leaned in, sniffed her neck. "Must be lonely without a husband. I can send my boys away. They'll understand. A widow needs comfort."

Rage blazed to life inside. It took everything in her to resist jerking the dagger tucked behind her back and jam it into Nymon's chin. Whether the Lech's lie indicated he had something to do with Hadir's death or not no longer mattered. A promise formed in the darkest part of her heart. *For mentioning my husband with such disrespect, you will die.*

"I hear Lah-Tsarene women are a feisty bunch between the sheets. A widow needs comfort..."

Her body screamed against the impulse to lean the other direction. Instead, she pressed into him. Her dark eyes bore into his, gaze unwavering. "For the right man, maybe." Nymon's vile grin stretched wider as her voice became a husky whisper. "My husband was tall like you. I like that. Sadly though, I'm on my moon's blood. You'll have to wait."

She stepped back, hand brushing up under his blond beard, against his neck, then trailing across his chest. "A woman *also* needs time." She turned and marched back the way she'd come.

As much as she wanted to look back to see if they followed, she kept her eyes forward. Her ears rang, listening for the sound of pursuit. She forced herself to walk normal. As if nothing was wrong. As if she wasn't trembling.

She knew Nymon watched her go.

When she was far from his leering eye, she doubled over, breaths tumbling in and out. She shook like a deer that had narrowly escaped being run down by wolves. Blood returning to her brain, the world grew brighter, and she stood up tall.

Minutes passed. Once the shaking subsided, she set out, eager to return.

The last rays of sunlight left the north wood awash in a blue-gray tinge. Night would be upon her just before she returned.

The entire way back, Nymon the Lech's face—his milky dead eye—haunted her. But there was something ever more unsettling about the man than his sexual advances.

He lied to me.

Distrust deepened. Men lied, certainly, especially those like Nymon the Lech. Yet, the man responsible for investigating her husband's murder was not only ignoring the duty, but lying to her about it.

Did Nymon kill Hadir?

All the way back to the wall, the question clawed at the back of her mind.

CHAPTER TWENTY-TWO

CALLING OF THE WAVES

G arlenna had departed early to scout. It went without saying that Barodane would remain at their secluded camp even though she'd agreed to
let him have a night in the next town.

"That doesn't mean we walk into a trap," she had said before leaving. Chainmen were notorious for laying traps along back roads where criminals were
most likely to stray.

"You really think word could have gotten to the Hammer that fast?"

"They're called birds," Garlenna said. "They fly. Horses don't."

Barodane had folded into his cloak, arms crossed. The persistent rains of
Digtown had receded, but the cold of late autumn marched across the duchy
of Lah-Tsarra. "All my years living in Digtown, I didn't see a single rookery.
Someone would need to be damn motivated, and it just so happens, we killed
everyone who cared about Hyram Olabran."

"Anything's possible." Garlenna swung onto her pale stallion. "Best not to
leave it to chance." She jerked the reins—then wheeled back. "You might consider giving the stone a try while I'm gone."

He stared at her flatly as she sped into the distance. Once she disappeared
through the wood, Barodane's sights fell to the stone. He looked away and
sucked his teeth in frustration. The stone sat just out of reach, mocking him
with every second he spent not attempting to lift it. Echoing back weakness.

"Fucking fool's errand," he muttered.

From the darkness came Meckin's eyes, fixed on the scorched rafters of the
Dregs. A muscle in Barodane's jaw twitched, another in his hand a second later.
He recalled the feel of the cutthroat's flesh parting—the pressure of it in his
hand as he exacted retribution for his slain friend. He thirsted to see them die
again. But his vengeance had been so disappointing, any sense of satisfaction
passing far too quickly to savor.

Just like Rainy Meadows.

If Garlenna hadn't been there, I would have died with Meckin. Maybe that would have been right. Lyansorca had lost an arm. Imralta a finger. Meckin and Jennim, their lives. *It's my fault. And yet, I live. Why?*

Skin crawling to release the sickness crowding his insides, he rocked back and forth on the stump he occupied. He tore off his cloak, exposing himself to the cold, and stood. He jabbed a finger at the stone. "Fuck you!"

He wandered into the forest. Scab, ever stoic, watched him go.

Impossible hopes dogged him. *Maybe there's godsthorn here.* Chances were next to non-existent, the sighting of the plant outside of Unturrus a rare occurrence.

Undeterred by logic, he hunted the damp earth for any spot of color. He kicked over sheaves of fallen bark. Swept leathery leaves into mounds with a boot to reveal rich, worm-riddled soil. He stalked the understory like he'd stalked the streets of Rainy Meadows, the ecstasy of escape his lone but elusive goal.

Sweat streaked from temple to chin. *The people of Namarr want me to lead them? A madman crusading for godsthorn where it doesn't exist?* He laughed. *If they're that stupid, maybe they deserve war. Maybe they deserve to die. Like me...*

He thought of his brother, Malath. Remembered the burst of awareness that had come with the news of his death. Like he'd been dipped in some acid that numbed the skin and ate the insides first.

I tried. He'd wanted to die at King's Crossing. The Twice-Burned's raek had clamped him in its jaws. Fangs punctured him, two in the chest, another in the thigh. Then the buffeting drag of wind filled his ears as he'd flailed through the air...the last thing he remembered before rising from the river, sputtering, drenched and dizzy, his wounds healed.

At least, that's what the memory had become. Perhaps ascending so many times thereafter had eroded the truth of events.

A cap of dark velvet caught his eye. He paused. Death dealer, a single stem. Something Meckin once said to him sprang to mind. *Death ain't a bad answer. Sure to get you where you want to go quickest. But it's only one answer, and I daresay, the least creative by far.*

Fists balled at his sides, he turned his back on the poisonous mushroom. "There's no fucking escape is there?" It took everything in him not to throw the velvet cap in his mouth and be done with all of it.

Where drugs and drink once barred the doors to pain, their absence now ushered it in. Dead faces, mouths stretching in shock, frozen in a final moan for help, flashed through his mind. The voices were gone, but the images...they rose with searing cruelty.

Memories, long-forgotten, were surfacing with increasing frequency. Worse than the violent ones were the days and moments that could never be reclaimed. Moments shared with his father and brother, and the rest of his friends. Moments with Omari D'Alzir...

He'd lost everything. Lost them all, forever.

Beyond the horror of his misdeeds, a truer pain thrived. Love now buried. Laughter's mouth filled with dirt and worms. Promises made in better days for better people—hollow words and hollower deeds. A grave he couldn't seem to stop digging...

And into that void, he fell.

Over and over, he fell.

The annual Singing Fields Tourney hums with activity. Knights and warriors from across Namarr have come to demonstrate their skill at arms and horsemanship. Those too gray in the beard or stiff in the knees oversee the competition.

It is the last one before the Great Betrayal. In less than a year, Barodane's father and brother will be dead and Rainy Meadows will be smoldering ash.

The memory of this day latches onto Barodane—the last time he was happy. He was seventeen...

Malath stands at his side, and together, they lean on a rail fencing in a dozen training yards. The Singing Fields, a six-acre plot with stone walls on every side, nested in the heart of Alistar's massive keep. Crowned by white puffs of cloud, the Dawn Tower throws a sword-tip shadow over most of those gathered.

"The races should be interesting this year." Malath is taller than his younger sibling, the closer of the two to their grandfather's stature. "Fancy you can beat me this time?"

Joy precedes jest as Barodane says, "You are aware, I assume, that fucking your horse doesn't actually make it faster?"

"Yes well." Malath exhales. "I imagine you'll strangle your cock later while thinking of your cleverness. Depraved bastard. Don't forget it's a tourney, brother, not the chamberpot. Do us the decency of waiting."

"You do that on the chamberpot? Disgusting." Barodane grimaces. "So that's what married life has driven you to?"

"Ha! Married life leaves my hips strong and my hands far weaker than your own." Malath shrugs and arches an eyebrow. "And I'll soon have evidence of my efforts."

Barodane rears back, scrutinizing his brother. "Ishra's pregnant."

Malath nods.

It is the last time he smiles at Malath. He claps a congratulatory hand on his shoulder. "Thank the Triune God. If it didn't happen soon, I was afraid I might find little centaurs roaming about the stables that looked just like—fuck!" Barodane stumbles back a step, clutching his side where Malath punched him.

"I really must speak with Father about getting you married to Omari. Nothing kills immaturity quicker than a woman to love and a child to care for."

Doubled over and wincing, Barodane spreads his arms. "Hence, my avoiding the whole affair."

"That's not what I've heard?"

The brothers twist toward the newcomer, Kaitos Barabi, swaggering over with a wolfish grin. "I saw you walking with Omari three nights ago in Admar's Grove."

Malath frowns. "The D'Alzirs are here and no one told me?"

"Come on." Kaitos prods Barodane. "Tell your brother your secret like a good little prince."

"I don't kiss and tell," Barodane says.

"So you kissed her?" Kaitos's muddy eyes glimmer with mischief.

Malath says, "Why wouldn't the D'Alzirs tell me they're here?"

Kaitos acts like he's whispering to Malath, but it's loud enough for Barodane to hear. "Kissed her *and* told her he loved her."

"That's my cue." Barodane slaps his hands down onto the rail of the fence, hauls himself up and over into the arena with a grunt. "I suddenly feel the urge to hit someone." He glares at Kaitos. "Volunteers?"

The clay-skinned knight's smirk withers but not on account of the challenge. He thrusts his dark bearded chin at someone behind Barodane, causing the young prince to turn.

Barodane's father, Crown Prince Kordin Ironlight, approaches. In his shadow, Pyr Syat, the White Flame, follows. All three of the young men at the rail, and a handful of others nearby, bend at the waist and salute, fists hammering honor plates.

Kordin dismisses a pair of combatants and a judge inside the fighting ring. Becoming a champion of the Singing Fields tourney fell to one's desires. Fights were conducted by challenge, empowering combatants to try for victory at their own pace over the course of two days. After a loss or two, most bowed out knowing they weren't likely to cover the points needed to win. Champions like the Beast of Anjuhkar, or in his prime, the White Flame, had to maintain a constant stream of bouts to stay ahead of their opponents. Whenever one warrior defeated another, they acquired half the amount of points the loser accumulated to that point, making the tourney a game of strategic numbers as much as it was a contest of martial skill. Often, jockeying for the right opponents carried the first day, while the most exciting match-ups came on the second.

Barodane promised Garlenna they would compete together this year. So far, she and Wolst led the tournament with twelve victories apiece with no losses or draws. Barodane took a lazier approach, enjoying long and frequent breaks between bouts—he knew he couldn't defeat either of the leaders. At the moment, he held a record of six victories, no losses, and one embarrassing draw against a teenage Scarborn girl who'd proved to be cat-quick and tough as granite, her eyes chunks of flint.

Wrapping an arm around his son, Kordin keeps his voice low. "You had a fine first day, didn't you?"

"If we're not counting the caravan-guard, sure," Barodane says. "You've arrived in time to see me call out my first opponent of the morning."

His father smirks. "Might I choose on your behalf? I was not so great a warrior as you or Malath—certainly not my own father—but my ability to choose favorable match-ups oft kept me high in points. Isn't that so, Pyr?" He looks to the First Sword of the Kanian Remnant for confirmation.

The White Flame bows, then straightens. He's short, all cheekbones above strands of long gray mustache that flutter in the wind like dirty cotton. Judging by skin alone, his age—though Barodane knows him to be old—is indecipherable. Not a wrinkle mars his face or hands. "His Majesty would make a better choice than you, my Prince."

Kordin glances at Malath and Kaitos, then at Barodane. "Shall I do the honors?"

Something is happening. Barodane can't figure out what. Suspicion blooms but he nods all the same.

"Excellent." Kordin claps his hands. "I've already notified your opponents. You'll have your pick from the three."

The furrow of Barodane's brow deepens. It goes slack as the first of his possible opponents leaps into the fenced-in ring across the way. Garlenna. Lips parted in outrage, he flicks a look at his father. "I'll take the second one."

Kordin chuckles as Wolst strolls up beside the prosort. Both wear fat grins and tournament regalia: quilted gambesons, leather jerkins, and blunted weapons.

Barodane balks.

Kaitos whistles low, and Malath shouts for his brother to try curling up in a ball.

"Who's my third?" Barodane mutters, "Okka Bael come back to life?"

"The first two don't suit you?" Prince Kordin beams with self-satisfaction.

"If I wish to end the day staring up at a Sister," Barodane says. "There couldn't be a more unfair—nay—more idiotic draw."

"Ah, so you're a lover then." An impish half-smile creeps into Kordin's cheeks. "Not a fighter?"

Barodane shakes his head. "If it means I don't have to challenge them, I'll be anything you want me to be." He pauses, overwhelmed with confusion. "What is this?"

Kordin takes Barodane's shoulders in his palms and forces him to lock eyes. A note of sadness fills his voice—a sound Barodane is familiar with. It's one that usually accompanies any sentiment having to do with his long-dead mother. "My son, just be yourself." He steps back, arm winging out wide in presentation. "Your third choice..."

Across the way, a clutch of D'Alzir knights step back in unison, admitting Omari D'Alzir forward. Her soft smile and gently parted lips beg him to go to her but he stays rooted in place. "What in the Maw's eternal dark?" he whispers.

The typical brocades befitting her station are absent. No jewels, pendants, or rings of any kind. She's stripped down to a plain silk shift. The outline of her hips swaying beneath grips him. The Singing Fields have fallen so quiet, Barodane hears the rustle of her skin against the fabric.

Omari takes the hand of a knight to either side and steps barefoot over the fence. A circlet of carved driftwood rests atop honeyed hair bound tight at the back of her skull. A single braid hangs down her neck.

Garlenna and Wolst leave the ring, smiles plastering their faces. Kordin, too, steps back. Someone presses a banha drum into Barodane's hands and tells him to play. Across the way, Omari waits, her spine erect, weight swaying from foot to foot.

Barodane gulps, then sits down cross-legged with the drum in his lap. He taps the nodule at the instrument's center. Omari moves, her wrist swimming down and then up with the note until it fades.

Barodane picks up the tempo without ever looking down. One thing holds his attention. Omari...exuding grace and desire and a willingness to experience it all alongside him. She bears the light. His light. No shadow can stand against it.

Slowly, she dances toward him. Naked feet cover the distance. Lunging, twirling, leaping. In the year since their courtship began, she told him that if he wanted to see her dance, it would have to be at their wedding. Her older brothers, Marus and Malus, always claimed she was gifted.

Barodane didn't realize just how gifted.

Desperation sets his hands to a faster tempo. He wants her badly and doesn't want to wait long.

She gyrates and whirls, motions that make her seem longer of limb than she is; motions that snap, a sail unfurled, an ocean wave cresting. Her body moves, swifter and tighter than any sword cut. The softness and exactness of sunlight tracing across the horizon in the first moments of dawn.

He strums the last note and she drops to a knee before him, head bowed to the ground. Seconds scud by, warmth in his chest—aching in his chest. She raises her head. Lips parting, her cheeks draw outward around a smile.

"Who taught you the Calling of the Waves?" he asks.

"Your brother," she pants, "and Kaitos. Now quit making me wait for an answer and say it."

Barodane swallows, emotions both heavy and light slithering into his belly. The words come out hushed, begging in their breathlessness. "You have found me. And in you, I am found."

They stand and embrace, a promise sealed. A promise that would soon be cracked and left to leak into histories better forgotten.

Cheering erupts across the Singing Fields as Barodane's palm cups the olive skin of Omari's cheek.

Crown Prince Kordin watches from a distance, pride evident in the lines of his face as Garlenna, Kaitos, and Malath close in, offering congratulations and heaping praise on Omari's brilliant performance of the traditional Kanian engagement dance.

"We're to be married," Omari says, unable to wipe the happiness from her face as she wraps her arms around him. "Odd, isn't it?"

He kisses her, which draws a second, louder round of cheers. "Odd indeed." He affects an expression of mock puzzlement. "Yet, my heart is full. Fancy that."

"Oh," she says. "I do. I do fancy it..."

The memory tilts with another kiss, a ship rocking on waves.

Solid ground a moment before now plunges out from under Barodane—drops him.

Back into the abyss.

Back to the present, and he's once more stripped of all but the blackest stretches of life, the screech of rusted hinges, and door after door slamming closed.

Barodane stood over the stone, rubbing his hands together.

If Garlenna can do it so many damned times, I can do it at least once.

When he started to remind himself of how he'd backed down from the Beast of Anjuhkar, he shook it away, and slapped his face. *Get it together and do it!*

He crouched, arms slithering around the massive stone for purchase. The angular surface was hard and dug into his forearms. He gritted his teeth then shifted his position. *Nope, still fucking hurts.*

He paused, coming around the front of the rock to see if there were any gentler arm holds. No luck. If he was to lift the thing, he would do so with some bruises to show for it.

Crouching once more, he clasped his hands together, inhaled, and then tried to stand. The stone moved so little, he couldn't be sure which of his muscles had failed him. None seemed to bear the load. A moment of breath held—a moment of strain. The rock hovered a hand-span above the ground.

A noisy exhale followed the rock back down. Barodane panted and fell to one side of it. He felt his eyes go wide as he recalled how many times Garlenna had lifted the stone earlier that morning.

The sound of hooves and a whinny sent Barodane scuttling back to his place on the stump.

Garlenna trotted into camp. "The road looks..." Halfway dismounted, she slowed, her eye drifting over the stone. "Clear." She glanced at Barodane.

He stared into his lap. "How far to the nearest town?"

In his periphery, he saw her looking from stone to prince. She spoke slow, voice belying suspicion. "Signs at a fork in the road say Breckenbright is five days' ride northwest. Halaleh in three, straight north."

"That's Mags Marwen's hold," Barodane said. "Nailmaker."

"Does he know you?"

"Never met him." Barodane rose to tend to Scab. "I figured you'd like hearing that."

"Indeed, I do."

On the morning of the next two days, Garlenna asked Barodane if he wished to exercise with her. He declined each time. "I'll be gone a while, scouting," she would say. "Perhaps try then."

He never did.

CHAPTER TWENTY-THREE

AWAY DEVIL

"They're shadowing us," Ash said.

Syn flicked the reins. "Nothing to fear yet."

Thephos cast about. A distant bird call echoed through the endless pillars of oak, cedar, and pine. He jerked his attention from one swatch of murk to the next.

"Then why are you picking up the pace?" Ash said.

They followed Syn at a trot. The big man shrugged. "Not every unwelcome house guest needs to be murdered if they make haste out the door."

Thephos leaned over his horse, eager to be smaller than he was. The invisible push of eyes traipsed over him.

Eight days they'd navigated the Ardent Heart. Eight days of peace and serenity. The first in all his life. Outside of the current moment, Thephos had reveled in the beauty of the Ardent Heart. Nature, he decided, was as good a way as any to come to know the self better.

His horse jounced him, making him bite his tongue. A trot was about as fast as he'd gone on the mare. He couldn't imagine what a gallop might do. *Bite my tongue in half? Toss me on my head and leave me for dead with the Kurgs?*

The last seemed most plausible.

"What clan?" Ash kept a hand on the reins, the other on her sword hilt.

Syn grabbed her by the wrist. Voice like iron, he said, "Don't do that. You know better."

Onward they trotted. Thephos's pulse drubbed his ears. Diaphanous light, thin like a spider's web, slid up and over Syn Backlegarm's bald head. "Rat clan."

"That rangy, old cunt," Ash muttered, too low for any of their stalkers to hear. "Next time I see Ioki Voidwalker..." The rest of the threat devolved into angry syllables.

Her familiarity with the Kurg told Thephos this wasn't something that had happened before. At least, not from the Rat clan.

Thephos raised his voice over the clomp and jostle of the horses. "Is it me?"

Ash stared at her husband, awaiting a reply, but Syn just encouraged them to continue riding.

The strident bugle of an elk sounded from Thephos's left. An answering call to his right came a fraction of a second later. The Rat clan Kurgs were keeping pace with the trio.

There was a handful of them crashing through the underbrush, snapping twigs, their mounts huffing. Alien tongues murmuring alien words, barely within earshot.

The fear in Thephos's belly curdled, became a sour chill. He frowned.

No, Theffy. No, no, no. You're strong. If you wanted, you could kill them all.

The fear started to burn. Heat pooled at the core of him. Sweat streaked from his armpits and temples. His heart became rolling thunder. He wiped his face with the back of his forearm—the flesh was hot to the touch, as hot as a horseshoe left in the sun on a midsummer day.

Angled off to one side, and behind Thephos, a Kurg shouted. No more than fifty paces. A mounted figure wove between the dense trees off the main trail, an indistinct blur of brown and gold amid the shadows.

Do you want to kill them, Theffy?

Sulfur tinged Thephos's mouth. He gagged. His eyes stung. His body suddenly weightless. Hands pulsing with strength—he crushed the reins. His mare whinnied, head swung out to the side to watch him with a single wild eye.

A cart-length ahead, Syn threw a puzzled look back at him. The Dominarri's eyes started to glow...

Thephos stifled the budding inferno at his center and focused straight ahead. The fire in his belly disappeared. His hands relaxed and the sulfuric taste was replaced with dryness as he gulped the chill air rushing past.

Sunlight stung Thephos's eyes, forcing him to squint, as the Kurgs chased them out into an open glade, shouting, "Kuan! Kuan roj'gal!"

"What are they saying?" Thephos panted.

"Away." Syn's expression was perplexed. "Away, devil."

The hairs on the backs of Thephos's arms stiffened. He glanced back. The Kurgs had stopped at the glade's edge, and now waited in the dim understory astride massive elks. They held no reins and strange weapons filled their golden-hued hands. *Would they have used them?* The way they seemed to watch Thephos was answer enough.

Then their upper bodies twisted back toward the dark forest—steering their mounts with their knees alone—and were swallowed by tree and shadow. He stared after them, catching his breath, when a whistle spun him around.

He'd urged his mount forward for only a few feet before he gasped and dragged hard on the reins, all the way to his chin. He'd been so consumed by their pursuers behind, so focused on the next patch of grass that could carry him to safety, that he hadn't looked at what lay ahead.

An immensity of white stone curved upward, inward, forming a dome of impossible magnitude. Granite, smoother than an infant's cheeks, showed no lines of placement between blocks; unbelievable as it was, Thephos could only assume it was carved from a single stone. At a height level with the towering tree line, the dome terminated as if some cloud-tall titan had beheaded it.

Thephos blinked, swiveled his gaze in either direction so as to take in its vast scope.

Syn sat astride his horse near a black pillar that split the distance between Thephos and the dome, a proud smile on his lips. "Pretty, isn't it?" he shouted.

That wasn't the word Thephos was thinking. In fact, he wasn't quite thinking at all. Coping was more like it. Coping in the way of those too awestruck by what their eyes perceived and failed to fit with what their mind knew to be possible.

Ash appeared at Thephos's side and nudged him in the ribs. "Welcome home."

Thephos gawped at her.

She offered a rare smile. "Enshai is Unti for 'welcome home.' Come on."

Together, they covered the distance to Syn. With the flat of his hand, the Dominarri gestured at Ash. "This is my lovely wife." That drew a coy smile from her. He gestured at the black pillar at his side. "And this is the Pillar of Orriok."

"The Pillar of Fire," Ash said.

The column was as big around as a wagon wheel turned on its side, though toward the top it gradually narrowed. Half as tall as the dome of Enshai, a sculpted flame crowned it.

Syn pointed to the other side of the clearing at a matching pillar. "The Pillar of Hrasdi." Then another in the other direction. Both were so far off, they were little more than a scabbed-over cut on the horizon. "And Noggu."

Ash Backlegarm looked at Thephos. "The Eye...and the Hand."

The Fire, the Eye, and the Hand. Each facet making up the Triune God. The words were Kurgish. Syn and Ash had educated him about unimism on their journey. Since Thephos might soon share their beliefs, he had listened diligently.

"Most Dominarri *are* unimists. Just goes with the territory," Syn said. "We've inherited a mission from our Kurgish predecessors. It's changed since then, but the principles are roughly the same."

"Enshai was a gift," Ash had said. "The Fire. The Eye. The Hand. Passion, truth, and duty. The essential qualities one must embody to move in parallel with their purpose. Their fate."

"External gods are great," Syn said with a laugh. "Whatever keeps people from killing and stealing and all the bad things in life. But where it goes wrong is institutions like the Sempyrium."

"Get used to praying to some outside force—to giving it the credit for all of the good and blaming it for all the bad—and eventually, it gets hard to stop doing it that way." Ash had fallen quiet, sullen, leaving Thephos to wonder if she had a history there.

"The Triune God is in each of us and in everything." Syn took over. "In essence, it's up to us to work in concert with the flow of life to maintain and protect it."

"And hold back that which threatens it."

Syn nodded at his wife. "Through love, truth, and duty...that's what it means to be Dominarri."

Thephos saw why the jump from Dominarri to Awakened came easy. So much of what he faced on Unturrus echoed what his friends were saying. He'd surrendered himself to the Mountain of Power, letting it flow into him and guide him on his ascent. Whatever lessons it had to give, he'd accepted without question. Even when it meant touching the fire of his suffering. Even when he'd molded and shaped his pain into truth.

He would continue exploring the life he'd never lived until he could do so no more.

A series of bells tied to a rope descended the length of the Fire Pillar. Syn shook it, sending out a deafening clangor. A few seconds later, a bell sounded from within the dome of Enshai.

Ash and Syn spurred their horses forward, beckoning Thephos to follow. As they approached the gigantic lens of stone, he scanned it for an entrance but found nothing. "How do we get in?"

"Lots of ways," Syn said. "Depends on who's on watch. I usually just keep going until it happens."

They aimed their horses at an ambiguous point along the curving stone and meandered onward. As they neared, Thephos saw that the dome of Enshai was, in fact, carved from a single piece of marble, or something akin to it. Solid white and unblemished, it possessed no lines, nor whorls of gray. Earlier when he couldn't see any lines, it was because there were none to behold. He picked over the expanse of it, eyes retracing the same pristine tracts, the same winks and halos of sunlight climbing its egg-like curvature.

At a dozen paces, subtle motion grabbed his attention.

A shimmer marred the perfect surface of the dome, an oval of evening sunlight dancing over a lake's surface. It reminded Thephos of the ghostly light that had filled the Corpse Gate moments before he'd passed through it.

The wall undulated but remained unbroken. Then it thinned, becoming a curtain of gossamer reality. Motion and images bled through it, resolving into a busy scene.

A tunnel.

They rode into the wall. At the littoral space where outside and inside merged, cold brushed over Thephos. The tunnel was dark, a portal of light a hundred feet beyond providing the sole source of illumination. Ahead, people walked past it. A hedgerow taller than Syn sat in the background.

Their horses' hooves echoed. Thephos looked up, discomfited by the amount of rock he assumed must be above him. *Is the dome truly this thick?* If the tunnel was a hundred feet long, the walls of the dome had to be of equal dimension. Being a pig farmer hadn't required much reading but he'd always needed a firm grip of numbers to build pens for the trotters.

Thephos huffed, echo splashing through the tunnel. *This is my home. A home for Awakened. For Dominarri.* His chest ached, excitement leaving him on the verge of panic. *What if they aren't like Syn? What if I fail them? What if they hate me?*

Sunlight drowned the courtyard in golden brilliance as they emerged. Standing at the mouth of the tunnel, a woman of fifty with crow's feet blinked gray vapor from her eyes. The portal through the dome's wall disappeared.

Syn nodded thanks to her and they dismounted. They saw their mounts off to a pair of youths who led them off through the labyrinthine hedges. The interior walls curved toward the opening at the top. Though winter lurked, the sky was a bright blue iris staring down at Thephos. It wasn't so azure and pure as the Mother when she'd come to him, but it stunned him all the same.

I am someone. Someone special.

Chosen.

The city of the Dominarri was a thing of myth and legend no common person had ever seen. The location was a well-kept secret. Kurgish allies in the forest enclaves handled whatever rumors couldn't. So to have not only seen it, but to be standing in it now...

"Thephos," Syn called. "This way."

The couple had moved off. Thephos had to jog to catch up. They turned a corner and traveled down rows of hedges of varying size.

Just as he reached his friends, the hedgerows dropped to shoulder-height all around. A handful of men and women were squaring off with sections of vegetation, long, slightly curved swords in their hands. All wore gloves and scarves around their necks.

One of them lunged forward, hips twisting, relaxed arms trailing the momentum of their strike. The woman's eyes, Thephos noted, did not waver from their target. Clippings of leaf and bark flitted through the air as they recovered and began measuring their next strike.

As they passed, Thephos peered at the hedge the woman had cut into. "It's—it's a cat."

The woman doing the cutting glared at him. "No shit, genius."

"Easy, lady," Syn said and pulled Thephos along. He lowered his voice. "These are all bladesworn. Like Ash. Artists and masters of the blade. Killer—"

"Assholes." Ash shrugged. "I'm one of 'em, I should know."

"They're not all assholes." Syn scratched his bald head. "But it tends to go with the territory. There's a lot of pressure to be the best among them. They protect their Awakened. Failure isn't an option when guarding such invaluable assets."

"Assets?" Thephos felt his forehead furrow. *Are we just weapons to be used?* The thought sickened him.

Syn seemed to notice Thephos's consternation. "Sacred might have been a better word." He looked around at the faces trimming the hedges, then ducked his head close to Thephos's. "Just don't cross the blond guy with the beard."

Brow pinched, Thephos made the mistake of turning to look. The man Syn referenced had a striking face, so perfect and chiseled of porcelain, a thing of alien beauty. The man looked bored as he flipped his sword increasingly higher in the air without looking, instead staring at his hedge. He laughed, caught his blade, and then executed a flurry of slashes. Where each stroke started and stopped was a difficult thing to recount.

"Now, he's an asshole," Ash said.

"Worse." Syn's brow darkened.

"Who is he?" Thephos asked.

Syn dismissed the question with a wave of his hand. "Don't worry about it. Just steer clear. We've got more important things to focus on."

The more important things Syn spoke of were underground. The city proper of the Enshai was reserved for the growth of food and care of animals, as well as a handful of necessary buildings that required ventilation. A great deal of it were the hedges; countless, endless rows of them.

Everything else was underground. That included Enshai's ruling body, the Skyfire council.

Two faces stared at Thephos from an elevated platform, the same type of mysterious stone as Enshai's dome. Syn and Ash had walked him through a network of connecting corridors cut into the bowels of the earth and then entered a hollowed-out chamber with enough clearance for a tree from the Ardent Heart to stand up in.

Rowed grandstands flanked the stairs leading up to the seats of power. At the center of the chamber was a pit, and at the center of the pit, a stand of marble thrust up from the floor, a basin as broad across as Thephos's arms could stretch wide poised atop it at chest level. A chill ran up his spine when he looked up. Suspended directly over the basin was a carved moth that descended from the ceiling by a file of stone.

"Syn, I'm surprised to see you here." The man who spoke had a pristine white beard, flowing hair of the same, and piercing blue eyes. Somewhere in his fifties, it was clear he'd been stunningly attractive as a younger man.

"Pintarith." Both Syn and Ash gave subtle bows to the man. Thephos followed their lead, and as he did, Syn whispered, "The Holy Sword." Then they angled toward an elegant woman with a swarthy complexion a few arm spans down the dais. She wore a maroon brocade etched with gold thread depicting tiny flames, eyes, and hands. "N'zara." This time Syn whispered, "The Holy Flame." Standing upright, Syn continued to address the woman. "I thought it time to check in personally."

"Half a decade is the limit, is it?" The man's sleek brow jumped. "We've found you and your bladesworn's reports to be satisfactory thus far. What's the occasion?"

Thephos found it odd for Syn's wife to be referred to as his bladesworn.

"Indeed. A lot of good years." Syn cleared his throat and stepped forward. "A Ruptured has escaped. He fell into the gap of our abilities, Your Grace."

"Too many," N'zara said in a rasping, smoky voice. "We bleed poison into the world with our folly."

Ash stiffened and looked at the floor. A pang of sympathy had Thephos cursing N'zara for admonishing his friends.

"So it has always been. This is nothing new." Pintarith eased to one side of his seat, piercing gaze boring down on Syn. "Tell me all you know of the Ruptured."

Syn did, and with every word, Thephos's astonishment grew.

By the end, Thephos couldn't hold back any longer. "The Wordfox?" he blurted.

"We've been calling him Shadowfox." Syn coughed into a fist. "For, uh, obvious reasons."

Pintarith regarded Thephos with narrowed eyes. "You know of the Rup-tured?"

Thephos stammered. "Only a little...Your Grace. Before we ascended Un-turrus, his mind already seemed broken." The empty room seemed to stretch, swell, make Thephos small in the yawning divide. The Skyfire council members maintained eerie silence until Pintarith nodded, a gesture Thephos took to mean that he should continue. "I didn't speak with him much. He was a bitter man, with a great deal of hatred for the House of Saud."

At the last, N'zara's head jerked toward Pintarith. She snapped her fingers at an Awakened by the entrance. "Fetch Filandir and his Awakened here now."

Syn inclined his bald crown toward Pintarith. "Wouldn't your son and Crowborn be a better fit for so dangerous a mission?"

Pintarith sighed. "Certainly, but at current, Pintarian is without his Awak-ened."

Ash gasped. "What happened?"

"Kashoggo crushed him. I don't wish to ruminate on it." Pintarith rubbed his brow. "Alas, my son's bond is broken and we've lost a good agent."

Tears gathered at the corner of Ash's eyes. She fell into Syn's arms.

N'zara leaned forward in her seat to leer at Thephos. Thick lips smeared with ruddy, waxen makeup. "Perhaps you've brought a worthy replacement?"

It was Pintarith's turn to level a shocked look at his counterpart.

Syn stepped back to pat Thephos's shoulder. "I believe our friend here has something special in him."

"What's his name?" N'zara purred.

"Thephos," said Syn. "Thephos of Carthane."

"So we'll see." Pintarith opened his hand and made a 'come hither' motion. "Demonstrate."

Thephos hesitated.

"Well. He's not sure of his power yet." Syn swept the room with a smile. "Which is another reason I've returned. I'd like to oversee his training."

A crease formed on N'zara's wrinkled brow. "You abandoned your post at Unturrus to parade an unproven Awakened before us? And this was after you allowed a Ruptured loose in the world?"

Ash stepped forward. "It wasn't his—"

"His appointment was your idea." N'zara waved a hand at Pintarith and crossed her arms. "He is yours to deal with."

A cloud of suspicion settled over Pintarith. "You'll oversee his training..." He drummed velvet-gloved hands on the marble-like stone arm of his chair. After a moment, he brought his fingers to his lips. "Take him to the chamber. Show him why we exist. If that doesn't stoke his powers, I'll expect you to take...more extreme measures."

"Even if this man had his powers, nothing about him says he can do this work," said N'zara. "It seems a waste of resources. And we keep your watchdog from his duties at Unturrus to do it."

Pintarith inhaled sharply and then spoke through clenched teeth. "You said it was my decision." He stabbed his chest with a thumb. "Mine."

"I *thought* you might make a wise one," N'zara said. "Now, don't be a child."

Pintarith purpled.

Before things escalated, Syn raised his arms to either side. "No problem, Your Graces. I'll just show him to his room and—"

"No." Pintarith's ire shifted to Syn. "Ash will do it. You'll come with me to my private chambers."

Syn nodded. "As you wish, Your Grace."

Something was afoot.

Trouble. Thephos had known it all his life. Heard it walking through the door, drunk and angry. Felt it as a set of eyes boring hatred into his back. Knew its burning ache on his body, a fist soon to fall. He was the cause of something dire, and like so many times before, he didn't understand why.

CHAPTER TWENTY-FOUR

DON'T BE STUPID

A nother night went by in which the girl from Womunger came to Ishoa's side. "He'll give you to those Orenese, or the Kons," she said. "It's now or never."

As the fiery-haired girl sat in ready silence, Ishoa shook her head. *Not without Arick.*

"Don't be stupid, Highness."

Ishoa flinched.

Wolst's death was her fault. He'd sacrificed himself for her because she hadn't listened—she'd chosen Rakeema. *Am I just sacrificing myself for Arick in a similar fashion?* If they ended up in Ghastiin, Joffus Kon's people would ship her off to the Warnocks in Jarik. At that point, Arick's execution would be all but assured. *She's right. I have to take a chance.*

Ishoa nodded.

A knife whipped up into Okki's hand. Banded moonlight played over the blade. "Be still." She wrapped a hand around Ishoa's wrists then huddled around them. Quietly, carefully, she started sawing.

Blood filled Ishoa's ears. She'd need to get the Fly's weapon away from him first. His ax. Perhaps together, she and Okki could deliver enough damage before the Shadowheart man knew what—

Fabric rustled nearby.

Okki's head swiveled to one side, her eyes gleaming and fixed on the last place they'd seen the Fly. There was no way to tell if he still slumbered there. Sweat tickled Ishoa's temples and raced between her thighs. She felt Okki's hand slacken around her wrists, felt the weight of the knife float away from her bonds.

A dull ringing at the edge of hearing, as if an ax were being dragged over blades of grass...

The girl from Womunger started to shake. Ishoa's heart pounded into the silence, louder with each stifling second that passed. Muscles clenched taut in fear, ached for release.

Okki hovered, motionless. Waiting. Ishoa imagined hot blood splashing onto her face after a few thudding footsteps. Expected it any second.

Yet the minutes passed without incident until a cough made Ishoa jolt—Okki too, one hand flying to her mouth to stifle a yelp of terror.

One of the crones smacked her gob, cleared a mass of age's finest excess from her throat, and then turned over with a noisy huffing.

Something in the darkness shifted then settled.

Okki slid off Ishoa a minute later and whispered, "Tomorrow," before creeping back to her sleeping place, low and lizard-like.

The next day, the Fly stalked off, a knife in each hand. Half an hour later, he returned touting a bloody squirrel. Ishoa swallowed hard at the sight of the dead animals, worried it might be the Fly's way of conveying a warning to the girl from Womunger. If Okki thought the same, she hid it well as she set about skinning the animals for the crones to cook.

Arick, meanwhile, remained delirious and weak. One of the crones changed his bandages and poultice as the Fly flipped Ishoa's gag down for a moment in order to press a slice of cheese into her mouth.

"I won't leave you," she said. His gloved-hand hovered, the rest of a hunk of pungent cheddar pinched between thumb and forefinger.

"I can't." Ishoa maneuvered her face to deny the next bite. The Fly kept her hungry, she assumed, so she would only eat and not speak in the short time he allowed her gag removed. "I won't leave him." She inclined her head at Arick. "I need you to carry him and we aren't safe without you. Untie me."

The Fly twisted around, appearing to consider her offer. He turned back to her and pushed the cheese into her mouth. Once she'd devoured it, he replaced the gag, and they broke camp, though the Fly let her trail at the back rather than forcing her to the front.

Small victory, I suppose. Whatever freedom he gave her, she'd take, for it could help her escape. Being out of his line of sight was certainly a benefit. Between the crones, the boy, and the girl, they might be able to drag Arick around. But still, there was the issue of protection. Without the Fly, they were vulnerable. Okki seemed familiar with a dagger, but even with Rakeema freed, Ishoa doubted their ability to survive against a group like the one the Fly had so easily dispatched.

Around midday, the road became bumpy with deep wagon wheel grooves and overturned rocks.

"Others." The girl drifted into place beside Ishoa. "Families carrying everything they can and fleeing to the nearest city they think might be safe." Wearing a frown, she kicked a rock. "Unfortunately, nowhere is safe."

Ishoa watched the girl. Grunted.

A pair of richly dressed men on horses pounded past, keeping one hand on the reins and one on their sword hilts as they shot wary glances at the Fly. A jangling chest was roped to one horse's flanks, and a bundle of flapping clothes trailed the other.

A leaning post with two splintered slats of wood nailed into it loomed ahead. One arrow pointed to Ghastiin over a slope that curved steeply down and away into valley. The other directed traffic to White Plains through a densely wooded area.

The creak of wagon wheels filtered into Ishoa's ears as they drew closer to the sign. Shouts and the bray of pack animals followed. The Fly slowed, tilting an ear skyward, but he didn't stop.

Ishoa and the girl from Womunger exchanged a look.

A train of wagons sprang up onto the trail coming from the direction of Ghastiin. Their lead drover half stood in the cab, flicking his whip across his lead animal's backsides. He shot them a look as he passed, snorted like one of his beasts, then stared ahead. At least fifty people and ten wagons filled in behind. There were a handful of children among the fleeing refugees clutching chickens or baby goats to their breasts and huddling into their mother's sides. From the stains of their clothing, these people had seen their fair share of bloodshed and ashen snowfall. Only a few had the hard faces of fighting men. Bulges under their cloaks at hip or shoulder proved Ishoa's conclusion.

The Fly moved at a steady pace as the wagon train trundled out of sight. He brought them to a halt at the crossroads.

"Ghastiin?" Okki pried. "Or White Plains?"

The Fly shook his head.

Ishoa's jaw tightened. *Shit. The farther we go toward Ghastiin, into enemy territory, the more dangerous and difficult escape will be. I have to act now.*

With his back to the group Ishoa watched him roll up his face covering around a mahogany-hued mouth to slug down water from a skin. Arick stirred and whispered to himself in the stretcher. For a stomach-fluttering second, she thought she heard him say, "Isha."

She chewed at her gag, wishing her teeth could cut through the dense cloth. She caught Okki's attention, inclined her head at the Fly's back, praying to her dead parents that the girl knew what she meant. *I'll distract him. You stab him in the back.*

After days and weeks spent ceaselessly fleeing for her life, Ishoa's feet were little more than deadened stone. She hobbled up to the Fly. The girl from Womunger followed at an angle.

At a half dozen paces, the Fly's head tilted as if hearing something. Ishoa hesitated then continued. *No stopping now. I'll throw myself at him, crying and distraught, to cover the sound of Okki's movements...*

A hand gripped her from behind and spun her around.

"Hey!" The boy. Her brow creased as she stared down her nose at him, acutely aware of the rapid swell and shrink of her lungs. The boy's eyes were narrowed. *Oh no.* He snapped his fingers, and nodded, pointing at her. Then he gestured at Rakeema and Arick, all tied up and leashed. "Ancestors take me, I can't believe it. You're her!"

Wide-eyed, Okki's hands slipped out from under her tunic—where she'd undoubtedly been gripping her knife—and took the boy by the arm. "I need your help with something."

"Wait a sec—" The boy fought off her attempts as she tugged at his elbow, now with two hands. "Damn you, just look at her, would ya'! It's the fucking princess."

"No it ain't, boy." The tone in Mittens's voice betrayed the truth of her words. "No it ain't."

The boy glared at her, twisting out of Okki's grip. "Blind old hag, you are. She's got the ice tiger. The eyes. Everything Ironlight."

The Fly drifted past Ishoa like an onerous raincloud.

Okki scuttled back from the boy to a safer distance, eyes downcast, though it seemed she was reluctant to leave the boy alone.

"What?" The boy blinked rapidly, naked chest pumping with the awareness of his mistake under the heavy hide he wore around his shoulders. The smile that had sprung onto his face at his discovery scattered to nothing, like autumn before the chill winds of winter. "What? What'd you think I said? I didn't say anything. Just a girl. She's—she's just a girl."

Ishoa's stomach lurched.

Calm and steady, the Fly pointed over the boy's shoulder. Knees quaking, the boy licked his lips and craned around—

Ishoa flinched as the Fly's hand flew in a sideways arc. Okki had stiffened, one cheek spattered in bright red droplets that matched her hair. The boy's head swung back around. Stunned, he stared at the Fly. For a fleeting moment, the boy's severed throat was a barren track, disparate flaps of leather yet to be stitched together, and then blood spilled out in a rush. Scarlet cascaded down his torso. He dropped to his knees, skin paling, death pulsing into him with every weakening heartbeat.

Once the boy fell to his face, he had yet to stop twitching before the Fly looked at Okki, exuding hostility. The crones fumbled their way into one another's arms, knowing they were next.

Okki raised her chin. Her nostrils flared, withered, flared again. "Stu—stupid boy." She booted his corpse in the hip. "Everyone knows the princess died at Jarik." Slow and methodical, the Fly stepped closer. Swiping the blood from her face, Okki backpedaled, words tumbling out in a final gambit to save her life. "My father said her head was placed over the Gate of the Tiger alongside her anjuhtarg's. We were with a wine merchant before you and he said the same, didn't he?"

Ishoa held her breath as she looked at the crones, hoping their corroboration of the lie might lend it validity.

Too scared to speak, the crones nodded vigorously.

The Fly was a deadly monster, yes, but far from stupid. Okki's composure crumbled as he stepped toward her, a dagger glinting in his hand.

The blade had moved so fast when he killed the boy. So smooth. A miraculously clean blow. Ishoa's chin fell to her chest in defeat, unable to watch. *At least it will be quick.*

A shout batted the air.

The Fly ignored it. His hand shot out, snaring the girl from Womunger by her crimson mane. He forced her to her knees in the snow and mud at his feet. Okki cursed, clawing at his grip and trying to stand, but he held firmly in place. The shrieking crones sheltered their eyes.

Run, you stupid hags! Ishoa clamped down on the gag and prepared to launch herself at the Fly to give them time to flee. The Fly raised his knife.

A horse screamed in the distance.

The Fly's masked face snapped in the direction of the sound. He released Okki. In the space of a single heartbeat, his ax-staff flowed from his back and into his hands. Forgotten, the girl from Womunger stumbled to her feet and out of the Fly's reach.

Hoofs thudded the turf behind Ishoa. She rounded and found a rider bearing down on her. "Out of the way!" He showed no sign of slowing or deviating. *He's going to trample me.*

She turned to run but slipped on a patch of slick. Slush flung up in an arc as she landed squarely on her ass. The Fly leapt past her brandishing his weapon.

The rider jerked the reins. A jingling chest strapped to his horse's rump slid askew but remained there, tied down by hempen tethers. A handful of silver and gold wheels shook free from a hole in the side of the chest to litter the road.

Twin arrows were embedded in the lid.

The Fly cut empty air before the rider, a warning more than anything, it seemed.

The man veered off with a curse, and then continued on, back in the direction he was coming from when they passed him the first time.

Ishoa squinted up the road. Plumes of dusted-snow trailed the train of wagons from earlier. They, too, were returning in the direction they'd come from. Right back toward Ishoa. This time, the wagon's driver was standing in the cab, arms flashing up and down in a rhythmic, frenzied wave. His ox team slavered at the mouth.

Shouts chased them. Armed men on horseback came into view over the rising slope, bedecked in purple tabards trimmed with fur. Furriers from Ghastiin, ten or more, waylaid the refugee train.

The world pitched into chaos.

The Fly slung his ax-staff over his back and gathered the ropes of Arick's stretcher. He ignored the cowering crones and Okki who now fumbled for her knife. He slashed Ishoa's gag and bonds. She flexed her hands and rotated her wrists, but when he tried to pull her into a run, she ducked his hand.

Okki was stumbling behind, still catching her breath from her brief fight for her life. Ishoa helped steady the girl, then pulled her by the hand after Arick's stretcher and the Fly, who'd broken into a sprint. With his cargo, especially with Rakeema thrashing every few bounding steps, he was slower, but still outpaced Ishoa and Okki.

"Die, loyalist dogs!"

Screams. Squawking. Bleating. Children crying.

Ishoa and Okki raced past the crones, a flapping, blubbering mass. The younger called encouragement to the older as they sped by.

A cacophony rumbled up behind, vibrating through Ishoa's nerve-dampened feet.

"Out of the way!"

A rush of sound filled her ears as the first wagon made its way past. Running hand-in-hand with Okki, Ishoa looked to her right in time to see a wagon wheel strike an upturned stone. A wooden spoke cracked, crumbled under the momentum of the rest of the wheel, and the bed careened out of control. The ox-team angled toward Ishoa, but Okki slashed out with her knife, slashing one along the withers just before it hit them. The beast bellowed, bucked in the hitch, then went down in a tangle with the other ox beside it.

Snow and steam and mud and grunts. The team stopped so abruptly, the driver sailed past Ishoa and Okki through the air, landing with a crunch against the hard ground. The man was dead on impact. Ishoa dodged around his body where it twitched in the road.

They sprinted for their lives. Ahead, the Fly seemed to have slowed, the extra weight he dragged finally taking its toll. Steel rang against steel. The sound of death dogging them.

Ishoa afforded a look backward.

A second wagon went off-road around the decimated first and was quickly catching up with Ishoa. This wagon was loaded with people. A man in the bed gripped a hammer, while one in the cab sitting beside the driver held the same along with a shield. The anvil and embers of Summerforge were emblazoned on their bronze honor plates.

A pair of the Kon holdguard soldiers closed with the wagon. "Loyalists!" they yelled with fevered malice. "Death to Namarr's dogs!"

One wearing a conical helm with a nose guard leveled a wild sword stroke at the occupants of the wagon. A woman screamed and tumbled into the waiting arms of the others, forearm rent bloody from wrist to elbow. A Summerforge holdguard stepped over a child to defend the rest as the wagon came abreast of Ishoa and Okki.

The smith from Summerforge scraped aside a blade stroke and dealt the Kon a hammer blow to the neck. Bone bulged sideways beneath the flesh of the furrier's throat as he toppled from his horse. The wagon humped up with a sickening crunch.

More holdguard from Ghastiin arrived to harry the wagon. Swords met hammers in sparking sprays, but there were too many Kons and too few men of Summerforge. Men, women, and children alike were cut down.

A slaughter.

The wagon rushed ahead of Ishoa and Okki, and then eclipsed the Fly as well.

A Kon galloped after, hurling a spear that struck the wagon's driver in the shoulder. He jerked sideways, dropping the reins. The ox team careened off the road in the opposite direction of Ishoa and Okki. The axle of the wagon stalled on some hidden object in the snow, a rock or root. Furriers swept around it as the Summerforge men sprang from the wagon bed to fight. A last stand.

Just ahead, the Fly dropped the rope, took his weapon in both hands, and stalked forward. They couldn't outrun the mounted holdguard, and wouldn't once they dispatched those in the wagons, but the Fly hitting them in the rear while they were distracted at least gave them a chance.

Without a word, Ishoa and Okki snatched up the rope of the stretcher. There was a stand of trees a short way from the road. If they hurried, they might be able to lose their attackers there.

Ishoa hauled the stretcher with Okki, their backs to their destination; it was far heavier than the Fly made it seem.

Facing the battle while dragging backward in tandem with Okki, Ishoa searched for the Fly. A Kon holdguard lay dead at his feet, the corpse's upper half separated from the lower, a smattering of innards covering the ground between. The dead man's horse was stumbling sideways, one of its legs severed at the knee.

The last of the Kons who'd attacked the wagon fell in a hail of hammer strikes from a Summerforge holdguard. But more were coming.

"Pull, Okki!" The muscles of Ishoa's thighs and back burned. Her lungs ached.

She watched the Fly spin about, eyeless mask hunting for the stretcher. They hadn't made it far. He spotted them almost instantly.

"Come on, Okki," Ishoa yelled. "Pull like your life depends on it."

But the girl from Womunger cursed and dropped the rope. Two Kons bore down on them. And all they'd managed to do was leave the Fly's protection.

Ishoa rushed to Arick's side to try dislodging his sword, but it was too well secured. Firm hands spun her around by the shoulders. A freckled face framed in a crimson mane.

"Go, Highness," Okki said. "You have to run."

Ishoa had been here before. She shrugged the girl's hands off and steeled herself.

Okki grimaced. "I killed my father for you. If you die now, it will have been for nothing."

"What?" Ishoa stared at the girl.

"My father was hold lord of Womunger. He made a deal with the Scarborn." Okki's lips twitched, gold eyes burning with the pain of her horrible deed. "He was a traitor."

"Your father was...Okka Womunger." It all made sense now. The knowledge of warfare. The dubious approach to the Fly. The way she'd known who Ishoa was. She killed her father out of loyalty to Namarr. *Loyalty to me.* Ishoa drew herself up tall. "I'm not leaving you."

Okki pursed her lips and then stepped so that she was shoulder-to-shoulder with Ishoa. "Then it will be my honor, Highness."

The pit of Ishoa's stomach felt as though it lay on the ground. Her jaw tendons tightened. "No, the honor is mine." Ishoa balled her fists as if it would come to blows. She knew it wouldn't.

A third rider appeared behind the first two, and then, they were on them. Horses thundering, yellow teeth clamped in snarls, blood-soaked blades upraised.

When they came within a lance's reach of the stretcher, a tied-up Rakeema leapt atop it, protectively straddling Arick. Horses, Ishoa had learned, didn't care for the ice tiger. The holdguards sawed their horses' reins as the anjuhtarg hissed and clawed the air. One mount reared, nearly throwing the lead rider.

Okki bolted past Rakeema, grabbing at an ax slung along the man's saddle as he fought to control his horse. "Bitch!" The furrier circled, raining down steel. But the girl was cat-quick and dodged every slash.

The second rider barreled around the wagon toward Ishoa. She backpedaled, ducked, and his blade licked space where her head had been. She threw herself sideways and landed hard on her shoulder. Her head clipped a corner of the stretcher. Ears ringing, a pinched feeling radiated from the base of her neck as she scrambled upward, disoriented. Glistening flecks hemmed her vision. She heard her attacker wheeling his horse around for another charge.

I'm too slow. She assumed that thought would be her last. That the holdguard would behead her before she'd had a chance to turn and face him. She blinked—braced herself.

But by the time she regained her orientation, a headless corpse swayed in the saddle where the Kon man had been—the Fly stepping clear. Crimson splashed the horse's flanks as it reared, throwing the body from its back before bolting into the woods.

Ishoa looked at Arick in his stretcher, seemingly unharmed. Rakeema, too, was unscathed. Relief was short-lived, however. The black-clad bodyguard from Shadowheart was at her side, propelling her toward the trees as he snatched the rope.

"Give me a weapon!" Ishoa cried.

The Fly didn't hesitate. He slapped his knife hilt-first into her palm. All thought of slaying the man suffocated. *He fights the Kons...keeps me safe.* He was taking her to White Plains, not Ghastiin. *Swords speak louder than words when allegiance is in question,* her grandmother had once said to a disgruntled hold lord in the High Hall. At the moment, nothing spoke louder than the Fly's ax-staff. His allegiance was clear.

"Little bitch!"

Ishoa whirled, dagger poised before her. Twenty yards away, the rider who'd been fighting Okki clutched at his thigh. Dark arterial blood leaked between his fingers. He strained forward in the saddle over the wound, grunting and red-faced as if he were shitting rocks.

The Womunger girl had covered an impressive amount of ground in her mad dash to the road, but a half-dozen Kons were zeroing in on her. "We have to help her!" Ishoa started forward.

The sky pitched into view as her feet were swept out from under her. She flung out her elbows by reflex to buffer the fall. Landing hard on her ass, she wasted no time with the pain and shot to her feet.

The Fly loomed.

"You're just going to let her—"

A bundle of her shirt filled his hand. He yanked her off balance, forcing her to grab onto his wrist or risk whip-lash. She was going to say die. *Of course he'll let her die. Why wouldn't he?* The boy's stunned expression as his throat spilled flashed through her mind. *Even if he's an ally, he's a monster.*

If the Fly wasn't already hustling away with Arick and Rakeema in tow, Ishoa could have done something. Would have.

Instead, she sprinted after her savior and captor, permitting herself a single look back before the woods swallowed her. A score of bowmen had arrived, the evidence of their work sprawled across the ground surrounding the wagons. Arrows riddled bodies still settling into death with twitches and spasms. Covered in a handful of wounds, the holdguard of Summerforge fought on, a brave but futile gesture.

Of Okki, Ishoa saw no sign.

CHAPTER TWENTY-FIVE

THE TRAP

A crownguard, with dark skin that marked him as a descendant of purer Lah-Tsarene blood, stepped inside the command tent. "We've apprehended thieves in the camp."

Gyr frowned at the young crownguard. A stiff wind billowed under the entrance flap, setting the candles on the table beside him to guttering.

Duke Malus clapped. "Congratulations, Caltheo. Your trap worked."

Gyr regarded his grinning cupbearer. *What trap?*

Malus addressed the crownguard. "Bring them here."

"My lord." Gyr pursed his lips. "Why wasn't I informed of—"

"This isn't the time." Malus sighed. "Caltheo proposed a plan to catch whoever was stealing from our wagons and I gave him leave to execute it."

They kept this from me?

Gyr chewed the inside of his cheek. "I'm still your prosort, am I not?"

"You are. And I am Duke of Lah-Tsarra." A storm gathered across Malus's brow. "Why do you find it necessary to continue down this path of insult and injury at every turn? I do what I must in the way *I* see fit." His chest swelled then deflated. His tone softened. "I love you, Gyr. Truly, I do. But you're getting on my nerves. In all but title, Caltheo is your equal now. I'm giving him opportunities to prove as much. Accept it, question it, whatever you will. But please, henceforth, do so in private."

A sudden chill penetrated into Gyr's bones. *Is the tent flap open?* Sodden were his movements as he swaddled himself in his fur-lined cloak. He glanced back. The tent's opening was lashed closed. *It's only me then.* A numb and frail thing. An old plow, gone to rust in a barren field. A broken blade after some forgotten battle, swallowed by earth and time.

What an old fool I've become. Useless. Childish.

With his hands clasped in his lap, he looked first at Caltheo, then at Malus, both men he considered surrogate sons. Both men he had pledged to protect and mentor. Both men now telling him to get out of the way.

The word *duty* rang in his ears, as hollow and empty as a freshly dug grave. Garlenna's face flashed across his mind. Now came his reckoning. Costs paid for sacrifices made. A father who left his daughter behind too easily. A father too easily left behind.

Gods, forgive me. Garlenna...forgive me.

He was thankful she wasn't there to witness his honor being tarnished.

"Of course, my lord. It will be as you command." Gyr saluted the duke. *Gratitude. The Sempyrean gods say I must show gratitude.* To Caltheo, he said, "You did well, Cupbearer. I'm honored by your success."

Despite the outward shift, the emptiness where purpose should be remained.

Three bandits were led in, bound at the wrists: a boy, a desiccated woman, and a hulking brute. Crownguard forced them to their knees in a row. A fourth bandit followed. Gagged, he thrashed between the straining arms of a pair of crownguard. Whoever had tied the cloth around his mouth had apparently done so with relish. A second length of rope stretched taut from the back of his head to a belt around his waist, forcing his head to arch backward at an awkward and painful angle. *So, he's bitten someone.*

"We did as commanded, Caltheo," a crownguard said. "Made it look like one wagon's wheel was broken and left it down the trail, away from the others with a hound beside it. Sure enough, they came for it. The half-dozen men waiting inside was on them quick but they killed one of ours."

Gyr cursed.

The crownguard shrugged as if to say it happens. "They also stabbed—"

Before the man could finish, there was a bellow outside the tent. Two of the crownguard turned in time to intercept a charging Halladorn. "You'll pay with your damn lives! Cut my dog—get the fuck off me!" The hound master shoved the dark-skinned soldier, but the rest of the crownguard were on him swiftly, securing him by the arms and neck.

"Cut—hurgh—my fuckin' dog!" The stump of a man managed to surge forward another step, fingertips brushing the hair of the kneeling boy's head.

"There will be justice, Halladorn!" Malus shouted over the ruckus. "But first you will calm yourself." The duke waited a beat as the hound master struggled and blustered. "Or would you like to be bound for the night?"

Animal wheezes issued from Halladorn's frothing mouth, flecks of white dappling his bushy red beard. "Fine! Fine, I say!" The crownguard eased their grips but kept themselves between the raging man and the captives. One snatched a dagger from Halladorn's belt, earning him a baleful look. The hound master hacked, spit a gob on the back of the head of the gagged man, who gave a gruff laugh in response.

"If there's justice," Halladorn said, "I want to be there for it. I want to see it done."

"You shall," said Malus D'Alzir. "Now, if you can't keep yourself under control, leave."

Halladorn straightened his tabard and beard, then nodded.

Malus stepped up beside Gyr, velvet cloak swirling about his legs. Dark hair tied back into a knot drew the skin of his face taut. *He would make a fine Crown Prince.* If Garlenna failed to find Barodane alive...

Gyr wondered if it might be a good idea to propose Malus as a replacement to the Ironlight line. Better him than a teenage girl, though still likely to end in civil war.

The duke leaned over to whisper in Gyr's ear. "What are the chances that these thieves stole from the mountain enclaves? Seems like that might be the cause of the Kurgish tracking party you ran across."

Before entering the life of a prosort of the Sempyrium, Gyr had served as a mercenary guiding merchants across the Shining Range. Sometimes they'd traded with the Kurgs of the mountain enclave, but on rare occasions, they'd been forced to fight off Outclan raiding parties. Excommunicated from the greater clans for crimes of spiritual dissent, these Kurgs banded together to survive. The common Namorite tended to associate the barbarous acts of the Outclans with *all* Kurgs. Gyr knew the differences between the groups all too well, and they were as different from one another as Kurgs were from any of the other Namorite races.

Gyr shuddered. Clever and ruthless, he'd watched a few men receive what was known as a "joker," a violent act in which a Kurg attempted to rip a man's jaw down hard enough that his mouth tore at the corners; it was rumored that the strongest Kurgs could tear it clean off. Those jokered weren't always dead first.

During the Great Betrayal, Gyr had seen Kurgs mobilize for war. No rag-tag group of savages. Honorable, brave, noble. Not disorganized, leaderless rabble, as historians would have Namorites believe. He'd watched them flank a Scothean sachar. Three hundred strong, the Kurgs moved as one astride their stout-legged ebhor, maneuvering down impossible terrain with such ease that many rested their hands on their thighs. They had rolled the flank as fast as parchment burned.

With a curt shake of his head, Gyr shot down Malus's theory. "No common bandits could steal from them. Certainly not ones who could then be caught so easily."

"What about the thing in the woods?" Malus whispered.

Gyr nodded. "We shall see if it was them soon enough. Though it may come to tactics unpleasant." They exchanged a long look. Neither flinched.

"So be it." Malus squared his shoulders to face the bandits, arms crossed. "Look at me." They did, and he pointed at the bone-thin boy on the end. "How old are you?"

"Thirteen," the boy's voice shook. "I'm sorry, my lord. I'm so sorry. Have mercy."

"Why are you raiding my wagons?"

"We—uh—we ain't had much to eat in a while."

Gyr motioned to the bull-necked giant. "How do you explain him, then?"

Wide-eyed, the boy gulped noisily. "Fullor, milord? You should have seen him before. He's gotten smaller since we left."

"Left from where?" asked Gyr. The boy stared dumbly, then his chin dropped to his chest. He cast furtive glances at the gagged man beside him. A bushy, drooping mustache rimmed yellowed teeth that bit down on the gag. *The boy's afraid of him. Their leader.*

"Tell us where you're from!" Gyr shouted. A guard slapped the boy's ear.

"Agh!" The boy spoke in a rush. "Kiyahd!"

"Are there more of you?" Gyr said. "Speak now and do not stop or my man will continue to drub you every time you hesitate. No lies!"

"Yes, milord. Uh—" A blow caused the boy to squeak. "No more of us. Kiyahd, we fled Kiyahd. I can't—agh!—I can't think, milord!"

Another heavy strike found his head. "Enough." Gyr waved a hand. "He's given us truth. These others can fill in the details." He pointed at the gagged man. "What's your name?"

When they removed both gag and lash that had been keeping his head craned backward, the mustached man stretched his neck. He jerked his chin to one side to crack his neck. "I'll tell you what you want, but if this filthy bastard touches my head, well." He glared at Malus. "You can fucking drub me to death cause I won't say another word. I done nothing wrong." He puckered his lips, then shot a stream of spit across the ground. The guard behind him drew a dagger as the gob hit the floor in front of Malus.

The Lord of Brighthaven arched an eyebrow. "Let him speak." After a pause, he added, "But if he spits again, cut his tongue out."

The man held Malus in a flinty stare. "I'm Durn. The Hardheart, these others call me. I don't got my honor plate with me, but I'm shadowguard. A farmer now, but I served in the Namorite regulars during the Great Betrayal as a pikeman." He looked Malus over. Chuckled and sneered. "You're Duke Malus D'Alzir. Ironic."

"How so?"

"Your Maw-spawned twat of a brother is who got me here."

"You insult my blood?" Malus said. "That's foolish."

"At least I didn't spit." Durn the Hardheart was hatred twisted into stone. "As I was saying, your brother needs my dagger between his eyes."

Malus cleared his throat. "I've heard enough."

Before they could get the gag onto the man, the Hardheart stood, forcing the crownguards to press him back down. Like a wild horse, he reared. "He doubled the taxes on my land. Land I bought with blood. Blood in service to Namarr, blood spilled by my friends, blood taken from foes on the tip of my pike and dagger. My damned own blood it cost me. And your regal pig brother fucked me out of it." Lord Malus gave no reaction, betrayed no emotion, only held up a hand. The crownguard waited. White flecks of spit rimmed the corners of Durn's mouth as he stopped struggling.

"You act as though taxes are uncommon."

Hardheart scoffed. "Protection against Kurgs, the tax collector said. Farms being raided on the outskirts of Kiyahd. So fucking what? No shiny cunt knight were going to come to my aid, so I told him I'd keep paying the same taxes I had been. That I'd defend my land my own damn self.

"So when the tax collector came back a month later with a writ to forfeit my land, I strangled him. Only the holdguard with him didn't think that was right, so they arrested me. The boy too just for being there. He didn't do anything wrong." Durn the Hardheart's volume rose, words cracking like a whip. "Now you tell me, standing there in your velvet fucking robes, how it's just that men like you get to decide for men like me when we should starve to death rather than die by a Kurg's club? How is it justice for you to tell me how I'll die, eh?"

The Hardheart's chest heaved, the tendons of his neck corded. The crownguard with the dagger wrapped his fingers more tightly around the hilt.

"You're right, Durn," Malus said. "You are the truest of heroes. Slaying a man so you don't have to pay a little more money to protect the lands of those less able to fight. Truly, the deepest sense of justice and morality."

Jaw clenched, Hardheart maneuvered the skin of his face around his mouth, making his mustache writhe. "All I know is if it weren't for Fullor breaking free of his bindings, we'd all be rotting in jail."

Gyr turned his attention to Fullor. "You broke your bindings?"

Blocky chin nearly touching the mounded muscle of his chest, the man gave a brief nod. Gyr exchanged a silent question with Malus. The duke dipped his head in assent.

"Go on," Gyr said. "Do it now, if you can."

The Hardheart's head snapped toward Fullor. Then he scrutinized Gyr.

Striated muscle clenched along Fullor's exposed shoulders. The cheesecloth shirt did little to hide the shape of him. Shoulders the size of spade heads bulged as the sound of stretching rope filled the pavilion. Fullor let out a quiet wheeze, the veins of his neck becoming cords of reddened rope, his body stiffening under the strain in a rictus of struggle.

The room froze. A crownguard gave some space and bent his knees in anticipation of a fight.

A marked twang. A sudden exhalation of breath. Fullor sat on his heels, arms drifting to either side from behind his back.

One of the guards whistled. Another said, "Fucking monster."

Malus stepped forward. "Indeed, he is."

"Strong. But stupid," said Gyr. "An intelligent man would have faked his attempt, then broke them later and fled."

Durn the Hardheart cursed. Gyr motioned for him to be gagged.

"I can't run no more, milord. Besides." Fullor glanced at the withered woman. "My wife's health...she's not been well since we fled."

It was then that Gyr finally noticed how pale and ragged the woman looked. It was hard to imagine the two to be well-matched even if she was healthy. She looked older than Fullor by ten years and drug addled. The type few sober men might couple with.

"What is your profession?" he asked Fullor.

"I owned a slaughterhouse, milord. Story similar to Durn's, 'cept I couldn't choose whether to give what the tax collector wanted. Wildrot took my whole lot of pigs two months ago. Me and my wife were arrested after that. I promise, I wanted to pay, but I couldn't."

"A slaughterhouse was it? For pigs?" Caltheo came to stand to one side of the man. "How long have you been following our wagons?"

Gyr knew his cupbearer inquired because of the pile of flesh in the woods.

"A few days is all," said Fullor.

Caltheo's eyes narrowed. "You lie."

Frowning, the monstrous man shook his head. A sword came to rest on his shoulder from one of the crownguard behind him, causing him to pale. "I swear to you. Only a few days. Before that—"

"My lord Malus," Caltheo said. "You heard him. He owned a slaughterhouse for pigs. Pigs! They're liars. I believe they followed us from Brighthaven and slew whatever was in those woods. The swift end of a blade would be the wisest course of action."

Gyr flinched.

All eyes turned to Malus D'Alzir as he took a pewter flagon of wine in hand, then paused, tapping a finger against the handle. "I'll take it under advisement,

Caltheo. Thank you. While I'm deciding the wisest course of action, why don't you attend to your other duties."

The skin around Caltheo's nose twitched, then he bowed deeply and left.

"My lord—" Gyr began.

Lord Malus slammed the pewter flagon against the table. When he turned back around, his demeanor was rigid. For a breathless moment, Gyr assumed Caltheo's extreme suggestion might have taken hold, that the order for summary execution was to follow.

"Who killed my man at the baggage train?"

Fullor looked sidelong at Durn the Hardheart, incriminating the man. Durn forced a laugh through his gag.

"And the dog?" Malus asked, eyes drifting from the Hardheart back to Fullor.

The hulking man hesitated. "Is the animal dead? If it is, I am sorry, milord." He puffed out his chest. "I will pay for it."

A crownguard scoffed. Gyr shook his head.

"I swear it, milord. I was a soldier once—will be one again if you'd have me. I've never done a bad thing in my life except this, and that's only because my wife is unwell. You see her, don't you? She's sick. You'd do the same if it were you."

The Lord of Brighthaven nodded. "I understand, and yet my hound master will not sleep again until there is justice for his animal. The dog is lame but not dead, correct? Yes, good."

The dark-skinned crownguard nudged Fullor's wife with a booted toe. "We found a bloody dagger on this one."

Fullor shook his head. "No, milord. I stabbed the dog. I'll take what punishment you have to give."

Gyr's heart sank. Fullor was a good man on the wrong side of luck. He held up a hand. "Perhaps we should let your brother deal them their justice. Consequences dispensed through the appropriate channels."

"Agreed," Malus said. "We'll take them to Marus for their justice. Since the big one cannot be bound, he will be kept at the front of the retinue under guard, along with the boy. His wife at the rear. If you break your bindings or attempt to flee, she dies. Understand?"

Fullor nodded. *A monster in size only.*

Staring at the back of the woman's head who'd wounded the warhound, Halladorn snorted displeasure.

"I'm not finished," said the duke. "There will be justice tonight." He nodded at Durn the Hardheart. "We cannot waste resources on a twice-damned murderer. This one will be dealt with. Now."

Malus squared his shoulders to the kneeling man. "Durn the Hardheart, for the crime of murdering a loyal crownguard in my service, as well as a tax collector in service to my brother, the lord of Kiyahd, I sentence you to death."

The Hardheart forced laughter into his gag. Terse. Grim. Muffled. All the while he held his glare on Duke Malus. The guards set to pulling their prisoners up by their hair and armpits. Durn kicked a cloud of dust from the carpet as he went.

"Let Caltheo know what is required of him," Malus said to the receding crownguard.

"My Lord," Gyr said. "Allow me. Caltheo has the camp to oversee. Allow me to do this one thing. For both of you."

Malus lay a hand on his shoulder with a somber smile. "So be it."

Chapter Twenty-Six

BETTER LEFT ALONE

A mile from Hawk's Keep, Zadani stepped off the trail in search of rising gold mushrooms.

Frog's finger looked similar except for the angle of the gills and that it grew in isolated patches away from other fungi. Rising gold mushrooms, on the other hand, appeared in tight-packed clusters. If Zadani ate the wrong one, she'd be sick for a week rather than experience the host of benefits, including but not limited to, increased energy, mental acuity, and faster physical recovery.

She needed all of those benefits and more.

A persistent ache clenched her low back. Around her knees and ankles, the joints had tensed to the point that she now walked with a limp. With night closing in and an urgent meeting with Jasso still ahead of her, she was in a sorry state.

Wind kicked leaves across her path and set the trees to swaying. Ivy-wrapped trunks met her hand as she traversed patches of sedge and lichen-covered logs. Behind a trillium flower, she found a cluster of rising golds.

Hunting knife in hand, she crouched to reap the mushroom, then stuffed a handful in her pocket. She withheld two, popping them in her mouth and eating them raw. Bitter and earthy, they slid down her throat.

A broad, gleaming cap to her left gave her pause. Using her knife tip, she tilted back the mushroom's top. Velvet truffles were a delicacy, the perfect garnish for Duke Malus when he arrived. But hunting the mushroom was quite dangerous. In low light, velvet truffles were easily mistaken for death dealer. This one was the latter, its frills squiggly rather than straight.

Trained by the royal cooks of Alistar, Zadani knew if one were to scratch the cap and then suck their fingernail, it would make them instantly ill, while more than that could cause death.

The hem of Zadani's linen shift filled her hand as she sawed a strip free with her knife. *Impeccable caution.* She wrapped a cap of death dealer in the cloth and then tucked it into a pocket.

The library smelled of paper and dust and the sweet, rosy scent of Jasso Jackolo. The Val scholar hunched over a book. Candlelight threw shadows into the corners, and creases into the face of a flustered-looking seneschal. The woman watched Jasso like a cat watching an injured mouse.

He spotted Zadani. "Ho there!" He waved her over as the seneschal shushed him and glared daggers into his back.

"Don't mind her," Jasso said. "She has a warped idea of what learning involves." His voice fell low, though still not low enough for the woman to miss what he said. "I spend much of my time in her silent little haven. To say she's tired of me is an understatement by degrees of magnitude. Isn't that right?"

The seneschal slammed a book down on the table.

The woman's ire seemed aimed solely at Jasso. When Zadani approached her with a smile and sweet tones, asking her to give them a moment alone, the aging seneschal left gracefully in the way of those overcompensating in their kindness to show hatred for another nearby.

The scholar laughed. "I feel for her, truly. I'd have caved my head in with a candlestick by now if I were her. Alas, she's too sensitive. A lovely woman I suspect. That is, when she's not being a persnickety crone about quiet."

"Jasso," Zadani said. "Have you ever known a form of shame you *didn't* leap into head first?"

He stood then bowed with a flourish. "Zadani Innan, you are a new friend but a very perceptive one. Because of the way I am, there are few in this world who seek to know me better. On two counts, you have struck target with arrow. The first, your manner of dealing with me—endearing rudeness—a bullseye. The truth of my shame-seeking nature, the second. Bravo!" He clapped as if mocking the seneschal in her absence. "Now, what can I do for you? I'm on a tight schedule."

"A tight schedule? Aren't you just reading?"

"Yes, and I have a great deal more reading yet. Two books a day, without fail. I've been doing it for decades now. The mind, as I see it, is no different than the muscle of a master swordsman. He trains regularly to become stronger, quicker, embedding the memory of movement into his bones so that reflex comes to him without hesitation in the moment of violence. I absorb information as fast and oft as possible to do the same. And then, I relax, trusting my subconscious mind to know answers before my conscious mind ever could." Jasso thrust a phantom blade into an invisible enemy. "My lunges and ripostes are wit and fact, unparalleled because of my training diligence. In my estimation, this is true intellect. A vast well of information one has access to combined with the frequency with which they draw from it. I know what others don't. Often, I find I know it before I know that I knew it."

Taking a seat at the table across from Jasso, Zadani smiled. "Quite impressive." She searched the room for anyone else lurking about as she reached into her boot.

Jasso raised an eyebrow. "You're acting rather serious. Has the seneschal rubbed off—"

"I need that well of knowledge you claim to have." She spread a crumpled roll of parchment out onto the table. Under grumbling protest, she pried his book from him and then grabbed another, stacking them on either end of the parchment. Then she recreated the hoof prints from the north wood with the piece of charcoal.

When the stylus dropped from her fingers, Jasso cocked his head, eyes darting back and forth between Zadani and the sketch. "The last time I helped you, my illicit drug activities were nearly shared before an entire court. Actually, it was almost shared that I violated a tomb on the burial grounds of one of the most powerful lords in Namarr." He crossed his arms. "So forgive me if I sprint suddenly from the room."

"It is the last favor I ask. I promise." Leaving her mouth, the words felt empty. *I'll ply as many favors from him as required if it leads me to Hadir's killer.*

Jasso drummed his fingers on the table. "You're lucky I've always struggled to say no. To all that has come my way, I've said yes. I'm far too curious for my own good. It's both my greatest strength and a thrice-damned curse, my curiosity. It's led me to great things I never could have dreamed of doing. Possibility is a door, I tell myself, the word 'yes' its key. 'Break into a tomb, Jasso.' Yes. 'Inspect my husband's body, Jasso.' Surely, for you are a grieving widow. Why not? 'Tell me what these tracks I've drawn are, Jasso.' A pleasure. More than happy to incriminate myself in whatever trouble I'm presented." He slapped a palm on the leather bound book before him. "I've just had a revelation I'll now share. A new maxim. No amount of intellect can serve as substitute for a pinch of good sense."

Zadani studied the man, twirling a curl of hair between thumb and forefinger. "You act as if I force you, Jasso. I, a commoner. You, a rich and powerful man. You could say no." She worried her statement might scare him off, but if she wanted his help, it might come easier if he saw it as voluntary.

Jasso slouched to one side and slung an arm over the back of the chair. "Sympathy. Foolishness. But more than anything, it really is my curiosity. I can't help my penchant for understanding. Finding answers is an obsessive impulse." Pale-blue eyes rose to meet Zadani's. "Are you a unimist, by chance?"

She shrugged. "I was raised as a Follower of the Sempyrean but I find unimist teachings more useful."

"Ah." He traced a circle in the air. "I do love the religious freedom of Namorites. Oppress a thing and it will eventually find its way free, won't it? Well, anyway, unimist monks talk of one's true nature. The triangle of being that connects the Fire, the Eye, and the Hand. Or in layman's terms, one's inner passion, one's inner truth, and the alignment of the two through actions taken. The concept is in some ways too linear for me. Nevertheless, it carries commendable value as a simple framework for living life.

"While humans are the most complex species, we can apply this principle to animals as well. Thunder angel jellies bob throughout the Sea of Psollus, giving off a nimbus of light that is easily spotted and easily avoided. However, that does not stop a territorial shark from attacking them when they light up, despite the fact that thunder angels don't compete with the sharks for food, nor are they a food source themselves. Of course, as soon as these sharks bite the jellies, they die, zapped full of paralytic poison. So why do they do this?"

"Stupidity."

"An argument can be made that you've hit the crux of the matter in its simplest form. But this is a unimist teaching, so I'll drag it out." He inspected a fingernail, chewed it. "Unimists say that sharks attack the jellies because it is in their nature to do so, even if it means doom. A territorial shark is—well—rather territorial. Born as a preeminent predator, it lives out said truth, and it ensures the promulgation of this naturalistic, preordained alignment. Thus, it attacks anything which fails to observe the boundaries of its territory. You, me, the sharks, the thunder angels...none of us can escape our true nature, Zadani." Jasso exhaled. "And not with all the intelligence in the world could I escape mine." A somber smile split his well-groomed beard as he leaned forward. "When I see thunder angels, I simply *must* take a bite."

Zadani was willing to lie, or kill, to see Hadir avenged. A passing question formed a lump in Zadani's throat. *What does that say of my true nature?*

Jasso inspected the image. "A shoddy rendering...but still informative. They look like ebhor tracks."

"Ebhor?"

He nodded. "It appears you've drawn the cloven-hoof prints of giant rams, bred for centuries to be rather large and rather smart compared to other bovids.

The Kurgs of the mountain enclaves ride them." He paused. "Why have you drawn them?"

Kurgs?

She told him of her dreams and her journey into the north wood to find the maple tree. Jasso listened intently, a hooked finger pressed against his lips. Zadani considered the moment in court when Sir Vallabathus had shared news from Staghill about Kurg mobilization. "Could it be that Hadir was killed by Kurgs?"

"If he was, it would make things...interesting."

"What do you mean?"

He shrugged. "How many tracks did you find?"

"I don't know. The tracks went in every direction as if they led their mounts in circles around the same spot, so it was difficult to tell how many."

Making a thinking sound, Jasso rubbed his palms together. "It takes a great deal for Kurgs to come this close to a stronghold. To commit murder on the doorstep of Kiyahd would be an act of open war. Furthermore, with nothing to raid for miles in any direction, and with no clear routes to their temples from here to the Winding Way, it makes little sense. Less sense still to kill a single man. No offense Zadani, but as good as your husband was at hunting and tracking, Kurgs are better. Even a party of twenty or more—which it sounds like this was—could have avoided him with little effort."

Zadani fought to contain her frustration. "You're suggesting it wasn't Kurgs who killed my husband even though their tracks litter the ground where he died?"

"No." Jasso studied the rafters and shook his head. "I'm saying it wouldn't make sense if that *is* what happened. To know whether the Kurgs and Hadir were there at the same time...I would have to see for myself."

She'd heard enough. "There's more." Against her better judgment, she told him of her interaction with Nymon the Lech.

Redness crept into Jasso's cheeks, a bloody contrast to his snow-white beard. He removed his hat, bald pate gleaming in the candlelight. He shook out his long hair, and with a grunt, tossed his wide-brimmed hat onto the table. "We should warn Lord Marus."

To overstep her bounds again would, at best, reveal that she hunted Hadir's killer. And that might stymie all progress. At worst, she might land herself inside a prison cell for subverting the investigation of Marus's holdguard.

"Warn him of what?" she said. "Of an imminent Kurg attack? Already, he sets patrols along the borders." She pushed off the table and stood. "Or should I warn him of some conspiracy I have no evidence for but my own scribblings? You already saw how that went. And remember this, Nymon and his men *are* holdguard. In his own words, Marus said he trusted them with his life—that they act and speak on his behalf. It would be the words of a paranoid widow against those of his own soldiers."

Jasso crossed his arms. "Zadani..." She could tell he meant to convince her to stray from her current course. "Your husband's passing is a tragedy—"

"Murder, Jasso. He did not simply pass. He was murdered."

Jasso pushed to his feet, then leaned onto the table with his fists. "You have a good life, Zadani. A safe life." She couldn't decide whether he pleaded with her or lectured her. "In all my travels, that is one thing I've known to be of value to all people, and yet, a rarity for far too many. You have a kind lord, worthy of your trust. You should be grateful—"

Her palm struck his cheek with a resounding snap. The scholar yelped then grabbed her wrist as she drew back to deliver another slap. Tense all over, fueled by rage, Zadani tried twisting out of the scholar's grasp to strike again.

"Stop!" he hissed. "Zadani, stop!"

She jerked free of him and thrust a finger in his face. "Tell me I should be grateful again and I'll do more than slap you. My husband is dead. If you think I care about my own life..." She harrumphed. "Death would come as a relief if it meant my love—my innocent, kindhearted love—got the justice he deserves. Until that happens, I trust no one. Not even Lord Marus."

A line split Jasso's brow. "You conduct shadowy business beneath his roof. You even gather evidence against his men."

"That is exactly why no one must know. Please, Jasso." Lips quivering, tears gathering, she locked eyes with him. "Please. I need this. For Hadir."

Jasso blinked then lowered slowly back into his chair. "What have you gotten me into, Zadani Innan?" He broke eye contact, refusing to meet her gaze again as he stared at the rows of books lining the walls.

"That's what I mean to find out. Starting with Nymon the Lech." She rolled up the parchment and stuffed it into her boot. "Have faith. As you've recently learned, a woman's rage is a dangerous thing to behold. All will end as desired."

"Right." Jasso stared at his limp hands, palms upturned on the table. "Right."

It seems our true nature is shared. We take bites of things better left alone.

CHAPTER TWENTY-SEVEN

THE FIRST SERMON

Teeming masses filled the grandstands of the vippedrome of Sesyrs. From dwellings low and high, they lined the oblong arena situated on a low plateau spanning the base of Darkfall's keep. Shrines to each of the Holy Instruments, Acramis, Jathos, Ikarai, Uhlvath, Niriti, Aurghov, and Guluhd, huddled around its rim.

Valka had few doubts the largest and most inglorious of them all would soon be Siddaia's. The god of truth, they were calling him. If Siddaia had allowed it, Rhul the Red, and the Awakened, Gishek Ghuul, would have already ordered its construction.

At the center of the vippedrome sat a columnar platform from which Scoth kings had viewed raek races each spring, as well as melees and contests of sachari during the other seasons.

Now, Valka stood atop it alongside Siddaia and his Blessed Cadre of Awakened. The people lining the rails of the arena stared down at a bristling wall of Grimshields arrayed on the dusty racecourse. Rhul the Red patrolled the space between.

A week had passed since the bloodshed. In that time, Valka hadn't heard from Essuhd or his Shadii.

From the Raeklord of Darkfall, he'd heard a great deal. Daily council meetings, in which Valka and Rhul saw to the transition of power, left the general with his fill of the traitor's face. A cloying taste tainted Valka's mouth whenever he sat in peace beside the duplicitous man.

Siddaia, meanwhile, had yet to be present at one of the meetings. "Contemplation" was the word used to excuse him upon each occasion by one of the Awakened from his Blessed Cadre.

Valka imagined him seated and smiling upon the steel-wrought flower throne. Now, he saw him for the second time. Right before he addressed his people, not as a newly crowned king or an aspiring emperor but as a demi-god. A messiah. A gift from the gods to their most favored children.

Valka saw the way the low dwellers looked warily at Siddaia's Blessed Cadre. Rhul had told him of each's history. Daimos, the footless woman who flew, had been a young cat burglar in Valat when she'd fallen from a building and shattered her legs so badly that a surgeon's apprentice from the Academies had needed to remove them.

The black woman, Zantheppi, was a Malzacy-born caravan guide. While Valka hadn't seen any demonstrations of her power, Rhul claimed she controlled water.

Then there was Gishek Ghuul. He'd been a prominent member of a family of ore barons at Stormwal before he'd gone missing three years prior. Easing through the air around Siddaia were a pair of lenses of hammered steel, six feet high and half again as wide. Gishek directed these protective shields to be on either side of Siddaia at all times.

And of course, the Black Hand Marionette was not to be missed. The salt-and-pepper beard and hair of the striking Namorite caught the gaze of every Scoth who looked his way. Except for an ample gut from ample wine, the man was powerfully built—a stout and imposing figure. Yet it was his hands, char-black from fingertips to elbows, that unnerved the multitudes.

Valka swept the crowd a final time. Terrace dwellers, the rich and powerful, were forced to mix in with those from lower dwellings. The poor. The starved. Those who had so recently tried wetting their knives with the blood of Valka's neighbors. Soldiers were on strict orders to keep the crowd affable, but that didn't keep the disgusted sneers off the faces of the rich, nor reduce the hard and covetous stares from the low dwellers.

Much to Valka's chagrin, Nera had elected to stay at home in her quarters, though now, seeing the tension in the crowd, he felt mild relief. Since their discussion, his daughter had enacted a moratorium on all communication with him. From Yanos's reports, it sounded as though she was doing well otherwise.

With Gishek Ghuul and his floating shields a step behind, the boy messiah sauntered over to Valka, his doe-eyed gaze never straying as he came to a stop before the general. His breath rolled up into Valka's face, odorless but for a hint of honey and lemon. "Would you do the honors of announcing me to our people, Ikarai?"

Without hesitation, Valka dipped his chin in obeisance. "Of course, my Light." He stepped to the center of the circular platform but before he could begin, a soft hand took his own, tugging him around. Valka surprised himself by not jerking free of the grip. Then again, he knew who it was.

The boy's eyes flitted over him. He squeezed Valka's hand reassuringly. "She'll come around."

Valka frowned. "Thank you, my Light."

"You are a great father to her. And to our nation." Siddaia smiled. "I am honored to count you among my allies."

Guilt skewered him. *By what measure do I count him criminal? My namesake, Ikarai the Golden Scepter, united Scothea by way of bloodshed, yet this kindly boy does it with his words.*

Betrayal spanned layers of immorality. A broken oath and a bloody knife, separated only by degrees of commitment. *Can a duty to one's nation supplant a duty to one's monarch and still be deemed the purer path?*

He inhaled slowly and turned to face the crowd.

The masses rumbled with disquiet. When they saw General Ikarai Valka at attention with the legendary Mournfang slung at his hip, a hush fell over them.

"Proud and worthy Scoths!" His voice boomed like scattered wind throughout the vippedrome. He shot a look over a shoulder at Daimos knowing she'd somehow amplified his voice with her powers. "Without the stability of tradition to hold you, you may now wonder at your future and worry. You may fear that more bloodshed will come to the doorsteps of your homes. You may hold your children tight with no way of knowing if you'll see them alive at week's end." Nera's pursed lips filled his mind's eye for a heartbeat. He didn't care if she was angry with him, so long as she remained alive. "Many of you—many of us—have faced these same dark thoughts. I am here to tell you that your fears may finally rest." *Last the Fire, that in the darkest hours unite...* "The Arrow of Light has come!"

A large portion of the crowd erupted, hands slapping skyward, mouths stretched into joyous gaps, bowing and kissing their fingertips in supplication, while the rest shot furtive glances at their neighbors.

Valka bowed and gave Siddaia the center of the platform. The messiah meandered up to the ledge and then shocked the crowd by sitting so that his legs dangled over the platform's lip. Shoulder-length hair caught the wind as he surveyed his people. Never had he looked more childlike. And yet, it worked.

He refuses the image of a conquering zealot, and instead, beseeches their humanity. He wants them to know he's one of them.

"I never wanted this," he said. Unlike Valka, the Arrow of Light didn't need Daimos to amplify his voice. Abject silence carried it farther than the Awakened ever could. "I really didn't. All I've ever wanted is peace. To see each of us love one another the way we're meant to."

The messiah's head drooped, shoulders hunching as he stared between his legs at the racecourse below. "But one who denies their gifts to the world, so betrays it. All the love and hope and contentment they could ever hold fades from reach. They become martyrs to their own selfishness. And make no mistake, fear *is* selfish. The withholding of one's gift is a crime against your mothers, your fathers, your siblings, your children. It is a crime committed against the entire world, for it is a better one when all give freely and wholly of themselves. Anything less is betrayal."

The final word struck at Valka's conscience like an adder snaring a rat.

The Arrow of Light's voice took on a condemning tone as he stood. "Hiding who you are is a poison that seeps from your cowardly heart down into the earth around you. Any who stand in your presence become tainted with your indolence. And the Sempyrean sees. Our Holy Instruments are disgusted by those who squander what they've worked to create for them. Do not let the low-minded convince you of anything different. I have starved! I have bled! I have been alone! My family is dead. Yet here I am, telling you..."

He paused, fists clenched at his sides. He dropped them, shoulders relaxing, and then leveled a finger at the crowd, moving it slowly from place to place as if picking out individuals. "You. Are. No. Different."

Siddaia started to pace, turning back to his cadre of war leaders and Awakened. "Witness the dawn of a new world," he whispered so only they could hear.

Tingles ran up Valka's spine as the messiah paced back to the center of the platform, the crowd held in rapt attention. *No matter how she feels about Siddaia, I wish Nera were here to see this.*

The crowd ringing the vippedrome seemed to hold its breath as if they feared to make a sound and miss an anticipated word. Valka was unsurprised to note that Siddaia had not once mentioned his rule nor King Rathon. He hadn't even acknowledged the grief or bloodshed caused in his name. *He sets their sights on the next horizon.*

"Do you see?" The messiah's hands drifted from his sides, palms upturned.

A strong gust brushed his hair over a shoulder and set his cuff to flapping. Valka glanced at Daimos. Her eyes bled white light perpetually so she could fly, making it impossible to tell if she'd aided in the theatrical timing of the wind.

"I can be only me. I am an innocent, devoid of impurity, for I live out my gifts. I see the truth of all things. I am guided by something greater. The Holy Instruments—the gods—protect me with Awakened so that I might share this sermon with you. So that *we* might change the world. My gifts brought me here to light the way forward. The way is illuminated for you to follow...if you listen."

He inhaled, calm smoothing the creases of his face. "All the human soul desires is an illusion, a path different from the one they walk. A path without suffering, without pain, without loss, without change. A path deviant from humanity itself. In order to transcend and know the true nature of your being, you need this very experience. Yet you try to avoid it. You strive and scuttle to amass wealth and power, but this makes you no king. You stalk the vapors of beauty, perfection, and admiration, but you are no deity. You sacrifice your soul on the altars of religion, but you are no slave. You fight for control of others, with whip and fist and blade, but you are no villain. You let your hearts be steered toward these fallacies out of fear, vanity, and avarice, out of desperation to escape death's inevitable touch only to be broken upon the shores of life's most inevitable truth.

"Let go your illusions of security. Allow me to show you what lies in the depths. There, you will find a shining pearl of truth amid the pitch-dark waters. The truth that you are human... Loss is your whetstone, suffering the cleansing fire, pain the tumbler ever polishing the jewel that is your soul. The entire world walks a path of illusion, but by my side, All shall be free of it. Through me alone *we shall awaken.*"

A dream-like feeling slid silken fingers over Valka's body and cradled his consciousness. A foreign entity, it seemed, but he knew it to be the potency of the moment. A clear, low ringing filled his ears as Siddaia's sermon came to an end.

Most wept. Many fell to their knees and begged. For forgiveness, he assumed.

Rhul, the mightiest soldier in Scothean history, sobbed like a battered woman, face buried in his hands.

Meanwhile, Siddaia smiled and watched them all like a grandsire in the dusk of life observing his grandchildren at play. Both high dwellers and low poured from the grandstands, the labels of station cast off, and together, they flooded the racecourse. Raek cavalry flanking the platform hissed, rearing in alarm. The knights mounted on them hauled on barbed reins for control as the masses swarmed the vippedrome's center.

The heat and energy of roaring adulation rolled over Valka. Dizzied, he stumbled a step then eased to a knee so that he didn't fall off the columnar platform.

Three makes one, but only one makes free.

A half dozen chroniclers with worry-etched features were clambering up the spiraling stairs leading to the top of the platform, but a score of Grimshields urged them back down. Valka looked at the Arrow of Light, who wore an expression of open concern. That, too, was different. So many monarchs put on a false face for their people. The boy hid nothing.

Now, Siddaia seemed to notice the shifting energy of the crowd. The dissolution of order to something potentially dangerous, and none but he could shepherd them back from the brink of chaos. "Brothers and sisters! Peace!"

While the crying persisted, all eyes fixed on Siddaia, and seeing him speak, they drifted back into subdued stillness.

Such control.

"All of you shall have my blessing...in time. Henceforth, you will find me standing in this spot on every Fifthday. For now, find your way back home. My faithful warriors have food and clean water for you at the shrines of the Holy Instruments." That idea had been Valka's, begrudgingly presented for it helped the boy-messiah, but it also helped the people who suffered. Throughout Rathon's reign, he'd wished desperately for some similar show of good faith from government to the low dwellers.

Cheers and wails of thanks spread among them. King Rathon's food stores had been rationed out to last for a few months of sermons and ensure that those most faithful among the populace would be nourished. Those who starved and teetered on the verge of loyalty, too, would have incentive to hear him speak.

So grew his following.

From the top of the platform, Valka surveyed the vippedrome crowd as it dispersed. There was nowhere near enough room for the numbers he predicted for the next Fifthday sermon.

"You spoke well, Ikarai." Valka turned to find Siddaia watching him. "It would fill my heart to see your daughter at the next."

"Of course, my Light." Valka bowed. A frown stole across his face as he considered how he might get Nera to attend, so he held the bent posture until the Arrow of Light moved on to confer with his Blessed Cadre.

When he straightened, his heart skipped a beat. He thought he spied Essuhd's hooded face moving through the crowd.

CHAPTER TWENTY-EIGHT

HARD OF HEART

It was an hour until dawn and Gyr hadn't slept. Shivering, he clamped the collar of his cloak around his throat. Whether it was the cold or the deed to be done that sapped the warmth from him, he couldn't tell.

He shut his eyes and breathed, gentle snowfall alighting on his face and hands.

Nearby, Durn the Hardheart growled into his gag. A pair of crownguards held him by the arms and hair. Two others bearing torches stood across from each other in the small glade a stone's throw from camp. The chosen execution ground. Flames danced in the dark pools of Halladorn's eyes from where he watched.

Within the ring of firelight, the snow glowed a white-orange, but beyond it, the sparkling crust was tinged blue.

They forced the Hardheart to his knees.

"The path to light does border shadow," Gyr intoned. One of the crownguard nodded agreement as puffs of breath billowed up from the damp rag fixed around Durn's mouth. "Remove his gag."

The criminal tested his jaw, opening and closing it, then working it side to side. He thrust at Gyr with his chin. "Glad it's you doing it. You seem a reasonable man, though I've never been one for the Sempyrium's horse shit."

They stared at each other.

"You were a soldier once," Gyr said. "For that you have my respect. I understand the call to duty." *Too well. It has taken my daughter from me, and now, it'll take your head.*

The farmer-turned-murderer stared at the snow.

"You've allowed unspeakable crime to overshadow your honor. For that, you must pay the ultimate price." One of the crownguard holding a torch handed Gyr an ax. He took it into both hands, the wood warming his palms. "Durn the Hardheart, you are sentenced to die. Have you any last words?"

"Aye." His face clenched, one side of his mouth hiking upward as if snared by a fishhook. Eyes closing, he ground his teeth. When the Hardheart opened his eyes again, there was naught but hatred there. His words slashed the frigid air. "I curse the D'Alzir family. I wish for them the torment of the Maw Eternal. Pain, suffering and a sharp fall to ill-fortune. Hear hear! To the poverty, famine, and gruesome death of Duke Malus and his vermin-hearted brother, Lord Marus...cocksucker and rat king of Kiyahd."

He drew a sharp breath through his nose, mustering a shot of phlegm before hacking it into the snow. "There's your words, Father. Go on now. End me."

"Do it," Halladorn hissed from the edge of the glade.

Gyr stepped to the side of Durn, sucking back gobs of bitter saliva in his mouth. Heart racing, stomach churning, he throttled the ax-handle. *It's lighter than I expected.* He hoped it would be heavy enough to cleave the man's neck in a single swipe. Second strokes always made the grizzly deed harder. The blade shone in the torchlight, razor-sharp.

Blessings upon me, Ozoi, righteous god of the flames. Let me strike true and clean. And may you burn away the icy grasp of Nacronus on Durn's soul.

Gyr raised the ax, a wickedly curved shadow hanging over the Hardheart's face.

Gods of the Sempyrean, I beg your forgiveness. Protect me from the stain of the dark god's touch on my soul, for I act in your name, a shield against evil, a righteous and unwavering arm.

As Gyr prayed, the Hardheart let loose with greater vitriol. It seemed that all the fear and sadness, every scrap of resentment or regret he'd ever had, were being channeled into volcanic rage. "Curse Lord Marus! Curse Lord Malus! Curse the whole lot of you who do their dirty deeds. You'll get what's coming to you...sooner than you think!"

Gyr lowered the ax, eyes fluttering open. "What's that?"

Durn's face twisted into a sneer. His drooping mustache glistened with fat droplets of spit. "I was gonna die out here anyway. Fullor...his dumb cunt wife. The boy. You and your lord. Your corpses are bound for the grave. Same as mine."

Gyr looked around the glade and then dropped to a creaking knee beside the Hardheart. "Tell me what you mean or I'll start with your fingers and toes." Gyr was so close he could feel the warmth of Durn's breath. Their eyes locked. Gyr's tone was flat. "It could be a long night for you."

The Sempyrium had trained him well in the ways of prolonging death. The moral trade-off of inducing suffering for one person in order to reduce suffering for many others was a necessary principle drilled into prosorts. Otherwise, duty became a clouded thing.

"Oh ho. I heard you prosort types were more spies than priests." Durn lowered his tone, all accusation. "Didn't know you were torturers, too."

"We do what must be done to bear the light in a dark world." Gyr rested the ax on the man's shoulder. "Even if it means occasionally walking in shadow."

A smile peeled back from ocher teeth beneath the Hardheart's drooping mustache. He gave a bark of harsh laughter. "You would tell yourself that, wouldn't you? Anyway, what I say won't change your fate a damn lick." He hesitated. "Tracks. Ebhor tracks. From here to Kiyahd. Hundreds of 'em. Lord Marus wasn't lying when he said he needed more money to fight the savages."

Stepping back, Gyr raised his ax.

The Hardheart grinned wide. "Got what you were looking for, *priest*?" His eyes danced with satisfaction. "It's coming! War is coming! War! War! War! I hope all you highborn cocksuckers drown in your own blood and guts!"

Gyr's voice was hollow and weak. "Where?"

"Everywhere. Nowhere. Let's just say I kept my group close to yours for safety's sake." Durn dropped his head forward, exposing a hair-matted neck. "Now best get to hacking, priest. I ain't got all night."

The path to light does border shadow...and someone must walk it.

Duty stomped a foot forward, sent the ax whistling downward in a cleaving arc. The Hardheart's head jumped from his shoulders, rolled, slopping gore into the snow as it went.

Like the torso, Gyr hung there for a heartbeat, rigid and unmoving. Then, he fell to one knee beside the body where it crumpled. Legs twitched and hands flexed as Durn's corpse coped with the loss of its head.

Gyr closed his eyes and prayed to the Sempyrean for their light, their und erstanding...their forgiveness. If they answered, he did not hear them. A single voice claimed his mind, that of Durn the Hardheart. *If he spoke truth, Sir Raius and his outriders are gone.*

The snow welcomed Gyr's fist with a stale crunch. In his gut, he knew the man hadn't lied. They needed to abandon their journey to Kiyahd. *We need to race south to the outpost at Staghill.*

Gyr pressed a cold, clenched fist to his forehead. The coolness felt good when nothing else did. Grounding. They needed to ditch their wagons, their tents, everything but their arms and armor and ride hard if they were to survive. Even then, those mounted might be the only ones to make it.

At any cost, Lord Malus must survive.

And at any cost, he will.

"Father." One of the holdguard looked at Durn's head in the snow, the frozen image of horror seeming to give a moment of breathless pause before continuing, hot breath gushing in the torchlight. "Lord Malus said to bury him."

"Yes." Gyr rose, searched for Halladorn but the hound master had gone. The thoughts lurking at the back of his mind lent every shadow an unsettling weight. "Do what you must but be quick about it. The shallower..." His gaze fell to the pained, twisted face of Durn. "The better."

"The deed is done." With his hands clasped behind his back, Gyr convened with Caltheo, an informal passing of the torch of command. The morning council with Lord Malus was still Gyr's while the evening had been relinquished to Caltheo days prior.

A splash of dawn light cut through the smoke of a nearby cook fire. There was a hurriedness to the retinue as they broke camp. Brazen bandits were no threat—not to a hundred crownguard accompanied by a score of knights. The violation of their space, however, felt like the first drops of rain before a storm, and pulled attention toward more dangerous possibilities.

Defensive stakes clacked atop each other in the bed of a wagon. Men whispered as they donned arms and armor. Those ready quickest bustled through the cook line, wooden bowls reaching for two scoops of spiced porridge and a hard baked trencher to eat it with. A hint of sweetness pierced the earthier scent. Even so, Gyr had no appetite. *There is dire work to be done.*

With a sleepless night behind him, and a soul burdened by murder and impending battle, Gyr expected to feel worse than he did. Yet his body felt stronger than it had in years. His cough, too, had diminished, something he accredited to the reduction in his duties.

Never was there better evidence of the toll they took than Caltheo standing before him. Bulging eyes now carried dark pouches beneath. Once tan, healthy Lah-Tsarene skin appeared paler and sallower, the creases in his cheeks and forehead deeper.

Despite the worn down appearance of his cupbearer, Gyr was proud of the man. The camp was running smoother than he would have suspected. *Once he acclimates to the long marches and long nights spent in council, he'll be a fine prosort. I pray he doesn't make my same mistakes.*

Gyr leaned close to his cupbearer. "When was the last time you rested?"

Caltheo scratched his beard, sending a flurry of flakes of dry skin drifting onto his dark green tabard and bronze honor plate. Gyr noted the four arrows of the gods of light facing outward from the fist and broken chain of Namarr.

The fifth arrow of the dark god pointed back toward the center. Gyr couldn't help thinking it should point at him.

In his mind's eye, he watched Durn's head roll through the snow, a thin layer of powder gathering in the drooping mustache and clinging to stubble and eyelashes. *I bore the burden of murder for you.* Already taxed with his newfound duties, adding a dark blot on the soul could have undone Caltheo's progress.

It's never easy, but what needs to be done rarely is. "The path of light does border shadow," Gyr said.

Caltheo shot him a quizzical look.

"If you can't remember the last time you rested..." Gyr inhaled slowly, spoke like a teacher giving a lesson. "Life is a balance. Shadow needs light. Life needs death. A forged blade needs both cold and heat to temper it. And our best efforts need intervals with no effort at all." The image of an army of Kurgs flashed across his mind. *It may be the last rest we get for a while.*

"Thank you, Father. I'll heed your advice." With a brisk nod, Caltheo made for his tent.

Gyr made for Malus's.

Like the rest of the camp, he hastened in his duties. Unlike them, he bore a harrowing account. A grave seemed to open up in his belly, the worms there wriggling in search of something to consume. Gyr hoped to see them starve. *Malus must listen. He must act in accord with what needs to be done.* If he didn't, there would be real graves with real worms to fill them.

A pair of crownguard stood sentry at the entrance to Malus's pavilion instead of Sir Qel. Gyr saluted them then ducked inside with a rustle of cloth.

Malus peered at Gyr through dark tangles. A row of melted piles that reminded Gyr of the fleshy thing in the woods were all that remained of the night's candles. They sat on a table, their flames casting Malus's seated silhouette tall across the canvas behind. He rubbed his eyes and yawned. "I hardly slept. Give me a moment, if you please."

Disobeying the duke's request was no way to start. He waited as Malus dressed. Velal prepared hot tea for the duke, then raced out of the tent to some other task.

Malus beckoned him as he eased into a chair. "The prisoners are taken care of in the manner I ordered, I presume?"

"Indeed, my lord." Gyr's heart pounded. "There are other matters to discuss."

The cup of tea in the duke's hand slowed as it reached his mouth, steamy tendrils winding round his nose. "Pressing matters?"

Gyr pinned his shoulders back. "Hundreds of them, actually. We rush headlong into battle with Kurgs. I have had reports that there are hundreds of them between here and Ki—"

"Reports from who?" The cup descended to Malus's lap. "If Sir Raius has returned, why hasn't he come straight to me?"

Gyr glanced at the exit, gaze lingering. *Let Faith in the Sempyrean guide you, and with it, transcend all fear.* "It is the morning of the fifth day since I sent Sir Raius and his outriders on their mission. They are not back yet. I fear the worst."

Malus drew dark tangles behind one ear as he sipped his tea. "I'll ask again. Reports from whom?"

Gyr cleared his throat. "Durn the Hardheart."

"Ah." Malus flashed a wooden smile. "While my knight-captain's continued absence rankles me—has rankled me since the start—I find the words of a bitter criminal before his execution far from useful intelligence."

"My intuition says he told the truth." Gyr took a step forward, palms upraised at his sides. "We must make for the outpost at Staghill."

"Head south?"

"Yes. We send messages to Kiyahd for reinforcements to attend our position on the Winding Way and at Staghill, both."

"Split our forces?" Malus frowned. "Are you suggesting we abandon our footmen and wagons?"

"You're in danger, my duke. I beg you. We take what supplies our horsemen can carry and cut through the trails with utmost haste. It's the only way we'll outpace them."

"The Kurgs, you mean? The peaceful ones whose leaders we have long-standing accords with? Has Father Alcor poisoned your ear, Gyr? Do you now harbor some cultural hatred for the Forgotten People?"

"What if it's an Outclan? What if the Hardheart tells it true and we rush to our doom? If I'm wrong—"

"You are." Sliding his teacup across the table, Malus leaned forward onto elbows, a finger pinioning his prosort. "You. Are. But you don't see it. Last night after sentencing, I had Caltheo question the other prisoners. There was no mention of ebhor tracks. Not one."

Gyr grunted. "What of the story you yourself heard? Your brother has increased taxes for protection. Against Kurgs."

"Again, you expect me to believe an admitted criminal? Odd that this is the first I've heard of such. When brought to account for their misdeeds, men will spin many stories to justify them."

Gyr raised his voice. "How can you deny the absence of Raius and the outriders, my lord?"

"They could be on their way this very second...or delayed. The terrain is unfavorable off the Winding Way's main trail. A horse with a thrown shoe or broken leg—carrying a second man would slow them considerably. They could also be lost. A number of reasonable explanations exist without assuming they've been murdered by allies. Besides, where are all these supposed tracks Durn spoke of, hmm?" Malus shook his head. "Dammit, Gyr, where is your mind lately?"

"My mind is where it always has been and where it always will be. Your safety and the greatest good of Namarr." Gyr tried rolling the tension from his shoulders to no avail. "Your question about the tracks has a simple explanation. They travel where only those with ebhor are like to see them."

"Then what of the ones you discovered with Sir Raius?"

Gyr's tone was low and slow, like water coming to a boil. "I fear that was intentionally done to draw our outriders away. Like I said..." He stood. "We *must* make for Staghill. Those left behind—"

Malus rose to match his prosort and slapped the table with his palms. "Enough of this! The paranoia stops here. We have problems. Oh yes, we have those in abundance, but ebhor tracks no one has seen except for some criminal isn't one of them. If any of this was true, Marus would have sent a pigeon."

"Unless the spy is still with us," Gyr said. "Or a network of spies. They could be shooting down any incoming messages before—"

"Silence! I'm still building to my command for you, Prosort." The way he used Gyr's title was like a lance through the heart. "Your illness, your age, your illegitimate fears. All of it makes you unfit to serve."

Gyr backed a step, a hand splaying over his heart. "What?"

"The threat of Scothea and a traitor in the Collective is dire. If we are to prevail, our focus must be unwavering. I need rational minds at my side—sound minds—not those dedicated to chasing specters. Caltheo has proven more than capable of..." Malus's lips pressed together. Sad eyes settled on Gyr. "Dammit, why must you do this? Henceforth, Gyr Renwood, you are no longer my prosort. Instead of abandoning half my men, we will continue to Kiyahd and arrive within the week—as planned. Today will be the last that you command my crownguard. By nightfall, Caltheo will be sworn in to replace you."

"Caltheo..." Shock gave way to rage. "How...how could you do this to me?"

Lank hair fell in a tangled cascade over Malus's face, making him look feral as he regarded Gyr. "Me? Doing it to you?" He scoffed. "You do this to yourself, man. I did my best not to fault you on account of your age and illness, but this petulance"—he indicated Gyr's fists clenched at his sides—"proves the rightness of my decision. Now, leave me. Your duty is done."

Face slack, legs wooden, Gyr turned away without so much as a bow or salute. *Unfit to serve as prosort.*

Harsh sunlight reflected off the snow, cutting at his eyes. He blinked, squint-ed back at the dark slit of Duke Malus's tent.

You're like a son to me...how could you? Gyr bowed head. *Now is not the time for sentiment.* Regardless of what his title may be, duty called, and only the gods of the Sempyrean could relieve him of his responsibility to do what was right.

He recalled the joy in Durn's eyes when he'd told Gyr of the tracks. The eyes of a man relishing truth. The eyes of a man comforted by the sweet taste of his idea of vengeance.

I will do what I must, when I must, for Malus's own good. He touched the leather thong where his mace hung. *Even if he might not recognize it as such.*

CHAPTER TWENTY-NINE

DEATH DEALER

Z adani watched.

An overcast sky at dusk painted the kitchen staff in a layer of shadow. Like ants, they crept in a circuit from hall to wagons, relieving drovers of their wares.

Thruna lugged a sack of flour up the short incline to the kitchens, grunting at every step, while Elmarie dug heels into soft earth as she hauled a handcart full of vegetables backward up the hill.

Zadani watched.

A holdguard who'd been at Hawk's Hall long before Nymon ever arrived strolled over to the Lech. The two exchanged the perfunctory manly snorts, brief chuckles, and finally, a pat on the arm.

So pleasant to see you mingling with the locals.

Glancing behind to ensure no one watched her, Zadani shuffled the inventory list behind another piece of paper.

She'd been rigorously tracking Nymon's movements—her latest note had been the last piece of the puzzle to fall into place. Every day, two hours before nightfall, the bastard disappeared from the grounds of Hawk's Keep.

The exact stretch of time he found me in the maple grove.

She'd learned it wasn't much different from tallying food orders from week to week. To a degree, she'd even acquired a decent understanding of the holdguard patrol routes at large. Need was ever the herald of solution.

Thruna approached, wheezing. Zadani shuffled the map of Nymon's schedule back into its hidden place behind the inventory lists.

The old woman pressed balled fists into her lower back to force an arch. Three articulated clicks later, she sighed. "Each time we bring in an order, I get flashbacks of the birthing table. Beautiful hags like me ain't cut out for this work."

"I've told you," Zadani said. "You don't have to help."

"My personality is burden enough for others. I'll not give 'em more reason to hate old Thruna by shirking duties."

Elmarie rolled a barrel of spiced wine up the hill. "This makes five, Mistress Innan."

With a blink of surprise, Zadani said, "I thought that was three."

"Five." Thruna thumbed her warty nose, then held up a hand, fingers outstretched as a visual aid.

"Oh, right..." Zadani eyed Nymon's back as he returned to the barracks.

"Mistress." Thruna raised a wiry eyebrow. "It seems you've been...distracted lately."

Zadani focused on the inventory lists. "I've just been, well, you know."

"You know, there's no shame in lying beside a man for comfort," Thruna said. "Never done it myself, but then again, I think all men should live in pens with the pigs. If I were Crown Princess, I'd have a harem of the fairer sex and send the men out beyond the walls to bugger each other and leave us in peace."

"I like men."

Thruna thumbed her wart. "So's your curse. We've all got one. Better to know what yours is than live in its shadow."

Locking eyes with Thruna, Zadani laid a hand on the old woman's shoulder. "Thank you. In hard moments, you've always been a relief to have by my side. The kitchens couldn't operate without you."

The old woman's genuine gap-toothed smile brought Zadani an unexpected jolt of admiration. Since Hadir's death, lying had come easier in her dogged search for his killer, but in moments such as these, the heartfelt truth also shined brighter.

Jasso's rant about unimism played through her mind, a guilty wheel about human nature that brought the lie around. "If I was considering bedding that man, would you keep it between us?" Zadani whispered. "I fear that if anyone found out I had eyes for another so soon after Hadir, they might think me a soulless harlot. The shame of it..."

Tears formed at the corners of Zadani's eyes. She was careful not to let them fall and draw unwanted attention. Kitchen staff *would* ask. This act was for Thruna and Thruna alone. "It would be too much to bear and...I get so lonely without him." The last bit was truth, the core of any good lie.

Thruna cocked her head. "Of course, my love. My own secrets have secrets that have secrets and I keep them locked tighter than Lady Daran's twat. I'll not give a grieving friend more to worry over."

"Thank you." Zadani rubbed the woman's arm then gave it a squeeze. As Thruna turned to leave, Zadani's loving grip tightened. She leaned, bringing her lips to the elderly cook's ear. "He's off duty now. Can you finish here and handle dinner clean-up alone?"

Thruna nodded, saggy neck flesh wobbling.

"You'll have a good lie, then, for my absence?"

Thruna shrugged. "In that, I'm well practiced. Don't worry, love."

During her week of mapping guard posts and routes to nail down Nymon's schedule, Zadani had managed to find a few blind spots in the patrols. The hedge she now hunkered behind was one such. Her neck and scalp tingled with looming danger as she sank deeper into the shadows and peered through a slit in the towering row.

The holdguard who'd drawn her a map leaned against the inside of the wall beside the path to the north wood. Nodding off, waking up, rubbing his face and kicking the dirt, the man was bored if not downright miserable.

Zadani was keenly aware she looked like some sort of spy, skulking in the dark and watching holdguard with a knife in her boot.

A loud rustle came from somewhere behind. Stomach jolting, she whipped around, a scream rushing to her lips but no farther. The wind tossed the dense foliage of the hedges, silvery tops shimmering under moonlight. *One mistake. That's all it would take. Impeccable caution, Zadani.*

Despite it being the first hour of night, the holdguard had fallen asleep again. His spear leaned against an ensconced torch. By the time tendrils of smoke wreathed the tip, Nymon the Lech clomped through the gap in the wall, torchlight peeling back the darkness as if it, too, found distaste in touching him.

"Wake up, you dumb cunt!" He snatched the holdguard's collar, shook him awake, then shook him a little extra.

What's this? A roll of parchment was tucked through Nymon's belt.

The holdguard shoved Nymon's hand off. "You're not my fucking captain." He squared up to the taller, one-eyed man.

"You won't do shit about it, so fuck yourself." A cruel laugh trailed Nymon as he walked past the place where Zadani hid and continued up the hill.

Where Zadani went, the shadows waited.

Weaving between the hedgerows, she followed Nymon to a wing of the keep. Narrow apertures lined the length of it, giving her a disjointed view of her target. Guttering torches made him little more than a floating silhouette.

She entered the wing, checked her surroundings, then peeked out from an alcove. At the end of the hall, Nymon was sliding a key into a door and cursing.

From what she understood, he'd been promoted recently, and so, had new quarters. He cursed louder and threw down his key.

Zadani flinched as he leveled a kick at the door. It didn't budge. With a wince, he leaned his weight onto his other leg before picking up the key again. Purple with anger, he jangled the lock until it gave a resounding click, and then entered.

He's probably reading whatever is in that scroll right now.

A thin strip of flesh parted from the inside of Zadani's cheek where she chewed it. Cloth swished and swirled around her legs as she rushed inside of a nearby drum tower. She took the steps down two at a time.

The kitchens were beneath ground level in the keep, and it sounded as though the day's business was winding to a close. She heard Thruna telling Elmarie to leave for the night. Zadani knew the way Elmarie was sure to come and waited for her there. Her lips were flour-dry, the rest of her, quite the opposite. A steady drumbeat in her chest drove her, every action now greased with urgency.

I must see what's in that scroll!

Elmarie rounded a corner. Zadani took a step to meet her. "Oh, Mistress Innan. I didn't see you there. Thruna said you were—"

"What good fortune." Zadani beamed. No time for chit-chat. "I am sorely in need of your assistance. Here's what I want you to do."

She took Elmarie by the arm and headed toward Nymon's room, speaking fast and giving no space for the young woman to get a word in. "I have something special in the kitchen I made for Master Nymon. I'm off to get it now. I need you to go to his room and tell him I have a gift waiting for him in my room. Escort him there if need be." They wound up the spiral stairs of the tower, Zadani locking elbows with Elmarie. "He may beat me there, but that's alright. Once he's at my room and waiting, you're free to go. I'm sure you're aware he's been a beacon of hope. Lord Marus has given him the task of investigating Hadir's murder, you know? Anyway, here it is—third door on the right—off you go."

"But...I..." Elmarie's mouth hung open, smooth, porcelain brow furrowed.

With a gentle push, Zadani propelled the beautiful young woman down the hall, then ducked back into the shadows.

Casting about, Elmarie pointed at one door, then another, finally a third. A shouted curse from within followed the girl's tentative knock. Zadani pushed down a sliver of guilt as a grimacing Nymon stepped into the hall and Elmarie cowered back.

They exchanged words, out of earshot, Elmarie all twitches and starts, Nymon all slithering lips and greasy confidence. Together, they walked toward Zadani, but peeled off into an intervening corridor halfway to her. Zadani's belly turned sour at the sight of Nymon the Lech adjusting his breeches and smacking his lips as he followed the young maid.

Inside his room, Zadani moved quick and quiet. Her pulse raced, throbbing in every limb. She'd known it would take something urgent to get him to leave the door unlocked. *And what is more urgent to that slimy man than a tumble?*

It took a few seconds to spot the scroll. A flutter of excitement shot through her. Upon closer inspection, it turned out not to be parchment at all but some kind of leather.

Hide. *Almost certainly, ebhor.*

She worked a loop of the same material free from what appeared to be a hook made of bone, then unrolled it...

Two brief lines were scrawled across the hide in a language she'd never before seen. Uncertainty crashed into her. She let out a whoosh of air, hands flying to her pocket where the charcoal stylus and parchment were to transcribe the alien letters.

The hide message whispered closed. For now, it would keep its secrets, though she would change that as soon as she could. She jammed her copy back into her pocket and left.

A low and throaty gurgle was the first sign that Zadani's plan wouldn't work. In her haste—her desperate need to see the scroll—she'd thought of the only thing she could in the time she had. The last part of the plan involved delay; it wasn't the best.

Around the corner from her room, Zadani clung to the wall, a sweaty mess. She had planned to wait until Nymon left, and then in the morning, whip up some pecan rolls for him with an excuse, or maybe blame things on Elmarie's inept communication—no harm done.

The second sign that Zadani's plan had failed was a distressed whimper.

"I've only had a few so sweet on the eye as you." Nymon spoke from deep in his throat, a lustful cooing. "Thinkin' bout that tight young mound makes my guts go all to mush."

"I was supposed to go...once I brought you." Elmarie's terrified words crashed into Zadani. *I did this.* "I was to go."

She thought of the shark and the thunder angel jellies. *Who have I become?*

She peered around the corner.

"I'm tired of waitin' for my gift." Nymon jerked Elmarie's head back by a handful of her hair and held her in place like a hawk snaring a rabbit. He pushed the index finger of his other hand against Elmarie's trembling lips and hushed her. "Maybe you're the gift she had waitin' for me, eh?"

The kitchen maid melted into the wall, frozen but for the rapid swells of prey-like breath. Nymon rotated her head to kiss her neck. The girl's slack and pale face was angled toward the ceiling, eyes fixed, glassy and distant by necessity.

Zadani ground her teeth.

Nymon's finger dragged down from Elmarie's lips toward her crotch, then suddenly, he was jerking at her belt. "Let's see my gift." Under the flurry of primal hands, Elmarie's head lolled as if she were about to faint. Then, seeming to wake from a bad dream, the young woman loosed a squeal, cut short by Nymon slapping the wall beside her head.

Like Hadir, Elmarie was innocent. *I won't let her be my sacrifice.*

Zadani swept from around the corner and was nearly upon them by the time Nymon registered. He rounded on her, fist cocked, expression a twisted snarl.

"I see you're ready for me." Zadani forced a coy laugh. Bile raced into her throat, but she swallowed it back, down into a seething sea of the shame in her belly. Three languid steps and she was there, hand sliding up Nymon's shoulder and around the back of his neck. "Go," she mouthed to Elmarie as she drew him into her embrace. "Trifling with girls who know nothing of a man like you." He smelled of horse and had the spicy stink of amply-sweated-in-smallclothes. Zadani rose onto her tiptoes and whispered in his ear. "Seems a waste of time when I'm right here."

Rank odor swirling, he turned, sucked at his teeth as he watched Elmarie slip down the hall, her thin, quivering arms clutching the wall as if it were the guy rope on a rickety bridge.

"A bit wooden for me." His face swiveled to Zadani. "I like 'em more eager."

"Come," she said.

The room was dark, ruddy light spilling in but a short distance from the torches in the hall. "One moment. I want you to be able to see your gift."

Nymon grunted assent.

Really, Zadani needed time to hide the copied message. That, and figure a way out of her situation; though the most likely answer to that was horrifying to admit. Mind reeling, her breath caught in her throat. A cold sweat beaded down her spine, dampening her backside.

This was their room. The bed she and Hadir had shared.

"Hurry up," Nymon barked.

I can't. I have to get out of this.

Prickles covered her, and she felt the room spinning. Hand shaking, she slid the scroll into a drawer of her nightstand, and as she did, a wad of cloth brushed her pinky. The one containing the death dealer. She froze. *A fingernail's worth, no more.*

"Fuck are you doing?"

She swallowed hard. In some dire instances, healers used death dealer to force out the contents of one's stomach. Sometimes, the person died. *If I do, at least I'll be with Hadir again.* Death was preferable to sleeping with Nymon the Lech.

By feel alone, she flipped the cloth open then scraped the nail of her pinky over the fleshy cap. She sucked the mushroom from under her nail—surprisingly sweet. Like a carrot.

She lit the candle. Turned.

Nymon stared down at her, awash in an orange glow and backed by blackness. His milky eye gleamed. A heartbeat of calm passed between them, a silent promise of violence to come.

And in the stillness, that flickering light, she saw something that sank a chill dagger into her. The first scar had taken his eye, but the other two were barely visible at cheek and chin beneath his thick blond beard. A beard similar to that worn by the rest of his men. Beards that covered the work of the Jurati.

They're Scarborn.

He gripped the cloth of her bust and tore the top of her dress apart. Zadani stifled a cry as the next jerking motion stripped her naked to the waist. The bed rose to meet her back with a whoosh of air and clap of breasts. Nymon fumbled at the laces of his breeches, breaths ragged with eagerness. Instinct made Zadani cover her breasts and tuck a hand over her crotch, but Nymon was quick to slap them away as he crawled atop her.

When their skin touched, she jolted.

Jolted again. Burning agony rifled through her belly and low back. "Uhh," she moaned.

Callused hands scratched over her skin as Nymon rubbed at her. "More o' that. Moan."

She did, but not for pleasure.

Shattered glass poured into her intestines. Flame rippled across her skin and climbed the back of her throat. Her mouth filled with a vile tang and a sheen of sweat lathered her. It felt like a badger was digging at her innards.

Nymon lifted his head from lapping at her breasts. Grinning, he moved his lips towards hers.

"Uhn." Her moan turned to a heave. A sickening rush—

Inches from her face, Nymon had begun to chuckle when a gout of hot vomit erupted, splattering his face, mouth, and chest. He gasped, sat back on his heels, arms winging out in stunned revulsion.

Zadani moaned again, spewed another gout of sick onto his lap.

"Ack! Plehk!" He shot to his feet, huffing and spitting. "Fuck—pleh—retched—bleh—bitch!"

He used the covers to wipe as much sick from himself as he could, grabbed his clothes, and then stormed out.

A satisfying last thing to see if I die.

Exhaustion, sudden and merciless, rolled Zadani onto her side. Labored breaths followed as a bladed viper coiled up in her insides. A wave of nausea forced her to sit upright and then quickly seek out the night soil bucket in preparation for another round of retching.

Arms wrapped around her belly, she purged, all night and into the next morning. And though there were a handful of times that the pain had her wishing for death, she remained alive and faithful to Hadir.

CHAPTER THIRTY

ALL YOUR YESTERDAYS ARE DEAD

T hephos followed Syn to an iron cylinder deep in the bowels of Enshai, a massive coin propped against the interior wall of a chamber with ceilings twenty feet high. To imagine such a structure could exist under the city stole his breath.

Then again, almost everything about Enshai shared the same quality of impossibility.

At Syn's command, a team of four young men and a heavy-set girl worked a crank connected to a spool of chains that slithered out of sight through a pair of holes in the cavernous rock wall. Thephos assumed they fed into some manner of pulley on the other side.

The cylinder groaned and clicked until a crescent of shadow wide enough to admit them appeared.

Syn beckoned Thephos to follow. "This is the best part."

With a rumble, the cylinder rolled back into place behind them.

"Syn?" Darkness consumed the senses. Thephos was no stranger to it. Darkness was more comfort than a thing to fear; in his life before, when he'd been a pig farmer, it had meant an end, or at least a reduction of the horrors brought about by daylight.

Before the first of his brothers had been born, he'd spent every night alone on a cot in the corner of the main room, plain winds roaring through the loose slats in the drab farmhouse. He only wished it had been darker, the wind louder. On unlucky occasions, he saw the devil savaging his mother through a crack in the bedroom door. Felt her pain in the shake of the floorboards. Worse than sight was sound—darkness did little for that. Capitulating grunts, a mix of his father's pleasure and his mother's fear, the first evoking the second into existence.

Mother was a prisoner to her circumstances, the same as me. Thephos grew up telling himself that. Blaming his existence for it. *If I wasn't there, she could have left sooner.* The muscles in Thephos's shoulders tightened. Ten years the devil had her before she'd summoned the courage to flee. To choose herself over her children.

His gums ached as he ground his teeth. *He would have killed her. That's why she waited until I was older. Big enough. Strong enough. She had faith in me and I squandered it...*

I let the devil kill Emmon...my brother's name was Emmon.

For so long, the shock of grief had numbed the wounds caused by the old devil. It made Thephos's own inadequacies a fact, carved from stone or wood or bone. But Unturrus had brought all of that festering, subconscious pain to the surface. He saw it clearly now. Daily, he followed its golden thread through the dark of his mind.

Who am I?

The question had come earlier that day when Syn woke him at dawn. "Come on fella, we have some important stuff to do."

"Where's Ash?" Thephos sat up, rubbing bleary eyes. As soon as Ash had shown him his quarters the night before, he'd fallen asleep. Road weary, sore from the saddle, and still shaking the shock of Awakening from his system, sleep had come and gone in a dreamless blink.

"Miss her already?" Syn chuckled. "She's grown rusty with her sword, so she woke early to count bees in the training paddock. If you're wondering what that is, you'll find out soon. One thing at a time. I know, all of this can be a lot."

Thephos couldn't agree more.

They'd sauntered down a hall, through interconnected corridors lit by luminescent ghost-flame. *What do I need of dreams when I live in one already?* Everywhere he turned, Tehphos found the awe-inspiring evidence of Awakened utilizing their powers.

Despite the swirl of discovery hiding around every turn in the corridor, Thephos listened intently to Syn. He tended to ramble, but more often than not, it was useful information.

"There's a lot coming at you right now. I'm being honest with you when I say it isn't likely to stop." Syn hustled down a flight of steps, Thephos at his heels and working to keep up. "We've all been where you are. You woke and found that all your yesterdays are dead. That your tomorrows could be anything. Power at your fingertips. Dread and adoration, your newest companions. All of it, just this weird feeling you're trying to settle into. Itchy clothes, too big, too small. Nothing quite right though."

He slowed to walk abreast of Thephos, chin tilted down to look him full in the face. "You might have realized that the past doesn't define you, but you've got no fucking clue how the future might."

The Dominarri waited for Thephos to reply. There was comfort in silence. Hope for others to speak in his stead. But this time, Syn, for all his talkativeness, would not cave.

"I don't feel broken. Not anymore." The words slid from Thephos. "But you're right. I don't feel whole, either."

"Exactly." Syn nodded knowingly. "We've opened the door for you, but first, you'll need to see what you're walking into. Then you decide if you want to stay."

Thephos chewed on Syn's words, mind racing toward vague possibilities.

"You have to know who you are," Syn had added as they entered the chamber with the cylindrical door. Thephos had deemed it a waste of words to ask where Syn was taking him; if the man was inclined to tell him, he would have—and at length.

Now, a sea of black engulfed Thephos. It reminded him of the one he'd been drowning in before the Mother arrived. He reached out. Angular stone brushed his palms—the wall. "Syn?" He turned around, directionless and disoriented.

A pair of burning gray orbs hung in the air a hundred yards off. "Over here." Syn's voice. Gray light burned the dark away as it expanded, reaching farther than normal in the voided stretches.

A path wound around steeples of rock, a field of spear-like stalagmites. Thephos was glad he decided to stay put. A dozen paces straight on and he could have slipped off a ledge and tumbled into a bowl where he'd have been a beetle on a needlepoint.

Syn waved him over.

They traveled along a ledge, like smeared butter in the desaturated glow. It led into a narrow opening, and then descended.

Between the eerie light and unfamiliar terrain, time became distorted theory; it trickled by, a wet streak on the walls every few hundred feet. All was painted ashen gray. Talons of rock threw shadows on the walls, fang-filled mouths taunting them as they walked.

Thephos looked back. His shadow followed.

Hours or minutes—it could have been either before they finally arrived at their destination. By the amount of sweat covering him and the rawness of the blister on his heel, he judged that it was more likely the former.

"Ah, here it is." Syn steered them under a brow of rock. He had to hunch over to clear the ceiling while Thephos dipped slightly.

A dozen paces in, Thephos paused. The floor glowed a faint azure.

His heartbeat quickened. The last time he'd seen that color...

They emerged onto a ledge coated in scintillating blue. Syn had relinquished his powers, letting the other source of light take over.

Thephos straightened to stand, heart catching in his throat. Memories poured into him, ecstatic and terrifying and beautiful. The Mother descending. Wings billowing in a thunderous, quiet rush. The disparity of motions so gentle, yet so titanic. He, a battered and dying husk, thirsting to be born anew. Ready. Thought and feeling clicking into place and echoing through him. He'd begged the Mother to release him from the pain of being what he'd been. Being *who* he'd been. Begged her to kill that part of him so unworthy of life. He'd asked for a glimpse before the end. A moment's look at what could have been had he been stronger, more courageous. *More.* To goad the man he never was forward into the light.

"Familiar, isn't it?"

Thephos wiped the tears from his eyes and nodded.

The cavern's ceiling had ruptured, giving way to a network of roots that hung hundreds of feet down into an abyss. A narrow, rough ledge encircled the pit. Thephos studied the roots, the longest of them as thick around as a drum tower. They pulsed with dizzying blue light. *The same as the Mother's wings.*

"Can't say I hate my duties right now. I don't often get to bring new recruits down here, but when I do, it's worth it." Syn gave a deep sigh. "This, Thephos, is what we fight for."

Thephos walked to the edge, closed his eyes and reached up, fingers stretching to the sides to let the light bathe him. For a moment, he thought he felt it rippling under the skin. "Is it her?" He opened his eyes.

"In truth, we aren't sure." Syn joined him at the ledge's limit. He leaned out and stared down into the abyss. "There are a lot of theories that have come up over the years. Obviously, the Mother is connected to it somehow. Whether she's the source of it, or a product of its existence, we don't know. What we do know is that Unturrus is an organism. Alive."

Thephos flinched. "This is Unturrus?"

"It is. These roots have been traced back to it. And there are more. Many more. Malzacor. The Sea Forest...other places we have yet to discover."

They were a week's ride from Unturrus. If what Syn claimed was true, the Mountain of Power's root system stretched for hundreds of miles. He frowned, recalling what Syn had said. "What do you mean, this is what we fight for?"

"The Dominarri." He squared to Thephos, the first of them to take his eyes off the roots since they'd entered. "You can have power. You can have riches. You can have fame. You can have anything the world has to offer that is normally reserved for those born to elite bloodlines." His tone was grave. "But what you will never have is a second chance to be a Dominarri."

A euphonious hum grew in the space around them. Thephos glanced at the roots, then back at Syn. The man watched him, a smile tugging at his cheek.

Don't trust him! The voice within startled Thephos. *He offers you suffering and will abandon you to it as your mother did.*

My mother. Not *the* Mother. "Will you kill me if I say no?"

Syn was taken aback. He shook his head, brow bunched. "Triune God, no. Come on, man. You're as bad as Ash with your paranoia. You can say no. If you do, I'll wipe your mind of all things Dominarri and set you on your way."

"Oh." Thephos frowned, waiting for the voice's rebuttal, but it had gone. Questions rose in its absence. *Do all Awakened hear a voice like me?* He looked at Syn, studied him, decided it was best to keep the thought to himself for now.

"I'm being transparent with you," Syn said. "I know you don't completely trust me, or us. Given your past, and the fact that I imprisoned you for a bit, it makes sense. So I wanted to give you the whole truth before you go down this road. I like you, Thephos. You need to know what you're pledging your life to."

Unlike the light given off by Syn's powers, the roots of Unturrus left no shadow. Somehow, it bent and curved and left no crevice unexplored. As if the light itself had curiosity. A purpose.

"Our duty is dangerous. It's not so glamorous a life as those Awakened working for a hold lord or earning fortunes in petty wars as glorified mercenaries. We have but one duty. Protect Unturrus and the Mother. Those entities are..." Syn choked down his emotions. "They are sacred and must be guarded as such. There are forces that would see them destroyed. *We* will never let that happen."

Syn stepped closer, looming. He poked a finger into Thephos's chest, held it there over his pounding heart. "In sight of the Mother's light, every Dominarri has pledged to give their life for that sacred mystery. If you wish to be one of us, you will too." The prodding finger drifted away and Syn stepped back. "Choose."

Thephos's pulse thundered in his ears. *Who am I?* The question loomed, feral jaws hovering at his throat, waiting to tear away everything he'd earned.

All that he could be.

Faith in himself lay within the door. His mother had thought she'd seen it when she left him in the devil's care. Thought he might rise up strong and take the bastard down. *That past is dead. I choose my future now.*

Hesitation and doubt were pushed to the edge of awareness, concepts once worn like gloves now slipping through his grasp. A pleasant letting go. *I have but to turn the handle and enter.*

He stared at the radiating light of Unturrus's roots.

He turned to Syn Backlegarm and lifted his chin. "I pledge my life to the Dominarri."

The tension left Syn in a gust, beaten out like dust from a rug. He looked relieved. "Excellent. Happy to have you, brother." He yanked Thephos into an embrace. A decade or more had passed since he'd been hugged by anyone. There was a memory of his mother doing so before she went, but it was distant. Untrustworthy.

Heat swept through Thephos.

No, the voice whispered. Hands locked around Syn, Thephos felt a sudden urge to jerk back and shove the big man into the pit.

Love only me.

CHAPTER THIRTY-ONE

MY LIGHT

V alka paused at the terrace leading to his manse and looked up at the Holy Chamber perched atop the peak of Darkfall's keep. Banners of white bearing a single golden arrow snapped in the wind above Scothea's much more elegant standard of old. The raek encircling the sun flew lower now. Less potent. The symbolism was not lost on him.

He surpasses in importance the very nation he now rules. To call the boy's ascent awe-inspiring was a tragic understatement. By his account, no historical figure had ascertained power so smoothly nor with such certainty except, perhaps, Danath Ironlight.

Echoes eddied up from the lower terraces where soldiers-turned-cultists drank and played sachari, and extolled Siddaia's name.

Valka took account of himself and felt unease. Day after day, his resolve slipped further into fantasy, and the facade of traitor grew into reality. A minor shred of his loyalty still lay with Rathon's line. *Why though? Can it be as simple as my conditioning? My oath?* After seeing what the boy was capable of, he wondered what kept him from releasing his reservations.

Reports abounded about the cruel acts carried out by the citizens of the lower dwellings. Those too slow to pledge homage to the messiah were being rounded up by their brethren and made to swear fealty under threat of death. Those were the better instances. Often, those suspected of remaining loyal to Rathon were publicly executed in a hail of stones and clubs. Although Valka and Rhul had acted quickly on Siddaia's orders to quell the violence, not a day went by without a few dozen mangled corpses showing up at the shrine of Acramis, the god of justice, or Nitriti, the goddess of malice.

The rich were no more dignified in their approach.

The night before last, screams had pierced the fog of Valka's dreams. Thinking Nera in trouble, he'd barreled toward her room, calling his household guard to arms. One look at an alert Yanos stationed outside her door with ax in hand, and Valka was mirroring his captain's puzzlement.

Then another scream had come—from outside. They went to a window and searched the rowed manses for the source, just in time to see a group of masked men piling out of the manor at the end of the terraced lane. The axes and daggers in their hands dripped dark. In the morning, the stench of blood and loosened bowel hung in the air before the manor as Valka passed it.

Now, a detail of his household guard trailed him past it once more. The hum of corpse flies and clank of plated skirts and chain made for a rotten symphony. *If Siddaia heard it, what would he think of his revolution? Would it be so righteous?* He thought of shoving the youth toward the corpse and shouting, "Are you their savior? Are you?" but the mental image devolved into the boy crying and Valka's defenses crumbling a bit more.

They were on their way to another Fifthday sermon at the vippedrome of Sesyrs. In light of the danger to those unwilling to entertain Scothea's new leader, Nera walked at Valka's side. The last thing he wanted was to return home and find her corpse bloating in the sun beside their neighbor's.

She seemed to sense his thoughts. "Another day in the messiah's paradise, father?"

"Careful what you say, daughter." He glanced back, only somewhat confident they weren't being heard over the marching din created by his guards. "Or at least, how loud you say it."

"Such freedom our new leader brings." She stared straight ahead as they walked but lowered her voice all the same. "We mustn't make too much noise about our butchered neighbors now, must we?"

"Change is difficult," Valka said. "It behooves us to be open-minded."

"And discerning. Let's not forget that part."

Valka's upper and lower teeth touched and pressed them together. An inhale later, and he felt himself relax. "If he was simply an Awakened, there would be a nimbus present when he accesses his powers. I've seen no evidence of such, yet he sees the heart of any matter without effort. Grown men wilt before him, tears in their eyes at truths imparted."

Nera craned her head to look him full in the face. "An unimpressive trick that women have managed for generations. Surely, you jest?"

"After today, you may shift your perspective on the matter." A thought came to him about the merits of things taken for the better, of a country on the brink of collapse riding the hope of new leadership, but he withheld it. His voice dropped to a whisper as he brought his head close to hers. "I'm not saying I believe, nor that you should. What he says and does, though, *is* convincing. If he is truly a messiah of the gods, then for the sake of diligence, we should consider that position as well."

She laced an arm through his. Together, they mounted a flight of stairs carved into rock and wound around a mile-long terrace. From there, they would descend another level to Sesyr's vippedrome. A bank of drab, dilapidated homes were clustered off to one side of the steps carved into the rock. A flock had gathered to hear a man in a soiled sack repeat one of Siddaia's missives. "Disciples of the Light" were popping up across Scothea.

The downtrodden disciple and his flock watched Valka's group pass. When they were out of earshot, Nera responded to her father's strategy with a quote from Jathos Wrathhand. "Proof is ever the woe of the unproven."

"You're welcome to come to your own conclusions, my daughter, but please, for the love of our Holy Instruments, if they're not favorable to Siddaia, keep them to yourself." *She is willful to a detriment.* Guilt had made Valka raise her with a soft hand. *Her mother's rebel-blood pumps within her, throwing her into actions premature.* "It's clear you've decided to be deaf on this matter. If my words fail to reach you, perhaps the voice of Uhlvath the Seer King can." *Though it is in truth a Kurgish shaman's work.* "Heed his prophecy:

"Three makes one and one makes three. In the shadow of great power will come the end of things unseen. First the Eye, bringing evil into the light. Then the Hand, ridding the world of its plight. Last the Fire, that in the darkest hours unite. Three makes one, but only one makes free."

"Catchy," was all she offered.

"Look for the signs and you may see." *Why do I fight so hard to convince her when I am undecided?*

Blood rushed to his ears, causing the back of his head to tingle. *Maybe I am decided.*

"I shall, father." She smacked her lips as if she'd eaten moldy mushrooms, then twisted around to beckon her bodyguard. "Yanos, I wish to arrive early and get a better seat. I don't have my father's station." Nera quickened her pace, the rustle of her silk wrappings sighing softly in her wake.

As Yanos lengthened his stride to keep up, Valka restrained him by the shoulder and locked eyes with his captain. "I apologize that you had to miss our Light's last sermon on account of Nera's fickle nature. Have you had a chance to read the chronicles?"

At each of the Fifthday sermons, scribes cataloged Siddaia's words verbatim. They were being called the "The Chronicles of Light" and distributed to citizens en masse. Valka had been tasked with having each sermon bound in gilded leather and sent to the leaders of the other major Scothean cities.

Captain Yanos's cheek twitched. *Is that frustration I see?*

"I did." A long moment passed between them. Yanos scratched a smooth cheek. "I would have preferred the real thing, General. This duty you've assigned me—"

"Difficult, I know." Valka's gaze flickered toward Nera's back as she opened more distance between them. "I've made you a glorified babysitter and caused you to miss vital teachings." Valka readied himself, eyes boring into Yanos. *Do you play the part as I do? Or are you a true convert?* "I trust no other with keeping her safe."

The captain gave no response for a handful of seconds, his expression stoic. He turned to Valka and saluted. "It is an honor, General." Then he moved to catch up with Nera.

Suspicion aroused, Valka watched them all the way to the vippedrome. Whatever Yanos believed, he would not betray it easily. The pair exchanged conversation, and at one point, Yanos even laughed.

Above all, he prayed Nera would be cautious.

The wrong word in the wrong ear and it might be her corpse in the street swarmed by flies.

A rare gloom spread across the sky, hung there like the graying murk of some fetid pond. Hot wind moaned through the vippedrome, throwing up chariots of dust that raced from one end of the arena to the other. Sweat damped the cloth under Valka's ceremonial white armor. He removed a glove and wiped his hand on the inside of his gold tabard. He looked at it, found trails of rolled-up dirt lining his palm and between his fingers.

He dragged the glove back on and ascended the platform, a knee popping at the first step. *Young enough to make the journey. Old enough to regret its merits.* The stairs spiraling the massive stone pillar gave him a better view of the field, where games of sachari were being played among some of the nation's best—another of Valka's suggestions. This one had been made in the hopes of Scothea remembering itself.

So far, it had done nothing of the sort.

One player held his ax beside his hip, focused on the stuffed leather sack resting on the blade. He paused, affording a glance at his opponent standing in a small circle a hundred yards away, and then looked down at his ax. In a single fluid motion, he exploded up and forward, ax whipping and sending the sack sailing in an arc. His opponent checked his feet, stepped to the circle's edge to ensure the throw was within bounds, then brought his own ax into the air, prepared to cradle the fast descending sack. If he caught it, he'd still be in, able to make a throw of his own. Already, this was the twelfth such exchange between the two.

Sack smacked metal with a quiet *whump*. For a heart-stopping moment, the sachari player had it poised on his weapon, but a second later, it tipped over the edge and off. His ax clattered to the ground as he spun away, hands covering his face in shameful defeat.

The crowd roared, a mix of approval and disappointment.

Valka smiled. A festival atmosphere had started to bleed into the Fifthday sermons. While the general questioned the way it deepened Siddaia's stranglehold on the people's favor, it also lifted his spirits to see them enjoying life once more.

They starve and yet they rejoice.

A raek knight pulled a horn to his lips and let out a deafening series of blasts. Siddaia joined Valka at the top of the columnar platform, accompanied by his Awakened.

Valka watched the messiah approach to face the crowd. "I suppose that means you wish to hear something from me?"

The teeming masses laughed. Even Valka smiled. Somewhere out there was Nera. Did she laugh along with them, or did she dole out mockery and cynicism? He prayed for the former but knew it likely to be the latter. He swallowed a lump of fear. *Be careful, Nera.* His daughter was as smart as they came, but her conviction on any matter was a wrathful thing to behold.

Before Siddaia could begin his sermon, a commotion at one end of the arena rippled through the crowd. Valka's hand fell to Mournfang.

People gasped and murmured, drawing back from a short file of men emerging from the shrine of Aurghov, the holy instrument of good fortune. They carried sacks over their shoulders. "My Light, wait!" the man in the lead hollered. "A gift for you!"

Soldiers rushed across the sand to intercept them. A light touch at Valka's shoulder brought him around to face Siddaia, his expression transfixed on those below. "Let them through, Ikarai."

Valka motioned for his men to stand down. The order reached his soldiers on the racecourse just as they were laying hands on the first of the five men. Argument ceased in its infancy. All of them were ragged. The kind of men that watched anyone who got too close to them like a dog guarding its meal.

It didn't bode well, Valka decided.

"Daimos, take me to them," Siddaia said.

By the time Valka had hurried down the spiral staircase and reached the sandy racecourse below, there were tears in Siddaia's eyes. The boy sniffled as he stared at the sacks the ragged men had unlimbered from their shoulders.

Flesh prickling along the backs of his arms, Valka understood with dawning horror what the "gift" would be.

Blood soaked the ragged men's grimy, moth-eaten shifts. The lead man seemed to register Siddaia's tears, his somber countenance, and started to tremble.

Already committed to his offering, he reached into his belt. "Here's the knife that did it, my Light. We thought—" He gagged on his words. "We thought it would make you happy. We thought it was what you wanted."

"I declared them free to go!" Siddaia raged. His voice cracked then slid into choked sobbing. The vippedrome fell deadly quiet. Siddaia's next, muffled words could be heard by all. "I did not want this."

Valka approached the sacks, arrayed from largest to smallest. Dark splotches marred the canvas the bodies had been stitched into. Blood dripped in a lazy rhythm at the edges of the two they'd murdered most recently. "Open them," Valka ordered.

When his soldiers made to comply, Valka waved them off and sneered, "No. Them." He pointed at the ragged low-dwelling murderers.

The lead man fell to his knees beside the largest sack, staring at the bloody knife in his crimson-flecked fist. He gulped and started to saw, the motion inhibited by his own pitiful crying. "I—I thought it's what he wanted. I saw them and...we weren't going to let them go free, were we?"

Rathon's face stared at the blasted gray sky. *We?* To be associated with such a vile creature made Valka itch from toe to nape.

A jagged wound as thick as Valka's finger encircled the dead king's neck. A dozen more crescent-shaped stab wounds covered his chest. Valka's gaze drifted away...traveled down the line to the smaller sacks. Children he'd spoken to. Children he'd tutored in warfare and history and how to be good leaders.

Children whose fates were separated from his own by little more than a knife's edge.

Before Valka knew what he was doing, he strode past a weeping Siddaia and withdrew Mournfang. The ax seemed to feel the general's vengeance pulsing through him; it glowed, splashing Rathon's assassins in radiating red light and turning Siddaia's tears into glistening jewels.

The low dwellers watched Valka approach, licked their lips and balked, eyes hunting for an escape. Two dropped to their knees. One started to beg. "Please, lord, please! I didn't do the cutting! I swe—"

The top half of the man was ripped aside, reduced to a sloshing portal of guts from the belly button up. A ribbon of blood splatted against Valka's chest, gold turned to red as the Gravequeen swept past. Rhul hung from the saddle, his wicked hakat scything three of the men in half in a blink.

The rest wailed in terror as the raek coiled back around, rearing over one of them with its fangs bared.

"No!" Siddaia cried, the sole voice of compassion lost amid the clamor of the crowd's approval.

The Gravequeen slammed her snout into the sand, eclipsing the man. Bones crunched and ground under the war snake's masticating jaws. A hand and foot were scissored free, flopping to the ground as she threw back her head to muscle the squirming mass down her gullet.

The remaining criminal pissed his pants and ran—stumbled over one of the bodies and started scrambling on all fours. Valka whirled Mournfang in his hand as he stepped to meet him. He swung, cleaving the man's skull from ear to ear with the ease of a hot iron through water. Ruptured brain matter and pink fluid trailed the ax from the steaming wound and flung it in a gory arc across the racecourse. The man's gaping head bounced off the canvas sack containing Rathon's wife, and then he slumped off to one side.

Breath and blood pumped through Ikarai Valka. He spat on the man's twitching body, then slipped Mournfang back into its leather thong at his hip. The ax's ensorcelled head dimmed, going cold as soon as it left his hands.

The crowd roared, bloodthirsty righteousness slaked.

Ikarai surveyed the masses—heard them calling his name. Rhul the Red's name as well. The raeklord hiked the barbed reins of the Gravequeen and raised the long-ax in his fist triumphantly.

Nearby, Siddaia stared at the bodies of the children. "I did not want this," Valka heard him say.

A keen sickness filled the general's gut. Many of those who'd sworn to the soldiering life developed a penchant for violence, but Valka never had. Justice, however, was another matter. Discomfited by the crowd's approval of his actions, he turned his attention to Siddaia. He went to the boy messiah and placed a hand on his shoulder. "I'm sorry, my Light. This...this should never have happened. The children..." The rest died in his throat.

No wise words from Scothea's ruler followed. No blinding truths or inspiring sermons.

Just the actions of a vulnerable, heartbroken boy.

Siddaia spun around, eyes squeezed closed, and threw his arms around Valka's neck. He felt the screams of sorrow more than he heard them. Felt the way Siddaia's heartbeat galloped from the suffering he felt responsible for.

Valka raised a hand to pat the boy's head. His hair was warm, damp with sweat from the heat of the violent moment. *Where is the insidious tyrant I seek to depose? The duplicitous one who wears a mask to better assert his power?*

Nowhere, echoed a wisdom from deep in the core of his being. *Your fear is a thing of the past. The future could be far brighter...if you allow it.*

The stone walls of Valka's cynicism broke, tumbled around the true nature of his lord and exposed him to dizzying revelation.

...my Light.

CHAPTER THIRTY-TWO

TRAITOR

G yr stood at the edge of a sheer slope, looking out over a sea of snow-capped evergreens falling rapidly under gloom. He was waiting for the moments before dawn, when Duke Malus was most certain to be asleep.

Scraggly brush reached from the untouched blanket of snow covering the Winding Way's shoulder like skeletal hands. Gyr turned about-face, gaze sweeping the encampment as it settled in for the night. Dense canopy shrouded the distant upper slope in darkness, boughs heavy with snow and shadow.

It had taken little to win Halladorn to his cause. The man had caught a few of his warhounds looking sharply into the woods over the course of the last few days. "They'll give half a mind to squirrels rushing about but with the bandits caught...it ain't sitting right with me. There's something else out there. I can feel it."

Gyr felt it, too. After a brief discussion, it was clear Caltheo could not know what was coming if they were to save Malus D'Alzir. The other men they gathered—nearly a score of them whose loyalty was without question—were fed the necessary truths to ensure their collaboration, plus a few lies for added urgency.

If they were to betray the duke, the case for doing so would need to be clear as a mountain lake's surface. Still, as Gyr waited, he felt a budding tightness in his chest, a steel shard lodged beside his heart.

If Halladorn, or any of the men, balk, it will bring endless shame to my name...to Garlenna's as well. He had less room for error than a crossbow's winch had slack. A single word of their plan whispered in the wrong ear would bring total ruin.

They'll think me the spy. Then, I'll be executed. Almost worst, his actions this night would see him betray a man who'd been like a son. One could even make the case he also betrayed the Sempyrium, but Gyr saw it as quite the opposite. *I honor both by doing what is necessary. The ultimate fulfillment of my duties.*

Night fell, plunging the camp into a simmering quiet. Gyr returned to his tent to wait until the appointed time. The hours slid by like a suckling pig onto a greased spit. Fear and purpose rotated in his mind all night.

Near dawn, a creak of boot leather and a crunch of snow broke Gyr from his ruminations. He stepped from his tent.

Halladorn had not wavered. Instead of a score, however, only a dozen fully armed crownguard were in tow. Gyr raised an eyebrow, lips pursed.

The hound master raised onto tip-toes to whisper in Gyr's ear, tumble-weed beard bright orange in the torchlight. "Only those who could be trusted. A handful of others are posted as lookouts along the way. Two whistles for warning, just in case."

Gyr nodded, then checked the straps of his armor and bracers. Despite his age, there was some small comfort in dressing for battle. Like the crownguard before him, Gyr wore a padded surcoat covered in chain but bore no helmet. All wore deep green tabards bearing the sigil of Namarr. In arms alone, Gyr differed from his men. They carried swords, spears, and rounded shields, while he gripped the four-pointed flanged mace of a prosort and carried a kite shield. One and all, they were prepared for battle, though Gyr was certain it wouldn't come to that. The retinue's crownguard were handpicked by Gyr. They respected him immensely. And Duke Malus would never see it coming. Once the Lord of Brighthaven was secured, the rest of the retinue would stand down.

"Come, we must move swiftly. He can't have time to react." Gyr turned to go, but a hand spun him around.

Halladorn stared intently from deep-set eyes. "We are putting a great deal of faith in you, Father Renwood."

"Faith?"

"Aye. A lot. I may not be a dreamer of fanciful gods and the like, but I do hold faith in people, especially good ones."

"I would not lead you astray. We do what is right." *I'm saving his life, as is my charge. And at any cost.*

Gyr motioned for the men to follow. Row upon row of tent fell away on either side as they passed. Within, most rested soundlessly, while a few snored. One pair who appeared to have been up all night crouched in the snow over an upturned helmet, flicking cards into it and drinking from a leather wineskin. Noting Gyr and his men's battle dress, the pair looked at each other in alarm and then stood. "What's—"

Gyr motioned him to silence. "All is fine. Go back to your game."

The men did as bidden, tongues darting over dry lips, heads drooping low between their shoulder blades as they stared at each other.

The lie made Gyr sink inside. This was not who he was, yet it was who he had to be. He gritted his teeth and carried on. *I will save Malus's life at any cost.*

He repeated the mantra. Few faces came and went, flickering in the firelight. Placid eyes, lowered chins, a slight widening or narrowing of the lids showing alarm or suspicion. Or something else. It all happened so fast, it was hard to say. Likely all of what Gyr assumed and more. Every time they crossed paths with one not in their retinue, Gyr's breath caught, heart beating fury in his breast.

None challenged them. Why would they? It was their prosort—the eyes, ears, and voice of the duke. And so, armed and armored, they moved without incident into a ring of torches surrounding the Duke of Lah-Tsarra's pavilion.

Velal stood over a small brazier, warming stones for Duke Malus's bedside. Gyr handed his shield over to one of the crownguard as he strode toward the man and drew a dagger. The groomsman glanced up at Gyr, smiling his fake smile. When he spotted the dagger, his smile vanished, mouth falling slack as he realized the situation marching straight at him. Before he could make a sound, Gyr lunged forward, snatching his hair in a studded-leather fist.

Gyr pressed the knife blade against the servant's throat. "Keep walking."

Velal attempted to warn Duke Malus, but it came out as a barely audible squeak.

They paused before Sir Qel. The knight wiped his nose and stash, nodded at them, then stepped aside. Gyr entered first, pushing Velal before him.

To Gyr's surprise, the duke was still awake. More surprising still was Caltheo seated across from him; it appeared the two had been up talking all night. *Like we used to.* Jealousy struck Gyr like an arrow. *No, this isn't personal.*

With his back to the tent opening, Malus twisted in his seat at the sound of shuffling feet and the jostle of arms. Mouth hanging open, eyebrows slightly raised, he studied the traitorous band. Caltheo eased back. He gave no inkling of surprise but for a slightly furrowed brow bent on solving a mathematics problem. Gyr locked eyes with his former cupbearer and something flashed across the young man's expression. A predatory calm. Even with the unexpected intrusion, Caltheo maintained his stiff, unflappable confidence, so recently gained.

"What are you doing?" Malus rose to standing.

Every part of Gyr begged him to lay down his arms, to plead for mercy for his betrayal.

Every part but the one that mattered. *I'm saving his life.*

Gripping Velal's hair tighter, Gyr pushed into the room, opening a space for the others to fill in behind.

Smoothing hands down the lapels of his velvet robes, Malus's mouth was a flat, hard line. "Gyr Renwood, you disgrace yourself and you drag these men down with you. Let go of Velal. Immediately."

Silence followed but for the shift of weight from foot to foot.

"You others," Malus said. "Arrest Gyr Renwood."

No one moved. The breath in the tent was warm and thick enough to choke on. Sweat beaded down Gyr's neck as he loosed a slow exhale, then afforded a quick glance backward. Every man in the tent watched him. Velal quivered under hand. *I'll see my duty through...at any price.*

Summoning his most commanding voice, Gyr said, "The duke's safety is our highest duty. Take them gently."

"Gyr Renwood!" thundered Malus. "What do you think you're doing?"

"Saving your life, my duke."

Crownguard crept along the edges of the pavilion. Malus cast about like a cornered animal.

Viper-quick, Caltheo snatched Malus's robes and pulled him backward, putting the table between Gyr's men and the duke. "Your sword!" he shouted at Malus, then drew an ax and brandished it. "Stay where you are, cowards!"

The men stopped in their tracks as Malus plucked a sword and scabbard from the bed and drew steel. Dread sat like a stone in Gyr's gut. Caltheo fixed him with an icy stare. "Arrest Gyr Renwood and Master Halladorn. If you do not, each of you dies a traitor."

Gyr pressed his lips together, chin dropping. "Take Caltheo as well."

"You'll take no one," Caltheo hissed. "This isn't some criminal. This is your rightful lord. Whichever of you touches him will be strung up for treason." He flourished his ax. "Unless you get my blade between your eyes first."

"Lay down your ax, fool!" Halladorn roared. Velal fainted, crumbling like a doll at Gyr's feet. He stepped over the man, mace swooshing from its thong. Distantly, Gyr heard shouts outside the tent. Crownguard were rousing.

We're running out of time.

"We won't go without a fight." Emboldened, Caltheo pointed at each crown-guard in turn. "Who among you will harm your lord? Think, you fools!"

"Men, take Caltheo with whatever force necessary," Gyr said. "Duke Malus is not to be harmed."

They moved to action, though still tentative. One poked at the air harmlessly, testing Caltheo, but the cupbearer didn't dignify the meager attempt with a reaction.

"Now, damn you!" Halladorn bellowed.

There was a crash of steel back at camp—far off—someone dropping their weaponry.

A decade ago, Gyr would have trusted himself to overtake Caltheo without spilling blood, but the cupbearer was a decent fighter, and much quicker than he remembered. *That reality is ten years gone.* Undaunted, he stepped forward, mace and dagger at the ready. A soldier nearby followed suit, naked blade in hand.

Caltheo pressed Malus against the back of the tent.

Something tugged at Gyr's awareness. He saw the confusion on the faces of those to either side. Then a heavy hand landed on Gyr's shoulder—Halladorn's.

"Listen," the hound master said. They froze and a hush seized the pavilion.

Over the hammering pulse in Gyr's ears, he heard it, sharp and sudden and terrifyingly clear.

"The hounds!" Halladorn hissed, then fled the tent. The fainter sound of men calling the camp to arms joined the chorus of barking dogs. Then a war drum boomed.

"Kurgs!" Gyr shouted. "Secure the duke!"

"No one touches him." Caltheo's voice was ice. "He stays by me no matter what. I said the Prosort's Creed. He's my responsibility now."

"Fine," Gyr growled.

Sir Qel leapt through the tent flap from outside. "Prosort, a hundred at least!"

"From which direction?" Gyr took his shield back from the crownguard who'd been holding it.

Sir Qel panted like the rest of them as they fought to remain calm. "The north end of camp and working toward center, but I hear fighting to the west and south as well."

Only the east remains open. The one toward Kiyahd.

"Mounted?" Gyr asked.

Sir Qel nodded curtly. "Many."

"We'll have to fight our way south toward Staghill. The safety of Duke Malus is our primary concern." Gyr took a breath. "On the ready, men! When I say so, we head for the wagons at the south end of camp. Lord Malus is to stay in the center at all times. Defend his life with your own at any—"

"The horses," said Caltheo. "We make for the horses."

"A trap," said Gyr. "They'll hit the horses first. The wagons are slow, defenseless—they'll save them for last. That means the draft horses may go overlooked. Whoever gets to the wagons alive takes Duke Malus straight for the outpost at Staghill."

As if confirming his point, a horse screamed in the distance.

When Caltheo didn't challenge the plan, Gyr turned to the tent flap, yanking at the strap on one of his bracers. *Tight is right.* His arms instructor at the Sempyrium always said as much. Hands wrapped around leather grips on both kite shield and the haft of his mace, so tight his fingers tingled.

A war cry pealed through the air outside the tent. The clash of arms. A curse from Sir Qel. The sound of struggling. A strange tongue...speaking Unti.

"I—I have a family," said a crownguard, voice quaking.

"We all have families," said Gyr. He thought of Malus and Garlenna—even Caltheo. "We fight for them. Remember that."

The snarling of Halladorn's warhounds finally ceased. "Malus and Caltheo to the center."

Ebhor bleated furiously amid a raucous din of cascading rock. Somewhere, a group of them were charging. "Ready..."

Shouts of battle raged closer. Outside the tent, the sound of fighting between Sir Qel and his opponent stopped.

Gyr lurched forward. "Move!"

He plunged into blinding gray light, into battle, into chaos, into screaming slaughter.

CHAPTER THIRTY-THREE

THE WRATH OF WIVES

Wind blew Hadir's hair flat around his face. Sunlight painted the surrounding treetops golden. Holding hands, Zadani stood with her husband on the tumbledown ruins strewn about the hill. The one he'd loved.

She watched him scan the horizon, thick features bunched into a smile. This was his place.

With a dagger of sorrow, she realized this might have been what he looked like before he died—one final, pleasant moment. The last before fear had sent him running for his life to the maple grove.

Hot, fetid air breathed down her neck like the unwelcome advances of Nymon the Lech, suffocating her, causing her to gag. Her stomach convulsed, a tangle of searing knots. The horror of it penetrated the veil of dreams.

Something told her it was real. That she was seeing Hadir before he died. "I'm sorry, my love."

He turned, said something indiscernible.

She shook her head. It was like he didn't know how it worked after so many dreams. Though they seemed to share this dreamworld, their perspectives could never align. That's where the pain lay, hiding in the gap between their understanding of one another. Even more than the space between the living and the dead.

Hadir's gaze drifted over Zadani's shoulder toward the stronghold of Kiyahd roosting on its hilltop. His smile disappeared. The whites of his eyes expanded with fear as his hand slid from hers, and then he raced down the hill.

"Don't leave!" Zadani wanted nothing more than to follow him. To tell him he was safe and that he'd be okay. But she couldn't move. And it was a lie anyway.

He would die like that. Like she'd seen him. Hadir would die afraid.

Zadani blinked, a tear rushing down her cheek as wind gusted over her.

She squeezed her eyes shut, wishing it could all go back to normal. Back to the way it was before. The wind moaned against her, louder and more frigid. Tears gathered at her chin and were swept away.

She heard a scream—her own—and woke to cold reality.

The trill of birds welcoming the day was cut short by Zadani stomping down the garden path. With a frantic flap of wings, they fled from the safety of the dense hedgerows, scattering to the wind before her purposeful strides. Strides intent on dispensing justice.

The strides of a wrathful wife.

After two full days and a third night spent embracing a bucket, Zadani was well enough to be on her feet. Thanks to Thruna bringing drinking water whenever she changed out the bucket of sick, the cramping had gradually diminished to a manageable level. Combined with a consistent dose of rising gold, Zadani awoke that morning feeling half herself again and ready to expose Nymon the Lech and his men. Between the unrest in Anjuhkar centering around the Scarborn, and the clandestine dealings with what seemed to be Kurgs during times of tenuous peace, Zadani decided she had enough evidence to inform Lord Marus.

Jasso will be pleased, though I'll keep his part in it to myself.

Mist bowed around Zadani's legs. The knife in her boot mashed her ankle bone—she'd promised herself to never go without it after the night with Nymon. Almost, she welcomed the stab of pain, a reminder of the safety it provided.

A startled heron cried out a warning. Her head swiveled sharply toward the willow tree it fled from under. Zadani paused...recalled something familiar. Part of its root system was exposed from the earth like a broken elbow breaching skin.

Breath came in paltry sips as memory snared her.

In their first year of courtship, she had watched Hadir do a handstand on the very same root. Watched his hand slip, heard his yelp of surprise during the subsequent tumble. With dirt smearing his forehead, he sprang to his feet to brush off bits of clinging earth, casting furtively about for those who'd seen the embarrassing feat. All the while, Zadani roared with laughter. While he hadn't been physically injured, his ego would end up wading through years of Zadani's jesting reminders of the incident. She wasn't sure he'd ever really recovered.

Tears dripped from one eye in a steady rhythm. She went to the willow and placed a palm against its trunk. Neither warm nor cold, but immutably firm. "I miss our walks, love." It was comforting to know the places where they'd shared their beautiful life together would remain intact.

More recent memories assailed her, whisking her from the warm bliss of the past. Rough hands seeking to violate everything sacred. A lying tongue, covering her in its sin. Greasy lips, smiling when they should be trembling in fear of what she knew.

At the end, he'll know it was me. Then it'll be me who smiles.

With a sharp sniffle, Zadani left the tree—a symbol of better days—and continued on her path to Lord Marus's chambers. The joy had died with Hadir. She barely knew that woman who she'd seen laughing in her mind's eye.

That Zadani is gone.

In the courtyard just outside the keep's main entrance, a sour taste spilled around her gums, a wave of nausea hot on its heels. The contents of Zadani's stomach threatened to rise. She swallowed, licked at her gums—spat. The flagstones tilted, opposite the sky. She slapped a palm against the wall to balance herself, then retched into a rosebush.

No amount of retching, no amount of washing will free me from the feel of Nymon the Lech's repugnant touch. The last, she'd already tried, but all it earned her were friction burns from over-scrubbing in places unseen.

To feel clean again, only justice will suffice.

In the hall outside Lord Marus's chambers on the third floor of Hawk's Keep, a dozen holdguard in purple and black tabards waited.

A good start. Though they'll need more when they arrest Nymon and his Scarborn.

The thrill of it all intensified in Zadani as she stepped up behind the nearest guard. "Excuse me. I must speak with Lord Marus immediate..." She froze, trailing off.

"Oh must you?" Nymon twisted around. Upon seeing her, he grimaced.

More heads turned. Thick beards, secreting the thin mark of scars. Out of instinct, Zadani stepped back. *No, I will have justice!* She puffed up her chest and reclaimed the step. "Yes. Immediately."

"Lord Marus don't want your sickness, wench. He's busy."

Stoic, cruel faces met her flitting gaze. She summoned her most commanding tone, one reserved for kitchen staff committing a grievous blunder. "This is an emergency. If he has to wait to hear it, I assume you'll be dealt with harshly."

Nymon's lip twitched. He craned around to look at his men, snickered into his fist, and then loosed a howl of laughter. The others joined in, and soon, the hall was ringing with mirth, needles in Zadani's ears.

A flush spread from chest to chin, the creep of dawning failure. *I was so close.*

The door to Marus's chamber opened. Lady Daran stepped out, her eyes a pair of dark pits. "Be silent!"

The Scarborn snapped to attention. Nymon sucked at his teeth. "Apologies, my lady."

Before Lady Daran ducked back inside, Zadani called out. "Lady Dar—"

A stinking hand seized her throat—a hand she vowed never to let touch her again. Pressure bloomed in her face. Dark spots bubbled into her vision making it look like the surface of a boiling pot. Slaver lined the corners of Nymon's twisted mouth as he squeezed. "Brainless fucking bitch," he hissed.

Air came in a strained wheeze, but she didn't need it. Hatred was enough to survive, and she had that in vast supply. She clawed his face, leaving a pair of vibrant weals next to his milk-dead eye. Her other hand flew, too, but missed. With a curse, Nymon lifted slightly then shoved.

For a weightless second, Zadani stared at the rafters...

Stone bludgeoned her backside. Her head snapped back. Pain shot down one shoulder, and into her elbow where it cracked against the unforgiving floor. "Ah!" Zadani clutched at the injury, lips pursed, sucking in stilted breaths.

"How dare you!" Firm hands hauled her up by the armpits to her feet from behind. "Lord Marus will hear of this." Genjin Hyrix stood at her side, cheeks bearing angry red splotches, his mouth pitted with disbelief.

Nymon hacked, showed the Awakened the gathered spit, then hawked it at his feet. "The little Lady Daran gets more of our lord's ear than you do, freak. Why, he's in there right now handling important business with Vallabathus and the rest of his family—all without you."

"I'm still a member of his council." Genjin hesitated. "I'll have you removed and in manacles by sundown."

Nymon laughed, cranked his neck until it gave a wet pop. "You ain't nothing more than a fancy ornament Lord Marus likes to dangle at court...Bloodrot."

The muscle's in Genjin's arm tensed around Zadani. The Awakened balled his fists and glared at Nymon. "What did you just call me?"

"What? Don't like your name, Bloodrot?" Nymon raised an eyebrow mockingly. "Not man enough to embrace the violent name you earned? I heard about you. Scary stories about your little trees—"

The air hissed around Genjin Hyrix. "I'll do more than tell you tales, fool." Pools of light glimmered in his eyes and coiled from his shoulders. Scintillating points of an alien glow emanated from his fingertips. A keening sound filled the air...

Zadani stumbled back. A few of the Scarborn behind the Lech did the same.

Not Nymon though. He doubled down and unlimbered a wicked-looking ax from his belt. "Try me, you queer fuck. Prove some shit to Marus and Vallabathus. They're in there right now, talking about spies." Nymon chuckled as Genjin gasped. "Yeah, that's right. No one told you. I hope you're quiverin' a bit wonderin' why that is. My boys tell me you get on real sweet with that fop from Valat. Take another step my way and maybe I tell our lord about it, eh? Spies always look for the weak ones. Easiest to turn."

Zadani flinched. *A spy?* "No, Genjin." She grabbed the Awakened by the arm and jerked him back with all her strength. The man was rooted in place. She may as well have been trying to remove an oak tree growing from a stone wall. "Don't."

Incandescent eyes regarded her.

"He's nothing." Zadani glowered at Nymon. "You've a better chance at getting respect from a swine."

Genjin's chest heaved. Nymon's men shifted. Zadani hadn't noticed they drew their weapons, yet there they were in ready hands.

The halos on Genjin's fingers and the glow in his eyes dimmed. The keening sound ceased.

Zadani pulled again. This time, Genjin came with her. Together, they stormed from the hall. Out of earshot and around a couple of corners, Genjin's anger subsided, though only a little. "That man—these new holdguard—I cannot stomach them."

That makes two of us. She patted his arm as he bent at the waist, hips pressed back against the wall.

"And I won't." He searched the floor, brow furrowed. "Not anymore. If Lord Marus wants to hire men such as these and leave me out of his council..." He straightened. "Jasso leaves in a month. I'll go with him if he'll have me."

Zadani considered sharing her discovery in confidence with Genjin. Their interactions over the years were limited, but the consensus was Genjin Hyrix was a good man. A loyal one.

But the trust simply wasn't there. And now, there was talk of a spy at Hawk's Keep. Everything she and Jasso had recently done made them look rather suspicious. She'd have to be careful when she posed her evidence of Nymon's treachery to Lord Marus.

Besides, if Genjin is willing to leave with Jasso, he may well be in love with the man. Love does strange things. It can change a person. It can twist them for the worse just as easily as it might mold them for the better. When in love, people are erratic. Dangerous.

No one knew that better than Zadani Innan.

Chapter Thirty-Four

RUN

Light splashed across Gyr's face. The men rushed out and around him from the tent.

It was dawn, depressing gray and snow drenched. All around were strangers' faces. Manes of jet were gathered into knots at the back of bald, thick foreheads. Grim expressions pulled tight over high cheekbones. Most were stodgy, short, and stumpy legged. Broader than a Namorite through the chest and thighs. A number of females raided with them from the look of it. Taller and leaner, but every bit as ferocious.

Bloody spear in hand, Sir Qel stood over a Kurg who thrashed and yammered on the ground, holding together a puncture in his gut.

"Finish him," Gyr commanded, "and follow!"

They veered through a maze of canvas, moving at a trot to avoid breaking formation while staying tight around Malus and Caltheo. Breath came in sharp flurries, reminding Gyr of his age and how distant he was from his days of rigorous training.

The instincts, however, were still there. They trickled into an open space where a cook had been preparing for breakfast. Now, his corpse lay over the fire, skin smoking and crackling, a trio of Kurgs overwhelming a soldier across the way. Blood poured from multiple stab wounds on the soldier's body. One Kurg pushed the weakened man onto his back, straddled him, knees pinning each shoulder. The Kurg reached down, gripped the man's jaw in both hands and then wrenched with all his might. Gyr couldn't see it. Didn't need to. The clipped scream and wet suck of tearing flesh told him the mouth was split into a joker's grin.

Sir Qel hefted his spear and hurled it into the buttock of one of the Kurgs. With a scream, he grabbed his hindquarter. The other two whirled to face the men of Brighthaven, brandishing chaswas, their deadly stone clubs. One had an ubley strapped to his arm as well, a long tube of lacquered wood that served as both a shield and missile weapon. With haste, the Kurg dropped a round stone into the oblong bowl, jerked back his arm and swung it. Gyr raised his shield. A resounding thud told him he'd done so in time to deflect the hurled stone.

Three more Kurgs joined the first two. They approached the larger group cautiously. One of them let out a loud whooping sound. Calling for help, Gyr assumed. "Quickly now!"

The men of Brighthaven charged. Gyr stopped short, shook a shoulder, baiting a Kurg to lunge. Instead, he sat back. Both swiped the air with their bludgeoning weapons then circled. The Kurg leapt, chaswa whooshing low then high. Gyr took the first on his shield, the second he caught with his mace. He was slower than his opponent, but a vastly more experienced fighter.

He swung his shield, catching the Kurg off guard. A wishbone cut split golden skin. Scarlet gushed from his brow. Gyr's opponent stumbled backward in a daze, knees wobbling, blood coursing, covering half of his face and dripping onto his chest.

Gyr glanced in his periphery. More Kurgs were flocking to the fray. Two of his men pinioned one, their blades ramming into either of his sides. One of his crownguard lie dead, bleeding from a deep, purple depression in his forehead, one of the Kurgs' lithe females shaking her arms triumphantly over him. It was a swirl of madness, of stone and shield and blade. Clanging, cursing madness. His men were dying.

The Kurg before Gyr wiped at the crimson covering his face, blinked dumbly at it. He fell into an unsteady crouch, chaswa raised. "Honor," he said in the Common tongue, then lunged.

Before the Kurg could cover the distance between them, a hulking figure filled the space. As easily as he might twirl a cat by the tail, Fullor snatched the Kurg by the hair, twisted his hips, and swung him overhead into the dirt. With his knees, he dropped onto the man's face with a sickening crunch, then took the dead Kurg's chaswa.

"Keep moving!" Gyr shouted.

Caltheo and Malus came into view, speeding into the lead. Gyr ran to catch up, Fullor, Sir Qel and four surviving crownguard bringing up the rear. Where the rest of their party went, he did not know. Everywhere he looked, there were pockets of fighting, the gurgle of death, the clang of steel against...steel.

That can't be. Since the forest enclaves' treachery during the Great Betrayal, Kurgs had faced an embargo on metals used to forge weapons.

Further considerations were fleeting. Another fight came and went, this time leaving Gyr with a cut along the scalp and one less crownguard. They raced onward to the south. He fell in beside Malus and Caltheo, noting the blood now soaking both their weapons. Caltheo's ax was gone and he now carried a sword.

Screams and the smell of shit filled the once crisp morning air. The crunch of snow under boots could barely be heard above the blood pounding in Gyr's ears or the chaotic breathing of their group.

Whenever they saw a solitary crownguard, they beckoned them to join their contingent. As they ran, their number grew. And then, after encountering pockets of the enemy, it shrank. "Keep moving," Gyr would command. And they did, Malus and Caltheo always returning to center.

Time moved fast, then slow, then fast again.

Gyr's lungs burned. His chest was painfully tight.

They weaved between tents, came across a handful of crownguard fighting back-to-back in a final stand against a score of Kurgs closing in around them. "Left!" Gyr hissed.

They moved over a line of defensive stakes as they cleared the main camp. The sound of fighting faded behind them. From the lack of blood splashed across the snow, it was clear the battle hadn't yet reached this area. Gyr looked up-slope and found what seemed to be a chieftain astride an ebhor executing an unarmed knight. A meaty fist held a longsword in a reversed grip as he plunged it through the man's mouth. The chieftain spotted them and pointed. The silhouettes of more mounted Kurgs materialized behind him in the morning mist.

He was armed like a Namorite. Bits of mail draped the Kurg's body and he had a sword. Someone had violated Bacot's Steel Embargo. Likely, the same someone he and Malus sought—the highborn traitor.

Unmolested wagons and draft horses were a hundred yards ahead. A thrill rifled through Gyr's chest. A soldier behind him whispered excitedly. Gyr's legs burned, his low back unyieldingly tense. After a short distance, one side of his gait shortened into a limp. "Keep going!"

Paralleling their movements, the silhouettes of mounted Kurgs raced through the trees to cut them off. Gyr beckoned his body to move faster. The rest of the group outstripped him in their mad dash for the draft horses. Gyr hacked up blood—pushed through the burning irons enclosing his lungs. He tossed his shield to go faster. Others did the same, eager to reach the wagons.

A half dozen Kurgs on ebhor burst from the mist-wreathed woods to their right. Dressed in chain and bits of armor, the riders leveled iron-capped spears and tucked ubley shields close to their ribs. Using only their knees to steer, they bore down on the men of Brighthaven.

Ebhor were massive beasts bred for rugged mountain terrain. Their stout legs pummeled the earth. Their chests were as thick as a horse's, though they stood only half that height. Horns curved backward, they lowered their heads. They were closing fast. None of their party would reach the wagons.

Duke Malus must!

"Halt!" Gyr shouted. "Turn to face!"

Hoofs kicked snow in furious white waves behind the mounted Kurgs as they charged. The interlocking plate armor draped across the ebhor's chests clacked as they sped closer. Gouts of steam rose from slavering mouths. Crag-faced riders crouched forward, murder in their eyes.

Gyr licked his lips, fingers tingling. He glanced back at a frightened Malus, Caltheo poised at his side. "We'll draw them in. When they're close, you two make for the horses!" *Dutiful sacrifice...for you, my sons.* Both men nodded.

A single war whoop drew the prosort back to the imminent chaos unfolding before him.

A sharp intake of breath rose from the men of Brighthaven as the Kurgs closed. There was a flicker of motion to Gyr's right.

The lead ebhor crashed into the snow a split second before collision, Sir Qel's deftly hurled spear sticking from its shoulder. The rider flew into their ranks and was cut down.

The remaining ebhor bulled into them, crushing armor and bone alike where they struck. One man was flung in the air like a doll, lifted by a set of ram's horns. Gyr leapt into the snow to dodge one beast's onslaught, its rider's spear ripping through his cloak as he hit the ground. Powder flew up around him as he rolled clear, mace still in hand.

Instinct told him to lie still for a moment as a rush of air, then a shadow, passed overhead. He staggered to his feet, lower back screaming.

He watched as an ebhor attempted to ram Sir Qel. The knight dodged the full brunt of its battering, but it caught his leg and flung him off balance. As he rose, the Kurg led his mount in a circle around the knight of Brighthaven then dashed his skull with a chaswa. Blood gushed from the part of his slick blond hair.

Gyr cast about. A hundred feet away, Malus and Caltheo neared the wagons.

He took off after them, looking back a final time. Fullor held an ebhor by the horns, attempting to grapple it to the ground. Its rider stabbed him in the shoulder, dropping him to his knees.

Seventy-five paces...

Gyr focused forward. Caltheo and Malus came to a stop at the wagons.

Fifty paces...

Gyr needed to cover the distance to the draft horses as quick as his body would let him. Once there, he could hold off any attack that might come so that Caltheo and Malus might escape.

Ahead, the duke and cupbearer slashed the draft horse's tethers, then mounted.

Twenty-five...

Gyr watched Caltheo close with the wagons, whirling his mount toward Malus D'Alzir's at the last second. The cupbearer brandished his sword. The motion caused Malus to search behind him for approaching danger. The duke seemed to notice Gyr running toward him. Their eyes locked—a flash of hope.

A vast emptiness opened inside Gyr as Caltheo plunged his blade into Malus's heart. Blood erupted from the duke's mouth. His eyes went wide as he looked down at the sword sticking from his chest. Gyr's legs failed him, causing him to stumble onto one knee in the snow, failed him again as he tried to rise. "No!" he shouted.

The Duke of Lah-Tsarra plummeted from the horse. Screaming, Gyr found his balance and rushed forward, mace in hand. Caltheo attempted to turn his mount and flee, but Gyr leapt, striking the beast in the leg, buckling it. He rolled onto his shoulder, felt a sharp pain in his collarbone. He gained his knees, struck out once more at the horse's hindquarters. A blade sliced the air overhead, tip barely missing him. This time, Gyr was rewarded with a snap. The draft animal pitched back, then forward, throwing Caltheo over its withers.

With a curse, his former protege moved like lightning to retrieve his blade, dashing any chances of Gyr attacking him unarmed. The bald cupbearer stood in a shower of snow, his face devoid of emotion. Dark bags clung underneath bulging eyes.

Gyr approached cautiously, mace at the ready. He looked toward Malus. The dead duke stared up from a snowy grave. Gyr loosed a pained grunt, glass shards pumping through his heart. He squared to Caltheo, sadness devoured by unbridled rage. Leather creaked between Gyr's fists as he choked the handle of his prosort's mace.

"Why, Caltheo?" he wheezed.

Caltheo whipped his sword in a perfunctory arc, casting Malus's blood from it and forming a scarlet crescent in the snow at his feet. "Who is Caltheo?" he said. The black of his pupils seemed to grow...to spread like spilled ink. Obsidian mist drifted from his face to dissipate overhead.

Gyr gasped, backpedaling in horror.

Oil-dark smoke rolled off Caltheo's skin. The flesh around his eyes sagged. A smell violated Gyr's nose.

The things in the woods. An intense sucking sound filled the air, along with the familiar, putrid stench. Caltheo's skin sloughed away, dropped into a stink-ing pile of offal with a wet slosh. Steam rose from the discarded husk that was

Caltheo at the Ruptured's feet. It was Duke Malus who now faced Gyr, a cruel smile on his lips.

Gyr shook his head, disbelieving. *That was not my Caltheo.*

A flicker of motion near the wagons caught Gyr's eye. His gaze darted to locate its source, but found nothing. The draft horses had fled, and the Kurgs were overcoming the last of the crownguard.

They'll come for the wagons next.

The assassin seemed to notice his situation at the same time as Gyr. Foul vapor emanated from the false duke's eyes and skin once more, evaporating moments after it burst from him. Steam rushed from split skin as the Ruptured's mask of Malus D'Alzir melted to the snow in slabs of slopping meat.

Gyr stared into the face of a Kurg.

Without a horse, he knows he can't get away. So he'll infiltrate the Kurgs.

There was little time to think. The Ruptured dashed forward, knocking aside Gyr's mace and then clipping his calf. Gyr grunted. More blows followed, too fast to track, each one scoring a cut. It was all Gyr could do to block half of them. The Ruptured's blade licked a thigh. Kissed a shoulder. Drew blood from his forearm.

Gyr dropped to a knee in the snow. In a matter of seconds, his hands were empty. Where his mace had once filled his palm, blood now pooled.

He stared into the assassin's face; it took only a moment to see his death there. Pain shot through Gyr's lungs as he coughed and spat a gob of crimson mucus at the false Kurg's feet. Shame crept into his shoulders. Malus's body lay nearby. Almost, he looked serene. "Gods...forgive me." A tear sped down his cheek.

"You are already forgiven by the only one who matters." The Ruptured's sword arm eased across his chest. No hurry now. A final backhand swipe and it would be over. "Soon, my Light comes to sing his Final Song. Then *all* will be forgiven."

Garlenna. I'm sorry.

The assassin's elbow rose, preparing for a downward slash. The killing blow, Gyr dimly realized.

"For Brighthaven!"

The Ruptured spun toward the war cry and brought his sword up just in time to parry the blade of a charging Sir Raius. Blood caked the diminutive knight-captain's hair from some unseen wound, rimming his hairline in a rusty red. Links of chain shone with the rents of battle and his lips were tinged blue and cracked from the cold, as if he'd spent too long in the elements.

Despite his dilapidated appearance, the swarthy knight-captain attacked with vicious precision. "For the duke!" Sir Raius moved swiftly, a series of tight strokes from high to low, then high again. The Ruptured was forced backward, the cruel smile fading from his lips. He sought an opening to launch his own offensive, but the knight's attack was unceasing in its ferocity.

A sound like thunder rolled through Gyr's chest. He wondered if it was the sound of him dying—the crimson curse finally come to burst his lungs—but then he realized it was in his legs, too. The ground trembled. *The Kurgs are coming.*

The back-and-forth clash of steel before him was all that mattered now.

Gyr tried lifting his mace to help Sir Raius but couldn't. He watched the world through a dim, hazy veil. Heard it through ears ringing with death. Felt it through numb and frail fingers. Blood-pinked snow surrounded him—his own. *I'm dying.*

His last wish in life was to see Garlenna once more but she was leagues away. He'd have to settle for seeing Malus avenged.

With a curse, the Ruptured gambled, abandoning his guard to deliver a heavy chop at Raius's sword arm, and as he did, the knight's blade flicked up to cleave off an ear. Despite the sacrifice, the risk worked. The Ruptured broke Raius's onslaught enough to piece together an offensive.

The knight-captain rushed to block a lunge and slipped. Gyr's breath caught. The thundering hooves of ebhor drew nearer. Everything Gyr could feel in his body, hurt. The rest, he no longer felt at all. His world darkened, became a narrow and faint thing. Warmth crept through him.

The Ruptured stabbed downward at the fallen Sir Raius.

From his back, the knight-captain rolled to his side and caught the blade in his cross-guard. In the same motion, his hand disappeared into the folds of his cloak and then shot through the air in a backhand arc. A dagger flashed in the dawn light as it sped upward into the roof of the Ruptured's mouth.

Sword falling from rigid fingers, the shapeshifter keened. Ripples moved beneath his skin. Black vapor poured from his orifices, as though he were trying to change skins again. Gaining his feet, Raius thrust his blade into the thing's chest, just like the Ruptured had done to Duke Malus. The creature hung there, skewered, and the knight-captain smiled through bloodied teeth on the other end of the sword. The shapeshifter withered, blood and smoke pouring from him in spurting gouts until all moisture had drained from him.

The corpse of a shriveled old man slid to the earth.

The rumble of Kurgs drew nearer.

"Run," Gyr wheezed. "Raius...run."

The knight-captain backed up to the edge of the Winding Way's path. A glacial calm seemed to fall over him in the face of the charging ebhor. Sir Raius closed his eyes, raised his sword in both hands overhead. There was nowhere to go. Before him, the ebhor. Behind, a deadly fall.

The first ebhor hurtled toward him. At the last second, Raius opened his eyes and cast his sword end over end, lodging it into the chest of a rider. The Kurg flipped backward off his mount. The ebhor continued on, butting an unarmed Sir Raius. Flung like a doll, he skidded to the edge of the path where nothing but a sharp descent awaited. The man cursed, grasped for any handhold of earth to halt him as he slid...

Then he disappeared over the lip without a sound.

Shrugging, the Kurgs turned away and approached Gyr, nearly twenty strong now. Some had tattoos depicting dog's paws, or snarling mouths over an eye or across their shoulders. Gyr squinted, racked his brain to remember which clan this was. His mind was foggy, slippery. Blood loss had taken its toll.

With a snort, one Kurg led his ebhor across the short patch of muddy, crimson snow. He swung a leg over his mount and slid to the ground. He was shorter than Gyr but nearly twice his width. Abnormally broad even for one of the Forgotten People. His hulking shoulders were bare, his nethers covered by stitched ebhor hide lined in wolf fur. Bullish, muscled arms hunched around a protruding belly and powerful chest. Like most Kurgs, this one's boots were cinched high, nearly at the knee, and he carried a menacing Namorite battle ax. He looked every inch a chieftain.

"It no matter, priest," the Kurg said. It took Gyr a moment to realize the behemoth spoke Common. Not well, but understandable.

"Wha—what?"

"Look all you want. It no matter." The Kurg gestured all around. "You go nowhere now. You know this?" The question sounded more like a statement. Gyr blinked, looked to where Malus lay.

The chieftain followed his gaze to the duke. Sorrow creased the lines of his craggy face. "Your lord is dead. This no matter."

Anger shot through Gyr. "Why do you keep saying that?"

"Because it is so. No enemy escapes Dog clan. I want to give you no..." The Kurg held up a stumpy finger as he searched for the word. "Hope. Hope no help you. Hope only make worse for you. If your lord lived, it no matter. He be dead anyway. You be just as rageful."

"Why?" Anger shook him, brought back some of his ability to focus. "Why would you attack us? We crossed no borders! We—"

Slowly, so slowly it frightened Gyr to the pit of his gut, the chieftain stepped close and laid his battle ax on the prosort's honor plate. "Listen for answer, priest. You no talk your way into answers. *Listen* for answers. Now keep silent or I will make you look the fool you are being."

Gyr pursed his lips, biting back a response. He knew "fool" meant "joker" and given the breadth of this Kurg, he knew his jaw would come clean off. He gulped. Nodded.

"Smart priest." The Kurg smiled, withdrew his hand. "Our queen suffers no ruler who is not herself. She is greedy. This she knows and accepts. We accept and we follow."

He looked to the other Kurgs, who laughed, some leaning over the horns of their stamping ebhor, others slapping their comrades on the shoulder. A few of the lithe female warriors spat. Gyr once heard Kurg women were highly competitive amongst one another. Animosity among them led to many fights.

"There is sadness in me for you, priest," the chieftain continued. "You not know you fight Queen of Dogs. How could know? The Dog clan is greatest. The fall of duke only first lesson we teach Namorites. We have more to teach. Come."

A hand like the lid of a cookpot fell heavily on Gyr's shoulder. Breath exploded from him. The wound in his shoulder made him dizzy as he was hauled upright. As if handling a child, the Kurg tossed him over the haunches of an ebhor.

In Gyr's last moments before he passed out, his eyes narrowed around Duke Malus's pale face. *I'm sorry. I failed you.*

Darkness stole the rest.

He knew only a brief and minor jostling, a wave of muscle moving underneath, the stink of shit so close to the ebhor's rear. In and out of darkness for an interminable time.

Dead faces. Blood-drenched snow. Here and there a joker. All passed under slow fluttering eyelids. Eyelids blinking like a butterfly drying its wings...

A sharp inhale. His own. He felt himself lifted from the ebhor. Felt the snowy earth crash into his side. He cried out as hard ground struck his wound.

Once the throbbing pain subsided, he rolled to his back. Snow fell slow and heavy. He blinked it from his eyes, wondering if he had died and joined the Sempyrean gods.

"Where?" he croaked.

"You are prisoner now. My leader comes to look at you."

Gyr lifted his head enough to spot the herculean Kurg from before. "You're not the chieftain?"

"Bubinga?" He laughed. "Bubinga is chieftain!" He raised his eyebrows and strutted about, massive belly shaking, his elbows bowed out in imitation of a chicken as he repeated his own name. "Chief Bubinga! Chief Bubinga! Here comes Chief Bubinga!"

The others laughed but were cut short by a sharp word spoken in Unti from somewhere out of sight. Then, in Common far surpassing Bubinga's, "Is this the priest?"

Bubinga nodded. A shadow fell over Gyr.

A lady Kurg stood over him. Everything about her was lean and powerful, elegant, and strangely beautiful. Three scratch marks were tattooed along both collarbones. High cheekbones framed a small plush mouth and a long muscular neck.

"He's old. He will not survive," she said, the same voice to silence the others a moment ago. "But if he does, he is mine." She crouched, her face coming to within an ax handle's length of Gyr's own. "Do you hear that, priest? You belong to Yashuu now."

She cupped a golden hand to her ear. "Who do you belong to?"

Swallowing hard, Gyr said, "Chieftain Yashuu."

More a flick than a slap, Yashuu struck him. "Princess Yashuu. Say it again. Say it right."

"Princess Yashuu," he blurted.

She smiled, teeth blinding white. "Come, it is a three days ride. Let us take the Queen of Dogs her gifts."

CHAPTER THIRTY-FIVE

THE HOLLOW PLACE

P ale-yellow light waved and flickered in the borderless glow of oiled window panes dotting the low hill where sat the town of Halaleh.

The place smacked of home. It sang of heroic deeds birthed from humble beginnings. Of neighbors and simplicity and everything slower. Of the kind of life veterans yearned for during times of war. A warm drink beside a warm fire, but nothing warmer than the cloak of family drawn tight around the heart.

That kind of place.

Barodane and Garlenna passed a handful of cottages spread out in the surrounding lowland. Those furthest from the hilltop were shittiest. A suspicious, grizzled face filled the wavy glass window of one, indifferent to any offense he might give with his stare.

Barodane swung his head to the other side of the rutted lane leading up the hill. First one set of eyes, and then three more popped up in a cracked window. Even with the fuzzy resolution of the glass, Barodane knew they belonged to children. Knew the much larger frame that swept up behind them and started cuffing them to be an adult. He wondered if the man was a veteran. One of the ones who'd longed for their fantasy safe haven.

Barodane supposed stories were stories for a reason. "Cozy place."

Smoke wound into the night sky from the surrounding chimneys in languid streams.

Garlenna drew the hood of her cloak overhead.

"After Digtown and weeks on the road, I thought you'd be happier to see a more...normal slice of civilization." Barodane lowered his voice. "Isn't this what you wanted? Me? The people? Together again and all that?"

She stroked her stallion's neck as muffled shouts came from the cottage with the children inside. "You know this isn't the course I recommend. Until we have more allies, we should be out of sight. The Hammer is hunting us. If we're caught, he's unlikely to believe a drug dealer's claim that he's the Crown Prince of Namarr returned from the dead. You'd be executed without trial."

"You think he'd let me ascend first? Or is he still a religious man?" Barodane exhaled. "I'd hate to die sober."

Garlenna's partially shrouded face swiveled toward him, the muscles around her single eye bunched tight. "This isn't a joke. Lives are at stake. Maybe tens of thousands. Have you learned nothing?"

I lived in seclusion for fourteen years and it took seeing my friends killed to drag me out of it. Have you?

He stared ahead. An old codger stepped from his door packing a pipe. Unperturbed, he stuck the flaming tip of a wood shaving into it until it glowed orange. He crossed his arms and blew out, matching Barodane's gaze from afar as they passed, path creeping upward.

"Working on it, Garlenna," the former prince sighed. "Working on it."

"From now until you bear Solicerames, you'll call me Ren of Farfield. What name will you go by? It can't be Kord."

The saddle creaked under Barodane as he shifted his weight. "Mal."

"Mal...Kord..." She peered at him with a flicker of recognition. "Your father and brother."

Barodane pushed Scab to a trot. "I hear music."

The hill leveled out onto a misshapen plane that made the town itself look drunkenly off-balanced. Barodane reined in, assessing the score of buildings haphazardly organized around a network of meandering dirt roads. Overlooking Halaleh from a low bluff sat a wooden fort in dire disrepair. A few holdguard with torches manned a stunted palisade, though only one actually patrolled it. Two others had set their spears aside between palings and sang bawdy songs as they passed a flagon back and forth.

Garlenna drew up beside him. "For a hold that makes nails, you'd think his fort would be held together by more than luck alone."

"A fair criticism." Music—badly played—murmured in the night air. Barodane jabbed a finger at a broad-fronted inn with a large stable beside it. "There. Come on."

Garlenna held him back with a hand on his chest. "You're sure you need this, Mal?"

Need? The longer he'd lived, the less the word had come to mean. Needs were for those who had something to live for. He hadn't needed anything but godsthorn, godsbrew, and a few quiet moments with Tyne when he'd had the pleasure of her company. After those early years, he hadn't even needed that. When Tyne left, he was free to roam deeper into the dungeons of his soul, to

feel his way along the walls, step by slow step, as far from the light as he could
go.

He answered Garlenna with a snap of Scab's reins. *I'm sure of nothing but my
thirst.*

Unlike the pair of stables he'd owned in Digtown, this one was spacious and
full of horses, and that meant travelers with basic means. An odd change of pace
compared to the company he'd grown accustomed to.

He passed under a sign that read *Rusty*, followed by a crooked nail as long as
his forearm. "The Rusty Nail."

"Good as any." Garlenna followed him inside.

Certainly better than the Dregs. Anywhere my friends haven't died.

The bar extended from wall-to-wall on one side. A dozen tables filled the rest
of the space. A hallway in one corner seemed to extend back into some rooms,
but what caught Barodane's interest was at the center of the dimly lit taproom:
a stage one step up from the floor and a few arm lengths wide. At the Dregs,
musicians and dancers had cleared the tables and chairs. Here, they gave a little
more care to welcoming the talent.

Barodane smiled.

A handful of glazed over expressions swung his way, then swung back to the
stage as a chord of music was struck—shattered glass in Barodane's ears.

Garlenna patted his back and whispered in his ear. "Are you still glad we did
it your way?"

One of many regrets I'll add to the list.

A young man with puppet-long limbs and a cavernous gap in his teeth drew
spidery fingers along the strings of his harp. He was better than the old man at
the Dregs, but that was akin to saying a pile of horse shit was preferable to a
dog's.

Smile gone, Barodane strode to the bar. "Godsbrew, and a mead. If you
have—"

"Busy at the moment," snapped the barman. "You'll wait."

Instead of feeling anger at the slight, Barodane noticed an odd sense of
comfort. The man wasn't Meckin, but he missed the curt talk of shit-town
innkeeps all the same. A liquid warmth curled in his chest. "Gladly."

Garlenna picked a spot in the corner, farthest from the stage and terribly lit,
and plopped into a chair with her back to the wall. From the bar, Barodane
watched her casual assessment of threats and exits. She summoned a yawn,
playing up the role of tired traveler.

A bump at the elbow. A splash of wetness.

Barodane looked up and found a pair of tankards had been rammed against
his arm, the surly barman already moving to the next customer. *And here*

I thought Meckin the crankiest of his profession. He took the tankards then joined Garlenna at the table. Every step of his journey across the room was accompanied by the clumsy farting of the harpist's song. As a prince of Namarr, he'd heard the best music ears could hear, but even at its best, harp play was soulless splashing.

Barodane plopped onto his seat. "Scab plays better."

Before Garlenna could respond, a young woman stepped over to their table, all skirts and hair and beaming sunshine. "Good eve, friends."

They nodded to her and she sat without invitation.

"My name's Wynna." The young woman's eyes were forced to slits by a broad smile pressing up her cheeks. "You're fresh to town?"

"And what a town it is." Garlenna leaned forward, waving a hand. Barodane had seen the tactic for seizing conversational control plenty of times. To occupy so much space before a person so quickly gave them pause. Enough for her to establish her own line of inquiry and ward off more questions. "Though I'm curious why Lord Marwen's fortress appears ill-tended to. If you've any insight on the matter..."

"Well." Wynna fidgeted with the lace of her bodice, maintaining a sheepish smile as if everything was a delightful secret. "That could have something to do with Lord Marwen's current state."

Barodane raised an eyebrow, prompting Wynna to clear her throat and hike a thumb over her shoulder. A short man with a dense red beard leaned to one side of a chair near the stage, head drooping over crossed arms. Four tankards, plus a fifth tipped onto its side, were all presumably empty and scattered before him.

"That's him?" Garlenna said.

Wynna nodded. "Ever since Roddic Olabran put the squeeze on."

Barodane frowned. "'The squeeze'?"

"Oh my." Wynna touched fingertips to lips. "You really aren't from around here. Either that or you've been living in a cave for a decade." *Not far off, I suppose.* "Every year, the magnates increase tributes for the smaller holds to keep their seats. They gain more power and assets, or simply absorb them."

Barodane frowned. "Doesn't the Collective step in?"

"What would the Collective do? Imprison Roddic Olabran?" Wynna slapped palms on her knees with a desultory laugh. "Goodness no. In truth, there's little to be done. The bites they take are small. Think of it like this"—Wynna batted her lashes—"the magnates are not sharks who consume a herring in a single bite. On the contrary, they are the ones eating the shark. A bite here and there goes unnoticed, but before you know it, a hundred days and a thousand bites later, there's nothing left but a floating skeleton."

"Even the small bites as you describe would call the attention of the Collective," Barodane said. "Danath Ironlight created the hold-system to maintain the balance of power."

Wynna made to respond, but Garlenna interjected, resting a hand on Barodane's arm. "It's as she says. Since the Shadowcrown has been in place, the magnates have capitalized on their opportunity."

"What?" Barodane said with a touch more vehemence than he should have.

His prosort's chin dipped. "The Ducal seats allow the magnates to cannibalize the smaller holds in order to assuage them until Ishoa Ironlight is crowned." The lines around Garlenna's eye was etched in sorrow. "Day by day and coin by coin, the Collective trades power for hope."

Cold, sickening guilt prickled Barodane's gut. He wanted to speak, but his throat seemed stuffed with filthy rags.

"Things have changed." Wynna pushed her heaving bodice forth and sat straighter. She glanced around, top teeth gripping bottom lip for dramatic effect. *I think she might fancy me. Must be the clean shave. Must not get that type around here often.* "My father received a pigeon three nights past from a friend in Anjuhkar. The Scarborn have deposed the Ice Maiden and may now hold the last Ironlight as their prisoner."

Barodane went rigid. He felt Garlenna stiffen as well. *My grandmother deposed?* Since the dawn of Namarr, Belara Frost had been a pillar of the United Lands. And his niece...

He muttered a curse as memory sprang to mind of a tiny hand clutching his finger, of innocent emerald eyes gazing into his.

"Shocking isn't it?" Wynna licked her lips. "They also say Duke Malus's death was..."

Malus's death?

The room started to spin. Barodane clutched his godsbrew tankard, desperate for an anchor. "Wait..." He closed his eyes and inhaled slowly.

"Duke Malus is dead?" Garlenna's tone was stern, threaded with disbelief. "When? How?"

"Kurgs did for Lord Malus a fortnight ago. The Scarborn rebellion happened then, too, if my father's friend can be believed. They think the Kurgs and Scarborn may be working together." Wynna stopped talking. The intensity of silence around Garlenna and Barodane set her to fidgeting, her smile sliding into a frown. "I'm sorry, ma'am—sir—we don't get messenger birds often these days. When we do, it tends to be exciting even if the news is harrowing."

Garlenna swept the taproom. "We?"

"Me and my da." Wynna twisted in her seat and pointed at Mag Marwen. "Don't let his drunkenness fool you. He's a wise man when sober. He says the insurrection is just beginning. The Scarborn have set the standard for the rest of Namarr. People are tired of the magnates' greed—the impotence of the dukes and duchess. Seems like the Kurgs are already mobilizing for war, and if the Collective wants to avoid the rest of Namarr joining them, they'll elect a new Crown Prince."

"Starved of satisfaction, they'll eat from the table of corruption." Garlenna leaned back in the chair while Barodane chugged his godsbrew dry.

Wynna perked up. "Peladon's teachings? How refreshing. We get so few learned types coming through." She noted Barodane's somberness and stretched a hand across the table to pat the back of his hand, fingernails lingering. "I know, sweetie, terrible news for the rest of us. Worthy of a drink...or five if you're my father. You'll be conscripted as holdguard, to be sure." She flicked a glance at Garlenna. "They'd probably take you, too. A woman you may be but you look stronger than most of the lot in here."

Barodane barely heard Wynna Marwen. *My grandmother and Malus are dead...because of my cowardice. Maybe Ishoa, too.* Tears welled in his eyes. He shied from them with a grunt

"I apologize for sharing such upsetting news with you. I thought it was common knowledge. Alas, word travels fast but reaches those travelers on long roads last." Wynna waved at a girl in the corner. "I originally set out this evening to bring merriment to my father's hold during these dark times. Do you think a song might cheer you?"

The summoned girl grabbed a leather case, large enough to fill her arms, and hastened over.

"A banha drum," Barodane said.

"Indeed." Wynna beamed at him. On the stage, the harpist bowed and the drunken taproom gave lackluster praise in the form of scattered clapping. Barodane assumed they applauded the end of the song rather than the performance itself. "Do you play?"

Garlenna's hand found his knee beneath the table. Using two fingers, she tapped out a single word of code: *No.*

Music had been Barodane's gift. Never had he won a tournament at the Singing Fields for horsemanship like Malath, or in battle like Garlenna. Nor did he excel in the ways of statecraft as his cousins, the D'Alzir twins, had. While he'd shown competence in all those areas, to claim the title of best had always been out of reach.

But by the Triune God, I can play the banha drum. All of his woes and insecurities, his hopes and dreams, expertly filtered from heart to hands to steel shell.

Again, Garlenna tapped twice, firmer than the first time: *No.*

He watched Wynna wave her servant away and then slip her plump hands under the leather cover. The cool touch of the burnished steel instrument would be pressing against her fingertips now. He knew the feeling...a taste, a sound, a luminous moment. Pure and cool spring water on a balmy summer day. The pulse of soundless and contented things, like first kisses, final breaths, and the smiles of loved ones.

Yes. I know that feeling well.

The drum slid out of its case, candlelight dancing over its smooth surface. Wynna strung together a few hand motions, rousing up a subdued thrumming.

For the first time in a long time, Barodane yearned for something other than godsthorn. He yearned to be connected to something greater than himself.

"I've dabbled," he said. "I wouldn't mind giving it a try once you're done."

She cocked her head, surprised by the request.

"They brew a strong drink here in Halaleh." Garlenna shifted toward him in her chair, crowding the space around Barodane, but he saw it coming and leaned forward over his tankard to evade her. Garlenna cleared her throat. "He does this in every town we go to. Makes a fool of himself on stage. You'll be lucky if he doesn't piss himself or get in a fight. I wouldn't give him the chance, milady."

"My travel companion is a funny one." Barodane's tone was cheery. In truth, he hungered to touch the instrument, to hold its vibrations in his bones and goad soft notes into his being. He'd do anything short of murder to play that banha drum.

Barodane shoved Garlenna in mock camaraderie. She moved very little. "Mal the Bard, they call me. Truth be told, Wynna, you couldn't have offered at a better time. I've recently had some difficulties and I've wanted nothing more to express them through song. Sadly, my own drum was stolen on the road. It would be a kindness I could never repay if you allowed me the honor of playing your instrument."

A flush leaked into Wynna's cheeks. *Ha! She* does *like me. You won't win this time, Gar.*

"Really Mal. Your style is... How should I put this? Not—"

"Ma'am, please." Wynna's smile disappeared. A thin line split her brow as she held up a hand. "You're clearly no artist. Out of respect to my father's hold, I can't let you finish that statement. It's never proper to prohibit the expression of one's chosen art form, no matter the quality." Lips pursed in haughty displeasure, Wynna pushed her drum across the table to Barodane. "I fully support your desires, Mal the Bard, and now insist that you perform. Kanians are said to be the best musicians in the world."

"Rightly so." Barodane shot his knee sideways into Garlenna's thigh then stood and gathered the drum.

An instrument both heavy and light, cold and warm. A conductor of whatever the one bearing it felt. Two sheets of steel hammered into opposing shells and then riveted together. Banha were difficult to make. Ever more difficult to make well. This one was middling at best, but he surmised it would do the job alright.

He threw a look over his shoulder at Garlenna. Stoicism greeted him there. *I'll hear no end of this.*

He stepped onto the stage then sat on the stool there. He kept the hood of his cloak up—at least in that, he might appease Garlenna. He hoped she would understand. He didn't act out of a desire for attention or to create difficulties.

This was for him and those he mourned.

Wynna took a seat closer to the stage. He nodded to her as he removed his gloves and dropped them unceremoniously on the floor. Cold steel pressed flush against his palms. He held them there, letting warmth flow into the instrument before tracing the gentle curvature of its circumference. Staring at it, he caressed the node at the center.

Clips of the past rushed to mind. Laughter. Smiles. Chases. Drinks and jests and bets and sweat and fun at any cost. The ones he loved too much and the ones he wished he could have loved more. The sweet thickness of those memories paraded past his defenses.

My grandmother and cousin are gone.

He flicked the node at the center of the banha drum. A drawn-out ringing...

The taproom, so bawdy a moment before, was drowned out by the droning note.

He closed his eyes. From the dark within, Omari watched.

An inward smile flashed through him, shattered and broke into a thousand shards of grief as he imagined her hearing about Malus's murder. *I'm sorry.* Barodane thought he was saving everyone—protecting them—by giving up the crown. *If I hadn't fled, would they still be alive?*

He stroked the node with his palm, his manner slow and repetitive, summoning up a resonating tone.

Loose fingers thumped out a pattern. The baseline beat hummed through him, a long note mixed with a rapid tattoo.

Malus D'Alzir argued with him over a goblet of wine. The argument, fierce but friendly. Barodane always lost. Always looked forward to it.

His arms crossed then jerked back to their original position as he thudded out flurries with thumb and fingertips while mixing in a swipe of his palm over the node. A deep, jumping rhythm plodded forth.

He saw his grandmother leaning over him on his fourteenth nameday. Danath had just passed away and Barodane had taken it harder than the rest of the family. His grandmother balanced a sword wrought in darksteel delicately on age-addled palms. "Fit for an Ironlight," she'd said with a sniffle. "Some honor the dead with words. Others do so with deeds. Let yourself be the latter. Train diligently. Make every blade stroke a testament to his legend...and his love."

Blood pumped through Barodane's arms, tension filling his muscles as he worked them around the drum, faster now, slapping out the pattern. He weaved in sounds both low and high alongside the persistently deep and rolling ring. Low, high, low. Low, high, low. Three, then five, then seven taps in lightning-fast sequence. Fury met sorrow and the tempo spiraled upward. A bead of sweat tickled his nose, then gathered at his chin. He forgot where he was. The steel drum bled beyond the limitations of its form, becoming an entity felt from the depths of his crippled heart.

Lungs heaving, shoulders aching, hands numb—he thrust his pain to the edges of awareness.

A skinned knee. Blood welling in the scuff of bunched skin. Wincing, sucking breaths. Malath hurrying over to haul him upright and asking him if he's okay. Barodane's tears had stopped there before they started, beaten back by a brother's permission to hurt. To experience the pain of living.

If Barodane had known that accepting such support, such love, such trades in vulnerability would drive him to the horrible deeds he'd done, he would have chosen to hate his brother instead. He would have made Malath a stranger. And he would have pushed away the rest of those who cared for him long before they'd died.

In so doing, he would have spared them rather than mourn them.

The drum worked itself now as he wove chaos on it, notes within notes within notes. Whatever panel of the shell he struck, the sound became a part of the whole, born in the last second and carried forward with the rest toward some unknown end.

Inexorably, he marched his feelings forth to be judged.

And just when he thought he could march no further, he reversed the pattern. A song, altogether similar but different.

Back he went, back into the past. Downward spiraling, deeper and deeper to dismantle all he'd built. A race out of the dungeons and into the light.

He cut the song apart, piece by measured piece, a butcher hacking at a carcass, winnowing it down into finer and finer cuts. Notes discarded in the exact reverse order of their birth. He stripped the song of flesh, muscle, and sinew.

Melodies dropped away like butterflies in a poisonous cloud as he flung it all back into the abyss from which it came.

All but that single, rolling note, spreading from his palm as he brushed the node at the center of the drum—the center of his being.

When the song ended, Barodane drew back his hand, hovered it for a count of eight and then flicked the central node.

It stung the air, a reminder of all that was gone...

All that he was...

And the nothingness that remained.

CHAPTER THIRTY-SIX

THE VIOLENT NAME

S omeone had died.

    After Zadani and Genjin parted ways, she'd returned to the kitchens, resolved to see Lord Marus that day even if she needed to announce the whole business at court. There was a sense of peace and relaxation imagining what might happen to Nymon after she outed him.

Death can bring peace after all.

Her hope for such peace, however, was soon shattered.

    Flanked by holdguard, Lady Daran darkened the kitchen doorway at mid-morning, absent her typical flashing smile. There was a flatness to her, the usual buoyant energy tamped down. Her raiment matched her demeanor—a black dress darker than the news in her eyes and cinched tighter than a noose.

    Intuition told Zadani what had happened within a split second of seeing the young woman.

    The kitchen fell silent.

    Soft and gentle horror stitched Daran's words together, a wound freshly dressed. "As you know, Lord Marus's brother, the Duke of Lah-Tsarra, was scheduled to arrive here for my seventeenth nameday." She stifled a sob, hooked finger coming to her lips. "We dispatched riders and..."

    There was a long pause. The young highborn cleared her throat and spit out the last words. "Malus D'Alzir is dead. My uncle—*our duke*—is dead."

    Errant gasps broke sharp against the collective hush. Frowns and cocked heads passed from person to person like wildfire. The duke was beloved even beyond the borders of Lah-Tsarra's duchy.

    I hadn't heard he was sick. When she'd seen him last, he seemed more a willowy librarian than a soldier but that did not mean he was unhealthy.

    The muscles in Daran's jaw trembled, accompanied by a twitch beneath one eye. "Murdered. By Kurgs. A hundred crownguard perished with him."

Hands covered shocked mouths. Elmarie wilted into a crouch, arms folded over her stomach. Mutters swept the room as awareness circled the dark implications like carrion birds.

"Are we safe?"

"My cousin was a crownguard at Brighthaven..."

"Will the Kurgs attack here next?"

Zadani thought of the tracks in the north wood, of Nymon and his Scarborn, and the message...

Daran held up a hand, beckoning silence. "There's nothing to fear. We've already dispatched birds to Alistar. Hawk's Keep is guarded by the finest soldiers in Namarr. Ten thousand Kurgs could not take it before the Crown's army arrived to aid us." She lowered her hand. "Court will be postponed until further notice while my family grieves." She turned and seemed to float from the kitchens, as if carried by the pristine image she held of herself.

In her absence, controlled turmoil rolled over the room. With heads touching, conversation frantic, the work of the kitchen staff began. They were scared. The size of their eyes told Zadani that much.

Many sought her input but she gave them little. The news sat inside her like a round cake in a square pan, stealing all other mental effort.

Duke Malus is dead, killed by Kurgs. Scarborn work as holdguard...and treat with Kurgs.

"With the Scarborn trouble in Anjuhkar, and the crown vacant so long, any kind of stability would be welcome," Thruna said. "Gods know, an old woman needs it in her dimming years."

Fear slid icy fingers between Zadani's shoulder blades. Butcher knife in hand, she dragged a chicken carcass onto a cutting board, and then swifter and louder than necessary, she hacked it into six pieces.

Thruna shot Zadani a puzzled expression before turning to Elmarie. "Kitchen's a good job for the emotions. Come, vixen, let's knead away our worries."

Zadani stared at the cutting board, listening.

"A war with the Kurgs *and* a civil war in Anjuhkar. With a Shadowcrown, Namarr won't survive. We'll be back to the days of territories!"

Zadani pulled another carcass across the board. Hack, pull, hack.

"Nay, deary. Won't be a Shadowcrown long. With these wars brewing, they'll vote one in next year. Have to."

Her movements were deft, the heavy blade separating thin muscle, pink flesh, and hollow bone with mechanical ease.

"Without a prince, there's no one to appoint a new Duke of Lah-Tsarra."

Head. Wings. Thighs. Breast. Six pieces—five hacks. Another carcass come apart.

"Not how it works, deary. In the absence of a prince's appointment, the ducal title falls to bloodlines."

Another limp fowl dragged forth. So vulnerable, so naked. Yet, the dead were anything but vulnerable—they were safest from the knife's descent.

With the back of her forearm, Zadani wiped sweat from her brow.

"So, Lord Marus will be the new duke?"

Using the blade's edge, Zadani scraped aside parceled meat to make space for more. At the final chop of the final chicken, she added extra force. Blade embedding in the cutting board, the knife's handle quivered.

"Indeed. Our very own Lord Marus. The new duke of Lah-Tsarra."

Realization stuck Zadani like a cleaver between the eyes. It took everything in her not to wilt as despair opened in the pit of her gut.

Lord Marus killed Hadir.

After the tumult that came with Lady Daran's announcement, an air of brooding gripped the kitchens. Lunch came and went, a flurry of mistakes, many of them Zadani's.

I must remain calm...act as though it were any other day.

Nothing said "normal Zadani" like a song.

"With a soul unafraid and a hand for the blade, came a fire-hearted man with ice in his veins."

She hadn't sung in the kitchens since the day they buried Hadir. But now, she had to play the role expected of her. She had to sing. And she was glad for it. The song kept her focused on something other than her racing thoughts. The sickening flutter in her belly subsided as her voice livened the space. Smiles rode the faces of the staff, filling her with a burble of joy long absent.

She sang like she once did when the world was right. One last time, she wanted to see them happy. To see their smiles. Hear their mirth. Stand beside them and imagine nothing was wrong. Thruna, with her wart and her barbs and the gap-toothed grin of a toddler. Elmarie, so fresh and innocent, and full of life. And the rest, all reliable hard-workers. Good people. Faithful servants of the D'Alzirs.

Hadir was a faithful servant, too.

Seeking justice for Hadir was a way of securing justice for every lowborn servant the world over, guilty of nothing but trying to live a contented life born under the rule of those with dark ambitions.

Soup sloshed over the rim of the cook pot Zadani stirred and into the fire; it sizzled and belched up smoke. She cursed, her song cut short.

Thruna laid a hand on Zadani's back. "Cooks faster if you don't put out the flames."

Zadani put on a smile. "A dream about Hadir last night has me all..." She twirled a finger in the air as if plumbing the final traces of pudding from the inside of a bowl. "Wound up."

Eyebrows raised, Thruna snatched the wood spoon from Zadani. "Details. Here, I'll finish the soup while you spill it—the steamy dream, I mean."

"I think I'll keep this one to myself for now."

Scratching her wart, Thruna pouted and began stirring. "Can't even get sex second-hand anymore. From a dream, no less. How boring life is."

When dinner was ready, Zadani went to the board Elmarie was preparing for the guest wing. The wing where Jasso Jackolo stayed.

Salted seal livers from Twilight Cape stuffed with grape jam from the Golden Silos of Peladonia. A hard seed bread and half a bloom of apple slices from the orchards of Kiyahd. Godsbrew, too, adorned the boards.

Zadani took Elmarie by the elbow. "Has Jasso Jackolo recently commented on the food?"

The young woman cocked her head. "No, mistress."

"He hasn't commented." Zadani nodded gravely. "Who's running for the guest wing today?"

"Thruna did lunch, so I'll do dinner."

"Take a break. I'll run it for you. I need compliments or criticism but neither is never good. Food should be remarked upon—with regularity."

Lugging the board up the stairs called for strength Zadani was sorely lacking on account of her recent sickness. *Thruna does this? How in the name of the Sempyrean gods...*

The old woman had to be made of iron under her robes. Zadani caught her breath at the top of the stairs and then made for Jasso's room.

When the scholar opened the door, white eyebrows bunched above a thin crest of nose. Zadani hushed him gently, causing the lines of his already furrowed brow to deepen.

Jasso watched her with annoyance until she pushed forward into his quarters. Richly embroidered cushions littered the floor. Lavish drapes befitting a prince were tousled and haphazardly situated. Silk sheets lay in a crumpled pile beside a bed big enough to sleep four.

"What are you doing?" he said.

"Delivering your food. Keep your voice down."

"Zadani, I'm very busy. There's a woman in the city I'm preparing to meet with tonight to arrange Genjin and I's departure. She's a disreputable sort. Does things she shouldn't, much like yourself." He shook his head. "Alas, she's the only one willing to take us to Alistar by boat. I can't fathom how you Namorites can trundle about in caravans so oft. Makes me sick."

Zadani made to speak but stopped when he crossed his arms.

"You've picked a terrible time to badger me. I seem to have lost my notes."

A cold tingle worked its way up Zadani's spine. She thought back to Nymon's comments about a spy and stiffened.

Jasso cast about, as if at mention of his notes, they might suddenly spring into existence. Noticing Zadani's shock, he slowed. "What?"

She pulled the message she'd taken from Nymon from her bosom and handed it to the scholar. "A last thunder jelly for the curious shark."

Jasso inspected the hide-scroll, shrugged, then unrolled it. "This is written in Unti, the tongue of the Kurgs." He tossed her a skeptical look. "Where did you get this?"

"Never mind that. What does it say?"

Jasso read in a whisper. "The duke is dead...a thousand more gold is owed...a thousand more pieces of steel needed..."

Suspicions confirmed, panic swept through Zadani. Specks of light entered the fringes of her vision, as her mind circled a singular truth she did not wish to face.

She locked eyes with Jasso. "Whoever wrote that killed Malus D'Alzir."

"So it says. But we already knew Kurgs were responsi—Zadani, what *is* this? What have you done?"

Marus is a traitor. A murderer. If Zadani had the time, she would have gone into Hadir's tomb and burned the wreath the D'Alzirs had him buried with. "I'd worry more about what my lord has done."

"I don't want this." Face slack with fear, Jasso pushed the message into her hands. "I don't want any part in it."

Stuffing the message back into her bosom, Zadani grabbed Jasso by the arm.

"You know as well as I that the D'Alzirs have both the gold and motivation to have Duke Malus killed. Think about it, Jasso! His tax hikes. The ebhor tracks." She lowered her voice. "Nymon and his men...they're Scarborn."

Jasso looked sad, a puppy who'd been caught chewing its owner's shoe. Color drained from his face.

"You and I both know Hadir died because he saw something in that maple grove. Just like you know it has to be Lord Marus. He'll be Duke now, dammit! Who else would benefit?"

Jasso shoved her hand away. "Zadani, we must burn that message. Now."

"No," she growled. The image of the wound between Hadir's shoulder blades assailed her. Rage crept into her jaw, burned through her chest and stomach. She tasted copper in her mouth—smelled it in her nose. "We'll do no such thing."

Jasso rubbed his temples. "Zadani, this is no game. If Marus paid Kurgs to kill his brother and is somehow involved with the Scarborn insurrection in Anjuhkar, we are in danger."

"If Lord Marus hired the Kurgs, then he is responsible for Hadir's death." Teeth gnashing, words biting, Zadani hurled herself down the path of vendetta. "For taking my husband, he'll pay with everything he loves. I'll take his wife, his daughter, his life!"

The scholar's mouth fell open. "You can't be serious." He drew back, skittish as a rabbit.

His crumbling resolve presented its own form of danger, one Zadani could not abide. "There's something you should know." *We're close to justice, Jasso, do not balk now. A more immediate danger might be the only way to sway him.* "They suspect you're a spy."

He recoiled. "What?"

The guilt of the situation was enough to buckle Zadani's knees. If not for her, he wouldn't be involved at all. She wasn't completely certain they thought Jasso the spy, but her intuition had brought her this far. "When did your notes go missing?"

He stepped back, the backs of his legs bumping into his opulent bed. "After breakfast..."

Zadani stepped after him, both hands alighting on his arms. "We have to go. If this message is true, we're not only in danger, but we're also honor bound to bring this information to someone who can—"

"No." He shook free of her touch and cut the air with his arms. "This is madness."

"Do you think it a coincidence that they suspect a spy and then your notes go missing? They're looking for anyone who might uncover their treachery. That's why Hadir died. He saw what he wasn't supposed to and they put a spear in his back for it. We must go—immediately. We must take the message to someone with the power to do something about it."

Disbelief etched Jasso's brow as he sat on his bed. "I suppose I deserve this. So many years spent riding the razor's edge of the law." He stared into his palms.

Zadani snapped her fingers. "Stay with me. We need to think."

He blinked up at her with sky-blue eyes. "Right. Right. The problem is you cannot simply accuse the lord of Kiyahd. No matter the evidence, he's powerful. No one will believe he paid Kurgs to kill his brother, nor that he breaks the Bacot Embargo."

"And yet, there you sit knowing the truth. A truth written in—"

"Your own hand. Weak evidence at best. It may rouse suspicions but to condemn one of Namarr's most prestigious families, we'll not only need to convince another lord of equivalent power about what transpired, we'll need to convince them we are not ourselves spies working for some foreign nation seeking to sow division throughout Namarr. Even if our accusation shines as true as the morning sun, it carries immense risk for any lord willing to back our cause. Marus is Duke of Lah-Tsarra now."

"We have no choice." Zadani leaned forward. "The man is a traitor, a liar, and a murderer."

"We're going to need an ally then." Connections with highborn were something Zadani lacked in earnest. Thankfully, after a few seconds of consideration, Jasso nodded to himself. "Onai Saud. He shares a bloodline with Val royalty. If anyone will listen to us, it's him."

"Then we leave tonight. When are you to meet with your woman...the disreputable one?"

Somberness flickered across Jasso's expression. He looked at Zadani, hopeful in the way of one prepared for disappointment. "What about Genjin?"

She glanced at the floor.

He gave a heavy sigh. "It's been many years since I've been in love."

She said nothing.

"Why can't he come?"

"You wish him to be implicated along with us?" Zadani stared out the window across the room. "I'd give anything to keep Hadir from harm." She looked at Jasso. "Someone has taken that choice from me—from him. Would you do the same to Genjin?"

Jasso punched the bedding. "I hate this."

"Good men deserve to live," she said. *And the rest deserve to die.*

Jasso's shoulders slumped. "So be it."

Short and dangerous was the path to freedom.

Zadani stood in her quarters for the last time, by the bed she and Hadir had shared. Calm moved through her, a wave of stillness as she closed her eyes. *For you, my love.* She touched her fingertips to her lips, kissed them, then pressed them on the place where Hadir used to sleep.

From shadowed alcove to shadowed alcove, she crept from the servant's wing. Luckily, holdguard didn't seem to think servants in need of as much supervision. *We do what we're told. Compliant without fail.* If stopped, she and Jasso had discussed what to say. Jasso opted for, "I go to shit in the chamber pot, care to join?"

Crude but effective.

Fatigue soaked through Zadani, making her every move molasses slow. Despite regular doses of rising gold, the aches left by the death dealer were proving difficult to shake. Once she and Jasso were safely on a ship bound for the House of Saud, she promised herself she would rest.

For now, there is too much demanded of me. The idea of Lord Marus and Nymon going unpaid for their crimes was an iron collar clasped around her throat. *I'll take everything he loves.* If faced with capture or a need to kill, Zadani was prepared. Hadir's hunting knife was slipped through her belt for easy access.

Moonlight filtered through the apertures, creating a stepping-stone-like path of panes of light before her. She hurried down the hall and turned down another.

Jasso met her in a passageway near the gardens. They stared at each other, half shadowed, half lit by the moon's dewy light, and said nothing. They knew what to do and where to go.

Zadani nudged him forward.

Hoods of their cloaks pulled overhead, they approached a pair of braziers that marked the archway leading out to the gardens. "I'll make sure it's clear," Jasso whispered and then took the lead. A half-dozen long, hurried strides grew the space between them rapidly.

Zadani spotted a flicker of torchlight through an aperture. Another came into view illuminating a familiar face—Nymon the Lech. Her heart skipped. *A trap.*

Jasso exited from hall to gardens, already out of reach. She pressed herself flat against the wall of the passageway, lips squeezed shut, blood running cold.

The scholar yelped. A cruel laugh followed.

"Jasso Jackolo. Brilliant scholar. Traveling philosopher." Lord Marus's voice was unmistakable but it sounded farther away than Nymon's. "And now, a spy of Valat."

Arms tight around her torso, Zadani felt the rapid swell and shrink of her breathing. Summoning courage she didn't know she had, she slid closer to the nearest aperture to peek out...to watch the horror unfold. A dozen holdguard were stepping from the hedges ringing the garden, Lord Marus at their center. Vallabathus stood at his side along with a handful of knights. Just outside the wall, near where Zadani watched from, she heard more men, while across the way, Genjin Hyrix stood at the head of Nymon the Lech and his Scarborn.

Jasso cast about, tongue darting over his lips. Trapped.

An animalistic impulse pushed Zadani to run, but she refused to comply. *My best bet for surviving the night and getting to Onai Saud is to stay still.* Besides, if Jasso ratted her out, she needed to know what was coming.

"You're a very clever man, Jasso Jackolo, but you already knew that." Lord Marus brought his hands from behind his back. In a black velvet glove, he held a leather-bound sheaf of papers—Jasso's notes. "Keeping tabs under the guise of study? Amnesty as an international scholar from the Academies, are you? Well, turns out, the paper you use is rather distinct. We matched your notes to a sheet of parchment found in the north wood surrounded by Kurg tracks. I chide myself for not detecting the ruse sooner. Though I still wonder...is it Valat or some other entity you work for? I suppose we'll know soon enough."

Lord Marus waved a hand and his men advanced.

"You're a righteous bastard, aren't you, Marus?" Jasso turned to Genjin, a spear's length to his right. Tears brimmed in the Awakened's eyes. Fists shaking, Jasso puffed out his chest and pointed at the Lord of Kiyahd. "You're the traitor, D'Alzir. You paid Kurgs to murder your own brother!""

Marus cocked his head, a raven inspecting a nut. Velvet-gloved hand up-raised, he called his holdguard to a halt.

"I—I have proof," said Jasso.

Zadani held her breath.

"Show us," Marus said.

Zadani had watched court oft and had enough experience running the kitchens to know the most confident voice in the room swayed the minds of those taking orders. None of these men looked remotely suspicious of their lord. Nymon and his impostors were stoic as they watched Jasso falter.

"Come on, then." Marus spoke with glacial calm. "Show us proof that you're not a spy. That I'm a villain."

He doesn't have it. Zadani touched the scroll tucked into her bosom. Guilt flooded her. Jasso would be arrested, tortured, and executed because she'd manipulated him to help her. He was a good man. *Like Hadir.*

"Nymon's men." Jasso's voice trembled. "They're Scarborn. The scarring rituals leave three distinct marks. Make them shave and you'll see proof."

Torch-flame danced in Marus's narrowed eyes. The shadowed creases of his face revealed a stranger. Zadani had never seen him appear so cold, so cruel. *He was a good man, a great lord.* Now, she seemed to watch a demon come to life.

"I've changed my mind," Marus said. "Kill the scholar."

The Scarborn at Jasso's flanks moved forward, grim-faced.

In the safety of darkness, Zadani shrank back, refusing to look. Rage begged her to draw Hadir's knife and die alongside the man she'd condemned. *If I do that I'll die. Then no one will know Marus's treachery.*

"Stop!"

Genjin Hyrix's voice.

Zadani craned around to look through the aperture, no wider than her palm.

Genjin had placed himself between Nymon the Lech's men and Jasso. The Awakened looked like a robed scarecrow in the torchlight. "Is it true, Jasso?" Anger etched his brow. "Are you truly a spy?"

"Of course not!" the scholar snapped. "Marus D'Alzir is the only liar here. A greedy traitor willing to commit fratricide so he can become a duke."

"Genjin Hyrix, I did not order you to interrogate the man. I want him dead," said Marus. "Now."

The Awakened ignored his lord. "Why didn't you tell me?"

"I couldn't." Jasso hung his head. "It was too dangerous."

"Too dangerous?" A fist flew up at Genjin's side. "You think I can't handle danger?"

"Genjin Hyrix, do as you're commanded!" Zadani had never heard Marus shout before.

Silence hung over the garden. Genjin didn't move.

Sir Vallabathus stepped in front of Marus, halberd in hand. A longbow was slung across his back, and a quiver of arrows was fixed at his hip. With the butt of the halberd, he struck the flagstone walking path. "Kill the scholar or face the charge of treason!"

"I loved you," Genjin whispered, desperation in his voice.

"I know," said Jasso. "But I had to. For your safety."

"My safety, Jasso? I would choose love over safety any day. I only wish you'd done the same."

Nymon the Lech rose behind Genjin. A scream clawed at the back of Zadani's throat as the haft of the Scarborn's ax slammed into him, pitching him to the ground at Jasso's feet in a tangle of limbs and flapping robes. "Go on, Bloodrot." Nymon's milk-white eye sparkled. "Kill your boyfriend."

The Awakened found his feet, his expression knotted with hate. To Jasso, he said, "Let me show you what I mean." He whirled to face the encroaching holdguard, scintillating light gathering at his fingertips.

Marus hissed.

"Wary, men!" Vallabathus barked. "Wary now!"

"The barracks!" Lord Marus snatched the tabard of a knight of Kiyahd in his fist. "Bring as many men as you can!"

Holdguard backpedaled, giving the Awakened space.

"Stop this, Genjin!" Jasso pulled at his lover's shoulder but failed to budge him an inch.

Tendrils of glowing vapor rose from Genjin Hyrix. A soft white brilliance grew in his eyes, then spilled, drifting into the heavens. "There can be no safety in love."

While others retreated, Nymon the Lech held his ground. He spat and shrugged his shoulders in a slow circle. His ever-present smile became a flat, hard line. Both hands wrung the handle of his long ax.

Genjin waited, wreathed in smoking ghostlight.

Prickles rippled down Zadani's spine as Nymon surged forward. "I'll fuck your corpse, Bloodrot!" His ax whistled.

Zadani closed her eyes, heard Jasso cry out. A resounding thud echoed through the garden air. The Scarborn leader's ax had found its mark.

Nymon cursed. Zadani's eyes shot open. The ax was buried in Genjin's forearm. Where there had been skin, thick bark now covered his hand and armored him to the elbow where it disappeared beneath his robes.

A dozen threads of eerie, coruscating light haloed the garden around Genjin, a luminous flood growing brighter by the second. It made a specter of Nymon the Lech's face as he stared at the Awakened in shock, his long ax embedded without harm into oaken skin.

Tracers of light trailed Genjin's fingers as he reached past the Scarborn's guard and touched the exposed flesh of his neck.

Nymon ripped his ax free and stumbled back, clutching at his throat. He gagged, wheezed, shook his head like a cat slapped on its nose.

Genjin watched him, radiating with mysterious power.

Nymon raised his weapon, took a step—spasmed. "Gah!" His ax clattered onto the flagstones. He dropped to his knees and vomited blood. He whined like an injured dog as he covered his stomach with both arms.

Zadani cringed, unable to peel her gaze from the carnage.

A terrified scream stretched Nymon the Lech's mouth into a cavernous pit. His skin became milk pale and then blotchy from excruciating pain. Bloody drool clung in ribbons to his blond beard. Both his normal eye and the clouded one were rimmed in red as he looked at one shoulder—

Watched it erupt.

A branch sprouted skyward, growing at an impossible rate. The snap and stretch of bark and the wet pop of skin spilled over the garden. Chunks of bloody meat were cast in all directions. The Scarborn mewled as his other arm shot outward, rigid and trembling before the elbow inverted with a crack of bone.

Holdguard and their Scarborn counterparts froze, fidgeting, hesitating. They looked toward their knight-captain for commands.

Twigs shot from Nymon's fingers, splitting them like overripe corn from their husks. Boot leather peeled back, his toes a second after. Roots drove down into the earth, blood pooling around them as flagstones lifted in a rolling wave.

Finally, the tree shucked off the fetid molting that was Nymon the Lech and stopped its growth.

"Run, Jasso," Genjin said.

"Kill the Awakened!" Sir Vallabathus commanded.

Chaos broke across the garden as D'Alzir holdguard and knights of Kiyahd overcame the initial shock of Genjin's powers and shot forward, wary but resolute.

A Scarborn leveled a sword thrust at Genjin's ribs that skittered off protective bark, the force of the movement propelling the man forward—a fatal mistake. Genjin touched his face as he flew past, the glow illuminating a thin scar under his left eye, which carried with it a look of certain doom. The man stumbled, staggered, dropped...

Zadani's mind raced. Sweat stung her eyes. She wanted to make a plan and follow it, but this...

All was a river of madness surging around her.

The man on the ground screamed and thrashed, then went plank-still. A branch exploded from his eye socket, carrying a pierced eyeball into the air, dangling scarlet flesh like the tail of a comet.

An arrow thudded into Genjin's shoulder and threw him back a step toward Jasso.

"You must flee," said Genjin.

"I..."

"I can't protect you here," Genjin shouted.

A towering knight of Kiyahd pushed through the throng of cautious soldiers, steel pauldron shining under moonlight. He hacked at Genjin, his sword sporting iron-wrought hawk wings that spread to either side to form the hilt. The Awakened caught the blow on a forearm and struck out with his other hand. The knight dodged, then circled in an attempt to get at Jasso.

Noticing the man's goal, Genjin sidestepped to cut the knight off. "Go!"

He's right. Flee, dammit!

Jasso saw it too. But instead of running back the way he'd come, along the route where Zadani hid in the passageway, the scholar bolted down a tightly packed hedgerow along a wall. If the D'Alzir men followed, they would be forced to do so one at a time or have to work their way down the steep hill in a wide arc to intercept him.

A pair of Scarborn raced for the escape route but Genjin cut them off. The tall knight slashed at his exposed back and sent a shower of slivers into the chill air. Noticing the blow did little against the supernatural hide, the knight frowned and retreated out of Genjin's reach, sword arm relaxed as if he was considering a problem of logistics rather than life and death.

Genjin planted himself in a defensive stance at the head of the hedgerows and wall.

Zadani knew where the narrow path led and hurried to meet Jasso at its end. The sound of arrows striking wood, of men being torn apart, faded as she ran.

"I want him alive," said Marus D'Alzir. "He may have information about Jack-olo's destination."

If the Val scholar was at all a skilled spy, he would have divulged little to Marus's Awakened. Then again, he wouldn't have been discovered quite so easily, either.

Genjin Hyrix caught a blade with an oaken arm, this time twisting the lodged weapon from his assailant's grasp. The man retreated, fell to his backside and scrambled backward. Before the Awakened could touch him, the towering knight, Sir Akaitys, leapt in, sword whirring. The blow hewed a shower of splinters from Genjin's arm. The Awakened lunged for the knight but Sir Akaitys proved cat-quick and danced out of reach.

A Scarborn dashed forward, ax swirling through smoking ghost-light to bite into the Awakened's shoulder. In a backward arc, Genjin Hyrix slapped the man. Death set in motion. Limbs snapping akimbo, flesh rending along marbled lines.

Another husk left. Marus sighed. *Another man I must replace.*

Vallabathus handed off his halberd to a guard beside him and unlimbered his bow. Arrow knocked, he drew as he spoke. "My lord, I don't think it possible."

Genjin Hyrix pressed forward from the alcove, turning sideways to pass between a pair of blood-drenched saplings, both slightly taller than the men they'd once been. Corpses lay in grisly piles around their trunks. Ichor dripped from their branches.

Vallabathus's arrow zipped past Genjin's blood-splashed face, casting up red mist in its wake.

"So I see." Marus loosed a frustrated sigh. "Fine. Kill him. The bark is but armor, albeit effective. Still, he's a just man."

Already, the Awakened had killed half his men. *And now he comes for me. It will take me months to find another to replace him.*

Bowstring creaking taught, Marus watched Vallabathus draw another bead. He exhaled slow—let fly. The arrow embedded into Genjin's arm, causing him to cry out. Few men could draw the poundage of Vallabathus.

"See, my knight-captain. You must think more positively."

Slow was the Awakened's progress toward Lord Marus, but determined, nonetheless.

Vallabathus told his men to use piercing weapons rather than slashing. All but the towering knight with the hawk hilt sword—Sir Akaitys—listened. As opportunity presented, he slipped forward to land a blow then exited the fray just as quickly.

Marus decided he liked the knight of Kiyahd who'd arrived a week earlier, fresh from training in Alistar. He fought with a calm, calculating strategy, untouchable but for the moments he chose. Much like Marus would fight if he were such a warrior. If Sir Akaitys survived the next few minutes, Marus decided he'd give the young knight command of Nymon the Lech's men.

The ones who survived, anyway.

Another holdguard perished in a fountain of blood and dripping foliage. Sir Akaitys leveled a sword stroke at the Awakened's leg and sent him foundering for balance.

"Lord Marus," said Vallabathus, "we must get you to safety."

The lord of Kiyahd shook his head. He would not sleep until Jasso Jackolo was caught and the Awakened subdued or killed.

The sound of skin tearing. A strangled scream. A gurgle cut short. A stirring rush of leaves.

Genjin chased Sir Akaitys. The big knight sidestepped, ducked, circled from threat of harm. The very moment Genjin paused his futile chase, the towering knight pushed off his heels and closed the distance. Wooden fingers flew across the courtyard. Genjin gasped, clutching at his reduced hand. Sap oozed from severed digits.

And then the fingers began to regrow.

How disturbingly unexpected, and yet, unsurprising. "Vallabathus, kill him now, please."

Genjin shot Marus a glare. It sent a jolt of fear through his belly but he lifted his chin, resolved not to show it. Fear killed confidence, and thus, undermined command. Besides, more men were due any second. If he left, his men might judge him harshly. If he stayed, they were sure to see him as powerful, a most necessary mechanism for loyalty.

A quality of particular importance for his imminent future as the new Duke of Lah-Tsarra. Once Genjin Hyrix was dead, only Jasso Jackolo would need be silenced to tie up loose ends. That, he hoped, would happen shortly.

All in all, a productive night.

The Malzacy-born knight-captain grunted. Fired. An arrow thudded into Hyrix's brow, rocking his head back, skin turning to bark on impact. "Too thick there," Vallabathus said.

Genjin deflected a spear thrust at his face. Only a pair of holdguard separated the lord of Kiyahd from death now. Less than fifteen paces. Hands folded at the waist, Marus took a single step back.

He's killed almost a score of men yet wouldn't kill the one I asked of him. An odd sense of justice, he has.

As the Duke of Lah-Tsarra, it wouldn't be hard to recruit more holdguard. Scarborn who didn't look like Scarborn would be tougher to come by. Kurgs, at least, were cheap. Steel weapons, armor, and a paltry tithe, and their lives were suddenly worth less than water.

Thousands will die by the time I'm crowned. Regret didn't enter Marus's mind. There was no room for it. Namarr was failing—would fail—without a strong hand and a capable leader, a man driven to triumph at any cost. Marus could think of no one better equipped than himself, and so, the gamble of lives became the burden of rule. Naught but the collateral of duty. Even the love of one's brother should not stand in the way of such momentously important callings. Great rulers were not something a nation simply happened upon.

Great rulers were forged by their own hand.

Vallabathus fired again, muttering something in Malzacy. This time the arrow entered Genjin Hyrix's eye, its feathered shaft shuddering in the socket. Trembling hands fumbled for the arrow as viscous sap pumped from the wound with a soft gulching sound. The light weeping from Genjin Hyrix's eyes and fingers dimmed—flickered—snuffed out. Face slack, the Awakened pitched forward onto the grass, barely an arm span from the feet of the soon-to-be-duke.

"Close." Marus patted Sir Vallabathus on the shoulder. "There's one down. Now, find me the other."

"Jasso! It's me!"

He looked a frightened animal, eyes wide, ready to react to any hint of threat. He rounded on her, fists raised as if he would fight armed men with them.

"This way," she said. "We must get you out of here."

Snatching a wad of fur-lined satin, she pulled him along. Shouts of alarm rang over the grounds as they wound through the hedges. Twice, they had to push themselves into the dense bushes to avoid holdguard running by with torches. To Zadani, they seemed to rush to their lord's defense more than they were looking for Jasso.

There was little doubt people throughout Hawk's Keep were waking to the clamoring alarm bells. They would be scared and curious, and most important of all, they would create further confusion. *That at least, might be in our favor.*

"Where are we going?" Jasso said.

Zadani pulled him close. They'd seen horrible things, and she suspected he needed some feeling of comfort to calm his nerves. Her own heart still beat painfully with the rush of fear. "We're waiting." She rubbed one of his hands in both of hers.

"What?" His voice was hollow. "We have to go."

"No, Jasso. *You* have to go. You have to reach Onai Saud. Find the disreputable woman, promise a gold wheel for the trip there, a gold wheel for her silence, and twice as much upon your safe arrival. And you have to take this with you." Pulling forth the message, she pressed it into his trembling hand.

"I don't understand." He stared at her, his face an inky blot of gleaming teeth and frightened eyes. "You have to come with me."

My mind is made.

She shook her head. "I have to stay. If we're caught together, Marus's crimes will go unpunished. I can't allow that. Our chances of getting this information to Onai Saud are better if we take different paths. Lord Marus suspects only you. I am still beneath his suspicion. I'm staying. I'll—"

"You're mad," he breathed.

Men's voices nearby silenced them. They waited, chewing stilted breaths. When the voices were gone, Zadani continued in a whisper. "I will see Hadir avenged by any means necessary."

"This is about more than Hadir."

"I know it is. There are thousands of innocent people across Namarr just like him whose lives could be in jeopardy because of whatever game Lord Marus plays."

After a moment of silence, Jasso nodded and took her by the shoulders. "You are a brave woman, Zadani Innan. If the world were full of more like you—"

"It is," she said. "Trust in that."

He sniffled, leaden hands falling away in somber acceptance. "Genjin's sacrifice won't be for nothing." He stuffed the scroll into his belt.

"Indeed." She led him to the end of the hedgerow. A short path led to the city of Kiyahd through a break in the stout keep wall. A pair of holdguard were stationed there. "When they're gone, make for the Salty Maid."

He squeezed her hand. "Good luck, Zadani."

She ran for the D'Alzir burial grounds, giving herself enough of a head start before calling out to the sentries at the gate. "Spy! The spy is here!"

It wasn't far to Hadir's tomb. Despite being beyond the point of exhaustion, she managed to pry open the thin stone door and then set it back into place once inside.

The torchlight of the holdguard pursuing her flickered through a finger-wide crack in the tomb's entrance, then passed.

Panting, and exhausted in every way one could be, she was now utterly alone. In the dark, she reached back, felt for Hadir's leg. Cold and nothing. She withdrew her hand, more comforted in the dreams of him in her mind than the reality lying nearby.

There was a truer solace now, one she'd not known since his passing. A solace in knowing who her enemy was. A warm wave of satisfaction settled in her chest.

Marus D'Alzir. The Lending lord of Kiyahd. A traitor to his people.

I will take all that he loves. His daughter. His wife. His title. His life! All of it!

As soon as it seemed safe, she would leave Hadir's tomb.

Then, her true work began.

PART TWO

ISHOA IRONLIGHT, THEPHOS OF CARTHANE, IKARAI VALKA, BARODANE IRONLIGHT

We are born to serve a purpose.

In concert with the gods of the Sempyrean, we move. By sacred gifts from the Sempyrean, we breathe. For the love of the Sempyrean's children, we act. With but one soul to give, we serve the highest good of all.

Worthy are we;

Just are we;

Wise are we;

Leading the way for those lost or unwilling. The hard of heart and dim of sight. We are lanterns for the souls of all Brothers and Sisters,

Who would perish beyond life, into the Eternal Maw.

A shield against evil, we serve

A righteous arm for the innocent, we serve

Lives given without reward,

We serve.

- Prosort's Creed

CHAPTER THIRTY-SEVEN

STRANGERS

Thephos watched ghostly armor coalesce around Syn. Scintillating light rippled along his greaves, vambraces, and across the visor of his helmet. Spreading from his hand, a glaive grew like molten steel poured into a crucible. "It's time, Thephos."

"I can't do it."

In a week, he would undergo the bonding ceremony necessary to make him Dominarri. With each day that had passed, though, Thephos felt less deserving of the post. He had yet to discover the extent of his powers. *Or any power for that matter. Maybe Syn is wrong. Maybe I'm nothing special after all.*

Ever since he'd pledged himself to the Dominarri before the roots of the Mother months earlier, the voice had gone quiet, and the sensation of his Awakened gifts along with it.

"Well, you need to." Syn twirled his white-hot blade, sizzling steam trailing it.

Thephos opened his eyes. Syn always gave him the freedom to come and go from their mental battlescapes when he needed.

On most days, between afternoon and evening meals, Thephos and Syn went to the training yard where the other Awakened agents and their bladesworn guardians drilled. At first, there had seemed to be so many other Awakened, it made the label seem less unique. But after seeing the same faces day after day, it became evident there weren't more than a score of teams.

The rest of Enshai was populated by those born to it who had no interest in the dangerous life of a bladesworn. Most acted as part of the menial labor force or as administrators, comforted by the fact that they lived in one of the world's safest, though smallest, cities. No more than a thousand people called the place home. Another hundred or so were on missions in lands both near and far.

Syn's voice echoed through Thephos's mind, even as his body sat statue-still beside him. "Thephos, we have to keep at it."

Other Awakened and bladesworn simulated combat scenarios against one another in the yard while Thephos sat next to Syn under a tree to conduct their training in his mind.

I'm special alright. The only Awakened who doesn't train like everyone else. Without a power, he would have been subdued or injured during a sparring match at the outset of any such contest. He'd always been left out in his previous life, but never had he felt so acutely abnormal as he did now. *I should be like them.*

"Fine." Thephos closed his eyes. Jagged peaks bisected by coursing lanes of lava rushed up under his feet as he dropped into the battlefield of Syn's mind.

"Thought I'd turn up the heat." Syn leapt, soaring ten feet onto an upthrust platform. "Couldn't hurt."

Thephos eyed the lava, then ran and jumped onto a second platform across from his mentor. The illusory armor Syn had given him clanged on impact. He stood and stumbled sideways. Martial combat was not his strong suit, even if it was imagined.

And so the beating started. Syn had tried a great deal of tactics to evoke Thephos's power. So far, none of them had worked. In lieu of this, Syn always said, "Time and pressure can make a diamond. So too could it wake your power."

If there's any power to wake.

Syn slashed with his glowing white glaive. Thephos blocked the first blow with a glaive of his own, but the butt of Syn's weapon slammed into his gut a second later. "Come on!"

Thephos retreated—not fast enough. Syn's fist collided against Thephos's chin with a crack of sparking light. Pain stabbed through his jaw as he was thrown backward, helmet winking off his head.

Something crashed into Thephos's side—a kick. Air gushed from his lungs.

Heaving, Thephos looked up from his hands and knees.

"What are you afraid of, huh?" Syn took a step back and waited for Thephos to rise. "It's like you don't want this."

He waits for me often. Nothing angered Thephos more. "I do." He wheezed as he stood and hefted his burning glaive. "I do."

"Prove it!" Syn lunged, carving space with his blade. Thephos lurched sideways then struck.

Syn slapped the blow away with ease. "I'm going to start projecting children in here to fight you instead. There was a pretty scrawny stable boy I met the other day. Might be a match for you."

A feeble war cry preceded Thephos sweeping the ground at Syn's feet with his glaive. The Dominarri hopped over it and laughed. "That's a better attitude. Still pathetic though."

Thephos glared, jerked back his arm and hurled his weapon like a javelin at Syn. The weapon blinked into nothingness. A flash of light exploded behind Thephos's eyes. He pitched forward, stone rushing up to strike him in the face. Salty blood spread from his sundered lip into his mouth. When he pushed himself up, a tooth lay before him.

He flopped onto his back, reeling and seeing double. Two Syns cast their glaives into the lava as they approached. Gradually, they blended back into a single man as the Awakened came to stand over Thephos. "You want to go without weapons? Let's do it. I'm just as tired of trying as you are."

He jerked off his helmet, tossed it away, and then fell upon Thephos, clutching for his neck. They fumbled at each other for a panicked moment. Thephos's back pressed against the stone, pinning him. A herculean fist descended. Black spots and an ache as if his cheek were broken. Another.

Syn's mouth was at his ear, encouragement veiled in threats. "Should I get your father here? Your dead brother? Maybe your mother. Bitch abandoned you, didn't she?"

Thephos blinked focus back into his vision as Syn reared back to dole out more punishment. A bolt of azure lightning pierced a distant bank of black clouds. Syn cocked his head, frowning.

"Don't call her that," Thephos muttered. He licked his lips, felt the snag of his cracked tooth on the bulk of his tongue. "Don't *ever* call her that."

Syn smiled. "What? A bitch? She was one. A dirty whore, too. Terrible mother. Let's bring her—"

"No," Thephos moaned. The voice that uttered the word was alien to his ears. Not his own. *The voice...*

Lightning left frozen blue branches in the sky. A serpent's forking tongue. Soot-black clouds rolled across the horizon, gathering speed. Coming for them.

Syn's brow furrowed. "Thephos?"

Rage swelled within, pressed outward, an unyielding force fighting for escape. Syn's weight became inconsequential, the hand holding Thephos down a leaf riding a tidal wave. He sucked the heat of the lava into his nose. Eased deeper into himself as he tasted the sulfuric air.

Time dwindled to a drip as mentor and student battled to a standstill of wills over a fissure between seconds, one fighting to close it, the other to pry it open. To drag it out to an eternity he controlled.

Thephos's fist erupted upward. Syn blinked, old-dog slow. He tried to dodge the blow as a blurred knuckles touched his cheek. The man's bone structure started to collapse, bowing inward with a sluggish crunching. Gelatinous blood filled an eye and the forked split in the skin where the fist made impact stretched open.

Keening filled Thephos's ears. The world snuffed to black. Memory fogged...

There was a face on the horizon—a horned skull in the clouds. Hatred brushed against his heart and cooled it to peace...contentment.

A silhouette wobbled over Thephos. He heard a sloshing, like he was being rolled along in a half-full wine barrel. A distant thud—someone slapping him. Dark fronds marred a familiar face. A bearded man appeared beside the first. There was a garbled exchange, drowned out by high-pitched ringing.

Then a single sound. A sound from within. A voice...

Tell them nothing of what you saw.

Prickles spread into Thephos's toes and fingertips. His cold lips were suddenly aflame. It felt as though an ax was buried in his crown and an ox sat on his chest. He gasped. A horrible sucking noise filled his ears followed by a roar of sound...his hearing restored.

"—ucking bring her!" Syn shouted at a man beside him then slapped Thephos's cheek. "Wake up. Come on, friend. Wake up."

"What..." Thephos croaked. "What happened?"

"Shit." Syn sighed the word and sat back, knees winging out akimbo with his head hanging between them. "Thought I killed you."

Ash supported Thephos's head as she helped him sit up. He winced, touched his brow. "I punched you."

"Yeah, you certainly did." Syn shook his head and used his tunic to wipe sweat from his face. "About obliterated me. I had to stop you."

"I thought you couldn't be hurt when you were in other people's minds?" Ash drew back from Thephos, frowning.

"So did I." Syn exhaled then smiled. "But who cares? The good news is that you accessed your power!"

I suppose I did. Thephos opened his mouth and then closed it as he remembered the voice's warning.

"Peerless speed and strength will come in handy." Syn's enthusiasm seemed to be rubbing Ash in all the wrong ways. Thephos saw it in the flat look she gave him, the downward turn of her pursed lips.

Speed and strength. Thephos looked at his hands. *Is that my power?*

Ash surveyed the training yard. "The Skyfire council will want to hear about this."

Thephos followed her gaze. Awakened and bladesworn watched them, and then drifted one-by-one back to whatever they'd been doing before the commotion.

All but the blond man, Pintarian. A cruel smile twisted his full lips amid a wash of golden, short-trimmed beard. "Like a baby duck trying to fly," he announced to anyone listening. Few laughed harder than he himself.

Ash shot him a baleful glare.

A young woman arrived. Syn gestured at Thephos. Plumes of white rose from her fingers as she moved them over his body. At his temples, she hesitated before nodding. "You're going to be okay."

Thephos wasn't sure he agreed.

"Syn told me what you did." The door to the infirmary creaked closed behind Pintarith. The Holy Sword wore a padded black gambeson, belted together at intervals from navel to throat, and flowing trousers stuffed into his boots. The unique sword of a bladesworn was strapped to his hip. "Impressive."

He'd never seen Ash without her sword, Death's Tether. Nor any of her kin for that matter. They wore their weapons at all hours. Walked around Enshai, their centuries-old home—a centuries-old fortress that had never been assailed—with their hands wrapped around sword hilts as if expecting danger at any moment.

Thephos sat on a stool, feeling one part guilty, one part worried. The power that had flowed through him had been scary yet thrilling. *I can do something!* And it had almost cost his friend's life.

The Holy Sword slung a foot up onto a stool beside Thephos. "We haven't long before N'zara arrives. Before then, I hope to strike an accord with you."

Thephos blinked at the man. "What for?"

He watched Pintarith repeatedly jerk Dire Jest from its scabbard by a half-foot then slip it back in. "It's funny the twists and turns life takes. The bitterness that seeps in at the edges of choices poorly made. Passion has ever been my undoing." *Shing—suph. Shing—suph.* Yellowed light glimmered on the naked length of steel. "The very strength that elevated me to my current station, and, the very weakness that cuts away at me."

Thephos searched the floor. *He fears N'zara.* "She is your bonded, isn't she?"

Dire Jest slammed into the scabbard and stayed there. Piercing blue eyes bore into Thephos. Truth was laid bare. *Not just his bonded...a lover or wife.*

"Why?" Thephos said. "Why do you hate each other?"

The Holy Sword gave a fake smile. "Fate of course. A dire jest indeed. Little did I know my blade's namesake would unravel into such a pointed meaning. Our son, Pintarian. He is all me and none of her. For an ego such as N'zara's that seeks control over so many things, this is a crime levied against her by fate itself. In that, none can escape her wrath."

Pintarith leaned forward, face hovering before Thephos. "You must follow my lead, for whatever I champion, she seeks to destroy, even at the cost of our mission as Dominarri. From what Syn tells me, you could be a vital asset. One I wish to nurture. N'zara hates me, hates Syn, hates our son. She is a woman of hate. She'll hate you too. I will protect you, but you must promise me something in return."

None of it made sense. *Conflict over me?* Frustration tightened at the hinge of his jaw. Ash and Syn should have told him about what he faced earlier. The pattern of withholding information was starting to grate on him.

Thephos shook his head. Jerked around as he was, the room seemed to be rotating, its shadowed corners shifting around him in the torchlight. "What would you have me do?"

Dire Jest sang from the scabbard. A second later, Pintarith's glove was off. "There's a Kanian proverb we Dominarri adopted. 'There is air. There is ink. And then...'" He nicked a thumb on the slightly curved tip of his blade, drawing a red streak. "There is blood.' Promise me you won't choose Pintarian at the bonding ceremony and I will ensure your protection."

When the Holy Sword of the Skyfire council offers you protection from a wrathful Awakened, in exchange for something you never planned on doing in the first place, agreement comes with ease.

Footsteps echoed down the hall. Pintarith glanced at the door. "Will you run naked and unarmed into the fray, or will you accept?"

"I accept." Before Thephos had extended his hand, Dire Jest split his thumb pad. So deft was the cut, he barely felt anything. Pintarith sank his blade home in the sheath, and then they shook, leaving thumb stamps of blood on the backs of their hands.

The door swung open.

N'zara's silhouette hung there, a diffused shadow of menace staring at the pair locking hands. "What's this?"

"Ah, N'zara my love." Pintarith's words were hollow, bordering on mocking. He slipped his velvet glove onto his hand. "I was just congratulating our newest initiate on discovering his powers. Peerless strength and speed—in a mindscape no less? Watch out, he may be a riverwalker like you someday."

N'zara strode into the room, grabbing a chair along the wall and dragging it noisily behind her. Satin robes, one panel of cloth white and stitched in gold, the rest black with fists embroidered in the same thread. She sat. "Leave us," she croaked, her words sounding as though they passed through layers of tattered canvas. "I wish to interrogate the prisoner."

Pintarith's leg swung off the stool. He towered over N'zara. She seemed not to notice. "You'll do no such thing. He's an initiate now. You need his consent to enter his mind." The Holy Sword gave a bitter laugh. "Dismiss me? Your ego never fails to astound."

Shark-like eyes, intent on their next meal, remained fixed on Thephos. He wondered if she heard her bladesworn's words. A thick smile curled her mouth. "My husband does you no service by making this seem a paltry conversation. You nearly killed one of our most powerful Awakened this morning. If you are not in control of yourself, I can help you."

Though she seemed kindly in that moment, the warning the Holy Sword had given of her hatred rang through Thephos. "I don't think that's a good idea."

"Oh?" she purred, eyes flashing. "Why not?"

Thephos flicked a look at Pintarith, then brought his attention back to N'zara. "I don't think it would help."

The torchlight became burning suns in the black of N'zara's eyes. "Help with what?"

Sweat broke across Thephos's hairline.

N'zara shifted in her seat. "Tell me, do you hear voices?"

Thephos flinched.

"You do," she purred.

Pintarith shook his head.

Thephos's brow bunched. "No. I only hear mine. Sometimes...my father's."

"A dreadful man, wasn't he?" she said.

"Consent," Pintarith growled. "You must have consent!"

N'zara shrugged. "I did no probing. I had my team that delivered money to his brothers do some...digging. What they unearthed was...unpleasant."

Thephos's throat went dry. One of his legs started shaking.

"You're strong. You know that now. But what happened today scared you." N'zara's words came fast, punching into Thephos's chest. "Whatever powers you have, you're not sure you can control them. And the last thing you want is to become your father—to hurt others. Today you hurt Syn. You don't want that to happen again, do you? What if you hurt the people you care about? What if you *kill* someone you love? What if you have to bury them like you—"

"Yes," Thephos hissed. He gasped, the breath stolen from him. "I consent."

Pintarith sighed, muttered something about N'zara being a crafty, dastardly hag.

The Holy Flame hooked an arm over the back of the chair. "Relax..."

Black vapor erupted from her eyes and rolled upward. A low, piercing sound washed away all other as the room stretched into the distance, darkness rushing to fill the peripheries. An unmoving Pintarith was suddenly twenty feet away, then fifty, then gone...

All winked into a lightless void. All but N'zara.

Thephos looked down. A cocoon of glowing thread held him paralyzed. The blinding light of it grew, consuming vision and sensation.

A finger twitched at the edge of Thephos's awareness like a spider's leg recoiling.

He sucked in a breath...cool, damp drool at the corner of his mouth like he'd just awoke from a heavy sleep. His head snapped up to find Pintarith and N'zara about where they'd been when the world had faded. "Did we start?"

"We've just finished," she said. "I found nothing."

A prickle swept from his ears to the base of his skull. *Nothing?* He swallowed, throat knotted. He watched N'zara studying him. Pintarith glowered at her. "The way you treat our initiates is not befitting of your station."

"I do what must be done!" she snapped. "Brook no caution when it's at your own expense all you like. I'll take no such chances."

N'zara whirled to her feet and swept from the room. Pintarith followed, muttering about mistakes he'd made.

Alone, facing an open door, Thephos hesitated.

The darkness pressed at him as he rose, groggy, a hand planted against the wall for support. A low laugh echoed faintly at the recesses of his mind. *Am I the creator of the demons I fear?* It sounded like something a Ruptured might ask themselves rather than an Awakened.

CHAPTER THIRTY-EIGHT

BETTER LUCKY

A tantalizing hush trailed Barodane's fingers through the silence as his hands slid off the banha drum. Bit by scintillating bit, torchlight entered his vision, revealing a darker world than the flowing river of harmony he'd stood in moments before.

He kept his head down and his hood up as he stared at the gapped floorboards.

He didn't need to see the room to feel their eyes on him. They pinned him in place, taking his measure, judging him, spinning tales of his past in the absence of knowledge. *If they knew what miseries I've wrought, they would not think my song so beautiful.*

The flare of connection leaked from him, a cracked vessel unable and unworthy of containing such admiration. His skin ached, like he was getting sick again, and his stomach turned sour. Sadness sloshed within, a gulp at the back of the throat that wouldn't go down. He stood abruptly to get ahead of it, stool screeching back then clattering against the floorboards.

In all his years, happiness was never more than a passing kiss of wind. The sense of something lighter, yet untouchable. It did little more than feed the flames of destruction smoldering within.

With the drum heavy in his hands, he stepped quickly off the stage and dropped it onto Wynna's table with a thud. All the way to the bar, their stares clawed at his back.

The barman was slow in coming over, as if he approached a feral cat rather than a man. Barodane laid a hand on the bar, palm gliding across the surface, and when he stopped, he gave it a few rapid pats. He glanced over one shoulder. A handful of people looked away. A low murmur began. Over the other shoulder, he found a frustrated Garlenna studying him.

The barman cleared his throat. Talk in the taproom resumed to a normal, bawdy level.

Barodane motioned the man closer. Every part of him was a tight edge working against itself. Twinges of pain in his neck and gut poured agitation into him.

The barman glared and leaned in.

Barodane whispered a single word: "Godsthorn."

The man flinched. He surveyed the crowd then nodded. "Not here." He hiked a thumb over his shoulder. "Stables. I'll send it your way."

"Much oblig—"

A figure pushed in at Barodane's side. "We're leaving." Garlenna wrapped a hand around his elbow; it didn't feel like the supportive or relenting type of pressure.

"To the stables then?" Barodane traded a look with the barman who sauntered off, eyes seeming to lock onto someone in the crowd. *My dealer, I hope.*

While Garlenna conveyed her urgency clear enough to Barodane, outwardly she kept her panic in check. "Indeed. The night is still young. Perhaps there's another inn you might regale with your stunning talent." She gave him a tug, and he had no choice but to follow or fall.

The stables were the place he wished to be anyway.

It wasn't yet midnight, but the cold felt far greater than when they'd first arrived in Halaleh. An attendant met them at the stable door and ushered them in. "Only take your horse. My mind's tighter than a Ghastiin furrier's trap, so if you take someone else's I'll surely know it." The young man tapped his temple. Barodane noticed a bell in the other hand.

"All is well," Garlenna said.

They entered the torchlit stable.

Barodane threw his back against a support beam as his prosort prepared the horses. "You should help," she said. "We have to go."

Barodane watched his breaths pool in the air before him, little dreams of peaceful days, each one fading fast. *It's like they have somewhere else to be. Someone else to be with.* "I need a second."

She snorted. Then Scab snorted.

Footsteps approached. Garlenna's face jerked toward the stable door. Muffled voices followed.

The door swung open, banged the outside wall, and shuddered. The attendant was gone. In his place, four men entered and closed the door behind. Garlenna drew up beside Barodane.

"You the one?" the lead man said to Barodane. Deep lines creased his cheeks, and he had dark hair chopped off level with a prominent chin. His eyes were narrow for a Namorite, and of the three who trailed him, he was the shortest by a head.

A brawny priest of the Sempyrean in smeared robes came to a stop at the group's flank. He swayed, deep in his cups. He cocked his head at Barodane and Garlenna.

"Depending on what you're after, I may be." Barodane said.

One side of the lead man's face coiled into a worn smile. "Vanavel the Black Blood, I'm called. While my dealings are pure, my lineage..." He moved his face in a circle, face bunched. "...Let's say it's somewhat Scothean."

"You're a thorn dealer?" Garlenna glanced at Barodane sidelong.

Eyebrows raised in question, Vanavel looked at prince then prosort. "Aye, lass. That I am." He shifted his weight, voice dripping menace. "And you be thorn buyers. That's what I've been told. That's what I expect."

Garlenna stepped forward, but Barodane laid a hand on her shoulder for restraint.

"Not another step." A looming man with a circle of beard around his mouth drew out a club.

"Be at fucking ease, Horse," Vanavel hissed, then sent a fist back into the man's gut. The brute named Horse barely acknowledged the blow. "A thorn deal is all."

The man watched Garlenna. She watched him in turn. Barodane broke the tension by jingling his purse. "What's your rate, friend?"

"Gold wheel gets you twenty."

Barodane stiffened. *That's over three times what I charged.* All the same, he dug into the leather pouch at his belt. His friends were presumed dead, and his grandmother and niece may have shared the same fate. He wasn't about to stir argument when necessity and opportunity favored his desires. Not to mention the three thugs at Vanavel's back.

He gripped the gold wheel in his fist. "I'll see the product first."

With her morality held in check by their need for anonymity, Garlenna did the only thing she could: scoff.

Taking her for a displeased lover, Vanavel laughed. "If your relationship is on hard times, my priest here can marry you. That should set your lass's ire to rest. Nothing steadies a woman like commitment."

Barodane blinked. Omari D'Alzir surely would have agreed with the man.

A Peladonian with blond whiskers, not yet twenty, reached into a bag at his hip. A pair of daggers were crisscrossed at the other.

Barodane inspected the product.

"If we only deal thorn, why bring so many men?" said Garlenna.

Vanavel tensed. "Do I fucking know you, lass?" A thick vein pulsed from crown to brow. "Or your man here?"

The nape of Barodane's neck prickled. A part of Vanavel's outrage rang true. The other part, though... *He's prying.*

"No." Garlenna rubbed one of Barodane's shoulders. "But you seemed familiar with him."

She sees it too. There was little Barodane could notice that Garlenna wouldn't, even with a single eye. So she played up Vanavel's assumption that they were a couple, to avoid suspicion.

Vanavel winced, lip twitching. "Right. Well, I don't know you. And sure as Nacronus's balls, I don't fucking trust you." With a smile as sudden as an adder's strike, he motioned the young man with daggers forward. "Better off being lucky in this line of work."

After swapping gold for godsthorn, it was Barodane's turn to smile. *Until we reach Matry's Isle, I won't spend a day sober in the saddle.* The pledge seemed to lack some of the push it might have had in prior years. It echoed empty, as if he already knew it would fail to hold against the forces he'd unleashed while wrapped around the banha drum. Doubt squeezed his spine.

"Luck's never been my strong suit." Barodane checked over the thorns in the roll, making sure none of them were fake. Godsthorn was a darker wood, almost cherry, with faint veins of blue marbling their base. A honey locust tree, common to Lah-Tsarra, was a touch lighter, and if shaved thinner by a steady hand, could resemble godsthorn at a glance. He eyed Vanavel's hands. "Not a whittler, I presume?" The name for false dealers.

"Not of thorns, no." He slapped a palm against the ax looped into his belt. "Just the occasional pinky."

From his periphery, Barodane saw Garlenna's hand disappear inside her cloak, the movement veiled and seemingly natural to those who didn't know her. Barodane cleared his throat to draw attention back his way as he tucked the roll into his belt. "Mostly harpists, I hope." He extended a hand to shake.

"Agh." The drug dealer stared at Barodane's hand, then waved it off, looking pained. "Sorry to do this to you—I saw you in the inn. Nearly cried at such a damn sweet song. But I must ask to see your sword."

"Why's that?"

Vanavel gave a shallow shrug. "They say some thorn dealer slew the magnate's son in these parts. A shadowguard with a fine blade, they say."

Garlenna sidestepped away from Barodane—clearance for her draw. "A big woman with him...did they say that, too?"

"Aye." Vanavel's voice simmered. "They did."

The song of crickets outside the stable intensified. Farther off, the harpists took up a tune in the inn, their pinkies too safe for Barodane's liking. Horse's chest was swelling rapidly. The man was a monstrous cock of throbbing veins looking for anyone to spill his rage on. The drunk priest breathed heavily, murmured something inaudible. *Pissants?*

The silence expanded, pummeling Barodane with regret about his most recent choice. *They've got us. Too much information to deny it.*

Closest to one another, Barodane matched the Black Blood's stony repose. Neither dared move.

The priest belched, dashing the tension.

"Here." Barodane unsheathed his sword, a decent enough blade, but not the one they sought. The sword of his family was securely wrapped in Scab's saddle bags. Well-shadowed at the back of the stable.

Vanavel blinked at the blade a few times, eyebrow arched. His gaze whipped back to Barodane and hovered there. The half-Scoth made a confirming sound in his throat and stretched out a hand. Dark crescents clotted his fingernails. "Well met."

Measured and cautious, Barodane reached forth like a thief removing a fortune from beneath the head of a sleeping king. The drug dealer's grip was weaker than expected. *Easier to pull free if needed—defensive.*

"You're a damn talent with that drum," he said. "Might be I'll trade you thorns for a lesson next time you pass through."

Cold sweat broke, damping Barodane's back. "You'll have to convince my woman, first." Smiling, he stepped back to wrap an arm around Garlenna's waist. "When it comes to where I spend my time, she's quite the tyrant."

Vanavel punched the blond-whiskered youth hard on the shoulder. "See? We've plenty of lords to bow to, but none are so demanding as the women we love." He hacked a gob of phlegm onto a hay bale. The group bade farewell amid knowing chuckles and left the barn. Horse cast Garlenna a dirty, slack-mouthed stare in parting. A few seconds later the stable boy returned, his face a shade whiter. He refused to make eye contact with Barodane.

Garlenna prepped their mounts for departure, muttering scathing recriminations on Barodane's character as she did. Stupidity, selfishness, and his lack of willpower topped the list.

Barodane helped, but unpracticed, he moved slower than his prosort. Sodden with guilt, the thorn in his trouser pocket made him a few degrees more sluggish still. "I'm sorry," he whispered.

"No you're not."

"I told you. I'm broken. Poison to those around me."

"Enough," she said, tone firm but low enough that it didn't carry to the boy manning the entrance. She stepped close, jerked a strap on Scab's saddle. "Give it to me. Now."

"Truly?" he spat. "You'd make me face the news we've heard sober? Malus is dead. My niece may be—"

"Malus was my friend, too. And you haven't even realized that my father..." She cleared her throat. She didn't need to finish for Barodane to know what she was going to say. Chances were, Gyr Renwood had been with his duke when the Kurgs attacked. Both of them knew her father. Knew he would defend Malus to his last breath. If the duke was gone, so was Gyr Renwood.

"Don't blame your weakness on anyone but yourself," she said. "This is your fight, Barodane. Yours. And *you* keep choosing poison."

Barodane's palm rested on the ax-wound wrapping around Scab's chest and neck, a bubbled line of hairless flesh. He traced the scar with his thumb, recalling the blood that had poured from it as he'd rode the stallion from King's Crossing. The wounds in Barodane's side from the raek's bite were much the same. Glossy divots reminding him of the miracle of his life.

That feeling had faded quickly, though, twisting into a curse he couldn't seem to escape. He'd never wanted to survive, which is why he'd headed toward Unturrus. He shook his head. *No, it was Nine Lakes I went to first..wasn't it?*

Gaps filled the days between Digtown and King's Crossing. Empty, vacuous stretches. Stains scrubbed clean. Memories forever hidden.

He still hadn't told Garlenna about the missing pieces of his mind. *If I tell her, she'll think me mad for certain.* Despite keeping her at a distance and gently pushing back against her desire to see him return to power, the idea that she might abandon him struck a note of cold fear in him.

The only thing worse than wearing the crown again was failing her.

"Fuck." He jammed a hand into his pocket, fished out the thorn roll, and handed it to her.

"One fight at a time. That's how you'll win." Garlenna hefted the godsthorn in her palm, then tossed it into the dark recesses at the rear of the stables. "The Hammer has gotten word ahead of us. The hunt is on. It's a race to Martyr's Isle now."

They mounted and led their horses from the stable.

The boy opened the door, then hurried off into the night.

Barodane frowned, "Odd of him to—"

A snarl from the left. A wooden pole of some kind flew into Barodane's vision—light flashed behind his eyes. Distantly, he heard a crack as half his face went numb from cheek to chin. Ears ringing, the clouded night sky tumbled over—then under—then over him. Earth slammed into his back. A frozen, breathless moment followed. He gasped. Shouts encircled him. Hands holding rope descended, a tight mouth circled with beard and spewing bad breath, behind. Horse.

Garlenna hurtled into view. Shoulder leading, she launched herself into the ribs of the man. The collision sent him flying, feet kicking up as he skidded down the slope. Garlenna landed on hands and knees, scrambled to her feet and drew her mace. "Up! Up!"

Barodane blinked hard, his head heavy and wobbling on a rubbery neck. Clumsy, disconnected fingers found his sword hilt—two sluggish attempts to unsheathe it. On his third try, he brought it free.

A hand ax chopped at Garlenna's neck. She danced back and deflected the blow. A second man with a polearm lunged at her from behind. She pivoted just as the blade's tip scraped past, shaving off a piece of the boiled leather armor protecting her side.

Barodane struggled to one knee. Head swimming, he pitched forward with blotted vision, falling onto his elbows near the feet of the man with the polearm. *Never stop moving.* That's what Pyr Syat had always said in training.

In a real fight, the stationary tended to stay that way...forever.

He swung at the ankles of the man with the polearm as he rolled away, hard and fast. He felt his sword drag on something—heard a satisfying howl. Like a barrel, he sped downhill, frost-crusted grass crunching under him.

He clambered to his feet then ran a couple of steps, flinging his blade in a backward arc to deter anyone who might have run up behind him. When he sensed he wouldn't be cut down, he spun to the fray.

Near the stable entrance, Vanavel and a recovered Horse bracketed Garlenna. The man with the polearm was on his knees, whimpering, and attempting to lever himself back to standing by planting the butt of his weapon in the dirt and hauling on it with both hands. Ankle tendon severed, dark blood sluiced onto the earth.

He saw Garlenna whirl her mace, lash out at Vanavel—

Motion to his right. The boy with daggers raced at Barodane, a determined expression etched on his face. The heavyset priest in tow brandished a cudgel.

Barodane backpedaled, keenly aware that the mustached henchman was Jennim's age. "I don't want to hurt you!"

With a snarl, the young man flew at Barodane, daggers raking empty air.

On second thought, fuck you. Barodane countered, ripping a hole in the shoulder of the boy's threadbare tunic.

"Get behind him!" the youth shouted at the priest. Barodane blocked a knife thrust aimed at his heart, then circled out of range. The boy cocked his arm and hurled a dagger at Barodane's leg. He jumped back—toes slipping on damp earth—lost his footing and landed on his belly. With no time to manage a defense, he tensed, breath locked in his chest as he prepared to die.

A heartbeat passed. Longer than it would take.

Barodane surged to standing in time to see the priest's meaty hand gripping a fistful of the young man's collar. A clipped syllable of protest was all the outraged youth managed before the priest bashed him in the gut with his cudgel. Eyes wide, veins bulging all over his face, the youth doubled over. The drunk priest planted a fist behind the boy's ear that sent him down to kiss dirt.

"Come on." Huffing, the priest gestured at Garlenna. Flickering torchlight at the stable entrance revealed a smattering of blood on her shoulder. She was hard-pressed.

Together, Barodane and the priest raced up the slope. The man with the polearm saw them coming and tried to bring his weapon into a defensive position, but Barodane swung his blade one way to knock it aside, and drew back the other way to slash open the man's throat.

The priest tackled Horse but the towering thug shrugged him off.

Barodane went for Vanavel. Sensing the tides had turned, the Black Blood tried to run. Barodane cut him off with a few quick steps. *Can't have you rallying the Hammer's men or the Crown's Justice and coming after us, can I?* It was a grim though necessary task. Barodane was no stranger to bloodshed. The crown and the many advisers who came with it had conditioned him to murder in the name of the greater good. It was never a matter of *if* a Crown Prince would kill someone. The only difference between an infamous tyrant and beloved monarch was intent.

Vanavel executed a series of tight chops at Barodane's head and neck. He parried each, then worked in a counter thrust that drove the Black Blood's back against the stable wall. Barodane was quicker, younger, larger, and more skilled than the godsthorn dealer. Barring an unlucky moment, it was a matter of time to the end.

Vanavel seemed to sense it too.

Barodane watched him brush back thin, greasy strands of chin-length hair. The half-Scoth's deeply creased cheeks bunched into a frown. "Never trust a fucking priest."

With a grunt, Barodane shifted his sword into one hand and drew a dagger from his belt. "I prefer them to Scoths."

Vanavel's lip curled back. "Lucky me."

From the corner of Barodane's eye, he spotted Wynna Marwen and the barman jog into the circle of torchlight outside the stables. The hold lady's head swiveled toward the convulsing body of the man with the polearm. "Rouse my father! Rouse the holdguard!"

The distraction nearly cost Barodane his head. Reflex saved him as sword met ax a few inches from his throat. Vanavel kicked him in the shin.

Barodane's heel slid on the frost-slicked grass, dropping him to a knee. He brushed aside a downward cut from Vanavel. The man snarled and hacked down again.

This time, Barodane caught it on his guard and twisted, locking the ax in place for a heartbeat as he rammed his dagger into the man's side with a rip of cloth and wet gulp of flesh.

"Ulck!" The drug dealer spun away, gripping his ribcage.

Barodane rose, stalking the wounded man to the stable wall where Vanavel lurched against it. His expression was slack, his skin chalky white, as he rotated to face Barodane. Drool trailed from his lips. To the man's credit, he mustered a war cry and raised his weapon one last time before Barodane stabbed him through the heart.

Bells clanged to life in the distance. This was no Digtown, where violence was an expectation that was given little attention beyond the moment that it ended. Shouting and the thud of bootsteps—holdguard answering their lady's summons.

Something slammed against the stable, causing the slats to shudder. Garlenna and Horse stumbled into view. Somehow, both had been disarmed. The priest lurched after them a second later, raining blows down onto Horse's shoulders but doing little to deter him as he throttled Garlenna.

Barodane knew his prosort well. She'd given the larger man a grip of her neck for a reason. Horse's arms were higher than hers, which meant she now had leverage. Clapping her hands together at the small of Horse's back, she threw her hips to one side and leaned her weight into him. The big man toppled, releasing his grip on her neck and flinging his hands to the sides to cushion his fall.

The back of Horse's head thudded off the ground as Barodane hurried up beside them. "Away!" he urged. "Give me an opening!" The man was unarmed.

Barodane meant to end it then but instinct had taken Garlenna to another place. She threw her legs over the man's midsection and began driving elbows down into his throat. Arms stiffening in the air overhead, Horse's eyes rolled back in his head. Windpipe caved in, he purpled and gawped. Finally, Garlenna pushed to her feet, allowing Barodane to relieve the giant of his last moments.

With a whistle, Garlenna called their mounts. Feet pounded down the lane toward them.

"I'll take a ride," the priest said, breathing heavily. "If you please?"

Garlenna started to speak but swayed then fell into Barodane's arms. Warm blood smeared his hands from a wound in her shoulder.

"She's hurt!" Barodane motioned for the priest to help him. "Quickly!" They grasped her under her armpits and rushed to the horses trotting towards them.

Garlenna lurched between them as they guided her onto her stallion. The priest gracelessly scrambled into the saddle behind her and Barodane leapt onto Scab. He wheeled his mount to point down the road they'd followed into town. "Not that way!" the priest warned. "The chainman's waiting for you."

"Shit." Barodane stared into the murky night as if he could see the trap.

"Come." The priest led Garlenna's warhorse around the stable and past a series of buildings. They found a goat trail and took it down into the dark.

Barodane slapped Scab's flanks, pulse flooding his ears. *Better lucky than dead, I suppose.*

CHAPTER THIRTY-NINE

AN INCESSANT BLEATING

A stone wall spanned one side of Ishoa's periphery to the other. Snow and persistent ash fall from the burning fields surrounded them.

"The Manger." Arick hobbled over to join Rakeema at Ishoa's side. The Fly hung back, ever watchful.

A glimpse of childhood memory...

Of Wolst and a swirl of holdguard approaching the very same wall. Despite a decade separating her from that moment, the Manger appeared to have changed little.

She turned to the Fly. Their escape from the slaughter on the road had preceded a night's dash through wild woods, frigid bogs, and a final stretch of open tundra. Somewhere amid the frantic flight, Arick had woken.

"He's helping us," he'd said. It had taken him the better part of the afternoon to puzzle out the presence of Megalor's bodyguard. "He's taking us to the Hines of White Plains."

"I know," Ishoa said before telling her cousin about the acts of villainy he'd carried out in keeping her "safe."

But Arick didn't flinch at any of them. "It's a war now, Ishoa," he'd said as if to excuse all of it.

He killed a kid and left Okki to die. The crones, too. She glanced at Rakeema who was watching a crow rattle and click in an evergreen tree. Outside of a little weariness, the ice tiger seemed in good spirits. When the Fly cut her loose, she bounded and scurried around with a kinked tail, happy to be free. Ishoa had rubbed her face against Rakeema's and cradled her in her arms, tears brimming. *And he hurt my anjuhtarg.*

Difficult as it was, she'd come to accept the Fly's presence, even if it left a bitter flavor in her mouth. "He has his uses," she'd said to Arick and then threw the giant a menacing look.

That was two nights ago.

Now, they'd finally arrived at the Manger. They stared at a wide gate. A discordant racket seemed to be coming from inside.

"No wains, no traders." Ishoa surveyed the road behind. A sharp ascent from a heavily wooded area. They stood on a crest of rolling lowland hills, surrounded by frosted grasslands stretching to the edge of sight in every direction. "Nothing but tundra."

"You'll see why in a moment," Arick said. "You may wish to plug your nose."

She glanced back at the Fly who shrugged.

A woman on the battlements blew into a curled horn. From within the Manger came an echoing groan and the clack of chains as stout, banded doors crept outward.

A line of holdguard bearing short bows sprang up along the battlements. Ishoa was pleased to find their weapons weren't trained on her, but on the distant wood as if expecting a trap.

In the widening gap between doors, dozens of spearmen waited in ordered ranks. Ishoa stepped back, bumping into the Fly's chest. He gestured forward, and reluctantly, she went.

"It's alright, Isha." A handle of the stretcher had been refashioned into a crutch by the Fly. Arick had it stuck up under a shoulder and now hobbled toward the gate. "The Hines are friends."

"So were the Kons." She watched the gathered soldiers. "So were a lot of those spilling Frost blood in the High Hall."

Fifteen paces out, Ishoa started to gag. It was like dung had been shoveled into her mouth and jammed up her nostrils. The smell coated her throat. "Ancestors, that's wretched." If she'd had anything more than a handful of rations in recent days, she might have heaved up the contents of her stomach.

The noisy tumult grew sharper in clarity. Beyond the ranked soldiers that bowed around Ishoa and her party, there was a brown and white flurry of movement. *Sheep. Thousands of them.*

Arick led them across the threshold.

Once inside, a man with a narrow face, shorn white hair, and a patchy beard parted from the spearmen. "Ishoa Ironlight." He raised a finger then slowly lowered it at her cousin, tone falling somewhere between confident conjecture and question. "Sir Arick Quinn."

Ishoa squared to face the man but said nothing. The Fly shouldered past her, ax-staff in hand, to put himself between her and the spearmen. Ishoa surveyed the bowmen along the battlements. They faced the distant forest until the gate groaned closed.

Even with the Fly on my side, we won't leave here alive if they're loyal to the White Wolverine Alliance.

Mud and shit squished under the stranger's feet before Ishoa, his pale eyes assessing. "You are among friends here. I am Sir Hollem Hine." He saluted, bowing in the process. Then he sidestepped, opening his body toward the keep at the center of the Manger's bailey, his palm upturned in presentation. "My mother awaits you in the Warming Place, Highness."

Arick laid a hand on the Fly's arm in restraint, which drew a blank, yet somehow reproachful gaze. Nevertheless, he lowered his ax-staff.

"Sir Hollem." Ishoa added a pinch of cheer to her voice. "The Warming Place, is it? I'd love nothing more, though a bath might be in order first."

"No time for that." Arick hustled forward on his crutch.

Ishoa fought to keep her face from bunching in displeasure. *Like a short bath will make the difference.* "I suppose you're right, cousin." *I won't have you talking over me in front of anyone else.* She looked at Hollem Hine. "Sir Arick requires immediate attention from a Sister of the Rose."

"I'm fine, Highness," Arick muttered.

"You've spent days in unconscious delirium. I won't have you live through all that just to die of infection."

Arick ignored her and continued on. An urge to shout for her cousin to do her bidding slipped into a vault of grievances, the majority of them pertaining to her age, gender, and general lack of presence. Frozen with insecurity, she summoned a petty scowl before following him.

The Fly stayed close as she knifed through the sea of bleating sheep. She'd adjusted to the smell, a thought almost as unsettling as the initial shock their scent had caused. *Hopefully, we won't be staying here long.* Lodecka Warnock held her grandmother captive—if she still lived. The Scarborn leader could, at that very moment, be sleeping in Ishoa's bedroom...

An image of the portrait of her parents being mishandled or destroyed flashed through her, a white-hot brand that left her sweaty with rage. The stain to her honor was already a deep chasm, and Ishoa often found herself at its bottom with no handholds to climb free but those of hate and vengeance.

She killed my uncle. Ishoa sucked in a sharp breath and turned her attention to the distractions of the moment to keep from a panic attack.

The Manger's bailey rivaled Jarik's own in terms of size, though it lacked in beauty by a sincere degree. Where there were flowers and trees and an inclination toward architectural aesthetics in the duchy's capital, here, there were sheep, sheep, and more sheep. Where the air was crisp and crackling with the bustle of hundreds of soldiers, courtiers, and castle servants, the Manger possessed a low-hanging cloud of beastly stench and an incessant bleating. Around the Sister Keep and the Ice Maiden's Keep, the people were richly garbed, a focus on prestige and elegance, living testaments to Namarr's prosperity. Ishoa studied those milling through the endless flock. Long, cruel-looking blades hung from the belts of the Hine holdguard under their woolen vests. Hideous, ballooning pants were stuffed into shit-caked boots. The citizens clearing way for their holdguard wore smeared, ill-fitting roughspun, and sheep-hide shawls.

One and all, the people of the Manger were dirty, stinky, and dour.

Yet, Ishoa couldn't be happier to be within stone walls again. She smiled at those she passed, sympathy mounting. *I would be frustrated too if I was packed in this tightly.* In Jarik, Ishoa could have ridden her horse around the bailey grounds with her eyes closed and never run into anyone. The Manger was a dilapidated huddle of slats, nails, and stonework. Most buildings were tucked under the wooden battlements but for a handful connected to the ugly gray keep at the bailey's center.

Of all she saw, Ishoa noted a single area she thought might be considered spacious. Toward the back of the Manger, there was an expansive training yard hedged in by aspens. A low fence kept the flocks from entering, and buildings clustered around the outside of it. If Ishoa was to stay longer than she hoped, she imagined she'd take Rakeema there to train.

Hollem Hine barked at the guards stationed outside a stake-wall encircling the keep. Up and out, a section of the wood pilings lifted to admit them to the inner bailey—the only place besides the training yard without cloven-hoof tracks.

More holdguard, wicked knives at their waists and shepherd staves sporting hooked blades, patrolled the keep's secondary entrance. One was working his way around the stone structure, tending to a handful of fires nestled into vents at its base.

Heavy doors were held aside. The thump of Arick's crutch preceded them through the twisting passages as the temperature increased. Vague flickers from childhood came to Ishoa in the dimness of those same halls.

She remembered clinging to Wolst's warskirt in fear as they entered a broad hall with a low ceiling and rows of flickering torches. Steam piped into the room from a dozen vents. Ishoa sighed, pleasure leaking across her skin. She'd been cold for so long out in the wild she'd forgotten how her body felt. Sudden drowsiness dragged at her. *Not yet.* She wrestled a yawn into submission. *Duty first.*

"Princess Ishoa Ironlight," Sir Hollem announced.

A thick slab of stone lay over a monstrous iron brazier. Smoke wended out in lazy curls from bolt holes around its rim and coalesced in a silken sheet over the room. Sir Hollem withdrew a chair situated around the stone slab for Ishoa; it was bedecked in lamb's wool and she sank into it with relish.

Once seated, Arick and three others who had stood upon her arrival sat back down in their chairs. One, an ancient, keg-bodied woman, did so with great difficulty stemming from what appeared to be an injured hip.

"Have not seen you in a decade or more," the aging woman said. "Had thought I might never again when news of Jarik's sacking arrived." In the way of those with too little life left for shallow gestures, she slapped a fist against an honor plate embossed with a ram's skull.

So this is the Matriarch of White Plains. Ishoa's memories fell short of recalling the woman. Near as old as Belara Frost, albeit with seemingly harsher years behind her, Rigga Hine didn't seem worthy of Joffus Kon's long-time rivalry.

Ishoa inclined her head. "Lady Rigga. I am in your debt."

The hold lady waved off Ishoa's platitude as if it were a gust of errant fart. "We'll talk of sentiments later, I'm sure. For now, you have needs to attend. Eat. Be warm."

An audible squeal of hunger erupted from Ishoa's belly at the smell of meat cooking on the stone slab. "I'm quite famished."

She took in the woman seated to her right. Not so old as Rigga, but neither was she young. The lines of her face were carved into her cheeks and her neck stretched twice as long as a neck should. Her spine was rigid, her legs crossed, and only a narrow portion of her backside rested on her wool covered chair as if she might need to leap up at any moment. Tight gray braids descended from a tight knot at the back of her head, and black velvet cinched tight at her wrists and ankles climbed to her throat. How the woman had managed to avoid mud or shit getting on her person meant she'd either been at the Manger a while, or she'd floated over it. Ishoa wondered if it might be the latter, for everything about her rested with the ease of a wound-up crossbow.

Rigga Hine unceremoniously flicked a finger at the woman. "The High Hand, Krhalka."

Ishoa saw it now. A steel claw hung from a thin chain on the woman's belt. *Jurati.*

"I met you when you were much younger." Krhalka's voice was butter-smooth, quiet and clear. She'd heard tales of forest spirits who lulled men to sleep with their sweet song. She'd always imagined they sounded something like this woman. "The circumstances of our reunion are sadly dire."

Across the table, a hunched man slapped a strip of veal onto the stone table where it crackled. Arick narrowed his eyes at the man then said, "What news of the Ice Maiden?"

The room resettled around the abrupt shift toward matters at hand.

"None, I'm afraid." Rigga Hine rubbed at the soft arm of her chair. "Of the White Wolverine Alliance, however, there is plenty. Despite being a hundred miles apart, the Kons and Scarborn have orchestrated their rebellion deftly. The fires in Jarik had nary become embers by the time a thousand furriers started their bloody sweeps of the Prince's Highway. At this point, they're mostly killing and robbing citizens who think it's safer to flee the larger cities and return to their smaller holds. Damn shame."

"They're sequestering our duchy from the rest of Namarr." Arick nodded somberly. "Getting Ishoa to Alistar will be...difficult."

"Black sails bearing Warnock crimson have come down the Gray River to attack Bleeding Point," said Krhalka. "So far, it seems they are coming to understand the namesake rather intimately. The Knight of the Hallow Moon sent them limping back to the Fringes."

"We saw," Ishoa said.

"Mmmmm." The man cooking the veal jabbed at it with a two-pronged fork then frowned at the seared meat. Whether the sound was meant to convey annoyance or realization, Ishoa wasn't sure.

"My jurati officers report short, dark-skinned mercenaries among the Kon holdguard sweeping the Prince's Highway." Krhalka sniffled. "Slave-gladiators from Oren. Bought and paid for."

"Joffus Kon's coin stretches further than I could have imagined," Arick said.

"Aye," said Rigga Hine. "Ti-Cora and her coven of bloodthirsty Orenese sluts give women a bad name. I've ordered those holds nearest to me to gather strength and burn their fields. Let Kon's coin stretch until it breaks, I say."

Ishoa barely heard the lady of White Plains's admonishment of the Orenese, so focused was she on the lord of Ghastiin's treachery. Joffus Kon had played Belara Frost for a fool. Tears stung at Ishoa's eyes, begging to fall, but Ishoa clenched her jaw and forced them away.

"A thousand holdguard," Arick said, "in addition to what it takes to defend Ghastiin is an impressive muster for a smaller hold."

"Joffus Kon said he'd been rationing his keep for years to finance expeditions to Mimbor for dragon skins," Ishoa said. "Now we know the truth of it. He was going to Oren. Raising an army all along. Right under our nose."

"Ah!" The man cooking veal produced a heavy knife from a sheath at his hip and cut a portion of meat. "There it is then."

No one afforded his outburst a stray look but for Ishoa. Thick funnels of gray hair nested atop his head, and a mustache longer than his beard descended from an uncommonly round face. He wore a filthy tunic that looked to have been tied to a wain wheel all the way from Jarik thrown over his bony frame. He caught her looking at him and smiled. Pollen-colored teeth, a handful of them missing.

"The Scarborn have split their army," said Rigga Hine. "Their foot march on Summerforge, supported by contingents from Baen's Handle and Prav, while their cavalry make for Shadowheart. The field fires ensure nothing larger than a company or two can attack us until winter's end.

"Well done, Lady Hine," Arick said.

She grimaced. "Thank my sons. Hollem's strategy is sound, for now. My other boy, Adus, has been tasked with mirroring the foot soldiers at Summerforge. He's to give us warning if they head this way. My horse archers will cut them to ribbons on the open tundra." Rigga Hine hacked up a gob of mucus and loosed it against the distant wall.

Stunning range for a woman her age. Enkita Vulkuu would be impressed. "What of Twilight Cape?" Ishoa asked.

"The Lady Enkita was taken prisoner," said Krhalka. "Her hunters will do nothing against the Scarborn until she is freed. Lodecka Warnock is no fool."

Wolst and Othwii were already gone. The thought of one of her heroes rotting in chains left a sour taste in her mouth. "Then we should free her," Ishoa blurted. "My grandmother, too. We *must* act."

She searched the faces around the room, much in the way Belara Frost would have done. Impassive judgment was writ all over the countenance of the High Hand, Krhalka. Rigga Hine rubbed at the spindly white hairs covering her chin and stared at the meat smoking on the Warming Place's stone table.

"I have no doubt your 'wait and see' tactic is sound, Lady Hine." Ishoa pursed her lips. "But while we wait, my grandmother and countless others vital to Namarr's future may die."

The feral man across the way was the first to respond. "Dance right into their trap." He shoved a cube of veal into his mouth and chewed, sucking air between bites to cool the steaming food.

Ishoa waited half a heartbeat for further explanation but patience wasn't her strong suit. "Explain yourself, stranger."

"Gladly," he said. "You, Ishoa Ironlight, have no army. Your armies are scattered or holding up for the winter. Giving in to your emotions will make Lodecka's job that much easier. If you die on some heroic mission, Namarr dies. Very simple."

Ishoa glared at the man. "If you think that, then you think Namarr weaker than it is. The ideals that bind—"

"Ideals!" The man's guffaw sent a flush creeping up her neck. "Common folk don't give a damn about ideals. Power is what holds them together, and without the Ironlight name hovering over their beds to offer a sense of stability, rest assured, they will look for the next name that does so."

Ishoa's fingernails dug into the wool on the arm of her chair. "Who are you?"

The man sawed free a chunk of meat and flicked it toward her. "Please accept my apologies for speaking tersely, Highness." Ishoa growled inwardly at the empty gesture but her eyes drifted to the browned, juicy, meat. Her stomach was more than willing to forgive the man's slight. A second of hesitation passed before she snatched up the hot morsel; it immediately set her fingertips to throbbing but she didn't care. Her mouth burned as she tore into it.

The man smiled. "I am the beastmaster, Gaern Yorek. I come from Akulsa."

Ishoa blinked. Chewed. Breathed out between bites in an attempt to cool her food even as she devoured it. Ishoa's Fjordsong was rudimentary at best but she knew enough to know Akulsa meant "Antler." Beyond the Fringes and across the border into the wild lands of C'Dath, there was a range of mountains called The Antler. Tales of the beastmasters who lived there would have been considered myth were it not for the very real anjuhtargs they sometimes ferried by barge across the C'Dathun straits to trade for the occasional small fortune. To imagine anyone living surrounded by trolls sent a shiver along Ishoa's spine. She glanced at Rakeema. Wolst had traveled to the Fringes to claim the ice tiger, she assumed, from the man now grinning at her.

As if to validate her theory, Gaern Yorek clucked his tongue, and Rakeema sprang to her feet. "Ah yes." He angled in his seat to inspect her. "I see she's grown a bit. No longer the rambunctious kitten I knew." His voice took on a somber tone. "Your uncle said she reminded him of you, Princess."

A sob rushed to Ishoa's throat.

Krhalka leaned forward, upper body a steady, flat plane. She cleared her throat. "I've dispatched messages to my contacts at Alistar but I'm still awaiting a response. The capital has had their own issues. Duke Malus D'Alzir is dead. Murdered by Kurgs, they say."

Arick shot to his feet. "That can't be. None of the enclaves are stupid enough to—"

"It's an orchestrated attack, boy. The Scarborn could not have their Rising under any other circumstance but total disarray. They work *with* the Kurgs." Rigga Hine snorted. "The lowborn do nothing but covet that which their betters possess."

Arick shook his head. "Ishoa *must* go to Alistar."

Ishoa flinched. *And let Lodecka win?* Wolst would never have stomached the sight of her if she willingly fled Anjuhkar while it remained in the hands of enemies. "I'm not going anywhere."

Rigga ignored her. They all did. "Best that she doesn't until my son, Adus, returns with the bulk of our knights."

"Better to gather information before she leaves," Krhalka said. "And allies."

The room moved past Ishoa's declaration as if she'd never spoken. Her fists clenched at her sides. "I said I'm not going."

Krhalka spared her a sidelong glance then launched back into the logistical fray. "The Collective's trust in Anjuhkar has been tarnished. I worry our ducal seats will be deposed. If that happens..." Her slow inhale seemed to hang on an image of proleptic disaster. "We'll get no help from Peladonia. Onai Saud and Haydees Cotter won't sidestep protocol. Prior to any decision, the Collective will need to meet."

"Too slow," Arick murmured. "Winter is upon us. By the time they convene, it will be spring. By then, the war for Anjuhkar could already be lost."

"In the face of Malus D'Alzir's demise, his brother will be named Duke of Lah-Tsarra," Krhalka said. "He sent a message stating that he believes in the strength of those holding Anjuhkar for Namarr's sake. Word has it, he sent two hundred holdguard to Shadowheart in a show of support."

"Brave of him to act unilaterally for one not officially yet a duke," said Rigga. *The banker lord gets praised while I am shuffled off into the shadows and ignored.*

"It validates our position on the matter, certainly," said Krhalka. "The White Wolverine Alliance has made its play. We lose nothing by waiting, consolidating power, and resources. When your son returns," the High Hand of the Jurati spoke across Ishoa to Rigga, "we can send her to Alistar with Sir Arick to establish—"

Send her to Alistar?

"We also gain nothing by waiting!" Ishoa's voice cracked as she bolted to her feet. Wolst, Stirmma, Othwii, Lodaris—countless loved ones had died on her behalf. Her grandmother and Enkita might still. And the council now watching her and judging her invalidated everything the dead had given their lives to preserve. A hope that still limped on...that Ishoa might still be Crown Princess of Namarr.

My voice will *be heard.* "We will take our remaining strength and make for Jarik."

"Less than five hundred holdguard and a hundred knights to retake the capital?" Rigga Hine snorted. "The shepherds of White Plains know their bows on open ground, and our staves rend flesh like any weapon, but what you'd need for a mission of that magnitude are gods. Magic and myth. Not going to happen."

Arick said, "It's not possible, Highness."

"I didn't ask if it was possible," Ishoa snapped. "I said it is what I wish to do."

"This is most unwise," Krhalka said.

"It's suicide." Rigga Hine scoffed, incredulous. "You'd die like your uncle. And you'd sacrifice my people in the process."

Agreement among them resolved into a discontented bickering. *They're convincing themselves they're right...that I am wrong. How dare they use my family and its legacy against me.* "I command you to listen to me!" she railed. Regret steeped in the silence that followed. She knew it wasn't the best approach but couldn't stop herself. Their dismissive air stung too much.

Ishoa felt them pulling back. It was evident in the way Krhalka's eyes dropped to the floor; in the way Rigga nestled into the crook of her chair, baggy wool swaddling the woman as she studied a blank section of wall; in the way Arick stared through her, wishing she wasn't the final hope of their nation. She knew the look. All her life, she'd courted that disapproving stare from him and the rest of her family. From her grandmother, especially.

Ishoa's knife jumped from its sheath into her hand. "We are called to war!" She punched the air with her blade. "And by my ancestors, I vow to bury the Warnocks before I leave my lands." It was supposed to be inspiring. A gesture like Danath might have made.

Gaern Yorek made a poor attempt to stifle a yawn. A holdguard coughed.

Ishoa bristled, knife drifting slowly back to her side. "Is it cowardice that allows us to give Lodecka all of Anjuhkar?"

Rigga Hine lifted her chin, the wattle of wrinkled flesh there smoothing. "It is offensive to be called a coward in my own hall. If her Highness is inclined to command a situation, she might be better served using a different tact."

Words flew, reason stumbling after them. "Her Highness has had enough of kindness and tact." Ishoa's anger had awakened and hungered for something more than veal to sate it. "My grandmother attempted diplomacy with fanatics. She thought to meet her problems in the shadows, with whispers and scribbled words and secret deals. Now she wears shackles and counts herself among the lucky. So if I offend you, Rigga Hine, it is because my feet ache from all the dancing around they've done."

None took up her passionate declaration. She was alone in her vehemence. Alone in her urgency. Rage hurled against the walls of shame and began flowing in a more vulnerable direction. *I'm weak, just as I've always feared.* Not only did they refuse her call to action, but they were clearly upset with her for making it.

I can't lead them. The realization punched her in the chest.

Arick rose, chair scraping the floor. Ishoa felt the sound in her bones. "My cousin has been under immense stress. We've lost loved ones and we've been fighting for our lives every moment during and since the Battle of Jarik." He bowed to the others, his voice husky with apology. "Please forgive and excuse us."

He turned partway from the table, eyes never leaving her. He waited.

Ishoa roamed her inherited council. No one wished to make eye contact with her. Not now. Not when there was a chance she'd take her cousin's offer of a graceful exit and leave them to discussions better had among adults.

She swallowed her pride and mustered what little strength she had left into her tone. "My apologies. It was a mistake not to rest before a meeting of such importance."

The Fly escorted her back to her quarters. When he turned to close the door, Ishoa said, "Do you think I could be a good leader one day?"

For a couple of heartbeats, the man's black hood stayed motionless. Then he closed the door, leaving her with an incessant bleating, not from the sheep outside her window, but that of her own voice demanding she be seen as something more than she was.

CHAPTER FORTY

THE WEIGHT OF THINGS

B arodane's circumstances seemed a joke. *What do you get when a former prosort, a former priest, and a former prince sit around a campfire together? Silence.*

A stream murmured nearby from a cluster of woods. A crow croaked. *Well, mostly silence. I'd say you get a guilty conscience, too, but I had that long before we sat down.*

Several leagues from the road, camped out in a marshy fen where no one would bother them, he still held no trust for the priest. Days had passed in silence but for the priest's singing and whistling. Yellow foliage surrounded them, rolled out like wool and spotted with murky puddles. Small animals worked the edges of the fen where it turned to woodlands, saving up for the coming gloom of winter.

It had been a few days of watching the priest tend to a nasty gash on Garlenna's shoulder blade as she sweated and moaned and slipped in and out of sleep. A few days of Barodane's hand wrapped around his sword hilt under his cloak.

"I saved you," the priest—Tohar, he named himself—said. "A little trust would be nice."

A fat roll of godsthorn would be nice too, but I'm not getting that any time soon.

"Why trust a man whose motivations are still unknown to me?"

Tohar shrugged. "Nothing a simple question or two won't unearth." He unrolled a fresh bundle of bandages they'd pilfered from Garlenna's rucksack. He removed the old, all rust-colored and dried. Half-conscious, she sucked in through her teeth.

"You dress the part of priest," Barodane said. "But act like a criminal. Lies come easier than truths, anyway."

Gingerly, Tohar dressed Garlenna's wound with the fresh bandages. When he finished, he wiped her blood on his robes, leaving scarlet streaks. "You don't understand how trust works, do you?"

Lying stretched out on a thick bed of moss, Garlenna woke and rasped for water. Tohar and Barodane stared at each other until the priest laughed, slapped a broad knee, then rose. "I suppose that's me. Can't be left alone with the lass. No, certainly not. I'm only keeping her alive!" He snatched up a waterskin and headed for the stream. Barodane watched Garlenna's eye following him. The man's mane of dark, lustrous hair bounced with every huffing step.

"Do you trust him?" Barodane asked.

Her eye closed, chest rising and falling with languid effort. "He's a priest of the Sempyrean."

"Not what I asked."

"He deserves as much of my trust as you do."

Barodane felt his brow crease. "What do you mean?"

"This." She hiked a thumb over the opposite shoulder, indicating her wound, then let her arm flop back down at her side. "Is your fault."

When Barodane didn't speak, she went on.

"Your moment of weakness almost cost me everything." She shifted her gaze to the darkening sky. Steam rose from her lips. She gulped against a tremor of pain. "We're hunted now and with many leagues left to cover before we reach Martyr's Isle. You jeopardized our nation's future. For what? A single sunset's reprieve from your grief?"

"It was ill luck, that's all," Barodane growled. "How could I know Vanavel would be chasing our bounty?"

"Let's not confuse stupidity with destiny. Only a fool stomps on a bear trap and calls it ill luck." She closed her eye. "Good things do come along once in a while, you know. It's okay to embrace them when they do."

Knifing wind pressed the fire low, squeezing out a flock of embers. Barodane turned his face to avoid them. "After all we've been through, you still think life is all juicy peaches and magic rainbows." He stood. "This may come as news to you—and I do hope it penetrates that fine layer of dusty brick you've walled your good senses behind—but the world is a terrible place."

"Lucky breaks do come. Happy moments. Special people. Helpful strangers. Sometimes, you have to let them be." Her voice grew somber. "You used to."

Barodane prised up a rounded stone with the toe of his boot. "Keep reminiscing about the old days—the old me—and see where it gets you."

"You were a careless boy." The violent thrust of Garlenna's words froze Barodane. "You were shallow, weak-willed. Talented, yes, in many ways, but a shell of what the Ironlights before you had been."

Barodane's mouth fell open.

"A new man stands here now. One who learns from his mistakes. One who knows the misuse of power and feels deeply the lasting cut it leaves." Pale-faced and wincing, Garlenna pushed herself to sit. "You think you're nothing. A worthless fiend, no more. But I see the possibility of someone greater. You cannot see the light without darkness. You cannot hold love sacred without losing it. And you cannot truly know who you are until you've touched the darkest part of your soul. Do you think—"

A whistling tune cut her short as Tohar returned. The priest's trilling song petered out when he noticed Garlenna seated upright for the first time in days, and Barodane standing, wearing a scowl. After an awkward moment, he said, "I can go—"

"No," Barodane said. "She was asking for your company. Preferable to mine at the moment."

Prince and prosort locked eyes, and then Barodane splashed off into the gloom. *There's your trust. Hopefully he doesn't cut your throat.*

A few minutes later, fear overtook anger as he considered the image of her being harmed. He'd stomped off a fair distance but glanced back. The pair were hazy silhouettes. Tohar moved about...

Barodane tapped the hilt of his sword. An itch blossomed at the back of his skull. Panic climbed his innards. *If she dies, it'll be because she pushed me to be more trusting. That's her fault.* The seconds ticked by, icy winter wind fingering the loose sleeves of his tunic. *Why would he kill her?* The thought was bereft of logic, yet he couldn't shake it.

He took a few hurried steps back toward camp.

A heron erupted from a stand of cattails and flaxen grass to his right, unleashing a discordant honking. Barodane whirled with a cry, sword drawn, heart hammering. Lazy flaps carried the heron across the fen as it threw abrasive bellows back at him.

"Shit." He exhaled. "Shit."

At camp, Tohar and Garlenna were in quiet conversation.

Barodane sucked in a breath as Pyr Syat's voice whispered through him. *Weakness breeds fear. Fear breeds weakness. Focus on your strength in here and neither shall hold you in their grasp.* The short Kanian had tapped his chest, a surprisingly gentle touch from the First Sword of the Remnant. Another thing the man liked to say was *the Hand of the Triune God is not idle...it practices or it pays.*

Barodane needed to practice trust. He thanked the heron for keeping him from looking an even bigger fool. If he'd gone stumbling back into their midst brandishing his sword, Garlenna would have shook her head at him. The priest, Tohar, had shown nothing but resolve to help them. *You lean on her more than a one-legged man leans on his crutch. No wonder you're so desperate to keep her safe. Without her, you're weak.*

Teeth gritted, Barodane slammed his blade back into the scabbard.

He let himself get somewhat lost in the fen as night closed in, searching for just the right size. A pool caught the orange-blasted sky in its reflection, a set of stones poking half up out of the mud on the other side. A thousand swarming gnats busied themselves over the water. Soon it would be too cold for them and they'd die or go to ground. His boots squelched in the mud around the rim of the pool as he picked his way around it to the stones.

Unclasping his cloak, he tossed it in a bundle with his sword onto a dry patch of moss, then spread his feet to either side of the largest stone. Fingers slid into freezing mud and found the bottom-most curvature. He settled back into his haunches—heaved upward, keeping his chest open to the sky like he'd been taught.

The ballast remained unmoved.

He exhaled, breath luminous in the layered gold of the setting sun. He adjusted his grip and his feet where they'd sunk a half-foot deeper into the muck, then resumed the strain. The stone didn't budge. Panting, he released it. Hands on knees, he gasped for breath. *Too ambitious.*

A rock half the size of the ones Garlenna had been training with lay beside the first. Dispersing a cloud of insects, he rinsed his hands in the pool, swiped them on his trousers, and then prepared himself to hoist the smaller stone.

He managed five lifts before his legs quivered like they were piped full of porridge. When he lowered the stone to rest, a cramp shot into his groin. The mix of cold and years of lethargy would make the night a difficult one.

He stretched his hips and massaged the cramp away before resuming. Another five. Another cramp, this one sharper and harder to shake. He cursed his feebleness. Cursed his reliance on those stronger than him. He hated himself for nearly getting Garlenna killed.

I said I'd never let it happen again. I promised.

Before his mind could spiral back into memories about the boy, he forced himself to focus on Pyr Syat. If he was to be strong like he'd once been—if he was to push fear from his heart—he needed something to focus on other than himself. And there were few moments in his life that had demanded his attention more than training for knighthood under the White Flame.

The First Sword of the Remnant slashed forward from the past...

A young Barodane retreated, barely raising his wooden blade in time to keep the man's thrust from knocking out his teeth. "Thrusts for the lazy defender," Pyr said. "No time to recover from a mistake."

The wood blade whistled around in an arc, then whipped forward. Barodane blocked the first blow, but a second, faster stroke he hadn't seen coming forced him to bend over backward to avoid it. "Tight cuts for the wary defender!

Always tight. Always at rising and falling angles. Aim for the outside of the closest leg or shoulder where their balance is least stable."

Master and pupil paused.

The White Flame gestured at him. "You must be sharp in all ways. Mind and body."

Barodane loosed the stone from his grip as he remembered his life before death.

A third set of five complete. His body was adjusting now, shaking out the rust. No cramps. Muscles warm and loose, he breathed rhythmically, gulping down crisp air. He didn't wait long and bent to lift the stone again...

Distinct in memory, Barodane watched Pyr Syat stalk forward a few steps and then change his stance. The White Flame winked and then dipped low to sweep at Barodane's ankles. "Keep your feet moving."

The prince avoided the stroke, but the trailing practice sword kicked up a cloud of dust. He blinked stinging sediment from his eyes—heard the shuffle of feet.

"Circumstances change," the First Sword said. "The wiser blade flows with them. The weaker blade fights against them. And so, you must be tempered."

A blow crashed into the elbow of Barodane's sword arm. Pyr Syat stood at an angle off to one side. "This is no game for children, Prince. You must hold the disposition of a surging tide. Attacking gracefully, retreating gracefully. Ebb and flow. This is the temperament required. To fight. To survive. To live."

Barodane had heard enough. He had growled and charged at his instructor. Young, impetuous, and a sore loser, he learned many lessons from the folly of his anger. More still at the end of the White Flame's practice sword.

"A lack of balance is your downfall." Pyr Syat's blade reaved the combat space, deflecting bullish strokes and viper-quick thrusts.

To his credit, Barodane had launched an attack one could call well strung-to-gether. He feinted, stabbing at Pyr's thigh, then flicked his wrists to whip his blade tip in an upward arc at the White Flame's chin.

The Kanian had seen it coming. A tight-lipped smile formed under his snowy mustache as he turned his face the few necessary inches to avoid being hit. He moved his wooden blade in behind Barodane's, forcing it to continue upward until Barodane's guard was stretched tall and his arms were extended overhead.

With ease, Pyr Syat stepped in and buried his fist into the young prince's solar plexus. "It is *you* who must be tempered. Beaten and battered by hammer and anvil until you understand."

Barodane folded, wheezing around the dark-knuckled fist.

"A blade is but a tool," said the First Sword. "*We* are the weapon."

Once Pyr Syat entered Barodane's mind, he struggled to put the man's words to rest. *If we are not sharp, nor tempered, nor balanced, we break.*

By Barodane's best estimate, he'd been broken long ago. He'd never been tempered; the Ironlights were a passionate people by nature. And whatever balance or sharpness of intellect he'd once possessed had been dulled by the events at Rainy Meadows, dulled further still by godsthorn and ample brew.

Am I really doing this?

Too much had changed in the past month. It was for the good of all, Garlenna claimed, but that didn't make it any easier. He'd left Digtown at her behest, yet the idea of retaking the crown was unfathomable. Disbelief followed him around like a shadow, poking at the thought every time it arose. After so many years spent altering his mental state, reality itself had become an overwhelming experience. The threads of his life had been slashed to ribbons by godsthorn, leaving him adrift in the present. Now the past reached forward, the future reached back, and he tentatively took their hands to see the bigger picture.

Whether or not he liked it, he wasn't sure.

There were moments. They came to him while he trained. Memories long suppressed that he'd once treasured, often accompanied by an acute stab of regret. But sometimes, they came to rest within...in a way that made him feel full, like a climbing tide that leaves the sand damp and heavy. Those memories gave him a sense of substance he'd been missing.

Pyr Syat's teachings, too, kept him focused. He mulled them over with ever-dawning clarity whenever he trained. And train, he did.

Over the course of the following week, Barodane returned to his place in the fen to bring his body back to life, or at least some semblance of his former constitution, just as Tohar worked in earnest to nurse Garlenna back to health.

His newfound practice, he discovered, served a dual purpose.

Sitting around a campfire with little else to do necessitated conversation, and Barodane was in no hurry to get to know the priest-turned-criminal. No hurry to have himself known, either, and so, he stayed aloof.

But today, Barodane had finished his training early. A part of him withered upon returning to camp and seeing Tohar's expectant face. *Ah well, it was bound to come to this eventually.* Barodane sat down on a log with a huff.

Tohar rambled for a while. Something about being assigned to some gods-brew operation, which he squandered. Barodane ignored the bulk of the bloated tale, catching only drips and drabs of the man's pointed attempts to relate until he said, "So you see, Mal, I'm like you. My love of drink cost me dearly. But I'm reformed." He pasted a smile on his face, but the way he wore it made Barodane think it somewhat regretful.

"Who said I loved drink?" Barodane asked. "Or that it cost me dearly?"

With a smirk, Tohar shrugged.

Barodane rubbed his palms together over the fire. The stone he'd been training with left them calloused and rough. A ghostly blister had formed at the base of his middle finger.

"You're less of a mystery than you think," Tohar said. "We're all open books. All it takes is someone who speaks our language to read us."

"Careful," Barodane muttered.

Tohar held up his palms in surrender. "Easy. I respect your past, friend. It's yours to keep, though I dare to say, maybe you should consider a bit more focus on where you're going. Cagier than a beaten dog, you are. The past can't be all that worthy of your ever-living attention."

"That so?"

Garlenna moaned, in and out of consciousness as her body fought a recent flare-up of infection. The priest's poultice was working to reduce her fever, but slowly.

Tohar went to her side and raised her head so she could take in a mouthful of water. "It *is* so." The priest hunkered back down onto the grass. "Can I tell you a story?"

Barodane withheld his response. People would do what they would regardless of his input.

"I'll take your silence as acquiescence then. You remind me of someone I recently met. A young man called to ascend Unturrus. For weeks, we were part of the same caravan, and in that time, he spoke with no one. It wasn't until the final days of our journey that I asked him why."

"Why?"

"Yes. Why ascend?" The priest stared into the fire. "Why condemn himself to a gruesome death? He never answered. I thought about that a lot afterward. I wondered what his answer, or any Ascendant's answer, could be. I never came up with my own. I was too focused on drinking myself into disgrace to think it out properly."

Tohar sniffled and swept a hand through his thick hair. "The Sempyrium strips you of all your possessions when they cast you out. Did you know that?"

"I didn't."

"Yeah, well, they do. They take everything you have. Sets you on the path of begging or criminality rather quick. When that happens, it's a select few willing to believe you were a man of the gods—they just assume you stole the robes and learned some scripture so you can swindle them." Tohar clasped his hands together between his knees. "Anyway, with nothing left, it didn't take long for me to team up with the Black Blood. If I wasn't a coward, I might have ascended Unturrus instead of letting my future open up before me like the legs of some diseased whore. Nowhere to go, nothing to do, no good to be had. Condemned to swim through muck forever, I thought."

Barodane flinched. With dizzying accuracy, the priest's words reflected his sentiment during his time in Digtown. *What do a former priest and a former prince have in common? A healthy dose of cynicism?* Barodane shrugged into himself. *Not much of a joke.*

Tohar continued. "That's when I figured it out. I never took *my* path. I've spent a lot of time looking back. As the years come, I do it more. They don't stop coming, do they? One day you're holding a faint little dream in your hands and hearing a faint little voice in your head asking you to follow it. A decade later, it's slapping you in the damn face and screaming at you to wake up."

The fire popped and shot a sizzling hunk of bark at Barodane's feet. *Not much of a joke at all.* He smothered it with his boot heel.

Tohar rocked back, keeping a hand on one knee and slinging an elbow across the other. "When I saw you play that banha back at the Rusty Nail...I *saw* you. Read you right through. As shiny and clear as an ocean sunrise. You've got nothing but damage and shame chasing you onward—just like that young man I met at Unturrus. You're walking forward, but your head's twisted around. Staring back at what happened. Blind to what could be. I'm no different. By the Maw, none of us are."

"You Sempyrean types sure love to share your opinions." Barodane tucked his cheek to a shoulder and stood. "So, we're your redemption?" He nodded at Garlenna's prostrate form. "You saw her mace. Figured out she was a prosort. Thought you could return to glory by doing a good deed for the Sempyrium."

Tohar's expression went rigid. He shook his head. "I'm a fool, sure, but not that kind. My days rallying Followers to the Sempyrium are done."

"What, then?"

Tohar relaxed. "I've heard rumors of a man at Martyr's Isle. A hero from the Great Betrayal. Goes by the name of Nserthes the Sophophant..."

Barodane froze.

"...He's somewhat famous in the halls of the Sempyrium. Whispers and all that—nothing the bureaucrats approve of. He served as prosort to Kordin Ironlight. It's said that the prince converted him to unimism in less than a year of service. He was excommunicated after. Some say he started his own monastery. As an outcast myself, I wish to see it. Decide if perhaps..." Tohar grunted, eyes roaming the ground. "Perhaps it's the path I was meant to take all along." He looked at Barodane and inclined his head solemnly. "For reminding me of it with your song, I thank you."

"Don't mention it." Barodane stepped into the frigid air beyond the fire's reach. He couldn't recall the last time someone had thanked him. The fact that Tohar thought Barodane had helped was a clumsy realization, a heavy sack filled with shifting sand. "I think I'm off for a bit."

"Aye," Tohar said. "A hard look inward requires a bit of time. May the gods of light quicken you to the path of your choosing."

Barodane framed his joke anew. *Former priest, former prosort, and former prince walk into the wilderness... Society is better off without them. Celebration ensues.*

CHAPTER FORTY-ONE

PUPPET MASTER

M igrants arrived at the Manger in a steady drip. Ishoa watched from the yard where she trained, her lone place of respite. A refuge from the council meetings where she spoke rarely and listened to voices much wiser than her own. Her quarters offered no reprieve. Each second of inactivity spent there reminded her of her complicity in the council's decision to wait. She'd come to see the error in her behavior that first day in the Warming Place but couldn't calm the turbulent sea within.

Thoughts of torture, of her grandmother falling under Scarborn knives and glowing tongs and...

She blinked, rolled out the shiver spreading into her shoulders, then looked to the gate where a handful of lowborn women and their children from the countryside were being admitted. A pair of men—presumably a father and teenage son—were separated from the group and escorted to an encampment outside the walls.

At the last council meeting, Arick had warned of the possibility of the enemy infiltrating their keep. While Ishoa agreed with her cousin's concern, she found the unequal treatment of men and women misguided. Lodecka Warnock, a female, had taken Jarik. If anything should have shown Arick his error, it was the amount of blood shed at the hands of women in recent months.

A streak of scarlet, old and dry, slashed the face of one of the girls held in her mother's arms. A testament to Ishoa's failure. To her weakness. To her inability as a leader. *Every one of them that comes through the gate lays another pebble of shame on the cairn of the Ironlight line.*

She whirled from the distant gate and clacked sword to shield rim. "First blood?"

Steam gushed from the black cloth covering the Fly's mouth. He raised one end of his ax-staff, pressed a finger gently to the blade, and then showed her.

Ishoa shot him a look of disappointment. "Cleverness won't save you."

He shrugged, flourished his ax-staff, then circled toward her. So many weeks on the road had caused her to wither, but since then, the Manger's bountiful meat had put healthy pounds back on her frame. *Needed pounds if I'm to train with the Fly.*

She was no match for Megalor Bog's bodyguard by any stretch of imagination, but still, she preferred sparring with him over anyone else. Opponents of lesser skill tended to fight harder and with less control than was safe. They strove to beat her immediately, which reduced the amount of desired repetitions. More practice meant more skill, a principle drilled into her by Wolst. "You become the motions of your life, Isha. So if you want to be a true death dealer at your core, you've got to practice until it drives down into the bone."

Clearly, the Fly understood the sentiment as well. He reduced his speed, power, and the complexity of his attacks to a level equal with hers. A single training session went as long as her lungs allowed.

She rushed in, stabbing high with her practice sword. He knocked it away, then dipped to one side, flicking a kick at her thigh. His boot thudded off her shield. Using the same pattern, she attacked again. And again, he executed the same response as if inviting her to try something different.

Back and forth they went, a fluid dance, until Ishoa's shoulder burned and her weapon sagged. "I yield." She dropped to a knee to catch her breath. Steam puffed from the Fly's hood, the same amount now as he'd started with. "You're not human, you know that?"

He tilted his head. *Maybe,* she interpreted.

"Why don't you train with your anjuhtarg?"

She spun to the voice behind her.

Gaern Yorek sat on the fence. Rakeema sat on relaxed haunches beside his dangling feet.

"She's not trained yet."

"Then train her," he said. "Not too hard to logic that one out, is it?"

Ishoa frowned. Wolst had taught her all the commands she'd needed to know in Fjordsong, but Rakeema had only ever responded to a few. "I don't know how. Most words don't seem to work on her."

A wave of agitation set Gaern to blinking. Between tangled locks of storm-cloud hair, the beastmaster grimaced. "Words. Words. No wonder you fail. You couldn't command a cow to eat grass with words."

Ishoa straightened. "I could command the Fly to rid me of your nattering mouth, hmm, how does that sound?"

The man from Akulsa snorted a laugh. "You've got the fire alright, but you have no clue what makes it burn." He leapt from the fence and strode toward her. Rakeema followed, an inch from his heel. He stopped, shuffled sideways, and backed up before moving forward again. The gap between his feet and Rakeema remained exact.

Ishoa gaped. "How?"

He waved a hand. "Lehrd." Rakeema pushed to her feet and bounded over to a row of buildings. Outside of a dilapidated chicken coop, she slowed to a creep. Where the slats weren't flush, she peered inside.

"She's hunting mice," Ishoa said.

The beastmaster nodded. "That's what happens when you tell your anjuhtarg to hunt."

"'Lehrd' means hunt?"

"It does." He watched her as she committed the word to memory by mouthing it. "But that part doesn't matter. If *you* say it, she's as likely to take a shit on your toe as she is to carry out your intent."

Ishoa glanced at the Fly as if he might help her. Instead, he went to one of the aspens edging the fenced-in yard and sat with his back against it.

"It's the same reason the council ignores you—even when you shout. You are conditioned to weakness. Conditioned to follow your perceived betters." He paused for effect. "You lack a sense of self. That is the place from which power is drawn. In order to fully bond with your anjuhtarg, you must access it. This is how one becomes Hulka'skara."

Ishoa stared at him, expecting a joke to follow. It didn't. "Oh, you're serious."

The muscles around one of Gaern Yorek's eyes twitched.

She blurted a laugh, covering her mouth a second too late to hold it back. "Sorry. But Hulka'skara... Does that mean you talk to C'Dathun trolls and...lie with animals?"

The beastmaster went motionless. "We do not *lie* with animals. The Hulka'skara are an ancient bloodline, deserving of more than your slander and suspicion."

"Apologies." Ishoa forced the smile from her face. "I was told they were a myth." *Because they are.*

"The only myth here is the one spread by the Frosts. You're descended from a treacherous lot of backstabbers and liars. What? Your royal tutor told you Caggathor was a noble uniter? That the first of your precious Ice Kings made Anjuhkar what it is today through diplomacy?"

Mouth open, Ishoa hesitated to respond.

"Of course they did. They educate you to their preferences." He waved a hand. "So do you wish to hear the truth about your ancestors or just stay ignorant all your life?"

Ishoa managed a nod.

"A wise decision. Fools stay fools because they seek comfort in what is already known. It takes courage to change one's perspective." He studied her. "A courage you seem to have." The beastmaster looked away. "Centuries before the Anjuhk tribes were driven north by the Kurgish Empire, my people ruled the lands around Akulsa in harmony alongside the C'Dathuns." Gaern ignored her shocked expression as he continued. "Your ancestors were as numerous as the fleas on a dog's back, though even thirstier for blood. Harsh winters made dying easy and decisions easier. Steal or die. Fight to live. Kill or be killed. And so, the warlords of the southern Anjuhk tribes fell upon one another.

"Your earliest grandsire, Caggathor I, was not the strongest, nor the wealthiest in resources, nor the cleverest. But he was the boldest. No other dared to cross the C'Dathun Straits, nor brave the peaks of Akulsa for fear of the trolls, and the mysterious warriors who called themselves Hulka'skara, living there. No other warlord dared...except Caggathor.

"Hulka'skara hold fearlessness sacred, and so, Caggathor made an impression on their king, Huunval the Bitten. Together, they subjugated the other Anjuhk tribes. Those who refused to surrender were slaughtered. Entire sub-ethnic groups were put to the blade. There one second, gone the next." The beastmaster snapped his fingers. "Two decades of peace followed. Trade lanes opened with the arrival of the first missionaries of Peladon from Valat. The written word was introduced and adopted...by most. Caggathor would take advantage of that, and so, take advantage of you and everyone else who swallows his lies today. But what came next was soon forgotten and stayed that way for as long as the Frosts have ruled Anjuhkar."

Gaern stared into a clump of snow, bitterness clouding his face. "The C'Dathuns and Hulka'skara were displeased with their share of the spoils. With their blades, the other warlords were defeated, and by their hands, Caggathor's legacy was made. Huunval the Bitten, especially, was outraged.

"A selfish man, was Caggathor I, and rapid was the wealth he'd gained from trading with the Mighty Isle. The man with the most to lose, fears losing it the most, so your grandsire's boldness leaked from him and fear wormed into his rotten heart. You see, Huunval the Bitten and his Hulka'skara terrified him—always had. In his eyes, their martial prowess and strange ability to command their war beasts was the greatest threat to his expanding kingdom."

The man from Akulsa fixed Ishoa with a stare. "So he did what most leaders would—he eliminated the threat. Caggathor invited Huunval the Bitten and his Hulka'skara to the negotiating table along with the most prominent C'Dathun war chiefs. With a promise of new lands, he lured them in and then murdered every last one. My people's entire history was reduced to ash overnight. Now, we are but an oddity. Beast trainers for the rich and powerful.

Honored guest, though few highborn recall why that it is, if any. Meanwhile, the C'Dathuns fell even further from grace. A horde of savage cannibals to be killed on sight. With none left who can communicate in their tongue, there's no evidence that they are a civil and noble race, is there?"

He spat. "Ice King Caggathor I, the great uniter of Anjuhkar." He spat a second time. "The Hulka'skara are gone but for scattered hamlets whose populations wither each year. Fewer and fewer possess the power we once had. Indeed, we *are* a myth in the making." The beastmaster made a fist, gnarled knuckles white. He released it. "Lucky for you, we never accepted the written word and maintain our history by oral traditions. Otherwise, there would be no memory of us at all."

Ishoa nodded, wondering what the old man wanted with her. "I do believe your story, and I feel terrible for what your people endured. Doubly so since it was my grandsire that caused so much suffering." She affected her most dignified stance, aping the way her grandmother might do it. "Therefore, it is my promise as a princess of Namarr that when I have access to Jarik's treasury, I'll give repara—"

"You think I tell you this for a handout?" Gaern snarled.

She froze. "Why, then?"

"Because it's only a matter of time before my people are all gone, and perhaps, the essence of our culture can live on in you."

"Live on in me..." Ishoa reflected the man's words.

"Yes. The Anjuhkar we fought for is dead but it has a chance to be born anew. The Hulka'skara can be revived, if we let go of our grudge—I've found they hold little value to the dying. We've kept our secrets so long we're bound to die with them. What's the honor in that? What's the point of keeping something sacred until it becomes dust? At least this way, someone might remember us. Someone might carry us onward. In this way, the spirit of our people lives on...in you."

"You want me to be Hulka'skara?" Ishoa shook her head.

"Yes. At least, try to be. Whether or not you succeed will be up to you." He picked at a dirt-crusted fingernail. "Any idea what it means?"

Ishoa racked her brain for the translation from Fjordsong. "'Skara'...is worry?"

"Close. It means 'fear.' And 'hulka' means master. If I train you to be one of us, I train you to be a master of fear. Something you very much need."

"A lofty proposition." She cocked her head. "What kind of fear? I'm already friendly with spiders, snakes, and mice."

A wicked grin spread across the beastmaster's face. "The real ones."

"Such as?"

"Death. Failure. Loss of control—that one in particular rusts a person's soul. You want it so badly, yet it drowns you." The man's bearing was as placid as a mountain lake. "You think holding your breath longer than everyone else will make you live longer when the truth is, it sinks you faster into an oblivion of your own making."

Her chin rose, her guard instantly raised at being called out.

He seemed to notice her mounting anger and scoffed. "To those who have not settled the scores within, wisdom from without does little more than agitate."

He's not wrong. It had been a week since the first council meeting, and her agitation over the result had yet to release its grip. She knew she couldn't rely solely on Arick to help her change the council's perception of her. Gaern, at least, seemed sincere. *I need allies. People whose motives I trust—who care. Those like Wolst.* The rest of them treated her like a piece on their game board. "If I accept, what then?"

"If?" he laughed. "You don't have many options. Look no further than your anjuhtarg. She cannot be better trained if she resists every command. She *must* surrender. Otherwise, she'll never learn. You're the same in that way."

"So, I'm to be a puppet."

"You already are, Princess. You just don't see it. Too busy chasing around your anjuhtarg, barking at her because you think louder is stronger, that louder is control. But what Rakeema and everyone else hears is a pitiful overcompensation from a frightened little doll." The beastmaster punched the air, just as she'd done at the council meeting, his tone mocking. "'I command you to listen to me!' That doesn't exactly inspire confidence, does it? Your entire life, you've danced on the strings of others because you were afraid not to. It's time to cut them."

Ishoa looked away, mouth twisting. *Is there anything I can do that won't be put under a magnifying glass and dissected?* The answer was as unpleasant as the question. *No, and that makes this man's guidance ever more necessary.*

She returned her gaze to her would-be teacher. "You spoke of scores being settled. I assume you refer to my need to kill Lodecka Warnock."

"Not at all." He did nothing to hide his sarcasm. "Now there's a fearless leader. A quiet poise that yanks men to a knee. No need for shouting when a stare will do. Something to aspire to, eh, Princess?"

The mere image of the woman's face in Ishoa's mind made her blood surge. "Indeed. And I will do anything I must to end her, including suffer you as my teacher."

"Excellent, for suffer you must. Meet me here tomorrow." He pivoted and trudged through the snow, calling back over a shoulder as he pointed at the keep. "They need you, by the way."

Ishoa was the last to enter the Warming Place. More and more, her attendance seemed an afterthought of sorts. She had dismissed the Fly to rest and entered alone, passing a pair of old men in rags on her way to her seat, the stench of smoke and cloying body odor forcing her to tuck a finger under her nose.

Arick, Krhalka, and Sir Hollem sat around the table. Since that first meeting, the embers had been removed, the stone allowed to cool. In place of sizzling meat, a sheepskin map of Namarr stretched across the surface.

All had stood when Ishoa entered but didn't wait for her to be seated before they eased back into their chairs.

"We're all here," said Sir Hollem.

"What about Lady Rigga?" Krhalka asked.

"Abed, resting," Hollem answered, pale eyes roaming the two men standing near the Warming Place's entrance. "This past week has taken a great deal out of her. She begs forgiveness."

With the courtesy of one who'd made an art form of ingratiation, Krhalka inclined her head. "Understandable. Give her my regards."

"Mine as well," Ishoa added.

Hollem nodded, first to Krhalka and then with a slight furrow in his brow, toward Ishoa. "I will."

"We have important business." Arick headed off further pleasantries, his focus on the bedraggled pair of men. "Proceed."

One had been picking at a callous but stopped when called upon, arms shooting down to his sides. "Yes, milord."

"I am a knight. You'll refer to me as 'Sir,'" Arick corrected. "Now, what news?"

The poor attempt at manners evaporated. "Bloody damn news, that's what," said the taller and far leaner of the two.

The short one hushed his friend to quiet. "I'll tell it proper. We come from Theren. Town's close to Bleeding Point along the Prince's Highway. Our lord's no named man to you, but he treats us well enough."

"Lord Ivarl," Krhalka said. "Are you fletchers by trade, then?"

"Aye," said the tall one.

The shorter one telling the story shook his head. "Not fletchers no more, milady. Weeks back, Ivarl and his knight—he's only got the one—they met with a group of furriers from Ghastiin in the town square." The man threw a nervous look at Sir Hollem, eyes lingering on the ram's skull emblazoned on his honor plate. "They wanted to see if Lord Ivarl wanted to switch sides."

"They produce the bulk of the arrows for our horse archers," Sir Hollem said. "I take it Lord Ivarl made a poor choice."

The men from Theren exchanged a look before the shorter resumed. "He said he would consider it. They gave him two weeks to decide and left. That night, someone else came..."

Hollem Hine shot forward, palms slapping the stone table. "Knights of the Wolf Banner."

The man from Theren blinked. "I didn't see no banner but I got a bit too close a look at one of their visors. Snarling wolf indeed. They was all dressed in black furs and steel. They set fire to Lord Ivarl's manor. Their leader was a monster, seven feet tall, every inch more dreadful than the next." The man gulped. "Well, he dragged Ivarl into the square...made him beg for his life. The Dread Knight—that's what we been callin' him—listened to our lord, alright. When the begging was done, he said, 'death to cowards' and slit his throat. Wife's throat, too. Afterward, they took everything we had. Food stores, best cloaks, blankets, feed. Went right back into the night."

"Left us to starve," the tall one said.

Ishoa frowned, watching Hollem Hine's reaction from the corner of her eye. The man eased back in his chair, face clenched with brooding.

"That's thrice now," Krhalka said.

Hollem snapped his fingers and ordered his holdguard to remove the men. "Give them each a silver wheel before you escort them to the camp."

With a holdguard clutching his elbow, the taller one twisted around. "They said we could sleep inside."

The doors worked open, then closed without acknowledgment of the claim. Ishoa considered when she'd fit it into her day to find the men and follow through on the promise, but her attention was swept back into the fray of matters more important.

"Thrice?" Arick asked.

There was a long pause from Sir Hollem as all eyes turned to him. "This... Dread Knight, he haunts the countryside. We've had numerous reports. They dress as the man said, embossed wolves on their plate. Furs. Most of their attacks come at night. They carry a banner bearing a black wolf."

"They're not Scarborn." Ishoa had deduced that much. "Another faction, then?"

Krhalka nodded. "Their attacks seem indiscriminate. Migrants along the Prince's Highway claim to have been robbed by them, though left alive."

"Unlike the Kons," Ishoa said, recalling the slaughter she'd witnessed along-side Okki.

"Yes," Krhlaka said. "My reports state that they've killed at least two detach-ments of furriers themselves. If not for this, we'd have marked them as enemies weeks ago."

"They *are* enemies," Hollem muttered.

"Warlords oft arise amid a power vacuum," Arick said. "If they're not our ally, we cannot trust them. That makes them just as bad as the White Wolverine Alliance."

Ishoa hung her head. *Another enemy. Another diversion.* Every day that Lodecka Warnock held Jarik made circumstances feel increasingly concrete and stripped her of any hope that they could take it back. "What are we doing about it?"

Sir Hollem hiked an eyebrow. "My brother was pulled away from his scouting endeavors in the east to deal with these wolf knights. He claims they do not sit idly. They move fast. Too fast for Adus's company."

"So we're doing nothing," Ishoa said. "Another brigand despoiling our homeland goes unpunished."

"As long as the Dread Knight is killing furriers, I say let him," Arick said.

"I don't like it," Hollem said. "But I see no fault in your logic, Sir."

"They killed a hold lord and his wife." Ishoa blinked, stunned to momentary silence. "They're hurting innocent people." Krhalka's weathered hand slid over Ishoa's, urging restraint. She gave Ishoa a near imperceptible shake of her head.

The council concluded and Krhalka leaned in to whisper, "War is an equa-tion that favors no innocents. A matter of trade-offs. The Dread Knight hurts our enemies much more than he hurts us." The High Hand stood abruptly, then bowed. "Highness." She left.

Ishoa found her feet. At the door, Arick waited for her. "Leave us," he commanded the holdguard. *A poor tone leads to a poor start, cousin.* Her grand-mother had taught her that.

His eyes locked on hers until just the two of them were alone in the Warming Place.

"The Knights of the Wolf Banner are but another reason for us to make haste to Alistar. Staying here is folly, Isha."

She looked away. "I suspect you've never crossed a decision opposing your own that wasn't folly."

"I'm serious. You're letting your hatred for Lodecka cloud your judgment. A ruler should not—"

"I tire of you telling me what I should or shouldn't do when you have no real evidence to know whether or not what I *would* do has merit. You undermine me at every turn. Speak over me as if I were a child. Tug the strings of influence in spite of me as if I were not an Ironlight princess. But you are right about one thing." She crossed her arms. "I *am* letting vengeance cloud my judgment, though at this point, I deem it more of a guide."

Hard-faced, Arick watched her, reclaiming some of the cool poise she knew him for. "You don't think that an issue?"

"No. Not really. Not when I intend to kill them all."

"Isha..."

"Save it, Arick. I could recite your reservations verbatim by now." Every day since they'd arrived at the Manger, he'd come to her masticating the same sad strategy: flee her people amid open rebellion. Find safety at Alistar. He wanted her to remain a child rather than live up to the name her ancestors had fought so bravely to establish.

"Indulge me," he said.

"Why? You're a distant relative, and at the moment, not a beloved one." She pushed past him.

"You're young." Arick's words froze her. "And Wolst is dead...that doesn't mean you have to bear the pressure by yourself. You need my guidance."

Whatever wisdom Gaern Yorek had imparted on her earlier that day was hurled into a soundless void of grief and rage.

You're not Wolst. She marched down the hall, holding back the impulse to run before the tears came. *No one is.*

CHAPTER FORTY-TWO

SHAME'S DEMANDS

N o matter the justness of the killing, Valka never slept when he took a life, an experience that had stood for all fifty of his years.

Yet the day King Rathon's family was slaughtered, he went to sleep without difficulty. The horrors of the day didn't fill his mind, nor did they jerk him awake with flashes of blood and gore pasted to the back of terror-rimmed eyes.

There was warmth. Compassion for himself and the people of Scothea. The Arrow of Light's gentle embrace.

Behind his eyelids, a glow persisted. He was at ease. The deeds of the day were condensed, made separate. He saw the actions and the man as two entities: one striving to restore balance while the other was a piece of the whole.

Those were the words Siddaia had shared with him. That was the blessing he'd given Valka to absolve him for his part in killing Rathon's assassins. "It is an inversive world we live in. To kill is to prevent murder. To deal harshly with what is wrong is to inspire the proliferation of that which is good. To feel your pain is to heal it."

Once the crowd had settled, Siddaia addressed the atrocities of the day. "I am sorry, my people. I do not control the wrong actions of others. If I could, I would have prevented this...I would prevent all the killing the world over. Rathon was already forgiven for standing against the light. So, too, were the men who..." Siddaia brought a hooked finger to the place beneath his nose. He sniffled and made a noise at the back of his throat. "Today is a shameful one. Shame for those who turned knives against innocents. And shame on all of you for praising their vengeance."

The sky seemed to inhale, sucking the air from the vippedrome.

Rhul dismounted, cast his gore-drenched hakat aside and fell to his knees. He stretched out his arms and touched his forehead to the sand. A tremor of motion went through the crowd—hundreds jockeying for space to grovel.

Ikarai lowered to a knee, but Siddaia seized him by the elbow. "No. Stand. All of you stand!"

They did, trading nervous glances. Rhul lifted his sand-dusted head.

"Shame does not demand that you give more of your power away. It does not demand that you find forgiveness...not from me. Not from any other." The Arrow of Light's tear-streaked face stared up at Valka. "Shame rises within, and so, must be dealt with in the arena of its birth. Forgive yourselves by action. By service to one another."

"And to you, my Light." Valka inclined his head obsequiously.

Siddaia released the general's elbow and stepped past. "Without a conquest, there is no conqueror. Without victimhood, there is no villain. Without weakness, there is no strength." He paused, words soaking into the assembly. "So suffer. Suffer all that you are and all that you have been. It is but your beginning on the pathway to absolution. Those who do not do this will remain blind. Would you live as a shadow of yourself?"

Valka's pulse had pounded in his ears as he listened, still reeling from the lightning strike of clarity within. *My light...*

A wave of sand gusted across the racecourse. "No!" someone shouted from the grandstands, and like a broken dam, a deluge of the same outcries followed.

Siddaia lifted his arms overhead. "Truth's light reveals all! Even that which leaves us in ruin. Do you see?"

Hesitation. Then meek assent.

"Have your voices been stolen? Hammered flat by the generations of kings who oppressed you? Or will you reshape yourselves, here and now?" Siddaia boomed, "I asked, *do you see?*"

Resoundingly, the crowd exulted, "Yes!"

Afterward, Valka and Rhul had led a meeting to establish a stronger presence in the city. Messenger birds were sent to the other cities of Scothea. None had responded since Siddaia had taken power, but they would. Of that, Valka no longer doubted. They would see. All would see.

By the time he arrived back at his manse, it was late. Yanos stood outside Nera's room and saluted.

Valka returned the salute. "Amazing day wasn't it, brother?"

"The light peels back the darkness to connect all things," Yanos said.

His understanding of the Light's teachings runs deep. While the reason for Valka's suspicions about his captain had changed, the desire to know where the man's loyalties lie remained.

Valka ordered servants out to retrieve new materials for his altar. A thick layer of dust covered the stump of stone carved from the room's sloping wall. Rare wood placards with images of the Holy Instruments, those Scoth leaders glorified as gifts from the Sempyrean gods, adorned the altar. Valka stacked them in a servant's arms then ordered them burned.

Another servant arrived with a neatly folded bolt of opaque cloth. Stamped on the top was a single golden arrow. Until Valka could commission a wood rendering, it would have to do.

Reverently, he situated it atop the stone and then went to bed. Aided by the soothing memories of his Light, sleep had swiftly arrived.

Now, he stirred.

Dim awareness touched a muffled sound...

Valka shot awake, vision narrowing around the thin tip of a dart an inch from his face. Orbs of woven wicker hung from the hands of two of his three assailants; they were filled with spirit lilies that cast the room in a blue-tinged glow.

A wicked smile plastered Essuhd's face from behind the sling-dart he held. "Call for your guards and you'll die like the traitor you are."

Like a cornered cat, Valka eased cautiously and steadily backward, silk sheets whispering under hand until his head and back struck stone.

Essuhd followed, the weapon in his fist like a cave viper's head. At the sound of string tightening, Valka froze, staring up at the poison-tipped dart a finger's span from his forehead. He swallowed; too dry, his throat burned with the effort. "Perhaps I might dress first."

Essuhd paid the request no heed. "You had a chance to kill the boy and didn't. In fact, you've had many chances. With Rathon's body—the bodies of his line—starting to stink at your feet, no less."

"You said to play the part," Valka said.

"Oh, you do more than play, I think."

Head unmoving, Valka looked to either side of Essuhd. Two more Shadii stood corpse-still at the foot of his bed. "Nera?"

"I should kill you now," Essuhd snarled. "Let you die wondering if we've taken her in for torture or merely slain her on the spot."

Valka licked his lips. *Even if I don't live...* "She's not a believer. Surely you know that. Surely your spies have—"

The dart drifted closer. The tip brushed his flesh. *No it didn't. If it had, you'd be dead.* "Please, Essuhd. I do only what we planned. I win Siddaia's trust. For the good of Scothea."

The Shadii master smacked his lips as if trying to clear a bitter taste. He let the sling-dart rest on a knee. Valka blinked focus into his eyes while Essuhd perched over his legs like some globular crow. "You console the boy for the good of Scothea, is that it? Try to convince Nera of his merits for the same reason?"

Despite the situation, Valka's anger could not be stemmed. These were the Arrow of Light's enemies now. *I won't let you harm him.* "You wanted me to kill him on the spot knowing I would sacrifice my life and my daughter's. Such easy expectations to meet." He waved at the Shadii hanging at the foot of the bed. "You seem capable of a great deal more than I. Have them do it."

Essuhd's face bunched. He seemed to be considering something. "Do not act as though that was your only pathway to success. You could be working on your soldiers, rallying them under the banner of the line of kings. Instead, you parade around the vippedrome suckling at the boy's tears."

Valka hesitated.

"Do you take me for a fool, Ikarai?" Essuhd stepped off the bed, came to stand between his men, moon-like face reaching no higher than their shoulders.

"No, but I daresay you're incompetent. I engage strategy rather than impulse to see Siddaia's rule reversed." The lie flowed seamlessly. "And for it, I'm called a traitor. You, meanwhile, with the might of the Shadii at your back, prove impotent. Why have you not done the deed yourself?" A cold sweat damped Valka's night shirt. *If anyone could kill Siddaia, it is this man. But I cannot let that happen.* A second thought struck him through with fear. *Standing against Essuhd could cost me Nera.*

The Shadii master scoffed. "He sees things...even my Shadii. Many have defected to him. It makes things difficult."

"So," Valka sneered. "The Shadii are at war?"

Essuhd bristled. "Indeed. Not a day has waned since his ascent that we do not battle one another in the shadows. Rathon's family was one such casualty."

Valka frowned. *He lies. Those men acted of their own accord. Not by will of the Light.*

"While the Shadii are busy looking out for other Shadii, you will fulfill your promise." Essuhd's voice dripped with menace. "Otherwise, your precious little orphan girl dies."

Valka stiffened. *How could he know about her?* He'd done everything in his power to bury that.

"Shocked, are you? Well, I wondered, why name her after a famous traitor?" Essuhd's smile could be heard more than seen in the dim light.

"It's a common name. My mother's, for one."

"Yet on her, it smells of something vile." Essuhd laughed. "And Nera's mother was just a whore in the Cyclone, right? I know the story. You lied then and you lie now. You are a despicable creature, Ikarai Valka. But you will make amends. Yes, you *will* make amends."

CHAPTER FORTY-THREE

PRECISION

Barodane's empty stomach screeched in protest. *Fuck off, I'm working on it.*

He searched the stream, toes soggy, boot leather stiff and mildewed. Weeks in the wetland had kept them safe. That didn't mean it kept them comfortable. They had tinder, firewood, flint and steel so they could boil water to eat, but the missing piece also happened to be the most crucial. Food was scarce. With Garlenna still recovering, it fell on Barodane to feed them. More accurately, his ability to provide food was scarce.

For the second morning in a row, he came up short and returned to camp.

Some people were born trackers and hunters. Tohar wasn't one of them, and unfortunately, Barodane's skill narrowly outshone the priest's. Malath had always been the better hunter.

At least in Digtown, I had regular meals.

They'd subsisted mostly on tiny fish from shallow pools around the fen. Frogs too, and once, a scrub jay he'd thrown a stone at. It had taken at least a hundred throws to finally hit it—scrawny amounts of meat, not nearly worth the energy wasted in getting it.

A single positive outweighed the negatives of their predicament. The fog of injury had all but lifted from Garlenna. She slept and woke at normal hours now. Even started moving around. Barodane made sure to chastise her for not bringing a bow whenever he could.

"Perhaps we should go," she said. "I'm sound enough to ride."

"Not sound enough to swing a mace though," Barodane said. "And that makes things risky."

Garlenna shrugged. "You've been training. So long as we avoid the main road—"

"They had a trap set at Halaleh." Tohar motioned for her to remove her cloak and tunic so he could look at her wound. "There's sure to be more."

She eased down next to the priest and stripped, covering her small breasts with a forearm. Barodane stepped behind the pair to inspect the wound. Flesh, once angry red and swollen, had become a finger's length of dull pink around a scabrous island. "It's getting better."

"Thanks to Tohar." Garlenna laid a hand on her own brick-like shoulder, fingers overlapping the priest's. The gesture was anything but mundane. Weeks of care and proximity had brought the two close. Once, Barodane had come awake in the night to find them cuddled together in the grass on the other side of the campfire.

"How much longer?" Barodane picked up a waterskin and slung it around his torso.

"Until she can sit a saddle?" Tohar helped Garlenna replace her tunic and cloak. "Now, I'd say. It might hurt but she's strong. Her muscles have become stiff, though."

"It'll take time to shake the rust off," Barodane said.

"Days," Garlenna said. "I'll start training tomorrow."

Tohar started to protest but Garlenna shot him a look. "Tomorrow. I've had enough of being coddled. There are matters more important than my comfort."

The prosort's resolve dashed any hopes the man might have had for something more with her. By the melancholic look on Tohar's face, it seemed the man knew their tryst would meet its end at Martyr's Isle.

"Sounds like my time as our provider is numbered." Barodane surveyed the land. The same boulders and trees he'd stared at for nearly a month were wreathed in morning fog. "It hasn't been too terrible a place to lie low."

"No." Tohar stared at the back of Garlenna's head. "No, it hasn't."

Sensing what was sure to be an intimate, but ultimately disappointing, discussion brewing between the two, Barodane left them to it.

Out of sight, he went in search of an open patch of dry ground to practice his blade work. In his mind's eye, Pyr Syat stood before him.

Precision is smooth, a great equalizer. Speed slows. Strength wanes. But precision, by its very nature, is faultless. You must make it your reflex. Conduct your strikes to the exact measure with every lunge and counter. Do this and you will be a master of the sword.

Barodane did a few sets with the boulder to warm up, and then drew his blade, slow and steady, embodying the effort of precision Pyr Syat had drilled into him. Weight rolling across his feet, he stepped within range of a row of cattails. The handle of his blade rested in his palms, its tip poised at a forty-five-degree angle from his hips.

Balanced.

He waited a handful of breaths, forcing himself to relax. *Precision is smooth, and so your body must be smooth—unhurried—if you are to be precise.*

"I am the weapon." He felt himself sink slightly. A tremor moved from jaw to shoulder, muscles sagging around a deep, easy breath. *Ah, there it is...*

A short step started the motion. The hilt did not move, not until his legs had built the necessary momentum and power. He turned his wrists, the tip of his sword weaving a shallow crescent as he lunged forward to slice the head off a cattail.

Just as quick, he returned to his original position, sidestepped twice, then repeated the motion.

Hours later, sweat dripped off his stubbled chin and beaded at the corners of his mustache. He exhaled sharply, then sheathed his sword with a smile. He wasn't sure when exactly it had happened but Barodane felt better. Better than he had since his betrothal to Omari, and while he groused about training and hunting often, he noticed that the words were more reflex than anything of substance.

While his blade work seemed to be returning to form, his hunting skills failed to improve.

He left the clearing, making for a stream a long jump in width a half mile from camp, right at the border of the woodlands. Frogs were one of the easier prey, he'd found, for the energy required to catch them. Spotting a heron hunting a cluster of pools nearby, he shooed it away and took its place, but couldn't find the reason it had chosen the spot.

He made his way back to the stream.

A wide cedar sat at the center, forcing water to split to either side of it. The canopy was a broken reflection on the stream's surface as it babbled over upthrust roots in the shallows and swirling pools in the deeper stretches.

Barodane picked his way along it, hoping to see a fish trapped in a fissure between roots or gulping its last after jumping onto a shelf of earth. A flock of sparrows descended onto the opposite bank, pecking at a line of ants traveling from a hole in the ground to a tree bole. Barodane's stomach squeaked. He considered searching for a rock to throw but stopped. *Pointless. At least someone can get their fill.*

Ahead, the stream curved into denser woods. Barodane wasn't willing to go farther. A mile of woods separated him from the main road. Without Garlenna in fighting shape, he didn't want to call undue attention down on them.

The clomp of fast-moving hooves sent Barodane ducking behind the nearest tree. A doe sprang from the wood ahead, two fawns trailing her. She panted, hindquarters shuddering. An ear twitched as she looked back into the dense forest she'd just emerged from. No wolf. No cougar. No bear.

He watched her circle away into the distance, looking for a reentry point into the woods that she deemed safe.

The leather hilt of Barodane's sword was warm underhand. *I don't even remember drawing it.* Pulse throbbing in his ears, he marked the direction from which the doe had fled.

Caution at the fore, he crossed the stream and made his way into the wood, stepping slowly from heel to toe and avoiding patches of daylight filtering through the dark canopy. He slid from tree to tree, turning himself sideways and peeking out before moving on to the next. He covered his mouth with a hand as he went to keep hot breaths from producing visible puffs of steam.

A snort came from somewhere ahead, freezing him in place. Voices followed. "The old woman said it was past the woods."

Barodane eased his head from hiding but pulled back when he heard a man's voice—not distant enough for comfort, but still close enough to make out what he said.

"How fuckin' far? I've got kids back home and this shit has already taken a month."

"Past the stream." A woman's voice. The clink of armor.

A man laughed. "Nacronus's balls! We've crossed a half dozen by now. Which one?"

The woman answered coolly. "The last one before we find them."

That killed further conversation.

Barodane ventured another attempt to locate them—spotted movement at an angle ahead and to the left. There were three of them, all busily setting up camp. They didn't have a fire going yet, nor did they appear keen on doing so. *Not their first manhunt.*

And from what he could tell, they'd just arrived.

One was a knight of the Crown. A brawny, bald man with a mustache that put Barodane's own to shame. Another was a holdguard from Breckenbright. Portly and weak-chinned, he tended the horses, preparing them for a night of sleep.

The third was a chainman who, oddly enough, was the woman. Female executors of the Crown Justice were rare, which could easily mean they had to be better than their male peers. Given her demeanor, Barodane felt confident in the theory.

Everything about her sat high. Angular cheekbones hovered over a pert mouth as she sat on a stump, her spine rigid. She was old enough to have wrinkles, but the ponytail blooming from the top of her cranium drew her thin skin taut and made her look younger and healthier than she might truly be. The green sash of office looped under her armpit was pinned to the front and back of a silver honor plate. Chainmen were knights—usually retired—with a knack for hunting criminals. Highly intelligent and capable. Dangerous foes.

Given her company, this one appeared to have come from Breckenbright.

Barodane sighed. The possibility of evading them this close to his own camp seemed unlikely. They would find his tracks and be on top of his camp in short order. *At least now, I know where they are...where they sleep.*

Grim realization lodged in his brain. *I have to kill them.* He racked his brain for other answers and came up empty. He could wait for nightfall and do it now, but knew that if he didn't return to camp, Garlenna might come looking. *No "might," she'll* definitely *come looking.* Tohar wouldn't be able to stop her.

Fuck. I have to. There's no other way. His skin crawled as he imagined the grisly work the night would bring. Even if he wasn't as good at sneaking as Garlenna, killing them in their sleep seemed the best plan.

He peeked out again, taking the measure of the trio. *If they knew I was their prince...*

He gave a heavy sigh. *If you'd wanted that to happen, you shouldn't have forsaken the crown. Now, you've got to kill your way back to it.* He considered Garlenna's plan to put Solicerames in his hands in order to give no doubt as to who he was. Even then, the forces conspiring to seize the crown would deny his claim and call him a pretender. *I've good and truly made a mess of my country.* The farther he traveled from Digtown, the more pressure the realization brought.

He recounted the dead and wondered if his niece still lived.

Who am I kidding, she's dead too. They all die. Vision dimming, his knees threatened to buckle. *And it's my fault. Now, I have to right the wrongs even if it means bloodying my hands.* If Garlenna knew about the chainman's crew and Barodane's plan, she wouldn't be talked down from joining him. He threw one last look at the Crown's Justice come to put him in shackles.

I do this by myself. Tonight.

He made his way back to his own camp, his hunger forgotten, replaced by a different kind of gnawing in his gut.

Precision, that's all it will take. Barodane had heard plenty of stories as a youth about bandits so good at their trade that they could cut an entire caravan's throat without making a peep. Confident in his plan, he said nothing of the chainman to Garlenna and Tohar. Foolish, he knew, but something inside begged him to do the deed on his own.

Desperation encased him as he lay awake by the dead campfire. He needed to gain some semblance of himself back—some semblance of self-reliance even if the risk was great.

Awareness prickled across Barodane's back. A moment later, Tohar gave a subtle gasp. Cloth slid over skin. Wet lapping sounds came next. Throat-tight sounds of pleasure sighed from Garlenna. Tohar grunted. The stroking of bare flesh and soppy clicks joined the hum of insects in the night.

Priest and prosort sighed. One of them whispered for quiet—too late. Barodane lifted the flap of hood covering his eyes and regretted the choice immediately. Moonlight bathed Garlenna as she hooked a leg up and over the muslin shadows of Tohar's body.

Broad chest fixed skyward, a flush spread from Garlenna's corded neck tendons down to engorged nipples that were the same luminous pale as the rest of her. Founded upon slabbed muscle, her breasts bounced minimally as she started to rock back and forth atop the priest. Thick, striated buttocks slid over Tohar's pelvis, gleaming in the splashes of moonlight. A singular dent of shadow filled the crevice of her hips. Under her, Tohar lay still, his fleshy, hairy legs jutting from under his robes. Garlenna pushed his chest, dense strips of triceps clinging to the backs of her arms like a trench-dwelling sea creature entwined with its prey.

Though only seconds, the image burned into Barodane's mind. He dropped the flap of cloak back into place. *Good for you, Gar.* It was pleasant for him to know she could experience moments of joy beyond her duty on occasion. He just wished he hadn't had to see it to know it.

A short while later, the scuff of skin against skin ceased. Despite doing none of the work, Tohar's breathless wheezing filled the night. They whispered to one another while Barodane waited. Tohar took a piss. Garlenna took a piss. Snores came next, and then Barodane was getting silently to his feet, scabbard in hand.

He crept away from camp.

Despite the distance separating him from the chainman, Barodane made his way carefully, checking for sound at intervals to ensure he produced little of it himself. He had all night, and caution was a free commodity.

Moonlight guided him, though a couple of times, he got lost in the obscurity of shadows. Chill wind bent the tall grasses surrounding him and flapped at his cloak. He shook in anticipation and the cold intensified it. Inside his clothes, he swam in sweat, his body a hearth of mixed emotions and sensations.

He switched his sword hands, wiped his palms dry. A slick grip could spell death. He had to be quick—efficient. Any mistake could cost them all their lives.

He entered the cluster of trees where the stream cut a path in the fen. To the best of his recollection, he retraced his steps. First, the cedar disrupting the stream, then a log he'd stepped over.

A ghost. A knife spreading butter. Be that. Be smooth.

His chest ached. His fingers, too, from gripping the hilt of his sword so tight. Three weeks, he had trained, prying stone into his arms and killing foliage for bladework—countless hours passing time. Yet his nerves were getting the best of him, pushing him to hold the sword like his life depended on it.

It does, fool. Now fucking relax.

He sighed, then hiked his shoulders up to his ears before releasing them, just like the White Flame had taught him.

He stepped lightly, each footstep feeling like it took a heart-pounding minute to complete. One of their horses nickered, hobbled a dozen feet from where their riders slept. Barodane expected one of them to be standing sentry, and so made sure to move through the darkest parts of the forest, but he saw no one. He waited a long time—heard no one. They hadn't cared about their campfire either. It smoldered now, smoke filtering into the moonlit canopy.

Confident as the hunters, are you?

Beams of moonlight broke through the overstory in patches, outlining three sleeping forms in silver. Barodane paused, gathering himself at the edge of their camp, his bowels watery with nervousness. The world had become eerily distinct, even in the dark. He pressed the soles of his feet into the ground. *Imagine your feet are cinder blocks,* the White Flame had taught. *Imagine your breath is a warm summer wind.*

But Barodane's breath was stilted, a trapped pain in his chest. At any moment, he felt he might float off into nothingness. A wispy, anxious nothing. He exhaled, brought his sword up in both hands to touch cold steel to his forehead—that helped.

A blade is but a tool. I am the weapon.

He entered the ring of their campfire. Smoke and horse filled his nose. He stared down at one of the inert forms. Raised his sword. It shook and he grit his teeth to bring it under control. *They've got children. Homes to return to...to drink and toast along with their friends. They're just doing their duties.*

He exhaled. *And I'm doing mine.* A tremor of calm passed into his arm and then into the darksteel blade. *Just another cattail.*

His sword sank. Cloth parted...from cloth. Spine tingling, he jerked his sword back and thrust down again. More cloth. He pushed the pile with his boot tip—a rucksack holding fuck-all lay within.

Footsteps thudded up behind him. He whirled and flicked his blade out as he sidestepped, scoring flesh.

"Gah!" The figure stumbled past. Barodane sprinted for the shadows. So many shadows. And twisting, distorting moonlight, playing with his vision and drumming up hulking figures to block his path where there was nothing.

Nope. That's the knight.

The chain of a morning star clinked as it drew tension. The deadly ball at the end whirred. With a curse, Barodane ducked and fell back onto his ass. These were professionals. *How stupid am I to think—*

The iron ball thumped the ground between his legs.

Barodane thrust, sword tip scraping up sparks from a plated kneecap. He rolled backward over a shoulder and stumbled to his feet.

"You're a quiet one." The chainman's voice tugged at him. She was somewhere near the horses. "Swing to injure, men. Not to kill. The Hammer needs him breathing."

A piercing sound and a brush of air past Barodane's neck. *A dart?*

Holding his side, the portly holdguard closed with Barodane. "Cut me, you fuckin' twat. I'll cut you!" He attacked with looping blows. Barodane blocked, parried and thrust, but his sword struck naught but air.

Reflecting the moon's glow, the hulking knight's bald skull came bobbing forward a split second behind the holdguard.

Barodane stepped behind a tree. He'd been lucky in Digtown when he'd fought the masons. Scab's ferocity had been an undeniable factor. And again, at Halaleh, the priest's betrayal had saved their lives.

This was different. The knight was big and composed. The stolid holdguard was no slouch, either. And the chainman...

A dart pinged off Barodane's sword near the hilt.

"Drive him into the light," the woman said.

The knight's morning star tore a chunk of bark from the tree where Barodane's calf had been a second earlier.

"Fuck!" Barodane shouted. It was only a matter of time before one of the woman's darts hit him, or one of her men crippled him, unless... He cupped a hand to the side of his mouth. "Help!"

The knight paused. The holdguard, breathing louder than a winded ox, did too. They seemed to be considering something. The chainman's icy tones came from behind him. "We'll deal with the others later." They surrounded him in a triangle now. Not good. He wouldn't run. They might think he would, but he wouldn't. To run in the dark was to trip, and to trip was to die.

Barodane feinted toward the knight, setting him on his heels, and then hurried toward a cluster of maple trees he would use to protect his rear. As he did, he felt a gush of displaced air.

The holdguard grunted. "Fuck, Merique, you hit me!"

"It will be over momentarily," she said. "We'll wake you in the morning."

The holdguard growled and sprang after Barodane.

That's it, charge me. Barodane angled backward, inviting the man into his guard and running him into the knight's path. He blocked a stroke from the holdguard as he sailed past and sidestepped. Then he lunged to engage the knight, effectively forcing his two assailants to switch positions. Now the knight's morning star would have to clear his comrade in order to execute a clean strike.

Barodane unleashed a combination of slashes that skittered harmlessly off the big knight's shield.

The holdguard recovered.

Barodane circled to the right, into the arc of the knight's morning star. He shot forward into the space between the pair, seemingly defenseless to a sweeping blow from the larger or a stab from the other.

The darkness proved a fruitful ally.

The knight angled his shield to absorb Barodane's thrust, obscuring his vision further. The holdguard saw the opening and took the bait; his sword flashed in an upward arc toward Barodane's flank just as the knight's morning star whipped around.

The side of the holdguard's head burst, fragmented bits pattering Barodane's face. The body thudded to the ground. Barodane sidestepped over it as the knight stared down at what he'd done and cursed.

"Merique!"

"Stay calm," she said. A hiss of air followed. Something pinched the meat of Barodane's calf. "He's hit."

Fuck. The holdguard had remained upright for at least a minute. That meant Barodane had that long to dispatch his foes. Somewhere in the dark, Merique drew steel.

Smoke from the fire still rolled into the canopy in a cottony pall. Barodane circled toward the smoldering rubbish. The knight pursued, moving in line with Barodane. The former prince kept his opponent at bay with probing stabs and backed closer to the coals. Heat flooded up his lower leg.

Barodane leveled a heavy, two-handed stroke at the knight's midsection to force him back, then booted the dying fire. A hunk of wood flew out, striking the knight's shield. Ash swirled through the air in a misshapen plume, a dense gray cloak that turned the knight into a hazy silhouette.

Barodane watched the man bury his stinging eyes into the elbow of his quilted gambeson. Partially blinded, he swung his morning star in wild arcs and retreated. Hazy moonlight beamed off his bald forehead.

A glimmering patch for a target.

Two precise steps, notes on a banha drum tapped out in rapid succession. Barodane thrust. Brain punctured, the knight dropped abruptly, nearly jerking Barodane's sword from his grasp. He was pulled forward, heard the blade scrape free as he stumbled past into the dissolving pillar of ash and light.

Merique loomed—aimed at his hand. He brought his sword up just in time to stave off being crippled. "Who are you?" she said.

He ripped his blade back into position. She stalked forward. Older, weaker, but her single blow had told him all he needed to know. With a blade, she was as precise as the White Flame himself.

She lunged halfway—reversed the movement—and weaved a shallow slash at his face that snicked off a wisp of mustache.

A tingling sensation rippled up Barodane's leg. His toes went numb. Cold crept into his knee.

The woman's reach was less than his, but then again, it didn't need to be longer. With seemingly little effort, Merique struck out, speed forfeited in favor of understanding. Wherever Barodane thought he might catch her off guard, he found her sword already there, as if she had predicted his attack.

"Who are you, a fucking seer?" He kicked dirt at her face, but she leaned to the side, letting it sail past with a stoic expression.

"Merique Inari. The Crown's Justice." She snuck past his guard, severing cloth. Her blows were landing closer to the mark with increasing efficiency. *She's toying with me.*

Barodane grunted, breathing soupy and sluggish. "Well, you're stupid."

"Oh?" She tapped his sword and then allowed him a counter lunge which she easily blocked. At any point, he realized, she could have ended it. "You sound tired."

"If you'd fought with your men, you'd have killed me by now."

"You were a surprise. The Hammer said you were only a drug dealer." She lowered her sword. Dawn licked the sky. The forest was brightening. "I don't recall the White Flame training any drug dealers in the way of the blade."

Barodane barked out a laugh, then wheezed, hunching over. A thread of drool raced from his lips to the dirt. She wasn't just a chainman. She was a Remnant. A Kanian blade master with highest honors. *Lucky me.*

His legs started to shake.

She squared to him, her mouth a tight, flat line. "Now, tell me. Who do I hunt? Who has killed my men and survived my blade longer than any other?"

Barodane's throat filled with cotton. His vision blurred, lips and tongue like wooden blocks. "I'm your goddamn prince, you stupid...uhh."

His limbs faltered, the words in his mouth dissolving into formless clay. He swooned—thumped to the earth like a lonesome drumbeat.

The last thing he saw was Merique's furrowed brow staring down at him.

CHAPTER FORTY-FOUR

THE LIES WE CARRY

W ord had come in the night that the Knights of the Wolf Banner were spotted on the plains. Shouted commands and the bustle of hasty preparation had roused more than just Ishoa. Mothers camped among the sheep mangers emerged with their children held tight, blinking out sleep and fear and the horrors that lay ahead whenever soldiers took to the saddle in full armor.

Servants scurried to help the horse archers of White Plains prepare to meet the threat on the open tundra, checking quivers, securing straps, and handing up spears.

Ishoa watched them line up at the gate in the gloom before dawn. Steaming breaths from beast and man formed a layer of mist around the ramparts. Once the gate ratcheted open, Sir Hollem raised a fist and led them through. Pale light glinted off bronze and steel honor plates. Ram skull brands marked the flanks of their lithe tundra coursers, trained for swiftness in the deep, winter drifts.

An hour later, when the storm had calmed, Ishoa climbed over the fence and into a quiet training yard. Sitting cross-legged in the snow, Gaern Yorek waited for her.

"So dramatic," Ishoa said.

The man ignored the jest. He fixated on the Fly behind her. One eye twitched with disdain. "Tell him to leave."

Ishoa twisted to her bodyguard. Without clamoring noise crowding the morning air, his silence was more noticeable. "Why?"

"You think I teach just anyone the secrets of the Hulka'skara? It is an ancient art not meant for outsiders."

Ishoa studied the Fly. "You're not an Anjuhk?"

He gave no reply.

"I know you can shrug...nod...do something."

The Fly shrugged, and with an agitated hiss, she dismissed him.

Gaern came to his feet.

"So what will it be today," Ishoa said, tone belying disinterest. "More staring at Rakeema under the tree? Or maybe you'll have me practice moving slow again."

Weeks had passed since she'd regrettably committed to the man's tutelage. So far, he'd given little explanation for what they did or why they did it but demanded her full commitment anyway. Most days he had her sit under a particularly broad aspen and watch her anjuhtarg. Staring at Rakeema for hours had made Ishoa feel insane. To anyone watching, she looked it, too. "I thought our goal was for me to learn to be a leader, not a laughing stock."

"No," the beastmaster had said. "It's to help you see who you are and become Hulka'skara. Whether or not you *are* a leader is for you to decide once we've finished."

A handful of other times, he had invited her to conduct her normal swords skills but at a tenth of her full speed. "And this?" she executed a lazy lunge over the course of her sentence. "Shall I lull my enemies to sleep?"

"You're learning to move with intention."

Out of the beastmaster's line of sight, she had rolled her eyes.

Now, with weeks of inane training behind her, she was less than eager to continue. Numerous times, she'd considered quitting, but the lack of mind paid to her voice in council meetings snuffed that thought. Each day that passed solidified her need for a change. And so she cast a tether into the shadows of herself hoping and trusting that this mean little man from Akulsa could help her salvage whatever merits she had left.

Only one part of their work kept her engaged. For the last fifteen minutes of practice each day, he would have her repeat the Fjordsong command for Rakeema to hunt.

"Feel into yourself as you say it." Over and over, for fifteen minutes, she would repeat it. For fifteen minutes, he'd shake his head, or snort in disgust, or laugh with contempt.

The day before, frustration had gotten the better of Ishoa. "Every crevice of Rakeema's ears knows this word. I think she gets it. Perhaps, we could try a different one?"

The man's face twisted into bug-eyed mockery. "I think she gets it!" He jabbed a finger into Ishoa's breastbone. "I'd say *she* doesn't. A new word is nothing compared to what I teach you. A few syllables strung together forms the bond between anjuhtarg and master, does it? Is that how you think this works?"

Like so many other times, Ishoa lowered her head before his cruel upbraiding. He snapped her face back to meet his, a curled finger striking her chin. Her eyes had widened with rage, hand drifting over her sword hilt.

"Look at me." His tone swung low, a farmer's scythe cutting her down. "Do you see me using words? If you knew how to do this, you wouldn't need me to teach you. You'd do it!"

"So I'm supposed to speak at her in my mind?" Ishoa snapped.

He shrugged. "Try it."

Ishoa tried but Rakeema didn't move. The beastmaster pressed her to try again to no avail. He laughed at her as she kept at it, each attempt deepening her sense of failure until finally, she gave up. "I can't do it without the commands!"

"Pfah! You can't do it with them, either. The words make no difference. Meaningless crutches for the weak." Hostility sharpened his words. "I let you use them out of pity. Whatever makes you feel better, right, Princess?"

Ishoa spoke through clenched teeth. "I seek guidance, not ridicule."

"Oh I think you've been guided plenty. Guided your whole life. Jerked this way, sent that way. Your betters have been battering you like an old piece of iron since the crib." Arms akimbo, he flitted his limbs about in a jerky motion. "This is you. Just a fancier class of marionette. Tell me, are you a puppet, Princess? A limp little doll?"

She hesitated, hands balled into fists. "No."

"Then choose your own path!" he roared. He glanced at her fists, mean smile plastering his broad face. "Anger makes you strong, does it? Nothing without it, are you? Rigga was right. You're doomed to repeat your uncle's failures. Lodecka plucks at your strings and makes you swing your sword arm." He waved a hand. "Go—Lehrd. Hunt your past to your contentment. Don't come back until you've had your fill."

Most of their training sessions had ended in a similar fashion. She knew he'd expect her back the next day, regardless.

Now, she stood before him yet again, numb to the predictable derision he was sure to level at her by day's end. "Shall I send her off?" Ishoa stroked Rakeema's ears. The ice tiger purred and pushed into her hand for more.

Wistfulness stole across Gaern's expression. "Do you wish to know her story?"

Ishoa's brow tensed. *That's a change of pace. Better than staring at her like a fool.* She nodded.

Gaern crouched before the ice tiger. Usually, Rakeema was filled with wild youngling energy and rarely sat still, but with the beastmaster locking eyes with her, she was statuesque. It was as if the man was telling her the story as much as he was telling Ishoa. And Rakeema seemed intent on listening to it.

"Her mother was the queen of Akulsa. A legend made flesh among the endless snow of the range. Magnificent. Deadly. She prowled those icy slopes without equal. Even with all the skill of my ancient lineage, tracking her was difficult. She was a gray phantom, impossible to pin down. Though she left plenty of clues of her existence—carcasses stripped to nothing but cracked-open bone. Her feeding patterns told me she was pregnant. It was what I needed to find her, and only luck let me do so in time. Neither before nor since have I seen a den so laden with skeletons. Bison, white elk, wolverine, C'Dathun..."

"Ice tigers eat trolls?"

"Oh, to be sure. She was the weight of a snow bison and twice as long. A creature so big eats anything and everything she can find."

"You stole Rakeema?" Wolst hadn't told Ishoa that part. In fact, he hadn't told her much at all except that he'd gone to the Fringes to get her. Having been orphaned at a young age herself, Ishoa felt guilt clawing at her guts at the idea of her anjuhtarg being taken from its mother.

"Traded for her is more accurate," he said. "A birthing mother is quite docile. While I could have walked in and pulled the kitten from her nipple without issue, I dragged a snow bison carcass into her den instead—an even trade. A bounty like that brings ease to the process. She wouldn't worry the sacrifice of a single kitten when the exchange ensures the rest of her litter's survival." The man paused. "Opportunities to bond with an anjuhtarg like yours happens once in a century. That alone made me wonder if fate itself was on your side...that you might be different. Worthy of something greater than the rest of your ill-gotten blood. Tell me, would you like to possess the power and agility of a fully grown war cat?"

Ishoa frowned. "That isn't possible."

The beastmaster did not waver. Hard, humorless eyes held her.

She glanced at Rakeema. The cat blinked slow, then set to rigorously licking a paw. *Is it possible?*

A tear sped down Gaern's cheek. "She was majestic, the mother. The most beautiful creature I've seen." Without breaking his stare from Rakeema's, he wiped away the tear. "Yes, she will be something to behold. If her master does what is needed. Come."

The beastmaster sped from the training yard, wordlessly dismissing Rakeema to hunt as he did.

Ishoa followed him down a row of ramshackle hovels, doors sliding past until they came to a graying one that clung to its hinges. "Do you wish to command your anjuhtarg? To operate as one with her? To know yourself to the deepest extent, and from that place, form an unbreakable bond with Rakeema?"

Ishoa made to say yes, but the beastmaster cut her off, gnarled finger upheld. "This is no fantasy, girl. Becoming a Hulka'skara is hard. Harder than moving slow and watching your beast play. Will you do what's needed...even if it kills you?"

Ishoa hesitated. *If I die, Lodecka wins.* She pinned back her shoulders. Besides her vengeance, Rakeema was all she had left. "Yes."

Gaern Yorek swung open the door and beckoned her inside.

A score of candles bled milky fat onto a table in the corner. A rug drew the room together. A pair of stools and a desk sat in one corner; a pack and scattered clothes in another. A drape separated the pair from an adjoining room—sleeping quarters, she assumed. Someone moved around quietly on the other side. A roommate forced upon the man from Akulsa. Rigga Hine wasn't one to value comfort over function. *Not even honored guests like a beastmaster get more than a shared hovel.*

The musty stench of animal hide shot up her nose. She jerked back, blinking rapidly, the smell familiar. "You've been letting in sheep for warmth?"

"Not quite." He motioned for her to sit down in the center of the room. "There's a shallow fire pit under the rug so watch your step in the middle there."

She did, and he sat across from her.

Palms riding his knees, her teacher drew in a deep, slow breath. Tangled hair framed his face. His eyelids hung heavy, forming slits. "Rakeema is an extension of the self. In all ways, she must be like another of your limbs. No different than your uncle taught you with a sword. The bond is an imposition of your will, of your certainty...a vision deep down in the bones that moves before you've a moment to think it into motion. Your anjuhtarg must know your every breath. She must sense you. Not your fear nor your self-doubt. *You.*"

Ishoa listened in silence.

Gaern rocked forward, chest over lap. "To command your anjuhtarg, you do so not with words, but presence. When you feel yourself in fullness, you have the ability to extend it beyond the borders of form. But if there is no sense of self, no innate knowing of who you truly are, there is nothing to extend. Your anjuhtarg easily ignores that which isn't there."

He rocked back, spine rigid, hips and shoulders square.

I have no sense of self, do I? She wanted to defend herself, to declare the man a crazy old fool and leave, but she held fast and watched the thoughts eddying in place. A child's thoughts, unworthy of all but the contrast in wisdom they yielded between distances of maturity. *I lose nothing by testing what he says. I'll prove him right or wrong, but I'll do so of my own volition.*

She bit back anger and saw the question circling it all.

So...who am I? The Ironlight name came to mind. Uttered to her from a thousand sets of lips over the years. Telling her of her past, of the exploits of those long dead and long loved. Telling her who she was by shared blood and nothing else. The lips moved, whispering of her measure, eyes watching for actions that validated their conclusions.

You're the last Ironlight.

You're a princess.

You're Namarr...

Wolst, Othwii, and Belara shrank into her sorrow, their voices replaced with less complimentary ones.

Naïve, said Syphion Muul.

Precious, said Ularis Warnock.

Lodaris came last, most condemning. *You do not see it, Princess.*

Eyes closed, a sob clamped her throat. *I'm trying to see...*

It struck her then. Her teacher had spoken true. Friend or foe, not a single person had ever asked her who she'd wanted to be. They heaped identity upon her. Molded her with their assumptions. Shaped her to fit the familiar forms of a past and future already agreed upon. And at every turn, she'd offered herself up to their making.

Her voice cracked. "I don't...I don't know who I am." The words peeled her open. Alone, orphaned, sheltered, she had never felt alive. Had never been more than an angry ghost rattling her chains and begging to be free.

"Are you your uncle?" Gaern asked.

Wolst had given her wisdom. Trained her to be an Anjuhk. Loved her like his own...more than his own. *But that's not the question.* "No, I'm not my uncle."

"Your great grandmother, then?" Gaern said, "Or Danath?"

"No," she whispered.

"Then why do they cloud your mind as if you are? Why do they take up the space you need to be free? You are torn. Diluted. A tattered and barren vessel. No one will follow you. You *must* break free from them to forge your own path. Let go."

Ishoa trembled. "I can't." The milky hue spreading over Lodaris's flesh filled her mind, a cold and disregarding Lodecka approving his death nearby. *I won't let my vengeance die too.*

And Wolst...her heart had grown to accommodate a man of such immense size and personality, and now, it echoed empty with an absence of the same volume. To forget any of those she loved was to betray their memory. They were a sacred part of her. Without them, she was nothing. "I can't. I don't know how."

"You see yourself as weak and unworthy." The beastmaster sniffed snot to the back of his throat. "An unchallenged assumption such as that is a dangerous thing. All of us play pawn to that which controls us from the shadows. You must shine a light on your beliefs about yourself, Ishoa. Those birthed from fear are the hardest to overcome, for each time they are accepted as truths, they burrow to safer depths and the wall they hide behind adds a layer of brick. But lie by lie, your defenses must be dismantled. One by one, these beliefs must be surrendered if you're to be free."

The beastmaster cocked his head. "So if you've got the courage, I suggest you start with what you say about yourself in here." He touched a temple. "There are a great many marionette strings to cut when it comes to your conditioning. Once free, you'll choose, by your thoughts, your words, your actions...you'll walk the narrow path of who you truly are. That is the moment when they will follow you."

Ishoa stared into her lap. *I can't.*

"Even now, fear claims you." A dark expression spread over the beastmaster's face. "Your real enemy is the lies you carry. Fed by naught but the poison of fear, they will continue to bear fruits of the same. Cut them out at the root, Isha. There is no enemy but fear."

She'd nearly forgotten the person on the other side of the drape as they shuffled over to it, their silhouette undefined in the flickering backlight of the candles. A chill ran down her spine. The stench of the room increased as they drew closer. "Who's there?"

"A single experience, no matter how horrible, does not condemn all experiences. Just like one failure on your part, Isha, does not condemn you to a life of failure. You *must* face forward to see your path." Gaern spoke in a hushed voice. "You must let the past go."

A gentle breeze—from a window in the other room, she guessed—billowed the drape. A familiar smell swept through. Musty hide. A pungent reek. Her hackles rose. *Not sheep.*

"Gaern Yorek," Ishoa hissed. Her body locked in place, overwhelmed by the danger budding in her awareness. Something out of the past...

The beastmaster's words fell into the bowels of hearing. "No enemy but fear."

Black, clawed fingers curled around the drape. Swept it aside.

Hands wreathed in snowy fur gave way to a narrow breast and long, goat-like legs. The source of the stench stared down its protruding nose at Ishoa. Cold tingles burst across the back of her neck as if struck with a snowball.

"No," she whispered. She dropped backward onto her palms, dug heels into the rug and scrambled away from the creature. Her back met the wall. "No!"

The C'Dathun troll took a step toward her just before she fainted. Gaern Yorek's voice trailed her into darkness. "No enemy but fear..."

Blood spurted from the man's side when the Sister of the Rose jerked the spearhead free, her hand shining crimson in the candlelight. The finger-length of steel plinked into a basin. Ishoa watched the woman's face fall as she hovered over the wound.

The Sister shook her head.

Pale and trembling, the injured man moaned. His head lolled from side to side. "Water," he rasped.

Most of what the Sister ladled into the man's mouth sluiced onto the table. He gagged, sputtered, then let his head drop back with a thud. "Easy now," the Sister said.

Ishoa's eyes locked onto the rags bundled at the man's side, sopping red and soaking through almost quicker than the Sister could replace them. *He's running out of blood.* Now, the Sister had stopped replacing them. Stopped pressing on the injury.

"It's okay," Ishoa whispered to the man. "The Sister's getting the bleeding under control. Shouldn't be long now."

The man nodded, eyes rounded and fixed on the ceiling. He gulped as if struck by some realization. Nausea seemed to pass through him and he pinched his eyes closed.

"Where were you attacked?" Arick stood at the man's feet.

Ishoa looked askance at her cousin. She wanted the dying man to rest but knew they needed to question him. *It's always a job for Arick. Never can he set it aside in favor of doing right by an individual.*

Ishoa's throat tightened. Weeks had passed since she'd fainted before Gaern's troll servant. Its name was Wiir. At least, that's what he called it. The beastmaster claimed it was a "he" but Ishoa felt more comfortable leaving it as an "it." Wiir didn't talk but for low grunts and a sound much like wind swirling among reeds.

"Must it watch us?" Ishoa had said during the only session she'd gone to since the incident.

"Must you care?" the beastmaster responded. "He's not hurting you, is he?"

No. But he would if given the chance.

Gaern's repeated promise that Wiir was harmless had done little to set her at ease, so she hadn't returned. She wished to become Hulka'skara but fear kept her distant...not just of Wiir. More than that, it was the beastmaster's words slapping at her in her worst moments of self-recrimination.

No enemy but fear.

Each time she heard Gaern Yorek's voice rattling in her skull, she wept. Wept for those lost because fate had chosen her as a princess of Namarr. Wept for those she would lead to their deaths every time she made the wrong choice.

He wants me to let go of the past...of my mother, my father, Wolst, and Lodaris. Everything she was lived there. And maybe, that was the point, to be something and someone different. By holding onto her loved ones, she held onto the horrible possibility of disappointing them. A fear that drove her and undermined any chance of confidence in her decisions.

That morning, she had risen from her bed wiping off the most recent torrent of tears and steeled herself, ready to meet with her teacher and face her fear of his troll. *If I don't, I'll keep tarnishing my family's legacy.*

The declaration had come a moment too soon. Wading through the shit-churned snow of the bailey on her way to the beastmaster's quarters, she found a wounded soldier, mounted but barely keeping his saddle, being admitted through the gate.

Now, stretched out before her, the man coughed up blood.

Insidious thoughts descended, hunting owls drawn to the squeak of prey. Ishoa tried to stop them. *I did not stab this man. It is not my fault. Not everything is my fault.*

With no victories in battle, no clever strategies, no celebrations from her council—without evidence of any successes—she found it hard to keep her self-criticism at bay. Even with her most recent insight, fear sank its talons into her nape and wetted its beak in her gut.

Sir Hollem watched from the head of the table. He repeated Arick's question. "Where were you attacked, soldier?" After leading out a sortie of horse archers, the eldest scion of White Plains returned days later having turned up no tracks nor signs of the Dread Knight's host. The man on the table was a Hine holdguard. Shining gouges in his bronze honor plate lent evidence to a series of spear thrusts. Apparent misses prior to the killing strike were visible near the collarbone.

"The forest...near Theren. Two days past."

"What livery?" Sir Hollem asked.

The man grimaced. "Wolves."

"The dancing kind?" Arick asked. Reports of the furriers of Ghastiin had diminished in recent weeks, with sorties from the Manger increasing.

The man shook his head. "Others. It was a trap."

"This is one of Adus's men," said Sir Hollem. "I sent a messenger bird telling him to hunt the Dread Knight." He raised his voice. "Does my brother still live?"

The man nodded. "My group was small. Sent to..." The man's gaze drifted.

Sir Hollem stepped closer to the table, pale, stony eyes bearing down on the holdguard. Ishoa eased back, thinking he meant to strike the dying man. Instead, he placed a hand on his shoulder. "Sent to what?"

The soldier gulped back pain. "To parlay with the Knight of the Hallow Moon's nephew, Camion."

Blankness overtook the dying shepherd's face. He stared at the wood beams of the ceiling, eyelids drooping. His hand brushed Ishoa's and she gathered it into a tight grip. She felt the others looking at her. *Judge all you wish.*

"Holding hands with a princess." The man's cheek twitched. "My father would be proud."

"What of Sir Gossryk's nephew?" Arick said.

"Dead. The wolf knights' leader flew a flag of truce...but it was an ambush." The man blinked, lizard-slow, voice weakening. "He killed them. Me...a handful from Bleeding Point...escaped."

"This Dread Knight won't fight Adus head on," said Sir Hollem. "He sets traps and winnows away our numbers. Draws us from the open plains. Adus's last pigeon said they leave no tracks on open ground. That they move among the trees."

"How many in your brother's host?" Arick asked.

"Father?" the man stared at Arick. "Father..."

Arick and Ishoa shared a somber glance as Sir Hollem continued. "Two hundred and fifty."

"At most, these wolf knights cannot number more than three hundred and fifty." A tear welled in one of Arick's eyes, a rare show of humanity as the dying man reached for him. "Otherwise, they'd have attacked your brother already. This is good news. It means they pose no threat of siege to the Manger."

Ishoa exhaled. "Can we not wait to discuss these things another—"

"Father." The tension of suffering in the dying man's face dissipated.

Ishoa squeezed his hand, noted the meek grip in response. A wet rattle rose from his chest. Then it deflated and never rose again.

Tingles raced down the backs of Ishoa's arms. She released his hand and pushed off the table as the Sister drew a soiled blanket over his face.

Sir Hollem sighed and turned from the table. "There are rumors that the Dread Knight gathers strength from the countryside. That he presses many of those his wolf knights don't kill into their ranks."

Ishoa's anger mounted as she looked at the outline of the corpse. Another life gone. Another day wasted while the body count continued to rise. "If you hadn't told Sir Adus to hunt the Dread Knight, would he have returned by now?"

Sir Hollem rounded, the hand that had been smoothing his white beard slowing.

Ishoa fixed him with a steady gaze. "If the Knights of the Wolf Banner pose no threat to the Manger and they aren't strong enough to challenge your brother's host in the field, why are we chasing them around? We could be retaking Jarik. Or contesting the Kons and their Orenese mercenaries to the east."

"Highness," he said, "a renegade force occupies our lands."

"I'm aware," Ishoa said. "But a far larger and more dangerous one threatens our nation. Call a council meeting. Now. And make sure your mother is there." Sir Hollem attempted to argue but she cut him off. "Immediately."

When the shepherd lord of White Plains found no ally in a silent Arick, he bowed to Ishoa. "As you wish, Princess." He left.

"See that this man receives a hero's burial," Ishoa said to the Sister.

Outside the door, the Fly waited. "How was that?"

The hooded face looked down the hall at Sir Hollem's back, hastened boot-steps echoing, and nodded.

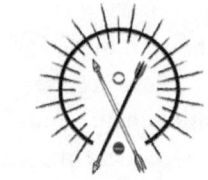

CHAPTER FORTY-FIVE

BLADESWORN

After his meeting with the Skyfire Council, sleep came in fits, the barrier between worlds a tenuous veil of agitation. Thephos tossed...found the horned skull from Unturrus's peak. It swallowed him, bone jaw and canine teeth clanging shut, enclosing him in its dark mouth.

And then it spat him out. Ribbons of drool hung from him, slathering his mouth, suffocating...

Suffocating...

He woke with a gasp, drenched in sweat, head aching fiercely. He heaved a sigh of relief. Brow clenched, he tried to go back to sleep but couldn't. "Enough," he said and went in search of fresh air.

Above ground, dawn was blisteringly cold. A gray sky engorged with rain stared down at him through the eyehole of Enshai's domed roof, winter watching and waiting to descend as autumn limped its last.

He made his way to the training yard. If he could make sense of what had happened, he might be able to control his power. To repeat it.

Or keep it from being repeated.

What he'd felt when he'd attacked Syn shortened his breath to recall. Surging power, surging hatred. A need to trade hurt for hurt. The glee of pain caused—the satisfactory give of Syn's face beneath his cinder-block hand.

But N'zara said there's nothing there. And Syn didn't notice it either. He did the Provocations. I'm okay. They said it was so.

He trusted the Dominarri in the same fashion he trusted anyone—very little. Lost and alone in his newfound powers, they were the only ones who seemed to understand what he might be going through. He'd heard snippets of conversation among other Awakened. Parts of what he was experiencing happened on occasion. All of them happening to a single person, however, was unheard of.

I could trust the voice.

Ecstasy stirred in the pit of his belly and a warm hand cradled the back of his neck, its palm velvet soft. *Yes,* it said. *You could. I want to give you power and ask nothing in return.*

Thephos bore down, clamping the muscles of his torso and folding his arms around his sides. *No. That's just my own voice. No other.* A tremor of agitation ran up his spine.

Focus on the good. Focus on the path forward. Soon, he'd be more than an initiate. After his bonding ceremony, he'd be a true Dominarri. The thought soured as he considered it; he hadn't connected with anyone yet. Most of the bladesworn reviled him, though none so vocally as Pintarian.

Ash likes me. Alas, she was bonded to Syn. He thought of his mother, earliest memories out of reach but for a phantom of longing. *Maybe...maybe I should bond with a woman?* Excitement fluttered through him, dying a second after it came. The Holy Sword had done so and it seemed to have led to nothing but resentment and bitterness.

Thephos sighed. Better to claim his powers more fully and hope one of them approached him to propose a bonding.

Slowly, he walked down a lane with hedges to either side. Footsteps from random passersby scuffed along, some near, some far. He soaked it in, appreciating his home. No one spat on him. No one lacerated him with contempt. And his brothers were being taken care of, the first of their sum already delivered to his old homestead.

The sky released its bloated contents.

Ahead, a figure strode across an intersecting lane, hood drawn up, files of blond hair poking out at the collar to cascade down his chest. He wore a blade at his hip and carried himself with an air of business. Thephos hadn't heard of any assembly at dawn, nor any other matter that might warrant such a hasty stride.

He looked back, then sped up to follow the man. At the intersecting path, he peeked out and saw the bladesworn disappear down some steps into the training yard.

Thephos followed.

At the far end of the yard, the man slipped through a set of doors just as the sky released its bloating contents in lazy drifts. Thephos hustled to the doors, paused at the threshold to listen, and when he deemed it safe, proceeded.

A series of doors lined the hall. He'd never been to this section of the city. One of them had just creaked shut. Thephos took a step—

Something slammed into him, hurling him against the wall. He cried out, light flashing behind his vision as his ribs shrieked. Blinking away the pain, he found a sword point staring him in one eye. "Who the fuck are you?"

A face hung next to the blade. A perfect face with eyes colder than the curved steel in his hand and a well-manicured beard of gold. Angular, symmetrical features balanced on a strong chin. A man assembled by the divine, it seemed. If his hair were white, he'd have been a near replica of the Holy Sword. *No wonder N'zara hates him. He's nothing of her, and all of Pintarith.*

He gulped. "Thephos...of Carthane."

"Ah, yes." Pintarian's blade was frozen in place. Thephos stared down the length of mirrored steel and wavering ghost-flame, and saw the orrastan—Pintarian's bladesworn oath—stamped along the fuller but he couldn't make out any of the words. "You're upright for once. Hard to recognize you without Syn and Ash Backlegarm cradling you like a babe."

The sword dropped to Pintarian's side. Thephos's chest heaved relief as he watched the bladesworn assess him. "You wish to watch me train, I assume," the man said. "Next time, ask. It's dangerous to follow someone like me."

Thephos frowned. "I don't—"

"No, you really *don't*, do you. You *don't* have powers. You *don't* have a bladesworn. You *don't* have anything at all except a couple of soft-hearted suckers whispering false praise in your ear."

"I never claimed to be special."

Pintarian scoffed. "You aren't dissuading their claims though, are you? That makes you just as guilty. One must wield a keen understanding of their strengths and failings if they're to amount to anything." He glanced at Thephos's feet. "We can cross skulking off your list of special talents as well. You're louder than a rickety wain wheel. You're liable to get whatever bladesworn unlucky enough to be bonded to you killed."

The muscles in Thephos's face were hardening with every passing word. *How can one carry so much vitriol for someone they don't know?* "Since you're so strong and I'm so weak, maybe I should bond with you?"

The abuse, at least, might feel like home.

The bladesworn's face split into a broad grin, a beam of light and joy. "Certainly!" The abrupt shift made Thephos flinch. "Come, let us train together and see if we are a true fit. I could be wrong—it's rare—but maybe you are special."

Pintarian stepped back and motioned Thephos down the hall. "Third door on the right. The servants prepare it for me every morning."

"I didn't know there were servants here."

The man laughed as he reached past Thephos to jerk open the door he'd indicated. "Apologies. The normal people." He steered Thephos within.

Thephos got the impression, Pintarian didn't fraternize with "normal people" often, if at all. *He thinks himself Dominarri royalty.*

A beehive hung from a pole at the center of a small, barren room, buzzing with activity.

The door clicked shut behind. Thephos rotated around to find Pintarian tossing a key into the far corner. "Keeps me from leaving before I've finished." The man's cheek twitched. "One must overcome the barriers within if they are to find greatness. Regardless of the pain."

Slowly, Thephos turned back to the hive. *I count bees with the best.* Ash's words chilled him. "What—uh...what do I do?"

Pintarian stripped off his cloak, tunic, and a padded gambeson. Long, lean muscle covered the man. He was broad of shoulder, narrow of waist, and every thew and sinew jumped when he moved. A hideous burn encircled his neck and trailed down his sternum as he passed by Thephos. "Watch." The bladesworn stopped short of the humming hive, his sword held before him and resting lightly in upturned palms like an offering to the bees.

Completing a slow, ritualistic inhale, he tossed his sword in the air, snatched it as it fell, and twirled it. The single motion was enough for Thephos to know the man was as limber as he was strong.

"Thephos of Carthane," the man sneered, any residual pleasantry gone. "Pathetic." He skewered the beehive and whipped it sideways. It was dashed against the far wall as it slid from his sword point.

Angry buzzing filled the room.

The man was a blur of motion. Forward and back, he danced at the edge of the growing swarm cloud, sword whipping out in flat arcs to send parted bees to their death.

Thephos raced to the door and pulled at the iron rung. Locked.

Pintarian laughed, a malicious promise.

A bee meandered toward Thephos. He swatted it, felt the subtle plink of its tiny mass rocket to the floor. It climbed drunkenly into the air once more as Thephos backed up to the wall. In terror and awe, he watched the bladesworn's prowess unfold.

Pintarian reaved life, his blade crisscrossing his frame and eliciting quiet clicks whenever it struck one of the enraged drones. With every cut and twirl, a half-dozen more were felled, strokes so accurate and swift as to be inconceivable. The man flowed behind his blade, every movement a purity of seamless energy without waste. He twisted, froze for a heartbeat, and then reversed to go the other direction, seeming to move time backward.

The cloud of bees thinned, the floor littered with their dead.

Thephos flattened himself against the wall next to the door as much as he could. The blade had come uncomfortably close a handful of times, and to be anywhere else in the room was to invite a severed limb or worse. "Why are you doing this?"

The man pivoted, slashed. Three successive clicks. Halved bees peppered the floorboards. "There is no room for dead weight among the Dominarri. My last Awakened was as selfish and lazy as you are. Soft as fresh-baked bread. But this path requires your full dedication. A willingness to suffer in service to something greater. I see it clear! Even with powers, you lack what it takes."

The swordsman spun around, flourished his blade to either side to slay the last two bees. Sweat covered his chest and damped the tufts of bronze hair peeking from his armpits. A dozen red bumps riddled his torso. Panting softly, he assessed the stings with disgust. Not his best attempt. Lighter specks, barely healed, told of the daily toll he willingly endured for mastery of his weapon.

From the corner of his eye, Thephos caught motion—a bee with one wing crawling up his shoulder.

A blur of movement. Thephos flinched and found Pintarian had pinned the bee to the wall with the tip of his blade, severing Thephos's tunic in the process. A shallow, red streak welled across the exposed skin beneath.

Keeping the sword in place, the bladesworn gathered up behind it, his face mere inches from Thephos's. "You're to renounce your pledge and leave Enshai. Understand?"

He's like my father. The two shared the same unpleasant quality of seeing the world through a narrow lens. What they thought others should or shouldn't do was the only reality that mattered. A demand to the universe that brooked no doubt, no disagreement, and certainly, no chance of changing their mind.

The man's eyes didn't waver as he frowned. "You've yet to agree."

I can't fail Syn and Ash. "I won't." More than that, Thephos didn't want to fail himself. *If I leave, the old devil wins. And I won't let any man like him dissuade me.*

Pintarian's lip curled. "Must I teach you a harsher lesson?"

With shaking breaths, Thephos held his ground, staying still as stone, aware that the bladesworn could slash him to ribbons at any time.

A moment later, Pintarian smiled, sheathed his blade, and dressed. "You choose your enemies poorly, fool." He kicked aside the husk of the hive and retrieved the key.

"Your last Awakened..." Thephos said. "He was killed by Kashoggo?"

The man swiveled feline-slow to stare at Thephos. One side of his face bunched into a sneer. "Is that the story my father's been spreading?"

Thephos remained silent as the bladesworn laughed.

The words that followed gouged at Thephos's freshly risen courage like a pressure point. "It was *I* who killed him. Kashoggo merely nudged me in the right direction."

"Why?" Thephos squeaked, a mouse in an eagle's talons.

"Because." The man's face went slack. "He was not fit to be Dominarri."

CHAPTER FORTY-SIX

PROMISES FOR THE DEAD

A thin film blurred Barodane's eyes as if he looked through a gossamer curtain.

Sitting on the ground near his feet, an older woman with a high ponytail ran sandstone along the edge of a blade in her lap. Barodane groaned around a cramp in his stomach. "Ugh."

The rasping notes of steel elongated as the swordswoman slowed her motion.

What was her name? Barodane blinked, made to rub his eyes clear, but found his hands bound. *Ah, that's right...Merique Inari. A Kanian Remnant trained by Pyr Syat himself.* He laughed, sending pine needles just below his mouth scuttling all directions over the duff. "I'm your prisoner?"

Merique Inari paused—resumed sharpening at a quicker pace.

"You may be good with that blade, but you're going to have an abysmal time throwing me over your shoulder and walking me to Alistar."

"I won't have to."

Barodane wormed up to his knees, then dragged himself upright. He rolled to his backside and sat hunched over with his legs splayed out like a woman giving birth. The body of the knight he killed had been positioned onto his back, arms crossing the morning star cradled on his chest. The holdguard had been pulled into place beside him, sword and shield similarly posed. Both sets of their eyelids were drawn closed.

Barodane shook his head.

"Does the sight of the dead discomfit you...Prince?"

Barodane worked his tongue, dampening his gums with what little moisture he had left. Whatever Merique had poisoned him with had dried him out. Sand filled his skull, his joints, and his gut begged for water. He tried to clear his throat but only strained it, making matters worse.

Fingertips gently buoying the steel, Merique inspected her blade. "I had been a Remnant five years when the war started. Bound as we are to Alistar's protection, we were unsettled by the idea of the Ironlights fighting in the field without us. Yet, tradition is maintained for a reason. Had you failed to defeat the Twice Burned's army, Scothea may have rallied at Breckenbright, and from there, descended on Alistar. We Remnant are strong but few. Namarr may well have found itself under the rule of snakes once more."

Merique sighed, then rested her sword across her lap. Her aquiline face rotated toward Barodane. "The Mad Prince. None were more conflicted by his actions than we. For levying the crime of genocide against our enemies—the same crime our people endured at the hands of the Scoths so long ago—the Kanian Remnant now wear the stains of his actions. And yet, he may well have prevented our eradication." She rose and came to stand over him. Barodane met her gaze. While she had the traditional dark complexion and warm hazel irises of a Kanian, her demeanor was as icy as his grandmother's. "So when I tell you we are conflicted about Barodane Ironlight, I hope you understand."

None is more conflicted about me than me, sister.

The sword whirled in her hand, tip gliding with fluid ease through the air before coming to rest against Barodane's chest. "If you are a charlatan, I shall gladly dispense justice."

He'd seen bluffs before. This wasn't one of them. Merique's arm and voice were unwavering. *As it should be. I shamed her. Smeared the efforts of my people to stand on higher moral ground than those who committed genocide against them. I sank them low...as low as our most hated enemies.*

He lowered his head. "If I am the Mad Prince, perhaps you should do it anyway." Cold soaked into his skin where the blade touched, and his eyes stared back at him, reflected in the polished steel. *Who do you see?* Before he could answer, the reflection disappeared along with the sword as Merique turned on her heel.

She stepped over the dead firepit, then cocked her head as if hearing something. "Clarity on the matter fast approaches."

Hooves clopped over the stony banks of the nearby stream, the hush of displaced water following. Despite the urgency Barodane assumed his prosort felt, Garlenna would be cautious in her approach.

The jostling of her warhorse—and by the sound of it, Tohar on Scab as well—grew louder. Before long, he heard the crush and scuff of forest detritus under hoof.

He saw them weaving through the trees at a trot, somewhat off course from Barodane's position.

Tohar pointed.

Garlenna angled her horse, flicked the reins, and charged to the edge of the clearing. Gouts of rich earth kicked up behind her mount as she jerked it to a halt. Bedecked in boiled leather armor, mace hanging low in one hand, she glanced at Barodane, then Merique, but said nothing.

"I got lost trying to catch breakfast." Barodane shrugged. "Guess I got caught instead."

Garlenna's eye tripped over the dead men. She assessed Barodane. "Are you hurt?"

He shook his head.

Tohar trotted up, cursing to keep Scab under control. The warhorse whinnied and stamped as the two women watched one another, neither willing to be the first to give away what they knew.

"I told her." Barodane's chest throbbed with panic. "She knows who I am."

Garlenna's mouth was a flat line. She swept off her stallion, the speed of the movement causing a shudder of pain. *She's not fully healed yet.* He hoped Merique hadn't caught the show of weakness but doubted it. The old woman missed little. Chainmen rarely did.

Garlenna stepped within a dozen paces of Barodane—fifteen of Merique. "Did she believe you?"

"No," Merique said. "But I believe *you*."

Trees swayed before a gust of wind, enveloping them in the hush of leaves and creaking trunks. Specks of sunlight appeared on the forest floor, worms of steam rising over them.

Garlenna echoed the Remnant, speaking without saying anything. "You believe me." It was a tactic for goading more from an adversary by feeding them what they'd already said.

"You did not die at King's Crossing like he did," Merique said. "And you are hard to forget. I've seen you about the castle on this or that errand for Archprelate Alcor. You are the prosort, Garlenna Renwood."

Tohar's face jerked toward Garlenna, mouth agape. Scab bucked, nearly throwing the man.

Garlenna's eye narrowed. "If you know who we are then why is our prince still bound?"

Merique looked up at the sun-dappled canopy. "These are dark times we live in. The Shadowcrown remains, and we Remnant hold that fact heaviest in our hearts while our enemies vie for a piece of a nation now fading in its greatness. Lord Malus killed by Kurgs. Anjuhkar tearing itself apart. And now, perhaps, the Sempyrium plays its hand for power with a fake sovereign."

Garlenna scoffed. "You would besmirch the miracle at your feet in favor of a conspiracy theory?"

"Conspiracy happens to be abundant at the moment—that is undeniable. Theory on the other hand, well, let's just say the word has become useful to those who wish to discredit their opponents as they seek Namarr's crown for their own."

"We aren't lying," Barodane said. "Show her my sword."

Under Merique's watchful gaze, Garlenna sheathed her mace and withdrew his sword from Scab's saddle. The blade sang free of the scabbard. The prosort placed it on the ground midway between her and Merique for the swordswoman to inspect—though only after the Remnant had made Tohar dismount Scab and step away from the horse. "In case you have a crossbow in the saddle."

Merique took a few steps, then leaned, peering down at the gloom sword. Her brow pinched together. "That sword was lost."

"Now found," said Garlenna. "Along with the prince who bore it."

"Barodane Ironlight..." Tohar's voice was a haunted whisper.

"Or he is an impressive lookalike who stole it." Merique reclaimed her place beside Barodane. "What of Solicerames?"

"We go to retrieve it at Martyr's Isle," Barodane said. "Without overwhelming proof that I am who I say I am, we'll face more skeptics like yourself upon my return. Now, if you please..." He rolled to one hip, gesturing at her with his bound wrists to cut him free.

Garlenna made to retrieve the Ironlight family sword, but Merique's blade whipped up, level with her stare. "No closer, priestess."

Garlenna's hand lowered to the mace slung at her hip.

"He comes with me to Alistar," Merique said. "Whether he is prince or impostor, he doesn't leave my sight."

Barodane growled, "We need Solicerames."

"We *need* our prince. Games for the crown are being played out as we speak. Absent an Ironlight—*our* monarch—the Remnant are little more than slaves again. I will not let that happen."

"Present him prematurely and you'll get him killed." Garlenna's mace slipped into her hand. "He needs time to gather allies. Resources. We don't even know who his enemies are, yet. You think you'll be able to defend him in the heart of the viper's nest?"

"An easy task for the Remnant. My son, Scieffa, commands them." Merique's mouth turned up at one corner. "As to his enemies, that too is a simple matter. Anyone without Kanian blood is not to be trusted. Right now, you and your Sempyrium top the list."

At mention of Merique's son, Garlenna flinched. "You're an Inari?"

Merique sketched a shallow bow. "Indeed. Mother to the First Sword, predecessor of the White Flame. And I taught my boy all he knows."

Barodane's gut soured. He'd seen what Merique could do with a blade. If it came to violence, Garlenna would be hard-pressed. Even if she wasn't recovering from her wound.

"Listen, Merique." Garlenna's arms drifted apart, beckoning peace. "I know you do not trust me. The Archprelate is no friend of mine. That's why I left. My duty aligns with yours. Duty to the Ironlights. If there was even a chance our prince lived, I was willing to forswear my allegiance to the Sempyrium—to my gods—to find him."

Thickness pressed up in Barodane's throat as he realized how much Garlenna had sacrificed on his behalf. Her lifelong vocation had been the cost of her loyalty. Terrible truth punctured his heart. All that bled out was guilt.

She's not a prosort anymore.

"Ah, Followers of the Sempyrean—martyrs one and all. While it gladdens me to hear you rubbing dirt in Alcor's eye, I'm afraid I must insist. You prosorts are notoriously skilled liars, and this is a hunted man. If he is my prince, I won't risk him being killed or captured or turned over to the Sempyrium."

Garlenna shook her head. "If he goes to Alistar, he'll die. I'd rather face a knife on the road than a hundred in my home."

"The Remnant will—"

"Fail. They will fail. You, Merique Inari, *will* fail."

The chainman's face twisted into a sneer. "You think yourself more suited to his protection than Kania's finest?"

If Merique was anything like other Kanians, her honor was a raw nerve best avoided. Garlenna's last comment had dealt it a stinging blow, but her assault didn't let up. "You're too old. You'll never make it there."

"Old?" Pride lifted Merique's chin a menacing inch. "Shall we let steel decide who is more fit to keep him?"

"No." Barodane shot Garlenna a look. Her nostrils flared, a flush creeping up her neck, readying to answer the challenge. "We don't have to do this, Gar. We're on the same side."

"Last night, I hunted a criminal. He killed two of my men. While I claim few friends, both of them were close to me. The criminal claims to be my long-dead liege. Then a known agent of the Sempyrium arrives to tell me, 'Thank you ma'am for saying hello, but we'll be on our way.'" Merique fixed Barodane with an icy stare. "I'll sooner die than act the fool. You're coming with me. With or without your spy."

Granite slabs leaned onto Barodane's shoulders. The weight of his ancestors. The weight of their hubris. The weight of their desperation. Crushed between a past paved by his own vile autonomy and a future lived as a pawn for Namarr's unity, he felt himself withdrawing. Wrong. All of it felt wrong. *No matter where I go...*

"So be it." Garlenna flourished her mace and then unslung her shield from her destrier's tack; discomfort tugged at her cheek as she slipped her forearm through the straps and hefted it.

Barodane's heart raced, chest aching. *Shit.*

Without a sound, prosort and Remnant closed.

Garlenna circled away from Merique's outstretched sword—circled to her weak side. The older woman was shorter and had a disadvantage in reach but remained stationary. With a snort, she switched sword hands.

Her tactic nullified, Garlenna stopped circling and lined her body up behind her massive kite shield, mace cocked overhead, flanged points angled down at her opponent. If Merique wanted to hit the prosort, she'd need to be quicker side to side or draw Garlenna into dropping her guard.

The older woman frowned. "Clever."

"One of my many qualities."

Tohar edged toward the fight, club in hand, but both women shot him a look of disapproval that stopped him in his tracks.

Adder-quick, Merique lunged, quiet thrusts hunting at the edges of Garlenna's shield. Unlike so many novice warriors, the prosort didn't take the bait. The shield remained steady as she stepped back and circled away from Merique's strong side. "You'll need to come closer."

The older woman broke off her attack. "Do I?" She bent her knees slightly and swept her sword behind her hips so that its point faced away from Garlenna. Weapon partially concealed, Merique moved forward, stepping in shuffling batches of forty-five degree angles, a deadly and unpredictable dance.

The distance between them evaporated. Merique's blade hummed through the air, cleaving sparks from hammered steel. Before the motion finished, she stepped off to one side then whirled—came to a stop off the prosort's shoulder—sword whipping around and down with her. Barodane's breath caught.

With a startled grunt, Garlenna twisted at the last second and sent the blow glancing off her shield as she stumbled out of reach. With the calm of a lioness, the Remnant followed her quarry, pushing her advantage against her off-balance opponent.

Before Merique could muster another assault, Garlenna recovered and launched her own. Rushing forward with her shield, her mace looped out in a series of tight, whooshing strokes. Merique ducked, slid to one side to avoid being run over, then deflected the last.

The two about-faced, squaring off once more. Merique breathed hard, but Garlenna was heaving. Sweat clustered her hair into ruddy coils about her face. A month abed had taken its toll.

"You're fading," Merique said. "Yield now or die."

Garlenna straightened, letting her shield arm go limp. She shook the tension from it and then inhaled, deep and slow. After a few cycles, she hefted her shield back into position and clapped the rim with the head of her mace.

Merique crept forward, heavy on the back foot, ready to dodge if Garlenna barreled toward her again.

Meanwhile, the prosort seemed content to let the fight come to her.

The Remnant flicked her sword at Garlenna's eyes then crouched deep, the angle causing the prosort to momentarily block her own line of sight with her shield.

Barodane's chest turned to ice as Merique lunged, grabbing Garlenna's shield with her off hand, sword arm cocked for a killing stab the moment it was cleared. "Your left!"

Merique ripped back the shield. Her blade slipped through Garlenna's guard—skewered air. Throwing back her hips, the prosort released her shield; it dropped to the earth with a clang as Merique's sword snaked past her belly.

Garlenna swung her mace at Merique's suddenly exposed head. Most other swordsmen would have died on the spot, but Remnants transcended the term. An expert of the highest order, Merique dropped to her side and rolled. The killing blow altered course, chasing her down. Dirt and dead leaves bounced from the ground where Garlenna's mace struck.

The older woman stumbled to her feet, throwing up her blade as she fell into retreat. Garlenna pressed the advantage, her mace a flurry of flashing death. Shield gone, her dagger filled her other hand.

Backfooted, Merique blocked and ducked and evaded, poise unbroken as she defended the relentless onslaught of knife and mace. Dust swirled at the combatants' feet, clouding beams of morning sun as they fought to and fro, a flood of razor-sharp steel and instinct, sharper still, that held no room for error.

Garlenna pressed her foe hard, unwilling to give Merique a moment to strategize. The older swordswoman had proved dangerous when setting the pace of the fight.

Barodane's chest felt as though it might split open. Garlenna was wasting all of her energy on one final push. *She's going to lose.* Her face was chalk-white. Sweat dripped from her chin in a steady stream and every blow she dealt caused her to wince.

Despite Garlenna's efforts, none of her attacks came close to winning through. Merique was on the defensive but still soundly in control. Worse still, she showed far fewer signs of weariness. Two plans for victory sang out in the repeated clash of steel: Merique, banking on her opponent to falter with time and Garlenna rushing to finish it before that moment arrived.

Suddenly, a mighty oak tree loomed behind the former Remnant. As back met bark, her eyes widened at the realization of her misstep. Garlenna opened her guard, giving the swordswoman an escape. Merique's blade missed no opportunity and shot forward to take the bait.

But Garlenna was already moving aside. Trap laid. Trap closed. Her flanged mace crashed into the Remnant's hand.

Sword flung from her grasp by the blow, Merique screamed and jerked her mangled fist to her chest. Blood and flaps of flesh hung from the wounded hand as she sagged in defeat.

Garlenna glanced sidelong at Barodane with her good eye, body swelling with exertion. The moment guttered like a candle flame. Barodane exhaled in relief. "Now that we have your submission, let's—"

Garlenna rammed her fist upward, planting her dagger in the woman's chest.

"No!" Barodane squirmed in his bonds.

Merique blinked in surprise, then folded around Garlenna's fist and knife. She grabbed the prosort's forearm, and locked together, the two of them rotated to the ground. They looked almost graceful as Garlenna laid Merique on her back, like a dancer dipping their partner.

Tohar sawed Barodane's hands free and helped him to his feet. They approached. Barodane fumed.

Ghost-pale, her diaphragm pinioned, Merique sputtered blood. Her breath scraped the air. Garlenna was looking down on her, a tear in her eye. The Kanian kept gulping, attempting to fill ruined lungs.

"Dammit," Barodane growled. "You didn't have to do that."

Garlenna didn't move.

Merique's hazel eyes flicked toward Barodane before locking on the sun-splashed canopy. "My pendant..."

Tohar unfastened the topmost button of the woman's boiled leather cuirass, then fished around underneath. A chain with a gold triangle fixed to the end came free, gripped in his pudgy hand. Etched into the gold was a flaming sword, the tip pointing downward.

Merique's quivering chin pushed at Barodane. "Wear it...to honor my deat h...Prince." *I cannot begin to reclaim the honor I lost for my people. Let this be the reminder of that.* He looped the chain and pendant over his head and stood.

"We will bury you in the way of unimists," Tohar said.

At his words, a wave of calm held Merique. Then a final breath rattled from her deflated chest.

"Dammit." Barodane kicked a clod of dirt at the dead campfire. "This didn't have to happen."

In the distance, someone whistled. Barodane swiveled toward the sound.

"She was stalling. Another group come to rendezvous," Garlenna said. "We need to go."

Tohar frowned. "But I promised her a unimistic burial."

Barodane grabbed the priest by the sleeve and pulled him toward Scab, Garlenna close behind. "Trust me, the dead have no use for your promises."

They mounted, turned north, and fled.

CHAPTER FORTY-SEVEN

YOUR TURN

Ishoa sat at the Warming Place table, a storm bottled in glass. "I want Sir Gossryk and the knights of Bleeding Point here within a fortnight."

Except for Gaern Yorek who picked the grime from a fingernail, no one moved. None were willing to voice their thoughts. Thoughts that went counter to the aims of their enraged princess.

Discomfiting silence dragged in the sounds beyond the room: a chorus of bleating, a baby shrieking, a seneschal ridiculing the kitchen staff. A holdguard at the door shifted his weight from one foot to the other and fumbled his bladed staff. It clattered to the ground and he snatched it up, cursing and mumbling apology.

"You were all eager to share opinions before," Ishoa said. "What happened?"

Arick moved to her side and spoke low. "We cannot abandon—"

"We cannot abandon Bleeding Point." Ishoa waved a hand of dismissal as she echoed his words for all to hear. "I'm not daft. I know what you think, cousin. When they finish digging the graves of this war, will Bleeding Point be all that's left? Our position grows weaker by the day and gives credence to the White Wolverine Alliance's claim that I'm unfit to rule. We chase phantoms in forests while our allies are encircled and culled. Our Duchess—my great-grand-mother—rots in a prison cell." One-by-one, she challenged her council with a condemning stare. "Am I hearing correctly that this is something you're okay with?"

More silence.

Spine rigid, shoulders level, Krhalka bent at the waist to peer at the map of Namarr spread out across the Warming Place table. "You would sacrifice the most important military position we have, Highness. Not just for Anjuhkar, but Namarr as well. Such a maneuver should not be executed without hearing the wisdom of one's council first."

"So, you're telling me it wouldn't be expected, then? I can't be the only one who's heard that the element of surprise is useful in war." Ishoa stood, tented fingers and thumbs propping her over the map. "The Scarborn were already beaten back by the Knight of the Hallow Moon once. Bleeding Point will hold."

Rigga Hine shrugged. "If all their commanders take a nap for a week."

"Spies watch, Highness," said Arick. "Any departing force larger than a company will draw the White Wolverine Alliance in haste."

"It will take time for them to mount another assault of the scale needed to take it." Ishoa's lips went dry, excitement prodding her forward. *I want my grandmother back.* If the Ice Maiden were there, she'd know what to do and how to do it. "What if we could rescue our duchess from Deephollow Prison? If we do that and Bleeding Point holds, we can end this." Life might even return to normal. The thought of handing power back to Belara Frost sent a tingle of relief through Ishoa, the weight of a nation sliding from her shoulders.

Krhalka regarded her coolly. "Your grandmother is beloved by many but she will not make the difference in this war. Not now." A long, leathery finger prodded Bleeding Point on the map. "This fortress most certainly will. In the hands of the White Wolverine Alliance, they can move unfettered from north to south. They'll dig in and establish an efficient supply line."

"Not to mention, they'll cut off ours," Arick said. "And they'll entrench at key crossing points along the banks. If that happens, the war will stretch for years. They'll have time to cultivate allies. You would give them the road to victory." Arick swept the audience. "I say we bring back Sir Adus and get the princess to Alistar before—"

"I'm not retreating," Ishoa snapped. Gaern sighed. "You have something to say, beastmaster?"

"Difficult to breathe with so much fear in the air," he said. "Crowns are easily inherited but hard to keep. Harder still for those unsettled by their burden."

Ishoa's lip curled. "I aim to protect my family's Crown at any cost."

"Funny." The beastmaster smiled. "I thought Alistar was Namarr's seat of power."

"I will not run! We've already lost too much." Scarborn spears dipped into Wolst's back. Blood leaked from a half dozen gashes in Lodaris's leg. Othwii's chest caved with a sickening thunk. The shepherd's grip failed in Ishoa's hand as he called for his father one last time. The sights and sounds of failure tainted her every memory. *No more.* "I want this war finished. People are dying."

"Sometimes, they die." Gaern rose then bowed. "If you'll excuse me, I need fresh air."

The words demanding he stay seated pooled in her mouth, a bitter serum. She let him go. *Ignore the old fool and focus on the matter at hand.* Unlikable though he was, the beastmaster's approval carried great weight. Without it, doubt threatened to creep in, but she bulled forward before it could find purchase. "We'll work fast. Surprise them at Deephollow and return before the White Wolverine Alliance has a chance to muster a counter attack."

"And if a larger host intercepts us?" Arick said. "Such as the Scarborn cavalry that's unaccounted for?"

"Or the Dread Knight?" said Sir Hollem.

Rigga Hine laughed, the ruffled flesh around her aging mouth pulling into taut lines.

Ishoa relaxed back from the table. "Something humorous, Lady Hine?"

Rigga eased her head back against the chair, chin thrust out. "You're going to do what you're going to do, Princess. What are the words of those wiser than you but jokes to be laughed at, eh?"

Ishoa bristled. She searched for a clever response to scorch the woman with but nothing came. "Fine. Out of respect for your hold, I will sit longer with my decision." Gaern wanted her to have temperance. To tame herself. So far, that hadn't worked. None of the Hulka'skara teachings had brought her any closer to seeing Lodecka Warnock pay for her crimes. "In turn, I expect you all to do the same. Look past your objections for a moment, and consider the potential rewards of the plan I propose. If we do this, we remove our enemy's best leverage. We *can* win. And we won't have to wait for the Collective to do it. That will show our strength—a united Anjuhkar under Namarr. Mistress Krhalka." Ishoa locked gazes with the High Hand. "I want whichever jurati spies you can spare descending on the northeast. They are to infiltrate enemy positions and sabotage weapons armor, and supply wains. Poison wells. Set fire to barracks—sow chaos at every turn, anything that will slow our enemies."

Krhalka inclined her head. "I'll send birds tonight."

"Good." Ishoa adjourned the council with the slightest of bows.

A whisper followed her to the door. Rigga, old and apparently incapable of controlling the volume of her voice, said to Hollem, "...Destined to die like her uncle."

The clumsy guard had pulled back the door a scant few inches when Ishoa slammed it open with a resounding bang.

Ishoa flew from the Warming Place, fists balled, insides bunched, unsure of the right choice but knowing that at some point something had to give or she would watch her nation crumble.

One week, that's all I'm giving them. Arick wanted her to flee to Alistar, to bide her time until the Collective convened and then play the game of politics with sycophants she hardly knew. *If I can't even gain traction in this shitheap, how am I supposed to do it with dukes and magnates?*

Krhalka seemed the only one capable of adjusting her perspective. *And I mean to deconstruct her Jurati when this is over.* There was a sliver of guilt in that fact Ishoa didn't like to consider.

The coattails of her cloak snapped in the wind as she made her way to Gaern Yorek's quarters. The delay in decision-making made her desperate for progress; if she couldn't get it from the external, she might find it by going inward.

Her fist rattled the gray door of the beastmaster's room. A few seconds later, it creaked open. A meek face peered at her from the shadows. Ishoa's breath caught. She stepped back, careful not to inhale too deep. "Where's your master?"

The troll watched her, eyes flicking up and down the length of her in unreadable assessment.

Knowing Rakeema was close by was all that allowed her to come face-to-face with the creature. Her hand found further comfort around her sword hilt. Despite Ishoa's limited interaction with Wiir, the troll didn't seem to share any of the ferocity of those she'd fought upon the Ice King's slopes.

Nevertheless, her knuckles went white around her blade hilt. "Bring me Gaern Yorek."

The door flew open. Wiir slunk off as the beastmaster replaced him. The old Anjuhk glanced after his pet, then at Ishoa. "You scare him."

"Oh, do I?" Ishoa scoffed. "Has he been strangled by a teen girl? Or maybe his friend was killed by a pack of wild princesses?" She waved a hand before her nose, warding off Wiir's foul scent. "Why do you keep him? Why not return him to the wild with the rest of his kind?"

She made to enter, but Gaern stepped to block her.

"What?" Ishoa blinked at the stunted man.

"Wiir has been through more than you know, Highness. If you insist on being cruel, consider your training over."

Her eyes narrowed. "And if I command it to continue?"

The beastmaster chuckled then slammed the door in her face.

She cursed. Rakeema stared up at her and gave a languid blink. As bereft of answers as she was, it seemed unlikely she'd become a Hulka'skara without a willing teacher. Already, she'd failed miserably with the few things the man from Akulsa had shown her. And that was when he wished for her to succeed. Guilt forced ghosts to the fore. *Lodaris would be ashamed to see me acting this way. He would never have tolerated such petulance.*

She choked down her pride and pounded on the door.

It flew open. "That was quick."

"I wish to tell it I'm sorry," she said.

"*He.*" Gaern's brow furrowed, a fleshy terrace framed in thick, snarled hair. "And there's no need. He heard you." The beastmaster stepped into daylight. A moment later, Wiir followed him out. The troll wore robes that dragged along the ground, and a cowl so deep she wondered how the creature saw anything.

The Hulka'skara hobbled over to an aspen beside the training yard and snatched up a fallen branch. "You want to move at a faster pace, do you?" After snapping off a few twigs to make it resemble more of a sword, he stood across from Ishoa and Rakeema. "I attack. You defend. Simple."

"I don't have a practice sword. Only steel."

He smiled. "I doubt we'll get that far."

Ishoa glanced at Rakeema. They hadn't done anything but talk in so long. Now, at least, they were training in a way she was familiar with. Wolst had taught her well. Her pulse quickened as she drew her sword. "Sajac." Rakeema stalked under her shield-arm, eyes honing in on Gaern.

He stared at the anjuhtarg, and then whispered, "Sajac."

Rakeema bounded over to him and whirled into a fighting stance. Ishoa locked gazes with her ice tiger. There was nothing of their year-long bond in evidence. A chill swept along Ishoa's spine. "Sajac!" she yelled.

He crossed the space whistling, Rakeema creeping along beside him, hackles raised.

"Rakeema!" Ishoa's eyes darted from beastmaster to ice tiger. "Rakeema, Sajac!"

Gaern dug at a gap in his teeth and spoke as if ticking banal items off a banal list. "Heeti."

Rakeema leapt.

Razor-sharp claws extended toward Ishoa's face, a parted muzzle with bared fangs just behind. Ishoa squealed in terror and stumbled backward, heaving up her shield in defense at the last moment.

A single word chased Rakeema through the air, neither stern nor soft, loud nor quiet. Weight slammed into Ishoa, hurling her onto her backside as claws raked the banded steel of her shield. The ice tiger landed on Ishoa's midsection, forcing the air from her lungs in a violent explosion and bearing her flat to the ground. Luckily, Rakeema's claws had retracted with the beastmaster's last command.

Panting, Ishoa stared into her anjuhtarg's unblinking, emerald eyes, vaguely aware of the burning pain in her stomach where the war cat compressed her insides. They watched each other. Rakeema appeared remorseless in her betrayal.

Gaern shuffled up to Ishoa and tapped her on the crown thrice with his stick. "Dead. Dead. Dead."

Ishoa shoved Rakeema off and scrambled to her feet. "So are you going to just keep lording over me, or are you going to teach me how you did that?"

"I have been teaching you. Well, trying to at least." The old Anjuhk shot her a puzzled look. "This was another invaluable lesson."

Ishoa studied her ice tiger. The little traitor sat at attention beside the beast-master, awaiting the next command. "Do share."

The man from Akulsa shrugged. "Your anjuhtarg is dangerous."

"I'm aware."

He held up a finger. "Your anjuhtarg is dangerous, but you are not. You think we're here to train a tiger but the truth is, she's here to train *you*, Princess." He left Rakeema sitting there as he hobbled back into position. "Let's try again. This time, be more dangerous."

Ishoa spat like Enkita Vulkuu would have done, then slapped her sword against her shield's rim. *Come on, Isha. Be dangerous.* "Sajac!"

Nothing.

"Sajac." Rakeema raced to Gaern's side.

Ishoa growled frustration. "How am I supposed to get better at this if you don't give me a chance?"

"I did." He gestured at Ishoa and Rakeema ran back over to her. "Again."

As the command left Ishoa's mouth, she saw Gaern's mouth move. She was louder, drowning him out. Nevertheless, Rakeema ran to him. "Stop doing that!"

"What's the problem, Princess?" he said. "Struggling for control of the situation?"

Rage burned in her breast.

"Anger is fear's ugly cousin. You think it will get you where you want to go, eh? Did you notice Lodecka Warnock showing her anger? No? That's because it's weak. If who you are is weak, then by all means, show me all your wrath." The Hulka'skara stepped back, squaring to Rakeema. "You're so in love with it, you may as well use it. Tell your ice tiger to rip my throat out. Here—I won't even fight back." He tossed his stick away and lifted his chin, then drew a finger and thumb across his mouth. "My lips are sealed. I won't stop you."

Ishoa glanced from war cat to beastmaster. Her heart bumped against her breastbone. The command sheltered in the safety of places better left in silence, but she dragged it from the depths anyway. "Heeti!" There was an edge to it like never before—petulant defiance. A child's hope for retribution, regrettable as soon as it was uttered, yet satisfying all the same.

Rakeema squeezed her eyes shut and then settled onto her belly in the dirt. She rolled over then twisted to scratch an itch on her back, her gray, striped fur tangling with bits of bark. Ishoa hung her head.

"You're no danger to anyone but yourself," the beastmaster said. "Not like this. Not while you covet your anger like a sacred idol." His voice was condemning. "You can't hide fear with anger. And you can't cover the past with whatever rash decision comes to mind next. You *are* a failure. A disappointment."

He gave a hiss and left the training yard.

Wind wrapped her cloak tight about her legs. The patch of muddy snow at her feet held her focus. In her periphery, she noted that Wiir had remained behind. "What do you want?" A sob clogged her chest. She wanted to be alone.

Wiir returned her stare a long moment before drifting away.

Ishoa rounded, turning her ire on Rakeema. "What a good little war cat you were! You're the disappointment." The ice tiger rolled onto all fours to shake dirty snow from her coat. Ishoa shooed her. "Lehrd."

Rakeema took off to hunt mice while Ishoa slumped in defeat. Gaern had proved her worst fears true. *No enemy but fear...and I'll never be free of it.*

The sound of footsteps brought her about-face.

"Princess Ishoa?" An unfamiliar face greeted her. Slathered up to the knees in filth, the man wore a deep cowl and heavy cloak. He had come very close—within ten paces—before announcing himself. One hand was held aloft in peace, palm facing outward at his waist while the other hid amid the folds of his cloak. He bowed low. The mirrored oak of Shadowheart was stitched to his breast.

"You're a treekin?"

The man nodded. "That's right." There'd been a tear in the armpit of his tunic when his hand was raised. A long gash of severed cloth. Ishoa searched the man's scruffy face. Puffs of steam clouded his features in the limp slant of his deep hood. "I have a message for you."

Prickles climbed the back of Ishoa's head. "From whom?" The flesh around her ears tightened. Ringing, faint at first but growing with every crushing heartbeat, filled her ears. She stepped back, putting a little distance between herself and the stranger.

He scanned the quiet yard, his side profile surfacing to the light. A beard of no more than a couple of weeks. Two thin, white lines along his cheek were hidden beneath it. Anyone might have missed the marks if they weren't intent on finding them.

Ishoa's hand flew to the hilt of her sword as the man jerked a blade from the shadows of his cloak and closed with her in a rush.

Her sword rose to meet his. Steel clashed, jarring her from wrist to shoulder. Their blades skipped apart and she nearly dropped hers from aching fingers. He hammered at her side, bowing her guard inward as her sword came slower to the defense. He was stronger. Faster. More skilled. Seconds remained.

Then she was dead. "Hel—"

The Scarborn assassin lunged, followed it with a kick to her chest that sent her flying into the wall. Stone slammed into her back, knocking the wind from her lungs. With a sharp gasp, she crumpled to hands and knees. His shadow fell across the snow before her.

Chest afire, arms numb, she raised her face.

The assassin brandished his sword—the cleanest part of him. Frenzied eyes drank in the satisfaction of a mission accomplished. "The message," he panted, "is from Lodecka Warnock." A scream for help died in Ishoa's chest, spasming muscles unwilling to release. Helpless, she wheezed. He hefted his notched sword for the killing blow. "She says 'die like the dog you are.'"

A blur of white and gray collided into the man's side. Taken off his feet, he hurtled sideways. Ripping cloth and a savage growl. Rakeema pushed off his thrashing form, alighting on the ground a few arm spans from her foe.

A pair of puncture wounds gushed from the man's shoulder where his tunic had been torn. Shreds of cloak flipped and twirled in the wind as he shot to his feet, arm limp at his side. Pale and sweating, he switched his sword from left to right hand. Twisted yellow teeth clamped together in a wince as he flourished the blade. "Here kitty."

"No," Ishoa wheezed—sucked in a whimper of air. "Sajac."

Instead of following the command, Rakeema squared off with the wounded Scarborn. Vision mottled with orbs of light, Ishoa struggled to stand—lurched sideways, off-balanced—and then launched herself at the man.

The assassin stepped back and pivoted, slapping aside her weapon. She sailed past and landed hard on her palms in the muddy snow. Grit jumped into her eyes. Acutely aware of her exposed back, she crawled forward, wiping at the burning sediment with the back of her hand.

Behind her, Rakeema yowled. Ishoa whirled onto her back just in time to see her anjuhtarg retreating, a front paw cradled in the air, a shallow cut dripping blood.

Ishoa staggered upright as the Scarborn spat and turned his attention to her. "Your turn."

Breath finally regained, Ishoa yelled for help.

Wild eyes bore down on her. She danced back from the Scarborn's flurry as a soundless shadow rose behind him. The assassin's blade cocked back to skewer Ishoa, but a clawed hand grabbed him by the elbow and dug in. The

Scarborn grabbed Wiir's white-furred forearm as it slipped around his throat. They wrestled for position, ribbons of blood flinging onto the snowy yard as the troll's claws dug deeper into the man's flesh.

With a wail of pain, the assassin dropped his sword and then shot his hips backward into his attacker's midsection. Wiir's hood jolted off his head, revealing an apish face and a set of stunted horns.

Ishoa angled for an opening, but the two moved too erratically for a clean stab. She couldn't attack without putting Wiir at risk, so she kicked the assassin's blade out of reach. The man growled and snapped his skull back into the troll's face.

The C'Dathun wilted.

Ishoa stepped and slashed, hewing flesh, tendon, and artery. The assassin frowned, eyes locking onto something in the distance as a ruby drape spread down the side of his neck. He tilted—stumbled to the side a step—then plummeted face-first into the stained snow.

Moments later, a bewildered Sir Hollem arrived accompanied by a handful of shepherds.

Dizzy and still fighting for breath, Ishoa leaned over the pommel of her sword stuck into the ground. Hine holdguard rushed over to Wiir, bladed-staves poised. Ishoa commanded they halt.

"This monster is with you, Highness?" They watched the troll, curved blades hovering over him as he regained consciousness.

"He saved me." She watched Wiir, hate leaking from her. *He saved me.* Defenses crumbled. Gratitude flowed.

Wiir wasn't her enemy. Her past was. The fear living there pinned her down and strangled her hopes. Time and again, it dragged her into the voiceless dark. Trolls trying to kill her while a Scarborn defended her. A Scarborn trying to kill her and a troll saving her. The stitches holding the terms of friend and enemy together burst apart.

Fear was not an evil to be avoided nor outmaneuvered. More so, it was a wild beast inside that acted as a guardian, protecting her from a past full of hurts rendered and possibilities reduced.

But the path forward belonged to Ishoa alone. And she would take it without fear.

She called Sir Hollem to her side as Gaern Yorek arrived. Rakeema was hurt and missing. The beastmaster shoved through the holdguard as they stepped back to let Wiir stand.

"I take responsibility for this attack," Sir Hollem said in a fluster. "There will be a harsh discussion with my men at the gate. I accept whatever punishment Your Highness deems appropriate."

She ignored his declarations. "Sir Hollem, send your brother a message. He's to return to the Manger without delay. I'll be sending a bird to Sir Gossryk as well. We leave for the north as soon as we're able."

She didn't wait for a response and went in search of Rakeema.

CHAPTER FORTY-EIGHT

THE HEADLESS SNAKE

There was a room in the bowels of Darkfall, heavily guarded by the Blessed Cadre, raek knights, and renegade Shadii. Essuhd claimed the key to deposing the Arrow of Light lay within, and so, tasked Valka with gaining access.

"What is it?"

"Think of it as your daughter's salvation," Essuhd had replied. Then he added, "All we know is that the measures taken to protect it far outstrip those of anywhere else in the keep. Siddaia visits it often. That says enough."

Valka had to agree, though questioned how he hadn't heard of it.

"Like I've been telling you." Essuhd had reached into the inky folds of his clothes. "Your messiah holds many secrets." He blew Mimborean sleeping powder from his palm.

Fine white dust billowed into Valka's face. He gasped, lurched to one side of the bed...

Valka woke some hours later with the dawn. *Praise the light.* While his gratitude that he'd not been slain was fresh, Essuhd's warning helped him resist the urge to give thanks through prayer.

He glanced at the golden arrow emblem resting on his stone altar. Woodenly, he dressed then swept from the room to attend a meeting with Rhul.

For two days, he delayed the start of his mission. If he could find a way out of it, he would. At that first council meeting, he nearly told Siddaia, a move that would inevitably start a manhunt for the Shadii master. But no matter how fast the forces of the Light acted, it wouldn't be fast enough. Nera would die.

After the next days' meeting, he'd tried a different tactic in private with the prophet. "Your sermon on truth, my Light. I've been ruminating on the subject and wondering which truth should be prioritized. Truth in relation to the self, or truth in relation to others?"

"What difference is there, Ikarai, when they are one and the same?"

Valka frowned. "I am trying to live out your principles, my Light, but finding it difficult to do so. My duties as a general inhibit them."

"Such dichotomous thinking breeds separation. You from yourself. Your true self from others. Truth is not some system we use to analyze all that passes through our mind, Ikarai. It is a clear place within, where silence reigns and peace grows. It is from there that we extend ourselves to others, and into that place that we invite them."

Silence hung between them. Valka cleared his throat, but Siddaia beat him to words. "You're lying now. Lying about your reasons...dancing past the truth when it would benefit you to state what you desire. You wish to know whether it's okay to lie sometimes, just as you're doing now?"

Shame poured over him, a molten iron cast that burned as it cooled, locking him in place. Meeting those hauntingly deep brown eyes, he fought the urge to flee and nodded. If he'd learned one thing of his Light, it was that all would be forgiven if owned.

"Your truth is what you make it, Ikarai," Siddaia said. "A perception of what is right."

"So...absolute truths don't exist." Valka made a show of thinking, reaching for something to remain afoot in the conversation. "In the hands of an exemplary liar, this sermon could be a dastardly weapon."

"So it could." Siddaia's expression was tranquil. "There will always be those who believe liars and those that don't. Fate finds the lucky, fate finds the fool. Such is the folly of dredging the answers of the soul from the hearts and minds of neighbors. The truth within, be it absolute or absent, expressed or suppressed, is what matters most, for perception is the ruler all."

The boy prophet took Valka's hand, enclosing it between his own, gaze unflinching, boring to the back of the general's skull. "You are eaten by doubt. Your trust shaken. Inside and out."

Valka's pulse pushed into his ears. "Have you lied to me, my Light?"

The response came with cutting speed. "Of course, Ikarai. Of course. But it does not shame me. I am truth. The absolute. I do what I must to keep you safe. And you, my brother, still stand on dubious shores. One foot in the sand, one in the tide. I fear if you had heard them, you would have been washed away—forever lost to me. You were not ready."

Hope pumped through Valka, abashed before his messiah, waiting to hear of the secret room and the lie he was not ready for.

Siddaia patted the back of his hand, then strode away, bare feet slapping the marble floor. Valka's hand dropped heavy to his side. *A fool's hope dies quickest.*

In his heart, Valka was a loyal follower, but Siddaia's declaration that he'd yet to prove himself shook him to his core. *I'm no closer to the room.* He wanted nothing more than to prove himself to his messiah, but time was dwindling and he refused to let Nera die.

It's as if I must choose between my daughter and my Light. I betrayed one king yesterday—betray the chosen son of the Sempyrean today. Will there be a tomorrow where I betray Nera? Competing forces tore at him, almost paralyzing.

But the price of inaction was too dire to allow.

The Blessed Cadre had been with Siddaia for years. To penetrate the confidence of that inner circle would take time he didn't have. And if Siddaia was truly a transcendental being gifted to Scothea from the gods, he would survive even Essuhd's greatest efforts, regardless of what Valka did or didn't do. He leaned hard into that line of thought.

He shook his head. *No, there has to be another way.*

But on the third morning since Essuhd's visit, he came awake to Nera's screams. Half of his household guard beat him to her chamber but they'd been ordered to stay outside by Yanos.

"What happens here?" Valka shoved his men aside to enter.

On one side of the room, the captain held a quaking Nera in his arms on the floor, her face smeared red. "She's okay," Yanos said and gestured with his chin to one of the tunnel-like windows ten feet above the bed.

The headless body of a rock viper was draped over the lip of the opening, blood draining from its graying corpse in a streak down the wall. Blood pattered onto Nera's pillow in a steady drip.

Valka went cold. "Who has seen this?"

"Only us," Yanos replied.

"Keep it that way." Valka hurried to his room.

"Father."

He pivoted and found his daughter's haunted eyes regarding him. A rare, cool blue. Once, long ago, the same eyes had watched him with abject fear. Now, they pleaded with him to keep her safe.

He crossed the room and knelt beside her.

Her voice trembled. "Who did this?"

"I don't know," he lied. "Could be that a hawk flew into your window with its breakfast and left it there."

"It's punishment, mistress," said Yanos. "The Holy Instruments see the lack of faith you've put in their son and send a symbol of their displeasure."

Valka's face whipped toward his junior officer but the man's gaze stayed fixed on Nera. Rage boiled in the general, his desire to strike the man mounting.

Nera shocked his wrath to silence with a solemn nod. "You've tried to tell me. Both of you have tried to tell me." Wiping away her tears, she pushed herself out of Yanos's embrace and sat with her back to the wall.

Isn't this what I wanted? Valka swallowed the stone in his throat, then touched Nera's arm. "It is good that you see the signs." *And better that you do not know how much danger you're in, if I fail to do my part.*

He addressed Yanos as he stood. "Dispose of the snake. Find a dumbstruck mute to clean up the mess. I'll not have word spread that questions my daughter's faith."

Yanos had followed Valka to his feet and saluted. "Her honor will be as my own, General."

"It is so," Valka said, and left.

A minute later, the door to his room clicked shut. First, he tossed his bedding. Nothing. He surveyed the chamber, hunting along its edges for clues or etchings in the stone. A thought struck him. He rounded. A pillar of sunlight filtering in from the tunnel-window over his bed illuminated Siddaia's banner on the altar.

Approaching, he drew back the first fold. A strip of rolled parchment sat within. The message was written in blood. Rock viper blood, he assumed.

Remember our deal, it said.

He lit a candle at the altar. A thin, black tendril trailed upward, bowed toward the window in the air as the note rocked on its curling edges until it was naught but blackened remnants.

Afterward, he prayed to the Sempyrean. Prayed to the Holy Instruments. To his namesake, King Ikarai, the Golden Scepter. He prayed for guidance, wisdom, and trust in himself.

Once finished, he plotted how best to betray his messiah.

A pair of Grimshields accompanied Valka down the steps to the raek burrows. Of all the paths he could take, this was the only one left to him. If Essuhd's Shadii couldn't gain access to the room by way of subterfuge, then Valka safely assumed he would have no better luck. They had broken into his home in the dead of night without alerting his household guard and done so again to plant a headless snake in Nera's room. Yet this room, they could not access.

The idea of force, too, was a laughable one. Essuhd had said that Gishek Ghuul, Zantheppi, and the Black Hand Marionette guarded the room in shifts alongside a dozen raek knights. Shadii loyal to Siddaia likely lurked somewhere nearby as well.

That left Valka with cunning.

The first thing he'd done was track Rhul's movements. While the raeklord hadn't been admitted to the room, he seemed to know of it, and monitored the guard shifts of his knights daily.

Valka's plan was quite simple. An honest lie. A naive curiosity. An explanation of happenstance he hoped might produce few enough foundations for suspicion.

It took a week for his plan to culminate in fruitful results. No headless snakes or other warnings had been delivered in that time, so he knew Essuhd saw the merits of what he attempted.

On his third trip past the raek burrows on his way to the dungeons, he intercepted Rhul the Red. If he'd timed it right, the man was on his way to oversee the changing of the guard at the door.

"Lord Rhul." Valka dipped, a shallow bow of equals.

The towering man returned the gesture, the knight behind him saluting as he would to any officer. Torchlight gleamed along the curves of their heavy plate armor in the dimly glowing hallway.

"Light be with you, General." Rhul angled away, his knight preparing to follow.

"A moment, Lord Rhul."

Twin horns spread from the sides of the great helm tucked into the crook of the raeklord's arm. He twisted around, white cape swirling about his legs. The majority of Scotheans were shorter, darker of skin, with narrowed eyes, but Rhul bore the markings of ancient blood. A descendant of the first cave dwellers, he was titanic in stature with mud-blond hair and a lighter skin tone.

Valka gestured at the raek knight beside Rhul. "If you're not using your man there, I may have need of him." He had rehearsed the story a score of times alone, playing out unexpected outcomes, and if necessary, developing last stand statements to get him out of danger. Though, doing so could mean failure, and failure likely meant Nera's life. *How far am I willing to push?* He prayed he wouldn't need to find out.

Rhul stared down at Valka, horseshoe chin unwavering. "Right now?"

"You've not heard?" He waited a heartbeat to see if the rumors he'd planted among his soldiers had reached the man. Normally, he'd have let such a story marinate longer to ensure an added layer of validation, but time was precious. "The most recent batch of voar have been struggling to adhere to commands."

"They're emotional creatures." Rhul gave a knowing nod. "They must sense the change in rule. The rising spirit of our people."

Valka grinned. *That may be so.* "Indeed. There are two we've been watching. Less predictable than the rest. I fear they must be put down."

Rhul looked back at his man, expression indecipherable. "Alas, my man is needed elsewhere."

Valka's heart thudded against his breastbone. "I promise, it will not take long." Valka turned halfway toward the descending stair. *Come on now.* When they hesitated, he frowned deeply, a false display of concern. "Is there something amiss? Is our Light in danger?"

Rhul spoke flatly. "You have only two with you to do the work of five. Why?"

Doubt snapped at Valka. He felt his cheek twitch. *Don't worry about his inquiry. You prepared for this.* "A violent outburst that killed a female—I've just heard. The beast must be destroyed without delay." In truth, he'd gone down hours earlier and given the weakest female he could find a pound of extra dog meat. Her end had been swift. Tongueless and docile, the voar made perfect set pieces in his scheme.

"I cannot spare him."

"A higher priority, then?" Valka arched an eyebrow. His tone dripped with offense. "Is there a council meeting I've not been made aware of?" He flipped his hand toward Rhul's knight. "One that a low-ranking officer has been invited to before I have, hmm?"

Rhul's gaze was implacable. "No." A cluster of seconds came and went, then the raeklord spoke over his shoulder to his knight. "Go ahead to your post."

The knight's great helm twisted toward his commanding officer. "Our Light said the room must be—"

Rhul's hand lifted slightly, a subtle but powerful gesture that silenced the knight. "Go. I'll be along shortly."

Without another word, the raek knight pivoted and marched up the stairs. Rhul swept past Valka and his Grimshields, leading the way down to the voar pits.

The work to be done was dirty and brutal. Each voar was chained multiple times over by a collar to iron beams driven into the stone wall. The practice was redundant, however. Since the Voar Uprising in the early years of the breeding program, Valka's distant predecessor had adjusted rutting strategies to ensure subsequent offspring harbored minimal personality traits resembling humans. The removal of their tongues, too, had been an ingenious move. Now, to revolt or disobey was to go without a meal, and the next meal was the extent of the creatures' forethought.

Valka and his Grimshields, along with the guards stationed in the pits, hauled taut the chains of a voar with a red X painted on its back. Sensing its impending doom, the beast thrashed and roared, but ultimately was subdued enough for Rhul to behead it. The second one they caught unawares and it emitted a single grunt before the work was over.

Winded, Valka thanked Rhul for his help as they ascended the narrow stairway out of the pits.

"Brave of you to do what those under your charge should," Rhul muttered.

Valka shrugged. "The Arrow of Light has given me new life. Why ask my soldiers to do dangerous work I'm unwilling to do myself? We are one, are we not?"

The raeklord stared ahead. "It's good to see you walking in the light, brother."

On that, we agree. Valka cursed the circumstances that had brought him to this dark path. Rhul had been the first of Siddaia's followers to welcome him into the fold. "For your part in it, I thank you." Valka's stomach lurched with every step, sick with guilt. Bile burned at the base of his throat. He swallowed. *Here we go.* "I couldn't help but overhear you speaking with your officer about a room he needed to guard...is this something I should be concerned about?"

Rhul claimed the next step, then slowed to a stop. Valka halted, expecting the explanation any moment. None came as the raeklord studied his face in the torchlit passage. "Something the matter, Lord Rhul?" To show anything less than offense at the raeklord's penetrating stare was to court suspicion, so he returned the man's gaze with measured tenacity, and his voice reflected the same. "The threat of a long-held look does not become you. If I've said something upsetting, do me a kindness and state it plain."

The men behind them shifted their weight uneasily from foot to foot. Valka's heart slapped his breast bone. Sweat trickled down the back of his neck.

Rhul broke eye contact and looked up the passageway. "Apologies, General. Allow me to show you the room."

A sliver of joy thrummed through Valka. Despite the thick padding under his armor, relief sighed cool across his skin.

As he started after Rhul, the man rounded. "Just you." He shot Valka's soldiers a reproachful look.

His pushback was minimal but he made a necessary show of it before ordering his Grimshields about other duties at the first intersection of tunnels they crossed.

Valka followed the raeklord along twisting passageways. Without Essuhd's intelligence about the room's location, he would never have found it on his own. They approached the tunnel leading to the cavern where the room was located...

And passed it.

Rhul did not slow.

Valka stared back at the shadowed avenue in puzzlement, then at Rhul. The raeklord's shoulders were square and steady; his gold-enameled pauldrons nearly scraped the arching rock walls of the narrow passage to either side. Another ensconced torch came at them, and Rhul maneuvered an arm backward to avoid it with the casual ease and grace of a Malzacy night devil.

They continued upward.

Wherever they were heading, it certainly wasn't to the promised room. Valka's mouth went dry. He slipped his fingers around Mournfang's hilt at his belt and shimmied it to a looser position just in case he needed to clear it quickly. If he were a younger man with the element of surprise, perhaps he could take Rhul. It mattered little how much armor and muscle the man had when Valka's ax could cleave through it like butter.

But images of the man lifting a bear and decapitating a voar in a single swipe dealt Valka a dose of bone-rattling reality. *Fighting will do little good.*

The dimness of the tunnel gave way to a growing portal of light ahead. The amount of steps they'd ascended had made sodden sacks of Valka's legs. He cursed his age, gritted his teeth, and powered through the pain. Wind moaned down the stairway's dark throat as they continued the climb.

A pair of raek knights, covered head to heel in gleaming gold plate, waited at the next junction, wind stirring their pristine white cloaks. Without slowing, Rhul gestured and they fell in behind a now wheezing Valka. Prickles swept up his neck as he was forced to let his hand fall from Mournfang. A foolhardy comfort, but a comfort, nonetheless. At any moment, and from any direction, he could be cut down.

Best to say my prayers. If he wasn't already desperately seeking an exit, a path to survival, he might have. He might have seen the smiling face of Nera and asked her for forgiveness. He might have begged his Light for another chance at redemption.

Instead, he searched the unfamiliar passage for the next dark archway to sprint down, as scared as the voar had been before in the final seconds of its execution. *Trapped like an animal.* His palm itched for the useless safety of Mournfang's handle.

They rounded a corner. Sunlight punched Valka in the eyes as he came to a stop and shielded his face. Wind heaved at a sky-terrace, a fungal disc inserted into the side of a cliff, drowning out his hearing.

He blinked rapidly, sight adjusting.

Backlit by blinding sun and azure sky, the silhouette of a lone figure sat cross-legged on the open-air marble platform. A hawk prowled the distant horizon over one of the boy's shoulders, his dark hair flapping lazy and banner-like over the other.

Unperturbed by the blinding sun, Rhul had continued forward to stand beside the boy. "My Light, it was as you predicted." The raeklord faced Valka, expression unreadable. "He asked about the room."

Rhul was a man willing to betray Scothea in service to a brighter future. A man willing to kill without hesitation. A man accustomed to a life of dangerous choices and bitter duties. A man like Valka.

Today, however, he was the better at it.

Valka laid calm over seething, cold dread. *Give them nothing to use against you...you're not condemned just yet.* "My Light. What's this about?"

Despite the activity swirling around him, Siddaia had remained motionless, facing the wind and the sun and the distant mountains with a serenity that could be felt by proximity alone.

The gravity of the moment, of Valka's likely execution, loomed. And yet, the overwhelming experience he felt as he laid eyes on his messiah was admiration.

A few seconds of peace gusted by. Siddaia's head turned to the side, not quite far enough to see his general. "It pains me to know you've been lying, Ikarai."

A spear of terror rammed into Valka's chest. They knew of his treachery, and now, they would close the trap. *I've failed everyone. My daughter, my nation, my Light.*

The hawk in the distance banked, shrieked, then descended.

So too would the headsman's ax.

CHAPTER FORTY-NINE

RECOGNITION

B arodane stared at Garlenna's back as they fled. Her cloak snapped and fluttered, the hem taunting him. He slapped it from his face then angled Scab farther off to the side. Sparse countryside stretched before and behind, a dried-out belly of land, well-bouldered, and broken by thin herds of stunted pine.

Upwards of five but no more than ten had pursued them from the forest marshland. All day, and now, into night, the gradient of their course gradually rose. With the landscape so stripped of foliage, their chances of escape faded by the minute.

But Barodane didn't have the ability to be afraid—not when he was still so angry.

Why the fuck did you do that, Gar?

Merique was beaten, disarmed. The agony on the older woman's face chased him as much as those hunting them. At least the men he'd killed had been armed. *Twist of fate, that, me the more honorable, and Gar the lesser.*

A twist of fate he hated. He needed her to be his rock.

Garlenna reined in her destrier and wheeled around. Scab flew past a few steps before following suit at Barodane's direction. Tohar nearly lost his grip on the prince in the sudden movement.

The man stunk of grease and sour drink despite never having a drop when they'd been in the marsh. But Garlenna was heavier, the least efficient for the horses to double up with, so Barodane had been gifted with the burly priest gripping his waist like an overgrown child. *Lucky me.*

Garlenna spoke between ragged breaths, her conditioning not yet returned. "So long as we keep riding in moonlight, we won't lose them." While they hadn't seen their pursuers but once along a ridge that morning, they heard them on occasion whenever one picked up the trail and whistled to the others over the distance.

Luckily, their pursuers showed more compassion than Garlenna had. If they'd have taken the time to bury Merique, they'd never have caught up, and if they'd left her, Barodane would have already been caught, so it was safe to assume they bore the Remnant's body.

"Well we can't ride in the pitch of fucking dark, now, can we?" Barodane spit the words, contempt poorly hidden.

Garlenna scanned the horizon, all heavy silhouettes in the moonlight. "This way."

She followed a path down a defile to their left.

Stone rolled up under Barodane as he descended after Garlenna. Pitch-black night welcomed him within like the endless throat of some titanic serpent. Scab's hooves clopped over the bowed, misshapen floor, a sound king to all others. In the blinding dark, Barodane's shadowguard pauldron grated against an unseen jut of granite.

Overhead, a river of stars filled the space between files of stone.

A minute later, they squeezed out of the rocky embrasure onto an expanse of tree-spotted lowlands. More of the same terrain but a step lower. A hundred yards to their left, the earth tapered off into a steep gorge. Forward and right put them back in the path of their pursuers.

Garlenna hissed frustration and cast about.

"Maybe you should double back, get behind our foes and dispatch them," Barodane growled. He stared back in the direction they'd come. "That's what you're good at. Put a dagger in your hand and—"

"This is no time. We need cover."

"She's right," Tohar said from behind, his breath a sour cloud. "We need to hide, my Prince."

Garlenna and Barodane spoke in unison. "Don't say that."

"The only trees I've seen are a half mile back," Garlenna said.

"That's a stupid plan. We'll run right into the masons...or the Crown Justice, or..." Barodane cursed. "Whoever the fuck that is back there."

Garlenna spoke in a strangled tone. "By the time they find our trail, we'll be behind them."

"You mean they'll be in front of us. Between us and Martyr's Isle. Genius fucking idea."

Scab flicked his mane back and started to search for food, but Barodane jerked the reins to keep him in line. The disgruntled horse swung his head back and clomped his teeth near Barodane's knee as if to say, "fuck you too."

"It may be a fight," Garlenna said, "but it's also our only way to slip past them."

"There could be ten knights back there." Barodane scoffed. "Sure you can kill an old woman in a duel, but even you can't survive those odds."

Garlenna shook her head and flicked her warhorse's reins. Riding up to the wall of rock, she skirted it, heading back toward a point where it converged with the last bit of land before dropping into the gorge.

Tohar whispered in Barodane's ear. "She didn't like that, my Prince."

Barodane clicked his tongue and wheeled Scab. "Shut up."

They followed the bulwark of tumbledown stone in silence, listening for riders.

"Her actions pained her more than they did you," Tohar said. "Give her grace. She carries the fate of Namarr on her shoulders."

"I thought I did."

"Until you wear the crown, it's her burden to keep you safe." Tohar paused. When he spoke again, his voice was thick with admiration. "I've never known a better human. You'd do well to be grateful for her loyalty."

The past snapped at Barodane.

Screams walked with Garlenna as she approached Barodane outside of the Rainy Meadows jail. Darkness and fire framed her ash-streaked visage. The gore on her clothes was not earned by valiant means. They echoed the bitter soul she served—a mad prince. *Do not forget, I dipped my weapon in the same blood you did.*

Never would he forget. Could not if he tried.

Barodane shrugged, leaned forward to create space between his back and the priest's chest. "Itchy business riding double like this."

Frustration burned at him. No matter who died at Garlenna's hands, it seemed she had a habit of shielding herself from the moral cost by naming it duty. *Duty to me—to my name!*

Barodane craned his head, popping his neck.

His prosort slowed as she reached the final strip of earth, then backed up her horse. "Here. The banks are clotted with forest below. There's a goat trail leading into the ravine." She eased her horse onto the steep path down, scree sliding around her horse's feet.

Barodane kicked Scab's flanks to follow.

Pillars of stone eclipsed their heads, thrusting them in shadow. They went slow to avoid injury to the horses. The sound of the wide stream meandering through the gorge grew louder as they worked their way down.

The trail opened and leveled out, spitting them out onto a shelf of stone just above the whispering waters. They entered the protection of the trees blanketing the banks of the gorge and waited for dawn.

They led their mounts with the current.

"These waters flow toward the coast," Garlenna said. "A day would be advantageous. Two would be better."

After traveling the shallow waters the better part of a day, even gifted trackers would be hard-pressed to find their trail.

"A gift from the gods," Tohar said. "That's what this is."

Barodane agreed it was a stroke of luck but struggled to celebrate. The streambed was mostly silt and mud, and while it made for easier footing and a faster pace, Barodane's boots filled with sodden grit. Add to that the simmering discontent he'd held all night, and he marched with a sour mood.

Hours passed, and the water level deepened but never submerged them past the waist. At midday, the stream widened into a series of conjoined pools, lazy and hemmed in by layered steps of dark lava rock.

Barodane recalled a similar place from youth, a place he and his brother Malath had frequented in Admar's Grove. One summer in his teen years in particular stood to mind. When the D'Alzirs had visited.

Malus had smoothed his velvet doublet and found the perfect spot to settle in with a book.

Barodane stripped off his tunic. "You're still going to get leaves up your arse," he said to his older cousin.

Malath was following suit. Warm summer wind pushed the pool's surface and sunlight rippled over the cerulean waters. Ruins of ruddy stone mixed with dense foliage to border the private swimming spot. Bent slightly forward, Omari D'Alzir clutched the hem of a purple and gold shift as she stepped methodically down into ankle-deep water onto the submerged stone platform occupied by Barodane. At the last, she slipped on the slick rock and wobbled.

Barodane turned to catch her—brushed the side of a still budding breast on accident before their hands clasped. Heat flared into his cheeks as he steadied her.

"Thank you." Omari's sapphire eyes found his and lingered. A smile bunched her cheeks, mouth parting indecisively as if she didn't know whether to inhale, exhale, speak, or...

"Easy, you two."

Before Barodane could react, Malath had snuck up behind him and jerked his breeches down to his ankles, then leapt into the water with his knees tucked.

Barodane's hands shot down to retrieve his underpants, yanking them back up to his waist in a flash. At the same time, Omari, suddenly relieved of her handhold, had lost her balance. She landed on her backside in the water, waves blossoming outward and then closing over her head in an instant.

Turning shades deeper red by the second, Barodane dove in after his older brother. The two struggled for position, Malath laughing hysterically as Barodane fought to dunk him.

From the shore, he spotted Malus looking at them from over his book with a smile. Doused from head to toe, a less enthused-looking Omari dragged herself back onto the rock she'd toppled from. "Wasn't planning on getting my hair wet."

"Wretched bastard!" Barodane pushed Malath off and swam to her.

Marus appeared a moment later.

"Ah! If it isn't the illustrious Marus D'Alzir!" Malath held his arms wide in mock welcome. "Pulled your face from betwixt the ass cheeks of the Collective for a breath of fresh air, have you?"

"Enough, Malath," Malus said. "He does well to learn the ways of court." He jockeyed with his elbows to sit higher against the tree. "We would do well to be so responsible."

Barodane had snorted. While all of them found Marus's brown-nosing ways off-putting, they still invited him to all their excursions. Rarely did he partake.

Marus gestured at Barodane and Malath. "Your father wants you at court this afternoon." He gripped a birch and leaned his weight from it to hang. "Daestro Anollio, the Ambassador of Valat, has arrived."

"Right now, I couldn't care less about some windbag from the Academies." Barodane swam up to Omari where she sat with her legs dangling over the rock shelf in the water. Both of them smiled broader as the distance between them faded. "Forget court and hop in, why don't you?"

Malath was already out of the pool to retrieve his tunic. "Come on."

"Court is a fascinating place. I count myself eternally lucky to have the opportunity to be a part of it." Marus straightened and started picking sheaves of white from the birch, either missing Barodane's attempted humor or purposely ignoring it. "It's important work, and when you're my age, you'll probably come around to appreciating it."

"He knows." Malath beckoned Barodane out of the water. "He's just being a brat. Let's go."

Barodane sighed, muttered, "I'll never be prince anyway" to Omari, and then got out of the pool.

A pool like the one he waded through now...

He knew the love of those from his past was long gone, but the feelings from the memory filled him as if they'd happened yesterday.

No, yesterday, you slaughtered a town. Yesterday, you were a drug-dealing wretch. Yesterday, your prosort murdered someone to keep you safe.

Barodane stared at the glimmering, sunlit surface of the pool surrounding him as Garlenna paced farther ahead. Halos of mottled light undulated up the walls of rock rimming the pool. There weren't as many trees as the one he'd swam in with his brother and Omari, but it was close enough that seeing it filled his gut with wrenching loss.

"Wait," he said.

Garlenna kept on.

"Wait, I said."

Hearing him this time, she stopped and turned. "What is it?"

"Well," Barodane said, "I was going to have a little chat with you but your tone has me reconsidering."

She let the dripping reins in her hand sink under the water. "Talk to me about what?"

"You know what."

Tohar rested a hand on Barodane's shoulder.

He shrugged it off and moved toward Garlenna as she, too, traveled the dozen or so feet to meet him. Their knees drove up out of the water, then plunged back down with a splash.

"You had her beat," Barodane said. "She would have submitted but you killed her."

"Oh, so now you're better than that? *Now,* you stop at killing?"

Barodane pulled up short, eyes narrowed. "What's that supposed to mean?"

Garlenna crossed her arms. "You won't get it."

Water babbled from a fissure in the nearby rock. Veils of light danced over his prosort, reflecting off the necklace Merique had asked him to wear. Milky light slashed Garlenna's face.

The eyes of Omari watched him from the past—right at the moment Malath had relieved him of his breeches. It was like that when he locked eyes with Garlenna. Naked, exposed.

Jaw clenched, he shook his head. *She's the one who's supposed to feel ashamed. Not me.* "Fuck this." He swiveled his face up to glower at her. "And fuck you. I'm done."

Tohar had come around the side of him, palms held up in entreaty. "Please. Best if we—"

Mist sprayed the air as Barodane's fist connected with the priest's cheek. Tohar's head snapped back, expression twisting into a frown at the blow. He reeled backward, stumbled—

The last Barodane saw before the world went dark. Water encased him. Sound reduced to gurgling, piercing shuffles. Filtered murk...the outline of a booted foot displacing white pebbles and thick silt on the stream bed. His chest tightened around held breath.

A hand yanked him above the surface by his hair—Garlenna's hand.

She spun him about by the shoulders as he gasped for breath. "Must I beat you senseless again?"

He shoved her hands off.

"Apologize to Tohar," she said. "He's done nothing but help."

When he delayed, Garlenna slid closer in the surf, fists balled and elbows cocked above the white foaming pool. Barodane held up a hand and nodded. "Fine. I'm sorry, Tohar. I should have hit *her*."

The priest rubbed his jaw. "For your sake, it's probably good that you didn't."

"A real 'beast of a woman,' some corpses will tell you." Barodane locked eyes with his prosort and waited for a reaction. She'd bludgeoned the last man who'd said those words.

Instead, she clapped condescendingly. "Bravo. Are you done yet? Ready to quit and go back home to your godsthorn and your whores and your dead?"

Barodane straightened, lip curling back. He could...if he wanted. Meckin's dead face stared at the rafters, a final questioning look. Then Omari's face was there, seeing something more in Barodane than he alone could see in himself. A look that held him to a higher standard because someone thought him worthy. Because someone loved him once for who he was.

He swallowed back the urge to walk to Digtown, breathing in a slow dose of calm instead. "Why did you kill Merique?"

Garlenna's chin dipped. Her hazy, distorted reflection stared back at her from the water. "I was preparing for a mission when I received word about you from my father. It was a special assignment from Archprelate Alcor himself. When I heard you might be alive, that you might be in Digtown, I packed what was necessary and left that very night. I never sent word to the Sempyrium..." She cleared her throat. "You know, you haven't asked how I've been. Not once. You haven't asked what it was like after you disappeared. Did you know there is an empty grave in Admar's Grove? Your grave." She choked on a sob. "We buried you between your brother and grandfather."

A flush crept up Barodane's neck. A tingle swept the length of him.

"I mourned you," she said.

When a warrior wept, it bred a special kind of sorrow in Barodane. A rare show of rawness and fragility offered up by roughened hands. There was no warrior greater than Garlenna, and so, the heat of shame licking across Barodane's skin as he watched her weep was greater than any he'd ever felt.

"For two years, I mourned. I was at your side every day. After a few months, they let me set up a tent near the gardens so I no longer startled the groundskeepers each morning when they found me waiting to hold vigil. I brought you almond flat cakes from the kitchens—you liked those most. I brought you flowers, but you never mentioned a favorite, so I just picked whatever ones I could find." She chuckled regretfully, as if she'd been made a fool, then rubbed the flesh under her eyepatch. "I've prayed, begged, fought, and nearly died to see you standing here now. Yet you haven't apologized for what you made me do at Rainy Meadows. You haven't apologized for abandoning me, either. You care more about that Remnant than you do me."

Barodane's head jerked away, heart feeling kicked. The urge to descend into a spiral of self-loathing slid up his neck like cold mud. At any second, he expected the voices of the dead to return and heap their shame...

Then he remembered he'd silenced them, and found his own voice on the matter was far from quiet. *That's what she's talking about, you egotistical ass! Stop focusing on yourself and listen!*

He spoke in a rush. "I'm sorry. For all of it. You're right. I never...I should have..." He sighed. "What I did to you is unforgivable. To my soldiers. To Kaitos. To my country. He threw up his hands. "Triune God, that's what I've been telling you! Don't you see? I'm not the one you want uniting a nation. I'm the one who rips them apart."

For the first time since they'd left Digtown, Garlenna didn't counter his negativity. She studied him a moment. "That may be true, but you're the only hope we've got." She arched an eyebrow. "Sullen and pathetic as you may be."

"Fuck off. I'm trying."

Her expression grew serious. "You are, but never do something that stupid again." It took him a second to realize she referred to him attacking the Remnant and her men. "Now that you understand the weight of what I've been through, I hope you also understand that I'm not going to let anything stand in the way of our mission. Merique had to die. We couldn't travel with her, couldn't leave her alive, couldn't do what she wanted us to. She was dangerous. We only get one chance at this."

"She was a potential ally." Barodane gestured at their surroundings. "And if you haven't noticed, we're in desperate need of allies. If we can't even outmaneuver the Crown's Justice, how are we supposed to reclaim Namarr?"

"By being smart, Barodane!" She lowered her voice. "Merique wanted to use you. You heard it. You would have been the Remnant's prisoner. A pawn rather than a player. Isn't that what you fear?"

"I...I'm not sure." Barodane pressed wet palms to his forehead. There had never been a moment without pressure in the courts of Alistar. Being an Iron-light ensured that. Marus had always been willing to engage, but Barodane had never gravitated to diplomacy and the nest of fake-smiling vipers who lurked there, all of them using each other in a quest for more riches, more influence, more power. Friends shaking hands while they plotted one another's downfall.

"You wanted to do the right thing by sparing Merique's life, Barodane. If I could have, I would have, but there is a nation full of innocent people depending on your survival. We're going to have to make harder choices than that if we're to succeed." She wiped her nose. "You have to trust me when I say it was necessary."

Barodane nodded. Insects zipped over the water, weaving in and out of sunlit swaths. Garlenna turned to leave, but reflex took over, spurred to life by an indecipherable voice calling out in the deep dark of him. It was tentative and hopeful when it shuffled forth to speak—but speak it did.

He took Garlenna's arm in a firm grasp, neither threatening nor relinquishing. She looked at his hand, then into his frowning face as he breathed, seized by the fear of his own desires for something better.

To be someone better.

"You'll need to trust me, too. I'm your prince. If I say a life can be spared, I don't care what your calculations tell you about the situation, we make it work or we go our separate ways." He let go.

As she turned away, he thought he saw recognition twitch across her brow.

"Well said, my Prince." Tohar slapped him on the back.

They continued upstream until they found a trail leading up out of the ravine and back onto dry, steady earth.

CHAPTER FIFTY

UNBOUND

R enuad the Ghost had been assigned to tutor Thephos and cover the gaps in learning he'd never had. Reading especially. Their daily lessons were the one place Thephos could forget everything.

The pressure put on him by Syn in training. The mistreatment he leveled at himself for being less than the Awakened he should be. The ridicule heaped on him by Pintarian and the other bladesworn.

Most days blew through Thephos like gales of broken glass. He was learning it was one thing to want to be Dominarri, and quite another to become one.

Since his meeting with Pintarian, the man had grown more vocal in his displeasure over Thephos's presence, and rallied other bladesworn to his mission of cutting the newest Dominarri to pieces as if he were a hedge in need of trimming.

To Thephos's woe, the man's influence was significant. He couldn't tell if it was because Pintarian was the offspring of the Skyfire council, or if the others respected him for his skills. The most likely answer, Thephos suspected, was that the others joined him in his derision out of fear. Pintarian's demeanor was one that drew invisible lines at every interaction, no matter how petty or unimportant. Lines that brooked no disagreement, and if crossed, helped him decipher friend from foe.

Thephos, meanwhile, held no sway among his peers, and so it was easy for them to deride him. Condemned in earnest by Pintarian, it was clear no bladesworn wanted him. Whoever he bonded with would be seen as unlucky. A tragic sacrifice so that the rest of them might be free of the burden.

Earlier that day, Pintarian's disgust had come with a joke like it usually did—rarely funny to any but himself. "For an Awakened, he's still mighty groggy."

Forced laughter followed.

In following the pattern they had all fallen into, Syn tried to instill hope. "Soon, you're going to be more powerful than any Awakened. They're fools not to want you."

Training proceeded, Syn eager to unlock what they'd touched upon in earlier weeks while Thephos avoided it at all costs.

After training, he'd asked Syn, "Does it always happen like this? Needing so much help to bring it out?"

Syn had watched him a few long seconds before responding. "No. Not usually." He smiled. More and more, Thephos concluded that his friend's kindness was fake, like a thief proffering a cut of meat to a guard dog. "But don't let that mean anything about you. The greater the power, the more effort it can take to master it."

No matter the man's words, Thephos didn't trust him—not anymore. He nodded assent but left their training session more sour than before. His own reservations were spreading, a cancerous mistrust embedding itself in all he did. It crept into his time with Syn, into his free time walking the grounds—crept into the displeasure evident on the faces of strangers he didn't know.

Malicious whispers followed him at the edge of hearing.

Unworthy to be Dominarri, they said. *Unfit. Sure to die a failure.*

Only the voice offered comfort. *I love you, Theffy...*

On a few occasions, while battling Syn in his psychic arena, Thephos had felt his ill-defined powers rush to the surface. But whenever the trickle of burning strength began, he plunged it down into the burning depths and ended the session. That first time he'd let go...it could have killed Syn. Would have, if the man had been any slower to subdue him.

To avoid the torments of his mind through the eyes of strangers, Thephos took to keeping opposite hours from most. He slept as long into the day as he could and stayed up late into the night.

Tonight, he roamed alone under the phosphorescent eye of the moon with naught but his thoughts accompanying him.

The cold was sharp but he didn't mind. He left his woolen cloak and scarf in his quarters below ground. The numbing air reminded him of Unturrus. The last time he'd felt free. The last time he'd felt strong.

They do not love you.

Ash had been called to other duties, the final diminishing flame of a presence already lacking in much warmth. And Syn...he promised a great deal that had yet to come.

Brotherhood. Sanctuary. Purpose.

Instead of those things, Thephos felt lost and reviled. Hardly of use at all.

Seated on a bench among the hedges with his arms crossed, Thephos's upper lip curled. *This self-pity won't get me anywhere.* Syn kept telling him he had to face the blocks keeping his powers from emerging, but what could he do when that was the very thing he feared?

Aren't you tired of letting them mock you? Don't you want to show them how strong you are?

Thephos's embrace tightened, fingers digging in behind his ribs on either side. *On my own terms. Not yours.* He'd been told what to do his whole life by others. It was becoming tiring. He didn't care how much the voice loved him. Although sometimes, he wondered if anyone else did.

He inhaled a gulp of crisp air. Tomorrow would be his bonding ceremony, and to most, he'd done nothing to prove he was worthy of it. *Unless I allow myself to demonstrate my powers...*

He hissed. *I can't. I won't.* Not when the entity begged him to. Not when he sensed its hunger to be freed behind the roiling waves of surging power.

Thephos descended the steps into the underground labyrinth of living quarters and administrative chambers. He moved quietly, careful not to wake anyone. Ghost-flame torches threw snowy light over the floor as he padded along on bare feet. Syn urged him to wear boots since he'd need to get used to it when he went afield. So he did—during the day.

At night, though, when no one was looking, he wanted to feel his skin against the earth. To feel as he had on Unturrus when he'd first glimpsed who he could be.

Heated whispering in a passageway to his left froze him.

Familiar voices.

"It's wrong to eavesdrop." That's what his father had always said before a stick or belt struck him or his brothers across the backs of the legs. Thephos did it anyway. *You're dead. You have no say.*

If he was placing the speakers correctly, they stood in the hall just outside of the Skyfire Council Chamber. He slowed his breathing so he might hear better.

Syn's words were the first he made out.

"...will happen."

"You play a dangerous game, Syn." N'zara's distinct voice. A throat full of honey. Words that rolled over brittle shells. "Letting an enigma into Enshai could compromise our work."

"You'd rather he stayed out there?" Pintarith said.

They're talking about me. Thephos's jaw tendon clicked. He knew it was odd for his power to be buried and inaccessible. The same feeling he'd had in the tent when Syn had imprisoned him came rushing back. *He lied to me. Said I was a normal Awakened.*

"Not what I'd propose." N'zara sounded somber. Like a father who'd just finished burying the family hound.

Something soundless passed between the three of them. The audacity of N'zara's suggestion was evident in the pinched tone of Syn's response. "You can't be serious. That's not who we are."

"If he's as powerful as you think, maybe it's who we *should* be. Need I remind you of what's at stake?"

"We're aware," said Pintarith.

"He isn't Ruptured," Syn added.

"And yet," N'zara purred, "we don't know what he is. You forget I, too, have been in his mind. I've seen what you have. I felt...something."

The implication of her words ran claws over Thephos's shoulders.

Syn sighed. "Whatever his power is, I think it operates fully in his subconscious. I'm not even sure we could kill him if we wanted to."

"If that is the case," said N'zara, "it's all the more reason we must."

"You would do this just to spite me? He could be a weapon of unparalleled value." A rustle of cloth—Pintarith shifting his weight or uncrossing his arms. "You dishonor your station—nay, the Dominarri."

In the silence that followed, Thephos imagined the married couple staring daggers through the other. The word "weapon" echoed in his mind. *So, N'zara wants to execute me and Pintarith wants to use me.*

Syn, too, seemed to be falling in with the latter. The claws on Thephos's shoulders dug into his chest, shortening his breaths.

"I've glimpsed a fraction of the power you and I both sensed, Your Grace." Syn attempted to soothe the budding war between husband and wife. "Thephos passed the Provocations. There's good in him. Enough to control what arises and wield it on behalf of the Triune God. I think it better to cultivate—"

"You *think?*" N'zara demurred. "You've been on Unturrus too long, running your games, drinking, and cavorting and gambling. Losing touch with the way things work. You do not advise me on opinions I'm perfectly capable of having on my own."

"But I certainly can," Pintarith said. "Syn is right. We cannot set a precedent for executing non-Ruptured just because you fear their power. We take the cautious path. We put our trust in Thephos, induct him into the fold, bond him with a bladesworn and send him afield. Something small. In fact, I have just the mission in mind."

"So you'll set a precedent for making them Dominarri instead?" The Holy Flame spit the rebuke at her husband. "What a brilliant idea. You are so desperate to be a hero in the war to come, you'll seal our fate with your narcissistic need for it."

"We have the bond for a reason," Pintarith growled.

"The blade that cuts both ways," N'zara said. The bond was for life. Bladesworn were meant to protect their Awakened, but also, were rendered immune to the powers of their counterpart. "Twenty years ago, I made a decision I would regret to the end of my days. I suspect you're doing the same now. So go ahead and make it, but know I will never forgive you for it if you're wrong."

Cloth swirled.

Her footsteps trailed down a hall in the distance, Pintarith's voice chasing her. "A stunning thing from one so forgiving as you!"

When the footsteps were gone, the two resumed.

"Ash and I have spoken. If it is for the greater good, we..." Emotion clogged Syn's voice. "...We will sever our bond. It will guarantee there is a trusted and capable bladesworn with him."

Ash? The prospect was less than thrilling. That Syn proposed it was no small sacrifice. Stories of the pain incurred by such a process were gruesome. Physical recovery might take months, but the emotional toll sometimes led to suicide or death.

"It is worthy of consideration," Pintarith mused. "You say he has not formed a strong relationship with any others?"

Syn hesitated. "Your son has ensured it. He wishes Thephos gone."

The Holy Sword cursed. "I told him not to meddle. I'll speak with him."

"Thank you, Your Grace."

"All the same. Prepare Ash. Yourself as well. Tell Thephos of the choice he's to make."

"I will, Your Grace," Syn said stiffly. They parted ways, boot strikes going separate directions.

Sweating in the dark, Thephos stood there a long time. If he didn't leave Enshai and renounce the Dominarri, it would be at the cost of irrevocably hurting the only two people he considered his friends.

It will happen to whoever I bond with anyway. I'm just going to die, and when I die, it will cause them unspeakable suffering. Even if Syn and Pintarith thought of him as some kind of weapon in waiting, he couldn't imagine being of much use.

His power was dangerous. Unpredictable. More than him, it seemed to belong to the voice, anyway.

N'zara and Pintarian are right, I should die and save them all the trouble.

Cold spread through him. By now it had become a familiar sensation, a herald preceding the entity within. Chill tingled in his fingertips and toes as the one who truly held the power arrived.

I'll never let them hurt you. Never.

Awakened and their bladesworn counterparts filled the grandstands of the Skyfire Council's chamber. The Holy Sword and Holy Flame had dawned their ceremonial garb.

Robes of a red so dark and deep they could have been black rested on N'zara's still frame. The symbols for orriok, hrasdi, and noggu were stitched in gold thread around voluminous cuffs and choking collar.

A simple brocade doublet of the same color adorned Pintarith's lean frame. His hair was bound in a ponytail that shimmered like the inside of a seashell under the luminous ghost-light.

All of the Dominarri were dressed in the likeness of the council.

Torches of white flame ringed the chamber. Silence throttled the room in its oppressive grip. Unsure what he would do, Thephos struggled to breathe.

Already a stranger to so many of those seated, and an enemy to a handful, he glanced down at his simple frock and dropped deeper into the skin-prickling realization that he was an outcast.

Someone to be manipulated. Something to be used.

A sheep they wish to be their lion.

"Thephos of Carthane," Pintarith intoned. "Approach."

Pulse thumping in his ears, Thephos walked toward the hanging statue of the Mother descending from the cavernous ceiling. Patches of light gleamed along the marble file's length.

Syn and Ash Backlegarm stood among their brothers and sisters in the front row of the grandstand to Thephos's left. Above them, in the back rows, were those bladesworn as yet unbonded. The supply of Awakened had always failed to match the number of Enshai natives who chose to train under the Dominarri's militant arm and become their protectors. A full third of those present were unmatched. Some as old as Pintarith and N'zara while some appeared younger than Thephos's nineteen years.

The common folk of Enshai were barred from the proceedings. For some, the risk of danger and death in the field as an agent of the Dominarri was worth it to be a part of the order. But Thephos imagined the smartest among them went about their daily lives beyond the chamber risking nothing at all.

Maybe that's what I should be doing. Why risk my life, even if it's for a worthy cause? Unturrus gave me a gift, a chance to do life a different way. Why squander it?

He wanted to run, denounce his pledge to the Dominarri and run. Like his mother had. There wasn't sense in her trying to be a hero. She didn't have it in her and he didn't either.

Syn Backlegarm had disagreed.

The previous night, he and Ash had come to Thephos and told him their plan to sacrifice their bond. "She'll be fine," Syn had said. "A new bond heals the old. But me, well, I'll have a tough time for a while. A few months of illness, sure, but I may be able to bond again after that."

"You mean, if you survive it," Thephos had said.

Syn shrugged. "There's a little risk in everything. I could die tomorrow, or you could—we all could. That doesn't mean we shouldn't do the right thing today just because it's hard."

I've never done the right thing. In his mind's eye, Thephos watched his brother's corpse roll into a shallow grave, then shuddered.

To his right, a familiar face caught his attention in the back row of the grandstand. Pintarian stared down at him, a smug twist to the corner of his mouth. He turned his gaze forward.

As he'd been instructed, Thephos stepped to the rim of the pit and waited to be called forward. He hovered at the top of the short flight of steps leading down to the basin situated right beneath the Mother's likeness. Shavings of Unturrus's roots were scattered throughout the water of the broad marble font, throwing up a glowing azure nimbus. Thephos stared into it...

Heard it calling. A murmur at the back of his mind. Not the one that told him it loved him; it was more of a sensation than that. An undeniable urge drawing him into its embrace. He hadn't been able to appreciate it when the same feeling had tugged at him to ascend Unturrus, but now, he had to fight not to descend to the basin before he was called to it.

N'zara's smoky voice jolted him. "Before we are born unto our true path, we must first let the false ones die." She raised her arms above her head, palms upturned. "We must all choose, and in so doing, commit ourselves to the death of all previous possibilities."

From the corners of his vision, Thephos spotted a few among the grandstands inclining their heads in respectful admission.

"For the one to be initiated today, a singular purpose remains." Pintarith swept the assembly slowly with a gray stare. "Thephos of Carthane, the Triune God calls you to step forward."

On the first of the short flight of steps, Thephos stumbled. Heat crept into his cheeks as stifled laughter echoed behind him. He threw a look over his right shoulder. Pintarian grinned back as the Holy Sword of the Skyfire Council commanded silence.

Thephos snapped back around and strode down the final few steps to stand before the basin. Overhead, the statue of the Mother watched, wings spread. He imagined many were inspired by the sight, a flash of memory that flooded their being with the ecstatic moment of their rebirth.

For Thephos, the contrast was crushing. Her warmth and love had stirred him to being. Now, the sight of her reminded him how far from that moment he was, here among peers who despised him or sought only to use him.

I will do you proud. I promise it.

Resolve spread into the hinge of his jaw, his balled fists, his spine...spread through him until he was almost a statue himself. *I will show them my worth, and one day, they'll accept me.*

"Today is an unusual one," said Pintarith. "For we welcome an Awakened whose powers are unknown into our service. An unprecedented event...or so I thought." N'zara's face swung calmly toward the Holy Sword, but Thephos could tell by the rounding of her dark eyes that her husband had breached some expectation she'd held. "I have consulted with our librarians and found that previous members of the Skyfire council have dealt with similar circumstances. Therefore, we shall choose a bladesworn on behalf of the Awakened."

Some bladesworn barked agreement, but more grumbled in dissent. That surprised Thephos. None of them wished to be bonded to him. The majority openly exuded loathing when he crossed their path. Any Awakened that couldn't control their powers was unpredictable, and unpredictable was dangerous.

"There is precedent!" Pintarith shouted. "He has forfeited his choice willingly!"

Thephos twisted to one side, spotted Ash and Syn in the grandstand to his left. Syn chewed his lip, a hint of terror etching the creases of his face. What hurt him more to see was Ash seated beside him. Mussed hair told of a night of restless sleep. Dark circles clung to haunted eyes. Shoulder rounded, back hunched, lips trembling and on the verge of tears, she nodded at Thephos.

He thought back to the night before.

The couple had embraced, a desperate tightness to the act. Minutes had passed as Thephos watched them, numbness spreading into his limbs, reminding him what life had been like before Unturrus. *I am not worthy, and she does not deserve it.* Shame seeped through him.

The same shame he felt now under the baleful looks of his supposed peers.

"Syn Backlegarm offers his bladesworn to bond anew," said Pintarith. "A courageous sacrifice."

Gasps from the multitudes gave immensity to the gesture.

N'zara lunged at the opening, words as poised and deadly as any bladesworn's steel. "He will be the one to announce his forfeiture before his peers. Not us. Those who serve this order do so of their own free will. It may be that if he doesn't wish to choose a bladesworn that he doesn't choose to be Dominarri at all." She turned feline regard on Thephos. "So what will it be? If you do not believe yourself capable of gaining mastery over your powers, you may leave Enshai. I'll even help you find a lord to serve. I know many."

Pintarith glared at N'zara, fingertips drumming the marble armrest.

"Or stay," said N'zara after a pause. "Sever Syn Backlegarm's bond with his wife. Accept Ash as your bladesworn and tether your success to someone more...*worthy.*"

Thephos's chin dropped to a shoulder. Ashen hair fell around his face, crowding his peripheries. *I am not worthy.* He stared into the basin of glowing blue water. Minutes passed. Someone cleared their throat.

Pintarian's words slashed at Thephos from the dark of his mind. *Because he was not fit to be Dominarri.* If Thephos left, he confirmed the man's judgment. Confirmed his father's, too. "A coward, just like your mother!" She had abandoned Thephos and his brothers to oblivion in the name of self-preservation.

I won't be like her...not anymore. The Thephos he'd been was dead. Taken by the Mother—his true mother. Now, he wanted to help people. He wanted to make the difference he never could.

"No..." he whispered.

"I'm sorry," N'zara cooed. "You'll need to speak up."

Thephos raised his head, his voice a thunderclap. "I'm staying."

Pintarith slapped a velvet-gloved hand down on the marble arm of his seat. "Excellent." He shot a look of smug victory at N'zara. "In love, truth, and duty you shall serve the Triune God. Ash Backlega—"

"Not her," Thephos said.

The Holy Sword's brow creased. "It has been decided."

"No." N'zara's voice lilted with uncontained glee. "Nothing is decided. If Thephos doesn't want to forfeit his choice, he doesn't need to. To deny him that right is heresy."

Pintarith returned his wife's jubilation with steely condemnation. Brow furrowed, he fixed his stare on Thephos. "You have leave to choose. Do so wisely."

Silence rang in Thephos's ears.

He looked to his left. Ash and Syn watched him with concerned expressions. Of everyone he'd encountered in his life, these were the closest people he'd ever had to friends. Regardless of Ash's agitation and grouchy demeanor, or Syn's half-lies and hidden truths, he'd witnessed a depth of love between them that had been alien to him for most of his life.

I can't. I won't.

He whirled. Pointed. "Him."

Every last one of the bladesworn thought him unworthy. Ash included. He'd held himself back long enough. Held back the power he sensed brewing beneath the surface. He knew what waited for him out in the world: more mockery, more shame, more of the same he'd always run from. He didn't want to run anymore. His mother had run—had left him and his brothers in the care of a devil. He would do his part in delivering the world from people like that. Something somewhere had given him the power to stand against darkness.

He had but to use it. And to do so, he would choose the best bladesworn available to him.

Pintarian glowered at Thephos, mouth working in rage. He flicked a look at his father.

The Holy Sword's voice betrayed his disbelief. "You have chosen...Pintaria n." The muscles in his jaw writhed under his snowy beard. "Are you sure?"

"Of course he's sure!" N'zara snapped. "We do not question the choice of an Awakened!"

A flush stained Pintarian's cheeks. "What if I refuse?"

N'zara sat back. "Banishment from the Dominarri, my son."

Pintarith stared at a point on the floor. His words rang hollow. "Pintarian of Enshai...approach."

"Father! You can't let this—"

"I am the Holy Sword of the Skyfire council," Pintarith roared. "Do not defy me!" At the last, the man's gaze stabbed into Thephos. "Pintarian is a *wise* choice."

Defiance wasn't in Thephos's nature and never had been. The act had been trained out of him by the old devil's fists. Defying the Holy Sword brought a wave of catharsis over him. *No one controls me. Not anymore.*

Pintarian spat curses and forced his way through his peers to stand beside Thephos. "You wretched fucking bastard," he muttered.

"Bring the chains," said the Holy Flame. Her hatred for her son seemed less than that she held for her husband, but not by much. A coy smile stole across her face at the sight of Pintarian's distress.

"Pintarian of the Enshai. Thephos of Carthane." Pintarith was no more pleased than his son, but the weight of responsibility and station propelled him onward. "In the sight of the Triune God, and by will of the Mother, I hereby bind you. May only death part you."

"Father," Pintarian growled. "Your Grace."

Thin loops of chain were slipped over their heads from behind. Thephos was surprised to see the bladesworn allow it.

"Mother," Pintarian hissed, "you waste me and you know it."

"All of us are bound by duty, my son," N'zara intoned, formality held above motherhood. "By the fire, the eye, and the hand, you will fulfill yours or you will reap a traitor's bounty."

Thephos glanced sidelong at his bladesworn. The man's ire bled into the space between them, eyes aflame in their hate.

A line of silver lowered across Thephos's vision.

The chain was cool around his neck. Heavier than it looked. He lifted it with a finger for inspection. Smoky gray in the shadow but holding pools of white in the light. From what he'd heard of darksteel, it matched the description.

The Holy Flame gestured at the fountain separating Pintarian and Thephos. "Pledge fealty and walk in the Mother's light."

Thephos placed his fingers in the azure waters. Cool energy sparked through his arm, racing from fingertips to chest where it percolated. He breathed, deeper than he thought possible, exhaled more fully than he ever had. A soft, steamy light emanated from his skin. Bliss stretched his lips into a smile.

Pintarian threw a withering glare at his mother and then jabbed his hand into the water.

Lightning struck through Thephos. His arm felt like it exploded. Heart racing, then seeming to stop. Everything faded until only blackness hung behind his eyes, freezing him in dim memory.

He oozed back into the present where he stood on rubbery legs. His heart thudded, chest aching, pulse droning in his ears. He found his hand attached to the fountain's lip, fingers smoking. He cried out as he pried them off with a steaming hiss, scraps of papery flesh clinging to the stone where he'd touched.

Beside him, Pintarian's head lolled, tracing a circle around his neck. The chain glowed bright white—flashed—then burst into ashes, leaving a brand in the shape of a chain in its place emblazoned over the scar from his previous bond. The one that he'd broken by killing his Awakened.

The reek of scorched flesh tainted the air as Thephos looked down and saw the chain brand through singed holes in his robe. He staggered, blinking away blurred vision.

The Holy Sword cleared his throat, emotion threatening. "Go from here as one." He pushed to his feet. "This ceremony is at an end."

Someone slid an arm under Thephos's shoulder and helped him from the hall. Pintarian shoved would-be supporters away and staggered out under his own power, expression drawn but wrathful.

I will show you my worth.

CHAPTER FIFTY-ONE

INITIATES OF THE OBSIDIAN HAND

Garlenna worried that a trap awaited them at every town along the way to Martyr's Isle, whereas Barodane felt confident they'd shaken their pursuers. Nevertheless, her caution won out and they took the necessary measures.

The biggest risk was letting Tohar go into town alone to fetch supplies. He could betray them for a reward, or barring such treachery, a chainman could detain him for questioning if they had his description.

Plenty could go wrong. But with a pair of near-death encounters now anchoring their relationship to the priest, it seemed the simplest course of action to trust him. And having won a horse out of the deal, the man was happy to do it. "The least we could do to repay his help," Garlenna had said.

Or do lovers shower each other in kindness and gifts? Barodane decided their tryst was fine so long as he never had to deal with the drama if things soured.

All the same, raccoons fought in his stomach whenever the deadline for Tohar's return approached. If the priest missed it, they would assume him captured and flee in haste.

Dogged by damp and cold, they camped whenever they found the cover of trees. Wool cloaks, tunics, and underclothes topped the list of supplies Tohar was sent to find, right beneath food and water.

By the time they traveled around to the northerly side of the Shining Range, Barodane was ready to sacrifice his left hand for a night of comforts.

At the crossroads to Brighthaven—fifty miles farther inland—they ran across a caravan led by a buzzardly old woman, twenty others in her party. Many wore clothing stamped with the sigils of Lah-Tsarene holds. A glinting sapphire on an emerald field for the Arazki. A lightning bolt setting a tree ablaze for the Stormcallers. Even a handful from Brighthaven, wearing purple tabards trimmed in black and stitched with the D'Alzir hawk.

Tohar led the conversation as he'd been instructed to keep attention off Barodane and Garlenna. "What news of Duke Malus? I heard he was slain near Kiyahd."

The lead woman brought the caravan to a rickety halt. Her knees were propped on the running board, elbows winging out to the sides atop them. She was all willpower and bones and hunched up like a fruit rind left to wither under the Malzacy sun.

"That's about all the news of a man come to his ultimate end, ain't it? What else you expecting? Him, risen from the grave?" She spat over the side of the cab, then drew a woolen sleeve across her puckered mouth. "Kurgs done for 'em. They say a big clan gone rogue up in the mountains. Violated Bacot's Embargo, bearin' steel and all that."

Tohar attempted to ask a question but the crone kept on as if conversing with none but herself. "Never been one for the Windin' Way meself. Colder than Nacronus's icy prick with winter so close. We go the long way round...as you can see."

Tohar's mount sidestepped then settled. He glanced back at Garlenna before addressing the woman again. She'd instructed him on the questions to ask if they met anyone on the road. Ways to discount or confirm information. "And what other rumors about who may have killed the duke?"

The crone frowned and leaned forward, chest between her knobby knees, to peer into Tohar's face, squinting as if she couldn't make out his features. "Rumors?" She looked at Garlenna then blinked rapidly at Tohar. "What's his excuse? He deaf? Kicked by a horse?" Her age-dusted voice cracked. "Not the dumbest man I met, but by the gods, you better hope he don't die."

A young woman came up alongside the crone, pleading for calm and hushing her. Judging by the embarrassed looks and frustrated sighs from the rest of the caravan folk, Barodane sensed it was a ritual that often needed repeating.

"Shshshshshshshsh!" The old woman went bug-eyed and flailed her arms madly at the girl. "Don't squeak at me, you little mouse. I'm not senile! This fatty ain't listenin' is all. You hear that, fatty?"

Tohar touched his belly, looking wounded. "Fatty?"

"The Duke of Lah-Tsarra." The old woman punctuated each word in stilted fragments. "Was killed. By Kurgs. Near Kiyahd. War brewing. Not safe. Beware." With a grumble she flicked the reins and the caravan trundled off.

Garlenna followed it a short way, riding alongside a man at the rear. She returned a few minutes later. "I asked if there were any survivors. He said a number of Duke Malus's people were unaccounted for."

Captured. Barodane didn't need to say it. All of them knew. "Did he say what clan?" Barodane once had good relations with the mountain enclaves. There was a chance he could barter for Gyr's life if they moved swiftly.

"He said no one knows." Garlenna shook her head. "He said Duke Marus means to declare war."

"*Duke* Marus?"

Tohar cocked his head. "I thought only the Crown Prince could appoint ducal seats?"

"Not when no one occupies it," Garlenna said somberly. "With a Shadow-crown leading Namarr, it falls to bloodlines. Lord Marus will be the next Duke of Lah-Tsarra. Officially sworn in at the next Collective session six months from now. His daughter, the Lady Daran, will rule Kiyahd in his stead."

Barodane remembered a clever man, older by a decade, but ever more so in his demeanor. Malus had always been the smarter; Marus the more ambitious. The more dedicated to Namarr. He would do well in the office. "The man I would have chosen anyway."

Garlenna flicked the reins. "I think I'd like to ride alone for a while."

Barodane's heart went with her. Gyr was a good man. A strong prosort. The fresh pain of Malus's death struck Barodane a moment later. *Too many good ones dying...*

The tightness in his throat remained for hours of silent riding.

At dusk, they crested a knoll and drew up short to stare out over the Sea Forest.

Rain sheeted them. Barodane felt a pang of nostalgia for Digtown and the misery of drenched clothing was almost welcome as they meandered down onto the beach. Gray waves pounded the shore.

Barodane looked at Tohar, his thick hair a nest of dripping beads. *Thank the Triune God we no longer ride double.*

Garlenna's leather armor had soaked through, swelled, and become a muddier shade of brown. A trail of dung plopped to the crusted layer of beach behind her stallion. Barodane covered his nose while veering Scab to avoid it.

Forked lightning lit the clouds. Thunder folded in upon itself with a rolling growl, a monster waking in the deep.

Barodane studied the horizon, a bloated wall of charcoal stretching the entire coast, spilling its contents back into the ocean from which it came. Farther out, another cracking bolt silhouetted the gnarled pillars of the Sea Forest. Legion rows of bleached gray trees, their trunks large enough to fit the entire town of Halaleh within, clotted the liminal boundary where sky met ocean.

Barodane gestured toward the Sea Forest. "Either of you ever been?"

Tohar and Garlenna laughed.

Ships traveling the northernmost waters of the world were forced to hug the shoreline. A few miles out and anything with a deep draft ran the risk of getting its hull punctured by a branch of one of the ancient, titanic trees hiding beneath the waves.

"Some say the Sea Forest is older than Unturrus," Tohar said. "Though there are a lot of fantastic stories about the place. I've even heard stories of a few pirates who made the journey through."

Garlenna slowed to fall in line abreast of the others. "There's a story for everything, isn't there?"

"No greater lot of liars than pirates." Barodane shrugged. "Except for politicians."

All of them nodded.

A bolt of lightning licked sky in the distance, its growl coming a few heartbeats later. Garlenna roamed the distance with her good eye.

The distraction from the news about her father was likely welcome, so Barodane was keen to keep the conversation going. "The Sea Forest might be mysterious, but those smarter than I claim it serves a mighty purpose."

A line split Tohar's brow. "How so?"

"This instructor I had during my years in the Valatian Academies..." Barodane rolled his wrist as he searched for the man's name. "...Jacko Jacko something. He said the Sea Forest blocks polar winds from C'Dath from reaching us on this side of the straits. That's why it's so damn cold at the Fringes and only a bit chilly at Martyr's Isle."

Garlenna stopped her horse and fixed Barodane with an incredulous look. "Do you mean Jasso Jackolo?"

Barodane snapped his fingers. "That was his name!"

"That was only the smartest man in the world, you dolt." Garlenna shook her head. "Digtown is a vacuum of current events isn't it?"

Barodane shrugged. "Why do you think I stayed there?"

"In truth?" Garlenna shifted in the saddle. "Probably because you didn't listen to Jackolo's wisdom. For someone trained by the world's brightest, you certainly turned out duller than expected."

Barodane muttered under his breath but smiled, glad that his prosort was siphoning some of her grief and pain onto him.

A bluff topped with lush grass forced them off the beach and into the surf. Sand sucked at their horses' hooves, creating a rhythmic *shluck* with every step.

Despite it being high tide, no more than a vanguard of bubbling foam crossed their path.

They meandered around the sheer cliff...

With a sudden intake of breath, Tohar's arm flung out, his pudgy finger indicating a black-enameled shield fixed to the rock wall of the bluff. "We're here."

Spikes had been hammered around the shield to hold it in place just above head-height. An inverted moth flew down and away from a crescent moon hanging above it. Both images were painted gold. Words circumscribed the shield's rim.

Barodane murmured them to himself. "Catch the darkness and hold it still. Breathe in light to break the seal." He looked down the beach in the direction they were heading.

A seawall stretched a hundred yards into the ocean, the jutting foot of a greater body that perched atop the coastal cliffs. A drum tower and network of parapets nestled highest among them. Martyr's Isle was no true island, but if Barodane recalled rightly, enough of the structures sat on the water that it formed a sort of artificial one.

They moved on, following a switchback trail up to the front of the fortification to arrive by nightfall.

A guard called down to them from the merlons crowning the drum tower. "Come back in the morning during trading hours. The portcullis remains closed till then. Thank you."

"We have business with Nserthes the Sophophant," Garlenna hollered. "He's expecting us."

"This very night? Doubt it. Lies won't help you here." The guard har-rumphed and pointed. "Listen, there's a lovely patch of wildflowers just beyond that stand of scrub over there. If I were you, that's where I'd go."

Barodane peered to where the man gestured, then at the dense black clouds marching steadily toward them from the east. It would be a night of heavy rain and unrelenting chill. Fourteen years he'd danced with the dreary gloom, passing the hours wet and shameful and high or drunk on godsthorn. He retracted his early sentiment about Digtown—he didn't miss it at all.

Enough of this shit.

"You listen," Barodane shouted. "I have a deal for you and the other lazy cunts in the gatehouse. Open this portcullis right now and I'll give you each a silver."

The man straightened. "That right?"

"What are you doing?" Garlenna whispered.

"What if there's twenty of them?" Tohar said. "Or more?"

Barodane waved a hand. "Place this size, can't be more than ten guards manning the walls at any time. Besides, it'll be worth it."

A second guard appeared beside the first. "You don't look rich."

"I'm a famous fucking pirate." Barodane tapped the saddle horn. "Explored every uncharted maiden's nethers from here to Scothea, your mother's included. Now open up."

"Well," said the second guard. "There's no need for such nasty talk is there?"

"Fuck it." Barodane drew Scab around and went off in search of the wildflower patch the guard had mentioned.

It was soggy, uncomfortable, and put Barodane in a black mood, but he was too road weary to care.

Sleep came fast.

In the morning, they led their mounts under the portcullis and into the town of Martry's Isle.

What it lacked in teeming commerce, it made up for in a unique commonality. The town spread down the cliff to either side of the main guardhouse, a series of stone walkways and wooden platforms descending into a large bay. Living quarters had been built into the inside of the thick walls or packed together above markets with narrow entrances.

A pair of piers connected the bulk of the town to a tiny island a hundred yards into the bay within the sea wall. The same symbol they'd seen on the beach of a moth fleeing a crescent moon looked over the circular harbor from the stained glass steeple of a floating monastery.

Barodane dismounted. Garlenna and Tohar followed suit.

As interesting as the town's layout was, the people of Martyr's Isle were more intriguing. Most wore gray robes. These too had a moth's likeness embroidered into the hood with gold thread. A couple wore black.

All were quiet.

A sailor bellowed from their ship out beyond the harbor. The town was peaceful enough that the sound carried all the way to Barodane as he gave three silver wheels and their mounts to a stablewoman beside the guardhouse.

They set out, working their way down the expansive network of platformed steps.

A pair of soldiers wearing gray doublets worked a crank atop the sea wall. A rusted iron gate ascended, giving a clutch of row boats clearance enough to slip underneath. The crews had to duck as a curtain of dripping water pattered them.

Once inside the bay, more robed Islemen extended a gangplank to connect the sailors to the interconnected flotilla of bobbing structures where they offloaded crates and goods with little fanfare.

Children weaved between Barodane and Garlenna, one smiling as the other gave chase.

"Even the children are quiet," Tohar said.

They passed a long line of vendors selling salted fish, mussels, and various tools carved from driftwood. Very little seemed beyond necessity. Nothing in fact that someone didn't need. It was a bare existence. Not a drop of drink nor caterwauling drunk among them. They whispered among themselves, offering naught but kindly nods and curious stares to the newcomers.

"You sure you want to live here?" Barodane swiveled his shoulders halfway around to face Tohar. "You're about loud as they come."

Grimacing, the priest bowed but said nothing, as if to declare his intent hadn't wavered.

Garlenna inhaled deeply, voice soft. "I like it here."

"You would." Barodane eyed a pair of young men locked in muted conversation walking toward them. He stepped into their path, speaking low. "Pardon me, friends. We're looking for someone."

Neither smiled, yet both seemed on the verge. "If you've come seeking light, you'll find it there." One of the young men nodded to the floating monastery with the moth and moon depicted in glass.

"I figured as much...thank you." Barodane fished for a silver wheel but the young men shook their heads and hurried on. "Well that was nice."

"A theme, it seems," Tohar said. "I imagine this was more or less what Peladon had in mind when he led his missionaries from Valat and came to these lands. More so at least than the abomination the Sempyrium has become."

Barodane noted that Garlenna withheld a response.

The iron-banded door of the monastery shook little as Barodane hammered it with his fist. Standing in its shadows, he spun slowly about. "More guards on the parapet than I thought there'd be."

Garlenna snorted. "Had that guard taken your offer, you'd be sorely in debt."

"Wouldn't be the first time I've done something foolish." If Martyr's Isle operated at a quarter of their day guards like most military outposts Barodane had known, he surely would have been. There had to be close to a hundred sentries patrolling the walls. "I don't recall Nserthes being a particularly wealthy man."

"Indeed, he wasn't."

Salt-weathered hinges screamed as the door to the monastery drew inward. A shadowy face hung just inside the threshold, half a head taller than Barodane. Whoever it was paused a second and then swung open the door. "Inside. Now."

Nserthes the Sophophant had changed little. Bald as an egg. Jaw like a lion's. The unwavering line of his mouth and ever-present bunching of his brows formed a steadier cut of stone than the rock Martyr's Isle was built upon. He exhibited scrutiny at all angles capable of piercing the confounding cloud around most any problem.

Jasso Jackolo may have been the smartest person in the world, but Nserthes the Sophophant was undoubtedly the smartest at Martyr's Isle. Learned through books, bloodied through experience, he was a stalwart and seemingly endless well of wisdom.

"Idiots." He whirled on them in the dark passage within, gray robes throwing dust up from the hem.

Barodane and Garlenna shared a look. Tohar shrank back a step.

Nserthes turned hard on eyes on Garlenna, waiting. Whatever it was he expected her to say died in the silence. He relaxed. "You've not heard, I take it?"

"We've heard many things, all of them unpleasant," Barodane said. "Malus dead. Ishoa too, perhaps. We—"

"You have not heard." Nserthes nodded to himself then motioned for them to follow him down a dimly lit hall lined with alcoves. "Come. We must speak."

They started to follow, but Nserthes rounded on them and pointed at Tohar. "You. Go with Amoni'Alu."

A diminutive figure in black robes with sable skin had appeared at the back of the group. She flashed a smile. "This way." She tugged at the soiled sleeve of Tohar's garment—they'd bought him a new tunic to replace his priest's robes but he'd managed to dirty it quickly—and gestured with her other hand to a hall splitting off from the main one.

They parted with their travel companion and followed the hulking back of Nserthes through a handful of twists and turns to his apartments.

Nserthes took up a stool on the other side of a driftwood desk then rubbed his brow. "Close the door."

They did.

Both Garlenna and Barodane remained standing as the latter said, "So...you're not surprised to see me?"

With a vein-marbled hand, the Sophophant made dismissive circles before him. "Yes, yes, you appear to be alive. I'm not blind and there's no point in dithering over facts. It's probably best that I bring you up to speed with the principles that form the foundation of Martyr's Isle so you integrate with undue notice. Then we deal with the potentialities that concern me. Specifically, her." He leveled a granite stare at Garlenna.

Barodane turned a puzzled expression on his prosort who shrugged, none the wiser than he.

Little space was given to rest in the confusion; Nserthes bulled it over. "I take it your father, Gyr, told you I know where Solicerames is? And you wish to retrieve it and restore an Ironlight to power?"

They nodded. Nserthes sucked his teeth. "It may be we are too late for that. The game is being played and you've yet to enter the field. Then again, maybe they kill each other and you swoop in at the end unscathed to snare order from the chaos. Either way, your father spoke true. I know where to find the Slave Banner. You'll need a ship, but more importantly, you'll need to survive long enough to get there."

"Are we in danger here?" Barodane said.

Nserthes was stoic, tone neutral but for the faintest hint of annoyance. He pointed at Garlenna. "You've brought the danger with you."

"Nothing you don't seem capable of handling. This fortress seems well pre-pared for war." Garlenna shifted her weight from one foot to the other.

"We defend ourselves, nothing more," Nserthes said. "War is only be waged by those committed to defeating their opponent."

"Then why such precautions?" Barodane asked. "And what has Garlenna got to do with anything?"

Nserthes leaned forward onto his elbows, sleeves sliding back to reveal smooth forearms corded with muscle. He nodded to Barodane, eyes stuck on Garlenna. "She is hunted."

"We're aware," Barodane said. "By the Crown Justice and Breckenbright."

Nserthes shook his head. "The Sempyrium."

Garlenna balked.

Nserthes eased back, jaw muscles twitching, and in that moment, Barodane realized why tension existed between prosort and Sophophant. Nserthes had been excommunicated by the Archprelate for his conversion to unimism. For that, Garlenna was sure to revile the former prosort, even if she kept it to herself. She held little space in her heart for those who forsook vows. Barodane alone seemed to be the exception.

Despite the subtle pinch between them, there should have been a resonance of purpose. Both had sworn themselves to Ironlights. In a way, Barodane won-dered if Garlenna was jealous of the man, for he'd taken his devotion a step further than she was willing to and adopted the religion of Barodane's father. After Prince Kordin was slain at the Bloody Beach, the Sempyrium had deemed Nserthes a dangerous radical. None hated the church more than he.

"They've named you a defector," Nserthes said. "Did you think you would simply slip away with a pat on the back from Archprelate Alcor? You're a spy of the highest order. When Duke Malus was killed, all agents of the Sempyrium were summoned. You failed to report during a crisis and are now considered a traitor. Some even claim you are complicit in the duke's demise, a theory owed to the timeliness of your disappearance and the link to your father. An obvious lie. They come so easy to the Sempyrium."

Garlenna's mouth fell open. "That can't be."

"It is so," Nserthes said. "But if we're lucky, a ship to Malzacor will steal you away before they come calling."

Barodane flinched. "Malzacor?"

"Aye." Nserthes folded his fists in his lap. "If you're lucky."

"How would the Sempyrium know I'm here?" Garlenna slipped back from shock and into strategy.

"You had to travel here, did you not? I imagine there's a description of you floating around by now."

"We weren't seen," Barodane said, voice betraying doubt.

Nserthes grinned. "Oh, you were seen, count on that. The Sempyrium will leave no stone unturned in its pursuit. And it just happens they keep a very tight watch on those who've wronged them. Namely me."

"You." The pieces clicked into place. Nserthes was infamous, one of the Archprelate's longest-held enemies. He would keep tabs on those he dealt with.

"We've done our best to diminish Alcor's spies, but our financial backing isn't quite on the same level." Nserthes cracked his knuckles. "Nor are our defenses. We need you gone from here. Quickly."

"So we must wait for a ship?" Barodane frowned. "There has to be a quicker way."

"We could brave the Corridor," Garlenna said, somberness leaking in at the edges.

Nserthes snorted. "I now see why you find yourself in the position you're in. Lack of forethought."

Garlenna glowered. "Better than waiting to die."

The Corridor of Storms was a notorious haven for bandit gangs. Even heavily armed and armored trade caravans struggled at times to make it safely to North Malzacor. It was a key reason Lah-Tsarene merchants were so rich. The same reason the Imperial Lights of Southern Malzacor had been waging a decades-long war against Kashoggo and his followers. They wanted the Corridor so they could trade with Lah-Tsarra, a foothold to greater wealth.

And wealth was ever the most notable ingredient in war.

"By ship, then," Barodane said.

"Where will we go once we land?" The hint of panic in Garlenna's voice made Barodane's gut tingle with anticipation.

Nserthes cleared his throat. "Kashoggo guards it. He is a champion of the values we—"

Garlenna surged forward a step. "He's a tyrant embroiled in civil war. His brutality—"

"Please, do not digest the Sempyrium's lies and spit them back up as truths." Nserthes's calm was unshaken by her looming. "I marked you smarter than the rest—though this day undermines that heuristic."

Garlenna's good eye narrowed.

"I understand your position," Nserthes said. "But so must you. What is best for Namarr no longer coincides with the Sempyrium, despite what you think. My acolytes and I prepare to defend our island at any moment because the Archprelate would attack us if he had leave to do so from the Collective. Furthermore, you and I both know he'd exterminate the Kurgs if he could. This is the man you trust?"

"I didn't say I trusted him." Her voice fell to a heated whisper.

Nserthes continued. "Meanwhile, the Dominarri remain sequestered, their influence isolated. The only reason they still live is because they harbor enough Awakened to level Alistar if they so wish. Otherwise, you can guess what the Sempyrium would have done long ago. As for Kashoggo, well, he falls into this same categorical imperative. He's an *enemy* whose influence must be quelled. His dogma silenced. Like mine."

The air simmered between the two of them. Nserthes's tone was neutral but the content of his words were flame to kindling.

Garlenna looked as though something worked its way to the surface and she was fighting to keep it down. "It's not just that." For a fleeting moment, her angry expression blurred into sadness as she glanced at Barodane. "My Prince...would you give us a moment?"

Barodane looked at the two of them. A pair of goliaths. Both former prosorts could deal death with any limb if so called. In this state of unrest, he questioned whether it was a good idea to leave them. Barodane shot a look at both in turn. "Are you sure that's wise?"

Shoulders deflating, Garlenna went to a corner and dragged out a stool. She sat with a sigh. "It's fine. Please just...give us a moment. There's something I must discuss with Nserthes. Alone."

The Sophophant flashed a stiff smile. "Matters of the Sempyrium, Your Grace."

Barodane stood, suspicion blooming. Then he went in search of...something.

CHAPTER FIFTY-TWO

A COLD AND QUIET FURY

The exchange of messages in the weeks between Ishoa's declared plans and their execution left a sour taste in her mouth. The unpleasant flavor, she came to find, was acutely that of Sir Gossryk Orr.

The Knight of the Hallow Moon had quickly established himself as an obstreperous ally. His temper dripped from the ink of their correspondence, his sentences brief. His lettering stabbed deep and dark onto the page. *My family has held Bleeding Point for five centuries of Ice Kings and Ice Maidens. If we leave now, we lose Anjuhkar.*

No signature. No titular address.

Ishoa's response was simple, though she had struggled not to include a threat. "Your concerns are noted, Sir. We leave in a fortnight to reclaim Anjuhkar, for she may already be lost. Make haste."

While she waited, she trained, and while she trained, she failed. Gaern Yorek repeated the same sentiments, adding little she might consider new information.

"Got a good grip on your hate, do you?" the beastmaster had said. "Making you stronger is it?"

She'd shrugged. "You'd have me be a gentle maiden?"

Ever watchful, the Fly stood by as they went back and forth, Ishoa demanding Rakeema's obedience and Gaern mocking her demands. After the attempt on her life, the bodyguard from Shadowheart never left her side.

Rakeema's injury had been a shallow cut that had scabbed over and mostly healed within days. Since then, training had become more intense. At one point, Ishoa had thrown down her practice sword and declared herself finished. Her teacher had laughed. "Frustration makes you quit, eh? I thought your desire for vengeance made you stronger than that."

She'd grimaced and scooped up her sword.

"You don't like to be proven wrong, do you?" He brushed a roll of thick hair from his face. "Is that what anchors you to your crusade to kill Lodecka Warnock? A fear of losing? If so, you've already lost. You're a shame to the Ironlight line."

She snarled and launched an attack, commanding Rakeema at her side. But the cat tangled with her feet, and together, they went down. Ishoa landed hard on her elbows in a way that jarred her neck while Rakeema twisted around and onto her feet with ease.

The beastmaster crouched, heavy brow and heavier attitude lowering her confidence into a grave. "You don't get it, do you?" He prodded her forehead with the tip of his practice sword, then held out a hand. Ishoa went to take it. "What? You can't stand on your own?"

Stung with agitation, she froze. "Don't offer next time." She slapped palms to the earth and got herself up.

"Don't lie in the dirt so long. You're a princess, remember?"

She refused the bait. "Sajac." Rakeema drifted to her side as she twirled her practice sword. Since they'd arrived at the Manger, the war cat had grown—most notably in the past weeks. Ishoa could still pick her up, but there was no way she could run with her as she'd done while fleeing Jarik. The steady diet of veal and mice was helping her anjuhtarg pack on too much lean muscle for that. Her back was level with Ishoa's hips now. Another year would pass before she reached her full size, but Ishoa was starting to see how large her anjuhtarg might yet become.

The Hulka'skara tossed away his wooden sword.

"What are you doing?"

"Giving you the first strike. You're mad at me, aren't you?" He raised his chin. "So strike me."

She hesitated. Then she got angry. "Must we do all of these theatrics? Why can't you just teach me?" Othwii had taught her with ease. *He knew how to handle me.* A touch of sadness built behind her heart. She missed him. Missed them all.

"You don't want me to teach you," he said. "That much has become clear. So, I must show you instead. Strike me. Here, I'll make it easier." Lips pulled back around ocher teeth. Hands balled into fists, he snarled and rushed her.

There was maybe a second to decide. Gaern Yorek was a short, old man, hardly imposing, but when she saw a gnarled fist cocked back with no signs of stopping, instinct took over.

Her practice sword swept up from her hip to crack him across the cheek. She gasped at what she'd done. Dazed, the beastmaster staggered away as if stumbling down a staircase on wobbly legs. A knee touched the ground and then he buoyed up again. Blood trickled from a cut nested in a splotch of ash and violet bruising.

Teeth rimmed in crimson, he squared to her, eyes wild. Primal. She'd seen the look before in the men who'd tried to murder her in the High Hall. The look in Sweet Ges's face when he confronted her at the base of the Ice King. Of the assassin. The eyes of a madman...a killer.

"Heeti!" Rakeema swung out to bracket the threat, and the beastmaster fell into the pocket between them. A claw slashed Gaern's thigh as Ishoa's practice sword struck him in the chest. He dropped hard and fast, lacking the gradual descent of the last time.

"Sajac!" Sweat slicked Ishoa's grip on her sword and the strap of her shield. Tongue lolling with effort, Rakeema returned to her side. "I demand you stop this madness."

Gaern stood, shrugging a shoulder. He cranked his neck to one side, emitting a gruesome pop. Rakeema's claws had left his breeches in shreds. Blood damped them dark. "As you wish, Highness."

His expression calmed. An eerie, unsettling calm. Brow and eyelids relaxed. He looked more like a man easing back in a chair after his first sip of morning tea than a warrior from an ancient bloodline. His level gaze found Rakeema. Silent command exchanged, the war cat spun around, head dropping between her shoulders.

She hissed.

"What are you doing?" Ishoa said. Ignoring his wounds, the beastmaster strode toward her.

Rakeema struck first, a swipe skittering off Ishoa's upraised shield. "Sajac!"

But the ice tiger didn't waver. She bounded into Ishoa's periphery, diverting her attention with another swing of her claws. Ishoa barely blocked the attack as the beastmaster surged forward to land an open-hand strike. The blow left her lips stinging and a coppery taste in her mouth.

Yet Gaern left himself exposed. She swung her practice sword at his unarmed side. If he blocked it with his arm, she'd likely break it.

A gentle whoosh trailed her sword, her target already gone. Ishoa's mouth fell open in shock at the man's blurring speed. So fast!

He nailed her in the gut with a fist. Through her boiled leather, the blow felt like a thrown cinder block. She doubled over, vomit rising to her throat. Swallowing it back, she fought to keep her shield raised and straightened.

What was it he'd said? Would you like to possess the power and agility of a fully grown war cat? She scowled at her mentor. *It's not possible.*

But it was and their attack resumed, fists and claws crowding the air. Rakeema was lightning, but so was Gaern. They weaved together, a single combatant sharing one mind, one speed, one ferocious power. Where one of their attacks stopped, the other's had already begun in a ceaseless flood of slashes and blows.

Sweating and panting and backing inexorably toward the stone wall of the Manger, Ishoa deflected fewer and fewer of their attacks. Most were aimed to toy with her. To make her look foolish, striking her somewhere sure to inflict pain but not damage or cripple. Devoid of emotion, their silent onslaught persisted, a cold and quiet fury.

A hundred pounds of ice tiger clung to Ishoa's shield. Rakeema left her feet, and when she did, the strap around Ishoa's arm bore her down—she released her grip and let the shield rip from her arm, leather and friction leaving her flesh raw. She threw up her hands, just managing to heave out the words, "I yield!" before he decked her in the jaw.

Gaern stepped close, voice low, breath reeking of garlic and mutton. "So too will your enemies. Hulka'skara don't need words barked in Fjordsong to guide their anjuhtargs. Nor hatred to guide their swords. Nor rage or fear to lead their warriors." He pounded his chest with a fist. "True power is here."

"I know," Ishoa said through gritted teeth. "You've said it a hundred times but nothing has changed. I was outmatched against a lone Scarborn. Rakeema and I almost died! So when, beastmaster, when will I have learned to be Hulka'skara? When will it work!" She threw her practice sword. Wood clacked against the stone wall then spun to the snow with a whimpering *piff*.

Gaern touched a temple, smug grin splitting his weathered-face. "Understand it here all you want." He tapped her chest. "It won't do you any good until you know it here."

"Great, so don't think." Ishoa huffed. "I can't just disregard my duties."

"No one is saying you must. On the contrary, this is your duty. You throw yourself headlong onto a dangerous path, one that will decide the future of Namarr. I know you understand what I tell you, yet in practice, you resist it in favor of what's comfortable. Familiar rage, familiar words in your head, crying about loss and warbling on about vengeance. But if you continue to stand on that ground, it will make you weak and it will make you stupid. Allow it to command you and you *will* die." Care smoothed his harsh visage, the first signs of it she'd seen from him. In that moment, she saw the truth. This man wished the best for her. Despite his abuse, his mockery, his recriminations, he cared for her. "It's time you found your own path, Isha."

Warmth flooded her, bringing a deluge of sweat with it. An ache started at the juncture of her jaw. "You want me to release that which is not mine." Lodaris's hand fell from the past into hers. Supple lips and eager breaths drawing nearer.

I love you. He'd said it. Even though she suspected he knew of her betrayal, he had said it anyway.

She swallowed hard. "My heart belongs to the dead."

She pushed past Gaern Yorek, entered the keep, and then ascended the cold stairs to her quarters to sit with old wounds, freshly opened and comforting in their familiarity.

Ishoa heard them coming.

One hundred knights leading four hundred holdguard made a degree of noise only the dead and deaf could ignore. She claimed the battlements to witness the knights of Bleeding Point arrive. Sworn to the defense of the riverine island where Gray River overtook Blue, the long column rumbled to a stop outside the Manger's walls.

Sir Hollem called for his shepherds to open the gate. Ishoa descended, her heart whipped to a trot. The council had already decided they couldn't house an entire regiment and leaving them outside the city left them vulnerable to attack. Word had it that Adus and his knights were a day behind. *Two days. We leave in two days.*

A contingent of soldiers from the Point had dismounted. In the lead was a tall, broad-shouldered man of roughly fifty years. Skull shaved bare, he waded through the press of sheep, a moon with a menacing leer painted onto a great helm tucked under his arm. A "bad moon" she'd come to hear it called. More moons, these dripping blood, were stitched into the livery of the knights trailing him. He leveled a kick at a sheep that bumped his legs, "Out of the way!" and sent it bleating for cover.

He searched the bailey, his hooked goatee a beckoning finger. Chaotic nests bunched together along his brow as he spotted Ishoa. Red-cheeked and bereft of manners, he headed for her, long strides carrying him at a pace that the wrong person in the wrong moment might deem threatening.

Ishoa wasn't concerned. The Fly stood behind her. Arick, too. While she doubted the Knight of the Hallow Moon—or anyone for that matter—stood much chance against The Fly, the worn grip on the hilt at his hip and the nicks in his armor told her a story of no meager experience. If she had to guess, he hadn't sat back and let his soldiers fight off the Scarborn assaults. *A man who leads from the front is worthy of respect.* Wolst had taught her that.

"Well." Sir Gossryk Orr let the word stand a while. Puffs of steam drifted from his slack mouth, expectation rather than physical exertion setting him to hard breathing. "I'm here. Half my fucking garrison with me."

Ishoa started to respond but Arick interjected. "Address her with honors, Sir."

The Knight of the Hallow Moon sniffed. "What's that, boyo?"

Arick covered the hilt of his sword. He was a devil with the blade—Ishoa had seen it first hand—but Gossryk had a larger frame and looked to be no stranger to violence.

Sir Gossryk spat. "Hurry up, head out, stand down, defend, attack. You order me around like a dog but show no gratitude when I show loyalty. I didn't come all this way to be treated like the enemy. I'd say I'm owed an apology before the honors start."

Leather creaked in Arick's tightening grip, but Ishoa restrained him with the back of her hand on his chest. "You're right, Sir. I've asked a great deal of you. You risk the fortress given into your family's care for generations. While I will not apologize for that which is needed, I can show my gratitude by making sure you're well rewarded."

His bushy brow wormed together. "You'll give me another fortress when the Alliance takes mine, eh?"

She kept her eyes locked on his. Grandmother had taught her that was important, especially with those questioning her command. *This country knight protects all of Anjuhkar. For that, he deserves a great deal.* "You're loyalty and ability are proven. Of all who've stood against the White Wolverine Alliance, Bleeding Point alone has defeated them. Whatever you wish that I have the power to grant, name it now."

Sir Gossryk sucked at his teeth. He grinned, long canines poking out from a bundle of rope for lips. "Ghastiin, for starters."

Ishoa looked back at the Warming Place, the seat of Rigga Hine's power. She and Joffus Kon had been jockeying to catch the windfall of the other's hold for decades. *Rigga Hine doesn't have five-hundred knights.* And she wasn't a war leader. She seemed to offer little to the efforts of reclaiming Anjuhkar beyond a safe haven, but even that was growing worrisome in its ability to shield them from danger.

Ishoa swung back to Sir Gossryk. "Yours."

The Knight of the Hallow Moon nodded. "I left my best back home. They may hold Bleeding Point after all. Wouldn't that be nice?"

"Indeed," Ishoa said. "I suggest you prepare your soldiers. We leave as soon as Sir Adus returns. Arick will see your troops are provisioned."

Sir Gossryk turned back toward the gate, "Come on then, boyo. Let's have it."

Arick slipped by, whispering in Ishoa's ear as he did. "Only time will tell if that was wise."

Ishoa whispered back, "If it wasn't, I won't live long enough to care."

CHAPTER FIFTY-THREE

THE ROOM

V alka drifted down to his knees, head hanging.

"There can be no secrets among us, Ikarai, if we are to share in truth." Siddaia stood then padded over on bare, grime-darkened feet. He glanced back at Rhul. "Do you keep secrets from me?"

"No, my Light."

Siddaia nodded. "Let us show our beloved general. Tell him about your original motives for joining my followers. Tell him what *you* would want him to hear."

Rhul's eyes locked with Valka's. "Siddaia, the Arrow of Light is the messiah of our people. He will lead us out of darkness and destitution. He will bring us into our closest alignment with the Sempyrean."

Siddaia's laughter caused Valka's brow to furrow. He glanced between messiah and follower, attempting to parse out the intent of the exercise.

"Now," Siddaia said. "Tell him your truth."

Rhul inhaled slowly but did not waver in his resolve. "I saw a pathway to victory and revenge. Danath Ironlight shamed my grandsire, Ravin Guhlkov. I begged Rathon to let me invade. General Valka, too. All but me thought it a ludicrous waste of lives and resources. My hubris saw an opportunity in my messiah, and so, I took it."

Siddaia stepped close to Rhul and stared up into his shadowed features. "You tried to secret this from me, didn't you?"

The raeklord nodded.

"Were you successful?"

"No."

"And you see differently now, don't you? You follow me because you are my most faithful servant, no other reason?"

Rhul shook his head. "I still desire to purge Namarr of its heathen people and retake what is rightfully ours. We are the chosen."

"Isn't this selfish? Despicable? Wrong, to be so driven by your ego?"

"It is, my Light."

"Yet you do it anyway?"

Rhul's face fell to the floor of the marble platform. "I beg your forgiveness, my Light. I've spoken my truth."

"It is one thing to have secrets..." Siddaia turned back to Valka. "And it is another to keep them from *me*. These are the false trails causing you to travel farther from your truth, Ikarai. Farther from me. Go too far and I cannot save you." His shadow crept over Valka. "Ever since you pledged your loyalty to me in the Holy Chamber, you have warred within. You have sought desperately to choose...to lay to rest the indecision so plaguing you. For love of *her*, you've delayed the answer you have known to be true."

Icy dread condensed around Valka's heart and spread slowly into his limbs. *Nera. If Yanos has acted as a spy for Siddaia, then he'll know of the headless snake as well. And if he knows of that...no. I would already be dead. He cannot know everything.*

The revelation bore mixed feelings. His messiah was not all seeing, not all knowing like so many asserted. Though it could not be debated that he saw and knew a great deal.

"You are my Light." Valka hung his head. "I have seen it and felt its truth."

A fragile hand slid under Valka's chin and lifted his gaze to meet irises so dark they drank all color.

"Stand," Siddaia commanded. Valka did so. "Anything you wish to know, I promise to share. But you must pledge yourself to do the same. Trust between us must be absolute. If you wished to see the room, you did not need to bandy lies of faith with me. You had but to ask." He touched Valka's face. Energy jolted from his messiah's soft fingertips into his cheek. The general flinched.

"We are in this together." Siddaia smiled. "Absolute trust from this moment onward."

Stunned to wordless silence, Valka nodded.

Siddaia walked past him. "Come. I will show you the room."

Torches ringed the cavernous alcove. A dozen raek knights stood at attention outside of a plain door. Gishek Ghuul leaned against a wall behind them, arms crossed. Somewhere between bored and disgruntled, he straightened when he spotted Siddaia approaching. "My Light, I thought you weren't coming today."

None of the raek knights bowed nor fell to a knee. *They've been commanded to be at attention at all times.* Whatever lay inside the room was being guarded with utmost caution.

Breath never full, brow never relaxed, stomach feeling like he'd swallowed a stone that couldn't pass through, a niggling sense of unrest circulated inside Valka.

My Light brings me into his trust, and now, I'll use it to aid his enemies. Unless this is all for show and he still means to kill me. The latter almost seemed the best option. *Maybe Nera survives that way. At least I wouldn't have to live in this hell between worlds any more.*

Valka followed his benefactor between the clutch of knights who stepped aside, long-handled hakats at the ready in their fists.

Gishek Ghuul pulled the door to the room open, fat face locked in a perpetual frown. For all Valka knew, it was a look of pleasure. Before his disappearance from Stormwal, the ore baron had been a staunch opponent of King Rathon's taxes, not out of love for the people who were cast one step lower on the rung of society, but because of what it would do to his family's wealth.

A shoulder-width antechamber led from the front door to a second one thirty meters farther in. Forced to turn sideways in the narrow space, Rhul led them to the second door—pure steel. A series of raps in a specific pattern resonated throughout the tunnel. Valka could have committed the code to memory but elected not to. Essuhd had him, but the general would not make things easier than necessary for the Shadii master.

From the other side of the door came a clamorous grinding, dense metal screeching against more of the same. The door idled open—it was at least a foot thick. The raeklord stepped through, and Siddaia motioned for Valka to enter ahead of himself. "My guest of honor shall precede me."

Valka ducked inside. After a moment, his expression twisted into a frown.

A dozen holes at head height honeycombed the vaulted chamber, each one covered by a slab of steel embedded into the rock. Torches flickered in sconces beside each.

In a blink, Valka formed his theory about their creation. Secret Shadii tunnels, now sealed off by Gishek Ghuul. *No wonder Essuhd knows of the room but cannot access it.* The room's value was clear: a nondescript, nigh impregnable launchpad for clandestine operations. Valka assumed each of the now barricaded tunnels led to somewhere of strategic importance.

This is the Shadii headquarters.

Siddaia's followers had come from every walk of life. The truth in his sermons appealed to those born to the highest terrace as much as it did to those wasting away in the filthiest quarter of the Cyclone. But the most pivotal of those brought into his fold had been the Shadii agents he'd managed to sway to his side.

But that wasn't what made Valka frown.

Near the back of the room, moans came from a dozen figures stretched out on cots. They wore the same drab, simple shifts Siddaia always wore. Some stared lovingly at the ceiling, while others thrashed as if stuck in a nightmare. Men and women—old and young. Along with a pan for their waste, their clothing was piled up beside their beds, some of it fine and expensive, some of it drab rough-spun.

All were bound by chains to an iron pillar driven horizontally into the wall.

"Greetings, my Light." Zantheppi, the black-skinned Awakened, waved her arms over a massive clay bowl at the center of the room. Her eyes and hands clouded gray as she accessed her power. Threads of glittering water rose from the bowl and twisted through the air on the way to the mouths of the people on cots. Sustenance wormed its way down their throats. Some choked, others took it with a smile, but all were eager to drink.

Valka inclined his head at the nearest. "Who are they?"

"I understand you are a bit of a historian, Ikarai." Siddaia meandered along the chamber's sloping wall, fingers tracing its uneven surface. "That's what Rhul tells me. Delving into the past has never been an impulse of mine. The future is of far greater interest. There is one matter, though, that I've long wondered about." He stopped just before a cot holding a young woman. Eyes pinched closed, the girl whispered incoherently to herself, sweat beading her upper lip. "Why did Namarr defeat Scothea?"

"There were many reasons, my Light. A lack of ability to maintain supply lines under duress. The enemy's numbers." Valka shrugged. "Disrupted communications despite New Scothea's independent ecosystem of command."

Siddaia placed a hand on the woman's head. "No, Ikarai. Even with all of those factors in their favor, they would have never taken Alistar."

The woman's eyelids fluttered, her chest pumping. Then she sighed and melted into a smile.

Valka swept the cots and their inhabitants, noting the excess of precautions to protect it. *Danath Ironlight took Alistar because of the Dominarii...*

"You see the truth." Valka found Siddaia watching him. "Don't you, Ikarai?"

"Awakened," Valka muttered. "You're...creating them."

His messiah's melodious laugh filled the space. "Awakened are already created, Ikarai. They have but to be nudged. Goaded forth from their fear, their pettiness, their selfish delusions. Nothing I don't already do." He smiled down at the woman and moved on. "Have you heard of the Cave Under the World?"

Valka shook his head.

"Few have, outside of the tribes of Mimbor, that is. Much like Unturrus, it is a deadly and mysterious place." He strode to a chest at the back of the room and hovered over it, his back to Valka. "Out of darkness comes light. Out of suffering comes strength. Out of death...life."

As Siddaia bent to the chest to unlock the clasp, Valka stared at an old man lying on damp, soiled sheets. Weathered and wasted legs shuddering. Mouth open and whimpering. He loosed a sudden shriek.

A shiver drew a line between Valka's shoulder blades. "How can this be?"

"With this." Siddaia had risen from the chest and now walked toward Valka, a dirty clump balanced in his palm. A patch of fibrous, cobalt flesh poked up from the clod. Siddaia brushed at the earth clinging to an azure-blue bulb. "We shall reclaim Unturrus, Ikarai. But first, I must raise an army of Awakened from their slumber."

They waited for Valka in the night garden.

Nera had been there with Yanos, praying before a wooden sculpture of a snake coiled around an arrow, her recent commission from the royal artist. The stalagmite had been hewn in half, the sculpture placed atop it; a honeyed glow lit its base, casting shadows into its crevices and light along its curves.

Nera and her protector knelt side-by-side, eyes closed. It wasn't the ideal vigilance Valka would have preferred to see in his captain.

Nevertheless, Valka had joined them without a word, his knees softly crushing the scattered earth as he lowered himself. *If anyone could use a quiet moment to think, it's me.*

The implications of his messiah's activities still staggered him.

Yanos and Nera suddenly stood. "Father," Nera said as Valka stared up at her round eyes. A stranger's blood had shaped them, yet it was he who had trained them to betray no emotion. "I wish to say I am sorry for being so cynical. I see the fault in my behavior. Our Light has shown me."

A frown threatened but Valka kept it at bay. *Can she truly have shifted so quickly? Or is it merely show for Yanos? For me?* He inclined his head. "That pleases me to hear."

Pulling her silk shift up at the hem, Nera led Yanos from the night garden. Once they were through, a guard on the other side of the circular door grabbed the rung and hauled it closed, leaving Valka alone.

Or so he thought.

"Four thousand and seventeen seconds, I held death in my heart and your daughter in my sights."

Valka jerked back from the sound coming from a swath of towering, faintly glowing, mushrooms. A familiar orb of flesh floated from the darkness and into the light of a patch of spirit lilies. Essuhd's face came into focus, pale and tinged with rainbow luminescence.

He held a sling dart at his side, pointed at Valka. Another Shadii slipped from the shadows after him, one from before, a bloody bandage wrapped around his crown.

Valka's kneecaps clicked as he stood. "You cannot hope to defeat him, Essuhd."

The Shadii master glanced at the wooden statue and scoffed. "Because he's a ...*god*? Honestly, Valka, I thought you were smarter than the rest of the stinking herd. They, at least, have the excuse of poverty for their whorish allegiance. You though, you're weak."

"On the contrary, Shadii." Valka spit the final word. "I move with the might of the gods on my side, so ask me what you will. I will not hesitate to tell you all you wish. It won't matter. Siddaia is the chosen Son of the Sempyrean. Your efforts will mean nothing at all." He looked at the injured Shadii. "You could say these are only words, but it looks like you've already come to understand the intimacy of their truth. Where's your third, hmm? Killed by the same one who dealt you that blow?"

Essuhd offered no response, only an intensity of regard. He settled himself as if seeking to align skin with bone, sling-dart still trained on Valka. "Tell us of the room or your daughter wakes up tomorrow without fingers."

What I said is true. They cannot harm the Arrow of Light. They've been trying and failing, and now, their impotence makes them desperate. With Siddaia on his side, Valka couldn't help but feel he had the upper hand no matter the circumstances. He smiled, let the information about the Awakened roll out with ease.

"So," Essuhd sneered. "How does it feel to know your messiah is just like all the others?" He laughed, a low wheeze. "He wants to invade Namarr and claim Unturrus as his own."

A wedge of uncertainty worked its way into Valka's mind. "Namarr is fracturing. The time is right to reclaim what's ours."

"Conquest, then, is it?" The Shadii's tone was beseeching. "Ask yourself what that makes him, Valka."

He wishes to win me to his side. That means Essuhd was losing the civil war among the Shadii. *He faces defeat and is desperate for my help. He's the weak one.*

A cruel half grin pinned itself to Valka's cheek. "You fool, Essuhd. Our people starve, and so long as Namarr holds Unturrus, they will continue to punish us with trade sanctions in Valat, Oren, and Malzacor. You'd let our people wither?"

"A never-ending war is no answer," said Essuhd.

"With the Arrow of Light leading us, it *will* end. Be sure of that."

"Consult your history books on this matter, Ikarai." Essuhd snorted derision. "Tyrants oft arrive in velvet slippers but they always leave in iron-shod boots." He hissed in frustration. "You know this!"

Valka drew himself taller. "There is but one history book I need to consult on the matter and it says, 'three makes one and one makes three, in the shadow of great power will come the end of things unseen. First the Eye, bringing evil into the light. Then the Hand, ridding the world of its plight. Last the Fire, that in the darkest hours unite. Three makes one but only one makes free.' That's him, Essuhd. The eye of truth, the hand of redemption, the cleansing fire. It is Siddaia that the prophecy of the Long Silence speaks of."

Essuhd frowned at his stoic minion standing at his side, then slowly, his face rotated back to Valka. "You risk a great deal on prophecy alone." He stepped close, but Valka no longer feared the sling-dart aimed at his heart. He pinned his shoulders back and thrust out his chin as the stunted Shadii studied him. "Such a student of history should investigate Siddaia's sermons of the Final Song."

When Valka gave no hint of understanding, Essuhd's cheek twitched, suggesting some forlorn sympathy. "A discerning man like you, Ikarai, you should know of your messiah's Final Song...if you're so willing to commit your life to his cause. In the early days, when it was mere dozens listening to his ravings, he spoke about it more. Now, I can't help but notice he mentions it little at the vippedrome. A less popular sermon, mayhaps."

"My Light carries the weight of all Scothea. When the time is right, I'm certain he'll tell us of it."

"Ah, but why wait?" Essuhd arched a razor-thin eyebrow. "Transcriptions of the sermons await you in your room at this very moment. Do not fear. They have been collected and bound into a book under the false title, *A Brief History of Warfare.* None should question your possession of it."

"And what if I do not believe you? What if I deem the transcriptions to be lies?"

Essuhd's chest shook in a soundless chuckle. "Mark my words. One day, you will know them to be true whether you listen to me or find out the hard way.

But you will know them to be true. Of that, I am sure. We Shadii have a saying vital to spy craft. 'If you did not choose the means, you are the means.' Do not be such a pawn, Ikarai."

Teeth clamped, Valka looked away. For a moment, he questioned if he might be better off burning the transcripts before reading them. "You mean don't be anyone's pawn but yours."

Slack disappointment wiped Essuhd's expression blank. "I see you aim to find out the hard way. So be it." The Shadii master and his assassin backed away and melted into the darkness.

A whisper trailed them—Essuhd's voice. "Choose your side wisely, Ikarai. Nera's life depends on it."

Afterward, Valka had the night garden searched and the fissure the Shadii had entered through filled and packed.

If only I could do the same to the fissure of doubt in my mind.

CHAPTER FIFTY-FOUR

GLORY

S ir Adus had followed the Dread Knight and his wolf knights all the way to the outlands of Summerforge before answering Ishoa's summons. Extra time tacked onto the handful of days it should have taken. To say Ishoa was frustrated was to say little. Seated in her chair around the Warming Place table, she fumed.

Servants wearing downy caps with iron-wrought ram skull clasps on their belts served a meal of peppered lamb pie stuffed with beets, carrots, leeks, and potatoes, swimming in gravy. The carrots were tough, the leeks rubbery, the gravy an under-spiced mucus. Ishoa scraped everything but the lamb to one side of her trencher. The shepherds did that well, at least. The meat was tender, buttery, and gushed with flavorful juice in every bite.

Candles as broad as Ishoa's fist lined the sills of the windows stretching from floor to vaulted ceiling. Braziers stood at intervals around the Warming Place table. Sir Adus filled the chair normally occupied by Gaern Yorek. The beastmaster from Akulsa had failed to answer the call to council, claiming it past his "bed time," and that he'd be of no use at such a late hour. Sir Gossryk Orr was also present, speaking in hushed conversation with Krhalka seated next to him.

Ishoa thought about eating another strip of lamb but found her stomach rolling. Anxiety set her fingers to fiddling in her lap. *Is this my last hot meal?* In the morning they would leave. Many were unlikely to return. She searched the faces around her, awash in a coppery glow. Not one of them did she know well. She had come to respect only Krhalka, yet the woman's profession plucked at the moral threads that stitched Ishoa together. Sir Hollem and his mother were as bland as the land they lorded over, though capable. Arick...was Arick. And her relationship with Sir Gossryk sat on a knife's edge. *If Bleeding Point falls, he may become an enemy.* If it withstood another assault from the White

Wolverine Alliance, and her rescue mission was successful, she suspected he'd be more than happy with his inheritance of Ghastiin.

She snared a piece of tender meat between thumb and forefinger, recalling the gift of seared bison from Ollo Bael's private stock. That seemed so long ago now. So many of her memories from that time had become punches and clips better forgotten.

She popped the morsel into her mouth, chewed without tasting it, then chased it down with honey-water. Across the way, Sir Adus leered at her. A tall man, with the same haunted eyes as his older brother. He wore an ever-present grin amid a bristling, fire-touched beard. "Forgive his stare, Highness," Rigga had said upon introducing him. "In the finer points of court, he's always been a failure. A capable mind for battle but little else."

Ishoa swallowed, disliking the taste trailing down her throat as she looked at the man. The prospect of talking to him made her belly crawl. She turned her head, sensed the Fly shifting his weight where he stood at her shoulder. It disturbed her to share a meal with a group of people she hardly knew, yet the greatest killer among them was the one that comforted her most.

I can't go on like this. Misery soaked her insides. *I miss him.* She brought a hooked finger to her upper lip and pushed, staving off tears as Wolst propped hulking elbows up on the table beside her. Her memory of the man rotated a slab of meat between bear-like paws and smiled at her. *They'd be damn proud of you, Isha.*

"Would they?" she muttered.

Rigga Hine grumbled up some mass in her throat, a sound no more unique to those her age as being blunt was. "Princess, I have news."

Hands hovered over meals, chewing mouths slowing as all eyes swiveled to the Matriarch of White Plains. She spoke. "I must ask forgiveness and admit that I'm the cause of Adus's lateness."

Ishoa frowned.

"Since you are so committed to your course, I had my son confirm with his own eyes that your great-grandmother still lives." The old woman's neck wobbled.

Not the chipper tone of one preparing to deliver good news. "And?" Ishoa's voice cracked.

"She's there," Rigga said. "And it cost ten of my shepherds to find out, so let's not waste it."

Excitement soared, straightening Ishoa in her seat. "I promise, Lady Rigga, their lives will not be in vain. We *will* take Prav. We will save the Ice Maiden. Both things only possible by the dutiful sacrifice of your shepherds."

Sir Hollem and Adus raised goblets of fermented sheep's milk. "White Plains," they intoned and then slugged back their drinks.

"Aye," Rigga said and followed their lead at a slower pace. "White Plains." She smacked her lips, licking milk from her mustache. She rapped the table with her knuckles then pointed at Summerforge. "There's more. I received a message but didn't share it with you for fear of it being false." She glanced at Krhalka. "The High Hand's spies are better than mine, so I failed to believe it could be true when she didn't bring forth the same information."

Arick flashed Ishoa a concerned look. Her gut slithered into knots.

"The Beast of Anjuhkar lives." Rigga paused to nod at the map. "He's at Summerforge."

Ishoa shot halfway to her feet, unable to contain herself. *Wolst lives!* Arick's face found hers, awe evident.

Meanwhile, Rigga had already launched into strategy. "Seems they're going to try leveraging him. Threaten execution if Hilkka Omenfaen doesn't open her gates. The bulk of the Bael infantry are there as well, along with a few hundred Scarborn."

"What word of cavalry?" Arick swiveled attention to the Lady of White Plains.

Rigga leaned back in her chair. "Adus."

The bearded man spoke in a heavy baritone fit for an ancient tree. "We crossed cavalry tracks heading northwest away from Summerforge. A thousand heavy horse."

Sir Gossryk whistled. "That's the combined might of Baen's Handle and the Fringes. Has to be. Prav can't put out anything close to that."

"My brother would agree with your assessment, Sir Gossryk." Hollem Hine turned to Ishoa. "It seems our princess has the opening she'd hoped for."

She pushed a braid of hair behind an ear, knuckles brushing the shorn patch she maintained in honor of Stirrma Omenfaen. Overwhelmed by the news of Wolst's miraculous survival, she took her time in responding. *Of course he lives.* She smiled to herself. If the myths surrounding her uncle could be believed, the Beast of Anjuhkar was nigh invincible.

She inhaled slowly. "I'm going to Summerforge. The Hine horse will have the advantage against the Scarborn camped outside their walls. So they'll accompany me and we'll carve their infantry apart."

Adus laughed and pounded the table. "We'll bleed them one by one from Crucible to Manger."

"Indeed," said Arick. "Without their cavalry, we'll own the open ground. The Omenfaens have no meager muster, either. Lady Hilkka will join the fray once she sees our upper hand. The White Wolverine Alliance has erred."

Smiling, Ishoa looked to Rigga Hine. "How many of your garrison must remain to hold the Manger if it's attacked?"

Rigga didn't seem to share enthusiasm for the plan, but it didn't bother Ishoa. The old woman had seemingly reached a point in life where the denial of activity superseded the enjoyment of all things. "I'll send my boys with two hundred of our finest. Fifty should keep me feeling cozy and safe here."

"A tragedy you can't partake in the fun." Sir Gossryk smiled impishly at the Lady of White Plains.

Rigga scoffed. "These days, my satisfaction waxes and wanes over bowls of stew and soft bedding. You and the princess and my sons can have all the glory to yourselves."

"Sir Gossryk," Ishoa said, pivoting the room. Her pulse pounded in her ears. Sleep, she guessed, would not come that night. Events were unfolding too quickly. For once, favorably. *Wolst lives!* "I'll be taking fifty of your knights with me." She peered at the map, traced her fingers along the road system, calculating—Othwii would have been proud. "We'll ride together until Bitterbridge. From there, you'll lead the assault on Deephollow Prison. You'll arrive at your location before we arrive at ours, so if things end quickly, hurry back to lend us aid. Together, we'll lift the siege. I'm sending you with the bigger host on the off chance you run afoul of the Scarborn cavalry regiment, or the Knights of the Wolf Banner."

Sir Hollem arched a brow. "That's clever, Princess. I was going to suggest the same strategy but you beat me to it." He twisted in his chair to address the Knight of the Hallow Moon. "From Bitterbridge, take Hallock's Bend to Deephollow rather than the Moaning Way. It will reduce your journey by half a day."

"Might make it back in time for the mop up after all," said Sir Gossryk. "I'd tell you to take it slow, but I know you won't."

"No," Adus said. "We won't."

A few more details were pulled apart and put back together over the next few hours before the council agreed on the plan.

Ishoa was eager for morning. Eager to share her success with Gaern Yorek.

Hinges screamed, iron grinding awake in the cold as the stout banded doors of the Manger trundled open. The disjointed clap of chains gave way to moaning winds.

Temperatures dropped sharply at night. Winter held them in its icy womb.

Ishoa recalled the first bites of it on the road from Jarik to the Manger as autumn waned, the way it latched on to her vulnerable parts like an ice tiger's fangs at the nape, never to let go but by the sun's grace. Inside the Manger's walls, among the sheep, she'd forgotten it. Now, she remembered why it was called the *dead* of winter. For those alone and unprepared, it was enough to kill. A pang of sorrow shuddered in Ishoa's breast for the displaced migrants who'd had to brave the elements on the open road to find safety.

She didn't envy the soldiers of Bleeding Point waiting outside the walls where the wind slashed cruelest to flense heat from flesh, either. To their credit, they appeared unperturbed. Hardened leather, encased in chain, wool, and steel—their stares harder still. None wanted to abandon their home to the Alliance but these men knew the price they might pay if their princess's plan failed.

If their friends and family were slaughtered, they would blame her.

White tabards, bearing a bloody moon with a river running beneath it, rippled over their padded surcoats. Here and there, knights emulated Gossryk Orr by painting emotive variants of the bad moon on their great helms. Smiles, winks, snarls...bad moons all.

Trailing Ishoa out from the Manger were a hundred mounted Hine hold-guard with short bows. Roughly fifty knights of White Plains preceded them, carrying blades fixed to staves in place of lances. They wore curved knives at their hips, and the flayed ram's skull was stitched into their surcoats and emblazoned on their shoulder pauldrons.

Sheep bleated in the wake of their departure like lamenting lovers.

That was the one thing Ishoa welcomed about the icy gusts beyond the Manger walls: the fresh air. The sudden absence of lamb shit in her nose and at the back of her throat. The sound of trees rustling. The persistent hum of bleating was finally gone.

Behind her, the gate groaned closed, and they joined Gossryk Orr's larger host. Rakeema ran at Ishoa's side. The Fly, ever present and ever silent, trailed her on a stallion.

If they were to succeed, speed was of the essence.

They traveled by night, hoping to stay ahead of the lazier spies across the land, and kept moving when it was coldest to warm the blood. They traveled light, two and a half weeks' rations per person. If her plan went accordingly, their hosts would reach their destinations in six and eight days, respectively.

Under Ishoa's command were the Hines, the lighter and faster of the two cavalry regiments. They would retrieve Wolst and lift the siege at Summerforge. Ishoa couldn't bring herself to leave his rescue to anyone but herself. In all but title, he was her father, and she'd be damned if she was going to let him die again.

Arick had suggested they locate Wolst by clandestine means, and then extricate him by night. Quick and quiet if all went well. If they didn't, they would conduct a more complicated maneuver using the Hine horse archers to execute a series of hit and run attacks to string out their infantry and whittle their numbers. Hollem Hine assured Ishoa that his men were the finest marksmen in Anjuhkar. Arick had heard the claim echoed elsewhere, and so approved the strategy.

Sir Gossryk would have the easier task. Deephollow Prison sat among the cliffs on the western edge of Prav; it was built to keep criminals in rather than enemies out. Sir Hollem suggested a regiment of three hundred could overtake it with minimal casualties, and Sir Gossryk, who seemed to have an exhaustive wealth of knowledge regarding all things militaristic, had confirmed as much. "Fifty guards, who if pressed, can summon up less than a couple hundred holdguard from Prav. Small, shitty place, Prav."

When Ishoa asked Gossryk how he was so sure of those numbers, he shrugged. "I'm no holder. I don't produce wool blankets nor wooden bowls. My worth is in war. My duty and title are a sacred and ancient one, bestowed upon my family line in good faith as protectors of Anjuhkar. Best that I know it all, girly—erm—Highness."

Throughout the days and nights marching at the double, Ishoa smiled to herself. Things were falling into place. Soon, she'd have her uncle and grandmother back, and with the core of Anjuhkar's leaders restored to power, the rest of the duchy would rally to the Ice Maiden's cause. The pressure of rule would revert back into Belara Frost's more capable hands.

And when that is done, Lodecka Warnock dies.

The thought spurred Ishoa to work through Gaern Yorek's teachings during their journey from the Manger to Hallock's Bend. It hurt her to know she'd failed so miserably at becoming a Hulka'skara. An entire people dishonored and left disappointed by her—yet another. She promised herself that if she survived, she'd set aside the time necessary to train with the beastmaster until the ancient skill stuck.

Despite his tutelage amounting to nothing, his parting words in the Manger's bailey had come as a comfort.

Accompanied by Wiir, the hermit from Akulsa had bid Ishoa a fond farewell. Or what equated to one from the harsh little man. "Rushing off to play the hero like your great grandfather, eh?" He snorted, then smiled. "Let's hope you're more like him and less like your uncle."

Ishoa had sighed. "Does nothing satisfy you? I finally rally my people, the very thing you and I worked to accomplish, and you throw it in my face."

He pouted mockingly. "Does Princess need a skein of warm, honeyed milk for her journey?"

"I'm sorry I couldn't honor the Hulka'skara. I wanted to." Jaw set, she shook her head.

The man seemed to soften. "Mastery is never a first step, Ishoa. Mastery is a path paved in failures. A path that leads you back to yourself." He rubbed her arm with a gnarled old hand. "You're not free yet, but I have faith you will be soon."

She touched his hand and he stepped back.

"You're not weak," he said. "Couldn't be if you put up with my training. If it comes to battle, remember—"

"No enemy but fear," she finished.

He gave a crooked half smile. "When you master the voice of fear, you find your true self. That is freedom." He bowed, first to Rakeema then to Ishoa. "No one is to be more feared than the free."

Ishoa returned the gesture from the saddle. *If only I could let go.* Without the identity of her family—the emotions anchored to their memory—she was nothing. To let go was to enter the abyss. Maybe that was what happened to her uncle, Barodane. After his father and brother died, his mind broke.

She curled her fist on the saddle horn. She'd known emptiness before. The yawning loneliness of disconnect that came with long nights in her keep, protected and safe, but sheltered because she was the last Ironlight. A routine in banality with none but Wolst and a picture of her dead parents to keep her company. Worse still, a routine of being educated on the history of those born to greater deeds. The pressure of it weighed her down in chains. *Will my mind break too?*

Fist tight, her knuckles popped. She was a storm, bottled and stoppered. *Lodecka has taken everything from me. She took my family, my love, my country... She's the one who will break.* Ishoa vowed to surrender no more to Lodecka Warnock. She drew that line in her soul. No matter what power lay on the other side—even if she never mastered her bond with Rakeema—she would not cross it and betray her loved ones. *I'm sorry Gaern, I can't let go. Not until it's finished.*

His Hulka'skara training would have to wait.

At midday on the sixth morning, her forces split. Ishoa and the Hines were set to reach Summerforge a couple of days after Sir Gossryk arrived at Deephollow.

The Knight of the Hallow Moon craned around in his saddle, eying his men with satisfaction. "You may have upended tradition by calling us from the Point but it's good to be out here and doing some fighting."

"I'm lucky to have you, Sir." Ishoa inclined her head. "When this is done, I look forward to bestowing Ghastiin into your care."

"Aye, Highness. I'll pay for it with Golthius Narl's head." He eased the reins to one side and clucked his tongue to lead his men away but Ishoa touched his elbow, holding him in place. "My grandmother, that's all I need back. Leave the traitors and their heads for scavengers."

Sir Gossryk assessed her, then gave a solemn bow. "Your will, Highness."

The men of Bleeding Point headed northeast, throwing up curls of powder and steam as they cut a line through the tundra. Ishoa's contingent went southeast. She hoped they weren't too late.

CHAPTER FIFTY-FIVE

CATCH THE DARKNESS

Winter slammed Martyr's Isle.

Evening winds came screaming in from the sea. The surf roiled and became a thrashing, bucking soup. Gangplanks were knocked into the water and had to be fished out. Initiates and laborers hustled through bowed curtains of pelting rain, squinting against the sting.

Barodane walked the circular harbor, gray cloak fastened at the neck. Between the persistent ocean spray and tumultuous winter skies, he experienced few moments without some part of him soggy. *Another month of this and I might just drown myself. Save everyone a trip to Malzacor.*

Now that he'd been free of Digtown's clutches for a while, the contrast had bred appreciation. He wasn't racing up the stone steps to the barbican with light feet and a ready smile, not nearly, but he no longer sought the depraved depths of his misery like he once had.

Besides, winter hadn't brought all bad tidings.

Ishoa is alive.

Embattled, yes, but alive. Word had it she'd taken refuge with the Hines of White Plains. Word also had it that the Scarborn-led White Wolverine Alliance was winning the war in Anjuhkar. Barodane chewed the inside of his cheek.

A guard at the barbican greeted him. "Evening, Mal."

As far as Barodane surmised, only Nserthes was aware of his true identity. Together, he and Garlenna had come up with a story that passed muster. All three newcomers were former Followers of the Sempyrean, fallen from grace, there by Nserthes's special invitation.

And now I'm an initiate of the Obsidian Hand. Splendid.

Barodane's vote had been for long-lost cousins. That way, he wouldn't have had to act like a monk. He reflected on where their ruse had landed him—cursed the disquieting banality of his new day-to-day. *Almost worse than the rains.*

Each morning at dawn, a skiff would row out to the center of the bay to ring a bell. Anyone in the city wearing a gray or black robe would file into the monastery for first session where they sat in silence with their eyes closed.

Brow furrowed, Nserthes would seize the front of the room, always looking like a man heading for war council as he beckoned them to recite the words of their order.

Earlier that morning, things were no different.

"To catch the darkness..."

"Hold it still," the masses intoned.

"To breathe in light..."

Barodane rarely said the words along with the others but he went through the motions all the same, even if he was off. "Break the seal," he had muttered, a half second delayed from the rest.

Nserthes had shot him a withering look, then left. Luckily, first session only went on until lunch. By the end of it, Barodane's knees were usually flattened by the pressure of resting them on carpet over stone for so long. He'd groaned to a standing position. "My hips and back still aren't used to it. Feels like I went to bed with a voar."

"I like it," Garlenna had said. She turned to Tohar. "Was it what you expected?"

"No, but that doesn't mean it's unwelcome." The ex-priest's face screwed up in consideration. "Change requires change. It's not comfortable for me to be quiet for so long but that doesn't mean I can't see the benefit."

A black robe had approached and they fell silent, nodding to him in deference as he passed between them.

Barodane watched the man disappear into a milling crowd at the end of the harbor's gangway. "My question is how does one make the jump from gray to black?"

Weeks later, the answer still hadn't been revealed. Whenever Barodane asked Nserthes about it, the Sophophant had changed the subject, or dismissed the topic entirely. As the de-facto lord of Martyr's Isle, he was exceedingly busy. Their meetings never happened on anyone's terms but the Sophophant's.

Barodane was tired of it. *You want to make me sit in silence all day, you better give me some fucking answers.* He shoved his chin to one side, cracking his neck as he followed a guard up a winding staircase to the parapet of the drum tower.

Nserthes stared out over the surrounding landscape, palms propping him on merlons. *If I don't get answers soon, I'll chuck him over the ramparts.* The scholar was rather massive though. Barodane doubted he'd have much success in such an encounter.

The guard dipped back down the hatch he'd let Barodane through with a clatter. Nserthes remained focused at a point in the distance, unperturbed by the sound. Wind howled over him, tugging at his gray robes and tumbling errant strands of straw through the air. "You're supposed to be at second session."

Barodane's mouth went sour at the thought. *More like two-hundredth session.* He glanced back at the hatch to make sure no one listened. "My niece is alive but under attack and you expect me to hum to myself for endless hours with a bunch of raving-mad monks?"

The bald man's shale slab of a chin hovered over his shoulder. "Raving?"

Barodane pursed his lips. "Listen, you were my father's best friend. You've served Namarr in ways that few others have had the courage to attempt. And you continue to do so. So forgive me when I say, I couldn't care less about any of this shit. I want to be in Malzacor yesterday. Ishoa's life—"

"Is in your hands." Nserthes turned halfway around. "And it's not the only one. Even if my agent arrived today, whatever is going to happen with your niece will be a foregone conclusion by the time you showed up. As to your training with my initiates..."

"I don't have time for it. Contact your agent again."

"Your training is vital."

"For old men seeking peace, or young ones fishing for purpose, maybe" Barodane said. "But I go to war, Nserthes. I go to reclaim an empire."

"And yet, you'd be defeated by a few hours alone with yourself?" Nserthes scoffed. "Consider my faith in you shaken. War is a patient man's game."

Barodane's rebuttal leaked from his open mouth. *You're a clever bastard, aren't you?* He thrust a finger accusingly at Nserthes, searching for something to say that would hamstring the man's superiority but it never manifested. With a defeated exhale, he let his hand drift back to his side.

"You have no idea what it is we do here. No idea about the importance of the sessions, the initiates—any of it." Nserthes leaned back against a square of stone and shook his head. "Your ignorance is no fault of your own. Grief and wrath stole you away before there was a chance to show you. This"—he gestured at the expanse of Martyr's Isle—"was your father's idea. I may be an intelligent man, but he was ever the more visionary. 'Imagine it Nserthes. What if one didn't have to ascend Unturrus to be Awakened? What if there was a way to unlock one's power without ever having to risk their life?' I thought it ludicrous. Many have tried similarly foolish endeavors. One cult in particular committed mass suicide thinking they might be resurrected as demigods, but alas, we've not heard from them in a century. There is no way to unlock the powers granted by Unturrus but by the means known. That's what I told your father."

Sorrow sloshed through Barodane as he glanced back at the monastery. At the stained glass moth and moon gathering beads of rain.

"Kordin Ironlight thought that if someone could court every part of themselves, integrate every aspect of who they were, they might unearth their innate power."

"The black robes..." Barodane's head whipped back around to Nserthes, scanning him from charcoal hem to shining skull. "They've done it, haven't they?"

Nserthes smiled. "'To catch the darkness, hold it still.' You must sit with yourself, Barodane. You must face your shadows. 'To breathe the light, break the seal.' You must open to the light within. Your strengths and weaknesses, your triumphs and sorrows, all must be explored. An endeavor that can take years, decades. A lifetime for many...if ever they should be so lucky."

Of the initiates Barodane had encountered, three wore black robes. "If you're preparing for a war, you might want to speed things up."

"You are not wrong." Nserthes lifted his chin. Rainwater slid down the thrusting curves of his jaw, pattering the bundled folds of gray on his chest in a steady rhythm. "You know the dangers Namarr now faces, my Prince."

In a handful of late-night discussions with Nserthes, they'd debated the political unrest descending on their nation, the civil war in Anjuhkar primary among them. Only in their most recent conversation a few nights earlier had the Sophophant surfaced the subject of Scothea, and it's newest leader, a child prophet.

"If we can hold Namarr together, a third invasion becomes a moot point, does it not?" Garlenna had spoken in the way of clever students questioning their teacher's methods. "A country so hampered by trade sanctions such as Scothea could not hope to conquer a unified Namarr."

Nserthes had drummed his fingers on his driftwood table. "Your quest to find Barodane has cost you the latest information. My agents—the ones who've survived, anyway—report something of a different Scothea rising from the ashes of the one led by Acramis the Twice-Burned."

"How so?" Barodane asked.

"It is not a king leading an army of nationalists anymore, but a god." Nserthes paused. "Or so his followers believe. On the backs of fanatics, swift is the ascent to godhood. Swifter still, the descent from intended light into darkness. Unfortunately, the ego it takes for such men to claim perfection also precludes them from having a scrap of sanity. Ever is this the relationship between religious institutions and their prophets."

While the man may not have intended to fluster Garlenna with his offhand comments, he gave as much thought to her feelings on the matter as a crocodile gives to the squeals of a fawn as it's yanked into the depths. Nserthes's conversational style was that of a giant stomping over a crowd, deaf to the crunching underfoot.

"He won't just raise an army," Barodane said. "He'll launch a crusade."

Nserthes had dipped his head. "So my agents tell me."

Now, standing there on the rainswept parapet and facing off with a man who looked as though he had voar's blood, Barodane was at his limit. *Ishoa's alive. Namarr's in peril. And I'm sitting here chasing shadows with a bunch of monks.* "Yes yes, damn dire situation we've got here. The Arrow of Light comes and all that." Barodane sniffed. Disdain edged his next words. "So where the fuck is our ride to Malzacor? You've got all these agents—a dozen ships coming through here every day. Does it matter which gets us there?"

The Sophophant hung there a moment, seemingly chiseled from the very stone at his feet, then closed the distance between them. He looked down his nose at Barodane, gaze unflinching. A wild moment passed where he thought the man meant to strike him—it wouldn't be the first time a prosort had done so.

"There is no going back, Barodane. Each step forward is a choice fast-buried, a decision made, and once made, you cannot reclaim it." Nserthes straightened. "This is something you, above all others, should understand. But patience was never your strong suit, was it?"

Without thought, Barodane's fist balled at his side, the other still pinching shut the mantle of his robes. "Oh, I'm doing a decent job of it at the moment, I'd say."

Nserthes noticed his white-knuckled hand. "You're living in the past, Barodane. Fighting with bone and thew and steel will not see us triumph against what comes." He tapped Barodane's forehead with a blunted finger. "This war will be won in the halls of the mind. The depths of the spirit. *That* is the true weapon of our enemy."

Nevertheless, I bet a foot of darksteel through the chest would do in the Arrow of Light just fine. Word had it, the prophet was more child than man. *History knows I won't balk at killing either.*

The Sophophant stepped back. "The winter seas are harsh. I have only one agent I would trust to take you to Malzacor—and bring you back safely. We cannot transport you, nor the Slave Banner for that matter, with just any ship's captain." He craned his neck to look out over the walls. Coastal shrubland and stands of shore pine stretched into the distance. "A pair of armed travelers asked for entry an hour ago and were denied."

"Masons?"

Nserthes shook his head. "Scouts for the Sempyrium, if I had to wager. They will come back." He turned a flat stare on Barodane. "If we're lucky, you will be gone when they do."

Lucky. The wind picked up and lashed Barodane. He huddled farther into his damp robes. *Now there's a strange concept.*

Hold it still...

Barodane knelt beside Tohar amid a score of others. Dim candlelight bobbed in the dark, netting the gathered initiates in its glow. Ever since Barodane had discovered that his father was the one to start the Order of the Obsidian Hand, he'd taken the daily sessions somewhat more seriously.

Emphasis on *somewhat.*

He practiced the way Tohar told him to. Slow and with ease. Self-compassion, too.

Barodane gave it his best shot for a few seconds before slipping back into a state of unnameable uproar. Bees swarmed in his skull, each one a thought, each one towing snips of memory pasted with regret.

Words he would have said to Omari had he given her the respect of letting her know he lived.

Forgiveness he would have asked for from Kaitos were the man able to stomach his presence long enough.

Words for his father and brother that weren't words at all. Just a humming mass at the base of his throat. An elephant's foot pressing on the top of his gut.

An itch in his face had him rubbing it like a cat where he knelt. A tremor in his chest threw off the cycle of his breath. In the juncture between shoulder and the base of his skull, an ache began, begging him to shrug—so he did. Then he quickly twisted his chin side to side, but his neck wouldn't pop.

A hand brushed his arm. He whipped to the side, face meeting Tohar's. The man pressed down on the air with an open palm.

His suggestion to calm down only made things worse. *I can't do this.*

No, you're afraid to do it.

Afraid? Ha! I faced a raek and slew the Twice-Burned in single combat!

Great, so then why can't you face the silence of your own mind?

Barodane hissed frustration and opened his eyes. Those in his direct vicinity shot him placid stares. One inched a few feet away as if it would make a difference in her ability to focus. *Where's Garlenna?* He looked over the crowd.

A platform raised up no more than half a foot sat at the center of the room, initiates of the Obsidian Hand arrayed in a circle around it.

On the opposite side of the room from Barodane and Tohar, Garlenna sat near the front, face serene, hands resting gently on her knees. Untroubled.

Barodane grimaced. A chasm had grown between them since arriving at Marytr's Isle. Her responses were near as gruff to him as Nserthes's were. Rather than be upset by it, Barodane did what he was best at. Letting things fester.

She's grieving, he told himself. *Gyr is captured or dead.* If Barodane knew nothing else, he knew the way loss could twist a person, and subsequently, the grace those experiencing it needed; and no one deserved it more than Garlenna.

A soft ring flowed through the room, the bell bringing the day's first session to an end. Most of them rose. A few remained behind. Some of the more stalwart initiates refused a break until after second session. These were the most dedicated of the order.

Barodane filed out behind Tohar. A heavy hand landed on his shoulder—Garlenna. "Northeast pier in five." She didn't wait for him to confirm before hurrying off to her quarters to prepare.

Leather armor creaked beneath his robes as he made his way to the deserted, isolated pier nestled behind a row of shacks. Nserthes had told them it was as good a place as any to train. Garlenna's back was to him when he arrived, a piece of polished driftwood and a wooden sword at her feet. Waves lapped in the space between sea wall and structural jetty, a sure sign a boat had entered the harbor.

Barodane stopped on the sequestered stretch of bleached gray planks and stripped off his robe, then unlimbered a practice blade from his hip. A seagull landed nearby, followed by another that chased it off screeching, like old lovers whose last bastion of love was the persistent nagging they exchanged.

Thunder rumbled in the distance.

Garlenna swooped, took up the wooden weapons in either hand, and turned to face him. She fell into a crouch and started to circle.

Barodane followed suit. Neither sought to be the first to engage. "You're in a serious mood. Being an initiate of the Obsidian Hand rubbing off on you?"

She gave a wan smile. "Funny as ever." She charged.

Wood clacked as he deflected a high, looping attack from her club, then dropped his guard to catch an incoming thrust of her sword.

"But humor will not save you!" She came in high again, followed it with a straight kick to his chest that sent him reeling backward to land on his ass. "They're younger than you. So you must train harder." In a blink, she stood over him, practice sword upraised. "They're faster than you. So you must be smarter."

He rolled away. Heard her blow shudder off a plank. Garlenna followed him as he tried to push himself to his feet, her attack unrelenting. "They're stronger than you. So you must be tougher!"

She stomped onto his ankle, pinning him in place.

"Fuck!" Barodane swung at her shin but she hopped over the blow. Favoring his left ankle, he stood, heaving breath. "What are you doing?"

She began circling him again.

Barodane flourished his practice sword. "Fine."

They traded a handful of blows, dancing back and forth across the pier. Garlenna recited the same mantra from before. "They're younger than you. So you must train harder!"

A glancing blow off his shoulder left it numb. In previous bouts they would have stopped. Not today.

"They're faster than you. So you must be smarter." She feinted, sent him chasing a blow that never came, then punched him in the gut. Air gushed out of him.

Garlenna gave no respite. With a wheeze, he barely managed to deflect her next strike as he retreated.

"They're stronger than you!" She dropped her practice sword, gripped her club in both hands and rained down staggering blows. Barodane held his sword horizontally in a high guard. Her full strength brought to bear, impact rattled up his arm until his fingers ached and it was all he could do to keep his weapon in hand.

"You must be tougher!"

He stepped back again—found his heel hanging out over open water. Nowhere to go. She'd backed him to the edge of the pier. He threw up his hands. "I yield!"

Absent any mirth, Garlenna laughed. "Of course you do."

Barodane glared at her. "What's got into you? You trying to kill me?"

With a resolute snort, she stepped back. "Wouldn't you prefer that?"

The furrow in his brow deepened. "What I'd prefer is for you to tell me what's going on."

"You aren't ready." She fired the words at him as if she'd been carrying around a loaded crossbow, just waiting for the right moment to pull the trigger. "I've seen you in there. You're not even trying."

Not trying? A need to defend himself surged to the fore. *Not fucking trying?* He'd been training with her every day. Doing every session like a good little fake initiate. Meanwhile, his niece and his nation were in danger and the pressure of it all fell onto his shoulders. Not only that, but he had to wait patiently and put up with Garlenna's sour mood for weeks without a single thorn or tankard of godsbrew to get him through it.

He bit back a response. That was what she expected from him. A childish case made against...a childish accusation.

She damn well knows I'm trying.

His shoulders softened. The coil of ire in his chest loosened. He leaned his head back and watched her.

Upper lip bunching, she looked away. Something was definitely wrong and had been since they'd arrived. *Since her private conversation with Nserthes that first night.* "You're full of shit."

"Me?" she laughed. The illusion was faltering.

He *knew* her.

All of it started to make sense. Fewer words, fewer interactions...less of a chance Barodane would suspect something was amiss. His mind went to Ishoa. The words stuttered out weakly. "My niece is dead, isn't she?" Last he'd heard, Ishoa was holed up at the Manger with the Hines, waiting out winter.

A subtle horror crept into Garlenna's expression. She shook her head. "She's alive. I swear to you."

"What, then? What are you hiding from me?"

Her eye fell to the lapping waves squirting up through gaps in the planks. A bolt of lightning flashed, its tracer frozen over her shoulder. A few seconds later, thunder gurgled, and under the heavy gray sky, Garlenna seemed to shrink.

"How can we do this if we're not honest with each other?" Barodane said. "I'm doing my part now, for fuck's sake. But you...you're somewhere else. If this is about your father, just tell—"

"It isn't." She looked up, truth lining her expression. Whatever she was withholding from him, it hurt her to do it. Her club slid from defeated fingers and bounced off a plank. "I can't tell you. I'm sorry."

She left him on the pier with more questions than answers.

CHAPTER FIFTY-SIX

TWANGING, HISSING

I shoa reined in her warhorse at the edge of a shallow valley blanketed in white. Summerforge rested over a hump in the earth, rowed buildings pushing up from the snow like the bones of a broken spine. Smoke girdled the city, columns of it tacked to a dozen smithies to form a persistent and frozen haze in the distance.

The rest of the regiment had remained behind, making a hidden camp in the forest while Ishoa, Arick, Hollem and the Fly had gone with a trio of scouts for a closer look.

Two concentric walls encircled Summerforge. The first, a meandering low thing that looked like it had been dropped around the city like a coil of rope. The second, higher and clearly more formidable, acted as an inner-ring around the Crucible, the home and keep of the Omenfaens. Over an icy lake, a drawbridge connected the inner wall to the heart of the city.

That meant Summerforge was still in the hands of their allies. And that meant there was a chance Ishoa's uncle still lived. In the days and nights drawing them closer to their destination, excitement had started to pool in Ishoa's chest at an increasing rate. Now, she brimmed with energy. The night before last, she'd hadn't slept.

"There," said Arick. Light bent around the charging bison on his honor plate as he thrust a finger at a line of dots moving away from a cluster of tents on the opposite side of Summerforge. "Scouts."

Ishoa studied the enemy encampment. Silhouettes, no bigger than spiders spotted on the other side of a room, scurried about. Somewhere in the teeming hive of infantry, Wolst was chained up and awaiting execution.

Sir Hollem and Arick wer discussing the dispatching of scouts to locate the Beast of Anjuhkar when Ishoa cut in. "Send as many as required." Then she wheeled her horse around to return to their camp. "This time tomorrow, I want my uncle back."

A hand shook Ishoa awake. She groped for her sword, fumbled it, blinked confusion from her eyes at the Fly standing over her. A shepherd stood at attention behind him.

He was tall—Sir Adus's height—but gaunt, and he swam in his sheep's wool and battle leathers. The bronze pauldron of a holdguard shone bright in the dim candlelight of her tent as he stepped forward and saluted.

She reclaimed composure with a sharp inhale and sat upright. "What is it?" Days on the road brimming with fear and anticipation had taken their toll. On the way back to camp from their vantage point, she'd been so tired she almost toppled from the saddle. Once she'd permitted herself to rest, her body had fallen hard into it.

If things had gone accordingly, a team of White Plains' best knights would be extricating Wolst at that very moment. If they failed, they would attack in full the following eve, or as opportunity presented. Arick and Sir Hollem had cautioned against the move. "You'll be exposed," her cousin had said. "The risk is too great."

Ishoa's counter had brooked no argument. "I'm done being protected. See to it."

The man before her stared at the wall of canvas above Ishoa's head as he reported. "The scouts have returned with news."

She hurried to dress. While the holdguard was tall, the Fly towered, black hood hushing against the roof of the canvas as they left.

Still buckling her sword around her waist, Ishoa motioned for the Hine holdguard to lead them. Rakeema mewled as Ishoa left. "Go. Lehrd." The ice tiger bounded to her feet and slipped into the night to look for a hare or squirrel. *Or something bigger if she's lucky.* Ishoa smiled at the thought of both of them soon finding what they desired.

Cold, hard ground crunched under their boots as they went, accompanied by the butter-smooth hum of the Fly's ax-staff slowly orbiting his hand. A light snow began. Ishoa thanked her ancestors they were surrounded by trees. They'd spent a handful of nights under the stars and she'd come to intimately understand how the Hine lands had come to be known as White Plains. Ishoa had needed an extra woolen vest, trousers, and a heavy scarf that started to itch whenever she warmed up from hours on the march, a discomfort far more welcome than the eviscerating cold.

Moonlight lanced through breaks in the canopy, its illumination amplified by crystalline sheets of snow. Just enough to make out shapes by contrast, but outside of markers like the Fly's height or the shepherd's pauldron, she was hard-pressed to make out who anyone was. Despite the cover of the forest, torches and campfires had been forbidden. This close to the enemy, they were taking no chances.

If Ishoa had to guess, it was a few hours until dawn. Only those too old or too nervous to sleep were awake. Most slept, but those who didn't wrapped themselves tightly in fur-lined cloaks and whispered to one another outside their tents, hot clouds of breath marking the speakers. They passed a long line of horses, snorting and stinking in the gloom. From the number of gaps between mounts, Ishoa ascertained that Arick or Hollem had decided to dispatch a score or more for Wolst's rescue. She frowned. They aren't back yet.

She hadn't seen Arick since the meeting overlooking Summerforge. If he'd decided to lead the raid without her consent, she would be livid. Her cousin's sense of entitlement often overwhelmed his dedication to her. She imagined the satisfaction of giving him a proper and public chastisement upon his return.

But if he comes back with Uncle...

Forgiveness would be swift. *What I would give to see Wolst again!*

In memory, they stood in the Sister Keep together during the Battle of Jarik, his hairy face beaming down at her. A final moment of pride and love before his supposed death. That was the man she'd known. Not the snarling beast he'd become as he hewed through pockets of Scarborn, nor the gloating pleasure of his bloody grin as he chopped Ularis Warnock's hand off. She didn't want the warrior back. She wanted her uncle. Her protector. Her guide.

Under her breath, she whispered, "I was so lost without you." The weight of her words lent a crippling pressure to her already shortened breaths. The glowing memory of Wolst consoled as much as it made saddened her. *They'd be damn proud of you, Isha. Like I am.*

The holdguard led them from camp and onto a furrowed path of deeper drifts. Time trudged by in long minutes and long strides. Her eyes now adjusted, Ishoa took in the fuzzing gray texture of the holdguard's back just ahead.

She pushed a branch from her face, spotting it in time to avoid a scored cheek. "If I'd known it would be this far, I'd have suggested horses."

"My apologies, Highness," the holdguard said. "We're almost there. The vantage from earlier."

Ishoa looked around, recognition of her environment clicking into place. The trees thinned. Bluish hues bathed the rolling white plains that concaved around Summerforge. Where the tree line ceased, four waiting silhouettes turned toward them.

Covering the last dozen paces, Ishoa failed to withhold her excitement. "What news?"

Sir Hollem's voice greeted her. "I'm afraid it isn't good, Highness."

Melting into the moonlight among the four figures, Ishoa stopped. She made out a pair of knights of White Plains flanking the Hine brothers. The mood was grim. Dread prickled at her nape. "Where's Arick?"

"Here shortly, I hope. I prefer not to repeat what I have to say." Hollem turned to one of his knights. "Go find out what's happening." The man bowed to Ishoa then ran off in the direction she'd come from moments before.

"Should I be concerned?" Ishoa twisted around to peer after the man into the surrounding woods. "Camp was rather tranquil when we passed through."

Hollem hitched thumbs into his belt loops and angled his face up at the full moon. "Out on the plains, we Hines came from meager beginnings. Huts of mud to walls of stone. A transition soaked with the blood, sweat, and tears of many generations of shepherds. For our earliest ancestors, life was harsh. Wolves were a constant threat. Sometimes we fought them off. Other times, we didn't. The shepherds of old said that on the bloodiest of nights, when the packs were thickest and most ferocious, they ate their fill and it turned the moon red."

A shiver clutched the place between Ishoa's shoulder blades. "Interesting story. The origin for blood moons, I presume?"

"Indeed. And on those nights, wolves do not howl, nor do they hunger. Their bloody triumph is a silent deed. No glee. No joy. No desire. Only nature and its necessity."

Ishoa adjusted her scarf so it reached higher on her neck. Frustration edged her words. "Am I to believe you roused me from bed to tell stories?"

"No." Hollem turned, orbs of moonlight painted onto his eyes. "We've located your uncle."

Mouth parting, a noise escaped her. She shot a look at the distant camp of Scarborn and cattlemen. "So he really is there." Her voice quavered. "I want him retrieved immed—"

"Nah." Adus laughed. "The Beast of Anjuhkar is fucking dead. Scarborn got him back at Jarik."

Ishoa whirled, white-hot rage swallowing her. "What did you say?" The grin should have slid from Adus's face. He should have looked ashamed for such rampant disrespect. Should have appeared anything but self-satisfied. "Explain yourself, Sir, or I'll be forced to..."

Her words crumbled away like ash in the wind.

Shadows sprang into motion on every side. Tips shining under moonlight, a ring of spears hemmed her in. At her side, the Fly fell into a crouch, ax-staff rotating into his hands.

It was like someone had jammed their fist into Ishoa's throat. She couldn't breathe, couldn't feel her fingers, her toes. Sweat loosed down her back. Her breath was hot and rapid, gushing out and moistening her nose and cheeks. The world bristled. Ached. All spear tips and her thundering heartbeat and the Fly's hooded face swinging toward every twitch of movement—shepherds surrounding them.

Violence leaned in. And all the while, crystalline planes of unbroken snow shimmered like magic, stretching out from where she stood to the place her uncle had never been. "What—what is this?"

"We're making history." Adus pulled sword from scabbard with the glee of a man withdrawing his member to release a long-held piss. "Putting the last Ironlight back in chains where she belongs."

No.

"Ah," Hollem said. "Here's your cousin."

A pair of holdguard tossed Arick to his knees in the ring of moonlight. Darkness stained the white braids on one side of his head, an echo of the blow that felled him. His rudderless gaze drifted about, seeing without comprehension, head lolling.

Muffled galloping from the nearby forest. A clutch of horsemen broke from the trees twenty paces off. Fear bled down Ishoa's legs at the sight of raised bows, arrows knocked.

Twanging, hissing.

She jolted. Flinched. Heard a series of rapid thuds, and for a moment, thought they'd hit her.

The Fly lurched, fletched shafts jutting from his side. Most had landed along his bicep as he'd angled away at the last second to give them less target.

"No!" Ishoa's gloved hand found her sword hilt and cleared a foot of darksteel before something bashed into the small of her back. Head whipping backward with the force, onyx sky raced past overhead, and then she slammed into brittle white snow.

The riders galloped past as Ishoa rolled onto her side. The snowy plane rocked and bucked like a ship's deck on turbulent seas. She blinked hard as vomit sloshed in her gorge.

Thirty paces out onto the plain, the horse archers reined in. The Fly had fallen to a knee but now struggled to his feet still gripping his ax-staff.

Before Ishoa could rise, a blade slapped onto her shoulder. "Don't move." She traced the length of curved steel up a haft to one of the knights of White Plains looming over her.

Movements jerky, the Fly lunged after Adus, ax-staff swooping but falling short of his target. Adus dodged it with ease and then hauled a vicious kick up into the Fly's gut. Pleasure gleamed on the widening stretch of the Hine man's lips. "Come on boys. Do for him."

"No!" The blade at Ishoa's shoulder slid to the side of her neck. She froze.

The holdguard who had escorted her into the clearing crept up behind the Fly, bladed-stave raised. He chopped at her bodyguard's back. The Fly twisted around, quiet in his pain, grabbed the haft in mid-descent, and in one fluid motion, swung his ax-staff in line with the man's throat. Night-black blood fountained from the gash. The man whirled halfway around, as if he'd meant to flee before dying.

Too late.

The horse archers had dismounted and two rushed the Fly. One paused to fire his bow. The Fly leapt sideways and rolled, fine powder dusting up in his wake. He came up swinging, deflecting a savage cut from the knight who reached him first. The man barreled into the Fly, a seeming attempt to tangle up the Shadowheart bodyguard so his comrades could finish the job. Instead, the Fly hooked an arm over and then under the knight's armpit, and tossed him to the ground. A second later, Ishoa's champion had stomped the traitor's neck to ruins with a booted heel. Eyes popping, the man thrashed for a breath that would never come.

A second knight arrived. A handful of thudding blocks followed as the Fly wavered, barely managing to raise his weapon in time to ward off the vicious attack. Dread prickled Ishoa's stomach as she noticed one of the arrows sunk to the fletchings in the executioner's ribs.

The Fly stiffened and dropped his weapon. Sir Adus stood behind him, blade buried between the Fly's shoulder blades up to the crossguard, sword point poking from his chest and dripping. "See, boys." Adus gave the handle a violent twist. "Easy."

"You'll pay for this!" Ishoa screeched. One of the knights removed her sword from its scabbard as Hollem Hine approached her. Icy tears streamed down her cheeks.

"More like be paid," Adus said, thinking himself clever.

"I'm sad for you, Princess," said Hollem. "Tragedy does not discern in its touch these days. I'm sure you don't deserve this, but alas, we Hines are sheep in name only."

"Why?" Ishoa asked but abandoned the question. *Because I failed, that's why.*

She glanced at a dazed Arick then back to Sir Hollem. "What will you do with us?"

Shouts from the direction of camp split the air. The fifty-man contingent of Sir Gossryk's men...dying. Chances were, only a few had escaped having their throats slit in their beds to fight.

"That's not for me to decide." Hollem Hine looked at Summerforge where it squatted at the center of the valley. "Hilkka Omenfaen will have that honor. If she does not open the gates by week's end, your cousin dies. The following week, you will. Either way, this war is over."

Ishoa spat. "Coward."

"A rich coward. And one that will live far longer than you. My mother is a shrewd woman."

"She's a black-hearted old bitch!" Ishoa shook her head. Rough hands lifted her and bound her wrists. "You'd fight alongside Joffus Kon, your sworn enemy...against your princess?"

Hollem's brow creased. "You?" He laughed. "You became the princess of nothing the moment you promised Ghastiin to the Knight of the Hallow Moon."

Ishoa's error struck her in the gut. She slumped in the hands of her captors. *What a fool I am. A greater fool still for believing Wolst lived. And I'll soon join him.*

She screamed in helpless hate. "Sheep fucking bastards!"

A sharp thump behind her ear—blossoming numbness. A tilting that wasn't quite right. A picture of snow and shadow shoved into her face then dragged heavenward. Ringing amid the dark...bleeding closer. An icy cold flush against her chest and thighs and stomach, and spreading, sliding down her throat with languid inhales.

A point of light. A single image, fading fast...

The Fly lay on his side, unmasked, a surprisingly boyish face staring back at her with surrender's empty gift.

There was no one left to save her.

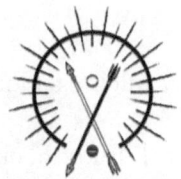

CHAPTER FIFTY-SEVEN

PROLEPTIC HURT

Thephos stood before Syn and Ash.

"By the Triune God," Pintarian sneered from horseback nearby. "Are you a man or a child?"

"Fuck off," Ash said. "This is what happens when you have friends. They want to say goodbye."

"What use would I have of friends?" Pintarian said, then steered his horse farther from the trio.

"What will you do now?" Thephos had wondered what might be next for the couple after his training was finished. Syn had spoken of returning to Unturrus.

"Not sure," Syn said. "Relax a minute. We haven't had that in a while. But if I'm being honest, we'll probably do something dangerous instead. Pintarith said he has a mission for us."

Somber, Thephos nodded. "That's the life, isn't it?"

"It can be, and often, it is." Ash stepped forward and placed a hand on Thephos's shoulder. "Not always though. There are moments of peace, too. Look for those."

With a beaming smile, Syn encircled Thephos in his arms. "I'm gonna miss you, buddy! You've got some special power in there. And you'll be protected by the best bladesworn since—ow!"

Ash elbowed her husband in the ribs.

Syn blinked at the pain. "Since my wife. Anyway...you're a Dominarri now. Don't forget it."

"And don't let that asshole push you around. He's all bluster and bullshit. The damn *cause* is everything to him though, so focus on your mission and things will go smooth." Ash pulled Syn off Thephos. "You're sweaty. He doesn't want that."

Syn laughed and dropped his arms.

Thephos wasn't comfortable with hugs but when it came to Syn Backlegarm, he had little choice. A protest would have gotten him nowhere. A sad truth he'd come to the night before his bonding ceremony—a truth that led him to ignore the Holy Sword's warning and choose Pintarian—was that he was far more comfortable with someone who treated him harshly. Someone more like the old devil. What did it matter if his bladesworn gave him compliments or barbs? If Pintarian was the best, the one most likely to help Thephos make something of himself, then he would choose him regardless of the cost.

After a handful more pleasantries were exchanged, Thephos mounted his horse and led it over to where Pintarian waited.

"Mommy and Daddy finger you like a good boy?" The bladesworn's smile was proleptic of the hurt he wished to cause.

Thephos shrugged and meandered past. If he was good at one thing, it was weathering verbal abuse. And the storm of it Pintarian had unleashed on Thephos was ceaseless since their bonding.

The man wielded his insults as well as his blade. Every interaction began and ended with a cut meant to bleed Thephos. Meant to assert himself as a superior. Most bladesworn allowed their Awakened to take the lead in their partnerships. Most placed their sacred oaths to those they saw as chosen above their own pride and preference.

But Pintarian wasn't like most.

Even among the conceited swordsmen and women of Enshai, he occupied a higher order of ruthless hubris.

Ahead of them, Renau the Ghost placed a wrinkled hand against the marbled wall. Glowing light suffused under his palm, the stone beneath losing density by the second and spreading until a tunnel entrance appeared.

Renau's voice was high and brittle with age. "Go with the Triune God."

"How could I not?" Pintarian said. "His greatest creation is at my side."

Renau frowned as Thephos followed his bladesworn into the hundred-foot path in the stone wall. Once alone inside, he continued. "Do not speak to me or I shall cut out your tongue."

Thephos didn't respond. Pintarian had threatened him before they'd been bonded and a handful of times since. Each time it happened, the promised outcome seemed less likely. It could be he was waiting to kill him as he had his last Awakened, but Thephos suspected that, too, might be a lie.

All bullshit and bluster, indeed.

A smile crept onto Thephos's lips, and though his head hung forward and his hood was up, Pintarian twisted in the saddle just in time to see it. He hissed and lashed out to deal Thephos a backhand to the temple.

The thud of it echoed numbly in Thephos's ears. Sparkling dots bobbed in his vision. After a few seconds, it dissipated.

"Don't let me see you either, wretch." Pintarian's laughter was as light as air. "If we're to play our roles, you'll need to stow the glower. You're my servant, remember? I'll strike you when I please."

Thephos glared and chewed the inside of his cheek as he recalled their last meeting with the Holy Sword in his private chambers.

"Come in," the tall, frosty-haired man had commanded. "Sit."

He'd arrived before his bladesworn, and so took a seat as bidden. Pintarian was later than he should have been. Because of the bond between them, Thephos felt the man wherever he was regardless of the distance. A tickle at the back of the neck. A bodily tug by some unseen hand.

The emotional state of his bladesworn could be felt too if he concentrated hard enough on their link. It didn't surprise him that many Awakened fell in love with their bladesworn, or grew embittered like Pintarith and N'Zara.

Seconds before the door jerked open, Thephos said, "He's here."

Hands clasped behind his back, Pintarian's father sighed as he entered. "Have a seat."

"Oh look here," Pintarian mocked. "There's one next to my Awakened brother." The man sat loudly then kicked his feet up on his father's desk.

"This will go faster if you behave," Pintarith said. "Now to it. There have been rumblings of—"

"I think we should start with farmers' daughters. We could help keep them from losing their chastity and all that. Right, Theffy? You know your way around farms *and* hogs, if I'm not mistaken. Though we shouldn't call women such names to their faces or they'll oink rather loud at us." For a moment it sounded as though there would be more, but Pintarian's casual rage clipped further words from surfacing. "Just making suggestions, father. Something I think my brother here can handle it."

Pintarith craned around, fixing his son with a look of displeasure. "You have no one to blame for this but yourself. You are a bladesworn, charged with keeping your Awakened safe. Instead, you let Kashoggo crush him. You, my son, are at fault."

Pintarian gave a smug grin and rolled his eyes.

Thephos decided not to mention that the man had claimed to have killed his own Awakened himself.

"Although..." Pintarith came around the desk to stand over Thephos. "You had better prove to be as much as Syn has said you are. You risk my son's life with your own, now. You went against my warnings—tied my hands in chains of my bitch wife's making. And worst of all, you've taken the best the Dominarri have to offer in the process." He leaned forward. "Do not disappoint me or I'll execute you myself."

Thephos straightened in his chair and fumbled out a platitude.

"Triune God save us," Pintarian mumbled.

"Enough!" Pintarith whipped toward his son. "You have a potentially dangerous mission ahead of you."

Genuine disbelief fell over Pintarian. "But he's untested."

"What better way to test him?" Pintarith paced around the room. "There is too much happening too fast. Too much at stake. If we are to find the best path forward, we must all be willing to take risks. That includes you, my son. For the cause."

Anger twitched over Pintarian's mouth, but he sat back in seeming submission.

"What would you have us do, Your Grace?" Now that Thephos was truly a Dominarri, there was an eagerness to feel like one in more than just name.

Pintarith watched Thephos a long second, then spoke quickly. "A hold lord has been slain—the Hammer of Breckenbright's third son, Hyram. Lord Roddic attempted to cover it up by saying it was a hunting accident, but I can smell the stink of his lies all the way from here. A one-eyed woman supposedly killed him. Others may have drawn the same conclusion as I, but I've also just heard that Garlenna Renwood has been exiled by the Sempyrean and is now hunted. I want you to get to the bottom of this and find the truth. See if these things are connected."

"Does anyone else hunt our quarry?" The ease of cruelty was gone from Pintarian's manner. Focused on their mission, his derision had been put on pause.

"Roddic Olabran is the only one we're sure of. There may be others though."

"So we may have to fight the wolves and carrion birds for our information," Pintarian said. "Where did the killing take place?"

"Possibly Digtown. Possibly Halaleh. We've heard accounts of both."

"We'll start at Halaleh," Pintarian said. "No one in Digtown will give us anything, even if we ask nicely."

Thephos felt a little lost, like his head was spinning around trying to track the conversation between the two. "Wait...so we're supposed to get the one-eyed woman...or just figure out what happened?"

Pintarian sighed. "Don't worry about it. I'll tell you what you need to know."

"You'll pose as a noble from Valat." Pintarith's velvet-gloved finger slid from his son to Thephos. "And you will be his servant. Given your demeanors, complexion, and skills, these identities seem to make the most sense."

"Couldn't agree more." Pintarian rose.

"You'll need nicer clothing." The Holy Sword stroked his fine white beard. "The projection of wealth will make gathering information easier. Thirty gold wheels from the quartermaster."

Pintarian nodded as if the sum of money were nothing, then patted Thephos's chest. "See to it, servant boy."

That had concluded their meeting. The start of Thephos's first mission as a Dominarri.

They'd taken a few days to gather supplies, and now, they were alone on the road.

"To Halaleh." Pintarian smacked his mouth as if tasting something vile.

Thephos followed like a good little servant.

Pintarian had to wonder why the dead weight that called itself Thephos even bothered. Of all the men he'd taken measure of, this one came up no higher than his boot heel.

"Must you mope so far behind?" Pintarian said without turning in the saddle. "People won't see you as my servant if we meet them and you're a league behind me."

Silent assent, like always. Then Thephos's horse trotted a bit quicker, though he stayed just out of Pintarian's sight.

Unturrus loomed ahead, a coaxing and malicious thumb of rock, tree, scree, and cloud. Rolling hills stretched to their right. To their left, giant boulders and clustered maples and firs encircled a large pond.

The road was a boring place. Nature did little to excite Pintarian, beautiful though it may be. It sat there, occasionally swaying or trickling or moaning. Nothing exciting at all.

He yawned, already tired of the road despite having cleared the Ardent Heart less than a week earlier. He preferred the bustle of a city or the booming motion of ship and sea. Better yet, the graceful chaos found in a training yard. Why his father had let him be stuck with Lord Wimpling and set him off hunting low-profile vagabonds was beyond him.

While it was his mother who'd pushed the ceremony of the bond, he'd waved goodbye to her love long ago. His father was the one he truly blamed. Fucking bastard. Pintarian's throat muscles clenched around the vitriol he swallowed back. *I'll never forgive him for wasting my skills on this ingrate.*

Pintarian had already resigned himself to bearing the brunt of the workload on their trip. The pig farmer was without experience, without a natural inclination for the work they were summoned to, and worst of all, seemingly without a power despite Syn's claims that it was there.

He smiled. Backlegarm was a capable spy. Pintarian knew he jockeyed to position himself as N'Zara's successor on the Skyfire Council, and if Thephos proved to be as powerful as Syn claimed, it could enhance his chances a great deal.

Pintarian glanced back. *If...*

A wet cat with broken legs carried itself with more pride. Thephos hunched in the saddle, spine bent at or near ninety degrees. Muttered commands were necessary to remind his horse it had a rider. Whenever they made camp for the night, Pintarian tested the Awakened's resolve, telling him to care for the horses, to cook and serve their meals, and to lay out their bedrolls. "And make sure mine is on the best patch," he would add. While it didn't surprise him that the younger man did his bidding without a word of complaint, it did unnerve him to consider whether it reflected his resolve in any type of conflict.

Crowborn, at least, could fight. A drunk, a gambler, and a shame to unimism and Dominarri both, yes. But he was useful in a scrap. Not that Pintarian needed any help. He'd proved as much when Kashoggo had discovered they were spies. The demi-god had blasted Crowborn's murder from the sky with a disc of summoned sunlight before stomping his head to a pinkish paste on the marble floor of his temple. Pintarian had been forced to carve his way through a dozen of the Awakened monster's cultists to escape.

Ah, that was quite the fun moment.

Sword whirring, the flesh around his neck boiling from his severed bond to Crowborn, he'd fought madly through the blistering pain. Afterward, he'd hidden in a nearby village until he was nursed back to health and no longer feared infection.

The information he'd gleaned of Kashoggo's actions against the Imperial Lights of Malzacor was chaff. And yet, not all was lost.

With Crowborn dead, he'd never felt more free. Hope swelled in him at the prospect of his father finally seeing the value in him that his mother refused to. From that moment forward, he prayed that he might be able to serve the Triune God alone.

Instead, I've been shackled to a sack of sad, powerless meat.

He rubbed at an itch in his gold beard with a velvet glove. "We stop here for the night." He angled off the beaten path toward the boulders ringing the pond. There came a sensation of emptiness at his back—Thephos hadn't followed. Reining in, he wheeled around to find his Awakened frozen and staring at the boulders from the road.

Thephos was far from easy to read. A plain, youthful face with sallow cheeks, stringy ear-length brown hair, and a slender frame. His expression varied from resigned to worried in most moments; neutral during his best. But now, fear gripped his eyelids and drew them wide. He didn't need to explore their bond to see something was clearly wrong.

"What?" Pintarian snapped.

Thephos blinked, shook his head, then flicked the reins. When he came within sword's reach, he said, "Nothing."

Preferring to speak to the man as little as possible, Pintarian left it at that.

They made camp at the edge of the pond among the trees, a drizzle of early winter rain having left the boughs strewn with glistening beads. Pintarian pulled a heavy padded coat treated with beeswax from his saddle bags, picked a place that would avoid the heaviest drip points from the branches, then lay on his back.

He watched Thephos. Unhurried and giving the rain no regard, he went about setting up camp, stopping on occasion to search the surrounding area as if hearing the sudden howls of a wolf pack.

But an owl's screech from somewhere out among the rolling hills was the only sound. Dusk settled fast—faster than Thephos worked. His slow pace was irritating enough to make Pintarian want to do the duties himself. "Your pigs must have starved often growing up. I daresay, I may, too. Go catch me a fish...if you can."

Thephos hobbled the horses. He studied the surrounding trees. "I think we should eat some of our hard tack instead."

Pintarian unclasped his hands from behind his head and shot to sitting. He'd become so accustomed to absolute rule in their dynamic that the pushback filled him with agitation. "I said I want fish."

"No." Thephos hung his head, resolve arising out of nowhere.

Add unpredictability to the list of shortcomings. Pintarian stood. "You would have failed anyhow."

After rifling through the saddlebag to find the fishing net, Pintarian swept off in a huff but not before saying, "If anyone sees a lord fishing in the stead of his servant, I'll make *you* cut their throat."

Thephos turned a cheek at him and said nothing.

Mud and gnats clogged Pintarian's path on the way down a gradually descending slope to the pond. If he hurled a stone with all his might, he could clear the other side. He slowed near the shore, navigating around the glassy pool in the gloomy light for a spot that wouldn't cause his faint shadow to startle any fish.

A low, clipped cough came from across the way. He glanced in the direction of Thephos. *Maybe he'll die of sickness and I can be bonded to someone more capable.* Harboring a narrow hope for Thephos's death, he resumed his activity.

He hovered over the water, net poised. A dagger of charcoal slid by—two bites of meat at best. Not worth scattering fatter game. Pintarian waited. Minutes came and went as frequently as the minuscule catches he refused. Oar bugs strafed the water's surface, dodging the great maws of death hunting below. Gnats hummed in a cloud as the sun eased farther down on the horizon.

Pintarian felt for Thephos through their bond. He sat at camp, unmoving, heartbeat slow. The bond between bladesworn and Awakened was an alien thing. A tickle at the base of the spine. The muffled, undulating sound of being under water. A faint knowledge just beneath one's understanding.

He sensed Thephos move.

Pintarian looked up and saw him step from the distant trees, his silhouette hazy. He walked with the urgency of a man who needed to find a place to shit.

Motion caught Pintarian's attention near his feet. A fat fish—six bites or more—twisted into view, cockily gyrating its body from side-to-side, a seductress swaying her hips.

The net dipped lower in his hand...

A sound to his left froze him. Boot scraping stone. Another scuffle somewhere else—bare feet trying to be quiet. Thephos hurried around the lake shore. He wouldn't reach Pintarian in time. Whatever was about to happen would be long resolved.

The bladesworn sank into a trance, flowing into the fish net in his hand. He reached out with his senses, snaring information from the absence of things as they should be. Crows scattering with a shrill cry. A small stone, tumbling. A gust of wind whistling through the rocks and causing a piece of clothing to flap. The stink of unwashed bodies tainting the air. A buzzing cloud of insects here—not there. Nor there.

There...

The larger presence behind was the most dangerous. A lesser threat would come in first from the left. A third bandit was farther off—in the rocks—possibly a bowman. *No, they'd have shot by now.*

Relaxed muscles were free. Smooth. Ready to explode into motion with ease.

He caught the drift of the first one's sulfuric breath, the man panting in nervous anticipation. Thephos's warning shout came a fraction of a second after the bandit sprang from hiding. Three lunging steps and then he was slashing at Pintarian's brow.

So slow. Gut-warming slowness. The world a thickening ooze.

The bladesworn shifted back just enough to catch the ax blade in his fish net, rotated his wrist to clamp the rim around the man's hand, and in one fluid motion, drew Last Breath. It left the scabbard with a velvety moan. Steel glimmered—swished up and down at an angle—a thing so deadly, yet so elegant. Two cuts too quick to see slid buttery smooth through the neck and leg artery of the rotten-mouthed bandit.

The ax the man had been gripping thumped into the mud.

A look of confusion, then burgeoning understanding. Rotten-teeth clapped a hand to his spewing neck and stared at Pintarian. Arterial blood sluiced through grimy fingers. Browning teeth milled together. He sucked in a hiss that turned into a gurgle.

Loose hair was slathered across his bald pate. *Wretched comb-over.*

Pintarian whirled from the dying. A Kurg rushed him, rusty sword in hand. The bladesworn pumped his head to the left, causing the Kurg to raise his weapon in expectation of a blow that never came. The curved tip of Last Breath skated down the length of the Kurg's notched blade, clipping bronze fingers free. They jumped into the air like kernels of threshed wheat.

Pintarian let his foe's weapon slide harmlessly past his ribs and stepped into the Kurg's momentum, elbow leveled at his jaw. A hush of impact followed. The Kurg's head snapped back. He dropped, sword tumbling from gripless files of slanted flesh. From a knee in the dirt, the Kurg noticed the gushing nubs where his fingers had been. He stood to flee—

Pintarian slashed his hamstrings, evoking a pained howl, and then kicked the man's shitty sword from reach. Sliding his heel in a backward arc, he rotated to face the boulders—eyed them hard. Not far off. Any second, he expected the third assailant to emerge, but the bandit hiding there proved smarter than his peers and never showed.

The one with rotten teeth thrashed weakly on his back in the water. *That'll do for the fish.* Pintarian sighed. The bladesworn stepped over him. "You ruined my dinner." He dipped his sword into the man's breast just far enough to puncture his heart. The bandit convulsed like a bug stuck with a needle, then went limp, lungs rattling one last time.

A moment later, Thephos arrived, winded.

The Kurg yammered in Unti and sought to stand.

"He's yours." Pintarian inclined his head at Thephos, then laughed. "Think you can take him? I trussed him up for you. You've slaughtered a sow or two, I'm sure. Should be easy."

Thephos stared, chest swelling like a panicked bird's.

"Come! Perfect practice for your powers. Look at him, paling from blood loss. Disoriented. Our next enemy may not be so stagnant."

The Kurg's eyes threatened to roll back in his head. Milky sweat lathered his golden skin. He caught sight of Thephos and his brow bunched...

What's this? Recognition?

Pintarian glared at Thephos, saw the way he wouldn't look at the bandit. "Do you *know* this Kurg?"

Thephos hesitated, then shook his head.

"Funny." Pintarian's gaze darted between the two. "He seems to know you."

A fly landed on the Kurg's sagging lower lip—darted off as he spoke. "Ascendant."

"He let me go," Thephos said in a rush. "That one..." He pointed at the dead man in the mud. "He—he wanted to defile me. But the Kurg made him let me go. He's a follower of the Triune God...like you."

"Like me?" Pintarian raised an eyebrow, disgust budding at the comparison. "The Triune God is so lucky to have bandits, murderers, and rapists as followers. A surplus, even." He leveled his sword. "Now, are you going to kill him?"

"He's incapacitated," Thephos pleaded. "We—we could let him go."

"You're right," Pintarian said. "We certainly can let him go." One step. The twitch of an arm.

The Kurg gulped as Pintarian's blade entered his throat. He had tried to jerk his head away at the last second but only managed a subtle movement that froze before it started.

Pintarian spoke with a playful lilt. "And here is how we trim the hedges for the Triune God." He stepped at an angle and heaved his torso around so that his blade erupted from the side of the Kurg's neck in a shower of scarlet.

Thephos caught flecks of the spray across his face—less than Pintarian intended, but funny to behold, nonetheless.

Gnats swarmed to escape as the Kurg face-planted in the mud. Pintarian swatted a path to the man's decrepit tunic, crouched, and wiped Last Breath clean with methodical care. The blade was everything. It had forged him, made him strong, made him someone worthy of duty, respect, admiration.

Someone worthy of fear.

Finished, he stood. He felt Thephos standing there, shivering from the cold. Gawking at the twitching corpses and questioning himself. "Not the same as watching me kill bees, is it?"

The pig farmer was quiet as Pintarian took his measure for what seemed the thousandth time. My best days of service are wasted on this soiled rag of a man. And I'm expected to swallow such bitter flavor with a smile?

"You've been misled." Pintarian locked eyes with Thephos. "By Backlegarm. By my father. By the Dominarri. But you already knew that, didn't you?"

Thephos hung his head.

I'd have a better chat with the Kurg's corpse!

Pintarian sighed and took a moment to survey the oasis among the rolling hills. Beautiful even with the murdered men littering it. He nudged the Kurg's body with the toe of his boot. *Too beautiful to let these unworthy wretches claim it.*

"You weren't ready and you know it," Pintarian said. "You have no idea what you're doing, or why you're doing it, for that matter. I see this with Awakened. Growing up in Enshai, we're taught to revere them and yet, they're often the most undeserving. Broken things, poorly mended, then elevated above those who've toiled all their waking hours to glean mastery from what little they were given." The words tasted like rotten fish, sustenance gone to poison. "Your purpose was not honed in earnest, and so, you must cling to the one given to you on a silver platter."

He stepped closer to Thephos, his broad, lithe frame eclipsing the dung heap. Words cut low. "I will never trust a man who does not choose his own path. Who commits by words alone when *actions* are necessary."

Pintarian tilted his head back at an angle, brought the tip of his blade to rest on Thephos's cheek. "Do you know why my blade is called Last Breath? Answer or I'll cut you."

"It will be your opponent's last breath."

"When I draw this blade, I fight for the Dominarri to *my* last breath. I will never give up. Never cede to whatever evil I'm pitted against. I give my life to the cause. That's what I was born to do and I've worked tirelessly my entire life to ensure my ability to do it well. Are you willing, *brother*? Are you so willing to die for this cause? To give your last breath?"

The boots of the bandit with rotten teeth scuffed up against stone, his leg flopping over in the water. Pintarian sank Last Breath back into its scabbard. "These men tried to kill me. Despite knowing they could be here, you remained silent—complacent. If you are Dominarri, you will never let your feelings get in the way of our business again."

He laid a gloved hand on Thephos's protruding collar bone, patted it once, then walked back to where they'd camped, mud sucking at his boots.

"I'm sorry."

Pintarian slowed to a stop.

"I just...I didn't want anyone to die."

"As I said, you were misled. The greatest good oft stands on the shoulders of darker deeds." Pintarian snorted. "You're a hero now, but never will you feel like one."

This time, he thought perhaps the Awakened would respond. No such luck. Then again, he'd rarely been lucky when it came to others. Whatever success he'd had in life was by his own hand, his own blade, his own hard work and determination. Other people amounted to little more than disappointments.

He rounded, found Thephos staring at his hands. "I'm no hero," the worm said.

"Good. Should be easier for you to drag those bodies to the other side of the rocks. They'll stink otherwise." Pintarian watched his Awakened mosey to the task, feeling sour to his core.

But if Thephos was to be useful to the Dominarri cause, it wouldn't be the last harsh lesson Pintarian taught him.

CHAPTER FIFTY-EIGHT

DREAD'S RIGHT HAND

Slaps of light woke Ishoa, dastardly bright and stabbing at the back of her skull. With every jounce and sway of the horse she was slung over, her breath caught with the pain.

"Wakey, wakey."

Wincing, she craned her head around. From the perspective of a chamber pot, Ishoa spotted Adus grinning down at her.

She strained against her bonds, rough rope gnawing tender flesh at wrist and ankle. She thrust with her hips, trying to roll from the horse's back but found herself fastened tight to the saddle. If luck favored her, there might have been a fray in the rope, so she forced her full body rigid. Heat pooled in her face. Tears pushed up behind her eyes and she fought the throbbing in her head just as much as she fought to win free. Black spots filled her vision...

A whimpering exhale. She went limp in defeat. *Luck abandoned me at the cradle.*

The Hines laughed at her futile attempt. She refused to meet their faces.

You've really messed things up, Isha. You gave Lodecka her damn Revocation and paved a road bricked in gold for Scothea to conquer all of Namarr again. And Rakeema...

Ishoa hadn't seen her ice tiger since she'd told her to hunt. She loosed a pinched howl of frustration that set the Hines to laughing louder.

Think of something, you naive, foolish girl!

She caught a fall of white braids on the flanks of a horse riding on the other side of Adus. Arick's bloody face lifted to meet hers. There was no sadness there. No anger. When stress came, Ishoa realized, her cousin retreated to safer places. Neutral observation pervaded his porcelain expression. *He's working out a strategy...that's why he isn't wriggling like a netted fish. That's a child's response. He's keeping calm and planning. Be smart, Isha, like Arick.*

She took in her surroundings. A column of horsemen trotted three abreast through the trees behind them and it looked like the rearmost weren't yet moving. *We're leaving camp.* She looked ahead. *And going where?*

She blinked back the fog of emotion veiling last night's betrayal and worked to recall useful information from the harrowing exchange. They were going to use her and Arick as bait for the Omenfaens. Arick would die first. *Then it's my turn.* The Ironlight line would stop with her, a foolish child too hell bent on vengeance.

Horror and shame smothered her to breathlessness. Sir Gossryk was likely leading his men into a trap as well. The Hines had planned it all. The White Wolverine Alliance would be waiting to crush them. Four hundred would die alongside the Knight of the Hallow Moon.

She retched. Bile filled her mouth and then spilled down the side of the horse. She gagged and sputtered. *I've become my uncle, Barodane.*

Warnings had abounded over the years, attempting to divert Ishoa from being like him. Though they were oft delivered alongside a bit of honey that sang the man's praises. Praises of who he'd been before his mind had sunk into grief's abyss.

I'm not the Mad Prince. I'm no one but myself. She ground her teeth, jaw popping on the side of her face where they'd punched her. A loose tooth bled salty warmth onto her tongue. *I'm Ishoa Ironlight—so act like it!*

Hollem Hine drew abreast of her. "You're awake. For a moment, I feared we'd squandered our most precious bargaining chip. Sir Ulth has a history of slaying men with his fists."

Ishoa glared up at Sir Hollem. *It's half a day to the Scarborn camp. That's where he'll turn us over to Lodecka, or Ularis, or whoever awaits.* There wasn't much time for idle chit-chat, nor sorrow, nor pity. Once Lodecka got hold of her...

Think, Isha!

Othwii's gentle avian face flashed through her mind. *Information is the shield that protects nations. Knowing what motivates your enemies, the killing blade.*

"How long have you followed Syphion Muul's teachings?" Her grandmother had taught her the tactic. Hazard a wrong answer to evoke the right one. People loved to correct others, especially when they thought they had the upper hand.

Mouth parted in surprise, Hollem said, "You think our loyalty so cheap that a few vehement words could steal it?"

Position him as a villain to afford another correction. "Your loyalty is cheap, Sir Hollem. The Hine name will sit beside that of Bacot the Traitor in the history books." She grunted. "Cheaper. At least the Scoths promised the mountain enclaves Lah-Tsarra."

Red crept into Sir Hollem's cheeks. "That's twice now you've slandered the name of our hold."

"What are you going to do, capture me again?"

The space beneath one pale eye twitched, some cruel resolve passing through his mind. "I can think of a few ways to exact retribution."

Fear puddled in Ishoa's groin. *No enemy but fear.* She spat. "You would do that. Treacherous whoreson. You heap dishonor on yourself and blame me for your villainy."

"If you think enraging me will do you any good, you're wrong." Hate slashed his face as he leaned over in the saddle. Hot breath damped the hair around her ear. "We have a full day before we must deliver you to the Scarborn. I can call a halt and have you tied to a tree so you and your cousin can get fucked by every man and horse under my command. Or, you could refrain from your slurs."

He grabbed her ear and twisted. Searing pain spread from crown to chin and forced her to crane her head along with the trajectory of the movement. "Do you hear me, Highness?"

"Yes," she breathed, tears flowing.

He let go. Blood rushed to the angered area. Heat and relief poured through her skull and down her neck. She exhaled, attempting to gain a hold of the ebbing pain. *What now?* "I just wish you'd given me a chance."

"We did. And you showed your gratitude by promising Ghastiin to the Knight of the Hallow Moon."

"I had to."

"Did you?" Hollem hissed. "Understand this, Princess. We were with you. Months we spent at your side without a word of reward for our loyalty. We kept you safe and would have continued to do so to our detriment. But the moment Sir Gossryk had an army for you, you bent over and gave him whatever he wished."

"I did what I had to do," Ishoa pleaded. "There's still time to do the right thing and prove yourself loyal to Namarr. I—I'll pardon you."

Hollem scoffed. Outside of huffing horses and clanking bridles, the column marched in silence. "I am doing the right thing, Princess. My mother deemed you weak, unfit to rule. With Namarr so embroiled, we all fear an invasion by Scothea, but what you may not have realized is that, with you wearing the crown, such a thing would be inevitable."

Ishoa felt her insides disintegrating. Like the weight of the world was smashing her flatter than a blade of grass underfoot. *I was so preoccupied with proving myself fit to rule, I did the opposite.*

I failed you. Almost, she said it aloud to Sir Hollem but bit back the words at the last moment. She would give this bastard and his stinking ilk nothing.

Sir Hollem had one last stone to place atop her funeral bier. "With you as our ruler, Namarr would be reduced to naught but ash and bone dust. Without you, we have a chance." He spurred his horse to the front of the column.

Ishoa cursed under her breath.

She tried a similar tactic with Adus. Promised him Ghastiin and more. Offered him a deal more lucrative than the Hines could ever hope to get from the Scarborn.

All the while, Sir Adus grinned down at her, unmoved by her honeyed words but seeming to enjoy the sound of her voice. Her negotiations were pitiful, scooped clean of confidence. Saturated by desperation. That's what he liked about it, she realized. The futility of her position—her powerlessness. Moist hunger filled his lecherous gaze, his fat, flaking lips encircling gleaming yellow teeth. It was near enough to make her vomit again. "Please. I'll give you whatever you want. Just listen, dammit!"

A hiss of warning from Arick. Reproach rimming his azure eyes. Dried blood and worry streaking his face.

Adus held a finger to his lips and hushed Ishoa. Then his mount shot forward to ride abreast with his brother at the fore of the column.

They were still in the trees when they came to a stop. It hadn't been more than an hour since they'd left. With such a short distance covered, it made little sense.

A change of heart? Ishoa withheld hope. Unchecked during dangerous times, it dulled the senses where cynicism kept one sharp.

Hollem and Adus turned their mounts to face back down the line. Hollem gestured, and Ishoa whipped her head to see the holdguard closest to her nod in return. He took the reins of her horse and split from the column.

Arick cursed, trails of dried blood flaking with the twist in his expression. Neck tendons ballooned as he attempted to pry apart his bonds. Like a wolverine uncaged, he fought, pale flesh turning a mottled purple.

The sudden brutality of her cousin's actions seemed out of place, better suited for the moment of waking to his fate like she had done.

I don't understand...

Confusion plummeted into her gut as she looked back. Terrible knowing marred the faces of the Hine holdguard. Disgust worn on furrowed brows, they watched the condemned. Watched her taken away. Approval curled upward on the lips of those who relished indecency, but it was those with unreadable expressions that were the worst for her to witness. The ones who looked away, unwilling to meet her eyes. The ones who showed no remorse.

The ones who would let it happen.

Understanding shattered against the back of Ishoa's mind, a pure white vase thrown to the floor. She felt herself lying heavier across her horse. Dead weight. Bloated with sick. A burdensome sack of flesh. She wondered how her mount could bear so much without buckling, how it could let itself be controlled without rebellion.

She supposed she'd find out soon enough.

Arick jostled the tack of his horse and hurled another threat. "I'll kill you!" His words died on the wind as the Hine brothers led her deeper into the woods. Farther from the rest of the column. Somewhere private.

After a while, Adus and Hollem dismissed the holdguard. She heard Adus's fat lips part with a moist click. Felt his glutting eyes crawl over her. He steered his courser close and patted her hamstring, hand lingering.

She heaved at her bindings, wishing desperately she wasn't tied up but knowing that when she wasn't, that's when they would begin to beat her.

Adus gave a hearty laugh. Ishoa drew phlegm to the back of her throat, loosed it—with him behind her, the angle was too difficult. It sailed in an arc and plopped in the snow.

"I've reconsidered our position," Hollem said. "I would have thought you'd be pleased."

Panic threatened to overwhelm her. She shook violently.

"Your offer to Adus was generous, so we're not going to take you to the Scarborn after all." He blew into a palm in an attempt to warm it. "It will be a different kind of exchange now. Dishonor for dishonor. We'll keep you captive of course—at the Manger. Nice and cozy until the Scarborn take Summerforge."

It sounded like Hollem was turning in the saddle, presumably to see how far they'd come. "Here works." They'd ridden in the opposite direction of the barren, white valley surrounding Summerforge. The trees were thicker here, and they were far enough from the column that they wouldn't be seen or heard by the rest of their soldiers.

One of them fumbled at the rope lashing her to her horse, then dragged her off by her feet into the snow. Wrists and ankles bound, she keeled over into a foot of powdery drift. She shrimped a few feet before Adus seized her by the bindings between her feet and towed her toward a tree. Clumps of snow slid into her tunic and under her mail, wetting her belly and back.

Gruff hands lashed her to the tree. She made it difficult for Adus, so much so that he dealt her a clubbing backhand that left a low whistling in one ear. Her jaw throbbed as she sagged in her bonds.

"What the Scarborn don't realize is we'll need a bargaining chip if the Collective of Namarr decides to take back Anjuhkar next spring. White Plains being so much closer to Alistar than Jarik, I daresay we'd be first on their list of targets."

He worked free the buttons of his heavy wool vest then stripped it back to reveal a fall of chain covering a sheephide tunic. Hairy fingers slid to his belt. "Fear of losing the last Ironlight, however, may have them thinking twice."

Adus pulled the rope he'd used to tie her to the tree, stretching her arms overhead. Then he lashed it to a root at his feet.

No...this...this can't be happening. Yet so many things had happened she didn't wish for. It fit the sordid pattern she'd rebelled against since birth. Suffering and loss of what was dearest to her had become her destiny. Only now, it wouldn't end at Summerforge. The loss of her innocence was to be stained into her, her suffering prolonged at the Manger for as long as the Hines wished.

Adus grabbed her hair, pried her head back, and nipped at her neck. The blood left Ishoa's body as his lips brushed her ear between fetid licks. "I'll take it slow. We've got the rest of our lives to—" He jerked back. "What the fuck?"

Ishoa followed his stunned expression to where Sir Hollem had been standing. It looked like someone was pouring wine down his gullet only to have it flow out at the neck in a skirt. Hollem fumbled at it, steaming blood soaking him to the elbow and carving lines in the snow at his feet. Another wound at his groin blossomed dark—the first wound by the look of it, the one that caused him to drop his defenses for the more fatal throat slash.

A short warrior covered in black enameled chain, leather, and plate stood behind Sir Hollem, a gory knife gripped in their hand.

Steel screeched from Adus's scabbard. His smile fled as he cupped the side of his mouth to call for help.

A shadow rose behind him, taller and broader across the shoulders. Adus slowly turned to face his assailant.

Death waited.

Clad in gleaming obsidian plate and a great helm fashioned into the visage of a snarling black wolf, the knight held a warhammer poised above Adus's head. "Traitor," the stranger declared. Darksteel flashed in the midmorning light.

Adus's skull split around the ears. Brain matter spewed outward. Salty droplets of ichor shot across Ishoa's face, a few finding their way into her open mouth. She blinked and spat. When she looked back, Adus's head had become a molten ruin. He crumpled backward to the snow, hands flexing like dying spiders.

The snarling black wolf visage swung toward Ishoa—nodded at her then to the one who'd killed Hollem. "Okki, her bonds."

A presence slid up beside Ishoa. A bloodied dagger sawed at the ropes knotted round her wrists. "You—you killed them." The knife slowed. This one, too, wore the snarling wolf helm. Red curls sprayed out from under it, tangling with the fur on their shoulders. They pushed back the visor.

Youth-smooth cheeks, green eyes, and a penetrating stare. Stern but pretty. A familiar face. "You're safe now, Princess."

"Okki," Ishoa muttered in disbelief. "Is it—is it you?" The rope fell apart. Blood rushed into her arms. She rubbed her tingling wrists, struggling to stay conscious amid the chaotic ebb and flow.

"It is Okki Womunger," said a booming voice. There was a familiarity there as well. Unparalleled confidence. "She is my right hand."

Ishoa studied her other savior. A black wolf on a filthy banner appeared in the hands of another knight behind him, as did dozens more well-armed and armored soldiers bearing the same attire as their leader. "You're the Dread Knight." Ishoa gulped, questioning if she'd truly been saved or if her fate had simply changed hands.

"That I am." The man gave his warhammer off to a wolf knight and reached up to remove his helm. The head of his weapon was shaped into the likeness of an anvil...

Ishoa's breath caught as the towering warrior slipped a head of dark curls free from his helm. His smile beamed. "My knights call me Dragga the Dread."

CHAPTER FIFTY-NINE

DARKENING DOORWAYS

B arodane resisted the urge to dog Garlenna's heels. If someone didn't want to talk about something, he found it hard to force them. Maybe a little of his own preferences in it, but he was content to ask once and let things lie. Most times.

If she was unwilling to address whatever was troubling her, he'd give her space. His prosort had done more than enough to earn her secrets.

Barodane passed his days investing in the silent practices of an impostor initiate. *At least she has the decency to send Tohar in her stead for training. A kind gesture, but a poor replacement.*

The priest could drub an unsuspecting youth from behind like he'd done at Halaleh, or hold his own in a fistfight, but the finer points of martial combat eluded him.

Tohar throttled his club in both hands and threw it about him like a spastic child playing keep-away from a smaller one. "Maw-begotten slick with that blade, you are!"

Barodane relaxed into the motions, demonstrating swordplay forms with seamless ease. "Still a little rusty but it's coming back."

Practice sword and club clacked off one another a handful more times before the priest called for a halt to catch his breath.

The sun's light ruptured across the sea, forming a glittering path along the inner wall of the bay. Barodane watched it for a heartbeat as Tohar hunched over to dry-heave.

"You and Garlenna have become close." Barodane felt he'd have more success using his station to pry information from her lover. "She must confide in you."

Suspicion crowded Tohar's brow. He dropped his club, voice conspiratorially low. "She said you'd ask me questions. I told her if I knew any answers I would tell you. That's why she also reasoned she couldn't tell me anything. 'If he pries, walk away.' She said that." He swallowed hard. "I promise, I won't though. If you wish to continue training, I will be your faithful—"

Barodane waved his sword at the ground and looked skyward. "No. It's fine." A pinkish hue had crept into the clouds. "It's time for third session anyway."

Outside the monastery, Barodane bumped into a porter wearing chain under his tunic. "Apologies sir," the man said. He wore the sickle and grain sigil of hold Cotter stamped on a doublet.

"All is well." Barodane scanned him up and down. "You wear armor?"

The man hesitated, then nodded. "Very dangerous on the roads. My friend was killed near the Shining Range last winter...by Kurgs. Eagle Clan."

"I'm sorry to hear it." Barodane bid the man farewell and went after Tohar.

"Rubbish," Tohar said. "Kurgs of the Eagle Clan would never attack an innocent caravan. Namorite bandits killed the man. Common sense knows it."

Before Barodane had heard of Marus D'Alzir's demise, he might have agreed with Tohar. Now, he wasn't so sure. "Odd times we live in."

The rowboat went out to the center of the bay and the bell for third session tolled just as they entered the cloister at the back of the monastery.

One of the black-robed initiates, a woman from North Malzacor named Amoni'Alu, claimed the platform typically reserved for Nserthes. "To catch the darkness..." she intoned. With distractingly smooth, sable skin and dark eyes that drank the confidence from a man, Barodane enjoyed it when she led the rites instead of Nserthes. A milky scar on the side of her neck was her lone blemish, and though most might think it marred her beauty, Barodane always found a bit of imperfection enhanced a woman's allure.

Omari was short. Sturdier through the ankle than many of the lithe women with aquiline faces who'd been paraded around at court. Yet Barodane had loved her more than any. His formerly betrothed possessed a beauty of personality and spirit that transcended any perceived shortcoming. Strength poured from her, as did a lust to know the core of matters both large and small. She wasn't just some puppet who squawked in thanks whenever a highborn complimented her looks.

She made me laugh.

Emotion lodged at the back of Barodane's throat. He refocused his attention on Amoni'Alu and fulfilled his part of the call and response, ending with, "Break the seal."

The resent with which he used to say the words was gone. Now, some small, quiet part of him, tucked away and long forgotten, looked forward to the sessions.

Silence descended and Barodane disintegrated into darkness on the other side of sound.

It was his prosort's face that floated into his mind first.

How can I trust her when she blatantly lies to me?

Consider what you've done. She still trusts you.

A fair point.

He sensed her somewhere nearby in the quiet. A few meters, no more. Kneeling. Like she'd done at Rainy Meadows...

Barodane drifted into the past.

Tears sting his eyes from smoke. Clog his throat. The screams of the dying and soon-to-be-dead dwindle to a vicious hum. Loyal to the last, Garlenna kneels at his side, equal parts victim and aggressor. Hero and villain. *At least she lives so that you can earn her forgiveness. What is one little secret she keeps compared to what you've put her through?*

Squalid faces streaked with ash and blood stare back at Barodane from frigid memory. Four hundred of his most faithful knights, heaving breath from pushing their mounts through the night and day to arrive at King's Crossing, the chosen place for Barodane's vengeance. Never would he have to hear the wails of the four hundred mothers they left behind.

"We hunt murderers," Barodane declares, jaw tensing, hands prickly as they strangle the reins of his horse. "Evil men from distant lands. They step on our soil. Kill our brothers. Our fathers. Our princes. They drive us to deeds as dark as those they commit."

He punches his own thigh, then raises a fist, armored and shining in the gloom light like something out of legend. "But they miscalculate our mettle. Our loyalty to see justice served. They think they can take from us and beat us down like the slaves we once were. But we are free! They do not understand the spirit of Namorites." His voice falls low, a challenge to any who dares question the assault at the ford. "They fail to understand that we would *gladly* give our lives if it meant every one of them was slain to the last."

The men's gazes do not waver; they are centered on their prince, trapped in the conceit of his bottomless pain. They have no choice but to trust him. Trust unearned. Loyalty begotten.

Barodane inhaled sharply and woke from the dreams of a dying past.

Now, he had a chance for absolution with Garlenna. A chance to give freely what he'd stolen from so many others. Warmth spread from chest to toes in a wave. Not once since he'd ridden Scab from the battle at King's Crossing had he trusted anyone. Not even himself.

It scared him more than death.

A nation entrusted you with a crown. Look at what you did with that.

Bitterness coated his tongue. Fourteen years she'd been with the Sempyrium. *That's a lot of time—maybe enough for her to change and grow into someone I don't know. Maybe Merique was right. Maybe she uses me.*

He shoved the thought from his mind. A cowardly attempt to justify the absence of his trust.

He leaned into a deep place, inaccessible in years past from the dampening effects of the drugs he'd consumed. A quiet echo from the young man he'd been, the one who knew his prosort beyond shadows of doubt or stirrings of mistrust.

I have to trust her. I owe her...that much and more.

Someone screamed.

Barodane's eyelids flew open. He was on his feet, hand hunting for steel at his hip—found nothing there—remembered weapons were forbidden within the monastery.

Across the way, Garlenna had risen, the other initiates of the Obsidian Hand a split second behind.

Heads swiveled toward a flurry of motion at the heart of the room where a woman in gray convulsed on the floor. Foaming white sputum dribbled down her chin. Her eyelids fluttered rapidly and her arms were locked to her sides at ninety-degree angles, hands rigid claws.

An initiate called for Nserthes.

Barodane dashed forward, stopping short of a clutch of initiates filling in around the woman as she bucked, skin slick with sweat. "He comes...all will be forgiven...he comes."

Then her eyelids flew open, milky white vapor clouding them for a gasping heartbeat. Her breast heaved like a rabid animal's, and her lips curled back around bared teeth. "He comes! He comes! He comes!"

One man shot back from her with a yelp of dismay.

Her voice echoed off the rafters, suddenly hollow, impossibly deep. "He comes! He comes! He comes!" A war chant. A promise of doom marching from her throat.

Prickles swept up Barodane's arms. Shocked murmuring followed a clamor of activity as those nearest worked to pin her down.

A door slammed open then closed. Nserthes bowled through his initiates. "Out of the way." The Sophophant gripped the woman's shoulders between concrete hands, lifted her slightly, then slammed her back to the hard floor. Her body went slack and she stared at the vaulted ceiling. The muscles of her face twitched and then settled as if her soul had crept back into its vacant vessel and all the humanity returned.

She started to cry, muttering, "He comes. He comes. He comes," and sucking in stilted breaths. She seemed a woman freshly violated, the moment of stabbing realization on her face akin to that of a soldier who'd survived their first battle, staring at their bloodied sword and wondering if they would ever be the same.

"You're safe, sister." On a knee, Nserthes cradled her head with utmost care, a thumb stroking her cheek. "You're safe. Now, tell me...what did you see?"

The first attempted word plunged the woman back into frantic horror. "He touched me." She curled up like a burning insect. "I was in a corner of the house I grew up in. My brothers were yelling at me and cursing me—blaming me for our dad leaving." A sharp wheeze escaped her. "I've never stood up to them before but this time, I did. I told them to leave me alone. Told them I would hurt them if they didn't...and then they were gone, just ash floating away. That's when the darkness came and swallowed everything. I could..." She squeaked and went stiff as if stabbed in the gut. "I could feel it. Swimming around me—inside of me. It was so cold. So empty. We used to play inside this cedar that'd been struck by lightning, my brothers and me. It was hollowed out and charred black. I felt like that. There but gone...filled with nothing but that darkness."

Awe lifted her higher into whatever fantasy held her. "A doorway, bordered in searing brightness, cut through the void. Then, *he* appeared, a crown wreathed in golden flames upon his brow. He told me I'm strong...that he needs me. He knew my every pain. He...he touched my face." Haunting gaze fixed on the ceiling, a mix of glee and rage twisted her cheek as she touched it. "He said I could Awaken. That through him, I would be forgiven. No more hate. No more cold. No more emptiness. An escape from life's waking nightmare—into power—into his light! He is coming. Coming for me. I just have to tell him where I am." Tears streaked down her face as her laughter rang out, brimming with bliss.

A shiver ran down Barodane's spine.

Nserthes breathed like a rabbit in the first few moments of finding its foot in the snare, chest and sides heaving, but otherwise, too afraid to move. "Who?"

Her head jerked toward the Sophophant. No semblance of humanity remained. "My Light. He comes! Soon, he comes!"

All sessions were canceled. Furthermore, all practices of any kind by initiates of the Obsidian Hand were banned. There were no complaints. Most had witnessed the attack, though few had understood. Until their leader could tell them what had happened and how they might deal with it, they would adhere to the declaration. Nserthes ruled Martyr's Isle, not by fear, but by having answers others didn't. When he needed time to think, the initiates gave it without question.

Barodane and Garlenna resumed their training in silence. Something had shifted for the prosort since the Arrow of Light's attack, and while she remained tight-lipped and distant, she no longer made Tohar do her work for her.

We saw what Siddaia can do. With the Arrow of Light able to reach them in ways they weren't prepared to deal with, Garlenna seemed to be reminded of the challenges they needed to overcome.

At the conclusion of their latest training session—a damn hard one—they went to find Nserthes in his apartments. Barodane lifted a rubbery arm in greeting as he and Garlenna entered.

Snapping a book closed, the Sophophant shuffled it aside without a word then crossed his arms.

"How is she?" Garlenna took a stool while Barodane leaned his back against the wall.

"Still recovering," Nserthes said, "under strict guard."

Barodane cocked his head to one side. "Are we questioning her allegiance?"

"The Arrow of Light targeted her specifically." Nserthes waited. He sometimes did this to allow them a chance to catch his meaning without explanation, but it didn't often take. Now was one of those times. He waved at the book he was reading. "I've been perusing the library's less popular selection of texts on Awakened and Ruptured to glean more about what Siddaia did. Alas, unanimity eludes the authors. Too few accounts stretched over too much time. Perhaps I query the wrong books, but either way, I'm left with neither direction nor consensus on the matter."

Garlenna shifted in her seat. "How is it that a boy from Scothea could have ascended Unturrus?"

A rare smile spread over Nserthes's face. "Ah." He held up a finger, dragged it down a tower of books at the edge of his desk and selected one to hold up for them. "On that, I believe I've managed a working theory. From our dearest xenophobe, The Lady Mavis of House Ippolo."

The wealthy aristocrat from Valat was a world-renowned historian, who hadn't just conjectured on the subject, but commissioned decades of exploratory ventures across the world. As a youth at the Academies, Barodane had been inundated with her works. Like most of those in his class, he found her writing easy to digest, her body of work dizzying, and her opinion on human nature deservedly harsh.

How do you decide humanity's worth? started the joke. *Fuck a man from every country.* That was the punchline. It wasn't funny. The rich Valatian brats populating Barodane's classes had a stunted sense of humor he'd never come to appreciate.

Nserthes opened the tome and found a place he'd marked. "'My first experience with a Mimborean was a bittersweet one. My Scothean hosts kept him locked in a cell, far from the other inmates. When I interviewed the man, it was clear by his persistent leer that he was raving mad. They told me he'd wandered into the city from the Mimborean jungles and attacked a woman. He'd eaten half of her face by the time passersby subdued him. Heinous was his crime, and yet, the fact that he survived the Pale Sands was intriguing enough that they kept him alive.

"'It should be noted that this Mimborean man was shorter than most Scotheans. If this is the norm for their race, it would rank them lowest in all the world by standards of stature—at least, the ones I've recorded. To an adult Valatian, they would seem the height of a child of fourteen. And just as lithe, as well. I assume their diminutive size to be a result of the heat and humidity of their jungle homes, an evolutionary necessity to combat lethargy...'" Nserthes flipped a couple of pages then resumed. "'Each question I asked went unanswered. Instead, the man prattled on endlessly about a glowing blue plant in a place my translator referred to as 'The Cave Under the World,' deep in the Mimborean jungle. A place where his gods lived...where his gods were made.'" He scanned lower down the page. "'It goes on to say the man had made claims that he was as strong as ten men combined."

Nserthes let the book drop and stared at Garlenna and Barodane. "To summarize, Siddaia did not *ascend* Unturrus. He *descended* into whatever this 'Cave Under the World' is."

Barodane scoffed. "A second-hand account of one raving madman and you're ready to proclaim the existence of a second Unturrus?"

"There are others with Siddaia. Awakened who follow him." Nserthes shut the book with one hand. "You wanted an answer, and so, I gave you one."

Footsteps moved down the hall beyond the door. Once they were long past, Garlenna said, "When will you resume practices?"

Nserthes shook his head. "I don't know, but like I previously stated, I believe the battlefield for this war will take place at the edges of the mind. Our enemy has dealt us a blow—a probing assault—and now, we must decide whether to charge in and hope it is no trap or hang back and trust we aren't outflanked."

"Resume the sessions." The flatness of Barodane's command drew a quizzical look from Garlenna. Nserthes leaned forward onto his elbows. "If what you say is true, then we're going to need 'soldiers of the mind,' as you put it. Anyone who proves vulnerable or too dangerous, you can send away."

"And if they come back?" Nserthes said. "If they continue the practices we've taught them, but they now have a teacher to guide them deeper into madness and power, what then?"

"That is the risk we take," Barodane said. "You said it would be a war of the spirit, so it will be up to every initiate to withstand the Arrow of Light's call. If they can't, well, I think it safe to say we've already lost then, haven't we?"

Footsteps moved down the hall once more. This time, they stopped at Nserthes's door. The Sophophant bid them enter. It was a guard wearing the moth and moon on gray livery. "A trade caravan just came through. They spoke of seeing a column of armed riders to the southwest."

Nserthes peppered the guard with questions. Except for how long ago the column had been seen, the man proved to know little.

"Four days. That was all the trader told me. I asked the same questions you're asking now," the guard said. "The trader kept his distance and moved past them quick. Big group like that with weapons...scared him senseless."

Nserthes dismissed the guard. When they were alone, he scratched furiously at his brow. "This is ill news."

"Let us hope your agent arrives soon," Garlenna said.

"Armed riders." Barodane straightened, stretched his arms wide in an attempt to loosen the budding soreness in his shoulders. "It's not a war of the mind and spirit quite yet is it?"

Nserthes fixed him with a damning look. No one laughed.

CHAPTER SIXTY

THE GOOD OF SCOTHEA

I n the weeks following his meeting with Essuhd in the night garden, General Valka sped further into the suffocating quiet of his own mind. The transcripts he'd found on his altar about Siddaia's Final Song itched in his hand.

Is my allegiance so facile? So easily swayed? So easily snared?

With mounting discomfort, he had stared at the thin, leather-bound book, its false title, *A Brief History of Warfare,* luring him to open it.

He hurled it across the room, and a note slipped free and drifted onto his booted toes. He thumbed it open. *If you did not choose the means, you are the means.* He burned the note with relish.

He glanced at his altar then at the book lying in a heap against the wall. The conversation about truth he'd had with Siddaia niggled at him. *Have you lied to me, my Light?* Valka imagined the prophet's response. *Of course, Ikarai. You were not ready.*

Unblinking for so long, Valka's eyes stung as he studied the book. *Perception is the ruler of all.*

Legs wooden, he rose, unlocked a chest at the foot of his bed and stowed the book there. The clasp closed with a satisfying click.

Meetings slid by in a rigid blur. He operated like an ant, moved by instinctual duty from place to place with disembodied awareness.

Each night, the book burned at his feet. When he woke to dress, he watched the chest as if it were a wild raek, wondering if that would be the day he finally caved to Essuhd's warning.

If you did not choose the means, you are the means.

Valka's teeth grated. Pesky little bastard.

In lieu of answers, actions, or anything resembling resolutions, Valka's agitation poured into his work. He analyzed the training schedule for the army and demanded it be tightened—earlier starts, later stops, twice as many war games. "Our Light must be protected," he told his captains. "Duty makes mighty."

Those were the words he sent them away with, a thoughtless adage he'd picked up from General Sahuhd when he'd been a captain himself.

He met with his other commanding officers, Rhul among them.

Military funding had been disrupted during the transition of power. Tributes from other cities of Scothea—Stormwal, Istaluuk, and Thundermount—were slow in coming, while those from Anzev Oghur and Mynsk never arrived.

"In time, they will see," Siddaia had said before retiring for introspection upon the sky-terrace.

Rhul and Valka, however, were of a more pragmatic mind. They ordered half the wealth of all aristocrats in Darkfall seized.

The first to be raided were Valka's neighbors. A woman three manses down from his own had shown up weeping at his door. Purple bruises mottled her face and forearms. "They savaged me!" Her pleas for vengeance filled his ears then meandered out, unheard. "Walk in the light of forgiveness, sister. Turn your cheek and be grateful. It is what our messiah would do." Unwilling to relent, he ordered her dragged back home. Scothea's future belonged to its people. Not those who sated themselves on the abuses of power and greased elbows prevalent during Rathon's reign.

After the most recent Fifthday sermon, one where Siddaia spoke of discipline being the quickest path to eliminating selfishness, Valka banned the army from using brothels and spirit dens. A single officer had pushed back on his orders. Valka snapped at the man. "What is more important, our Light, or your comforts? Our Light, or your pleasures?" The man made a hasty salute, color draining from his face. Valka demoted him to sergeant and had him shipped off to Thundermount to watch the border with Oren.

Unsettled energy jerked the general to-and-fro. He thought his litany of pious commands would do...something. Anything to quell the rats of doubt gnawing inside of his skull. *An action taken in concert with belief, is a belief expressed in its truest form.* That's what Siddaia said. That's what Valka *wanted*.

Yet seeing the luster of Nera's personality so dulled in her newfound faith added weight to his dilemma. His inhales grew shallower, and his desire to read the transcripts about the Final Song grew harder to resist.

Valka missed his chance to join Nera and Yanos for their weekly walk to the Fifthday sermon. Long hours drilling his army at the parade grounds left him without time. Accompanied by a score of Grimshields, he arrived at the vippe-drome of Sesyrs.

Hours earlier, seated amongst Rhul and the Blessed Cadre, Valka listened to their messiah's promise of a special announcement later that day. To those given over to such emotions, a buzzing sense of excitement permeated the meeting.

"My Light," Valka had said. "It would be best for security reasons to know the nature of your announcement."

The other members of Siddaia's inner circle regarded Valka with amusement.

"Have faith, Ikarai," his Light said. "One does not grow wheat by jerking it from the ground before it is ready to fruit."

Nevertheless, Valka's pulse throbbed as he stood beside a Grimshield captain, surveying the crowd. "If our Light's announcement increases their fervor to a worrisome degree, stay calm. Trust in Him."

Captain Paranthese, a titan with a beard of gray stubble and a thinning horse's mane of hair, saluted. "We shall shed our own blood before theirs. As our Light would want."

Dedication to Siddaia ran ever-deeper.

Files of the populace scrambled into their seats ringing the vippedrome, and when the stone-carved grandstands were filled, they spilled onto the patches of rust-colored earth to either side of the racecourse, rustling up plumes of umber dust.

Valka nodded to Captain Paranthese then climbed the stairs to the top of the pillar where he watched for Nera and Yanos to arrive. Since his daughter's dedication to the Arrow of Light, she and the captain had become inseparable, causing him to wonder if the pair now traveled past the boundaries dictated by custom, station, and command.

Perhaps it would be best if Yanos was reassigned. It wasn't the first time Valka had considered the idea. Nera was of marriageable age, and by all measures, she should have been betrothed already. There was no shortage of suitors, but Valka had denied them all out of fear of her true parentage being discovered. In many ways heavy to the soul, it might indeed be better for her to have an affair with Yanos and mark herself unworthy of marriage.

That way, at least her secret would stay safe.

Gasps of wonder rose from the masses as a pair of dark silhouettes descended from the sky above Jatho's shrine. Entwined with Siddaia, the legless Daimos landed atop the pillar, joining Valka, Paranthese, and a handful of Grimshields. Rhul was mounted upon the Gravequeen at the pillar's base alongside Zan-theppi and the Void.

Gishek Ghuul ascended the steps. Three large shields, hammered flat, floated behind him as if towed by invisible rope. Threads of tenuous light rolled off the portly man in ghostly waves. He lowered the shields with a clang into upright positions at the peripheries of the platform. Dust gushed outward into empty air.

The crowd fell to quiet murmurs, and then silence as Siddaia sat cross-legged on the lip of the pillar. Hair whipping, he faced the sunset, eyes hanging above the crowd but never looking at them.

Valka's chest suffused with warmth at the sight of his messiah. A moment later, Essuhd's words assailed him. *If you did not choose the means, you are the means.* He hadn't chosen Siddaia, not initially, but he did now. He fidgeted with Mournfang at his belt and chewed the inside of his cheek. Coppery blood coated his tongue. As a general, he'd come to covet his cynical nature as a strength, but as a follower of the Son of the Sempyrean, it had become a detriment.

I shall go to him and ask forgiveness. He swallowed hard and scanned the silent crowd for Nera and Yanos. The families of officials had been forced to intermix with low-dwelling citizens, but they'd always congregated in the same place in the grandstands. Today, though, his daughter wasn't among them. A thought rang through his mind with the jarring impact of a mace battering armor. *Tell Siddaia...tell him of Essuhd.*

Voice projected with Daimos's aid, Siddaia seized the attention of his followers. "Today will be a short sermon." He spoke at a languid cadence, eyes closed as if tapping into something only he could hear. "And, it will be a sorrowful one."

Valka's brow knit. Worry babbled from the masses.

"Today is the last I shall speak publicly for some time." Siddaia's eyelids fluttered open. He studied the shocked faces of the thousands gathered with an intimate look. Like a lover saying goodbye. "I am as saddened by this news as you are. If it were up to me, I would sit and speak plainly with you for as long as my years allow. Alas, I am not your creator. I am a tool through which the gods speak. And now, they call me elsewhere."

He rose with deliberate slowness. In recent weeks, he'd begun wearing a pair of fine sandals, and traded in his drab homespun and rope belt for a white silk tunic and a sash embroidered with his emblem. A carved pendant depicting his flaming arrow swung from a silver chain around his neck.

He stared at his dusty hands, lips parted, eyes widening. Wind stirred his dark hair and pressed his clothing tight against his lanky frame. "The mouth starves without the hand..." He drifted off in thought. Brow and voice tightening with resolve, he looked up. "The time for words is over. I have said what I must, and I have prepared you in the way the gods would have wanted. We have rejoiced at the awakening light within, and celebrated the same revelation in our loved ones. Now..." Eyes of burning night swept the crowd. "Now is the time for demonstrations. Now is the time to earn your mantle as followers of the light. The Sempyrean speaks, and I listen. So, too, must you. It is the gods' wish that I perform three miracles.

"The first, I shall restore the might of our raek burrows. The counts of the other cities have already been invited to bear witness." He held up three fingers and ticked them off, one by one. "The second, I shall reunite our continent..."

Disquieted murmurs drowned out Siddaia's amplified voice. War with the Orenese had happened before, and while Scothea had won the last conflict at Thundermount, it had taken a ghastly toll. A quarter of the mothers in Scothea still mourned the loss of a son. Ti-Cora ran her nation with unrivaled ruthlessness. One might think a nation run solely by women would be peaceful, but to keep it, they'd had to overcompensate for their apparent vulnerability to make would-be conquerors hesitate.

Scotheans were rightly displeased by the idea of a war with their sister nation.

Long minutes passed. Arguments and fist fights broke out in the grand-stands, requiring the attention of Grimshields.

Siddaia waited for order to be restored, as stoic as a stone. "And the third," he said, lilting orator's tone snapping like a whip, "I will unlock the secrets of Unturrus and lay them bare for all the world!"

Valka flinched and locked eyes with the nearest Grimshield whose mouth hung open. After a moment of shock, the assembly erupted into shouts and whistles, their fists beating the air. At first, Valka worried his messiah might have fumbled his credibility on a single, lofty declaration.

But the Arrow of Light knew his people better than that.

Men, women, and children dropped to their knees where they could in the grandstands to bow and pray. Tears sped down bunched cheeks, following the curves of cheering mouths. They were not thrown off by their messiah's claims—not in the slightest.

This was the confirmation they'd wanted. Despite Siddaia's claims of being a simple vessel for the gods, they saw him as more than just another Holy Instrument worthy of a shrine. He was one of the Sempyrean's own. A god. Who else could make such a claim? Who else could deliver that which was darkest and unknown in the world into the light?

My Light.

Valka's hands tingled. Almost, he dropped to his knees to offer obeisance, but Essuhd's words held him by the nape. *Is this what he spoke of? Is this the Final Song?* To invade Oren was task enough to bring any general to his breaking point, but to add Namarr to the list as well...

The mind of a military commander overwhelmed that of faithful follower. Doubt sowed with renewed life on the heels of his messiah's miraculous claims. He hated himself for lacking trust but he needed to see the deeds done before he would call the man a god.

The crowd boiled over the grandstands and into the Grimshields forming a defensive line along the racecourse. They begged for blessings, begged to be touched by their messiah. Valka stepped up beside Siddaia who watched the surging mass impassively. "My Light, will you go down to them?"

Serene and innocent, Siddaia searched Valka's face. "Yes, Ikarai. For the last time, I shall."

Daimos stepped up beside Siddaia and bore him aloft. Gishek Ghuul, Valka, and the Grimshields cleared the platform. They arrived at the base a minute later. The general motioned for his men to allow the people through their line.

A trickle of raving followers darted across the sands, heading for Siddaia as he lowered toward the racecourse. Daimos weaved her hands, pools of light filling the air around her. Cross-legged, Siddaia floated over the crowd, an undulating field of air protecting him. The faithful packed in beneath their messiah, clamoring to be touched. Siddaia reached down to either side and let them brush their fingertips over his.

Valka led a contingent of Grimshields through the throng.

The crowd thickened, a stinking hot soup of begging humanity. "Move aside!" Paranthese bulled through, Valka trailing as they carved a wedge toward Siddaia.

A woman shrieked.

Icy panic stabbed into Valka's heart as he saw Siddaia and Daimos suddenly rise to hover a dozen feet over the crowd, heads swiveling toward the sound. The flying Awakened shot out her hand, slapping aside a thin projectile from the crowd with a concussive burst of air. A hail of darts followed the first. Like the first drops of hail on a pane of glass, they pinged off the swirling ward of air protecting Siddaia.

Chaos exploded across the racecourse.

Darts from behind peppered Daimos's shoulder and buttocks. A dagger thrown with expert precision took her in the small of the back. The Awakened arched backward, mouth frothing. Blackening veins bulged along her neck and forehead. A plume of blood shot from her mouth. The poisoned darts of the Shadii worked fast.

Mournfang was in Valka's hand. "To our Light!"

Paranthese and the Grimshields slammed their axes into the squealing tangle of humanity before them to clear a way. The crowd devolved into directionless panic.

Daimos plummeted from the sky and Siddaia followed a split second later.

"Protect our Light!" Valka shoved after Paranthese. Somewhere nearby, steel sank into flesh. He glanced back. Two of his Grimshields were down. Blood spattered their breastplates and warskirts as they wilted. The ax of a third—a traitor—dripped scarlet as he squared to another Grimshield loyal to Siddaia.

Paranthese reversed his ax, no longer working the butt into those too slow to move. He lashed out, carving a bloody path through the innocents.

Desperate to reach Siddaia, Valka followed suit. Mournfang bit through the flurry of flesh, sizzling blood and crackling bone. Smoking, stinking, acrid scents filled Valka's nose. His arms were hot and thundering blood. He swung and swung and swung.

Violence on all sides. A boom shook the vippedrome, and the citizens of Darkfall fled like smoke before a mighty wind, the crowd thinning as precious seconds evaporated.

Barren pockets of inactivity surrounded Valka now—thirty paces to his right, Gishek Ghuul and the Void ran toward the place Siddaia had dropped.

A dying man passed by underfoot, clutching his throat and foaming at the mouth. A woman with her throat slashed came and went. A young man, freshly slain, gaped at an ax wound in his shoulder still bailing blood. A few heartbeats remained before the boy died.

Gishek Ghuul reached their prophet first. The massive shields he commanded smashed through the crowd, leaving a trail of wailing Scoths cradling shattered bones. Siddaia was just ahead. A pair of determined-looking men wearing homespun tunics and breeches hustled toward him, silver gleaming in their hands.

Valka saw Gishek throw out a hand. His shields sped into position around Siddaia and started to orbit him at blinding speed. A dart from one of the plain-dressed men clinked off as Siddaia fumbled up to hands and knees, looking dazed and holding a palm to his skull.

Ax upraised, Paranthese charged, outpacing Valka. One of the assassins turned at the last second and side-stepped. His arkiev met Paranthese's armpit in a viper-fast thrust and the Shadii's foot hooked the bullish captain's. With a clipped shout, Paranthese stumbled headlong into Gishek's whirring shields. Ichor erupted like a flagon of wine slammed onto a table as his head met spinning iron. The gore-streaked shield flipped away and clattered to the ground.

Valka closed with the Shadii who'd killed his captain. The man slashed at his face, then danced out of reach. It seemed he was fully aware of Mournfang's capabilities. From the corner of Valka's sight, he saw more Shadii filtering from the crowd.

Here, a woman shoving a child off her hip to draw an arkiev.

There, an old man letting his crutch fall aside to aim a sling-dart.

The Shadii had come.

A flash of blinding light preceded a deafening boom. Valka and the man he faced were hurled apart. Mournfang slid across the sand to disappear among the hustling feet of the crowd. Ears ringing, Valka rolled to a side and stood up. Snatching his arkiev from its sheath, he whirled. One of Gishek Ghuul's shields now smoked, cracked open at the center and melting.

A hundred feet from Siddaia, a stunted woman robed in the way of a chronicler held her arms overhead, white light haloing them. A raek knight cut through the red sand of the vippedrome, but a bolt of death from the heavens grilled the rider in his armor and blasted the war snake in two.

Not all of the Shadii in the crowd were Essuhd's. Some belonged to the Arrow of Light. The two factions warred, darts and arkievs and puffs of powder.

Valka watched a familiar figure stride casually toward Siddaia. If Valka hadn't known the bastard, he might have discounted him as a threat for the unassuming, easy manner with which he approached.

Essuhd.

Valka sprinted on rubber legs, tripped over a dead man and fell to the ground. He looked up as a third lightning strike split the air and left a crater where Siddaia had been a moment before. At the last instant, the boy had leapt away, landed in the dust and rolled, limp arms flopping to his sides as he came to a stop, unconscious.

Another bolt of lightning. Two charging Grimshields crumpled, blackened husks of boiled guts.

Valka shook an ache from his leg and ran.

Ahead, Zantheppi lunged, eyes winks of blazing dawn. Ribbons of gray coiled from her flesh. She clapped her hands together, fingertips blurring. In the distance, the Awakened who'd called the lightning staggered as a foot-long shard of ice impaled her shoulder. Energy crackled over a shaking hand as the lightning-caller pointed at the onyx-skinned Awakened.

But Zantheppi was faster. She splayed her fingers. The ice shard buried in the Awakened's shoulder burst apart. Fragments scored her cheek and outstretched arm, while a sliver the size of a dagger's blade lodged in her chin. The woman's wounds welled with blood as the Gravequeen slid past and Rhul's hakat sent her head bouncing across the racecourse.

The injured Shadii from the night-garden appeared before Valka. Reaction alone saved him. Arkievs met, high, low, and then they were locking hands and wrists and snarling into one another's face. The man was taller than Valka, stronger and younger. His blade tip angled down at Valka's chest.

They held their breath as they strained against one another.

Valka stepped back and tried to jerk the Shadii off balance, but only managed to give him an opening to plunge his arkiev closer, now inches from Valka's eye... Drawing closer with every heartbeat.

His shoulder burned—demanded he let it happen. Spittle flew from Valka's lips onto the man's bandaged face, but the assassin gave it no regard. No smile. No gloating. Just a mission nearing completion.

A ball of black energy shot through Valka's periphery. The Shadii gasped as obsidian light flashed in his eyes, then left them hollow. The man's strength was sucked from him. Cold and limp, he collapsed. The stink of death clogged the air.

The Black Hand Marionette had entered the fray.

Valka sped on, scintillating orbs of onyx humming past. A random citizen was struck and dropped like soiled laundry. A Shadii drank dust moments later when a sphere splashed into his back. Puppets with their strings slashed, flopping dead on all sides.

Ahead, the sling-dart in Essuhd's hand was steady as stone as he pointed it at Siddaia's unconscious form.

"No!" Valka cried, too far to make a difference.

A spike of hardened blood sped past and thudded into the Shadii master's gut, doubling him over. The sling-dart fumbled from his hand. Valka reminded himself to thank Zantheppi when he got the chance.

A dozen steps later, Valka booted Essuhd to his back with a whump of dust and then slammed a knee down on his arm as he groped for his sling-dart.

"Agh!" Blood ran from the sides of the Shadii master's pale mouth. Tears of pain flooded his eyes as Valka brought his other knee to rest on the man's wounded gut.

I could spare him. Save him for questioning. Wait to see the truth of my Light's miracles...or read the transcripts of the Final Song as he begged me to do.

Valka risked a glance back just in time to see Gishek Ghuul's last shield flip over onto Siddaia. The fighting had ceased. Essuhd was the last. Valka watched the man's beady eyes take him in. Let him absorb the gravity of the moment. "You've lost."

The Shadii master coughed and then gasped, eyes rounded in anguish. He let his head drop back, death fighting to claim him as he stared at the sky. "Promise me, Ikarai." Essuhd wheezed, his voice faint. "The Final Song. Promise me..."

Everything in Valka tightened around the words, and in that moment, he knew the feeling would never leave. Not until it was satisfied. The seed of doubt had taken root and Valka damned the man for planting it there.

"I'll do what I must." He rammed his arkiev into Essuhd's heart, blade sinking through rubbery flesh and fat and scraping spine on the other side. "For the good of Scothea." The Shadii whimpered, gritted teeth barred, eyes bloodshot and welling with tears.

Valka ripped the slender dagger free and stood. Expression vacant, Essuhd watched the sky. The man had died for his beliefs. Died hoping Valka would read the transcripts. Died fearing he'd lost.

Siddaia's followers had no such fear.

The general spun slowly in a circle and took account. Daimos was dead. Fifty Grimshields as well. A score of Shadii impostors and their lone Awakened desecrated the grounds of the vippedrome. And what remained of the Blessed Cadre tended to Siddaia as he came awake.

They almost got him.

Siddaia inhaled and exhaled rhythmically, utilizing one of his breathing techniques for calm. Zantheppi moved her hands over him, her powers offering some minor healing.

The Son of the Sempyrean...nearly killed by a handful of mortal men.

Valka glanced at Essuhd's corpse, then back at Siddaia. *If you did not choose the means, you are the means.* If Valka was to be his messiah's means of conquest, the least he could do was grant a dying man's wish.

CHAPTER SIXTY-ONE

THE FRAYED END

U naccustomed to riding a horse, Thephos dismounted clumsily and near-ly fell into the mud.

A memory flashed in his mind... Of him placing a finger to his lips as he tried to ride one of the sows. His little brothers had snickered into their dirt-dipped fists, careful not to disturb their father who snored in the nearby farmhouse. It hadn't worked, of course. The pig squealed, then squirmed from under Thephos before speeding away and leaving him on his backside. The joy on his brothers' faces had been worth the soreness.

Scattered moments like that one, hard to touch and harder to hold onto, were growing easier to recall of late. A smile tugged at his lips as a stable boy took their horses.

"Pay him," Pintarian commanded. Posing as a lord from Valat, the bladesworn affected the accent of one from the Mighty Isle, smoother and less pronounced around consonants.

"Wealthy Val do not touch their own money," Pintarian had told him. "That's what servants are for." He had gone on to tell Thephos of Val society, of how those who handled money less often were seen as more confident, more trusting, and more prestigious. "But as a minor lord, it will be a balance between us. The poorest nobles who try to never touch their money are seen as fools, for they're easily robbed. 'A careless rich man loses nothing, but a careless poor man loses it all,' they say." It was the first time Pintarian had talked to Thephos about anything outside of his shortcomings or the mission at hand.

Pintarian snapped his fingers.

Thephos fumbled at the fine leather satchel slung around his torso and withdrew the right amount of wheels for the boy.

Pintarian swept past him up to the inn. With a hand shielding his mouth, he twisted back to Thephos and whispered, "Follow at my heels like a dog and do nothing unless I tell you to. Understand?"

Thephos nodded. His bladesworn was a dangerous man, and while he wasn't the old devil, he wasn't Syn Backlegarm, either. Killing the bandits had been an unnecessary cruelty; if he was capable of that, he might not think twice about doing the same to Thephos.

He watched Pintarian run a velvet-gloved hand along the wall of the inn's landing, then reach up to tap a sign. Thephos tried reading the word. "Roosty."

"Rusty," Pintarian sneered. "Fool."

Thephos blinked at the image of a long, bent nail under the word. "Rusty. ..nail."

Pintarian shook his head and entered the inn.

Within, hazy pools of light hung around the bar and a slightly elevated stage. A pair of harpists, one old and gray and wobbling drunk, the other, a gap-toothed youth with spindly arms, sent a soft melody tapering into silence. Half-hearted applause followed. The harpists bowed and grinned as if they'd just played for Danath himself.

Thephos was vaguely aware of being watched as he trailed Pintarian to the bar. He glanced back at the other patrons in his periphery. His skin crawled under their attention—almost the feeling before godsthorn took hold.

Pintarian ignored everyone. He strode up to the barman with an imperious swagger, produced a pair of silver wheels between his fingers, then slapped them down. "Drinks all night for my servant and I." At first, fury flashed over the barman's expression, then his brow jumped at the sight of the money and he set to pouring. Two deft swipes of the head cutter later and he pushed drinks into Pintarian's hands.

He gave one to Thephos who stared at the tankard. "I've—I've never drank before."

"Stick your mouth to the rim and tilt backward. Surely you can manage." Pintarian locked eyes with Thephos, taking a drink as he did. His voice fell low. "Personally, I hate the stuff. I'd much rather have a couple of thorns. Better than slugging down this piss. Alas, we don't wish to call attention to ourselves."

Thephos cradled his tankard in both hands like a sacred chalice. "Aren't you being a bit loud, then?"

"It's fine so long as it meets their expectations," Pintarian said. "Let them see a brash noble. A demanding bastard. A fiendish philanderer. Anything but a Dominarri. If I were sneaking about at the back of the bar, staring at everyone without touching my shitty godsbrew... Now that would draw the wrong kind of attention, wouldn't it?"

Thephos dipped his head in assent. "Yes, master."

"Good." Pintarian stretched, elbows bending back to rest on the bar. He smiled broadly, vanity and confidence shining through. "Tell me, are there any young ladies looking my way?"

It took a moment for Thephos to register his meaning but when he did, he scanned the room, trying his best to make the act casual. A short, sweet woman with good posture and a glow about her glanced sidelong at Pintarian—gaze hanging on for an extra second of appreciation. She grinned, cheeks taut, apple-round and brushed with red. Her face fell to her lap, smile lingering, as she smoothed her dress over one leg. "Thick brown hair...near the stage...at the table with the harpists."

Pintarian patted Thephos's chest. "You're not so useless after all. I'll take her. You take the Sempyrean fools at the back of the room."

"What?" Thephos started to turn.

Pintarian grabbed his face and hissed a warning—turned it into a laugh. He patted Thephos's cheek mockingly to cover his actions. Just a drunken master treating his servant with a normal amount of denigration. "Don't be a fool about it. There are three paladins and a bishop. There's an empty seat at the adjacent table. Sit there and listen. I want to know why they're here, and if we'll have a fight on our hands."

Thephos sagged a bit. "If we do, am I to be the sacrificial lamb?"

"Only if you're unwilling to be a lion." Pintarian threw back his tankard, drained it, ordered two more, and then moved off.

Thephos stared into the murk of his drink. Ratty, ashen hair hung around his narrow chin in the dark liquid's reflection. *Do I look like a spy?* He wasn't sure what a spy was supposed to look like but at the very least, he didn't look like an Awakened. No one worthy of notice, for that matter. *Pintarian doesn't look like a spy. He looks like a lord.* Thephos's gaze hovered over his cup. *So long as they see a docile servant, I'll be okay.*

He sipped his drink. Nut and oat mixed with the acrid tinge of something akin to urine. Flavorful to be sure, just more so than he preferred.

Legs trembling, he willed himself past the men of the Sempyrium. It was darker on this side of the room, farther from the stage, a dim coat of light amid shadows. Spear tips of candle flame lit the center of each table, just enough to shine off armor, gleam off yellowed-teeth, and fix haunting embers in patrons' eyes.

The back of Thephos's skull bristled with awareness. The men at the next table were the mortal enemies of the Dominarri. Three warriors and an administrator, all within spitting distance. Platters of half-eaten food sat at their elbows. The smell of wine wafted from their cups. Hesitation and expectation gripped Thephos as he sweat, waiting for one of them to look up and declare "Awakened!" at any moment.

None gave him any mind as he pulled out a chair to sit.

Across the room, Pintarian held the young woman's wrist in his hands as he traced a fingertip along the lines of her palm. He leaned close, their faces inches apart, ignoring the harpists who spoke amongst themselves. The girl looked to be enjoying herself. The bladesworn was the statue of a god made animate. Clean, charismatic, well-spoken, and dangerous.

Nothing like Thephos. He made a show of looking around the room while drinking as little of his godsbrew as possible—just enough to keep suspicion at bay. Under the surface, his nerves danced on shattered glass. More than once, he thought the Sempyrium's men looked in his direction. *A trick of my fears, no more.*

It took a moment for him to bring his pulse under control and listen. They spoke in hushed tones. Mostly the bishop, or so he thought. He didn't dare look.

"Gather along the coast. Archprelate Alcor's edicts are unquestionable. He stands highest among the Sempyrium. His ears are closest to the gods' own lips. His word is final."

"Pardon, bishop, but a prosort? A whole town? It seems..."

The thought was left hanging in the open.

"Speak your worries now," the bishop snapped. "There is no way to handle the dark god's touch but to bring it into the light."

"Namorite citizens, bishop...fighting them just to retrieve a renegade prosort seems wrong."

"Not just any prosort, my son. Garlenna Renwood. Her mind holds the secrets of the entire Sempyrium. What if she falls into enemy hands, hmm? Nothing could hurt Followers of the Sempyrean worse. It would make the insurrection in Anjuhkar look like child's play. The entire backbone of Namorite society is at stake."

Liar! You only care about yourselves. Thephos bit back the urge to scoff aloud. "Lofty fucks, the lot of them," the old devil had always said of the Sempyrium. On market days, Thephos had never seen any of the priests give him or his battered younger brothers a second glance. Followers of the Sempyrium claimed they did right. He'd never seen them do anything.

One of the men whistled low. "Martyr's Isle. It'll be—"

"Justice," interrupted the bishop. "A *righteous* cleansing. Our informants say it is a breeding ground for terrorists who seek to overthrow the Sempyrium. That, we cannot allow. Even if our mission is...*unsanctioned*. We serve the gods first, Namarr second."

Thephos perked up. *They carry out violence against Namorites without the Collective's knowledge.* Somehow, he didn't think this was the kind of information Pintarian would expect.

"So we are to spread rumors about what happened?" said one of the paladins. "We aren't actually there though."

"It's called a lie, and you'll tell it for the good of the Sempyrean. These people cannot handle truths they do not understand...look at them."

Shifting weight. Chairs creaking. A pause.

Too long. Thephos felt his ears tingle. He took a frantic sip of his drink and stared at the table. Listening. Heart pounding.

"What are you doing there?"

Thephos swallowed hard. *Not me. You're not talking to me.*

"You there." Same voice. One of the paladins had risen and was now coming to stand at the edge of his table. He tapped it firmly with a fingertip. Thephos refused to look. "I'm speaking to you, patron. What business have you sitting so close to our table? There are plenty of others available."

Thephos didn't look up. He licked his lips. "I'm sorry," he whispered.

"Sorry?" the man leaned down. A square jaw and smooth face—of an age similar to Thephos—but gnarled hands told of a far different path. Practiced at arms. Prepared for battle. Trained to protect the sanctity of his gods at any cost. "*Why* are you sitting *here*?"

Thephos released a shuddering breath. He met the man's eyes. "What's that?" He dug a finger into his ear and stared intently at the man's lips. Having accidentally laid the groundwork for his ruse, he barreled forward with it.

Suspicion spread across the man's expression. He looked back at the rest of the Followers at the table. "Hard of hearing."

"He seemed to be listening just fine a minute ago," one of them said.

The table bucked under Thephos's arms, sloshing his drink. Pintarian laughed as he bumped into it, the young woman under his arm joining in and pointing at the mess they'd made. "Lem, we need our horses, we're going for a night ride."

Lem? Oh right, that's me.

Pintarian acted as though he were noticing the paladin standing there for the first time. "Trust me, your gods don't want him. Terrible personality. Not much for menial tasks, either. Can't follow a command without me repeating it a half dozen times—and still sitting there!" Pintarian kicked Thephos in the shin. "Horses, I said! Fuck's sake, get to it, Lem."

"Don't hurt him." The woman landed a playful punch on Pintarian's chest.

"This is your servant?" the paladin said, suspicion shifting from Awakened to bladesworn. "Did you tell him to sit by us?"

With a smile, Pintarian pressed his lips to the woman's ear and whispered something. Covering her mouth, she blew a raspberry, then cleared her throat and said, "Gods no."

"Hey!" The paladin covered the hilt of the sword sheathed at his hip. "I asked you a question."

Pintarian arched an eyebrow and scratched his finely wrought beard. The joy on the face of his female companion faded. She unslung Pintarian's arm from her shoulders, gathered her hands at her waist and straightened. "Take your ungracious mit from your weapon or I'll have you thrown in a cell. These are my guests, and in case you weren't aware, I am Lady Wynna Marwen."

Hand dropping from his sword hilt, the paladin mumbled an apology.

Wynna held up a hand. "This is my family's hold and if I must send you into the countryside to sleep in order to keep it peaceful, I'll do just that."

The bishop stood, grabbed the paladin by the collar and hauled him gruffly into a chair. "Humblest apologies from the Sempyrium, my lady. We did not mean to offend you or your hold. There was an attack at Martyr's Isle, you see. Cultists conducting human sacrifices. Given the bloodshed, our Followers are a bit on edge. Please..." The man rummaged in his robes and drew out a pouch of jingling coin. "A pittance for troubling your guests."

Wynna Marwen snatched it and bid Pintarian and Thephos to follow her as she strode from the inn wagging the purse over a shoulder.

Thephos fidgeted and looked away. Pintarian was groping the lady of Halaleh's broad backside and sliding a hand down the front of her bodice.

"Your servant...he's right there," she said breathlessly before swatting his hand away.

Thephos glanced sidelong at them.

A wolfish grin spread across Pintarian's face. "If you don't wish him to see, we should find a more private place."

She shook her head but agreed anyway, and then led them through the wooden gate of Mag Marwen's hold.

A row of sharpened stakes swung inward to welcome them into the dilapidated fort. The reaction of holdguard to their lord's daughter bringing two strangers home in the dead of night was mixed. Disgruntled for those honorable types, and too-drunk-to-care for those seated in alcoves with their spears cradled in the crook of their arms, an empty flagon curled up in the other. From what

Thephos had gathered, the nailmaker lord of Halaleh was running his hold into extinction.

Musty tapestries and iron-sconced torches lined a simple great hall, three wings branching off into separate parts of the hold.

They took the hall to the right. After a short walk, they pushed past a door guard into Wynna's room. Thephos cast about, wondering where he might sleep as Pintarian wrapped an arm around Wynna from behind and nibbled her neck. With a voice of disembodied pleasure, she pointed at a door at the back of the room, husky words swaddled in satin. "Servant's...uh...anteroom."

"Yes, milady." Thephos shuffled past, giving the impassioned pair a wide berth.

For over an hour, Thephos's pulse pounded as the room rocked and vibrated. Old planks in need of replacement jiggled in their struts as if a small army marched through the fort. Moaning, and breathy whimpers. The slap of pelvis against pelvis. The sensuous crinkle and slide of sweat-damped flesh. The rhythmic vibration traveled from floor to bed, from bed to body. Thephos felt himself aroused but he corralled it into the bog of oily guilts and other intimacies he'd been trained since childhood never to express nor appreciate.

Never had he witnessed sex. Never had he heard it. And certainly, he'd never experienced any form of it.

Eventually, the jostle of their coupling faded. In the quiet lull that followed, Thephos's flesh buzzed as he finally drifted off to sleep. Dreams darted past quick, dark fish in darker waters...

The voice arrived like the shadow of a shark amid the murk. *Someone is here.*

Half-conscious, Thephos tossed on his straw-stuffed mattress, brow knit. Wood creaked. Delirium handed him back into his dreams—

A second creak of wood. Anxious anticipation split his awareness like an ax cleaving a log, accompanied by the thought, *I hope they're not at it again.*

No. Someone is here.

Thephos shrugged a shoulder, slipping it from the grasp of a clawed hand that wasn't really there. A hand trying to wake him.

Creak. Creak. Creak.

A soft metallic ring resonated in his ears.

Someone is here. Wake up!

He sat bolt upright, chest heaving, eyes immediately finding the figure webbed in shadow. Hunched over and seated on a trunk at the foot of the bed, Pintarian gently held the hilt of his sword in one hand and spun it with the other. Tip touching the floor, it revolved quickly at first, then slowed. He spun it again. Steel ringing. Then again.

His bladesworn was naked from the waist up. Tufts of blond converged between striated chest muscles. Shoulders chipped from granite bunched with each spin. Twin burn patterns encircled his neck, one for each Awakened he'd bonded with.

Thephos waited, dimly aware of the voice's warning. Why had it warned him?

"Well?" Pintarian didn't look up.

Thephos worked the cotton from his throat. "Well what?"

Pintarian stopped the sword mid-spin and flipped it up to rest on the back of his hand. He balanced it a moment, then tossed it into the air before touching the tip back down to the floorboards. "For a moment, I thought we were Dominarri. You know, gathering information. On a mission. All of that." Affect flat, he stared at Thephos. "Do you think I fucked that annoying sow because I wanted to? Because we're on a vacation in the countryside?"

Thephos's mouth fell open. He hadn't considered his bladesworn might couple with Wynna for any reason other than pleasure. "You...you don't like her?"

A snort of disgust. A pause. A subtle shrug. "I've had worse, lied more, and learned less. Alas, nothing outshines the wealth of rumors held by a willing maiden. I prefer a single night sacrificing my chastity to days or weeks of scrimping about this unsavory town suffering ingrates their conversations about the weather. Now..." He spun his blade, light winking off its length with each revolution. "What did you learn from those Sempyrium fools?"

Thephos thought back. Parts of the conversation were hazy while some were more distinct. "They were hunting someone. A prosort."

The bladesworn let his sword come to rest. "Garlenna Renwood?"

Though Thephos had forgotten the name at first, it came back to him when he heard it said aloud. He nodded. "It sounded like they knew there was going to be an attack on Martyr's Isle. They were supposed to cover it up afterward...to lie about what happened."

A crease marred Pintarian's brow. "Conspiracy." He resumed toying with his weapon. "No lord died here, so we can cut that from our list of concerns. A drug dealer did, however. A man named Blackblood Vanavel. I think that is where our rumor stemmed from. A lord killed, the event conflated with the death of a prominent local thorn dealer."

Thephos nodded. "Who killed them?"

"Ah, the interesting part. The answer to your question is where our work begins. Two of the Blackblood's thugs died alongside him. Killed by a musician and a woman with an eye patch." Pintarian watched Thephos, seemingly awaiting a realization that never came. "I forget, you've lived under a rock your whole life. While there are plenty of veteran women who fought during the Great Betrayal, there are few with an eye patch. Fewer still who could survive a scrap with three hardened criminals, much less kill them." He held up a finger. "Yet, there is only one who could draw the attention of both Followers and the Crown's Justice."

"A chainman was after them?"

"So I'm told," Pintarian said. "A group of them came through over a month ago, presumably tracking those who killed Vanavel rather than the thorn dealer himself. I think it is Garlenna Renwood, former prosort to the Mad Prince. If the Sempyrium and Crown Justice hunt her, we would be wise to find her first. Something is happening. I don't know what, but the Dominarri would do well to know."

Excitement thrummed through Thephos. *I was a pig farmer not so long ago.* He'd never felt like an important person despite his ascent of Unturrus or becoming Dominarri or Syn's attempts at convincing him otherwise. At most, he was an Awakened whose powers remained a mystery. It was no wonder his bladesworn didn't trust him. He wasn't an asset, he was a liability. And the game they played involved someone connected to a former prince of Namarr. Doubt sank talons into his spine.

Can I do this?

Pintarian looked out the row of arrow slits letting in moonlight. "Dawn approaches. We should be gone before the sun is up."

Someone is here.

A wave of nausea made Thephos clutch his belly. Grinding discomfort in his bowels. A rabid itch under the skin, impossible to scratch.

The voice sounded eager. *Prepare for violence.*

Pintarian turned toward the door and cocked his head. "Do you hear that?"

Faint shouts of alarm. Booted feet hurrying through the hall outside Wynna Marwen's quarters. Thephos thought he heard someone yell, "attack."

"Come!" Pintarian was already out the door by the time Thephos drew back his covers. Everything in him wanted to stay put, to stay tucked safely in his hidden room, but an unseen force, an indomitable urge orbiting the core of his being, compelled him now.

Satin robes flowed from Wynna Marwen's stout form as she jerked the iron rung of the door to her room. Sword in hand, Pintarian was a step behind her. A holdguard filled the doorway. "Stay where you are, Lady." He held out a palm to stop her and spotted the bladesworn a second too late.

Pintarian leapt, knee swinging upward into the man's chest. The holdguard shot back into the far wall of the hallway. Head colliding with stone, the man crumpled and lay inert.

Thephos followed his bladesworn to the great hall. Moth-eaten tapestries billowed amid guttering torches. The heavy, banded door to the fort's interior was open. Slumped to one side of it, a holdguard clutched a gash in his neck and coughed up blood. An icy gust blew in, snuffing out the closest flames and throwing half the great hall into darkness.

A blood-chilling scream tore from Wynna's throat.

From the wing opposite them, a pair of holdguard dragged Mags Marwen between them by the elbows into the great hall. The man's nightclothes were soaked deep crimson. Deathly pale in the flickering torchlight, a dozen wounds perforated his torso. They laid him on a soiled carpet as a score of holdguard arrived in answer to the cries of alarm throughout the keep.

"I didn't see anyone!" one of those dragging Mags said. "Search the grounds!"

A dozen armed men rushed off to obey, leaving the rest to protect their lord and lady should the attacker return.

Mags's voice was weak as he fought to remain conscious. "Shadows..." Scarlet bubbled from a wound on his chest and his bushy red beard was coated in pinkish slaver.

He's here, the voice crooned. Tingles scurried spider-quick between Thephos's shoulder blades. *Release me. I will protect you.*

Thephos ground his teeth against the surge of hate and rage pooling in him. He shoved that condensing storm—that presence—back into the depths. His shoulders convulsed with the effort. His fingers spasmed.

A holdguard stepped up next to Pintarian. "Lay down your sword, stranger. You're under arrest."

"Don't be a fool," Pintarian squared to the man. "I'm here to help."

Movement behind one of the tapestries caught Thephos's eye. Wind from the open door causing it to billow?

Release me, Theffy. Please.

Thephos stared at the tapestry. "Someone's here." From the corner of his vision, he saw the holdguard frown then track over to the spot he stared at.

A fox mask, fractured down the center and restitched together by bands of shadow, leaked out from an impossibly thin space behind the tapestry. A hearty cackle seized the hall. "Oh lord! Oh lord! Of larders and lording and futile little meaning. One falls, from riches to rags, then gladly dies...screaming!"

The fox mask sank into the shadows and disappeared.

A moment later, a skeletal hand rose from the floor at Lord Marwen's side. A curved dagger flashed, driving into the man's heart. Holdguard shot backward from their lord, crying in alarm as Mags gasped and kicked, heels digging the rug into ruffled folds. He twitched, then fell into death's embrace with a rattle.

Laughter cascaded, bouncing off the flagstones and echoing everywhere at once as holdguard cast about for the enemy.

"Oh lord! Oh lord! They multiply, these greedy beasts, rutting about and nutting about. One must die for another to rise, a succession of wits...or a drought?"

A holdguard standing behind Wynna Marwen was flung back—or rather jerked back against the wall. A pale, sinuous forearm passed across his throat, knife trailing. His neck split and gushed like a slashed wineskin.

"Ware the shadows!" shouted the captain of the holdguard.

"It's him," Thephos said. "The Shadowfox."

"Torches!" shouted Pintarian. "Bring more torches!"

The Ruptured hiding in the shadows cackled. "More light, more light, they clamor in fright, while one by one, succumbing to *my* shrouded might."

A holdguard grabbed for a torch resting in a brazier. From its shadow, silver flashed at his leg, severing hamstring with a rasp of bone. He bellowed and dropped, clutching at his tattered leg. Once there, his body started to jolt, and Thephos realized the unseen Ruptured was stabbing up from the pooled darkness on the floor into the man's back and hips. "Die," the Shadowfox grunted. "Die, die, die, die."

"Stop!" Wynna Marwen wailed. Streaming tears framed her cheeks. "Stop this now!"

The Shadowfox repeated her words in mocking tones, then waxed poetic. "Ah, the floweriness of powerlessness. So sweet to smell, for a frightful spell. Sweeter still, to see...when it comes from *me*."

Thephos's gaze darted from shadow to shadow. A holdguard near the wing leading to Mags Marwen's quarters bolted down the hall. Another made for the open door to the outside. But from the man's own shadow, the Ruptured rose like an actor elevated onto the stage by crank, platform, and lever to block his path. The Shadowfox snatched the collar of the stunned man's tabard in wraithlike fists, and then plummeted into the abyssal dark at his feet like a ship's anchor. The man was yanked down, his face colliding against the stone floor with bone-shattering force. Blood leaked into a pool around his head as his legs started to twitch.

The Shadowfox's poetry told Thephos one thing very clearly: the Ruptured was committed to killing these highborn. *Wynna Marwen won't leave this place alive.* Pintarian guarded her now, but even the bladesworn could not contend with the amount of shadowed recesses surrounding them. Dawn was coming—still minutes too far to make a difference.

Release me! I will end this.

Another guard ran for the open door and died. The Shadowfox seemed happy to slaughter them one by one. To savor Wynna Marwen's horror to the last drop.

"Now would be a good time to use your powers," Pintarian said.

Yes, the voice cooed. *Release me.*

Afraid of the tumbling strength of the thing within, Thephos girded himself against the urge. Instead, he eyed the tapestries, and then took off, snatching a torch in each fist as he went. He stumbled, nearly caught himself on fire—lunged and pressed a flame to the hem of a moth-eaten old hanging. A few heart-pounding moments passed—he expected a dagger in his back any second as wispy smoke thickened to a fat wave of gray. Flame crackled up the cloth and began to spread.

Light poured into the hall.

He made for the next, but the Shadowfox stepped from behind it, long knives clutched in each hand. The fox mask tilted to one side. "I *know* you." With a cackle he sprang at Thephos.

"Ah!" Thephos retreated. A loose stone grabbed his heel and hurled him onto his backside—a knife ripped air where his chest had been. His hands flung backward to catch his fall, and in the process, the torches tumbled, splashing embers and rolling out of reach.

The Shadowfox loomed, daggers poised. By the time Pintarian arrived, Thephos would be dead.

I don't want to die. He realized the words weren't true as soon as he thought them. What he really meant was that he didn't want to die a weakling.

Release me!

Fearing death, fearing his own cowardice, fearing the truth of a sad life squandered—but most of all, fearing he might die with his father and Pintarian's claims of who and what he was hanging over his grave for all eternity—fearing all of that, he opened himself to his power.

The merest crack...

A rushing feeling, somehow both heavy and weightless, gushed into him.

Light encompassed all.

Welling energy hurtled outward from an infinitely dense place at the center of him. Thunder clapped in his ears. The world lit a brilliant blue. Howling rage woke in the deepest part of him, roiled up and out only to be lost in the deafening peals of power unleashed.

The blinding light of everything dissipated. Tracers of arced lightning filled his vision. Enormous wings wreathed in the smoky hue of nightmares spanned the ceiling in its in entirety. Thephos squeezed his eyes shut...blinked them open and found the wings had vanished.

Orange light surrounded him. Every tapestry burned. The carpet too, was aflame. Heat gushed over Thephos as the shadows were swallowed by blossoming flame. Invigorated muscles threw him to his feet, a blur of iron motion and snapping strength he'd never known. If the Shadowfox still stood before him, he sensed he could have slain the cretin with ease. But the Ruptured had disappeared.

Thephos spun around, teeth clenched. Eager. Hungry for the bastard's heart.

His bladesworn wasted no time. Pintarian stabbed at the closest shadow, sword rasping against one of the few remaining inky pools large enough to hide the Ruptured. He swung the blade backward at Wynna's shadow on the floor, sparks splashing around his feet from the tip. Then he whirled and brought his reversed blade up in both hands to strike downward at his own shadow between his legs just as a dagger was rising to slash his ankle.

Something soft squelched and the unseen Shadowfox howled in pain beneath the bladesworn. Pintarian pulled his sword free, tip wetted in blood.

A keening whine followed by a snarl filled the great hall. "You'll pay for that!"

More...please. Let me have him, Theffy. We'll tear him to pieces. Please.

Thephos shook as he fought for control of the power coursing through him. He resisted the entity engulfing him in its ancient and endless hate. *No.* Tears brimmed, blurring his vision as he snuffed out the surging chaos within and sealed the monster back down in the deep.

Fire and heat spread. Before light fully eclipsed the hall, the Shadowfox sprang from the silhouetted blot of a dead holdguard next to the open door. Cradling a sinewy arm, the Ruptured flopped against the opening, smeared a splotch of red over the stone, and then staggered outside.

Thephos and Pintarian gave chase outside into the crisp morning chill. Thephos squinted and shielded his gaze from the rising dawn light, breaths steaming.

The Ruptured was gone.

A few huffing holdguard trickled over. Pintarian directed them within to Wynna who'd become a blubbering heap.

"Best we go." Pintarian's eyes lingered on Thephos. Measuring, unsure of what to say. Unsure of what he'd witnessed.

Thephos touched his bladesworn's shoulder. "To Martyr's Isle."

"Yes," Pintarian said, composure returning. "Yes."

Thephos sensed a hint of respect in the man's tone. *I can make something of myself. I can be important and make the Dominarri proud.* He knew it now. *I just saved our lives!*

Somewhere dark and silent and unseen—somewhere on the other side of Thephos's will—the source of his power sighed in contented pleasure.

CHAPTER SIXTY-TWO

CREATURES OF NECESSITY

They sped toward Deephollow Prison, the Wolf Banner leading them night and day over the endless tundra. Dragga the Dread's ranks had swollen since Sir Hollem had given Ishoa an estimate weeks earlier—back when they were seen as an enemy. Having lost two score in a brief but furious surprise attack on the Hine regiment, they now numbered just under five hundred.

After killing Hollem and Adus, Dragga had given Ishoa into Okki's care along with a clutch of guards, and then swiftly orchestrated an envelopment on the unaware horse archers of White Plains.

Dragga had returned from the day's reaping, a thin cut on his cheek as if he'd allowed the enemy a single strike out of sympathy before slaughtering them. Blood soaked the black wolf pelt draping his broad shoulders, singing of his handiwork. Gore and strands of blond hair clung to Stirrma's warhammer, bits of the same here and there on his darksteel armor. Gone was the wistful youth who'd once sought Ishoa's hand in marriage. Gone was his effervescent hubris. In its place, a paragon of violence remained, an idol placed upon the altar of war. A hint of his sister's malice danced at the edges of his eyes now. Grief, it seemed, had stolen Dragga's heroic veneer and allowed a darker creature to emerge.

A creature of necessity. A creature of violence.

Ishoa knew it all too well.

When they finally had a chance to convene, she and Arick had done most of the talking, a drastic change from her previous interactions with Dragga.

"Deephollow is a trap for Sir Gossryk," Ishoa had said, wrists, ankles, and spirit still raw from the attempted rape. "The battle may still rage. If we hurry, there's a chance we can make the difference."

Dragga's black stallion stepped sideways and flicked its mane, its rider's eyes trained on Ishoa. Nose upturned, expression twitching with resentment, he watched her with a sort of smug condemnation.

He thinks he'd make a better ruler than me. "You seem displeased," Ishoa said as she took in the hard-bitten warriors flanking him. Men and women of Summerforge, mostly. Well-armed and armored. But there were others as well. The oak of Shadowheart. A woman wearing a pauldron emblazoned with a winged fish. A handful of what appeared to be Frost holdguard. Some others without the mark of any hold at all; these were seemingly plucked from the populace. A scrawny boy. A scrawnier girl. An old man. All dressed in drab and bits of pilfered chain.

All wore wolf furs.

Dragga finally spoke, "When Jarik fell, my mother tasked me with your protection. I wanted to stay at Summerforge. To help her when the siege came to our doorstep. But she was adamant that Summerforge is not easily won—that you were more important. Because Stirrma died to save you, she refused to let such a sacrifice be in vain."

The reins of his stallion rested in one hand while the other gripped his weapon, anvil head hanging a foot from the ground, dripping what was left of the Hines onto the snow. Ishoa wasn't sure Stirrma would have approved of her twin. Dragga had taken from her yet again by pouring himself into the shape of her hostility. None but the dead could say whether he honored or disgraced his sister's memory.

"So you've been riding around the countryside raiding caravans and razing townships looking for me?" As Ishoa said it, she saw how it fit with the reports in a spark of clarity. The Knights of the Wolf Banner never engaged unless their advantage was certain. They attacked caravans to stay supplied. They fought the enemy as opportunity presented, but it was never their primary mission. She frowned at the thought of the fletchers who said the Dread Knight slew their lord—traitor or no—and she thought of the Hine holdguard who'd hoped his father was proud of him as he died, his hand going cold in Ishoa's. "You killed innocent people."

"I eliminated threats to your reign." He shrugged. "What does it matter if they were armed? Empty hands one day can easily carry swords and spears the next. Call me proactive."

"You slew Camion Orr."

"A traitor," Dragga declared. "Conspiring with the Hines."

"Do you have evidence of your claim, Sir?" said Arick.

Dragga stared wistfully to one side. "Besides the host of lambs I just slaughtered?"

"Yes," Ishoa said. "Besides that. The Hines did not falter in their allegiance until—"

"You would assume the innocence of a traitor over my word?" Dragga tsked. "A sentiment I'd not throw around, Princess. Else my soldiers here may feel unappreciated."

Ishoa's words were bound in iron. "*My* soldiers."

Mouth parted as if to speak, Dragga exhaled instead and left his counter unspoken.

"You're Namorites, aren't you? Or have you decided to try carving out a little piece of my nation for yourself like everyone else?" Face angled upward, Ishoa stepped forward. *I tire of your pompous air.* "Swear fealty. As an example to your knights."

His thick neck strained against his gorget as he watched her, then he craned around in the saddle. "Should I do it?" He twisted back, a condescending smile on his lips. More than a few of his wolf knights laughed. "I've never been one to disappoint my mother, so I suppose I will." He turned his destrier broadside, hand reaching down to Ishoa's.

Her lips pushed into a hard line. The man spoke far less than before yet managed to gloat just as loudly with his offer of a handshake—a gesture of equals. *He wants to show everyone he's in charge regardless of what is said.*

With displeasure, Ishoa assessed Dragga's outstretched hand. Balled-up dirt and blood lined the creases of his palm. She was reminded of the time Wolst had crushed Unalor Bog's hand for scaring her with his hawk. *It would be easy for Dragga to do the same with me.*

She scanned the gathered soldiers behind him. Contempt, poorly hidden, thrust them to silence. But she saw it clear for the lack of anything else. She was the reason they'd been fighting a guerrilla war for months now, and she had the gall to be demanding of their leader who'd seen them through it.

She took Dragga's hand. A firm and nonthreatening shake.

"Allies are hard to come by these days, Princess," Dragga whispered down. "Yet so very important to maintain."

On the second night of their headlong rush to Deephollow Prison, they had made camp on the open plain, so far from anything resembling a city or town, that Dragga allowed cook fires. The Knights of the Wolf Banner were used to fast flights and short spans of sleep. To hear some of them tell it, they'd been fighting a war all on their own. No force had ever gotten the better of them because no force could ever keep up. They were fast, efficient, unpredictable, and they knew the land well.

A singular mission drove their success: slay any who stand against Namarr. Sow havoc. Conscript those loyal to the Crown. Finding and protecting Ishoa, she had learned, had become a secondary purpose after so much time had passed. Most had assumed her dead.

Their tactics were ruthless, and in any formal setting, Ishoa would have condemned their behavior, though she couldn't deny its efficacy.

Dragga killed Gossryk's nephew, Camion. That, more than anything, unnerved Ishoa. Another report claimed the Dread Knight had murdered a caravan of migrants just for having Prav sigils painted on their wains.

Ishoa asked a knight about the truth of it. The man had inclined his head in merest respect, then shrugged. "Spies are good at acting like innocent folk. We're too careful to let that go."

I steer a pack of wolves by the ears. I pray they've had their fill of blood.

Anger boiled in Ishoa. She was surrounded by allies who acted like enemies, yet she didn't have the backing to depose their leader. Not when his allegiance seemed so tenuous. It was like she was back at the Manger fighting to be heard all over again.

And yet, it became clear Dragga still held hope of marrying Ishoa. The mix of scorn and flattery he directed at her could be interpreted differently, but it was Okki Womunger that chiseled her theory in stone. Anytime Dragga drew close to Ishoa, the girl stiffened or went flush. Given that the two seemed to be intimately familiar, Okki's behavior belied a deeper sense of her mate's intentions. If it came to it, Ishoa would tell the girl she had nothing to worry about. Until then, she'd keep away from the man unless necessary.

In the dead of night, Ishoa's teeth chattered her awake. It was biting cold upon the plains. The Knights of the Wolf Banner traveled light, a single fur blanket for each of them which led to most cloistering for warmth. As princess, Ishoa couldn't allow for such, and so suffered the chill.

If only Rakeema were here. A piece of her heart had stayed back at Summerforge, not knowing if her best friend still lived. Chance and logic declared she was dead, though a deeper hope prowled inside Ishoa. A wakening sense that her anjuhtarg had simply been scared off in the commotion and was, even now, striving to return to her.

Wind moaned into Ishoa's small tent, the lashings failing to hold down the entire entrance flap. A gust cut through the bottom half of the opening and over Ishoa.

She sat up, unwilling to brave the blood-curdling cold to retie it so it stayed closed. The back of her neck prickled, and somehow, heat bled over her, into face and torso and toes. Frustration and fear crumbled to dust and blew away. Hollowness like she'd never experienced replaced it, not the pain she'd known when Lodaris and Wolst had died, but a complete emptiness. Blissfully open—like everything would be okay even if it wasn't.

Ishoa threw off her blanket, skin humming, insides tight with anticipation. She stared at the tent opening. A lip of canvas flapped aside, revealing crisp darkness and a line of glittering stars. Ishoa's heart thudded.

The canvas dragged against itself then whipped outward.

Rakeema pushed in through the tent opening. Ishoa lunged at the same time, meeting her ice tiger with an embrace, uncaring of the snow-crusted fur, or the icy, wet tangles falling onto her bed roll. Abrasive licks pummeled Ishoa, swiping her chin, cheeks, and nose.

"I missed you." Ishoa wept and rubbed her anjuhtarg's ears then planted a batch of kisses on her frozen snout. "I missed you."

She beckoned her ice tiger under the blanket and clung to her as a scabbard clings to the sword within it. Tears dripped and she promised to never let her ice tiger go again. To never be without her.

Warmth emanated between them, rebounding and amplifying and filling that empty place of serenity she'd felt moments before their reunion. Rakeema was the one thing that always seemed to go right. The one who was always there for her. The one whose intentions were never malicious nor conniving—never anything other than her friend.

She was Ishoa's anchor to peace amid the chaos.

And their bond was unbreakable.

CHAPTER SIXTY-THREE

FROM BAD TO WORSE

A hand shook Barodane awake in the dead of night. "What's so damn urgent?" Barodane mumbled. He'd been having a lovely dream of he and Omari sharing a kiss in Admar's Grove. Every day spent at Martyr's Isle returned a piece of himself he'd thought lost. And with it came a steady increase of thoughts about his formerly betrothed.

She was alive. That much he'd gathered from Garlenna but that didn't mean she'd ever be pleased to see him. *She's probably married by now.* Even if she wasn't, there was nothing he could do to earn her forgiveness. Of that, he was sure, and it fell across him like a white hot blade to hamstring hopes unspoken.

The sweet feeling of the dream started to fade...

"Hey." Garlenna kicked the sleeping mat. "Did you hear me?"

Barodane frowned—shook his head. "What?"

"The captain is here." Garlenna's travel pack was slung onto a shoulder and her kite shield was strapped to her back. "Come. Bring your things."

A handful of hallways and a set of steps separated their quarters from Nserthes's. Without knocking, they entered the room. A tall man turned to regard them, arching a fine eyebrow. Tattoos spiraled around a sun-bronzed neck. When he smiled, a dimple appeared on one cheek beside a tightly kept salt and pepper beard. His hair was shorn close to the scalp. *A Kanian.*

The man's easy confidence bled throughout the room. "Captain Kaltes Kasjeri, my loves." He gave a courtly, but somewhat mocking, bow. "In some waters, I'm known as the pirate lord, Armada."

Barodane was struck with a sense that the man before him was both hateable and lovable all at once. He glanced sidelong at Garlenna. A splotchy flush crept up from her collar. *Smitten, are we?* Barodane suppressed a grin as the captain adjusted the folds of his salt-stained cloak and sat with a clink of metal. *A pirate that wears armor? So his smooth manner covers up something dangerous underneath.*

Garlenna cleared her throat, tone ingratiating. "I am Ren of Farfield. This is—"

"Lord Picks Lillies of Dirtyarseland." Kaltes laughed. "I know who you are. The Mad Prince and his renegade prosort."

For seemingly different reasons than before, Garlenna purpled.

"Apologies to you both. We do not always get to choose our allies," Nserthes grumbled. "The most willing and capable can sometimes be the least pleasant to suffer."

"My brawny, bald friend, your words cut deep." Kaltes slapped his heart, then flowed into a stretch. Rows of daggers were strapped neatly under his cloak, his armpits, and around a thigh. He yawned.

"Took you long enough to get here," Barodane said.

The man's demeanor shifted, smile falling faster than the underpants of the legion of maidens he'd undoubtedly bedded. "I came the very night the bird arrived. And I assure you, my ship is the swiftest on the sea."

Garlenna scoffed. "It's been nearly two months."

"Coming from Scothea, that's about half as long as it should take." Kaltes turned to Nserthes. "Which reminds me. There was an assassination attempt on the Arrow of Light. Don't get too excited. He survived. Wiped out a good deal of his opposition's Shadii in the process too, the little fuck."

Barodane stiffened. *Wiped out the Shadii?* Beside him, Garlenna's mouth hinged open in astonishment. If one Shadii wanted someone dead, it was usually a foregone conclusion. They were the most notorious assassins in the world, and now, Siddaia had killed "a good deal" of them.

Nserthes rubbed his forehead, calluses stirring up a great rustling sound. "You leave tonight."

"We're ready to go now," Garlenna said. "We only need to retrieve our mounts from the stables."

"Very well. Kaltes, are your sailors—"

"Drinking themselves to death or very well near to it?" Kaltes said. "Yes, I believe with absolute certainty that they are."

"I told you to keep them at the ready." Nserthes rose from his chair, knuckles planted on the whorls of lacquered driftwood. "What about that order did you not understand?"

"The nature of orders, for starters." With a sigh, Kaltes used the back of his hand to brush away splinters tangled in the fibers of his cloak. "What *you* don't understand is that I'd have better luck getting sharks to eat seaweed when there's a big fat bucket of chum on their snout. My sailors are loyal to a fault, yes, but they're still men."

"The comfort of sailors is of no consequence." Garlenna stepped forward. "*This* is your prince."

Kaltes Kasjeri eyed Barodane. "So it is. And his flesh uneaten by grave worms, no less." He clapped a few times and then let his hands drift back to his sides. "A master magician. As fate would have it, he'll still be my prince on the morrow when my sailors have had a chance to rest and play and blow their ample amount of hard-earned wheels on whatever they so wish. I pay them to traverse predatory waters, their potential slaughter lying in wait on every ship that passes. I pay them to make port under false guise with our most hated enemies. To intermix with snakes—purest black bloods." He spat the last, face twisting into a snarl. "And I pay them to follow me without question, manning sails day and night with scant rest for nearly two months to get here. I pay them damn well, but even wheels made of gold will only carry a man so far. The Great Betrayal may have ended fifteen years ago, but I assure you, we have not stopped fighting since. So when I say my crew needs rest, trust that I am right."

Under Kaltes Kasjeri's peacock exterior, a dire man emerged. Barodane had seen his likeness before in his erstwhile friend, Kaitos Barabi. These men who towed the edge of danger just to feel alive had to know the balance between what would break them forever and what was just enough to keep them on the trail of the next thrill. If Kaltes Kasjeri said it would be detrimental to his crew to leave as soon as they made port after a long and harrowing journey, then Barodane was inclined to agree. "We leave tomorrow." He nodded to the captain. "Your men can enjoy themselves at least one night."

Nserthes exhaled angrily. "This is foolhardy."

"A result never measured, is a measure never needed," Kaltes said. "One of my favorite pirating mottos."

"Idiotic drivel," snapped Nserthes. "A pathetic excuse for wisdom in the absence of strategic forethought."

"And so it is." Kaltes slapped his knees and shot to his feet. He bowed to Barodane then Garlenna. "Sixty-four 'thanks' to you, Your Majesty. One from each of the sailors on *Anthera's Revenge.*"

Barodane was taken aback by the name. "An unsung hero of the Great Betrayal. Interesting choice."

"I've a soft spot for the type." Kaltes flashed a rakish smile. "Now, I must be off. Dear Nserthes, what's the quickest way into a maiden's pants from here?"

The Sophophant crossed his arms.

"Ah. Never been, I see. Pity for the ladies." The ship's captain paused in the doorway. "Your confidence in me finding it on my own is all the inspiration I need." Finger drumming the doorframe, he drifted from the room, cloak billowing up behind in his going.

After a minute spent complaining about the Kanian, Nserthes dismissed Garlenna and Barodane so he could "soak in his chagrin," as he put it.

They made their way to the stables to check on their horses and woke the stableman, telling him they'd need their mounts groomed, reshod, and the tacks repaired by the morrow.

As they walked back to the monastery, Barodane took in the bobbing boats in the bay, the bucking of the maze of piers, and the lapping between planks amid the quiet. Fog coiled around the inner sea wall, cold and damp it nipped at his nose. He wrapped himself tighter, grateful for his warm clothes keeping him from the worst of it. *Nothing breeds appreciation like contrast.* Tranquility pervaded the bay. Even the late-nighters, few though they were, enjoyed their drink and festivities in relative silence. "I'm going to miss this place," he said.

"Yes." Breathy reverence cradled Garlenna's words. "Me too."

I wonder how much of that longing is for the place, and how much has to do with the man she leaves behind? In the intervening months between Halaleh and now, she and Tohar had grown close. Most nights, they shared a room. From what Barodane had picked up from each of them, there was a consensus as to the short-term duration of their coupling, sad though the parting would be.

Barodane patted Garlenna's shoulder. Her chin dipped toward her chest, the burden of a love soon to be lost anchoring it. "Thank you," she said.

Torchlight ringed the harbor. A hazy silhouette stood just beyond it, swaying at the mouth of an alley. Barodane squinted. A man in gray robes, unfamiliar to Barodane. "Evening," the man said.

Barodane returned the gesture. It was well past midnight and the town was mostly asleep. Manners dictated those with friendly intentions should greet each other with so few others around, even in a smaller town like Martyr's Isle.

They crossed from stone walkways to wooden piers with a slosh. Flinty voices filtered from the windows of the tight-packed homes shoved up against the land-wall. It was a dreamlike place, Martyr's Isle, though not the kind of dreams he usually had. More like the kind he wanted. Belonging and contentedness. Trust in one's neighbor. The opposite of Digtown.

Peace murmured up from a calm, steady heartbeat. A sensation he suspected would be few and far between in the journey ahead. He sighed.

Near the monastery doors, a pair of merchants sharing a bottle in an alcove saw them coming and shuffled out of the way. "Pardon us."

"You're alright," Barodane said.

A few steps past where the men huddled, Garlenna grabbed Barodane's elbow, stopping him.

"Excuse me," she said as she turned, "but did you happen to come in on Captain Kasjeri's ship?"

"That we didn't." The shorter of the two had a drooping mustache. "We arrived yesterday from Inyre. You're not in the market for some varnish are you? We've sold less than predicted, so there's a good deal more to offload."

Barodane smelled it now. The biting scent of varnish, but also a heavy dung smell mixed with it. He shielded his eyes from the torchlight and peered at an outline in the dark behind the men that rested against the building.

The taller of the two traders, a hairless man, stepped into the light abreast of his peer. Flipping aside the lapel of his jacket, he revealed a sigil with a spoon surrounded by five droplets. "Lacquer lord's lackey's, we are."

The one with the drooping mustache grinned broadly. Barodane grunted a conciliatory laugh but kept his focus on the object propped against the monastery. *Arm-length. Definitely not barrels.*

"Interesting," Garlenna said. "I've never seen that sigil before. Inyre, you say?"

Barodane's eyes adjusted, shapes taking form behind the men. Three sticks. He'd smelled the elusive scent before he realized...when he'd laid Rainy Meadows low. *Not sticks—torches...soaked in varnish and saltpeter.*

The mustached man took a step. "Indeed. Here, take a closer—" Silver flashed out from his cloak in line with Garlenna's throat. Instinct saved her. She leaned back, letting it sail within inches, then bobbed to one side as a thrust followed the slash. The man's smile became a murderous snarl.

Barodane had already ripped his sword free as the tall, beardless man drew his. "Attack!" he shouted. "Attack!"

He angled for an opening but Garlenna was blocking his path. Hands open, she stepped out of range of the man's dagger, then launched forward off the balls of her feet, stiffened fingers crashing into the man's throat. He gurgled and hunched, eyes agog. She snatched his wrist and punched the blade from his hand; it skittered over the planks and fell into the harbor with a plop.

The tall merchant lunged over his comrade's shoulder. Garlenna ducked and yanked the mustached man's wrist so that his neck slid along the length of the other's withdrawing sword. Then she kicked the mustached man in the side of his knee. Bone crunched under the force of the blow. Blood spurting from his neck, Garlenna's foe stumbled over the edge to join his knife in the drink.

The tall man bolted.

Barodane stepped to the chase but Garlenna reined him in. "Look!"

Armed men surged up the stone walkways to the ramparts and began assaulting the heavy, iron-banded door of the drum tower. Dressed like traders, musicians, and robed initiates, their shoulders were a bit too broad...a bit too boxy to belie anything but armor underneath. Barodane recalled a man he'd bumped into a week earlier that had been wearing chain under his clothes. "The Sempyrium."

The door to the monastery flew open. Tohar's face swam out from the dark, hair wild, a club fixed in his hands. "What happens?"

"An assault," Garlenna said. "Gather the others. You'll have a better chance in numbers."

A young man in gray robes came up behind Tohar, a round shield and short sword in hand. He gawped at the weaponry carried by Barodane and Garlenna. "Brother? Sister?"

Barodane turned toward the fighting along the concourse. "Stay here with Tohar and guard the door if you want to live." By the numbers, things weren't looking good for Martyr's Isle, but the monastery would serve as a keep in a pinch. The narrow gangway to its entrance made it highly defensible.

Garlenna led them toward the drum tower.

To their left, a building burned, belching up plumes of black smoke. Steel clashed along the ramparts. No time to think, they headed for the gatehouse where the fighting was thickest. Halfway there, the portcullis clicked upward a few feet and then stopped. A heavy wooden beam was lodged up under the gate. From the outside came a steady stream of dark figures, crouching and dipping underneath it in a shadowed blur.

Shit.

A salting house erupted in flames to their left; curtains of fire bowed outward with a gust of wind that forced them to hunch over as they passed. In the distance, gleaming armor seethed at the gate in the firelight, shouts of "For the Sempyrean!" claiming it for the paladins who'd already won the struggle there.

"We've got to get that gate closed," Barodane said. He looked at Garlenna, her expression grim, the doom of Martyr's Isle in her eye.

A man and woman rushed at them from an alley. Flames licked up the side of the building where they'd been setting it afire. In response, Garlenna didn't hesitate and accelerated into the Followers with her shield, flinging them back. The woman's head bounced off a stone wall and she crumpled. The man brought his sword up in time to block Garlenna's mace, and just in time for Barodane to run him through the ribcage. The Mad Prince twisted the blade, making the man squeal, then jerked it free.

A silhouette loomed in the path ahead, mace in one hand, kite shield in the other. Barodane braced for another attack, but a relaxed Garlenna at his side gave him pause.

The figure strode down to them from the darkness. Nserthes materialized. "What are you doing out here?" He wore battle leathers, a steel helm, and gauntlets. Every bit the vaunted warrior of his youth.

"You'll lose if we don't retake the gate," Barodane said. "We can't let—"

"You must go. Now." Nserthes swept past them, ignoring the singeing flames licking at him from the burning buildings that lined the wall. "Come! Kaltes's ship awaits."

Barodane gripped the hilt of his sword in both hands. "I'm not running." He whirled. A paladin engaged an Isleman on the ramparts at the top of the stairs. Barodane started toward them but Garlenna spun him around. "Get out of my way, Gar."

"Barodane—"

He dodged past her and found the Isleman had spitted the paladin. Barodane altered course, surging up the walkway as he hunted for the next attacker he could cross blades with.

The cloth at his throat went taut. He rounded. Garlenna held a wad of his cloak. "Stop this!"

He chopped the cloth with the back of his hand, ripping it from her grip. "Never again," he hissed, and with those words, the past rose in him.

Not the horrors he'd done, but the good he hadn't. Not the lives taken, but those he'd refused to save when he'd given up the Crown. Here and now, another city burned in his name. "We can help them, Gar." This was a chance to be on the right side of history for once. *A chance to make amends.* "I...I will help them."

Nserthes had followed them the short distance. "Now is not the time for chivalry. We cannot risk losing you."

Fire pulled down a building across the bay. Innocent Isle folk were piling into boats to escape the bloodletting. In the distance, he saw Amoni'Alu guarding a fleeing family, ghostly light rolling off her like smoke as she corralled a plume of fire from a building and funneled it into a clutch of attackers. They screamed, flesh falling off in crisping sheaves, and jumped into the bay.

He looked back to find Garlenna barring his path. "Let it go, Barodane." She laid a palm against his chest. "You have to let it go."

He knew she wasn't talking about Martyr's Isle anymore. Nor Rainy Meadows and those he'd killed. She spoke of Malath's laugh. Of the proud smile of his father that he'd never see again. Of Kaitos's barbs. Of Omari's graceful dancing and warm lips. All the splintered memories of youthfulness and joy.

Let it go...

The world that had been. The one he'd loved. *I miss the man I was. The one who laughed with Kaitos, and loved Omari with ease.*

The near fatal wounds of his past had scabbed over, but now reopened.

Let it go. The shame and guilt of the bad, but more, the regret and sorrow of the good—all of it. That's what Garlenna was saying. *Let it go.*

If he was to wear the Crown again, he had to release everything he'd lost including the man he'd been. Only then could he accept who he had to be for the good of the many. "I can't, Gar. I can't let this happen...not again."

Never again.

"No matter what you do, this doesn't end tonight," Nserthes said. "It only ends when you take back the Crown and unite Namarr once more. You can't do that if you're dead."

Garlenna's eye bore into him. "I know you don't want to but you have to. You have to let it go."

Barodane's shoulders sagged. Neither prosort was going to budge, stubbornness being one of their least pleasant but most persistent qualities. And they were right. The screams, the fire, the smoke, and death. So many would face the same if war returned to Namarr.

Pyr Syat's voice reached through time to find his ears. *Circumstances change. The wiser blade flows with them. The weaker blade fights against them.* He looked down at his sword, rotated it, and saw himself in its reflection. *A blade is but a tool. We are the weapon.*

"Fine, dammit," Barodane said. "We'll go. But you better win, Nserthes."

The former prosort gave a shallow bow, then saluted, mace touching opposite shoulder. "Only the living can honor the dead, my Prince. Take what you're feeling and shape it into something powerful. Use it when the time is right."

Barodane hesitated, then nodded.

They sped down the gangplanks toward the harbor, Garlenna bringing up the rear and Nserthes leading.

A skiff knifed through the open gate of the sea wall, a score of armed inhabitants bristling with steel and plate. With a roar, Nserthes launched himself at the first to unload onto the wooden pier, mace whipping through shadow and milky firelight.

Two steps behind, Barodane and Garlenna closed with the enemy.

"For the Sempyrean!" a bearded face bellowed. Barodane hacked at it—was blocked—felt the tremor of the blow travel up his shoulder. A counter came flat at his head. He ducked, stepped past, and twisted, slashing at the joint under the paladin's armpit. Darksteel severed dense padding and the softer flesh beneath. The Sempyrium warrior keeled over into the drink.

Another stood behind, a replica of the first. This one stabbed at Barodane's face. He met the attack, steel singing its ancient song as he muscled it away. Blades clashed again, ground like millstones against each other, faces inches apart. Spit flew from the straining man's lips—hot breath gushed out, dampening Barodane's cheeks. Both men's pride to prove the stronger took hold for a moment before the prince remembered he was trying to kill his foe. He spun, let the man push past, off-balance. Barodane cleaved downward, slicing a flap of meat from his unprotected flank. The paladin inhaled sharp as if dunked in ice water as Barodane whirled toward the fray.

Garlenna and Nserthes had formed a shield wall at the pier's edge but they were being pushed back as more and more Sempyrium soldiers disembarked. Broken and leaking bodies littered the planks about their feet, but the renegade prosorts couldn't kill fast enough to stem the tide. The boat was only half-emptied, and still, they were gaining ground on the pier.

Soon, they would envelop the prosorts.

Barodane attacked the enemy's flank, driving his blade low at the nearest assailant. The man warded him off with a flurry of hammering strokes—backed him up enough for another paladin to clamber up from the boat to stand at his brother's side.

They spread out, approaching cautiously as more dragged themselves onto the pier, a trickle that now hemorrhaged like a rent artery. A third, then fourth paladin crowded the space between Barodane and the prosorts. Seconds remained before he'd be cut off from them. Then he'd be good and truly fucked.

This is bad.

Forced to back up, he contested every inch, a tiring dance equal parts attack and defense. He risked a glance at the harbor. If it came to it, he could jump in. A few heartbeats thudded past. The dark waters were looking better every second as his vision crowded with gleaming pauldrons stamped with the four arrows of the Sempyrean gods and the inverted fifth for Nacronus. He imagined it like a middle finger, the Valatian gesture for people to fuck themselves.

In that moment, it seemed a fitting tribute.

Strength in numbers grown to a comfortable five, the paladins launched their offensive push. All they had to do was back him off the pier. A sword swished air and another clanged against Barodane's warding blade.

A couple more seconds, then the drink. *Shit.*

A knife thudded into the side of one of his attacker's necks. The man spat blood, tongue jabbing out as if it could escape the pooling death soon to drown him. A second man turned—a second knife zipped through the dark to bury itself in his cheek. His head snapped back, knees faltering, and then he slammed face-first onto the planks.

The remaining paladins swiveled toward the new threat at their flank.

War cries split the air. "Fuck you!" and "Die, bastards!" the most common among them. A wave of armed sailors poured over the pier like ants, cutlasses chopping and hewing. They lacked the finer points of martial combat but it didn't matter. They fought with the fury of a storm and the glee of men born to good old-fashioned brawling.

But it was their leader, the one who'd saved Barodane, that drew his attention. Kaltes Kasjeri's men flooded around him. The captain's eyes were absent pits, his hands moving within clouds a shade of black deeper than the night. He swung his hands in violent arcs, vaporous obsidian trailing like a comet's tail. A knife sped forth—hilt quivering in another paladin's chest—as fast as a crossbow bolt.

With the aid of the sailors, they finished off the remaining paladins.

"Into their boat!" Kaltes motioned his men into the skiff. They maneuvered a pair of armored corpses over the sides, depositing them with a plunk into the threshing harbor to clear space.

Once all of them were loaded, a heaving Nserthes stood alone upon the pier. "Hurry now. They may have already taken your ship," he said to Kaltes. To Barodane and Garlenna, he said, "May the Triune God guide and protect you."

Rowers locked gnarled hands onto the oars and hauled back.

Barodane called out to Nserthes. "What will you do?"

Nserthes the Sophophant's jutting chin rose in defiance. "What I can." Then he ran to where the fighting was thickest near the drum tower.

Two more skiffs—stolen and filled with Kaltes's sailors—joined them in their escape as they made their way under the sea wall and out onto open water where *Anthera's Revenge* was anchored.

Barodane sat back in the skiff's stern, Garlenna at his side. Standing at the prow of the longboat, Kaltes Kasjeri smirked at them. "Worry not lovelies, I'll keep you safe."

Smug as it was, he was true to his word.

A pair of Sempyrium rowboats had launched from shore and moved at an angle to intercept.

"Captain!" yelled a sailor over the din of counted oar strokes. "Turn her to fight?"

"No time," Kaltes said. "I'll handle this."

Absent of all light, the Kanian's eyes and hands became an ethereal black. He swung his arms. The first rowboat bounced, the nose flung upward and away as if struck by a whale breaching into its bow. A handful of the Sempyrium's warriors were thrown into the water as the boat whirled around from the force of the attack.

The Awakened pirate focused on the second boat, his cloak snapping where he stood in the prow. He shot out a palm. Wind stirred Barodane's hair, and in a matter of seconds, it increased to a roaring, persistent gale. The sound of a single high-pitched note dragged long in his ears. Stinging salt spray kicked up all around, forcing Barodane's eyes to slits. He glanced at Kaltes's target.

A long divot carved the water between their boat and their pursuers'. The rushing winds deepened the rift. Strain spasmed through Kaltes's face as he contorted his hands. The last row boat drifted flush with the watery trench, then capsized into the gap. A mere eight feet, but it was enough. Kaltes dropped back into his seat, sweat dappling his brow. The wind ceased and the ocean swallowed the Sempyrium boat.

By the time the first skiff regained control, they'd seemingly thought better of fighting the Awakened on the open sea and rowed for shore.

Minutes later, they were being tethered to the side of *Anthera's Revenge* and filing aboard. Crawling up the rope netting to the rail, Barodane looked back. Flame and darkness, smoke and screams. A reminder of a past that would never let itself be forgotten—a reminder of a future he could never seem to grasp.

Sorrow lodged in his breast. *Why? Why must all that is peaceful be stolen and all that is beautiful be slain?*

For a long held breath, he watched Martyr's Isle burn. Then he threw a leg over the rail and stepped to safety.

CHAPTER SIXTY-FOUR

A ROCK AND A HARD PLACE

I n the early morning, they found the first of the bodies leading them on a trail north past Hallock's Bend, the path to Deephollow Prison that Hollem Hine had suggested. The one Gossryk Orr had taken.

Not long after, they came upon the sight of the battle, a road cutting up between humps of rolling grassland to either side.

"A perfect place for an ambush," Arick said.

Crows were already wetting their beaks among the twisted landscape of dead. Shattered lances jutted from backs and necks and ribcages, and occasionally were lodged in the visor of a helm. Broken swords and spears caked in dry blood lay in limp hands. Waxen faces drained of color. Mouths stretched into shrieks that could never end, and yet, ended all the same. At the center of the body-clogged road, the earth was churned to mud a foot deep.

They weaved through the carnage, careful not to trample the stiffened bodies.

Countless knights and holdguard wearing Bleeding Point livery formed a morbid thicket at the road's center. The white and brown checkers of cattlemen interspersed one edge.

A veteran riding beside Dragga that Ishoa didn't know said, "Ollo Bael's men come o'er from Baen's Handle. A couple hundred. Nothing to sneeze at. Attacked first to suck our boys down to the low side o' the road." He smacked his gob and scanned the higher side, an elevated bluff blocking sight from anyone below. "Scarborn only scattered among the dead o'er there. That musta been the bulk o' the attack. Big charge o' horse right into the Knight o' the Hallow Moon's back. Broke 'em. Fucking scum." He spat onto a dead man of Bleeding Point and muttered a hasty apology.

"A third group—from Prav—struck the rear." Arick covered his nose with cloth. "There was no escape."

"Maybe two hundred from Baen's Handle," Dragga said. "Much less from Prav. And the bulk of the Scarborn cavalry."

The air was soup thick, the acrid scent of the dead clawing down Ishoa's throat. Carrion birds cawed and rattled over their feast. Most of Ishoa's allies had been stripped of their arms and armor, half-naked bodies sporting ragged wounds in papery flesh. Some had crawled a short distance before dying. Long drag lines in the tundra marked them.

Ishoa gagged. Someone farther back in the column spewed vomit with a hiss into the snow a moment later. Wherever Ishoa brought her gaze to rest, she could not escape the glassy-eyed stares of the dead.

"The middle bit o'er there surrendered," said the veteran, tongue dipping into the bottom of his cheek. "That's why there's so few bodies. Most o' them survivors headed west. The rest went on t'Deephollow."

"How long ago?" Ishoa said.

The veteran smoothed his long beard. "A day'er two past. Tracks filled in with last night's dust'n."

Ishoa shot a look at Arick. "We must hurry."

A half day later, they reached the crags surrounding Deephollow Prison. The city of Prav hugged the coastal inlet a mile beyond. Ishoa, Arick, Dragga, and a few guards had left the rest of the regiment behind.

From the vantage point they now claimed, they were greeted with a sickening splat coming from the canyon below. Ishoa's gut lurched as she found the source. At this distance, the sound was delayed for a full second after the execution was carried out.

Golthius Narl, Lord of Prav, laughed, and it echoed throughout the gorge. His holdguard untied the corpse of one of Sir Gossryk's men from an enormous boulder. What was left of the man's crushed skull oozed a trail as they hauled him over to a pile of corpses stacked chest-high.

The rest of the knights from Bleeding Point knelt in the dust, disarmed, disrobed to their smallclothes, and bound with their wrists behind their backs. Thirty holdguard surrounded them, their tabards stamped with the slavering mouth of the bakers of Prav.

Helpless, Ishoa watched as another of Sir Gossryk's men was plucked from the group. Less than half of those who had set out from Bleeding Point still lived. Battered faces told of resistance after capture, but as the corpse pile grew, Ishoa was certain their spirits were dwindling.

The Bleeding Point man paled rapidly, knees going weak on his death march to the boulder with a puddle of human dross at its base. Golthius stood off to one side, apish palm resting on the ball of his long-handled mace. He'd taken the pleasure of doing all the executions himself, it seemed. Dark stains marred his fine pink surcoat, tabard, and the glittering gold chain encircling his blubbery neck.

His holdguard forced the knight's arms apart, notched rope to his wrists, and then tied them to stakes on either side of the boulder. He was fastened over the top of it. At most, he could lift his head by inches. Nowhere to go but the afterlife.

Golthius rolled his shoulders then hefted the two-handed mace into his pudgy mitts. He nodded at someone to his left. Ishoa traced his eyeline to Sir Gossryk who stared blankly back at the Lord of Prav. *Narl taunts him with every death and saves him for last.*

The heavy ball swung up in the air, its gaping mouth stained with blood and hovering. Futile squirming led to puffs of dust in its shadow. A desperate plea...

Descent.

A soupy thunk and clatter as chunks of shale split from the boulder, ichor raining down with it. A moment later, the rose-colored mass of the Bleeding Point man's brain eased down into the gore below with a wet plop.

Ishoa found herself frozen, buzzing with incredulity. *How could he do this?* She had only to reverse the roles of fate to know the horrible truth of her answer.

She recalled the slash dealt to Lord Narl's son during the fight in the High Hall. *I hope your son is dead and rotting in his grave.* If he was, Ishoa imagined he likely smelled better for it, and she vowed to send his father to join him soon.

"The host that went west...they went to Bleeding Point, didn't they?" Ishoa said.

Arick thought a moment. "If I were Lodecka Warnock, I'd send them there straightaway."

Dragga whistled low. "Not good."

"No." Arick turned a look of disgust on the scene below. "Far from ideal."

"Circumstances are what they are." Ishoa's tone brooked no response. "We work with what we have and deal with the rest later."

"You're lucky you have me," Dragga said.

She ignored him and studied the prison below instead. A handful of uneven platforms were separated by short flights of stairs carved into the cliff face that led down into the prison. It was an architectural technique known as "Scothean step work," for it was they who'd invented it for their slave quarries. "Tell me, cousin, how would you approach this?"

"In truth, Prav has no military value," Arick said. "I suspect Lodecka will focus her resources on Summerforge, Bleeding Point, and Jarik. Prav is of little value and its defenses will reflect as much."

Dragga confirmed her cousin's sentiment. "A prison does no good when slaughter is the only way to win the game."

"Yes, indeed," Arick said. "I suspect the town itself is garrisoned solely by Narl men."

"It seems unlikely to be a trap." Dragga smirked. "We can take it."

"They think I'm captive." Ishoa gestured to Dragga. "Clueless to you and yours. We attack both town and prison simultaneously. I could care less about caution at this point. Men are dying." *And it's my fault.* She sensed Arick hesitate. "Say what you have to say, Sir."

"A lack of caution is what got us here, Highness. We should proceed in a more rational manner if we're to see a better outcome."

He was right. She'd almost thrown away everything with her impulsiveness. And yet, in this instance, he was wrong. "Your wisdom is sage as always, cousin. When this is done, I promise you we will go to Alistar." The time had come to abandon Anjuhkar, to abandon her pride and do what was right. "However, my plan is sound. Attacking Prav cuts off reinforcements to the prison while a direct assault ensures Golthius Narl won't slip past us. Their forces will be divided."

"I agree with the princess," Dragga said.

Mind working, Arick saw the futility in his cause and relented. "Aye."

Dragga peeled away to ready his knights for the assault.

Another of Sir Gossryk's men was being dragged to his doom. Ishoa turned to go but Arick's voice held her in place a few seconds longer. "I should trust you more, Isha."

He never calls me Isha. Her fists balled at her sides. One thing she counted on with her cousin was that he would always be objective. Choices from a place of emotion were as foreign to him as a lighthearted jest. Through it all, he'd stayed at her side, fighting for her to keep her crown. She supposed she should be grateful for his admission. That it might mean something since it came from him.

"Thank you, Arick," she said. "We'll know if it's warranted soon enough."

Arrow fire swept the bowl of earth, cutting down a dozen Narl holdguard before they found cover inside the caves at the base of the cliff. A trio of rusted gates banged closed, their prisoners and their dead brethren abandoned without.

"Do not hit Golthius Narl," Ishoa said to the fifty wolf knights tasked with guarding the horses. Using bows stolen from the Hines, they would act as the first phase of the assault and rain suppressive fire on the enemy from above while the rest followed Ishoa and Dragga down the stairs carved into the cliff side.

As soon as their descent began, the twang of bows and screams of dying men filled the shallow ravine. Not far off, Arick and Okki Womunger led a similar assault on Prav.

Halfway to the basin, Ishoa realized there was no hurry, despite fear slapping the flanks of her heart. The entirety of the Narl holdguard had sequestered themselves.

Now unguarded, the Knight of the Hallow Moon surged to his feet. "Princess!"

Throwing apprehensive looks back at the gates the Narl rats had swarmed into, the knights of Bleeding Point ran to a safe distance. The man strapped to the boulder awaiting execution cried out, a mix of joy and desperation as he called to be released.

Wolf knights slashed away hempen rope, freeing the men of Bleeding Point. Weapons and armor had been cast into a pile beside the corpses of the less fortunate. That which hadn't already been stolen by Narls was reclaimed and immediately fitted. It didn't matter whose was whose so long as it fit decently. The urge for protection on the heels of assured death was an overwhelming instinct. Pickings were slim. Some managed a single helmet, pauldron, or fall of chain. A good many straps had been slashed in the disarming process, and a great many swords claimed as spoils of war by the Narls.

Ishoa met Sir Gossryk as he slipped vambraces onto his wrists. The man chewed at an invisible cud in his cheek. "Bastards stole my helmet." He glared at the prison. "Narl... Fat whoreson made me watch. Wanted me to see them all go before he did me the same. I'll have his fucking head."

She put a hand on his bicep. The Knight of the Hallow Moon glanced at it. "It was the Hines."

His lips trembled. He looked away. "I've a long list of people to repay."

"You and I both." Ishoa strode past him, Dragga in tow, a tidal mass of darksteel and menace. Sir Gossryk, she noticed, locked onto the Dread Knight. Ishoa winced internally. He'd slain Sir Gossryk's nephew, Camion Orr. *I'll need to deal with that soon.*

Dragga lengthened his step to come abreast of Ishoa. "I've a score to settle with Narl."

You act as though you have a score to settle with everyone. Ishoa remained facing forward as they wandered closer to the barred gates. Torches within highlighted dozens of shadowed forms. "Your score is no more pressing than my own. Nor Sir Gossryk's. Be patient. And let me do the talking."

From the corner of Ishoa's eye, she saw the snarling wolf visage whip in her direction, studying her for a handful of hasty steps before returning forward. "As you wish, Princess."

They came to a stop a stone's throw from the gates. Ishoa glanced back. Tendrils of smoke drifted up from the city of Prav in the distance. *Good luck, Arick.*

She turned her attention to the prison. "Lay down your weapons and surrender."

Golthius Narl's voice echoed from the cave. "Come and take them, bitch!"

She waited. The sound of battle filtered up the ravine from Prav. She let a minute pass. Then another. When she was certain those inside Deephollow had heard it, she spoke. "You think reinforcements are on their way to save you but you're wrong. No one's coming. Your city falls to my cousin as I speak. That leaves you with your own choices to make. I do not speak to your lord Golthius anymore. I speak to you, his holdguard, and to the knights of Prav. Not long ago, you were my subjects, but your traitorous lord misguided you. Delivered you into the hands of lowborn wretches."

The last word hung in the air. She gave it space for emphasis, room to breathe and find purchase among the Narl's men. "You have been deceived by no fault of your own, and so, I pledge on my name as an Ironlight that you will not be harmed." Venom dripped into her last words. "If you bring me Golthius Narl."

"She's lying," the baker lord hissed—the sound more resonant than before, as if he spoke to someone behind him in the cave. "You open these gates, we're all dead."

Ishoa tucked integrity out of sight. The lie came with ease. "You thought the Hines would deliver me to the Scarborn at Summerforge, but they have been subdued, their lives spared."

A different voice hollered back. "The Knights of the Wolf Banner don't take prisoners!"

"I command the Dread Knight." She looked at Dragga, a silent tower at her side. "He will do my bidding." The snarling wolf crest on his great helm dipped in obeisance. "The choice is yours."

Bickering broke out inside the cavernous prison, whispers pushed like bucking waves about the shallow canyon. Steel rasped. Clashed. Someone screamed. Golthius Narl's voice sifted to the fore of the fighting. "Fucking cowards! Here—"

Another scream, clipped this time.

Ishoa cupped a hand to her mouth. "I want him alive!"

"Bracket him!" A different voice. "Wary. Wary now!"

Golthius grunted. "Traitorous fucking—die you fucking dogs!"

Curses and the sounds of exertion peaked and then settled into quiet. A moment later, the central barbican embedded in the base of the cliff screeched open, rusted hinges tearing the air. Three holdguard wrestled an unarmed Golthius into daylight. From a sundered lip, crimson leaked over his pallid double-chin. Buttery sweat lathered his face as he wheezed like a wounded ox. From the sound of his breathing, Ishoa imagined his men had broken at least one rib, though how they could generate enough force to impact it through the mountainous fat that enrobed his torso eluded her. Flesh hung in a flap from the back of Golthius's hand, a nodule of bony knuckle crowning. Blood dripped from the ruined appendage in a steady stream to patter the dust.

One of the men carrying Narl licked his lips as he took in the legion of wolf knights that awaited. The three holdguard grunted and heaved—Golthius Narl dropped to broad kneecaps in the dust. Sucking in ragged breaths, he blinked and then recoiled at the sight of his brutalized hand.

Ishoa pointed at the holdguard. "Drop your weapons and go."

They looked at each other, unbelted their scabbards and swords, and then sprinted for the stairs. A pair of Sir Gossryk's men snatched up their discarded blades.

Ishoa looked to the caves. "The rest of you—surrender!"

Hesitation preceded those who remained, but seeing their brothers allowed to flee, they exited the prison all the same. Around sixty men and women filed out, dropping their weaponry in a stack beside the mouth of the caves. They raised their arms in surrender. Dragga's wolf knights descended, corralling and forcing them to their knees.

With Dragga and Sir Gossryk flanking her, Ishoa approached the lord of Prav.

Golthius rocked back on his heels, folds of belly swaying out from under the cover of his mail shirt. "I have...information."

The Knight of the Hallow Moon flourished his sword. "Allow me the pleasure of gutting this slug, Highness."

"Information you..." Golthius gulped and fought to stay conscious as his lax gaze flickered between Sir Gossryk and Dragga the Dread. "Information you need. Lodecka, she'll—"

In a single fluid motion, Ishoa drew a dagger and pressed the point under his chin. Teeth gritted, she resisted the urge to drive it up into his brain. "Tell me all you know. Now!" The blade tip sank a quarter of an inch. A primal alertness possessed the lord of Prav as a drop of blood ran down the steel.

"She uh—she's..." He stared at the sky.

"He doesn't know anything," Gossryk sneered. "Kill him."

Ishoa planted her feet, readying to ram the blade home. "Last chance."

Golthius Narl blubbered, eyes rolling back in his head a second before snapping back into focus. A pungent reek assaulted her nose. She assumed he soiled himself. *Pathetic. This one deserves no mercy.*

She withdrew her dagger and replaced it at her hip. A sigh of relief trembled through Golthius. Tears and sweat poured from him as he muttered repeated thanks.

"Dragga." Heart stone-hard, veins pumping ice, Ishoa stared at the Lord of Prav. Observed him as if from a great distance. Watched him with someone else's eyes. Condemned him with someone else's mouth. The command passed her lips, flat with resolve. "Strap him to the rock."

Golthius Narl blanched as Dragga's wolf knights hurried to comply. They trussed him up like a pig and tied him down in the same fashion as he'd ordered done to Sir Gossryk's men. The baker lord whimpered as they hauled his arms tight and immobile.

"Fine justice, this." The Knight of the Hallow Moon had a glint in his eyes.

"The Scarborn are working with the Kurgs!" Golthius shouted. "It's true. I—I'll tell you more."

Sir Gossryk scoffed. "Lies to save his hide."

It's too late. Ishoa held wolves by the ears. She knew what her men wanted. They would tolerate nothing else. She gave Dragga the command.

Stirrma's warhammer rested over the Dread Knight's shoulder. "Give your bastard son my regards." He raised the cruel anvil head.

Ishoa forced herself to watch. *I cannot shy from my own justice.* Still, the look on Golthius's face unnerved her. It was as if who he was had vacated his body. He trembled and stared at a bare and pointless patch of dirt between Dragga's feet.

A wet resounding pop, the sound of a tree falling onto the surface of a lake.

And then one of Golthius's eyes was sliding down the side of the boulder.

Ishoa retched. Some others did as well. None of the Narl's men though—they'd been properly conditioned.

"Now the rest!" Dragga bellowed.

Before Ishoa could comprehend what was happening, screams and shouts drowned out any chance she might have had at undermining Dragga's orders. His wolf knights heeded his command without question, even when it ran afoul of Ishoa's.

Ribbons of blood leapt through the air as the wolf knights hewed into the unarmed men of Prav. Like farmers at harvest, they moved in scything rows, a methodical reaping of panicked men.

One minute the Narl's men were alive, shouting and begging, and in the next, they were reduced to a morass of disembodied limbs. Those coughing up blood or still wailing were quickly silenced.

"What have you done?" Ishoa hissed.

"What was needed," Dragga said. "What you wouldn't."

Ishoa bristled and fingered the dagger at her hip.

"The way is clear now, Highness. You did not break your word. The fault is mine and mine alone. Your honor is still intact." Dragga dropped to a knee, head bowed before her. "I beg your forgiveness."

Nothing of his tone *begged*. She scanned her surroundings. A veritable sea of wolf helms watched the mockery transpire. *In function, I am nothing but an old dream to them. Dragga is their true leader. Their future. He does what must be done to win this war.*

She decided it best to play her part in the illusion. "You are forgiven." Then she gave him a look as he rose that told him they'd be talking later.

She strode toward the prison entrance in furious disgust, leaving Dragga to clean up his mess.

Impotent torchlight left black stretches among the twisting tunnel system of Deephollow Prison. To little benefit, Ishoa snorted out her breaths and inhaled as quick and shallow as she could to avoid the tainted atmosphere of musty stone, human waste, and something tougher to pinpoint. *A mix of anticipation and fear...or hope and despair?*

She saw it as much as she smelled it.

Grime-matted locks of hair piled around shrouded faces. White-knuckled fists gripping the bars of their cells. Hands blackened by unwashed time. They awaited Ishoa's orders in silence, witholding their urge to beg her. Their impulse to shout for joy at their liberation. These criminals had lived under Narl guard. Nothing was guaranteed, least of all good fortune. She sensed that they'd been treated with a pointed lack of compassion even the condemned did not deserve. For them, the only assurance they could rely on was suffering.

As a result, those crowding into the light of their meager cells hesitated, swaying anxiously from one foot to the other. Ishoa slowed and turned to face one such group.

One man with sandwiched-together features, his eyes mere slits, his cheeks ponderously full, bowed. The others eyed her nervously. "How many of you are down here?" she asked.

A voice from the filthy huddle. "A hundred."

The clutch of prisoners erupted, each fighting to be heard as they shouted down the first guess and offered their own numbers. Five hundred, two hundred, a few dozen...

"Silence!" One of the wolf knights slammed the butt of his weapon against the bars and the criminals devolved to muttering.

"Thank you, Sir." Ishoa rested a hand on the knight, beckoning him to ease. "Now, one at a time. Where are they keeping the prisoners from the battle of Jarik?"

The man with slitted eyes raised a hand.

"Speak freely," Ishoa said.

The man's voice was melodious, soft and even, a velvet swath stroking her ears. "A right at the next passage, Highness. Another right after."

This one is different. The wolf knights escorting her sensed it too. She heard the rustle of chain coifs as a few behind her exchanged glances. Ishoa motioned for them to lead the way, and they plucked torches from the walls.

"Excuse me, Highness," said the velvet-voiced man. "Would you like to know our true number?"

She swiveled. "I do."

"We are three hundred and twenty-six," the man said. "Seventy-one are prisoners of war from the Battle of Jarik. Mostly Frosts. A handful of others."

Ishoa blinked in surprise. "That's rather specific. You're a perceptive one, aren't you?" She took a step, attempting to make out more of the man's features but a wolf knight held out a warding hand to keep her from getting too close. "Are you...Kanian?"

The man's chin rotated over a shoulder as if revealing a shameful secret. "I am, Highness. On both counts."

"Your name?"

He hesitated. "Velvet, Highness."

Ah. Fitting. "You are well-spoken and well-mannered. So what landed you in Deephollow?"

His gaze fell to the cave floor. "Forgive me, Highness, these things are better left unsaid in the presence of—"

"Tell me now. I've no time for games."

"Murder. Piracy. Theft." Velvet sighed. "I served on a vessel called *Anthera's Revenge.*"

The name sounded familiar. One of the wolf knights cursed under her breath. Ishoa threw the woman a look. "Terror of the Sea of Psollus, Highness," she said. "Terror of the Dolgn Ocean, too. Still sailing, last I heard. Under a treacherous bastard who goes by Armada."

Velvet gestured confirmation. "That is correct, ma'am. I was her captain for a time—she had a different name then—before I was removed by the current one. He spared my life, but in a truly dirty yet clever move, turned me over to the Crown's Justice at Toros. Fifteen years of crime attached to my name and my name alone."

"You've led men before, then?" Despite the day's victory, the fight against the White Wolverine Alliance was far from over. Sir Gossryk's host was depleted and the Hines had switched sides. *The Crown's presence in Anjuhkar is fast weakening. I have need of good men with combat experience. If I can't trust a Kanian...who can I trust?* "Swear fealty to Namarr and sign on as soldiers, and I promise not one of you will spend another day in that cell."

As one, all criminals within earshot roared in exultation. Once it died down, Ishoa said, "Velvet, I'll look to you to tell me of those who can't be trusted and need to be left behind bars." To the rest, she said, "From this day forward, you're conscripts in my army."

The flat line of Velvet's mouth reeled up on one side. "This is a debt I cannot repay." He bowed deep. "But I will try."

Ishoa started down the tunnel, raising her voice as she went. "Hold Prav until this war is over and I'll consider the debt repaid."

The boots of the wolf knights echoed in a rhythmic thud and scrape. They came to a tube of granite leading down a dim path with a rope riveted to the wall for balance. The soldiers with Ishoa shuffled down it, armor jangling. Heeding Velvet's directions, the torchbearers in front took a right at the next passage toward a clutch of cells.

Scores of prisoners greeted them. Among those wearing clinking chains, she saw the soiled tabards of charging bisons, inverted oak trees, embers and anvils, and a handful of sigils from lesser holds.

They cheered as a wolf knight swept forth to turn the key to their freedom.

"Arm yourselves and await further instructions on the surface," Ishoa said. "I hope you're all eager for vengeance. Your duties resume immediately." Most nodded grim assent as they saluted, fists slapping starved shoulders where honor plates should be.

They flooded up the steps, all but a rugged, bruised woman, naked but for a gray tabard bearing the three black spears of Twilight Cape. She tugged at the cloth, moving it to cover one area even as it exposed a strip of flesh in another, a fruitless carousel of indecency. The hard look in the woman's eyes confirmed Ishoa's suspicion that she'd been ravaged, a fate Ishoa had only glimpsed as the Hines roped her to the tree. If Adus and Hollem had managed to carry out their deplorable act, Ishoa's world would have been painted different. Seen different. Felt different. Like this woman's.

Her anger at Dragga for slaughtering the Narls vanished.

"This way, Highness." The woman hustled past, arms wrapped protectively around her torso.

A streak of dried blood traced the back of the woman's inner thigh, mapping a recent assault. *Now I wish some of the Narls were alive.* Hatred nipped at Ishoa's neck, grabbed and throttled her guts. Looking at the abused woman who now led her down into the twisting bowels of Deephollow, Ishoa would have paid a small fortune to bring the Narl's men back to life so she could execute them again.

Thoughts of revenge disappeared as Ishoa arrived at a ledge overlooking a wide open pit. The sheer walls of the earthen bowl descended twenty feet. At its base, a tiny form lay in the fetal position, seemingly asleep, strands of long, lank hair splayed around her head.

"Wake up!" the Twilight Cape holdguard shouted.

The scrawny form stirred in the echoing bowl and struggled to her feet. She raised her face to the torchlight, revealing a jaw and throat tattooed black.

"Enkita?" Ishoa stammered.

The Lady of Twilight Cape smeared her face with the back of a hand, looked at it with her brow drawn together, then wiped it on the bedraggled pelt draping her. "Weak little princess survives. Saves Enkita. Maybe not so weak."

They found a rope and hauled the woman out of the pit. Hooked to plates bolted into the rock wall, a set of empty manacles hung from chains. *Enkita wasn't restrained.* Puzzled, Ishoa asked why.

Enkita snorted, the gesture more sorrow than disdain. "Your grandmother. They lock her there. Think I turn into bear and eat her. I disappoint them."

Ishoa gripped Enkita's arm. "Where is she?"

"Gone, little princess." Enkita swallowed, jaw muscles flexing. "Sick after Jarik. She last few days. No more."

Ishoa stared into the pit. Empty manacles stared back at her.

Enkita patted Ishoa on the back. "Belara is true hero." The diminutive woman ushered the rest of the group up the carved stairs, leaving Ishoa to privacy.

She's gone.

There was no more Ice Maiden. The champion of the Unification Wars and the Great Betrayal was dead. Belara Frost wasn't to be freed, nor would she rally those Anjuhks loyal to Namarr to victory over the White Wolverine Alliance.

Gone. Forever.

Memories of being alone in the Sister Keep and staring out a window at the servants, knights, and holdguard beyond invaded the sweeter recollections she had of her grandmother educating her in the ways of statecraft.

The low-born get to choose their lives. She'd had the thought a thousand times. Felt the jealousy of it in too many instances to count. They wouldn't be royalty no matter how hard they tried, but Ishoa could be nothing else. A smith, a baker, a musician, a soldier, a wife...no possibility but one.

"You were born to be a princess. To rule over the greatest nation the world has ever known." Belara had looked proudly down at her one night as she'd fallen to sobbing and wishing her parents were alive. "Take comfort in that, my dear."

For as long as Ishoa could remember, she'd never felt comfort in the fact. She'd been trapped. Bound. Abandoned into a life she hadn't chosen. A life she could not deviate from.

Ishoa raised her wrists, gaze darting between the manacles her grandmother had died wearing and the raw lines left in her flesh by the Hines. A knot at the center of her being loosened.

She dove into it. Gnawed at the feelings rising in her like a feral beast chewing its leg free of a trap. She'd hated when the Fly had tied her up. Hated the helplessness of it. The violating theft of self-control.

Ishoa seethed, heat pumping up her thighs and into her belly. Sparkling blobs crawled into her peripheries. Sweat bloomed down her back. Everything she was had been dictated to her in ink and blood. Histories won and kept by the edge of a sword. A concrete future laid before her stretching from cradle to grave.

Every step.

Now here, now there. No choice at all—no matter her feelings. All of it. No choice but to comply. A nation and all its people, the weight of them, hanging by a strand of silk from her brow, bearing her down.

Always bearing her down. The price of her freedom.

I never chose any of it!

Something boomed within her, a dense orb of budding energy that pooled and then rushed to fill her limbs. A source of strength, untapped and unwilling to see the light...out of fear.

The fear that she might *choose* the very thing she resented above all else.

The Crown. Recognition dawned, rippling over her skin. The weight of history and legacy lifted. She mourned Belara Frost, a woman who'd carved evil from the world so she could cement foundations of prosperity against it. A woman Ishoa was proud to share blood with. And yet she felt her great-grandmother's final sacrifice deep in her bones and knew it to be a necessity.

My path is my own. I choose it!

The shackles in the pit glinted in the flickering torchlight as the Ice Maiden's voice penetrated through the swirl of emotions. *And what will you choose, dear Isha?*

The child long guilty of resenting others from her tower window died, and her fear of responsibility—her fear of power—died with her.

The chains of Ishoa's past fell away with a hollow rustle and descended into the abyss.

CHAPTER SIXTY-FIVE

THE MIRACLE OF LOVE

T hey watched the smoking city slide past in the dawn gloom.

Busy getting the warship under way, Kaltes and his sailors paid Garlenna and Barodane no mind. The pair were left to themselves to watch the flames rise, the smoke thicken, the screams drain away into the plunging creak and boom of waves breaking on the prow of *Anthera's Revenge*.

"Nserthes seems too resourceful," Barodane said, attempting to turn the mood.

Garlenna shook her head. "There was nowhere to go. The Sempyrium will be thorough. Nserthes knew that. Martyr's Isle will fall."

Heavy silence crouched over them. The clattering and shouting of the ship's crew did nothing to lighten it.

Fuck.

Garlenna eyed Barodane. "What?"

Lips pursed, he slapped a palm on the rail. "Scab."

"He'll be okay," she said. "I saw the stablemaster free the horses before the flames claimed the building. Many escaped through the gate once they'd levered it up. I saw my mount among them. Chances are, Scab escaped too."

Barodane snorted out a laugh. *Might take more than a little fire to kill old Scab. Ugly, bitter old bastard.* He blew a raspberry. "Malzacor, then. Kashoggo. I admit I've always wanted to lay eyes on him. Fifteen feet tall, I've heard. Do you think..."

Garlenna was turning away, her back to Barodane.

"Not a fan of the big bad rebel leader, eh?" He tried to laugh it off, hoping their brush with death had set things back aright. Having lost Scab and Martyr's Isle, he'd hate to find he'd lost the special dynamic he'd shared with his prosort as well. The one where laughter and truth could chew up anything that threatened to come between them.

Defeat dragged every line of her face into a frown. She gave no reaction beyond a worn expression, her palms clapped to the handrail.

A lance of agitation drove into Barodane's forehead. *I've about had it with this shit.* He grabbed his prosort by the shoulder and spun her square to face him. "For weeks now, I've given you space, I've given you time, and I've given you my trust. But right now, we're on a fucking pirate ship on our way to meet with a—a whatever the fuck Kashoggo is—and you're *still* hiding something from me. I can't have that. Not with what's at stake."

She sucked in to speak but her rebuttal died in her chest. Her sides swelled and then deflated with a sigh.

"Must I command you?" Barodane waited. Kaltes knew who his cargo was, but the rest of the crew had seemingly been left in the dark on the matter, so he and Garlenna had agreed to maintain their identities as Mal and Ren. He rubbed the outline of his mouth as he whispered. "Very well. Your *prince* commands you to—"

"You know I dislike lying. Even moreso to you. But I had to. I had to do it or..." She pursed her lips. "I was afraid you'd fall apart."

Barodane froze, watching her like a mongoose watching a viper. Waiting to dodge a deadly bite or attack.

Garlenna lifted her face skyward and Barodane followed her line of sight. Gulls circled. A few split off from the flock, banking toward Martyr's Isle to scavenge. The town was little more than a dark smear on the horizon.

"If I told you what awaited us in Northern Malzacor you would never have come along willingly," she said. "Our whole mission would have been in peril. Namarr back on course with doom...just because I didn't have the strength to keep you in the dark awhile."

Prickles crept up the nape of Barodane's neck. The boom of the bow breaking waves penetrated his awareness, causing him to jolt and setting his own heart to booming. A chill spray thrown to the peripheries of the ship whenever it crested had left his gray initiate's robe sodden. Yet, the cold spilling over him was nothing compared to the dread anticipation he felt.

After all I've fought through to force myself to be here, what could she possibly think would stop me? The question sent fear slithering into his guts.

"I suppose we're still on course with doom. Returning you to throne and crown is a narrow hope, so perhaps I should have told you and saved my soul the torture." She faced him, drew in the will needed to speak, azure eye searching his face.

She said something...

A dull roar flooded Barodane's ears. His head was light—disconnected feeling. A splintering sensation, as if he were dissolving, worked into his hands and feet. Garlenna blurred. He blinked and emitted a soft gasp. Awareness was slow in returning to his body for those dim and disembodied seconds.

"Did you hear me?" Concern lined her face.

"Omari D'Alzir," he mumbled, "is a follower of Kashoggo." *Damn.* As much as he'd been longing for her since he'd stopped ascending on godsthorn, he never thought he'd actually have to face her. It was a conversation he could do without.

Garlenna's voice dropped lower. For a heart-stopping moment, she hesitated, another hard truth hanging on the verge.

"What is it?"

She cleared her throat. "Kaitos is with her."

"Kaitos Barabi?" That didn't make any sense. "My Kaitos?" *Of course, you jackass. Who else?*

"Yes. And as far as I know, time has not improved his opinion of you. He refused to come to your funeral. He sent a letter condemning me for going."

Barodane nodded, agreeing with Kaitos's sentiment. "Wait." His expression skewed, brows furrowed. "What do you mean he's *with* her?"

"They're married, Barodane. That's what I mean."

So my best friend has married the woman I loved. He went numb. *It figures.*

He closed his eyes. "Indeed, you were smart to withhold that from me." He patted Garlenna on the shoulder and moved past her. She called to him, but the world had dilated into a singular tunnel with a lone image hanging at its end...

Kaitos took Omari in his arms, wolfish smile beaming, muscular arms holding her tight. And she, a face as open and inviting as her heart had always been, staring up at him in the same way she'd looked at Barodane. Blue eyes that drank the breath from him, that felt a shameless indulgence of the spirit for how long they held his own. Those same eyes, out of blissful memory, ignoring him now and favoring the friend he'd betrayed.

Not just him. Her, too. I betrayed them both. Best to keep tabs on such matters.

A few strides from his cabin, tears burst forth. He lunged at the door—flung it open—flung it shut. His back rattled the wooden wall as he slammed against it and slid down to the floor. "What have I done?"

Out of bitterness, he'd driven Kaitos away. Out of selfishness, he'd left Omari to suffer the consequences of his broken promise alone. Their last memories were of a man who'd done unspeakable acts. And somehow, in the vacuum of pain he'd caused them, the two had fallen in love. They found what he'd lost. Treasured what he'd buried and damned.

What have I done?

Madame Gratha and the memory of her strange, healing light kept him from walking down an all-too-familiar path bricked in gravestones. *You will honor those who've suffered by your hand with better deeds.*

But that seemed like the kind of thing that required love to accomplish. A love he'd thrown away. A love he kept throwing away. That's where his hate came from...the death of love.

He inhaled slow and let his skull bang against the wall behind. Musty air tinged with the acrid scent of lantern oil crept up his nose.

What will I do?

The answer haunted him across the sea.

CHAPTER SIXTY-SIX

THE COLD KEEPS LONGER

Rakeema stared up at Ishoa. Ishoa stared back. The world was distant, time vague and boundless. A smile stretched across Ishoa's heart. Rakeema's own beat faster than hers. She felt that too.

There was a faint ruckus at the edge of hearing. Men cursing. Nothing important.

"Ishoa..."

Pressure against her elbow. She ignored it. *No more chains to break.* Her grandmother was gone. Wolst was gone. Lodaris and Othwii, gone. So few left to fear disappointing. *But not you, girl.* Since she'd found the empty shackles the Ice Maiden had died in, her bond with Rakeema had grown. Awarenesses entwined like reflex. Almost, she could touch it...

"I'll gut you, boyo."

"Ishoa," Arick whispered. "Do something."

Ishoa shook her head. Sir Gossryk's men and Dragga's wolf knights were at it again. Two days they'd been gone from Deephollow and already fists had flown—more than a few times. Spit, more often. Once, a dagger was brandished but didn't find flesh. For that, at least, Ishoa had been thankful.

After listening for endless hours to the insults, the quibbling, and the out-right dismissal of her commands to get along no matter the cost in pride, Ishoa had slipped into a tooth-grinding, sword-pommel-strumming state of full-bodied contempt.

Arick leaned in at her side where they sat on stones to form a ring around a cook fire. "It's getting worse."

Wind howled over the tundra. They were en route to the Manger, but Ishoa worried they might not arrive as one army. Her goal was to go to Alistar but not before paying Rigga Hine a visit. "I'm aware," Ishoa muttered.

On the other side of the crackling flames sat Dragga, elbows propped on knees as he gnawed at a chicken leg stolen from the storehouses of Prav. They'd left the prisoners of war from the battle of Jarik in charge, with Velvet as the point of command buffering them from the criminals meant to bolster their numbers should an attack come. "The more distractions for the Alliance, the better," Arick had said once the orders were given. "Well done."

Dragga had smiled at her in a way that pressed down. Truth was, his smile had always done that before, but after ordering the Narls slaughtered, it did so with ever greater effect.

And he smiled at her now, full-lips shining with grease. Jet ringlets reached down past his ears, framing smudges where sweat displaced dirt at his temples. He was stripped to the waist of armor, his head tilted with smarmy ease.

Ishoa locked eyes with the man as he ignored the knight of Bleeding Point challenging one of his own. The targeted wolf knight—a young warrior with misshapen eye sockets—sneered and clutched his cock. "Gut your mother with this."

Gossryk's man surged toward the wolf knight. "Black-blood cunt!"

Rakeema jolted at Ishoa's side as Dragga flew to his feet and backhanded the Bleeding Point man with the chicken leg. The struck knight dipped, knees faltering, and then buoyed back up, stumbling and unsteadied. Angry curses were fired between factions. Sir Gossryk entered the fray, pounding the shoulders of his men and damning them to calm while Dragga watched with indifference.

Ishoa stroked Rakeema's head.

Dragga raised the flayed chicken bone and tossed it experimentally at a man of Bleeding Point. The goad pattered off the man's shoulder. Sir Gossryk whirled. "Doing your level fucking best to keep the order here, Dread Knight?"

Dragga scratched the patch of black scruff that dappled his chin. "*An* order of sorts."

The Knight of the Hallow Moon glowered, chin tucked, forked beard hooking upward like a bull's horns. Ready to charge. "I don't catch your meaning?"

"I can provide a lesson, if you need clarity. We can't all be swift of intellect."

"Isha," Arick hissed.

A vein in Sir Gossryk's neck jumped. The side of his mouth split, revealing a canine. "You think playing at war and executing a few ambushes on weaker forces makes you invincible?"

"Hard to refute when I've not died yet."

Sir Gossryk snorted. "Yet."

Dragga's face twitched a few times then went slack. "Killed a good many though. As you're aware."

Sir Gossryk stiffened, face going flush.

Arick cursed at Ishoa's side. "This has to stop."

"That's enough." She eased forward from her seat. *Dragga thinks himself above, not only Sir Gossryk, but me as well.* "Both of you, stand down." Ishoa surveyed the Knights of the Wolf Banner arrayed behind their leader. Not a set of eyes was on Ishoa. Not one saw her as important when the men were speaking. Not one expected her commands to stop whatever was about to transpire. Mere words, lacking in power and unimportant, were an annoyance to the real decision makers.

The Knight of the Hallow Moon stared down his hooked nose at Dragga. "You'll find I'm quite a different beast than my nephew."

"Will I?" Dragga picked a mealy mass of white from his teeth and flicked it away with seeming disinterest. "Terrified."

"Piss and prance all you like, but you'd be right to fear me, boyo."

"Not if it was you who taught your nephew the blade." Dragga feigned a yawn. "A boring affair, killing traitors."

"I said that's enough." As Ishoa's command went unheeded, she pet Rakeema and evoked a rolling purr. She would not proceed frantic, nor angry, but she would have their attention one way or another.

Sir Gossryk had recoiled as if slapped from Dragga's last insult. He started ripping at the leather straps securing his honor plate. "To settle the account of Camion Orr's honor, I challenge you to a duel, Dragga Omenfaen." Spittle flew from the Knight of the Hallow Moon's lips as he flung the pauldron at the Dread Knight's feet. "To the death, I hope."

"I accept." Dragga laughed. "Do give your nephew my regards when we're done. You can ask him about his betrayal for yourself."

It looked as though Sir Gossryk had eaten something bad. A purple hue crept up his neck. They wouldn't make it to the duel if things continued.

Ishoa stood and spoke loud enough for all to hear. "I shall fight in Sir Gossryk's stead."

The Knight of the Hallow Moon swung stunned eyes on her. Brow furrowed, Dragga followed suit. Ishoa didn't spare a glance at Arick. She knew what his face looked like. The same disapproval she'd always seen there. She no longer cared.

But more importantly, she no longer feared. "Dragga Omenfaen, you have wantonly killed my subjects in the name of duty to the Crown—my Crown—and so, you will face me in combat."

Some of those gathered around had the decency to stifle their laughter, while others openly let loose. Even Sir Gossryk smiled, her interference more ludicrously wild than a thunderous fart could have been. "You can't be serious, Highness." He looked around as if someone might leap out to let him know it was all a joke. "Forgive me but you're—"

"Not finished. Furthermore, Dragga, you denude your family's legacy that was hard-won by the steadfast allegiance and brave acts of your ancestors. If your sister were alive today to witness your rash and arrogant disregard for the Crown of Namarr, she'd spit in your face."

That wiped the humor from the Dread Knight's expression. Cold eyes narrowed at her.

"Do you accept, Dragga, or do you concede and forfeit all right to call yourself a man?" Ishoa looked to the faces behind him. "I daresay some might be excited by the latter prospect. You are rather handsome."

One man's chuckle shifted into a cough. A few arched their eyebrows. Dragga didn't move but for a single spasm at the corner of his mouth as he painstakingly growled, "Accept."

"Good. Sir Gossryk, have your men construct the ring," Ishoa said. "We cross steel at dawn."

Baffled muttering joined the sizzle and pop of the logs on the fire. Before Arick could speak, Ishoa faced him full on. "Trust me, Arick. You said yourself that you should. So do it." She turned back, flicking a glance Dragga's way. Twice her weight. Nearly a foot taller. The teen had already slain C'Dathun trolls, knights, and even a few lords.

Will he hesitate to kill a princess?

The winds of White Plains tousled Ishoa's hair as she stepped inside the ring of stones. The Knights of the Wolf Banner and men of Bleeding Point crowded in, their animosity momentarily set aside in favor of the spectacle. A handful tripped over the loose barrier of rock as they shouldered and jockeyed for a better vantage.

Dragga spun Stirrma's warhammer around a fist, caught it, spun it again around the other. He wore full armor, the embers of Omenfaen emblazoned onto his darksteel chestplate. A snarling wolf snapped out from the visor of his great helm. He raised it. "Would you like a second to join you, Highness?" He gestured at the men ringing them. "Plenty to choose from. I know it's less of an Anjuhk custom to use seconds, so I'll happily forgo one to even the odds."

He leaned abruptly to one side and threw out a gauntleted hand to right himself. "Woo now!" He laughed, then took a horn of something from a knight in the crowd and slugged it back.

He's drunk. That's how worried he is about fighting me. Ishoa let the slight go. She needed to be clear of mind and nursing her pride over someone else's choice would do her no good.

She scanned the crowd, meeting the gaze of as many of the men—and the rare woman—as she could. Okki Womunger fidgeted with the pommel of a dagger at her belt. Arms crossed, Sir Gossryk brooded.

"In the days before Namarr," Ishoa intoned, "duels for kotarg were fought with anjuhtargs at their master' sides. Does any here deny me this right?"

"Kotarg?" Dragga frowned.

"It means honor." Sir Gossryk spat. "Your ignorance surprises us all." The sarcasm set the men of Bleeding Point to laughter.

When it died down, Dragga said, "A poor choice for a second, I say." He smiled at Rakeema. "Fine. Have your cat. But if it dies, it will be no one's fault but yours. Tell them you will seek no retribution."

"Aye," Ishoa announced without looking at Rakeema. "I will seek no retribution."

Dragga clapped the visor of his great helm into place. The chivalrous youth she'd known disappeared. She faced the Dread Knight now. A bloodthirsty animal leading a pack of the same.

Tame your fears, Isha. She let her next breath slowly fill her lungs.

At the center of the ring, Arick raised a fist. "Combatants, may the ancestors be with you." He dropped it.

Dragga advanced, warhammer whirling in a dizzying display of speed and skill at arms. An image of him killing a white wolverine in one swing flashed through Ishoa's mind. *He didn't have to do that. He shouldn't have.*

Where rage would have once moved her hand, it was that hollow place that did so now. Naught but the wind and the rhythmic thud of her pulse existed as she gripped the stiff leather hilt of her blade and drew it forth.

"Dragga, I do not fear you." The words left her, and as they did, she knew them to be true. Peace coalesced in the empty place where fear had been. A peace born of deepest knowing. A peace that came to those who flowed in concert with their truth.

No enemy but fear.

The Dread Knight slowed his showmanship for the crowd. He raised his visor—a smile smeared his face. Laughing, he unbuckled his helmet and tossed it to a knight in the crowd. "No need."

"Dragga," Ishoa said again. "I do not fear you."

He studied her, a hint of curiosity passing over eyes glazed by drink. He grunted.

At Ishoa's side, an unmoving Rakeema watched the man. Ishoa opened her mouth to give a command and paused. Instead, she closed her eyes and slid into the emptiness within. Into the word itself. And from that quiet place of blossoming power, where fate and action converged, she pushed herself *into* Rakeema.

Distinct, almost overwhelming, she smelled the warriors around her. The ones who'd most recently urinated. The ones whose sweat stank of worry and excitement. She felt the wind caressing her every fiber. Every bristling strand of fur.

A vibrating sensation met Ishoa's consciousness—a question about the man across the way. In answer, she sent a wave of iron resolve flooding back to soothe it. Resonance bloomed in the space between anjuhtarg and master. Understanding. Equal ground, now shared.

Ishoa opened herself more. *Let go. Let go of control.* The manacles had fallen away. Kept falling, down into the abyss where the prisons of her past lay.

I am free.

Power siphoned into her. Her sword and shield became feather-light and she felt as though she floated over the tundra on the balls of her feet. Muscles brimming with strength, demanding to be loosed. She was dense and agile, air and steel, princess and war cat.

I am a Hulka'skara.

"Well, I can't just kill you without a fight." Dragga's voice.

Ishoa's eyes snapped open. Every line and plane of Dragga's visage, every blackhead on his nose, every bit of his stone-carved face was a clear mosaic.

She lunged.

The Dread Knight jerked back as the tip of her blade scored his armor near the neck. A second stab, faster than the first, slipped into a joint of one arm and left a shallow gash.

Dragga stumbled out of reach, gaping at her in shock. Gaping at the wound she'd given him. He grimaced as the burn hit him, then muttered, "Little bitch."

The crowd went crypt-silent.

Breath, heavy with spirits, washed over Ishoa as she dropped into a crouch and started to circle her prey. Rakeema weaved between her legs, a threat in constant motion.

Hand over hand, the Dread Knight passed his warhammer behind his back and then brought it whistling around in a flat arc. Ishoa raised her shield to absorb the blow. Wood chips splintered along the banded rim, shock compressing the bones in her arm even as she positioned herself for the counter.

Now, my girl.

Rakeema lashed out, claws shredding boot leather. Ishoa followed with an attack of her own—two looping chops at Dragga's midsection, another at his head. Overextended from his initial blow, he was forced to throw himself backward in retreat.

Ishoa returned to her crouch, blade resting on the rim of her battered shield and pointing at her foe. She waited.

"You all saw, the princess means to kill me." He wiped sweat from his brow. "I shall give no quarter."

"None needed." She felt the pattern within her, the threads of unity binding her with Rakeema, forming them into a single entity.

Ishoa raced forward ahead of her war cat and feinted low—Dragga dropped his guard to meet her slash just as Rakeema pounced, sailing over her shoulder. Jaws clamped around the mail protecting Dragga's uninjured arm. The crushing strength of her bite made him cry out as Ishoa rained blows into the gaps in his guard. Sparks and shattered links of mail showered the earth.

With a single hand, Dragga raised the haft of his hammer to deflect a chop that would have beheaded him. Ishoa's sword bit into the wood and lodged there. Dragga slammed a knee into her chest plate. Teeth clacking, she was hurled backward.

To me!

Rakeema released Dragga's arm and returned to the space beneath her master's sword arm.

Not wanting to let the Dread Knight recover, Ishoa launched forward to keep him on his heels. Rakeema slipped from one side to the other, harrying his flanks, claws raking at his legs. Dragga cursed, face purpled, breathing heavily through his mouth.

He cursed and snatched Ishoa's shield in a firm grip, then flung her aside.

The shield disappeared into the mob of spectators, but the wall of humanity caught Ishoa and stood her upright. Rakeema bounded to her side.

Panting, Dragga surveyed the damage to his weapon, his armor and arm. A tattered mess. Blood dripped from his fingertips.

Ishoa took account of herself as well. No more shield. No protection. Her thoughts bled into Rakeema's, drank in the quiet echo of the ice tiger's awareness. Her anjuhtarg wanted to attack, to finish the man off. Ishoa agreed. *No quarter.*

They flew at Dragga, a silver-and-white blur of steel, tooth, and claw, driving him back. He managed a single sweep of his warhammer but Ishoa ducked it with ease. As much as Rakeema fed off Ishoa's calm and confidence, her strategic direction, the war cat's power and speed filled her in turn. They melded into one, a being of primal fury and icy resolve.

Ishoa's sword bit through mail on Dragga's forearm. She was quicker—quicker than the Dread Knight! Rakeema erupted from between Ishoa's legs mid-lunge to barreled into Dragga's lap. Claws hooking to his belt, she wrapped around his thigh. Off-balanced by the ice tiger's weight and digging claws, he fought to stay upright.

Ishoa launched a frenzied assault.

Unable to fully defend against Ishoa for fear of being pulled down by Rakeema, nor against Rakeema for fear of being skewered by Ishoa, Dragga roared in frustration. A roar that became a shout of anguish. He faltered.

Ishoa's blade licked out, severing chain and flesh high on his ribs. Dragga seized, eyes bulging. He dropped his warhammer and buckled as Rakeema bore him to the ground. As soon as his knee touched, the ice tiger squirmed out from under him and returned to Ishoa's side.

Injured and paling, the Dread Knight didn't look so dreadful anymore. Lungs heaving, Ishoa cocked back her sword to deliver the final stroke to the kneeling man. At this range, she would not miss.

Okki Womunger threw herself in front of Dragga, the point of Ishoa's hovering blade near to touching her nose. Ishoa had almost spitted the girl. The muscles of her shoulder tingled with the effort of reining in the motion.

"Please, Princess." Face downcast, hands upraised in surrender, Okki begged, "Mercy."

Ishoa blinked at the girl with flame-kissed hair. Behind her, Dragga sucked in ragged breaths. One of his massive hands found the shoulder of the girl protecting him. "Okki..." he rasped.

"I need him, Princess." Fat tears gathered on Okki's lower eyelids. Her voice quavered. "Please. Spare him."

She's in love.

Ishoa would have given anything to be at Lodaris's side when he'd passed. She swallowed the regret and lowered her sword. "Dragga Omenfaen, swear on your sister, your mother, and the Omenfaen name that you will serve and obey me without question until your dying breath. Do that and I will spare you."

The crowd was so quiet, every hitching spasm and pinch of pain in Dragga's breathing could be heard. He glanced at Rakeema, then Ishoa. Lips parted, he hesitated, sweat beading his brow. A flutter of recognition crossed his expression, that glimmering moment that oft preceded a smile. Ishoa couldn't help but recall the way he had looked at Stirrma every time she spit barbs at her brother. *The very same way...like he respects me.*

Ishoa was still open and extending herself outward. She wondered if somehow it gave her access to unspoken things in people the same way it did with Rakeema. A sort of sixth sense. *If he sees Stirrma in me, I accept the honor.*

"Surrender." Ishoa raised her blade to Dragga's chin. "In the old way."

A tremulous smile, then a nod. The Dread Knight kissed the flat of her sword. "I swear my fealty, Highness. Uck—" He clutched his side. "Until my dying breath."

Her duty done, Ishoa sank sword into scabbard and headed for the ring's perimeter. Knights of the Wolf Banner and Bleeding Point peeled back before her to form a path.

A path of her own making.

To say the feud between Dragga and Sir Gossryk was dead and buried would be woefully inaccurate. In light of Ishoa's ascent to leadership, not just in name but function, they conceded not to kill one another for the time being. The two stayed far from the other's reach rather than interacting with the silent hope of a bloody altercation.

Ishoa didn't care what they did nor how they felt, so long as they followed her commands. If anyone understood the sacredness of harboring vengeance in one's heart, it was her, so she let them keep it in secret.

After Dragga's defeat, Sir Gossryk had found Ishoa outside of her tent. His request for an audience was polite—more polite than he'd ever been toward her until that moment. "You stole my vengeance, Princess." He nodded as he scanned for anyone listening. "A hard thing to accept for a man of my well-rusted years. But you've given me something else instead. A bit of hope." A wide smile broke across his weathered face, pointed canines gleaming. "I follow an Ironlight once more. Your performance honored my nephew. Camion was gentler than myself, and I imagine he would have approved of your methods." The Knight of the Hallow Moon cleared his throat then bent at the waist to sketch a deep bow. "Princess."

"Sir." She saluted. Sir Gossryk straightened up and she fixed him with a steady gaze. "I promise, we *will* get Bleeding Point back."

His tongue filled the lower left of his mouth. "Aye."

She'd left him there and swept past the guards with Rakeema at her heels for a much needed rest.

When she woke the next day, the bite of animosity no longer tainted the air. All eyes were on her, and she supposed they saw a person they'd never thought to see again. As Sir Gossryk had said, an Ironlight was among them. Not some doted-upon girl. Not a teen, who needed men to fight for her or save her or advise her. Not the princess who was unfit for the Crown.

An Ironlight.

Half human, half myth. She caught whispered snippets preceding her wherever she went. Eyes staring, then looking away when she noticed them. With a rare smile, Arick had reported the gossip. "They say you fought your way free of Jarik. That Rakeema is a demon from C'Dath."

Ishoa chuckled. "That's ridiculous."

"They say you beat the Fly in single combat and made him swear fealty to you just like you did with Dragga. Some are even claiming you have ghost blood."

"An Awakened?" Ishoa waved a hand of dismissal. "People will believe anything."

Arick's smile faded, azure eyes regarding her beyond the point of comfort. "What?"

Another second of something unspoken studied her until his gaze landed on Rakeema and remained. "Nothing else, Highness. We should arrive at the Manger by tomorrow night."

Ever since she'd left the comfort of the Hines' fortress, Ishoa had been riding at a blistering pace, weathering severe cold and sleepless nights. Tack on her duel with Dragga, a rape attempt, the grief of losing Wolst a second time, and her grandmother's death, and she felt nothing short of complete exhaustion.

And the journey to Alistar was a long one yet.

"Good," she said to Arick. "We'll allow our soldiers a rest. They've earned it. A small contingent will go to the Manger to parlay." She would pay a great deal for Gaern Yorek's release. The man was of almost no political value, so she assumed Rigga Hine could be convinced to let him go for a paltry ransom.

The next morning, scouts discovered the churned earth from a column of heavy cavalry. Sir Gossryk grimaced at the report. "The Scarborn fucks who handed us ours."

"Does it intersect our path?" Ishoa asked. The scout reported that it didn't and Ishoa doled out commands to her council.

A dozen knights accompanied her on the trek to the seat of White Plains' power. Dragga and Arick gradually slid back from riding alongside her, and in their place came Okki. For a long time, the girl from Womunger seemed to be fretting with something to say. Ishoa waited patiently, catching turns of Okki's head and parted lips in the interim. Finally, the girl said, "Thank you, Highness."

Then she peeled away to let Ishoa ride at the fore alone.

When they entered a dark forest laden with deep drifts, half the knights spurred ahead to encircle her. An hour passed before they spotted the Manger through the trees. The same trees she'd exited months earlier, bound up like a gift by the Fly.

They drew in their reins, forming a line. Okki and Arick to either side of Ishoa, with Dragga once removed beside the Lady of Womunger.

Smoke no longer stained the sky around White Plains as it had months prior. The inky touch of battle had settled and sifted to the earth, sowing the lands of Anjuhkar with the seeds of some foreboding doom. The fruits of something final.

Snow poured on them. A cooling salve for a wounded land with no hope of healing.

They stared at the Manger's battlements in somber silence. Scanned the line of grotesque warnings—a score or more. Prickles swept Ishoa's arms. The whole of her felt laid open.

Where is Krhalka? The High Hand of the Jurati had either turned her back on Ishoa or escaped. Sadness welling, Ishoa grunted. Sorrow clogged her throat like soiled cotton. She had an urge to be warm, to be snuggled under a blanket with Rakeema.

Warmth...they'll never have that again. Just the cold now.

From the look of the impaled heads, the frigid air would keep them longer than if they'd been spitted in summer. It would be a slower, more elegant rotting.

A gust of wind moaned up from the hillside backing the Manger to stir Gaern Yorek's thick, funneled locks. The way they moved atop the battlements made it clear they'd stiffened. Tar or blood, or perhaps a mix of the two, now frozen after so many days left in the elements. Her beastmaster's lips had been stitched shut, while Wiir's mouth had been left gaping to reveal apish canines.

Wooden stakes had been driven up through their chins. A gift of fear to the populace warning them to stay loyal to the Hines of White Plains. A message telling any who saw that the Ironlights no longer held sway in these lands.

In truth, that didn't seem entirely wrong. The beastmaster and his servant were holdovers from an Anjuhkar long forgotten, a people whose hands felt the mud in their palms. Who let the cold leech their warmth knowing it made them stronger.

Ishoa's horse nickered and she realized she'd been squeezing her legs too hard. "I failed them," she whispered. *Anjuhkar is lost.* "I failed you all."

Okki placed a hand on Ishoa's leg. Even that was a shame to her—a sign she was weak. A princess who needed comfort from her subjects. A princess with subjects who would console her without consent. Both screamed of weakness. *I'm not a girl anymore. Such debates of worth and weakness and strength are for those as of yet untested. I am an Ironlight. A Hulka'skara. My path is forward.*

She patted Okki's hand, appreciation and suggestion to remove it conveyed all at once. She inhaled. "I will not fail you again. We go to Alistar and when we return to this place, it will be with an army at our backs."

She turned her horse and beckoned the others to follow her.

EPILOGUE

The Scholars

D awn threw fingers of light through the battlements surrounding Martyr's Isle. Thick smoke rose to meet it, creating a golden cloud above the carnage. Nserthes's underclothes were soaked through with sweat, his limbs heavy from battle. He laid his shield against a smoldering ruin then took a ladle from one of his initiates.

"They've claimed the barbican." He was a young man—maybe a teen—with eyes rounded to their limits, absorbing the endless horrors the night had brought and dawn revealed. "The entire upper city. Most of the—"

"I am aware." Nserthes dropped the ladle back into the bucket. A soldier shambled over, breath ragged, gaze locked on the water within.

Nserthes hefted his shield, taking a moment to indulge in the words circumscribing the rim and the moth and moon emblazoned on the steel. He'd labored for years to establish the sanctity of Martyr's Isle and establish the Order of the Obsidian Hand. And the Sempyrium would burn it down in a single bloody night.

Catch the darkness and hold it still.

Nserthes unlimbered his mace. Vindication surged through him. He would be a righteous hand and use the very weapon issued to him by the Sempyrium to kill their Followers.

Breathe in light to break the seal.

He accepted the darkness. The urge to be violent. To prove in combat what could not be accomplished by word alone. He shrugged. Though his armor had fallen to disuse over the years, wearing it now, it felt like a second skin.

If this is to be my last time saying the words, my last time fighting for my cause, I will make a mighty show of it.

He arched backward to face the sky, arms at ninety degree angles to either side and loosed a thunderous howl of rage at the Sempyrean. Where rain gathered. Where lightning brushed the world. Where mountain peaks scraped sky. Where the lie of gods held back the dark god's touch.

I will show you where darkness truly lies. I will show you it lies within each of us.

He faced forward.

The gold and black tabards stamped with moth and moon and smudged with ash were being driven back in droves. Tight clusters of Martyr's Isle initiates fought desperately along the parapet against paladins. Most of the trained holdguard had already succumbed to the enemy.

Sempyrium forces filtered into the bay by boat, but their leadership rode in under the gate by horse. There they sat, directing their superior force. Spreading their insidious virus at blade-point.

Nserthes rushed toward a line of his students' backs. "Make way!" A few startled faces in the rear rank glanced back to find their leader. They stepped aside as he shouldered to the front.

Bulk huddled behind his shield he slammed into the paladins. Iron screeched. Shields ground together. Splintered wood and sparks rained as Nserthes shoved into the thick and fell to his side.

Mace sketching circles overhead, he clipped a man's unprotected knee. A spear loomed over him. He yanked his shield into place, heard the metal point scrape. Bashed the man in the shin with the rim. A satisfying crunch and the man toppled down beside him. Nserthes caved in the fallen paladin's face with a backhand blow of his mace.

The Sophophant leapt to his feet and shoved off sideways into a pair of men that knocked them down and off-centered a handful more.

A knife swung toward his gut. He bashed it away. A bearded face pressed up close to his in a cloud of hot breath. His forehead jerked forth to collide with the man's nose—missed. A sharp crack told him he'd shattered a cheekbone instead. Surrounded, Nserthes swung his mace in wide arcs—hammered something soft to one side, then twisted around. Keep moving!

Fire exploded in the meat of his shoulder. He pitched away from the agonizing pain, slipped and stumbled to the blood-drenched gangplanks below. He rolled onto his back. A man holding a sword that dripped crimson stepped over him, blotting out the sun.

The narrow window Nserthes had to protect himself had already fled. The paladin's motion already started—sword cocked to plunge into Nserthes. *Catch the darkness and hold it still. Breathe in light to break the seal.* The leader of the Obsidian Hand inhaled sharply through clenched teeth.

A man with a shield bearing a gold moth struck his executioner in the ribs and the two went down in a tangle. Nserthes's initiates had followed him into the breach and were breaking through the enemy ranks.

Nserthes flipped onto all fours and barreled into the sea of legs. Grabbing as many as he could in a bear hug, he rolled like a crocodile. The world spun around him, a disorienting whorl of shadow and light and violent momentum.

Grunts and shouts of dismay trailed in his wake. One ankle he'd latched onto gave a wet pop. His mace rammed into a gap in the planks and started to crush his hand—he let it fall away. Jaw locked, he wrenched a knee cradled in his arms until it snapped, the foot suddenly facing the wrong way. The bracers on his shield snapped, and it, too, disappeared.

Daylight beat down. With no more legs to grab, he stopped rolling and stood, unarmed. Hands on knees and lungs afire, he watched his initiates flood into the lane of havoc he'd wrought in the Sempyrium's line.

The neckline of Nserthes's chainmail hood jerked as he was pulled over backward. Head striking hard wood planks. A numbing lance shot through his skull and light flashed at the corners of his vision. A knife descended.

"Black blood!" the man hissed.

Nserthes grabbed for a wrist, caught it with one hand but his other ran the length of the blade. He gasped as the flesh of his palm parted, but held on.

The man groped at Nserthes's face, seeking an eye to gouge. In one fluid motion, Nserthes stopped resisting and angled the blade into the man's own exposed forearm. The dagger bit deep, slid along bone to the bottom of the paladin's wrist with a gruesome whisper. Blood pumped hot onto Nserthe's neck and cheek. The paladin keeled back in stunned silence to stare at the hilt jutting from his arm. Bright arterial red spurted from the wound with every heartbeat.

Nserthes kicked the man in the chin, stood, and then stomped his face with a booted foot until his jaw broke, coming unhinged. Blood filled one eye as the dying paladin brought a shaking hand to hover over his ruined, tread-lined face.

The Sophophant yanked the knife embedded in the man's forearm free and whirled.

Initiates of the Obsidian Hand had swarmed up the plaza, pushing for the next cluster of Sempyrean Followers waiting in ready ranks in the mercantile quarter. Nserthes followed, snatching up a shield along the way and trading out his knife for the first long blade he found.

At the gate, the Sempyrium leaders appeared to be scrambling to direct more forces to the sudden push from the Islemen.

Shoulder burning cold, Nserthes threw a look back at the sea knowing it would be his last. A place he'd loved. A place that had loved him back for as many years as he'd found peace living in its embrace.

The white sails of Kaltes Kasjiri's ship were far from reach now, little more than bleached and broken leaves on the horizon. The Sempyrium's skiffs would never catch them, though Kasjeri was letting them close and giving them a false sense of success. To draw forces away from Martyr's Isle, Nserthes realized.

He nodded thanks to the insufferable Kanian, however in vain his help might be, then turned back to the fighting.

An explosion rocked the earth. Flame and smoke and fragments spewed from the window of a home. Cracks in the plaster snaked down the building's side as wood groaned and then crumbled. Dust rolled over Nserthes and his initiates in a blinding cloud, forcing them to shield their eyes. A column of stone and mortar toppled across their path, stymieing their assault.

When the dust cleared, a thickset man strapped from shoulder to heel in boiled battle leather sauntered down the steps from the Sempyrean command post. A steel plate was riveted into the bone of his face at brow, lower jaw, and cheek. An oval of wired mesh covered one eye.

The man pulled a thin, stoppered vial from a bandolier of interlocking metal plates hung around his chest. As if he were doing no more than feeding bread to ducks at a pond, he cast the vial under hand at the front line of Islemen. It spun, arcing over them. Their knotted brows stared at in confusion as they tracked its trajectory. It fell, disappearing into the mob.

A tinkle of shattered glass, like a chime—

Deafening explosion. Nserthes was thrown back. His head ricocheted off something unforgiving—the pier bludgeoning him senseless. Cries of pain spiraled around him in the darkness. Nausea at the rolling hand that held him. He blinked away acidic tears that stung his eyes. Gray, smoke-clotted sky came into focus.

Men begged for water, for their mother, for both. A vacillating ring engulfed Nserthes. He tried to rise, but his head lolled, nausea pounding his gut. *Concussion.* He swayed onto one side to vomit, and then steadied, staring from under his brow at the chaos surrounding the bay.

Vision mirroring itself, he watched a group of paladins move among the dead. Crackling white flame ate at black-and-gold tabards on the smoldering bodies of gray-robed initiates and armored Islemen. For those left alive but too injured to stand under their own power, the paladins offered them the blade. For those who made it upright, shackles awaited.

A pair of paladins spotted Nserthes trying to stand. He drooped forward then pitched backward onto his ass. Miraculously, his soot-smeared fist maintained his grip on the sword he'd found and it slapped down on the gangplanks for balance as the earth bucked to one side in his mind.

The first paladin to reach him swung a gauntleted fist.

Nserthes's nose and cheek went numb. He fell.

Kept on falling...wondering why the fist wasn't breaking chains instead.

Bellator Gova looked out over Martyr's Isle. A smoking ruin of fading screams. Gulls circled, waiting for the chaos to die down enough for them to pick at the dead. He pointed with the iron-wrought hand pinned to his stump wrist, permanently shaped into a fist. "That one. I want him."

The big bald man seemed to be a leader. If he wasn't, he was at least a capable warrior and those types tended to hear important things in the company of greater men.

The Sempyrean bishop frowned. "I will have to ask the Archprelate if—"

Bellator angled his face toward the man as Las Furio stepped up on the other side of him. Inwardly, Bellator laughed. Few men held to their convictions with Las Furio staring death into them.

He watched the bishop shrink back from Las Furio's skeletal frame, but the killer stepped with him. Like a hound watching a hambone in their master's hand, Furio's gaze tracked the bishop.

"My man doesn't like you," Bellator said. "He'll cut your throat tonight if you don't do as I say." Although the bishop had chain clinking beneath his vestments, Bellator guessed he had donned the armor for show rather than function. The godly man was paling under the intensity of Las Furio's stare. The bishop had the right sense of the situation—Bellator's prediction was not idle. Las Furio dealt in promises. "A smart man would do as I say."

"Fine." The bishop spit. "Heathen Val maniacs."

"Vile words, unfit for a man of your station." Bellator exulted at the chance to subjugate the peons of the Sempyrean. "I did what you couldn't. You should be kissing my hand. Isn't that what you do for your betters?"

A bony hand shot from the folds of Las Furio's cloak to hover before the bishop's lips. The holy man recoiled, but the Val mercenary kept calmly pushing it toward him.

"Remove your hand, cur."

Bellator twisted. Archprelate Alcor's own prosort strode toward them. Karuu Lafiq had joined the assault party at dawn, adding fifty more paladins to their number to ensure success. The man was a wall of charred brick come to life and given a mace and shield. Silver, penetrating eyes were anchors of tranquility amid a wild mane of flowing argent hair. Bellator held as much love in his heart for Malzacys as he did for the pious. By his count, that was two valid reasons to hate the man.

Las Furio whipped out a hand-crossbow and pointed it at Karuu. The prosort slowed and turned his body sideways.

Smart, a smaller target.

"How is your aim?" Karuu asked.

Arm unwavering, Las Furio said nothing.

"Even if it is true," Karuu said, "your first shot will be your last."

"It would be better to let your bishop kiss his hand," Bellator suggested. He wiped a bit of spittle dripping from his mouth where flesh met steel faceplate, a regular annoyance for its constant seepage. "Furio will die before he relents. Better to kiss his hand."

The bishop huffed, incredulous, but when he realized Bellator wasn't joking, he flicked a look at Furio's hand and then at Karuu Lafiq.

The sable-skinned prosort glared at his brother in faith. "By the gods, do not—"

The bishop pecked at Las Furio's bony knuckle. "That's the last time I abase myself," he declared in clarion tones. "The next time I'm backed into a corner, there will be blood."

If he had the capacity to feel joy, Bellator might have smiled at the concession. At the wrong time, in front of the wrong people, a display of weakness was all it took to destroy a man. He saw it in Lafiq's eyes: disgust. Shame by association. The prosort would have never given in to such intimidation. It wouldn't take long for Archprelate Alcor to find out about the indecency and remove the bishop from leadership.

Bellator cocked his head at the pious weakling. "Abase yourself for a man who will kill you and it's foolhardy. Abase yourself for gods that are naught but farts on the wind and you'll kill for them. You religious types make little sense."

The man purpled. "I do not know why Lord Olabran hired you. Godless heathens."

"Because of this." Bellator Gova slipped a vial from his bandolier and thrust it toward the bishop. "*This* is my god. More real and more deadly than any of yours. Real fire. Triggered by little more than air and agitation. You've seen its capabilities?"

The man gulped, clearly regretting his proximity to the combustive substance.

"Then you know my partner and I are worth every penny." Bellator replaced the vial in his bandolier.

"A creation from the dark god, no doubt."

Bellator scoffed. "You Namorites have no sense of education. This is but basic chemistry."

The bishop thought about it for a moment. Bellator saw the light in his eyes and knew his conquering thoughts. "If it is a simple thing..."

"I did not say it was simple." Bellator tapped his faceplate. "You'd blow yourself up like I did if you tried to make it. That is, if you're lucky. If not, well, you'd meet your precious gods. Chemistry requires intellect. That thing you dither away on..." He mulled the bitter concept in his mouth. "Scripture."

"The Hammer told me you were a professor in the Academies of Valat." The bishop sighed and tried to sound confident in an attempt to save face in front of the Archprelate Alcor's prosort. "I would expect a man with such a pedigree to have a more favorable outlook on studies, regardless of their origins."

Las Furio's voice was a haunting thing, a specter that arose infrequently. But when it did, it lodged a shiver in the spine. "The Hammer also told you not to speak of the Academies to my master, didn't he?"

Bellator Gova laid his flesh-and-blood hand on the bishop's shoulder and looked across at his sinewy companion. "Ease, Furio. Ease." He beckoned the bishop to follow him.

Karuu Lafiq spun around in a swirl of navy cloak, and barked orders about gathering prisoners.

Las Furio also remained behind, predicting what Bellator wanted without needing to hear it. The symbiosis of their relationship was a wordless thing. A matter of presence. Bellator's invention of nitritus—his success at managing chaos in a bottle—had helped him understand Las Furio. The deadliest things in life required the utmost care. The most respect. Such weapons had to be treated gentlest of all.

"Your man offends the Sempyrium." A vein in the bishop's forehead pulsed. "I'll be speaking with the Hammer about this. For the transgression of indecency toward a representative of the gods, your friend will be appropriately disciplined."

Bellator let the weakling's words dribble in his ear as they walked down the broad steps of the plaza. The "terrorists," as the bishop called them, had been quelled, their remaining number rounded up into bound and bloodied clusters. Women and wailing children were being separated from the men. These would be press-ganged into service to the Sempyrium. Nestled away in a place where the rest of Namarr would never hear from them again. Brainwashed. Conditioned to serve the gods.

It was evil, yes, but knowing such atrocities would occur wasn't reason to forgo the fortune Roddic Olabran had promised Bellator if he found his son's killer. While the Sempyrium wanted Garlenna Renwood, the Hammer wanted the man she rode with. To Bellator, the former prosort was an obstacle between him and his quarry, nothing more. Unless he beat the Sempyrium to her. Then he'd ransom her to the Archprelate and collect a second fortune. The living side of his face, the one not fried to the nerves, tugged into the ghost of a grin—more grimace, really.

"You find what I'm saying funny?" the bishop sneered, courage seeming to return to him the farther away they moved from Las Furio.

"Eagles do not heed the squawk of pigeons unless hungry."

The bishop's brow tensed. "What's that supposed to mean?"

Bellator approached the man he'd pointed at. The large, bald one who'd broken through the Sempyrium's line. The one who'd forced Bellator to join the fight. Paladins were helping him to his feet. A tear at the shoulder of his gray robes was damp with blood—a shallow wound there.

Bellator motioned the man brought over. One paladin shot a questioning look at the Sempyrium lickspittle.

"Lord Roddic's man." The bishop made a face. "We're forced to work with him. For now."

The partnership smelled like shit to both sides. Only out of function, and the necessity to follow the Hammer's contract, did Bellator suffer the god-nursing fools. Neither side was pleased that they'd had to camp together. But especially Furio. He'd been peaking on a godsthorn bender in Breckenbright's finest whorehouse when the summons from the Hammer had come. The last thing he'd wanted after that was to interact with Followers.

The paladins shoved the warrior to his knees at Bellator's feet. The terrorist was bull-necked, stained by the bruises and scuffs and filth of battle. Yet he didn't have the haunted look like so many others. He was keen behind the eyes. Sharp of mind. Alert. Before he even began, Bellator sensed his efforts to gather information would fail.

But curiosity had ever compelled him.

Bellator brought his good hand behind his head to scratch at the thick folds along the back of his neck. He lifted his promontory chin at the kneeling man. "It seems we share the same barber."

The warrior's eyes narrowed as he picked over Bellator's attire. Then he looked at a group of paladins in the distance herding his people up the plaza toward the sundered gate. By nightfall, Martyr's Isle would be empty.

Revulsion twitched along the man's jaw.

"Perhaps we share more than a fine sense of fashionable haircuts," Bellator said. "A hate of the Sempyrium, maybe?"

The man's face jerked up to meet Bellator's. "Who are you?"

Bellator pulled a vial from his plated bandolier. A group of young terrorists similarly garbed in gray had been left roped together at the end of a solitary pier jutting into the bay. He nodded toward them. "You think I can hit them from here?"

Silence expected.

Expectation met.

"You saw what this does, so you know what it will do to them." He held the vial up for the man to see. A thread of maroon liquid flowed from one end to the other as he tilted it, points of sunlight freezing along the length of the glass. "Agitation mixes the compounds. End over end toss does the trick. Air triggers the explosion. Impossibly unstable in large quantities. But I assure you, this will slaughter the lot of them. Now." He lowered the vial. "Who are you?"

"Nserthes the Sophophant."

"Ah. So you *are* the one in charge." Bellator put the vial of nitritus back in its place. Hands on knees, he hunched so that his face was a few inches from Nserthes's. He glanced over a shoulder at the bishop, who stood there, seething in his pristine brocaded vestments draped over useless chain. "The god-lovers know you. They hate you. They will not be kind."

Nserthes raised his blocky face. "I am prepared...have been from the very moment I forsook the gods."

Bellator nodded. "We are brothers of a sort, you and I. The..." He hunted for the word, a rarely used one in the Common tongue, but its simpler translation in Val was widely known. "'The Sophophant,' they call you. A creator of wisdom. A *scholar*. Like me." He straightened. The stump of his left wrist itched where his hand should be. Saliva peeked from what remained of his lip and he wiped it away. "Yet here we are. Men of books become men of war. Pitted against each other when we should be uniting in our intellect to overcome the disease of ignorance that plagues this world."

A line split Nserthes's brow. The look of a man deciphering madness from brilliance.

Bellator recalled his peers at the Academies who claimed he fell into the former category. Fools, one and all. "Alas, your judgment is a wedge between us. Cannibalistic we are, we scholars. And so the world falls to ruin because you're unwilling to see the truth." He ran a finger over the stoppers of the vials adorning his chest. "A man can only fight against ignorance so long before he gives in to the base animal within. I had thought myself above it. Elevated myself to be master of the herd through my studies. But I ask you, who is the human in this scenario? Those who aspire to rise above their nature, or those who give in to it?"

For a moment, the Sophophant seemed to have forgotten he was bound and defeated, the stimulus of the conversation sweeping him to a time and place preferred. "The spirit tames what the mind cannot. Your philosophy smacks of one born to power, a seed whose predetermined blueprint grows into a hierarchy of life that favors him. You speak of nothing more than a propaganda used to justify your merciless greed. Intellect twisted to evil ends and in evil's name. Meanwhile, you blame the world for not providing you with more of your own to heal its wounds. Another justification. But in your case against humanity, you forget that choice alone is what separates us from who we truly are and the men we fear we may become."

"Merit." Bellator grunted, lone eyebrow raised. "Merit. I concede, I may not be your equal in this line of wisdom. Still, I am pleased to find another of my kind among..." He gestured at the pier full of terrorists with his iron-wrought fist. "The herd."

Nserthes's lip curled. "You and I are people, just like them."

Few were the moments when Bellator felt the spark of kinship, but Nserthes's wanton attachment to his sheep snuffed it out. The man hadn't yet grasped what Bellator had about the world. Ignorance claimed even the mightiest minds, it seemed. Demonstrations, he had learned, provided the best means for understanding. "I track a man and woman on behalf of Lord Roddic Olabran. The woman, I suspect to be the renegade spy, Garlenna Renwood. The man, I do not know." Bellator withdrew a vial once more. "Tell me who he is."

Nserthes lowered his head, searching the deck for a lie. "Kord. His name is Kord, a drug dealer from Digtown."

"Good," Bellator said. "And the ship they boarded. Where will it berth?"

Nserthes went wooden.

"I give only two chances, Sophophant. Its berth." He pinched the vial between thumb and forefinger. They locked eyes. "The berth, and I'll make sure the Sempyrium spares your life. Your followers' lives, too." Bellator pointed at the half dozen prisoners seated on the pier. "Tell me the ship's berth. Or say goodbye."

Nserthes stared at the men and women on the pier. They were looking at him, seemingly puzzled as to their leader's intense gaze and Bellator's pointing. A thickset man with lustrous hair struggled against his bonds and spat into the bay in the direction of his captors. When he spotted Bellator watching him, he shouted, "May a horse fuck you to death, you Maw-begotten pissants!" Then the man gave a nod of solidarity at Nserthes. A promise to win free. To find a way out.

Perseverance. Bellator almost envied the fool his misplaced optimism. He'd never acquired a taste for false hope himself. The concept was illogical, a danger to self-preservation.

Nserthes eyed the nitritus. Bellator took no pleasure in necessities of violence. If there were not a fortune weighing down his mind and a bishop gnawing at his patience, he would have loved nothing more than to continue his discussion with the Sophophant. "Alas, you're wrong on one account, my friend." Sounding bored, Bellator was resigned to a demonstration of his final point instead. "In a world run by beasts, there is no such thing as choice."

Nserthes surged to his feet. "Don't!"

But the vial was already spinning. End over end. Beginning and end and beginning again in the flashing sun. A dainty thing—not some looming horror to behold. Just a splash of flame and heat and a clipped burst of sound, and then the darkness would come. As it would come for every one of them. In that, there was no choice at all.

End over end.

End.

Over.

End.

Over...

...end.

ACKNOWLEDGEMENTS

Book two went smoother than expected, so I'll have to save all of my apologies for book three's acknowledgments.

Until then, I'll do what any author lucky enough to be married should do: extoll the endless and multitudinous virtues of my goddess-in-the-flesh, wife, Jess. She deserves a sainthood for dealing with me on a daily basis.

The Skull King Quintet: Josiah Rosell, Andy Peloquin, Zack Argyle, and Michael Webb. Ya'll are the best. Our retreat had a huge impact on my author career that's likely to make ripples for years to come. Not sure what I did to deserve your camaraderie but I'm grateful for it.

Furthermore, JA Andrews, Ryan Cahill, Rob J. Hayes, Aaron Hodges, and Michael R. Miller. Your mentorship and guidance has been massive. You can count on me to be your second in a duel if ever find your honor besmirched.

My beta team is the lifeblood of my writing process. Without you, my books would suck. I know many of you question your contribution. Don't. It's vital, even if you only mention a handful of moments you liked. That's just as important as telling me what you despised. Each of you will forever be a champion in my heart.

My friends and family who took support a step further and integrated reading my first book into their busy lives. You deserve friendship medals. Gold goes to ZB Steele for being "First Ear" of the series.

To the Rachels. Rachel Marchesi, my editor, I'm so lucky to have found you first. Your care and thoroughness were the whetstone I needed to make this baby shine. Rachel St. Clair, I'm still stunned by how much your typography and cover layout enhanced Chris's amazing art. You didn't just nail this project, you made me a huge fan of the art form.

And Christopher Cant. Whoa, dude. It didn't take long to see why you came so highly recommended. Just when I wasn't sure I'd ever find "The One," you saved the day.

Petrik Leo, you're a king. Your suggestions were pivotal in giving my book the perfect artistic representation I was hunting for.

To those lovely Kickstarter backers who opted into being in the Acknowledgments, you are the highest order of dream makers. Your support makes a monumental difference. A huge thank you to: Arild Tvedt, Bruce Harpham, Dave Becker, Stephanie Wokan, Joe Deckert, Señor Neo, Kristopher Ecklof, Sheena R Butt, xor, Sebastian 'Sonny' Sonnhalter, Dead Fishie, Kris M, Mc-Moogle, Megyn "Crimson" MacDougall, Tom Deannone, David Kirlin, Jon Auerbach, Quint Ashburn, Michiel Stade, Serdar Rakipovski, C. A. Maxwell, Jeremy Moss, Johan Berts, Aaron Granofsky, Kurt Boulianne, Marte Myrvold, Lahman Marcel, René Schultze, Pamela Hamlet, Martin Jackson, L. Haymond, Sean Willson, Christian Holt, Amanda Auler, Heiko Koenig, A.P Beswick, CMT, Schon Duncan, Karyne Norton, Kian Ardalan, Adam Barnes, James N, Emily Cass, Dylan Kistler, Simon Dick, K Stoker, Michał Kabza, and Cypress.

ABOUT THE AUTHOR

Michael Michel lives in Oregon with his wife and their "mini-me" children. When he isn't obsessively writing, he can be found exercising, exploring nature, enjoying comedy, or playing Warhammer. His favorite shows are Dark, The Wire, and Scavenger's Reign—clearly, he loves his heart to be abused. If you are foolish enough to challenge him in table tennis, he will gladly destroy you.

REVIEWS: If you enjoyed this book and feel it should be spread far and wide, please leave a review on Amazon, Reddit, Goodreads, your socials, or wherever you feel called to share. I would greatly appreciate it!

michaelmichelauthor.com

Instagram @michaelmichelauthor

TikTok @MichaelBookCult

Bluesky @michaelbookcult.bsky.social

Twitter/X @MichaelBookCult